KARL MAY

WINNETOU,
THE CHIEF OF THE APACHE

A modern unabridged English translation
of the full Winnetou Trilogy in one book
by M. A. Thomas

CTPDC
Publishing Limited

CTPDC
Publishing Limited

CTPDC Publishing Limited, 28 Ashfield Road, Liverpool,
L17 0BZ, United Kingdom

Translation and editorial material copyright M. A. Thomas 2014
Cover illustration Spotted Bull - Mandan by Edward S. Curtis,
Library of Congress Prints and Photographic Division, Edward S.
Curtis Collection LC-USZ62-83602

Printed by Lightning Source

TABLE OF CONTENTS

THE TRANSLATOR'S FOREWORD

KARL MAY was born in 1842, and over 35 years he wrote a huge number of adventure stories. His popularity has been unbroken in many countries around the world, especially among the youth, in spite of his misfortune that Hitler named him as his favourite writer.

He wrote his books in the style of village story tellers. A focus is on the adventures, and nothing restricts the flight of fantasy. There is no fully developed story line in May's Western books: it is the series of escapades that give the impression of fullness. The characters in his books do not change as the plot develops, and there is very little analysis of the psychology of his heroes. Yet, in spite of these literary shortcomings, the popularity of his books has not suffered.

This enduring popularity, apart from the dare-devil adventures, could partly be explained by the basic moral foundation. In the world of May's books the good and the evil struggle with each other, and the good always wins even if the positive heroes sometimes have to pay a heavy price for their victory. This moral stance and the adventure are united in the heroes. The positive heroes are men who have no shortcomings. They are not only just and honest people, who are ready to act for justice, but also strong and clever men, who can shoot and ride as nobody else. The evil is represented by villains who are overpowered by their own wickedness, and defeated by the heroes at the end.

The aim of this English translation was to retain these characteristics, while modernising the style, and editing parts that were erroneous or could evoke bad associations. Therefore, this English translation is an unabridged, but edited version of the Winnetou Trilogy.

As to the style, the editing involved some minor structural changes. May often used extremely long dialogues to carry the story forward. Without changing the content, these were made more concise, or were replaced by summarising paragraphs. Interjections (e.g. "said", "asked", etc.) were also introduced where they were appropriate. In some cases descriptive paragraphs were transformed into dialogues.

Geographic errors, such as names of rivers, mountains, settlements, and forts were corrected, and these names now follow the current conventions.

Tribal names (sometimes names of various bands) were also corrected and transliterated to the currently accepted forms (for example Oglala instead of Ogalalla). In Volume II, one of the villains is described as the "Athabaskan chief". Athabaskan is a language family (the Apache language is a Southern Athabaskan language). I replaced this with Arapaho, because of the area where the events take place, and also because the Arapaho tribe formed an alliance with the Comanche in the South, thus would have been enemies of Winnetou.

The word "Manitou" was avoided. It is an Algonkian name for a transcendent being, thus the Apache chief would not have used it. Instead of confusing the reader by using different names, the expression of Great Spirit was preferred. Similarly, the word "wigwam" was replaced. Some of the tribes mentioned by May built wigwam-like huts, but they did not call these wigwams.

Unfortunately, most of the ethnographic errors could not be removed. The reader will not have a true picture of the life of the Native Americans' from May books.

The social order of the Native Americans were very different, and much more varied. Here I list only the most important ones. Most tribes did not have a supreme chief (May assumes that both the Apache and the Comanche had such an office). War chiefs (peace chiefs are never mentioned in Winnetou) were elected, and the office was not inherited by the son. Many tribes followed a matrilineal system, that is, the children from a relationship belonged to the mother's clan. Therefore, the father and the son belonged to two different social groups.

May described the Mescalero Apache as a quasi-pueblo Indian tribe (leaders living in the pueblo, and the rest of the tribe in a tent village, which is a projection of European feudal social structures onto the Native American tribes). In reality the culture of the Apache was similar to the Plains Indians' mode of life.

No peoples buried the man with his horse as May described in Volume I, and suggested in Volume III. In reality, the animal was skinned, and the bones put in the skin, and buried with the person. This was corrected by making the scenes more concise.

The religions of the Native Americans were more varied than it appears in the book. May, essentially, projected a version of Christianity onto the Native Americans. This could not be fully removed, but wherever it was possible, it was toned down. The passages in which May described his own religious moral were removed, because these seem to be forced upon the heroes (Winnetou's quasi-conversion to Christianity in Volume III in particular) and also because most of them are bound to the perceptions of the 19th century. They actually weaken the story.

The editing of sensitive issues, words and passages that could be perceived as insulting to nations or races, involved different tasks.

In May's books many, if not all, important heroes are German, and Karl May often, quite clumsily, wrote about German superiority. This had to be addressed. These parts were either removed or toned down without removing the nationality of the heroes.

Prejudicial or racist comments by May were deleted. The "comical" role of Bob, the black servant in Volume III was eliminated. However, it was impossible to completely achieve this aim about certain Native American tribes. In May's stories the Apache are the noble people, and any tribe hostile to them are mean, cruel, etc. Various Sioux tribes (especially the Oglala), the Comanche, and to some degree the Kiowa are described in a particularly bad light. It was possible to tone down these comments somewhat, but they could not be fully removed without breaking the story.

ix

Finally, the spelling of Indian names was changed to approximate the English pronunciation. Hawkins's name was changed. May spelt it as Hawkens, which could have caused confusion for an English speaking audience. For the same reason the spelling of Old Shatterhand's first name, Charley, was changed to Charlie, and one of the minor character's name from Hoblyn to Hoblin.

I believe that with these changes the core of May's world, the action, the adventure, the dreaming of heroic deeds, and the struggle justice have become more emphasised, and more accessible for the reader.

M. A. Thomas

VOLUME I

THE GREENHORN

I DO NOT want to detail why I left Saxony in 18--, and went to America to make my fortune in the New World. The poverty in my homeland was the main reason, but I do not want to deny that my desire for adventures also played a role. I was not twenty years old yet when, with big hopes, but with empty pockets, I arrived to New York. From there, driven by my desire for the Wild West, I went to the bank of the Mississippi, to St Louis. I found a job there as a private tutor with a kind family of German descent.

The family was frequently visited by a Mr Henry. I learnt that this rosy-cheeked, grey-haired man was a celebrity of the town, and he was also a philanthropist. He was a gun designer, who loved his work, and introduced a number of innovations to rifles. The rifles that he produced fetched a triple price. People thought, in spite of his philanthropy, that he was eccentric, because his manners were abrupt and rough even to his customers. Only later I learnt of his deep sadness that probably caused this behaviour: many years earlier his wife and his only son had been killed in a raid on his farm in his absence. Mr Henry's gloomy, introverted manners started then. Then he had moved to the town, and had returned to his original profession. He developed gun-making into a real art.

I, however, was lucky with him. For some reason he liked me from the first moment. He immediately invited me to visit his workshop. Of course, I accepted.

'When will you come?' he asked.

'Maybe tomorrow evening.'

'I will expect you.'

However, I visited him only three days later.

Instead of greeting me, he started with, 'Where were you yesterday, young man?'

'I was busy.'

'And the day before yesterday?'

'I didn't have time.'

1

'You didn't have time! But you promised that you would visit me.'

'I didn't think it was so important.'

'Of course it's important! And it's important for you, and not for me, young man!'

'Why?'

'You'll see. For the time being let's talk a bit.'

It was a third degree interrogation. He wanted to know what I had studied, what career I had wanted to pursue before leaving my homeland for America. I answered his questions openly. I told him that I had wanted to become a teacher, but I had to leave school to earn money, and I had tried every honest way to do so. I also told him that my favourite hobby was sport, and added that I was good in all branches of it.

'Have you mastered guns too?'

'I think quite well.'

'Quite well? Only a greenhorn can be so self-confident! You flicked through some books, and you think you have the knowledge. You swam about a bit, you wrestled, and maybe even boxed, and you think of yourself as a great sportsman. But the school of life is much more difficult than your previous education. In the forests, and on the prairies you have to know other things too. Sport isn't a game there. Wrestling isn't for a medal in the West, for example, but for life or death.'

As if he felt that he said too much, he suddenly became quiet. He took out a cigar, and lit it. He was silent for at least ten minutes. I did not want to disturb his train of thoughts, so I also remained quiet. Finally he stood up, went to his workbench, and picked up a gun barrel. He kept the barrel towards the light, looked into it, and examined it carefully. Then he turned to me.

'So you said that you know a lot about guns. Fine. Then take that gun from the wall! Yes, from that hook. Show me how you would aim it. It's a bit heavy, it's a bear slayer, but it's the best.'

2

I took the gun from the hook, pressed it to my shoulder, and aimed with it.

'Uh!' exclaimed Mr Henry 'You picked it up as if it was a walking stick. It's not visible on you how muscular you are. So have you mastered weightlifting too?'

As a reply I grabbed him by his belt, and lifted him above my head with one hand.

'Damn it!' he shouted, and kicked about. 'Put me down, right now.'

I put him on his feet, and apologised for the dumb joke.

'No problem,' he said. 'I can see that you are stronger than my Bill used to be.'

'Who is your Bill?'

'He used to be my son, and died like others. He was very promising, but he was killed while I was away. He was your age, your countenance, and carriage remind me to him.'

Deep sorrow ran through his face, and he changed the subject of our conversation.

'Let's talk about the gun. I would like to see how good your aiming is. I have a fenced plot not to too far from here. I use it as a shooting range to test my new guns. I'll be there tomorrow. Do you want to join me?'

'With pleasure, Mr Henry. At what time?'

'You start your class at 8 am, don't you? Then come to me for 6 am.'

'I will be here.'

Mr Henry put the barrel aside, and from a cupboard he took out a many-plane iron piece. He started to file it. He was so deeply involved in his work that he forgot that I was still there. Occasionally he carefully examined the piece. He looked at it almost with love. It seemed that this piece of iron meant a lot to him.

'Is it a gun component, Mr Henry?' I asked curiously.

'I hope it will be,' he answered, and looked at me as if he only now recognised that I was still there.

I noticed that a hole had been drilled in every plane of this iron piece.

'I have had many types of rifles in my hand,' I said, 'but I've never seen such a component in my life. What type of gun is it for?'

'There's no such a gun yet,' he replied, 'but there will be!'

'Your invention?'

'Indeed.'

'Then I sincerely apologise for my curiosity. I know that such things are secret.'

He looked into each of the holes, and finally attached the iron piece to the barrel that he had in his hand earlier. He appeared to be contented as he looked at it.

'Yes, a secret,' he said, 'but I tell you about it. Even if you are a greenhorn, I can also see that you can keep your mouth shut. I'm designing a completely new breech-loading gun from which twenty-five bullets can be shot.'

'There's no such a cartridge that can hold twenty-five bullets,' I remarked doubtfully.

'This iron piece will hold the bullets, and it will feed the gun. There are twenty-five holes on it for as many bullets. The structure is not yet ready. I've been working on it for years, but now I'm close to the solution.'

'And also close to a bad conscience!'

He looked at me with an astonishment for a while, and then asked, 'A bad conscience? Why?'

'Do you think that a murderer has a bad conscience?'

'Come on, what do you mean that I'm a murderer?'

'Not just yet.'

'Will I become a murderer?'

'Yes, because aiding the murderer is almost as bad as the murder itself.'

'Damn! But I'm not an accomplice in a murder!'

'Not just one, but of a mass murder.'

'I don't understand you!'

'If you make a rifle that can shoot twenty-five times without reloading, and give it to any rascal, who then rides out to the prairies, the forests, and the mountains, there will be gruesome murders, I'm telling you. The poor Indians will

4

be shot as coyotes, and in a few years' time there will be no more of them. Do you want to have this on your conscience?'

He stared at me, but he did not answer.

'And,' I continued, 'if anyone can get such a dangerous gun for their money, you will sell thousands quickly, and the mustangs, the bison, and all the game will be extinct, and there will be nothing for the redskins to live on. The blood of humans and animals will flow in streams.'

'Did you really come over the Ocean only recently, and you have never been in the Wild West?'

'Yes, this is the truth.'

'So, you are a greenhorn, yet you talk like the ancestor of all Indians who have lived here for thousands of years. Young man! Your words warm my heart indeed. Yet, even if everything happened as you described, it would not apply for me because I'm a lonely man, and I don't want to build a gun factory with a hundred workers.'

'But you can make money by taking out a patent for your invention, and sell that.'

'Until now I have always had what I needed, and I think that I will suffer no hardship even without the patent. But it's enough of this for the time being. I don't want to judge a bird's chirping before it's fully fledged; before knowing if it can really sing, or it can only whistle.'

I knew very well what he meant. He had grown fond of me, and he was certainly willing to be a fatherly friend to me. We shook hands warmly, and I left.

When I said good-bye to the good gunsmith, I could not have suspected how big a role the heavy "bear slayer" gun, and also the Henry-rifle, which was born in the front of my eyes, would play in my life.

On the following morning I entered Mr Henry's workshop punctually. It was 8 am.

'Good, young man,' he said. 'We can go. You'll carry the bear slayer, and I'll take a lighter gun.'

In ten minutes we arrived to the plot that Mr Henry had transformed into a little shooting range. Now he loaded both guns. First he shot, then waved to me to take my place on the shooting bench. As I did not know the bear slayer gun, my first shot was not perfect, but already the second one hit the middle of the target. The subsequent bullets flew precisely in the same hole.

Mr Henry's eyes showed great surprise, but he only said, 'Good … Surprisingly good, considering that you are a greenhorn.'

He gave me the other gun to try. After the fifth or the sixth hit he said, 'Very good. Not even a marksman could do better. If you can ride like this, I would say, in a few years' time you would become a man who can stand up in the Wild West. So, what do you say about riding?'

'Not a big thing,' I replied, 'only getting on the horse is difficult. If I'm on the saddle, the rest is just fun.'

He looked at me searchingly. He could not be sure if I was joking, or I was serious. However, I put on such an innocent face that made his suspicion vanish.

'You are right,' he said finally. 'Getting on the horse takes some effort, while dismounting is easier because the horse also helps.'

'You mean that it throws the rider off?' I asked.

'It can happen even to the best.'

'Not to me,' I stated proudly. 'There's no such a horse that could throw me off.'

'Do you want a trial?' asked Mr Henry.

'Willingly,' I replied.

Mr Henry glanced at his watch.

'There's enough time,' he said. 'We'll visit Jim Corner the horse trader. He has a pinto that he cannot sell. It's a bit stubborn, if you understand me.'

'Let's go,' I said.

There was a huge yard behind Corner's house surrounded by stables. The horse trader must have been Mr Henry's old acquaintance, because he welcomed us very cordially, and after the mutual greetings he asked how he could help us.

6

'This young man says that there is no horse that can throw him off,' said Mr Henry, 'and I remembered the pinto that you mentioned to me. What do you say, Mr Corner?'

The horse trader measured me up, and finally he nodded contented. 'He looks muscular, and his bones look strong,' he said. 'If he wants to try my pinto, I don't object.'

Following his instruction, two stable boys brought the saddled horse from the stable. The animal looked very nervous. Mr Henry suddenly changed his mind, and wanted to dissuade me from the trial. However, I did not share his view, and I had no intention of retreating from the challenge. I only asked for a whip and spurs. I put the spurs on, and jumped on the horse. However, I needed several attempts to sit firmly on the saddle, because the horse did everything to destroy my intentions. When I got on his back, he stretched his four legs, jumped up, and then tried to lean on his side to get rid of me. However, I held him firm by the reins, even though my feet were not yet in the stirrup. When I finally managed that, the horse rose so violently that the two stable boys stepped back with fright. I stayed on the horse. The clever animal rushed to one of the walls, and tried to squash me. My whip explained that it was not a good idea. At that time I was not an experienced rider, so I had to substitute my lacking in skills with the strength of my thighs. Their strong pressure forced the pinto to accept the situation. After a great struggle I won, but when I jumped off the horse my legs were trembling. The surrendered pinto was sweating, and his mouth was foaming.

Mr Corner ordered the stable boys to cover the horse with three blankets, and walk it slowly until it cools down.

'I couldn't have imagined this, young man!' he turned to me. 'I was sure that the horse would throw you off in the first minute. You won't have to pay a cent, of course. Just the opposite, I would like to ask you, if you have time, to come again, and tame this beast. I don't mind paying ten dollars to you for this. I bought this pinto at a high price, and I can sell him only if it's a bit tamed.'

Mr Henry recovered from his fright only now, and he joyously shook hands with me.

'If you knew how happy I am,' he said. 'I have to say, you are an accomplished rider. Where did you learn it? Where did you practice it?'

'It was an accident,' I answered. 'I was once given a fiery Hungarian horse. Its homeland was the plains, and it didn't let anyone on its back. It took me weeks until I tamed him. It was hard, but since then I'm not afraid even of the most stubborn horse. But now I have to hurry, because my class is about to start.'

When we parted, Mr Henry shook hands with me, and asked me if I had a free afternoon.

'A week today,' I replied.

'Then please stay at home if you could, and wait for me,' said Mr Henry, 'because I'd like to return your visit.'

When he arrived on the agreed day, I wanted to offer him something to drink, but he did not even want to sit down. 'I came to take you.'

'Where to?' I asked.

'To some gentlemen who want to meet you.'

I saw that he had a new surprise for me, and I did not resist. After a short walk we stopped in the front of a big house. There was some office on the ground floor. Mr Henry grabbed my arm, and he almost pulled me in. I did not have time to read the gilded letters on the glass door. It had to be some sort of an engineering office.

There were three gentlemen there. Mr Henry introduced me; they offered us seats, and as we sat down, they stared at me curiously. It seemed that Mr Henry had talked about me to these gentlemen.

I looked around. I saw some drawing boards, and all kinds of tools. I was curious about what they wanted from me.

The talk started with indifferent things, among them they asked how I liked St Louis.

'Nice town, but I have to admit, I don't particularly like town life,' I replied.

'I agree with you,' said one of the three gentlemen, 'if I was younger I wouldn't sit around in an office either.'

He was a greyish-haired man and he wore golden-framed glasses. For a few moments he seemed to be lost in his own thoughts. He was drumming on the table with his fingers. Then, without any transition, he asked me, 'Tell me, do you like maths?'

'I've always liked it, but never had enough time to go deeper into it.'

'And geometry?'

'More so,' I replied, 'because in one summer vacation I wanted to earn money, and I worked for a land surveying company for two months. I learnt a bit of geodesy.'

The three gentlemen exchanged curious looks with each other. The eldest pushed his glasses higher up on his nose.

'Geodesy?' he asked slowly. 'This is our business too, but from a very practical point of view. When I saw you, I thought you were a very sympathetic young man, but also that you wouldn't know anything about geodesy. Look at that tool there. Have you seen such a tool?'

'Of course,' I replied right away, 'it's a theodolite. I have worked with it.'

After this, questions came after questions. It felt like an examination about binoculars, chains, steel ribbons, angle mirrors, trigonometric height measurement, levelling, and everything. The three gentlemen kept on nodding to my responses, and Mr Henry was rubbing his hands.

In the beginning it had amused me, but then I started to get a bit peeved. It seemed to me that Mr Henry had boasted about me to his friends, and he wanted to show off with me.

"Thank you," I thought, "that was enough to me."

'I don't want to hold you up,' I said aloud, and stood up.

After the friendly good-bye, when we were already on the street, Mr Henry stopped; turned to me; put his hand on my shoulder, and with a beaming face he said 'That was perfect. I was sure that you wouldn't let me down, but I didn't expect such a success.'

'What success? I'm not a comedian or some eccentric to be shown off. I don't know why you did this whole thing.'

'Come on, my friend! One has to be among people! And you surely don't want to take away from me the joy of trying to help your career. Since I cannot help my son's …'

I regretted my impatience. I did not want to remind him to his sadness.

To change the subject I remarked: 'Do you know that the pinto is quite tame now?'

'What? Have you visited Jim Corner again?'

'More than once. I went to him to ride some mornings. It felt good, not to mention the ten dollars that I earned.'

'That's a good work! And it's good for Jim too. I really would like to know how much he would charge now for the horse. Well, good-bye! We'll meet again soon.'

About three weeks later my pupils' mother asked me not to go out in the evening, but have dinner with them. She added that Mr Henry would be there, and also Sam Hawkins, the famous hunter, whose name was well known in the Wild West. When she asked me if I had heard of him, I had to excuse myself that I had been around for a very short time, and that I was rather uninformed.

I arrived to the dining room a bit earlier than the agreed time. My little pupil, five years old Emma, was going around the laid table. When she caught sight of me, she rushed to me, leant to my ear, and whispered, 'It will be a farewell dinner. We're saying farewell to you, Mr Teacher.'

I didn't understand it.

'Why?' I asked.

'Secret,' replied the little blond girl, as she put her index finger to her lips.

Even if I wanted to, I couldn't question her any longer because I could hear voices in the hall. The guests had arrived. Mr Henry brought two gentlemen with him.

'This is Mr Black,' he said, 'and this is Sam Hawkins.'

I was not interested in Mr Black at all. Sam Hawkins caught all my attention. I could hardly wait to meet a real

Western man, but my first impression, because of my false expectations, disappointing. Sam Hawkins was a small, lean man, that is, not what I had expected, a broad shouldered, tall giant. His face was round and friendly, and not at all weathered. His small eyes were bright, and I could see that they constantly scanned everything around him. He was surely a clever man, and his bravery, inventiveness, and consciousness must have coped with the trials thrown at him. I knew he must have been strong and tenacious, but his appearance did not show any of these qualities.

When he put down his gun, whose name was Liddy, and put his hat on the barrel of the rifle, I noticed with a shock, that there was no hair on his skinless, red skull. The lady and the children screamed.

'Please don't be frightened ladies and gentlemen! There's nothing to be startled about. Once I had my own hair, and I wore it honestly all my life until one or two dozens of the Pawnee captured me, and took my hair and my skin from my head. It was a horrible experience, but I survived it, hehehe! Then I got a new scalp for myself, a toupee for which I paid three thick bundles of beaver pelts. The toupee is more practical than my old hair, especially in the summer, because I can take it off when I sweat, hehehe.'

He put the toupee on his head again. He then took off his coat, and laid it over a chair. This coat had been patched, and repaired many, many times by fixing one leather scrap on top of the others, and thus his coat gained a stiffness and thickness that probably could resist even an Indian arrow.

He was clearly interested in me just as much as I was interested in him. After some observation he turned to Mr Henry and asked, 'Is he the greenhorn whom you talked to me so much about?'

'Yes, this is the one,' said Mr Henry, 'don't you like him?'

'Just the opposite,' answered Hawkins smiling, 'I'm very contented. I hope he feels the same about me, hehehe.'

Sam Hawkins had a surprisingly high pitched voice, especially when he laughed. When I heard this laughter for the first time, I could not really appreciate it. But later I learnt how many times this laughter had encouraged his comrades in situations when nobody had the desire to laugh!

'Madame,' said Sam Hawkins as he turned to the hostess with his eyes gleaming with craftiness, 'I think we can tell our young friend what this is about.'

The lady nodded, and she turned to me saying, 'The man standing by you is Mr Black. He's the new teacher of the children, that is, your successor.'

'My successor?' I was stuttering, and I felt that my face looked rather stupid.

'Yes. As we are saying farewell to you, I had to look for a new teacher. In fact, I should have insisted on a notice period, but I didn't want to obstruct your career. We are sorry that we have to part with you because you have almost become a member of the family, but what could we have done, when you are leaving tomorrow?'

'Tomorrow … Leaving?' I was still stuttering because of my confusion about all these words. 'Where to?'

Sam Hawkins, who was standing next to me, slapped me on my shoulder, and answered with laughter, 'With me, to the Wild West! You passed the examination, hehehe! The whole expedition is leaving tomorrow, and you are coming with us. I will be the scout with two of my good friends, Dick Stone and Will Parker. We are going along the Canadian River to New Mexico. There you will quickly forget that you are a greenhorn.'

Now I fully understood the situation. These good people conspired for my benefit without letting me know any of their plans. They meant it as a pleasant surprise. I would now become a surveyor in the Wild West, a member of the avant-garde of the building of a great railway. It was an interesting job, and it was made for me.

After some silence it was Mr Henry, who picked up the conversation, 'You worked for a very kind family, but I saw immediately that you desired something else. It seemed to me that these were the forests, to the prairies, and all the adventures! I can understand all these desires. This is why I turned to the Atlantic Pacific, and I offered them your services. You passed an exam without knowing it. They gave you an excellent mark for your performance, and here's your appointment.'

He took a paper from his pocket, and gave it to me. It was a job offer. I scanned through its content. When I got to the salary, I could not believe my eyes. It was such a sum that I would never have dreamt of.

Mr Henry smiled, and continued, 'You will have to go on horseback, so you'll need a good horse. I bought the pinto that you tamed. This is my present to you. And as you can't go without a gun, you will get the bear slayer from me. So what do you say, young man?'

I could not say one word; I grabbed his hand, and then squeezed it so much that he hissed. It was the hostess who helped me out, because she sat down, and thus we had to follow her example. The dinner started. It would have been rude to bring up my own issues, so I remained silent, and gave all my attention to the excellent food.

I said good night to the hosts early, as I had to get up early to pack, and to sort out my most important affairs. I also wanted to visit Mr Henry again to thank him for his help and goodwill.

On the following morning when I visited him, I found Sam Hawkins there also. At last I learnt what I could expect. The corporation had started a huge venture. It wanted to build a railway from St Louis to the Pacific Ocean through the Indian Territory, New Mexico, Arizona, and California. They broke up the planned route to phases, and the surveying of these phases started at the same time. The phase on which I had to work was situated between the Canadian River and the Pecos River.

The boss of my group was Engineer Bancroft, and there were three surveyors apart from me. We were responsible for evaluating, measuring as well as mapping the land. Sam Hawkins, Dick Stone and Will Parker led us there. We would meet a whole group of Westerners, and we could expect them, and the forts to protect us. By the time I had been given all this information, the moment of farewell had arrived.

'I don't know how,' I started an attempt to express my gratitude, 'could I thank you, Mr Henry.'

'What?' he interrupted my speech. 'You don't want to pay homage to me, do you? What do you think, Sam? He's a greenhorn, isn't he?'

He slapped me on my back, squeezed my hand, and then he turned away his head quickly. I could see that his eyes were filled with tears.

KLEKIH-PETRA, THE WHITE APACHE

THE INDIAN summer was coming to an end. We had worked for three months, but we were well behind the other team that almost completed their work. There were two main reasons for our lagging behind.

Firstly, our landscape was particularly difficult. The planned line ran along the Canadian River, through the forests and prairies, to New Mexico, and we had to find the best direction for the track. This required a lot of riding, and countless comparative height measurements before we could actually start the work. We also had to be alert, because Indian bands wandered around the area. The Kiowa, the Comanche, and the Apache considered our work a hostile act. We had to be careful even with hunting when we wanted fresh meat for our kitchen. Our supplies arrived from Santa Fe on ox-pulled wagons.

The other reason was the composition of our team. Half of the team was made up of lazy men, who wanted to make money quickly and easily, but did not like working. They did not feel responsible for our task. I recognised soon that I was the only one who approached the job with any responsibility. I not only did my work, but theirs too, and for this they looked at me with mocking contempt.

Mr Bancroft, the engineer, was skilled, but he was an alcoholic. He got his brandy from Santa Fe by the barrels, and he was more interested in these barrels than in the tools. Sometimes he lay on the ground all day drunk. As we shared the bill for all the food and drink, the three other surveyors, Riggs, Marey, and Wheeler, made it sure that they would have their right share of the brandy, and competed with their boss in drinking. You can imagine what their state was some mornings. I did not drink, so they despised me even more.

Upon arrival to our area of our work, we had found the Western hunters who had been contracted to support us. It did not take me much time to recognise that I could not expect anything from them. They were adventurers, the scum of the West. I do not have to emphasise that in such circumstances the discipline of work, on which our success depended, had become non-existent.

On paper Bancroft was the boss, but nobody obeyed him. They simply laughed at his orders. On such occasions he swore, and then went to the brandy barrel to restore his psychological balance. The three other surveyors were no different. Step by step I became the real leader. I had to be careful and crafty, like the wife who manages her drunkard husband without the man ever recognising it. I was called a greenhorn a dozen times or more a day, but in reality I led the whole team.

My situation would have been hopeless, had I not been supported by Sam Hawkins and the other two scouts, Dick Stone and Will Parker. These three men were solid and honest, and helped me. We made an informal alliance against the others. I was particularly grateful to Hawkins. He was my first teacher in the skills that one needed in the Wild West. His first lesson was to teach me how to handle the best, and most dangerous weapon: the lasso. The little man made me exercise the throwing of the lasso for hours day after day. The target was his horse. He did not let me rest until he was sure that all my throws were successful, even when my horse was galloping fast. After the exercise he always made it sure he had had some encouraging, and positive words.

'This is quite acceptable, young man!' he would say with a challenging good humour. 'But don't imagine that you know everything. You still have a lot to learn. But if you continue like this, you won't be a greenhorn in six or eight years, hehehe!'

In spite of all the difficulties, we advanced with our work, and now we were able to make contacts with the other teams once a week.

We needed to send a messenger to one of them, and to my surprise, Bancroft said that he would ride over to them with

16

one of the men, and inform them of our "achievements". We occasionally received couriers from the other teams, thus we knew that they had progressed very well, and that the team was led by a capable man.

Bancroft wanted to ride over Sunday morning. First, of course, the farewell glasses had to be emptied. Everybody was invited, except me. Hawkins, Stone and Parker found excuses to decline the invitation.

One glass followed the other, and it ended with Bancroft not being able to even totter, let alone get on a horse. I knew it would happen.

I am disgusted by drunkards. To avoid seeing them I went for a walk in the forest. I was musing whether I should go over to the other team instead of Bancroft.

I discussed it with Sam, who pointed to the distance. 'I don't think you will need to ride there, Sir, because two emissaries are coming from them.'

I also spotted the two riders. One was an elderly scout. He had visited us before. The other was a young man, who looked clever, and strong-willed. I had never seen him before.

He greeted me, and asked me who I was. As soon as he heard my name, he exclaimed, 'I know you! You are the young man who works conscientiously, and even instead of his colleagues. I know about you. Let me introduce myself. I'm Mr White.'

He was the boss of our Western neighbour team to whom Bancroft had wanted to ride that morning. I did not know why Mr White had come, but obviously he had a reason.

'I would like to talk to you,' he said. He got off his horse, and joined me. We were walking back to our camp. We had not yet stepped out of the forest when we saw the brandy barrel as well as the drunkards around it on the ground.

'So this is how it is?' he asked. 'Nice ...'

'We are over the most difficult part of our work,' I said, 'and they had to celebrate the success. Mr Bancroft wanted to ride over to you this morning. I'll wake him up.'

17

'Don't bother. Let him sleep it off. It's probably better if I talked to you anyway. Who are those three men at the edge of the clearance, separated from the others?'

'Sam Hawkins, Will Parker, and Dick Stone. Our three most reliable scouts.'

'Ah, Hawkins! He's a strange man! Excellent! I've heard many good things about him. Call them over.'

I waved to them to join us, and then asked the engineer, 'Is there any trouble which is why you visited us, Mr White?'

'Nothing really. I just wanted to have a clear picture. Your work is related to ours. If you are lagging behind, it affects our work too.'

I tried my best to excuse my colleagues. I referred to the difficult terrain, and other problems.

'I know, I know,' he interrupted, 'but I also know that if you had not worked for four people, Bancroft would still be where he started.'

'I don't know why you think this, Mr White. I can assure you that the whole team worked and …'

'Come on! My couriers have been here many times, and had the chance to observe everything. It's good that you are modest, and cover up for your boss, but I will ask somebody else, for example, the excellent Mr Sam Hawkins. Let's sit down somewhere!'

We sat down on the grass in front of my tent. Mr White questioned Hawkins, Stone, and Park thoroughly, and they told him everything honestly. I tried to interrupt, and excuse the lack of progression in vain. Finally the engineer asked for the work journal, and the draft maps. I did not have to obey, but I did, as I saw that he had the best of intentions.

He examined everything carefully, and then said, 'It's obvious that all the notes and drawings were done by one person: you. The rest didn't contribute at all, not even by one letter or one line. The journal,' continued Mr White, 'doesn't list how much work each member of the team carried out. Solidarity is a virtue, but, I think, you take it to the extreme.'

Hawkins showed a crafty face when he remarked, 'Just dive in the inner pocket of this young man's jacket if you don't mind, Mr White. You'll find a tin box there that once upon the time contained sardines in oil. The sardines were consumed, the oil dried, and now there are papers in the box. I would call it a journal, a secret journal. It surely says more than the official journal that attempts to cover up the laziness of his colleagues.'

Sam knew that I kept a diary, and that I carried it in the tin box. I was annoyed that he had disclosed it, but now I had to show it to Mr White.

He flicked through it, and noted, 'In fact I should send these pages to the company's head office. Your colleagues are loafers, and they don't deserve their salaries, while you should get a triple wage. But you do what you want. I can only advise you to keep these notes, because they could be useful one day. Now, let's awake this glorious company!'

He stood up, and started to clap loudly. The men tottered up somehow, and looked at us with uncomprehending faces.

Bancroft complained with lots of dirty words that we had dared to wake him. When he learnt that we had guests, he became a bit more polite. His first action was to offer a glass of brandy to the other engineer.

'Right,' said Mr White, 'we are on the same managerial grade, and I cannot give you any order. There were sixteen drunk men lying around the brandy barrel. I counted them! I suppose you will say that it's none of my business. But you cannot prevent me from reporting to the head office what I have seen here for two hours.'

'For two hours?' Bancroft was shocked. 'Have you been here for two hours?'

'About so,' answered Mr White, 'and so I had enough time to gather information. I've learnt that the whole team here lives as if it was a holiday camp, and only one person works here, the youngest.'

Bancroft jumped to me, and hissed in my face: 'This is what you told him? You rascal! You mean, liar, slanderer.'

'You are wrong,' said Mr White, 'your young colleague behaved like a true gentleman. He didn't complain about you, just the opposite, he tried to excuse you. You should apologise to him.'

'Apologise to him?' laughed Bancroft mockingly. 'Come on! He's a greenhorn. He can't distinguish a triangular from a square, yet he calls himself a surveyor! We would have finished the work a long time ago, had this idiot not been here, and made one mistake after the ...'

I could not keep my cool any more. I had coped with his injustice in silence for months, but this time my blood boiled. I grabbed him by his shoulder, and shook him so much that he could not finish his sentence.

'The brandy is speaking for you, Mr Bancroft,' I said, 'and if I didn't consider that you are completely drunk, I would make you swallow your ugly words.'

Bancroft was not a coward, but he recoiled. Probably my countenance frightened him. But in the next moment he recollected himself, and he immediately turned to his men, the Westerners, for help.

'Mr Rattler,' he shouted to his main bodyguard. 'You, and your men were hired to protect me! And you remained passive while this man attacked me!'

Rattler was a tall, strong, broad-shouldered, and brutal man. There were many stories about his strength, but he was also feared because he was the drinking companion of the boss. He had disliked me for some time, and now he was happy for having the opportunity to challenge me.

He stood next to me, and said: 'Of course, I won't remain passive. This puppy, just because he can lift his hind leg, thinks that he can quarrel with grown men. I will make him think twice before he lies and slanders next time. Take your hand off the engineer, right now!'

The last sentence was meant for me. He grabbed my arm, and squeezed it. I turned to him. As I had two opponents, I had to start with the stronger one. With one motion I freed my arm from his hand.

20

'Did you call me a "puppy" and also a "liar slenderer"? Apologise for these, Mr Rattler, or you'll regret it.'

'Did you hear him?' croaked Rattler. 'He is a complete idiot, isn't he?!'

In the next moment I hit him on the temple with my fist, and he fell on the ground like a sack. For a whole minute there was complete silence, then suddenly one of Rattler's men bellowed, 'Boys! Do we just watch this and do nothing? Let's beat him to death!'

He jumped at me, and I received him appropriately: with a good kick in his stomach. It is a good defence if one stands solidly on the other foot. My kick was rather successful, my opponent bent forward like a penknife, and then collapsed. By then I knelt on his chest, and kept on hitting him. He lost his consciousness.

Then I jumped up, pulled out both of my revolvers, and shouted, 'Who's next?'

Rattler's gang would have liked to take revenge for their two companions, but they looked at hesitatingly at each other. I warned them, 'Listen! Whoever makes a step towards me, or tries to get his weapon, he will be shot dead!'

Then Sam Hawkins stepped next to me, and announced, 'My revolver may go off too, if necessary. Remember that this greenhorn is my protégé. If someone tries something, he will be shot dead. And I mean it, hehehe.'

Dick Stone and Will Parker also joined us indicating that they would not let us down either. This was sufficient caution for the group to turn away from us, and pretend as if nothing had happened. Bancroft considered it better to retreat to his tent.

White looked at me with admiration. 'It's unbelievable. I wouldn't be surprised if the story of this event went around the prairie, and you would be called Shatterhand.'

Hawkins really liked the idea.

'It's a great name,' cried Sam, 'this Shatterhand, hehehe! Excellent! If Sam Hawkins starts to teach a greenhorn, he becomes somebody. Shatterhand, Old Shatterhand.'

White touched my arm; he pulled me aside, and said: 'I really like you. Would you like to join my team?'

'I would like to, but I can't.'

'Why?'

'Because of my responsibilities here.'

'No problem, I'll arrange it.'

'No, Mr White. If I left, the work of this team wouldn't be finished.'

'Why do you care? You have so many enemies here that you would have to leave at some point anyway.'

'So far I've only defended myself. And I'm not afraid of them anyway. My fist gained me some respect. They will think twice before they seek a quarrel with me again.'

'As you wish, my young friend. The man's will is his heaven, but often it's his hell. You would have been useful in my team. Would you accompany me for a while?'

'Are you leaving already?'

'What I saw, I saw. I don't have any inclination to stay here any longer.'

'Would you eat something before you go?'

'I'll eat on the way back, I have enough provisions.'

'Won't you say good-bye to Bancroft?'

'I don't feel like.'

'Didn't you want to discuss something with him?'

'I did, but I can tell you what I wanted to tell him. I wanted to warn him that there are more and more Indians around here.'

'Have you seen them?'

'Only their tracks fortunately. This is the season when the mustangs and the bison migrate to the South. At these times the Indians leave their villages to start hunting. We don't have to be anxious about the Kiowa as we have an agreement with them that they won't interfere with the construction of the railways. But the Comanche and the Apache refused to agree. It's not a concern for me as I'll finish my work here soon, and move elsewhere. But you should hurry. It'll become hotter and hotter around here.

And now, please, mount your horse, and ask Sam Hawkins if he wants to join us.'

Of course, Sam wanted to join us. I entered Bancroft's tent to inform him that Sam and I would accompany White for a part of his journey. As it was a Sunday, I did not need to ask his permission.

'Go to the devil, and I wish he breaks your neck!' he said, and turned his back on me. I could not have imagined how soon his wish would almost come true.

My pinto happily received me when I put the saddle on his back. We had become friends, and it was an excellent horse. I hardly could wait to tell this one day to Mr Henry.

It was a nice autumn morning, and we joyously rode in the beautiful forest. At noon we found a stream, where we rested, and ate a bite.

This is where White departed, while we continued our rest. Before getting up to return to our camp, I leant forward to drink from the crystal clear water of the stream. I noticed something in the bed of the stream. It looked like a footprint. I called Sam, who examined it thoroughly.

'Mr White knew,' he said, 'what he was talking about. We have to be prepared for an Indian attack.'

'Do you think, Sam, that it's an Indian footprint?'

'Definitely. The contours of an Indian moccasin are very distinct. How do you feel about it, young man?'

'Excellent.'

'Are you not afraid?'

'Not at all!'

'Not even anxious?'

'I'm not!'

'Clearly, you have never met Indians.'

'Then the more interested I am! Surely, they are like us; they like their friends, and hate their enemies. As I've never caused them anything bad, and I don't want to in the future either, I have no reason to be fearful of them.'

'This is how a greenhorn talks, hehehe,' mocked Sam. 'You will learn that you'll have to deal with the reds very

23

differently. What will happen won't depend on your will, and I sincerely hope that your experience with them won't cost you a shred of your flesh or your life.'

'What do you think,' I asked, 'when was the owner of this moccasin here?'

'About two days ago. We will find his other footprints if the grass hasn't stood up since then.'

'Was he a scout?'

'Yes, scouting after the bison. As there is no war among the tribes right now, they don't send scouts against each other. This scout was a young man.'

'How do you know that?'

'An experienced warrior wouldn't have stepped in the water where he would leave a highly visible footprint. He is just as stupid as a white greenhorn. Let's go.'

He looked at me grinning, and thus I did not become annoyed, because I understood what was behind his words. He only teased me, and called me stupid, to express that we were friends.

We should have returned to the camp on the path by which we had left, but as a good surveyor, I wanted to study the landscape, and so we made a detour.

Soon we arrived to a pretty valley. It led almost precisely to the North. After some riding Sam lifted his hand above his eyes, and carefully peered to the distance.

'Yes, there they are! The first ones!' he exclaimed.

'Who?' I asked curiously. I also tried to see what he saw, and soon I could see twenty or twenty-five slowly moving dots in the distance.

'Considering the distance, they are too big for deer. Also deer don't live in a herd larger than ten animal,' I said.

'Deer, hehehe,' he laughed, 'by the Canadian River! That was a wonderful guess from you. But otherwise not bad. These are much bigger animals.'

'Bison?'

'That's it! Bison! They started their migration. These are the first to arrive. So Mr White was right in this too. Of the

Indians we have seen only a footprint, but we can see the bison in full living size. And what do you think, young man, what will we do now?'

'We get closer to them.'

'Then?'

'We'll watch them,' I answered, 'because I've never seen bison, and I want to look at them.'

'Watch them, hehehe! You're very modest, but I'm not. Watching them is not enough to me. I also want to hunt them. Don't you know how tasty roast bison is? The ambrosia is nothing compared to it. And I will eat a fillet of bison even if it costs my life! The wind blows from their direction. This is good. One side of the valley is sunny, the other is in shadow. We will hide in the shadow so that they wouldn't notice us too early. Let's go!'

First though he examined his double-barrel gun, Liddy, then he jumped on his horse, and rode on the shadowed side of the valley. I also examined my bear slayer gun, and then rushed after Sam. When he caught sight of me, he waited for me, and asked, 'You don't want to participate in the bison hunt, do you?'

'Very much so.'

'I advise you against it. The bison is not some canary that picks the seeds from your hand. It won't take much, and you'll be trampled into a mush.'

'We will see.'

'Shut up!' shouted Sam at me as ferociously as he had never done before. 'I don't want to take your death on my soul. Other times you can do whatever you want, but now you must obey. Do you understand it?'

'I heard it,' I replied smiling.

'There are about twenty of them, if my eyes didn't cheat me,' continued Sam. 'But some time ago thousands migrated through the prairies. I've seen a herd that consisted of ten thousand animals. Once these were the bread of the Indians, but the whites deprived them of it. The Indians were careful. They killed only as many as they needed. But the whites carried out a real massacre among them. They did it brainlessly, without any reason. And unfortunately, the bison will be extinct. The same thing will happen to the mustangs. Once thousands roamed here, now if we are lucky, we can see a herd of a hundred horses.'

Now we were approaching the herd more carefully, and soon we were about four hundred steps from them. We stopped again. The bison advanced up in the valley, while they were grazing. In the front an old bull walked. It was so big that I was truly impressed. It was about two metres tall, and three metres long. At that time I could not estimate the weight of a bison. Today, I would say it was more than a metric ton. A fantastic amount of flesh and bone! The bull reached a puddle, it lay down, and happily rolled in the mud.

'This is the lead bull,' whispered Sam, 'he is far the most dangerous in the herd. I will aim at the young cow on the right. Watch where I'm aiming: under its shoulder. Then the bullet penetrates its heart. This is the best, moreover, the only safe shot, except if you can hit it between its eyes. But who can be so mad to aim at a bison face to face? Move back to the bushes with your horse. Then you can watch it. But for God's sake, don't come out until I call you.'

True what is true, I was excited, even if I did not show it. But I also felt: why one cares for the cow, when the real challenge was the huge bull.

My horse showed his fear as he had never seen a bison. He was rising and kicking. He would have liked to run away, and I needed all my skills to hold him back.

Meanwhile Sam got to about three hundred steps from the herd. Then he spurred his horse, rode past the bull towards the cow. The cow got frightened, but did not have enough time to run away. I could see that Sam aimed, and shot. The cow trembled, but I did not have enough time to see whether it collapsed or not, because my attention was caught by a more exciting scene.

The bull jumped up, and he stared at Sam Hawkins. What a huge animal this bison was! It had a massive head, broad forehead, and short, but strong upward bending horns. There was thick and bushy hair on its chest, and around its neck. It was surely a dangerous animal, but any hunter must have felt the urge to challenge such an animal.

Did stubbornness make me leave my hiding place? Or did my pinto jump out because of its fear? I do not know. But suddenly I realised that I was galloping towards the bull. It heard my approach, turned towards me, and bowed its head to spike me with its horns. I heard that Sam was roaring something to me in his fright, but I could not understand what. I did not have time to lift my gun, and aim at the bull, so I had to be contented that I had avoided the bison's attack with a quick turn. The horns did not hurt my horse, but they almost touched my leg. My horse made a long leap, and then fell in the middle of the puddle from which the bison had got up. I was very lucky because I could jump off the saddle in time, and in the next moment I was next to my horse with the gun in my hand. The bull approached, and for a moment it turned its side towards me. I aimed, and pulled the trigger. The bull stopped suddenly. Without hesitation I pulled the trigger again. It slowly lifted its head, and roared. Every part of my body trembled. The bull swayed to the right and then to the left, and then collapsed. This was the first time the heavy bear slayer gun saved my life.

I almost ejected a shout of victory, but I also recognised that I had more important tasks. My horse had got out of the puddle, and ran away. I did not care with it for the time being as I was anxious for Sam Hawkins. I noticed him as he was riding up the slope of the valley being followed by a bull that was not much smaller than mine.

The bison, if it is angered, would stubbornly follow its enemy, and can be as fast as the best horse. Sam certainly saw that the distance between him and the bull was reducing. He kept on changing directions to mislead the bull, but these sudden changes exhausted his horse. It was time for me to help him, and with great leaps I ran up on the slope. Sam noticed me, and wanted to come closer to me.

This was a mistake. The bull caught the side of the horse. I saw as it lowered its head, and with a huge upward thrust it raised the horse and the rider into the air. When they fell on the ground, it charged at them, while shaking its head, to trample them to death. Sam cried out with fright I was about a hundred and fifty steps from them, and every second was important. I would have been able to aim better from a shorter distance, but it was clear that any hesitation could cost Sam's life. Even if I could not hit the bull, maybe the sound of the shot would distract him. I stopped, and aimed at the left shoulder of the bull. The shot popped. The bull lifted its head, and it slowly turned. It caught sight of me, and charged towards me, but slightly slower than earlier. This gave me time to quickly load my gun. The bull finally stopped about thirty steps from me, and starred at me with bloodshot eyes. Then he lowered his head, and approached me like the bad fate from which there is no escape. I knelt down, and pushed the butt of my gun hard into my shoulder. Because of my motion the bull stopped again, and it lifted its head. Its mean, threatening eyes were at the same height as the barrel of my gun. I quickly pulled the trigger twice. One bullet went in the left eye of the bull, the other to the right. Its huge body trembled, and then collapsed.

I jumped up to hurry to Sam Hawkins if he needed my help, but he was approaching me already.

'Thank God, you are alive!' I greeted him joyously. 'Are you wounded?'

'Only some strain in my right hip. Or is it the left? I'm not sure,' he answered, 'but it's nothing.'

'And your horse?'

'That's finished, the poor thing. The bull cut its side open. I'll shoot it dead so that it won't suffer anymore. Damned bull! He really made me sweat!'

'Why did you start with that bull?'

'Start! Didn't you see it? I aimed at the cow, and killed it with the first bullet. Then I saw that the bull rushed after me. I quickly shot the second bullet at it, but the only result

28

was that it became angrier. I didn't have time to load my gun again. I had to throw away Liddy so that my two hands would be free to direct my horse better. The poor thing did its job, but then it became the victim.'

'Because you turned too quickly, Sam,' I said, 'if you had turned on a bit larger arc, you would have avoided the bull.'

'Just look at the greenhorn! He teaches the experienced hunter! But I have to admit, you are right. And I thank you very much, because without you I would have ended up like my horse.'

'Come on, Sam! Let's check your horse!'

The horse was in a sad state. Sam searched for his gun, found it, loaded it, and gave the coup de grace to the good, faithful animal. Then he took off the saddle and the reins.

'Now I have to carry these,' he said angrily. 'This is the punishment for the hunter if his passion carries him away.'

'Where will you get another horse?'

'Don't worry! I will catch a mustang. If the bison started their migration, the mustangs will follow soon.'

'I hope I can participate.'

'Yes, you have to learn that too. Now, let's check your bull if it's still alive. Such an old Methuselah is very tough.'

We arrived to the spot, where I killed the first bison in my life. It was dead. As it lay there, I could really see what a colossus it was. Sam leant forward, examined it, and then shook his head.

'Unbelievable!' he said, 'You hit him at the best place. You aimed like an experienced hunter. But apart from the praise, you deserve some scolding too, you know. It was an unbelievable recklessness that you challenged such a bull. Tell me what happened.'

I gave a detailed report to him. He shook his head while listening to my story, then he said: 'Find your horse, and bring it here. We'll put some of the loot on it.'

By the time I found my horse, and returned, Sam had already been kneeling by the cow. With great expertise he skinned one of the legs, and cut out the fillet.

29

'This is how it's done,' he said, 'we will have an excellent dinner. But of this only us, and Will and Dick will dine. If the others want some bison meat, they have to come here for it.'

'If the vultures aren't quicker,' I remarked laughing.

'You are right. Let's cover it with branches, and put heavy stones on the top.'

We covered the whole carcass with branches, and put big stones on it that only a bear could have moved them away.

'And the bulls?' I asked. 'They have much more meat on them than the cow! We shouldn't waste it!'

'What about them?' asked Sam shrugging his shoulder. 'You don't shoot a bull for food, you clever young man! This is at least an eighteen or twenty years old animal. Its meat is so hard that even if we cooked it for days, you could still not chew it. It isn't worth the trouble.'

'And the skin?'

'What about it? Are you a tanner?'

'I've read about a method ...'

'You read! And because it's in a book, it's true, hehehe! There are Westerners who kill animals for the hide, but we aren't one of them right now. Let's go home!'

The road to home was long on foot. I walked next to Sam, leading my horse by the reins as, apart from the meat, it also carried Sam's saddle. When we arrived to the camp, we were surrounded, and their questions rained on us.

'Where have you been? And why did you come back with only one horse? Where's your horse, Hawkins?'

'We went hunting for bison, and a bull stabbed it with its horn,' answered Sam sadly.

Hearing the word "bison" more men came to us.

'Bison? Where? Which direction?'

'About an hour from here, over there,' pointed Sam. 'There were about twenty of them. We killed a cow. We brought only a part of it; you can go for the rest if you want.'

'Of course, we will!' shouted Rattler. 'But how come you killed only one cow from a whole herd? What kind of hunters are you?'

30

'Just go there, and you'll see something else,' replied Sam. 'This young man also killed two bulls. One is at least twenty years old. It was a very dangerous beast.'

'Only a greenhorn can be so stupid to hunt a twenty years old bison!'

They were all laughing.

'I don't think he could have done anything else with the first one. The other was chasing me. This greenhorn saved my life at the last moment.'

'Saved your life? How?'

'I don't want to talk about it,' declined Sam. 'But if you want to eat meat, go, because it's imprudent to go for it in the dark, and it's sunset already.'

Rattler rode away with his mates. Sam waved to Parker and Stone to stay. Four of us started to make the dinner. In the meantime I had something to do in my tent. On the way back to the fire I heard that they were talking about me. My curiosity prompted me to hide behind a bush, and eavesdrop.

'Did he really kill the two bulls alone?' asked Parker.

'I was surprised too,' answered Sam, 'but you'll see this lad will become such a hunter who has very few peers. And it will be soon! His strength is amazing.'

'I know,' nodded Stone, 'last week, after the big rain, he pulled out a loaded wagon from the mud. Still you always scold and criticise him.'

'Because I don't want him to become overconfident,' answered Sam. 'He is excellent material, but a lot has to be chiseled out of him. Overconfidence would do no good to him. I want to be proud of my student.'

'But I think some praising words here and there would be alright,' opined Parker.

'That time will come,' laughed Sam, 'but I really don't want to spoil him. He thinks that I'm a scoundrel, and an ungrateful bloke, but I don't care. The most important is the outcome. Still, tonight he'll get the best part of the fillet. And tomorrow I'll take him to catch a mustang. I know that with this I'll give him the greatest pleasure.'

I stepped out of the bush at this point.

We made a fire, and when it burnt well, we pushed one forked branch into the ground on the right hand side of the fire, and one on the left. We laid a nice, straight stick across them, and it served as a spit. We fixed the huge piece of meat onto it.

Sam Hawkins turned it around above the fire slowly, patiently, and with a great skill. His otherwise serious face gleamed with joy. I was not sure if he was joyous for the excellent dinner, or for the fact that he could show me how to make the perfect bison roast.

He really gave me the best piece of fillet. Its weight was about three pounds, and I ate the whole lot easily. Those who would consider me a glutton for this, do not know the life of the hunters of the Wild West.

Apart from other things, food contains a certain amount of protein and carbohydrate. A civilised kitchen would give both in appropriate quantities. But in the prairies and the forests there is nothing else but meat, and the hunter, who struggles with the vicissitudes of nature from the morning to darkness, sleeps in the open during the night, and has to expand a lot of energy that a townie could not even imagine, has to eat a lot of meat. I once saw an old trapper who ate eight pounds of meat in one meal, and when I asked him if he was well-fed, he smiled, and replied, "What can I do if I don't have more?"

Two hours later the gang arrived, and they started to roast the meat. Their dinner was not peaceful like ours. Although they also had enough food, they argued for the best pieces. They were so hungry that they did not have the patience to wait until the meat was properly cooked. They ate it half raw, and then hurried off to the brandy barrel.

On the following morning I pretended that I wanted to start my work as at other times, but Sam came up to me, and said: 'Leave the tools for today, young man! Get your horse ready, I'm taking you for a little excursion.'

'And my work?'

'Leave it! You have worked hard enough. Anyway, I hope that we will be back by lunchtime. Then you can measure the land as you want.'

I informed Bancroft while Sam borrowed Stone's horse, and we rode away. I asked Hawkins where we were heading to, but he only smiled mysteriously, and replied, 'You'll see, but keep your eyes open.'

After one and half hours we arrived to a prairie that was cut through by quite a broad brook. Because of the brook, the grass grew vigorously there.

After crossing the brook, Sam jumped off his horse, and examined the tracks in the grass for a long time. Then he whistled contented.

'Follow my example, and tie your horse tight to a tree. We'll stay here.'

'Why should we tie the horses?' I asked, although I knew very well what it was about.

'So that you wouldn't lose him forever,' he answered, 'because in certain situations it could easily happen.'

'In what situations?' I continued the play-acting.

'Don't you know it?'

'How would I know it?'

'Don't you even suspect it?'

'Not at all.'

'Then why did we come here?'

'Hm …'

'Try again!'

'Surely not for catching a mustang?' I asked with the face of a simpleton.

'Exactly for that,' he answered.

'Now I understand you,' I nodded, 'because in such a situation our horses could be carried away by the mustangs.'

'How do you know that?'

'I've read about it.'

'Damn you and your books!' he exclaimed, irritated. 'I thought it would be a surprise. I really should meet people who are illiterate!'

'I'm really sorry, dear Sam,' I said laughingly, 'but last night I eavesdropped. So I knew what I should expect today. So, what did you read from the tracks?'

'That the mustangs were here yesterday. But these were only the scouts of the herd. These mustangs are very clever. They send out small groups to the front, and to both sides. They have officers like in an army. The lead horse is always a strong, brave, and experienced stallion. When they graze or migrate, there are stallions on the two sides of the herd. They keep the mares, colts, and fillies in between to protect them. Do you want to catch one?'

'Thank you, but no.'

'Why not?'

'Can you remember when you talked about the stupid, unnecessary slaughter of the bison that also deprives the reds from food? The same applies for the mustangs. They should be free, so thus I would have to have a reason, like needing a horse, for taking the freedom away from one.'

'Right! Let's try it differently. I've taught you how to throw a lasso. I hope you haven't yet forgotten it. You'll have an opportunity now to try your skills. You can consider it an examination.'

'I'm ready.'

'Good. I need a horse, and I'll get it today. I have to tell you that the most dangerous moment is when the lasso is stretched. Then sit tight on the saddle, and make it sure that your horse stands solidly with all its four legs so that you wouldn't simply be dragged away. The horseless man on the prairie is a pitiful phenomenon. I don't want to end up with two horseless men at the end.'

He went quiet suddenly, and pointed to the northern edge of the prairie. The prairie had a slight slope towards that direction, and it was bordered by some hills. From among the hills a horse appeared, a single horse. It was not grazing. It was stepping up on the slope, and turned its head to the right and to the left, and kept sniffing with its wide nostrils.

'Can you see him?' whispered Sam very quietly, although the horse was far enough not to hear his voice. 'This is the forward. It was sent to scout the area. A clever stallion. Just watch how he looks, and sniffs in all directions. Fortunately the wind blows towards us. This is why I chose this place.'

The mustang started to gallop. First forward, then to the right and the left, and at the end it turned around, and soon disappeared behind the hill from which it had arrived earlier.

'Excellent!' Sam was enthusiastic. 'How cleverly it used every bush and the terrain to remain under cover. Not even a red scout could have done it better.'

'Why did it turn back?'

'To inform his four legged general that the route was clear. But he was wrong this time, hehehe! I bet that they will be here in ten minutes.'

'What are your orders, as I don't know anything about mustang hunting?'

'You will ride to the southern end of the prairie, and hide there. I will gallop down on the slope, and hide behind the hill, in the forest. When the herd comes, I'll let them pass, and then I will chase them from behind. If they get to you, charge at them, and chase them back to me. We will drive them up and down in the valley until they get confused. During the chase we will choose the two best horses, and catch them.'

'But we need only one as I have one.'

'Fine. We'll check them, and I will keep the better one. The other can go. But let's start, otherwise we will miss the moment.'

We got on the horses, and departed from each other. Sam galloped to the North, while I rode in the opposite direction. Although my heavy bear slayer gun slightly obstructed me in riding, and I would have liked to hang it on a tree. Sam though had told me many times that a true Wild West hunter would never part with his weapons, because a predator, a bandit, or an Indian might appear at any time.

So, instead of parting with my gun, I only tightened the belt so that it would not dance on my back.

On the top of the hill I hid behind the trees. There I tied my lasso to the saddle, and then I put it in the front of me to be by my hand. I excitedly waited for the arrival of the mustang herd.

In a quarter of an hour I saw small dots at the other end of the prairie. They became bigger and bigger as they came down on the slope. First they looked like sparrows, then cats, then dogs, then calves, and finally they appeared in full size. They were mustangs in gallop.

What a beautiful scene it was! The horses' manes and their tails fluttered in the wind. There were about three hundred of them, and the ground resounded under their hooves. A dun stallion ran at the front. It was a beautiful animal, and probably it would not have been difficult to catch him, but I knew that a true prairie hunter would not choose such a horse, because its colour would be noticed by the enemy from a distance.

It was time that I showed myself. I leapt out of the woods. The dun stallion stopped suddenly as if a bullet had hit him. The herd stopped too, and the horses snorted. Their fright was visible. They turned around as if they had been commanded. The dun stallion galloped to the front of the escaping mustang herd, and soon they all disappeared to the bottom of the valley.

I followed them slowly, and knew that Sam would drive them back to me. However, something hit my senses. When the herd stopped, it seemed to me that there was a mule among them. I could not see it clearly, but it seemed to me that one animal was different from the other horses. So I decided that at the next turn I would investigate it. The animal galloped in the first row of the herd, right after the dun stallion, and it seemed that the mustangs considered it as a deputy leader.

After a short time the scene repeated itself. The herd was heading towards me on the slope. Now I looked at the deputy carefully, and I could see that my eyes had not misled me. It was a light brown mule with darker stripes on its back. I really liked it: in spite of its big head and long ears, it was a pretty animal. Mules are less demanding than horses, their steps are more secure, and they do not become heady at the edge of a cliff. All these are advantages that should not be underestimated. On the other hand, one must know that they are very stubborn. I saw a mule that rooted its legs, and would not move forward. It did not obey even to the whip, or even to the threat of being killed.

It seemed to me that this mule was livelier than any of the mustangs. Its eyes were clever, and its movement was light. I decided that I would catch it. Surely it had had a master before the wild mustang herd swirled it away.

The herd approached for the third time.

I saw Sam Hawkins as he chased them. The herd split up, and tried to escape to the left and right. The mule stayed with the larger herd; right behind the dun stallion. It was a very fast and enduring animal. I started to chase the larger group, and saw that Sam had the same intention.

'Let's take them, you from the right, and I from the left,' he shouted to me.

We spurred our horses, and rode up to the mustangs, and soon we were among them. They fled in all directions like the chicken when a hawk strikes. The mule and the dun stallion broke off from the herd, but stayed together.

'Are you after the stallion? Then you're a greenhorn, hehehe,' he shouted, 'I'll go after the mule.'

I did not enlighten him about his mistake. He would not have heard my answer because of his own laughter. I gave the mule to him. Sam had got close enough to throw the lasso. It was a perfect throw, as the noose fell on the neck of the mule. Now Sam should have done what he taught me so many times: stopping, raising the horse, and gathering all the strength not be torn off from the saddle by the jerk. He did all these, but a moment too late. He flew out of the saddle, and rolled onto the ground. His horse almost fell over too, but regained its balance, and obeying to the pull of the lasso, it ran after the mule. I hurried to Sam to make sure that he was in one piece. He was already on his feet, and looked after the animals in disbelief.

'Damn it,' he swore, 'now I lost Dick's horse too.'

'Did you hurt yourself?'

'Get off the saddle and give me your pinto!' he shouted.

'What for?'

'To go after them. Get off!'

'I won't,' I replied, and spurred my horse to chase after the two animals.

I had little hope that I could catch up with them, but I was lucky. There was a disagreement between the mule and the horse. One wanted to go to one direction, the other to another, however the lasso connected them. I caught the lasso, and I twisted it several times around my hand to reduce its length. I let the mule run for a while, but then I kept on pulling it back with the lasso, and it had to give in, otherwise it would have strangled itself. There was one more jerk, and the animal collapsed on the ground.

'Just hold the mule until I get there, and then let it go!' Sam shouted.

The mule was kicking around wildly, but Sam was not frightened, and got very close to it.

'Now let it go,' he said.

I dropped the lasso. The mule gained air, and jumped up, but Sam leapt on its back. The animal stood motionless for a few seconds. However, it did not last long. It started to kick again. It raised its front, then its back legs, and finally it jumped up with all four legs to throw Sam off.

'You can jump about, mate,' laughed Sam. 'Just watch it, greenhorn! It will gallop away with me. You just stay here. I'll bring it back in ten minutes nicely. By then this mule will be like a lamb.'

Sam was mistaken. The mule devised a different tactic. It lay down suddenly, and started to roll. Sam had just enough time to jump off otherwise the animal would have broken all his bones. I quickly dismounted, picked up the lasso, and with lightning speed I twisted it around a nearby tree. The mule wanted to escape, but the lasso stretched, and the animal collapsed again.

Sam made a few steps back, felt his ribs, then he showed a face as if he ate sour cabbage with plum jam.

'Let's forget about this rascal,' he waved with despair, 'It's a waste of time to try to tame it. It's so stubborn that we won't get anywhere with it.'

'Come on! This is a mule! Its father was a donkey, and it won't make us ashamed! I will teach it obedience.'

I took the lasso from the tree, and stood above the mule with my legs spread. When it regained its consciousness, the mule jumped up, but by then I was already on its back. I knew that everything depended on my ability of pressing it hard enough with my thighs. The mule tried to throw me off in all possible ways, but I was holding the lasso by the noose. Whenever it tried to throw me off, I just pulled the noose. With this I told the mule that its challenges would not go unpunished. It was a real wrestling match. The sweat was rolling off me, but the mule was sweating even more, and its muzzle was foaming. Its challenges became weaker and weaker, its angry snorts gradually softened, and finally it surrendered. I took a deep breath as I also felt being at the edge of my strength. All my muscles were aching, and I felt as if my tendons were torn.

'What a man!' exclaimed Sam with an honest respect in his voice. 'You are stronger and more stubborn than a wild mule. If only you could see yourself in a mirror!'

'Why?'

'Your eyes are goggled, your lips are swollen, and your face is bluish!'

'The greenhorn deserves it,' I replied mockingly, 'for not letting the mule throw him off, as the experienced hunter showed him!'

'I deserved this, hehehe,' grinned Sam. 'And how are you with your ribs and other bones? They are all fine?'

'I don't know yet, I'll check them later. What a beast! I hope I managed to teach it to be obedient.'

'That's for sure. It lays here so weak that I feel sorry for it. You can put a saddle on him. I have to say, I'm envious of you. It's a much better animal than the dun stallion.'

'I wasn't interested in the dun stallion at all,' I replied. 'I wanted the mule from the first moment because even if I'm a greenhorn, I know that this mule is worth much more than a dun stallion.'

'Just look! Did you learn this from books too?'

'Yes, Sam! But console yourself. I didn't tame the mule for myself, but for my dear teacher. Please, take it.'

The two of us made the exhausted animal stand. It stood quietly, and its legs were trembling. It did not resist even when we put our reserve saddle on it. Sam mounted it, and the mule, which had been so wild just before, obeyed to every command.

'It already had a master,' remarked Sam, 'who had to be a good rider, and knew about horse training. I'm very happy for this mule. You know, I already have a name for it. It will be Mary. I once had a mule, and its name was Mary. At least I don't have to think of a new name.'

'So, the mule is Mary, and the gun is Liddy. Very good.'

'They are sweet names, aren't they?

'I'm happy that everything ended so well.'

'Not really. If the gang learns in the camp how I got this mule, there'll be some mocking and teasing.'

'They won't learn it from me,' I replied. 'Let's not waste time on this. Surely I won't expose my teacher and friend to the mocking of stupid blokes.'

Sam's small, crafty eyes twinkled, and I almost thought that he was shedding tears. We shook hands.

'Then it's all great,' exclaimed Sam happily. 'And I'm your friend too. We can now head home. Let's go.'

I tied Dick Stone's horse to mine, and we rode away. Sam did not stop being mesmerised by Mary's obedience. 'She had a good school,' he kept on repeating, 'she's not more than five years old, and she's not only a quick learner, but also a character.'

'Like me?' I asked jokingly.

'There's something in that,' replied Sam seriously. 'I had two bad days, but they were very good learning for you. You got acquainted with bison and mustang hunting. Did you expect them to happen so quickly?'

'Why not? Here in the West one must be prepared for everything. Of course, there are more dangerous animals to hunt than bison,' I opined, 'like bear hunting.'

'You mean the yellow-nosed black bear?'

'No, I meant the king of the mountains, the grey bear.'

'What? A greenhorn, like you, shouldn't even think of it. The grizzly on its hind legs is two feet taller than you are, and with a single bite it can mill the head of its victim. It's undefeatable.'

'There's no such animal that a man cannot defeat with his mind and strength,' I argued.

'Did you read this too?' asked Sam.

'Yes.'

'I think these books have to bear the blame for so many irresponsible actions,' Sam teased me.

I let his remark go, and then said, 'Of course, it depends on the man. The brave would face it, the coward flees.'

'I tell you, fleeing from a grizzly is not cowardice. Just the opposite, not fleeing is suicide.'

'But there are situations when fleeing is impossible. If the bear surprises me, and there is no time for fleeing, I have to face it. And I cannot flee from it if it attacks my friend, and I have to help him. Then it is a struggle for life or death. The victory, the bear paw, the ham, and the fur are even more pleasing then.'

'You are an incorrigible man, and you really frighten me to death! But it's true, the bear paws are the best food in the world,' added Sam, 'better than the best bison loin.'

'But we don't have to be concerned about this. There are no grey bears around here.'

'You are wrong,' laughed Sam. 'There are grey bears in the mountains. Sometimes they come down to the prairies along the rivers. I don't want to talk about this!'

Neither he, nor I suspected that this conversation would become horrifying reality on the following day.

Our talk had to stop as we got close to our camp. The team, it appeared, had pulled themselves together while Sam and I had been away. Bancroft probably wanted to show that they could advance without me. They had made a good progress, while we had been after the mustangs.

'Look, what a nice mule!' shouted someone, when we arrived. 'Where did you get it, Hawkins?'

'Got it by mail,' answered Sam morosely. 'Do you want to see the envelope?'

There were some who laughed, and some who swore, but Sam achieved his aim: they left him alone. I did not know what he told Dick and Will, because I immediately started my work. By the evening we had advanced so far that I knew that the next day we would work in the valley, where we had hunted the bison.

Indeed, we moved camp early in the morning. Hawkins soon disappeared, as he wanted to train his new mule. Stone and Parker joined him for some riding.

We, the surveyors, set up our measuring rods, and tools. During the work we got to the place, where I had killed the two bison. To my surprise, I could not see the carcass of the old bull. A broad track showed in the grass that it was pulled to the bushes.

'How can it be possible?' Rattler was clearly surprised too. 'I examined it, and it was dead, but perhaps it still had enough strength to pull itself away.'

'The pest!' I exclaimed. 'When I saw it last time, it was dead. Somebody pulled it away. Perhaps the Indians. We saw their footprints.'

'That huge, heavy carcass? Only a greenhorn can say such a stupid thing. The bison recovered, and moved to the bushes to die there,' trumped Rattler rudely.

I shrugged my shoulder, and returned to my work, while Rattler, with some of his men, followed the track, and they disappeared into the bushes. I barely touched the tools, when frightened cries resounded from the bush. Three gunshots popped in quick succession.

'Climb up on the trees, otherwise we are dead,' shouted someone. I could recognise Rattler's voice. 'Fortunately it cannot climb on trees.'

"What is he talking about?" I mused, but I did not want to abandon my work. Then one of Rattler's men rushed out of the bushes in mindless fear.

'What's up? What happened?' I shouted to him.

'A bear! A huge grey bear!' he answered panting, and then rushed away.

In the next moment I heard a scream. 'Help! Help!'

Such a scream is ejected only when one is in the throat of death. I did not know who it was, but I wanted to help him. I left my gun in my tent, which was not irresponsible in the current situation as it was the hunters' task to guard us, so that we could work safely. I had only my Bowie knife, and two revolvers with me. These were ridiculous weapons against a grey bear. It is nine feet tall and it weighs eight hundred pounds. Its strength is beyond imagination. It can carry away a deer or a colt easily. Not even a rider can escape from it, as it can outrun any horse. This is why the Indians consider the killing of a grey bear to be a heroic deed.

Following the tracks, I rushed among the bushes. The bear carried the carcass there. As quickly as I could, I broke through the thicket. The screams came closer and closer. But I also heard something else: the hum of the bear. In fact, grizzlies do not hum, but eject short snorts, and strange hisses when they are angry or wounded. This was the sound that I heard.

At last I arrived. The mauled carcass of the bull was in front of me. On the trees Rattler's men stooped. However, one of them obviously climbed clumsily, and the bear caught him. He held himself on a strong branch. His torso was safe, but the bear was tearing of his legs and thighs with its horrible claws. The fate of the unfortunate man was sealed; he was beyond help. But I could not watch his death without doing something. Without hesitation, I picked up a gun from the ground and, as it was discharged, I held it by the barrel, and jumped over the carcass of the bull. I hit the bear's head as hard as I could with the butt of the rifle. The butt of the gun splintered on the hard skull. My only achievement was that I distracted the animal from his victim. It very slowly turned its head as if asking: who could be the stupid being that dared to attack it. It seemed that it hesitated if it should finish off his victim or deal with me. This moment saved my life at least for the time being. I pulled out one of my revolvers, and jumped towards the bear. It stood with its back to me, but when turned its head I shot four bullets into its eyes. Then I jumped aside, and pulled out my knife.

I was very lucky that I instinctively moved. The blinded beast quickly turned away from the tree, and leapt on the place where it had seen me earlier. As its paw hit the air only, the bear started to search for me, and hissed in its mindless anger. Standing on four paws it clawed at the ground. Maybe its anger prevented it from utilising its smelling sense. Its searching for me lasted for a good ten minutes. In the end its pain forced it to deal with its wounds. The bear sat down, and reached for its eyes with its paws. This was my moment! I jumped at it, and stabbed it twice between its ribs. The bear tried to hit me again, but I quickly moved away. I missed its heart with the knife, and now the bear hit about with doubled rage, and tried to find me again. However, it had lost a lot of blood because of the stab wound, and it clearly had become weaker. It sat down on the ground again, and rubbed its eyes with its paws. I used the opportunity, and stabbed it again. The bear tried to get back on its paws in vain. After a few more attempts it stretched out, and lay motionless.

'Hurrah! The beast is dead!' shouted Rattler from the top of the tree. 'It was hot!'

'For me, not for you,' I replied angrily, 'but you can come down now.'

'Not yet! Check if it's really dead.'

'It won't hurt anyone anymore.'

'Don't be so sure! You don't know how enduring such a beast can be. Try to turn it!'

'You should turn it! You're the famous hunter, and I'm only a greenhorn.'

I rather turned to the victim. He was still hanging from the branch, and looked at me with glassy eyes. He was in a terrible state. He was not screaming or jerking anymore.

'Come and help me with this unfortunate man!'

Nobody moved. The famous hunters had not come down from the trees until I turned the bear several times, thus convincing them that they had nothing to fear. They climbed down, and helped me to take down their companion from the tree. His hands held the branch so tight that his fingers had to be straightened one by one. We put the poor, horribly devoured man on the ground. He was already dead.

I was indignant that his mates turned away from him so indifferently. They were grouping around the bear. Rattler was rubbing his hands.

'Now comes the reward!' he cried. 'It wanted to eat us, but now we'll eat it! I'll cut out its ham, and paws.'

He pulled his knife to carry out his plan, but I stepped in his way.

'Why didn't you pull your knife, while it was still alive?' I asked angrily. 'That would have been more honourable! Now, it's too late!'

'What? Do you want to deny me my share?'

'I do, Mr Rattler!'

'On what ground?'

'On the ground of the indisputable right of the hunter: I killed the bear.'

'It's a rotten lie! What do you think of this greenhorn?' he turned to his companions. 'He wants to make us believe that he killed the bear with his little knife! We shot it before

45

we climbed on the tree! There was barely any life in the bear when he came.'

'Put your knife away, Mr Rattler,' I shouted at him, 'or I will teach you to respect my words.'

He ignored me, and leant forward again with his knife in his hand to stab it in the skin of my bear. I grabbed him with both hands by his waist, lifted him, and threw him towards the nearest tree with such a strength that all his bones were crackling. Then, cautiously, to be ready for all eventualities, I pulled out my other, still loaded, revolver.

Rattler got to his feet. With bloodshot, rolling eyes he looked at me, and held his knife towards me.

'You'll pay for this, you greenhorn!' he roared. 'You've attacked me twice! I'll make it sure that you don't try it for a third time!'

He approached me while swinging his hand that held his knife. I aimed my revolver at him, and said, 'One more step, and you'll get a bullet in your head. Throw your knife away! I'll count up to three and if you don't obey, I'll sort you out in the same way as I sorted out the bear! One, two ...'

He did not throw away the knife, and I think I would have really shot him, even if not at his head, but at his hand at least, because I could not step back from my words. Fortunately, I did not have to carry out my threat, because a strange voice sounded from the direction of the trees.

'Are you mad, gentlemen? Two white men fighting each other in the wilderness? Put your weapons away!'

We all turned to the direction of the voice. From behind one of the trees a lean, hunchbacked man stepped out. His clothing and weapons were similar to that of the Indians'. Indeed, at first sight we could not decide if he was a white man or an Indian. Only his suntanned face showed that he was born as a white man. His dark hair reached his shoulders. He wore Indian leggings, a hunting shirt, and simple moccasins. In spite of his hunchback, he did not look strange, and his exceptionally clever face and eyes attracted me in the first moment. Unfortunately, there are stupid

46

people who can laugh at other people's disabilities. Such a man was Rattler.

'Look who's coming there,' he shouted. 'Is it a dwarf or an elf? What a mongrel lives in this forest, hahaha!'

The stranger measured him up from top to bottom with a contemptuous look, and replied calmly, 'Thank your fate that you were born with a healthy body. But it's not all. The heart and the mind are more important than the body, and you cannot challenge me in knowledge, bravery, and character.' With his foot he touched the grey bear, and continued, 'This is the bear that we wanted to hunt. Unfortunately, we arrived too late!'

'Have you met this bear?'

'We saw its track the day before yesterday. Since then we have followed it through bushes, forests, and on the most difficult terrains. And now we have to accept the fact that somebody else killed it.'

'You are speaking in plural. Are you not alone?'

'No, I came with two of my excellent friends.'

'Who are they?'

'First, I would like to know who you are, and what you are doing around here, because there are more evil men than good ones,' he said calmly, and glanced at Rattler and his men before turning back to me.

'We are surveyors,' I felt no reason to doubt that he would know the meaning of the word, 'under the direction of an engineer. Our team consist of four surveyors, three scouts, and a dozen prairie hunters for protecting us. The commander of the prairie hunters is this gentleman there,' I pointed to Rattler.

'Gentleman?' the stranger repeated the word with an emphasis. 'Anyway, I can see that you don't need protection. And what's your work about, if I may ask? Why do you survey the land?'

'For a railway line.'

'Which will cross here?'

'Yes.'

'So, have you bought the land?' he asked in sharp voice.

'I don't know anything about that,' I replied, 'I've got the commission to do the work, and the rest has nothing to do with me.'

'Is it so? But you surely know that this land belongs to the Indians, more precisely, to the Mescalero tribe of the Apache, who did not sell it, and did not allow anyone to build railways across it.'

'What are you harping on about?' Rattler shouted at him. 'Don't interfere with us, and with things that are none of your business.'

'I do interfere, because I'm an Apache.'

'You? Ridiculous! Everyone can see on your face that you've never been an Indian.'

'I was born as a white, that's true. But I belong to the Apache. I'm Klekih-Petra.'

At that time I did not know that the two words of the name meant "White Father" in the language of the Apache.

Apparently Rattler had heard the name before, because he bowed mockingly. 'Klekih-Petra, the famous teacher of the Apache,' he said. 'Too bad that you are a hunchback, because the red rascals must laugh at you a lot.'

'You don't have to worry about that, Sir,' said Klekih-Petra. 'I got used to being ridiculed by rascals, but not by good people, like the Apache. As now I know who you are, I'll tell, or rather show, you who my companions are.'

He shouted something in an Indian language, and two men stepped out from the forest. With slow, gracious steps they approached us. They were Indians, and I recognised right away that they were father and son.

The older was medium built, very muscular man. His face was characteristically Indian, but less emphasised. His eyes were calm, almost gentle. His noble face showed thinking, reflection, and a rich internal life. He tied his black hair to a helmet-like shape. A huge eagle feather stood out of it. It was the symbol of the office of the chief. His fringed leggings, moccasin, and coat were simple, but finely

48

produced. There was a knife in his belt. Many bags, with the necessities that he needed in the forest, hung from this belt. His medicine bag and his peace pipe, whose head was made of the sacred clay, hung from his neck. He held a double-barrel rifle whose wooden parts were decorated with silver nails. Later his son, Winnetou, inherited this gun, and there was no man in the West, who had not heard of the famous silver gun.

His son's dress was similar, but more elaborate. His moccasins were decorated with porcupine quills. His leggings, and coat were embroidered with red shapes. His medicine bag and the calumet hung from his neck on a string, just like his father's. He had a knife in his belt, and a double-barrelled gun. The most striking was his hair. Many ladies would have envied such a hair. It rolled down onto his shoulders in bluish-black thick waves. The colour of his face was like dim bronze. It was lighter than his father's.

Later I learnt that he was born almost on the same day as I. He impressed me deeply from the first sight. I felt that I met an exceptionally intelligent young man, who was equipped with special skills and talent. He also looked at me searchingly with his serious, dark, velvety eyes, which lightened up for a moment as if he was greeting me.

'This is Inchu Chunna, that is, Good Sun, the chief of the Mescalero Apache, recognised as the top chief of all the Apache,' said Klekih-Petra pointing at the older Indian. 'His son, Winnetou, has carried out so many heroic deeds that would not be misplaced even for an experienced warrior.'

Rattler laughed scornfully, and exclaimed, 'You should have said he "committed" these acts as the reds' deeds are thefts, robberies, and knavery.'

The three men simply ignored the serious insult. They leant over the bear, and examined it.

'A knife killed it, not a bullet,' announced Klekih-Petra. So, he had listened to my argument with Rattler!

'What does a hunchback schoolmaster know about bear hunting!' cried Rattler, 'Once we skin the bear, everybody can see which wound killed it. A greenhorn won't cheat me out of my rights!'

Winnetou pointed at one of the blood stained wounds of the bear, and asked: 'Whose knife made this wound?'

'Mine.'

'Why didn't you my white brother use your gun?'

'It wasn't with me.'

'I can see many guns on the ground.'

'They aren't mine. Their owners threw them away when they climbed up on the trees.'

'Did the squirrels run on the trees, abandoning their companion whom the bear attacked, and caught?' asked Winnetou surprised. 'Their action was inglorious. Why do they still mock you as a greenhorn?'

'I've been around only for a short time.'

'The palefaces are strange people. The Indians are more just. We can differentiate between bravery and cowardice.' He spoke perfect English.

'This young paleface deserves praise, and not criticism, especially from those who climbed on the trees in their fright,' said Winnetou's father. 'He's no longer a greenhorn. But let's look around a bit, what are the palefaces doing on our land?'

He headed to the clearing, where we had left our tools.

'What are you doing with these rods,' he asked turning to me, 'and why are you measuring the land?'

'We are making the preparations for the path of the Fire Mustang,' I replied.

His eyes flashed. 'And do you belong to these people?'

'Yes.'

'And why are you doing it? Are you paid for it?'

'Yes.'

He measured me up with a contemptuous look, and then he turned to Klekih-Petra.

'Your teachings sound nice, but the facts often show something else. Here is this brave-hearted, open-faced, honest-eyed paleface, of whom one could believe that he is different from the others. But he doesn't deny that he is ready to commit any villainy if he's paid for it.'

I remained silent in my shame, because I felt that he was right. I could not refer to any moral principle or right to excuse what I was doing.

The engineer came out of his tent with the other three surveyors. He looked at the huge body of the bear, and the Indians perplexed. Before he could have asked what had happened, Rattler stepped up to him.

'Bear paws for lunch, and bear ham for dinner today! As you can see we had a special prey today. I killed it!' he said.

The three strangers looked at me expectantly for my reply to this shameless lie.

'You shouldn't believe a word of this, Mr Bancroft,' I said, 'I stabbed the bear to death. When Sam Hawkins returns, he will tell us if a bullet or a knife killed it. I think nobody can doubt his expertise in this.'

'I don't give a whistle to his expertise!' shouted Rattler. 'With my men I will skin it right now, and whoever wants to obstruct us, he will get half a dozen bullets in his body!'

'It would be better if you buried your companion, whom you let down,' I said.

'What? Did the bear kill someone?' asked the engineer frightened.

'Yes, Rollins has died,' replied Rattler, while shrugging his shoulder. 'The poor man! He died because of this stupid greenhorn.'

'How? I don't understand it.'

'He wanted to climb on the tree, like we did, as this was the only thing that we could do then. Then this greenhorn came, and made the bear angry. Rollins was the closest to the bear, so it caught him. He's responsible for his death!' He pointed at me.

'So Rollins would have escaped if I hadn't intervened?' I cried angrily.

'Yes,' said Rattler, and pulled his revolver, because he expected an attack from me.

'But he was already mauled when I arrived!'

'It's a lie!'

'Then you can hear or feel the truth now!'

I knocked the gun from his hand, and I slapped him on his face so hard that he flew for six steps. He quickly got up, and came rushing at me with a knife in his hand. With one blow I knocked him out, and he lay at the front of my feet unconsciously.

'Uff! Uff!!' said Inchu Chunna with appreciation, while one of the surveyors, Wheeler, murmured, 'He deserves the Shatterhand name.'

'I have to ask you, Mr Bancroft,' I told the engineer, 'to make order here. You can see what happened. You know that Rattler always seeks to quarrel with me. I could now kill him according to the law of the prairie. I don't have to spare someone's life who attacks me with a knife, or a revolver. Something though holds me back from killing a human. However, my patience can also run out!'

'I'll talk to him, when he recovers,' said the engineer unwillingly.

Inchu Chunna turned to the engineer: 'I can see that you are the boss of the palefaces. Am I right?'

'Yes,' answered the engineer.

'Then I have to talk to you.'

'I'm listening.'

'Not like this. We are all standing. Men sit down when they have a council.'

'Do you want to be my guest?'

'How could I be your guest, when we are standing on my land, in my forest? But I allow you to sit down for the council. Who are those palefaces, who are coming there?'

'They also belong to us,' answered the engineer as Sam Hawkins returned with Dick, and Will.

Sam immediately saw that serious things had happened while they were away. He pulled me aside.

'Who are these Indians?' he asked.

'The chief of the Apache and his son,' I replied.

'And the third?'

'His name is Klekih-Petra. Rattler referred to him as a schoolmaster.'

'Klekih-Petra, the white teacher of the Apache,' nodded Sam. 'He's a very famous man, you know. He has lived with the Apache for a long time, and he's as respected as their greatest magic men. How did they get here?'

With a few words I explained the events, and showed him the body of the grey bear.

'What a grizzly!' Sam whistled. 'A really huge one. How did you dare to fight with it, tell me!'

'I didn't have a choice,' I replied.

'With a knife against a grizzly! A true greenhorn! Tell me, why did you bring your heavy bear slayer gun?'

'It wasn't with me.'

'In the most important moment? Remember, young man, a true hunter never parts with his gun! It was a good lesson to you, even if it ended luckily.'

The two Indians, and Klekih-Petra sat down on the grass opposite Bancroft. They had not started the council yet as they were waiting for Sam's opinion of the bear.

'It was very stupid to shoot at the bear, and then climb up on the tree,' he said. 'If the hunter is not certain that he could kill the grizzly, he shouldn't shoot. If the bear is left alone, it rarely attacks humans. But if it's angered, it will want its revenge. Who shot at the bear?'

'I did,' shouted Rattler. He had by now pulled himself together, and joined us as if nothing had happened.

'Where did you aim at?' asked Sam.

'At its temple,' replied Rattler.

'True,' announced Sam, 'I found the trace of the bullet.'

'Did you hear it?' Rattler looked around victoriously. 'The bear is mine, Sam Hawkins said that I hit it.'

'Just a moment!' interrupted Sam. 'Your bullet only grazed its ear. The grizzly wouldn't die from that, hehehe! No, Mr Rattler! It died of a stab in its heart. You hardly could stab it from the top of the tree. Who did it?'

'I did,' I said quietly.

'Then the bear is yours. But good hunting manners require that you share your loot with your companions. The skin is yours, the meat is common, but you have the right to decide on the distribution of the various parts of the animal. Am I right, Mr Rattler?'

'Go hang yourself!' growled Rattler at him, and went to the wagon, where the brandy barrel stood. I knew that he would drink himself drunk.

Bancroft now turned to the Indian chief, and asked him about his wishes.

'I don't have wishes, but commands,' said the Apache chief proudly.

'And we don't accept commands,' replied the engineer in a similar manner.

'Then I would like to put a few questions to you,' said Inchu Chunna after he had suppressed his anger over the engineer's words. 'Do you have a house?'

'I have,' replied Bancroft.

'Does it have a garden?'

'Yes.'

'And if your neighbour wanted to build a road across your garden, what would you say?'

'I wouldn't allow it.'

'You answered correctly, my white brother. The land beyond the Rocky Mountains, and on the left bank of the great Mississippi River belongs to the palefaces. But they have come to our country in search of gold and gems in our mountains. They also chased away our mustangs, and slaughtered our bison. And now they are building a path for the Fire Mustang to bring even more palefaces, who will take away what the others have left to us. Is it just?'

Bancroft remained silent.

'Don't we also have the right to live?' continued the chief. 'We were chased away from our land, and soon there will be no place where we can lie down to sleep. Why are you doing this? Don't you have enough room back home? Klekih-

Petra, who's sitting next to me, has spoken a lot about your holy book, which is the law of love. But is it love when you want to destroy us? Your law has two faces: it allows everything to you, and nothing to us. This land is ours. Who allowed you to build a path on it?'

'I didn't need any permission.'

'Why? Is it your country?'

'I think so.'

'No, it's ours, and I forbid you to survey this land.'

The engineer could not answer.

As the chief's logic pushed him into the corner, he turned to me. 'Explain it to him that he's wrong, and we're acting lawfully.'

'Don't expect this from me, Mr Bancroft,' I replied, 'I do the work that I was contracted for. I'm not a solicitor, and I cannot make speeches.'

'There's no need for speeches,' stated Inchu Chunna firmly. 'I'm leaving now with my son, Winnetou, but we will come back in an hour's time. You can think it over. If you leave in peace, we'll remain brothers. If you continue, we'll dig up the war hatchet. Haw, I have spoken!'

He stood up, and Winnetou immediately followed his example. The two Indians left through the valley, and they soon disappeared. Klekih-Petra remained seated. He rested his head on his hand, and he was deep in his thoughts.

'Where have they gone?' asked the engineer.

'To their horses,' answered the hunchbacked man.

'Did you come on horseback?'

'Of course, but when we saw that we had caught up with the bear, we hid our horses. One cannot approach a grizzly on horseback.'

'And are you not joining them?'

'I will. But I want to make a last attempt to persuade you. The chief is not joking. He is very angry. I advise you not to ignore his words.'

'This is stupid,' said Bancroft impatiently, and waved the argument away. 'It's all in vain.'

'Then I give up too,' said the little man, 'but you'll have to give your answer to the chief when he returns.'

He sighed deeply, and left following his two companions. There was an infinite sadness on his face. Something spurred me to hurry after him.

'Would you allow me to accompany you for a while?' I asked him.

'I'd be very happy,' he replied. 'For some reason I have good feelings about you. You are at the beginning of your journey, and I'm at the end.'

'Do you like Indians?'

'I like humans. In the Indians I like what is nice, good, and noble. You can find these in every race, every people. But you can find the opposite too, unfortunately.'

'I can see that you're an educated man,' I said. 'How did you get to this wild part of the world?'

'I was a revolutionary in Germany when I was young. I was one of their leaders. Many, many fell in battle! Others died behind prison walls. I escaped. In the morning before I reached the border, as I was hounded by the police, I ran through a little garden of a cottage. There two woman, a mother and her daughter, hid me for the sake of their husbands as I was a comrade. The young husband fell on the battlefield, the old was sentenced to prison. I had a bad conscience as I was their leader, and I led them to defeat. I fled from the world, and from the people. Then I saw the red men in despair. I knew that their fate was sealed, and that I could not save them, but there was one thing I could do. I went to the Apache to teach them. I wish you could know Winnetou better! He actually is my own work. This young man would be a great military leader or a ruler in Europe if he had been born high in the social ladder. He is my spiritual child; I love him more than myself.'

He fell silent, and lowered his head. I was deeply moved, and said nothing. I took his hand in mine, and pressed it warmly. He understood me, and gave me the opportunity to recognize this by a slight nod, and a return squeeze. After a while he asked quietly, 'Why do I tell you all these things even though I met you only today? It seems that there are moments, when opening your heart to someone is a necessity of life. Or do I feel that this is the last time in my life when I can tell these things to someone? The old men are like the dry leaves, the slightest wind can tear them from the tree, and swirl them away ...'

The time had passed quickly, and we saw that Inchu Chunna was approaching with his son. They were coming on horseback. Winnetou led Klekih-Petra's horse by the reins. They exchanged a few words with Klekih-Petra, then they headed towards our camp. They passed by the wagon. Rattler was sitting there. His face was red and swollen from my blows. He stared at us. I involuntarily felt my revolver, so vile and threatening were the debased man's eyes.

The two Indians got off from their horses, and walked to the centre of the camp. The engineer came to them.

'Have you, my white brothers, thought over what I said?' asked Inchu Chunna.

The engineer gave an evasive answer. 'I cannot decide alone,' he said, 'I'm sending a man to Santa Fe to ask for an order what to do. The answer will be here in a week.'

'I can't wait until then. You should give the answer now.'

'For the time being we are staying,' said Bancroft.

'Then we will leave now,' said the chief, 'but the peace between us has ceased.'

They headed for their horses.

Rattler approached with a tin cup filled with brandy. I thought he had it in for me, but he went to the two Indians and said with a slurred tongue, 'If the redskins drink with me, we will leave, otherwise we won't. Let's start with the boy. Here you are, have the fire water, Winnetou.'

He held out the cup towards the young Indian. Winnetou made a repellent gesture.

'What? Do you refuse a drink with me? That's an insult. Then you get the brandy in your face, cursed redskin. Lick it off, if you don't want to drink it!'

Before anybody could have intervened, he hurled both the cup, and its content at the young Apache's face. That was an insult for an Indian, punishable by death. This time the punishment was not so severe, but came very quickly. Winnetou's fist hit Rattler's face so hard that he fell on the ground. He staggered to his feet. I was about to intervene as I expected him to assault Winnetou, but he did not. He stared at the young Apache, swore, and then tottered back to the wagon.

Winnetou dried off the brandy, and then showed the same rigid, immobile face as his father. Nothing was visible on him of what was going on in his mind.

As they were going, suddenly Rattler's voice resounded from the wagon.

'Go to hell, you red dogs! I will send one of you, the young one, to hell myself!'

He picked up a gun, and aimed at Winnetou, who was the closest to him.

'Winnetou, look out!' cried Klekih-Petra frightened, and jumped in front of the young Indian to protect him with his own body. The shot popped, Klekih-Petra jerked his hand to his chest, swayed, and then crashed on the ground.

All this happened in half a minute; so suddenly and unexpectedly that nobody could understand the situation at first. Everybody was paralysed. Then the silence of the shock changed to excited shouting and running. Only the two Indians were quiet. They silently knelt down by their friend, who sacrificed himself for his beloved student. They examined his wound. The bullet entered the ribcage by the heart. From the wound the blood shot out. I leant over Klekih-Petra who was lying in the grass. His eyes were closed and his face was losing its colour at a frightening pace; it was sunken and pale-yellow.

'Take his head on your lap,' I asked Winnetou, 'because if he opens his eyes, and sees you, his death will be lighter.'

The young Apache did not say anything, did not look at me, but he obeyed. Not one of his eyelashes moved when he

58

sat down on the ground next to his teacher, and with a gentle movement took his head on his lap. The dying man opened his eyes, and saw Winnetou as he leant over him. There was a happy smile on his tortured face.

'Winnetou ... my dear son ...,' he whispered so quietly that it was barely audible.

His eyes fluttered as if he was looking for somebody else. Finally his eyes found me, and they rested on my face. He started to speak in German, 'Stay with Winnetou ... be his faithful friend ... finish my work, and look after him!'

He lifted his trembling hand. I held it tight. 'It will be as you wanted,' I said in German, 'I promise it to you.'

His face was now bright, and his forehead smoothened. 'The leaf ...,' he whispered, 'falls down ... and then the wind swirls it away ...'

He put his hands together. From his wound the blood shot out once more, then his head fell. He was dead.

I recollected the long talk we had. He had said that he would sacrifice his life for Winnetou. Surely he had not expected it so soon. Or had he suspected it, felt it?

Winnetou put the dead man on the ground. He stood up, and looked at his father questioningly. I went to him, and put my hand on his shoulder. 'I'll be your friend and brother,' it broke out of my lips. 'I will go with you, and I promise to you that we will revenge this vile murder together.'

With a violent movement he shook off my hand from his shoulder, he spat in my face, and then, with an infinite contempt, he said, 'Mercenary! Mangy coyote, land grabber, stinking dog! Don't dare to come after us, because I'll crush you with my foot!'

I felt I had been insulted unjustly even though I was an intruder on their land. I wouldn't have taken these insults from anyone else without responding with my fist, but to Winnetou I could not even reply. The others waited for the Indians' actions. However, they did not reach for their weapons, they did not even look at us. They brought their horses, lifted Klekih-Petra's body from the ground, and tied him on his horse. They did not cry, they did not threaten us, and they did not promise revenge. Their silence was the most threatening. Then they mounted, and supporting the horse that carried the body from both sides, they slowly rode away and disappeared.

'Terrible,' whispered Sam, 'but what comes will be even more terrible, you'll see.'

I did not answer. I got on my horse and galloped away. I felt I needed loneliness and physical extortion to shake off the experiences of the last half an hour from my soul. I returned late in the night, deadly tired and exhausted, both physically and emotionally.

THE BOUND WINNETOU

IT WAS late in the night when I returned to the camp, but everyone was still awake, except for Rattler, who was intoxicated, and was lying in the grass.

I had not even jumped off my horse, when Sam rushed to me, and said, 'At long last, Sir! We've been very impatient and hungry for roast bear. We carried the grizzly to the middle of the camp next to the fireplace. We needed ten men for it, because it was so heavy. I skinned it, but I did not allow anyone to the meat without your permission.'

'Share it as you wish,' I said. 'The meat is for everyone.'

'Very good. But the most delicious parts are the paws. There's no better food in the whole wide world, hehehe! In fact, it should be ripened to make it even better. But we cannot do that because the Apache may return, and then there will be no feast! But it's edible even when it's fresh.'

'Then do it!'

Sam skilfully cut off the four paws of the grey bear, and distributed them among us equally. I wrapped my share in a cloth, and put it aside. I was hungry, but I had no appetite whatever strange it sounds. The others gathered around the fire to roast their share.

I pulled aside, sat down under a bush, and stared at the fire from there. I was thinking of Klekih-Petra. The leaf of his life did not just fell; it was torn off. His murderer was lying there, still drunk, almost unconscious. What held me back from going over, and putting a bullet in the head of the coward villain? It was the disgust. The same disgust was on the faces of the two Apache, apart from their deep sadness. They were well aware of the situation. They would not have achieved anything by immediately jumping on the murderer. His mates would have gone to his aid, and there would have been more victims. With their amazing self-control they postponed their revenge cleverly.

Klekih-Petra told me that he would have sacrificed his life for his student. And this is what happened. But why had he asked me to look after Winnetou, and be his faithful friend? Could he read people so well that after one hour's talking he knew he could trust me, and that I would carry out his last will?

And why had I nodded to the dying man reassuring him? Was it because I felt pity for the dying man? Or was it because I had already considered Winnetou a good friend, and a brother? His seriousness, his calmness, his intelligence, and the bravery gleaming in his eyes had captured me so much that not even his last insulting words had raised anger in me against him.

Sam interrupted my musings, when he sat down next to me, and asked: 'Why aren't you having your dinner?'

'I don't feel like eating.'

'So are you musing about what happened instead? You have to get used to this. We are in the West where life is cheap, and there are more rascals than wild game.'

'What do you think, Sam, what will happen to Rattler?' I asked, looking at him.

'Don't worry, the punishment will catch up with him.'

'Shouldn't we do it?'

'What do you mean? Should we arrest him, and then transport him to Santa Fe or San Francisco to put him on trial there?'

'We could hold court over him here.'

'You're talking like a greenhorn. You don't know the law of the prairie. Are you a relative of Klekih-Petra or a close friend of his?'

'No.'

'You see! Here in the West, the attacked man has the right to take revenge immediately. Eye for eye, tooth for tooth, as it's written in the Bible. Close relatives also have the right to revenge. But a stranger who barely knew him? If you killed Rattler without further ado, you would also become a murderer.'

'So, will he get away with this?'

'Calm down! He won't. Trust the Apache.'

'And till then, do I have to be with him day after day? Couldn't we chase him away from the camp at least?'

'You have no right to do that either, and I tell you, it's not advisable. Most of the hunters would take sides with him, and you'd lose. Not to mention that it's better if Rattler is among us. At least we can keep an eye on him.'

'You are right,' I admitted, and sighed 'but sometimes it's so difficult to listen to the rational words.'

'You don't have to wait for long,' Sam consoled me. 'The revenge of the Apache is only a question of days. But I'm afraid we won't have much joy in it. They will consider us to be the same as Rattler. The construction of the railway made them angry. They think we are all land grabbers. The best would be to clear out of here.'

'Leaving without finishing our work?'

Sam was thinking for a while, and then he asked me, 'What do you think, how many days do you need to finish your work in this area?'

'I think we can be ready in five days.'

'As far as I know, there is no Apache village nearby. The nearest is about three days' hard riding. They will take the body there, and they will bring help to finish us off. They can't be here in less than a week. If we finish the work in five days, they'll only find our empty camp.'

'And if you are wrong? They could meet an Apache band on the way, and they could return earlier. The migration of the bison has started. Inchu Chunna and Winnetou could have arrived here with a hunting party, and have already agreed on where they would meet them.'

Sam Hawkins's small eyes twinkled.

'Damn it!' he exclaimed. 'You are a greenhorn, but what you said is not silly! Not at all! Well, sometimes the chick teaches the hen. You are right. We have to be more careful than I thought. You know what? I will ride out tomorrow morning, and look around a bit. I may learn something.'

'Good, I'm riding out with you,' said Parker.

'Me too,' joined in Stone.

'No, you have to stay,' said Sam, and glanced towards Rattler, 'when he wakes, it could be unpleasant here.'

'You can't go alone!'

'I could if I wanted, but I don't want to. I'm taking this greenhorn here. I'll talk to the engineer.'

It did not go very smoothly. Bancroft agreed that Sam should go out on scouting, because he was afraid too. But he did not want me to go with Sam, because then he would have to work too, and still they would not have progressed much.

'See, Mr Bancroft, this is the best solution,' Sam pushed his point. 'Scouting is dangerous. If I met Indians, I could easily kick the bucket, and then somebody has to bring you the news, and warn you of the danger.'

'That's true. But you could take Parker or Stone.'

'I thought of that, but it's not good,' said Sam. 'Firstly, I need someone brave. You saw how strong this greenhorn is. And there is something else. Tomorrow, when Rattler recovers, he would probably quarrel with Shatterhand as he hates him. These two men cannot co-exist; they are as the red rag to the bull, to each other. And if they fought, what would be gained from it? Let's keep the two men separated at least for tomorrow. After then, things will calm down.'

This argument finally worked. Sam returned to us, and told me, 'We'll have a difficult and tiring job tomorrow. We need strength. I'll roast your share, and you'll eat it, right?'

'I can try,' I said.

'Try, hehehe,' grinned Sam. 'Once you tasted bear paws, especially if I roast it, you won't stop eating it until you have any left! Give me your share that you put aside!'

My appetite returned as Sam foretold. This was the first time that I had bear paws, but on this first tasting I became a fan of this food forever.

Sam watched my eating with joy.

'You see,' he rubbed his hands, 'it's better if we eat the grizzly than the grizzly eats us. Now I'll cut a piece of its ham, roast it, and we'll take it for the road, hehehe. But let's go to sleep because we'll get up early.'

'Right. Tell me, which horse are you taking?'

'What do you mean? Mary, of course.'

'Mary is a mule, and not a horse.'

'So what? Do you have a problem with this?'

'You have ridden her for only a short time. What will we do if she suddenly bolts, or does not want to continue, or snorts in the most important moment? For scouting one needs an animal that can be trusted unconditionally.'

'Really? And how do you know this? From a book?'

'Of course.'

'I thought so. Reading such books must be very pleasant. Once, when I'm retired, I will stretch out on a sofa, and I will read Indian books. But only to have a good laugh!'

'Why?'

'Because these books are written by people, who have never been in the forests and the prairies, among Indians, and you can see this on every page.'

'And if there was someone, who lived here for a long time, and wrote up his experiences?'

'There's no such a man. Firstly, you see, the forest and the prairie are like the sea. They won't let you go. I didn't mean it seriously either, when I talked about the sofa. If you get used to the West, you won't feel at home anymore anywhere else.'

'So, we cannot expect such books from you, Sam?'

'From me? What makes you ask this? I can read, but my hand has forgotten writing. It has held the reins, has turned the knife and the lasso, and has pulled the trigger for so many years that it cannot draw letters anymore. I'm glad if I can write a letter now and then, but not a book.'

'Then someone else will write it.'

'Who? I would like to see that man!'

'Then look at me.'

'You? And why would you do that?'

'For many reasons. Firstly, to write up my memories. Secondly, for the readers to learn from it. And finally, to make money from it.'

'Learn from you? How? You don't know much; you are a greenhorn. There are enough teachers and schoolmasters in the world, why do you have to increase their number?'

'Sam, teaching is a sacred profession!'

'Hm! And you talked about money. How much would such a book cost?'

'A dollar or two. Maybe three.'

'You see, if you became a hunter or a trapper, you would get a hundred times more for the furs.'

'You don't understand it, Sam. Not I, but the publisher would sell the books.'

'What's a publisher?'

'I will explain it to you at another time, Sam. But look out! You may find a book in which you meet yourself.'

'What do you mean? Do you want to write about me? I wouldn't have assumed such meanness about you. I forbid you! Excuse me!'

Sam was almost raging. I could hardly calm him down. Slowly he understood that it was not shameful to be in a book, and that it could even be honourable.

The good Sam! He was a simple soul, but golden hearted, and he was a true friend!

Sam woke me at dawn. Parker and Stone were also up to help us with the preparations. The rest of the team were still sleeping; Rattler the deepest. We ate a piece of meat; drank water; looked after our horses, and then started off. Just before leaving, Sam pulled Will and Dick aside, and gave them instructions on how they should act if Rattler was seeking a quarrel.

The Sun had not yet risen in the East, when we rode out of the camp.

My heart throbbed with excitement. My first scouting! Later, over the years, I had many more such adventures, and I got used to them, just like a townie to walks. We started off to the direction in which the Indians had left our camp, that is, towards the valley in the North. When we got out of the forest, we arrived to the prairie.

'Strange that they headed this way,' said Sam, 'because the large village of the Apache is to the South.'

The track soon turned, and led straight to the South.

'They went around us, hehehe,' said Sam. 'A simple Indian trick, but they wouldn't mislead even a greenhorn with this.'

Greenhorn again! I was peeved, but I did not say a word.

The prairie became broader, and in the middle of it the tracks of the three horses were clearly visible. They were heading to the South.

'I don't like it,' said Sam. 'The track is too visible. As if they did it deliberately.'

'I like it,' I said.

'Why?' asked Sam. 'Because you don't understand it. When you have spent as many years on the prairie as I have, you'll pay attention to such small details. The Indians are experts in removing their tracks. Why didn't they do it this time? They want to lure us in a trap.'

'I'm sorry, Sam, but I have to tell you: I don't believe in this trap.'

'Really? You don't believe in it! Can you tell me why?'

'I think they didn't remove their tracks because they were hurrying. They wanted to get to their village quickly to return with a larger band. And they also had to carry a dead body in this heat.'

'Are you so sure that they were carrying him? They could bury him on the way.'

'I don't think so. Klekih-Petra was highly respected as the great wise white man, the teacher of the Apache. They would bury such a man in the presence of the entire tribe. And the most appropriate ceremony would be if they could torture his murderer to death at the same time. It would be a satisfaction to them if the murderer did not live much longer than the victim.'

'Oh! Were you born in the Apache country?'

'Nonsense!'

'How do you know all these things?' asked Sam.

67

'I have read about them in the books that my friend Sam Hawkins despises so much.'

'Well,' he said, 'let's continue.'

Half an hour later we arrived to a savannah. The grass was much lusher here than elsewhere on the prairie. At the headwaters of the Canadian River and the Pecos River there were many savannahs like this. The tracks were even more visible there. There were three tracks, as if the ground had been raked with a huge three-pronged fork. The three horses rode next to each other. It had to be difficult to keep the body straight on the middle horse. I was thinking about this, while Sam gave me a whole lecture on reading hoof prints. He explained how one could recognise if the riders rode in steps or in gallop. It was all very clear and clever, and I made it sure that I would remember it.

At one point a little forest expanded into the savannah from the right. At the edge of the forest there were some oak trees. Near the trees the grass lay flat as if the Indians had rested at this spot. We jumped off the horses, and inspected the area. We found freshly cut twigs and branches on the ground. It seemed that the Indians cut strong and thick branches from the trees, and then cut off the smaller ones from these branches.

'What do you think, why did they do this?' asked Sam, and looked at me like a teacher at his pupil.

'They made a sleigh to carry the body.'

'How do you know it?'

'I thought it would make their journey easier.'

'Good thinking. It's difficult to transport a dead man on horseback. Let's see if we were right.'

'It's important,' I noted, 'that they must have reached this place yesterday evening. We have to ascertain if they spent the night here, or only made the sleigh, and continued their journey.'

We examined the area again, but did not find any sign that the Indians had spent much time at this place. So we mounted our horses, and followed the tracks. There were still three lines, but they were very different from the earlier ones. On the two sides there were narrower tracks, while the prints of the hooves were between these.

'The base of the sleigh was made of two thick poles, and they fixed smaller branches across them,' said Sam. Then they tied the body on these. Finally they made one of the horses pull the sleigh, and led it by the rein.'

'Hm....,' I hummed doubtfully.

'You are humming again! What do you want to say?'

'Only that between the two side lines there isn't enough room for three horses. The tracks of the hooves are in the middle of the track, and not on the sides. So, one rider went in front of the horse with the sleigh, and this was followed by the second rider.'

'In a file, hehehe,' mocked Sam, 'Why would they do that? It seems to me that your books let you down this time!'

'They must have had a reason. Maybe they thought that if they couldn't advance quickly enough, then one could ride ahead, to their village. They would gain time to gather their warriors, and to attack us.'

'No!' exclaimed Sam. 'I'm telling you, remember it, that they won't split up!'

Soon we arrived to a dried out brook. Its bed was broad, but shallow. The tracks led that way, so we followed them. I was looking at the pebbles, because they creaked under the hooves of my horse. It occurred to me that this would be the ideal place for the separation of the Indians, if that had been their plan. The tracks were not visible on the pebbles, so if they were followed, there would be no trace of the fact that they had separated.

After about a hundred steps or so, we got onto grassy land again. Sam wanted to follow the track, but I called him back, because it seemed to me that it was left by one horse only. After some resistance Sam followed me, and we rode about two hundred metres along the river, where we found another track of horse hooves.

'What is this, Sam?" I asked proudly.

69

His little eyes goggled, and his face stretched. 'Hooves,' he replied in astonishment.

'Where did they come from?'

He looked along the dry bed, and he knew that no tracks would be visible there, so he said, 'Here from the river bed.'

'Yes, and who was it?'

'I don't know.'

'No, but I do,' I said teasingly

'Then who?'

'One of the two Apache warriors.'

Sam exclaimed, 'One of them? Impossible!'

'Oh, it is!' I continued teasing him. 'Just as I said. You can see that the tracks come from two horses.'

Finally Sam had to agree that only one horse crossed the brook, the other two continued on the bank.

'It happened as I said,' I remarked. 'One rode to the village. Probably Inchu Chunna. As a chief, he could gather his warriors by the time Winnetou arrives with the body, and they would be ready to ride out.'

Sam looked at me silently for a long time.

'Tell me, greenhorn,' he burst out at the end, 'why do you want to send me up the garden path? Why do you want to make me believe that you've never been on the prairie? A greenhorn cannot have such sharp eyes, and, without doubt, such a sharp mind! And you call me "master"? I have to blush, really.'

He stared at the ground for a while musing, and then he said, 'I would understand that your eyes are better than mine, because you are younger. But how could you find out what these Indians had done?'

'By a chain of logic.'

'What's that?'

'I will explain it through an example. Hawkins comes from the word "hawk", doesn't it? Hawks eat field mice, thus Sam Hawkins eats field mice.'

I meant it as a light hearted joke, but it went wrong, and Sam was genuinely angry, and indignant.

'What? That I eat mice, more over miserable field mice? It's a lie and a slander! I won't talk to you.'

He spurred his horse, and left me behind. I followed him, and then I rode next to him. Ten minutes passed without a word. Sam was stubbornly quiet, and I decided to break the ice, and make peace with him.

'Sam,' I started, 'I can't offer you a duel. So I'll give you satisfaction in another way. I decided that I will give you the grizzly fur!'

'What? That beautiful fur? I'm really happy with this satisfaction. Thank you, greenhorn, thank you! Do you know what I will make of it?'

'What?'

'A hunter fur coat that everybody will admire. You can see my skills on my coat.' He pointed at his many times patched coat, then he added, 'But I'll give you the teeth and the claws of the grizzly. Few hunters can boast with such a trophy. I'll make a beautiful chain for you. I know how to do this. And now I don't even mind if you say that I eat mice. Field mice! Rats! Everything is fine. I'll have a wonderful coat, and you will have a wonderful necklace.'

After a short ride Sam started to speak again.

'As to the books ... I have to say, you can learn from them indeed ... Will you write one?'

'Maybe ... Maybe more than one.'

Sam hesitated, but then he asked, 'Then, when you write about these tracks, would you not mention that I didn't notice the change? The mice and rats can stay, I don't really care what people think of my food, but that redskins so easily tricked an experienced scout like me, that's no good.'

'No, I won't do that,' I replied, 'because I want to write up everything as it happened. I would rather leave you out.'

'Don't! You are right. The readers can learn more from the truth, and then they wouldn't make the same stupid mistake, hehehe!'

We rode on. An hour later, just before midday, Sam stopped his horse.

'This is enough,' he said. 'We are turning back now. We know that the Indians didn't stop for the night, and they hurried. We have to be prepared, because their attack will come much earlier than we expected.'

In such circumstances we had to hurry back. My pinto easily coped with it. Mary, as a mule, was also enduring. At half way back to our camp we arrived to a little creek. We watered the animals, and decided on an hour-long rest. We stretched out in the soft grass among the bushes.

I was staring at the sky, and I was thinking of Winnetou. It was difficult to accept, although it was highly likely, that I would have to fight him, and his Apache. I did not know what Sam was thinking about, because when I glanced at him, he was snoring with his mouth open. True, he had slept very little during the night. Why should he not have slept a bit now, when he had the opportunity, and there were no signs of danger?

The mule pulled back to the bushes, and disappeared from my vision. It seemed that she liked loneliness. My pinto was grazing a few steps from me.

Suddenly the mule gave out a short, strange, or I should say, warning snort. Sam jumped up immediately.

'Mary wants to say something,' he said. 'Where is she?'

'Among the bushes.'

We climbed in the thicket, and we saw that Mary was watching something among the branches. Her ears moved lively, she repeatedly lifted her tail, and then slapped it down. When she saw us, she calmed down. It was clear that the mule had been in good hands at some point, and Sam was right to be glad to get such a well-trained animal.

We also peered out. Six Indians were approaching on horseback. They were following our tracks from the North.

Their leader, a stout and muscular Indian, never moved his eyes away from the ground. The Indians wore leather leggings, and dark-grey woollen shirts. All had a gun, a knife, and a tomahawk. Their faces were gleaming with fat, and they had a blue and a red stripe painted on each cheek.

I looked at Sam anxiously, but for my surprise he cried out loudly, 'We are lucky! They'll rescue us!'

'Be quieter, for God's sake!' I whispered.

'I want them to hear me. These are Kiowa. Their leader is Bao, his name means Fox. He's a brave and crafty fellow. His chief is Tangua, also an old acquaintance. It seems they are on the warpath, although I haven't heard of a war. They are probably scouts of a larger group.'

At that time I did not know the different Indian tribes well, but I knew that although the Kiowa were moved to the Indian Territory, some of their bands wandered in Texas. They had many good horses, and thus could travel rapidly. Their main enemies were the settlers, but their relationship with the Apache was almost equally bad. I also heard that the Kiowa were robbers. Their only excuse was that the white men debased their character.

The six Indians approached. I did not understand Sam's joy. Six Indians could easily finish us off, but they were not enough for saving us from the Apache. Sam stepped out of the bushes, and called their attention with a sharp whistle. For this they put their horses into a gallop as if they were charging at us. We waited for them calmly. A step from us they stopped their horses suddenly, jumped off, and let the animals go.

'What are you doing here, Sam, my brother?' asked Bao.

'My red brothers cleverly followed my tracks,' said Sam giving an evasive answer.

'We thought that we followed the tracks of the Apache dogs,' said Bao.

'Apache dogs? Is there a war between the Apache and the brave Kiowa?'

'We dug out the war hatchet, and will punish the dirty coyotes,' replied the Kiowa.

'I'm happy to hear this,' said Sam. 'My Kiowa brothers should sit down with me, because I want to tell them some very important things.'

Bao looked at me searchingly.

73

'Who's he?' he asked. 'I've never seen him before. He's young and muscular. Maybe he'll become a good warrior.'

Sam pointed at me ceremoniously. 'This young man is already a great warrior. He arrived only recently, and he had never seen bison or a grey bear before. But he already killed two bison bulls, and stabbed a grizzly to death with his knife to save my life.'

'Uff, uff!' exclaimed the Kiowa, and he looked at me with surprise.

'His bullets always hit the target,' said Sam, 'and his fist is so strong that he can knock out his enemies with a single blow. This is why the whites call him Old Shatterhand.'

It was still unusual to me to hear my war name. Great hunters are called by their war name, while their real names are not known even by their friends.

Bao offered me his hand, and informed me in a friendly manner, 'Then you will be our brother from now on, Old Shatterhand. We appreciate people like you, and we happily receive them in our tents.'

I immediately responded to this, 'I also like the red men, because they are the children of the Great Spirit just as the white men. We are brothers, and we will fight together against everyone who doesn't deserve our friendship.'

A contented smile fluttered through Bao's painted face. 'You spoke well, Old Shatterhand,' he said, 'and we will smoke the peace pipe with you.'

They sat down with us at the bank of the creek. Bao took out his calumet. Its terrible stench hit my nose immediately. He filled it with a mix that, in my view, was made of grated wild carrot, ground acorn, hemp, and sorrel leaves. He lit it, breathed in the smoke, and blew it first to the sky, and then to the ground.

He said, 'The Great Spirit lives above, the plants and animals, which the Great Spirit gave the Kiowa, live on the ground.'

He smoked again, and now blew it to the four cardinal points. 'In the North, the South, the East, and the West our

74

brothers and enemies live. We'll help our brothers, and kill and scalp our enemies. Haw, I have spoken.'

He believed he had made an excellent speech. It was clear from his words that he considered the flora and fauna to be the property of the Kiowa, thus if they took it, it was not a theft, but a just action. And I had to become the friend of such a man! But I had to accept it for the time being.

Bao gave the pipe to Sam, who also blew the smoke to the six directions, and then said, 'The Great Spirit looks at the men's heart, and not their skin colour. The heart of the Kiowa is brave and faithful. I'm so attached to my Kiowa brothers like my mule to the tree to which it's tied. I'm sticking with them. Haw, I have spoken.'

His speech was also greatly appreciated. I looked at him smiling, but my good mood had gone, when he pushed that stinking clay pipe in my hand. There was no such bad tobacco that I would have refused. I had even smoked the infamous "Three Men" tobacco; named so, because two men had to support the smoker. But this kinnikinnick, as the Indians call it, challenged my bravery. But I had to do it. I stood up, put the pipe in my mouth, and breathed in. I immediately recognised that they must also have milled an old moccasin into the mix.

I blew the smoke to the two directions, and made the following speech. 'From the sky the rain and sunrays come. The ground gives us the bison, the mustangs, the bear, the deer, the marrow, the maize, and the wonderful plants from which the clever red men make the kinnikinnick so that its smoke could be the symbol of peace and brotherhood.'

I sucked the pipe for the second time, and now blew the smoke to the four cardinal points. The smell was more composite than I had thought earlier as I recognised two more ingredients now: rosin and cut fingernails. After this discovery, I continued, 'There are countries to the North, West, South, and the East, and if these were mine I would give them to the Kiowa warriors, because they are my brothers. May they, in this year, hunt ten times as many bison, and five times as many grizzly bears as many warriors they have. The grains of their maize may be as big as gourds, and their pumpkins so big so that they could make twenty canoes from the shell of one. I have spoken. Haw!'

It did not cost me anything to wish them these glories, they were just as happy as if they were really getting them. This speech was the most successful one in my life probably because these Indians had never met a man, especially a white man, who just wanted to give them more and more. The appreciative "Uff, uff!" cries did not stop. Fox shook my hand, and he repeatedly assured me of his lasting friendship.

I grabbed the opportunity to give him his pipe back.

Smoking the peace pipe is an important ceremony. It is done on important occasions, and its consequences are taken seriously. But in this ragtag Kiowa company I felt that the whole thing was a comedy. To get rid of the smell of the pipe, I took out a cigar from my pocket, and lit it. Bao looked at it with longing.

We received the cigars from Santa Fe and I had plenty of them. They were cheap, and while the others spent their money on brandy, I bought cigars. Before leaving for the scouting trip, I had filled my pockets, and now I gave one to each Kiowa warrior. There was heavenly happiness on their faces when they smoked the cigars. With this present my reputation also increased. Now we could start the council.

'When did you dig up the hatchet, my Kiowa brothers?' asked Sam. 'I haven't heard of wars.'

'The time what the white men call a fortnight. You must have been in a remote place, my white brother Sam.'

'I thought my red brothers have lived in peace around here for a long time. Why did you take up your weapons?'

'The Apache dogs killed four of our warriors.'

'Where?'

'At the Pecos River.'

'Is it where the Kiowa's tents stand?'

'No, the Apache live there.'

'Then what did your warriors do there?'

76

After a brief hesitation Bao admitted honestly, 'A few of our warriors attacked an Apache village one night to get their horses. But the mangy dogs kept their eyes open, and killed four of our bravest warriors. This is why we stepped on the warpath.'

"So they wanted to steal horses, but were punished," I thought, "and now they are angry with the Apache."

'Why did the Kiowa need the horses of another tribe?' I asked. 'I know that the Kiowa tribe is rich, and has more horses than warriors.'

Bao answered with a superior smile, 'You have only recently come over the Great Water, my young brother, and thus you don't know the customs here. We have enough horses, that's true. But paleface traders came to us to buy horses. We gave them our surplus. They said they wanted more. We told them that we didn't have more. Then they told us to get them from the Apache, and then they would give us a barrel of Fire Water. This is what happened.'

Yes, just as I thought. Greedy whites had persuaded the Indians to this villainy, and were responsible for the four dead, and those who would fall in the war.

'Are you scouts, my red brothers?' asked Sam.

'Yes.'

'Where are the others?'

'A day's riding behind us.'

'Who leads them?'

'Tangua, the great chief.'

'How many warriors does he have?'

'Twice a hundred.'

'And do you think you'll surprise the Apache?'

'We'll strike at them like the eagle at the crows,' replied Bao proudly.

'My brother is wrong. The Apache know everything.'

'How? Do they have ears in the tents of the Kiowa?'

'We have met two of their scouts.'

'Then I have to return immediately to Tangua to inform him. We thought that we would surprise the Apache, and thus two hundred warriors would be enough. Now we need many more,' stated Bao.

'Chief Inchu Chunna is a clever man. When he saw that his warriors killed four Kiowa, he knew that there would be a revenge. Thus, he came as a scout with his son, Winnetou.'

'Uff! We must return to Tangua. You'll come with us.'

'Indeed, we will ride with you,' replied Sam, 'but not to Tangua's group.'

'What do you mean? I don't understand it.'

'Listen then! What would you say if you could capture Inchu Chunna alive?'

'Uff!' exclaimed Bao enthusiastically. 'With Winnetou?'

'Yes.'

'Impossible!'

'You've known me for a long time. You know that I don't speak hot air.'

Then he told them that we were working on building the railways, and that our camp was near. He told them about our meeting with the Apache chief. He told them everything.

'At first I believed,' he added, 'that the two Apache chiefs were on bison hunting, and this is how they got here. But now I know that it's much more serious. It was only by accident that they came to our camp. But they would return to revenge Klekih-Petra's death. He will send a small party against us, and a larger one against you. The chief will be with the smaller one. First you have to come with us to know where our camp is, so that you could find it later with the main group. Inchu Chunna will bring not more than fifty warriors, and you will have two hundred. There are also twenty white men, so we can easily overpower the Apache.'

'Then let's go!' said Bao impatiently.

I wanted to protest, but Sam had already leapt on his Mary, and went ahead of the Kiowa to lead them. I had to go with them. On the way I tried to pull Sam aside a few times, but the crafty little man avoided me. My heart was full of anxiety that Winnetou, this noble and young Indian, would be entrapped in such a way. Sam knew my sympathy for the two Apache chiefs, and his avoidance kept on increasing my anger. As we would arrive to the camp soon, I would not be able to hold council with Sam.

We made the journey without stopping. The men in the camp were frightened at first when the Indians arrived, but then they were even more joyous, when they heard that these were our friends and allies, and they would protect us from the Apache. The Indians were treated in a very friendly way, and they even got some of the bear meat. They did not stay long as they had to leave to take the information to their chief. When they had gone, Sam came to me.

'You are showing a very peeved face, greenhorn. I can see that you aren't happy with me.'

'Not at all happy,' I replied gloomily.

'Would you tell me the reason?'

'Can't you find it out?' I asked.

'My soul is clear,' announced Sam with surprising calm.

'Even if you could become the cause of Inchu Chunna's and Winnetou's death?'

'What do you mean? I sympathise with the two Apache chiefs just as much as you do, believe me. I don't want them to be harmed.'

'Isn't it enough that they would be captured?'

'It is! As this is the only way that they wouldn't kill us, and they would also survive.'

'I'm warning you, Sam,' I stated without really listening to his words, 'that if Winnetou is attacked, I would take side with him, and protect him even against you. I gave my word to a dying man, and a good man must keep such a promise.'

'Why don't you listen to me,' asked Sam as he scratched his head. 'I want to achieve the same as you do, but not stupidly as you want to, but in a successful way. The Apache want to attack us, it's not my fault. And I want to survive the attack, which is not my fault either. Nobody else can help me, but these ragtag Kiowa. If the struggle starts, they would kill your favourite Winnetou with his father. Isn't it better if they are captured?'

'Then they are tortured, and then they are scalped!' I hissed raging in anger, yet quietly enough, so that others could not hear it.

'No, I have a plan.'

'What plan?'

'So you would like to know it? Hm, yes. Your old Sam Hawkins noticed that you wanted to talk to him. But he couldn't let you, because you would have destroyed his beautiful plan. I don't want to let everyone see my cards, hehehe! Judging from how the Apache chiefs rode their horses, we know that they hurried. I suspect that they'll be here tomorrow night. So we are in great danger as we didn't expect them so soon. Fortunately we met the Kiowa. They will bring their two hundred warriors here, and ...'

'I will warn Winnetou before the Kiowa can capture him,' I interrupted.

'For heaven's sake! Don't!' he exclaimed. 'That would only harm us. No, they really need to be captured, and see death before their eyes. If we then liberate them secretly, they have to be grateful to us, and give up their revenge. At most they will demand Rattler, and I wouldn't deny them that. What do you say now, you angry gentleman?'

I offered my hand to him, and replied, 'This is fine, Sam. You have a good plan.'

'You see, Sam Hawkins is a man about whom a certain someone even said that he eats mice for lunch, but he has good sides too. Are we friends, greenhorn?'

'Yes, old Sam.'

He grinned at me.

'Then lie down, young man, and sleep tight, because tomorrow we will be very busy. I will inform Parker and Stone of the plan.'

"The good old Sam," I thought. Of course, the "old" was just a rhetoric adjective. He was not more than forty years old. In the West those people were called "old" whom were liked and respected. This is how Old Firehand, the famous hunter, got his name. First they called him Firehand,

80

because all his bullets hit the target. Then he had become Old Firehand. I was particularly lucky because I was called Old Shatterhand immediately.

It took a long time until I fell asleep. Sam's plan, which sounded so good at first time, now made me anxious. Would we be able to rescue the father and the son if they were captured? It would have to be done secretly without any suspicion falling on us. Would they surrender at all? I doubted it very much. How could I prevent their death in the battle? I was determined to be alert.

On the following day everybody was busy. We wanted to finish the phase. We worked as never before, except for Rattler, who was idle, although he was not drunk this time. Everybody talked to him in a friendly manner. I could see again that they were from the same type. If I had another quarrel with Rattler, I could only rely on myself, Sam, Will, and Dick.

A day later, the work started just as early, but then at lunchtime the Kiowa arrived. Although our camp moved in the meantime, they found our tracks easily.

The Kiowa were well armed, hard men. More than two hundred arrived.

Their leader was a frightening giant. His dark face and predatory eyes did not promise much good. His name was Tangua, which simply meant Chief. I felt a tug in my heart strings when I thought of the possibility that Inchu Chunna and Winnetou were captured by this beast.

He came as our friend and ally, but he did not behave like one. He did not even get off his horse, when with a motion he ordered his men to surround us. Then he rode to our wagon, and he lifted the canvass. It seemed that he liked what he had seen, because he jumped off his horse to examine it more thoroughly.

'Oh!' whispered Sam who stood next to me. 'It seems he considers our belongings his prey even before greeting us. He wants to get us after the Apache. I'll have a few words with him about this.'

'Be careful, Sam!' I warned him. 'He's got two hundred warriors.'

'But much less brain,' remarked Sam, 'just watch how I twist a rascal like him around my fingers.'

We went to the wagon with guns in our hands, and Sam asked Tangua in an anxious voice. 'Why do you want to move to the happy hunting grounds so young, Tangua, the great chief of the Kiowa?'

Tangua, who was standing with his back to us, and leant under the canvass, straightened up, turned, and looked angrily at Sam.

'What a silly question, my paleface brother! You know it well that Tangua will lead his people to battles and hunting for a long time.'

'And if that long time is only a minute?'

'Why?'

'Come away from the wagon, then I'll tell you.'

'I'm staying here.'

'Good, but then you'll be blown up!'

Sam turned, and pretended to flee. Tangua caught up with him with one leap, and grabbed his arm.

'Blown up? Why do you say this?'

'To warn you.'

'How? The death is in the cart?'

'Sure.'

'Where? Show me!'

'Later. Have they not told you why we are here?'

'You want to build the path for the Fire Mustang, I was told about it.'

'Yes, through mountains and valleys. We'll have to blow up rocks. Do you know what it is?'

'I know! What does it have to do with me?'

'More than you think! Have you heard how we blow up the rocks in the way of the Fire Mustang? No? With a little white powder! But there is more power in the powder than in hundred times hundred guns.'

'I believe it. The palefaces have a lot of magic.'

'We keep this white powder in packets in the cart. But those who don't know how to handle these packets could be blown up just by touching them. They would be torn to hundreds of small bits.'

'Uff, uff!' cried out Tangua frightened. 'Was I very close to those packets?'

'So close that if I had not hurried here, you would be on the happy hunting grounds. But how? In pieces of flesh and bones. You wouldn't even have your medicine bag, and the ghost horses would trample all over the pieces of your body'

He could not have said something more frightening to an Indian. Tangua quickly pulled Sam further away from the dangerous wagon.

'I'm only fearful that if one of your warriors start to look around in the wagon,' said Sam, 'and then he would cause an accident, because the white powder affects as far as ten times hundred horse-lengths.'

'I'll tell them,' said Tangua, 'that they mustn't go near the wagon.'

'You can see that I care about you,' said Sam, 'because we are friends and allies. But you don't really behave as if we were allies. When friends meet, they greet each other, and they smoke the peace pipe.'

'You have already done that with Bao.'

'Yes, with me and this white warrior here. But not with the others.'

'We are on the warpath,' said Tangua to try to avoid the request, 'thus we don't have kinnikinnick with us.'

'But I can see it next to your calumet.'

'You can be sure that the smoke of the peace pipe is extended to all of you.'

'As you wish,' said Sam, 'but then you won't capture the Apache!'

'Why, are you betraying us?'

'No, not at all, but I won't tell you how you can do it.'

'I'll talk about this too with my warriors,' said Tangua after a short reflection.

He called his deputies to hold council with them.

'He pretends as if he didn't want to do anything bad to us,' whispered Sam to me. 'He's the biggest horse thief in the world, and his men are no better.'

'And who brought them here?' I asked with reproach.

'Just wait till the end,' said Sam to calm me.

The result of the council was visible: for Bao's order the Kiowa dismounted, and dispersed. The ring of the warriors that had surrounded us hostilely earlier, now broke up. Tangua came to us, and he smoked the peace pipe with Sam. Then all the white men shook hands with all the Indians.

After this ceremony Tangua told Sam, 'You won't have any reason to complain, my white brother. Soon we will have another council, and discuss how we receive the Apache dogs when they arrive. Three of you can attend the council. You will be one of them. Bring two of your companions.'

When we were alone, Sam said that he would take Dick Stone, and Will Parker. 'Why not me?' I asked surprised.

'It will be better.'

'What if I don't endorse the outcome of the council?'

'Endorse? There's only one person who makes decisions here, and it's Sam Hawkins.'

'I mean if the plan endangers the two Apache chiefs,' I explained myself.

'Don't worry. You carry on with your work. It could be some days until the Apache arrive, you may even finish this phase.'

I had to agree with his opinion, and so I returned to my tools. My work involved three main tasks. I had to make measurements, keep the working journal, and draw maps. I made these in two copies. I gave one to the engineer, but I kept the other in secret. I do not know why I did this, but I thought, it could come useful.

The council, as I expected, was long. It was followed by a feast. There was still some bear meat, and the Kiowa also brought dried meat, thus there was plenty of food. Sam Hawkins even gave them brandy; he distributed the

84

remaining half a barrel among them. Rattler fortunately was not around, because otherwise there would have been an argument about this too.

I could hardly wait until I could speak to Sam.

When he sat down next to me to eat, his first words were: 'Don't worry, greenhorn. Nothing bad will happen to your favourites, and more importantly: to us either!'

'What is your plan, Sam?'

'Very simple. My aim is that the two good Apache chiefs would survive, but we too. It can only be achieved with the help of the Kiowa. But the Apache mustn't know that the Kiowa are here. It's better if they think that they have to deal with only us. I'll go out tomorrow. Surely they'll send out scouts, and I'd like to meet them. I'll make sure that they will see me.'

'Isn't it dangerous?'

'Not at all. They won't hurt me. If they see me, they will think I'm out for a walk, while the others are working. They'll be happy, because they want to attack us when we don't expect it. Why should they warn us by killing me?'

'And then?'

'The scouts will return to their chief, and will report that everything was as expected. Meanwhile we'll prepare for receiving the Apache. Not here, but in a better place. We'll move our camp, and the Apache will follow us.'

'Where to?'

'I don't know yet. To a place where the Kiowa can hide, and appear at the right moment. I discussed it with Tangua. He agrees with me.'

'This is not enough for me,' I shook my head. 'I would like to agree too. What's the plan?'

'The essence is that we'll make a big fire in the new camp, and with that we lure the Apache. When they arrive, what will they find? Our cold place, hehehe! Because in the last moment we'll also hide. We'll turn things around. The Apache want to surprise us, but we'll surprise them. Do you understand?'

'No.'

'You'll know everything at the right time. You'll also learn your task.'

'And how will we rescue the Apache?'

'Just trust me! We will rescue the two chiefs.

'And the others?'

'I don't know yet. Let's sleep now.'

His showing off peeved me, but I did not question him further. I saw that I could not do anything else, but wait for the events.

It was an unpleasant night. There was a raging wind, and by the morning it became so cold that we almost shivered, which was rare in that region, as we were further to the South than Sicily.

Sam looked at the sky in the morning.

'It will rain, which is good for us,' he remarked.

'Why? I don't like being soaking wet.'

'I understand that, but it's good, because after rain the trampled grass straightens, and it won't tell the Apache that there were more than two hundred people here.'

We could not continue this conversation because Bao was approaching. Tangua sent him to invite Sam. After a short discussion the Kiowa mounted their horses, and rode away. Of the whites they took only Sam, Stone, and Park. I knew that they went to choose the place that was the most advantageous for the battle with the Apache.

At noon the rain started. It was a deluge. I thought that the whole prairie would become a sea. In the middle of the shower Sam returned with his two friends, but without the Indians.

He immediately went to Bancroft to discuss the tasks with him. The only thing he told me was that we would move to a new camp later on the day.

The rain stopped as quickly as it had arrived. The Sun fought its way through the clouds. We packed up, and left led by Parker and Stone. Sam had disappeared already before the rain had stopped, because he had gone to scouting again.

He went on foot, as it was easier for him to hide without his mule, Mary.

After one and a half hours' riding we arrived to a long clearance which was surrounded by forests from three directions. The fourth side ended at the bank of a creek. I did not see a single footprint, although the large group of the Kiowa had passed through there in the morning. Sam was right when he talked about the straightening grass.

The creek had swelled from the rainwater so much that it had burst out of its bed. It had become a real lake. The clearance rose above the water level, and it had become a kind of peninsula. Behind the creek, the rising ground was covered with thick forest.

'This is the place that Sam chose,' said Stone, and looked around appreciatively, 'and I have to say, he couldn't have found a better one.'

'And where are the Kiowa?' I asked.

'On the other side, in the forest,' answered Dick. 'They hid themselves well.'

'I'm really curious what will happen,' I remarked.

'Let me tell you,' said Dick. 'Consider the peninsula as a mouse trap. We'll lure the mice in, and when they are in the trap, we will knock them out.'

The engineer joined us, and shook his head anxiously.

'Let's hope that they won't knock us out,' he remarked. 'I don't like it at all. Getting into the middle of an Indian battle! I won't wait for it, but I'll escape as soon as I can.'

'Then you can be sure that the Apache will capture you, Mr Bancroft,' replied Dick. 'The only way to survive this is by staying with us. I don't want to say that our situation is desirable, but let's hope for the best. The Kiowa will chase away the Apache, and we will be left alone. The Kiowa scouts are on the top of the tallest trees, and they will give the signal at the right moment to start the dance.'

'Nice a dance!' complained the engineer. 'What good is it that the Kiowa are on the other side of the creek? By the time they get here, we will be finished.'

'Come on! We'll hide in the bushes, but first we'll lock the entrance to the peninsula. It's thirty steps from here.'

'How will we close it?'

'With the horses.'

'With the horses? I've never heard of such a thing.'

'You won't hear it, only see it. We will tie the horses to trees close to each other. By the time the Apache chase them out of the way, the Kiowa will be here.'

'But some of our men may die,' sighed the engineer.

'That could happen,' answered Dick, 'but don't forget that we are in the Wild West! Bloodshed happens here! You have time to consider things, Mr Bancroft, because I think the Apache won't arrive before tomorrow evening.'

I was almost as nervous as the engineer, but not because of fear for my own life. I trusted to my luck and bravery that had helped me through many difficult situations. I was anxious only for Inchu Chunna and Winnetou.

I wished Sam Hawkins would arrive, and then tell us something encouraging. This wish was fulfilled only in the early afternoon of the following day.

Until then we worked hard on surveying. However, the work did not ease my anxiety, and I almost cried out when Sam Hawkins appeared among the trees. The little man was visibly tired, but his small eyes twinkled joyously.

'Did you bring good news, Sam?' I asked.

'How did you know? Did you read it from my nose?'

'From your eyes really,' I replied.

'So my eyes betrayed me. It's good to know for the next time. I'll be careful about this. Otherwise you're right. My journey was successful.'

'Did you meet the scouts?'

'Met them? I even went after them. I watched the main group, and listened to their discussions. But now I have to go over to the Kiowa to report. I'll be back soon.'

We waited for him impatiently for a whole hour, when suddenly he appeared next to us as if he had grown out of the ground.

'Here am I, gentlemen!' he cried, rubbing his hands. 'So you didn't hear my steps? You didn't notice me? I'm proud. This is how I approached the Apache.'

'Let's hear the news then,' I growled at him unkindly.

'I'll sit down first, if you don't mind,' said Sam, and sat down. 'There are many miles in my legs today. I don't get tired on the saddle, but I don't like walking. It's more prestigious to be in the cavalry than in the infantry, isn't it?'

'Let's hear the news,' I repeated my question angrily.

'It will be over tonight,' answered Sam.

'So soon? I thought they would arrive only tomorrow.'

'I did too. But in the Apache villages they already knew what the Kiowa were planning. They sent out a strong group against them. Inchu Chunna met them. This is how he could arrive earlier than expected.'

'What did you learn?' I asked.

'Patience, my friend, patience, let's be methodical. First, I had to go out in the rain, and I could do this, because my coat is impregnable. I scouted around our old camp. I hadn't even started when I spotted three Indians, and I knew that these were the scouts of the Apache. I thought I would grab the opportunity, and show myself to them as I planned. I don't know why I changed my mind, and hid in a bush instead. Maybe I was curious what their plan was. Well, they sniffed about, searched for footprints, then they sat down under a tree where there was a dry spot even after the deluge. They were waiting, and so was I. They sat there for two hours, and I did the same. Finally a group of riders arrived. Their faces were painted to war colours. Inchu Chunna and Winnetou led the war party.'

'And then?' I asked, excited.

'The scouts showed themselves, and reported to the chiefs. The group, after a short break, started off again, but now to the direction that we took two days ago. The rain washed away the footprints, but it was clear to them. It was a joy to see how well they found their way. I've always said that the Apache is the most outstanding Indian tribe. Their leaders are excellent too! How carefully they led their group! They were silent, and communicated in sign language. I don't have to say that I followed them.'

'On foot? After the riders?' I asked questioningly.

'They rode very slowly because of the sunset. They didn't want to be exposed to some surprise. They could also have been tired as they had a long journey. Inchu Chunna chose the resting place well. They set up guards, but I got through, and stole up to them. They were careful not to make a fire, and this made my job easier. I couldn't see them, and they couldn't see me either.'

'You didn't listen to their conversation Sam, did you?' I asked amazed by his bravery.

'I know it's not the right manner, but what can I do with this bad habit of mine?' laughed Sam. 'Even if I don't speak the Apache language well, I understood most of what they said. They spoke briefly, in an Indian manner, always about the essence only.'

'And what was the essence? What do they plan?'

'They want to capture us alive.'

'Nice of them. So they don't want to scalp us?' I asked quite surprised.

'Not now, hehehe. Of course, later they want torture us to death; this is their plan. In their village, on the bank of the Pecos River, they have probably set up the torture stakes to be able to poke, and burn us more comfortably as we would be tied to the stakes. But we'll have a few words about this, hehehe!'

He stared at the ground for a while, then continued.

'They want Mr Rattler especially, yes, you, who sit there. Yes, Mr Rattler. You will be impaled, poisoned, stabbed, shot, knocked out, and hung, always one after the other, and always in a way that you can survive it. And if you're still not dead in spite of all this, then you will be put in a pit with Klekih-Petra whom you shot, and you'll be buried alive.'

'Good Lord! Did they really say that?' asked Rattler. His face was pale like death.

'Of course they did. And you deserve it. So, with all these kinds of death behind you, you won't again commit such a heinous crime. But you will have a lot of time, because the body of Klekih-Petra has been handed over to a magic man, who knows mummification. So they aren't in a hurry. They'll wait for you to be able to participate in the funeral ceremony. I wouldn't like to be your skin, I have to tell you.'

'I'm not staying here,' exclaimed Rattler. 'I'm leaving! They won't get me!'

He wanted to jump up, but Sam Hawkins pulled him down, and warned him, 'Not one step away from here if you value your life! The Apache may have occupied the whole neighbourhood here. You would run right into their hands.'

'Is there anything else?' I asked.

'I learnt other things too,' continued Sam. 'The Apache gathered a big army against the Kiowa. Inchu Chunna met them. He chose fifty men to capture Rattler and, of course, us. When they have finished this job, they would join the main army.'

'Where?'

'I don't know. They didn't mention that. But it's none of our business. We only have to deal with these fifty.'

The good Sam was wrong. The coming days showed that we had an interest in the main army; more than we thought.

'I learnt most of the things that I wanted to know,' said Sam, 'and I was ready to pull back, but I didn't dare to move. I had to stay in my place until dawn, when they got up, and left. Their direction was the same as mine. I followed them for six miles, then with a big detour I got here. This is all.'

'So, you didn't show yourself to the scouts at the end?' I asked slightly mockingly. 'But you said ...'

'Yes, I know,' he interrupted, 'but I didn't need to. One has to adjust to the circumstances. And ... Oh! Listen!'

His words were interrupted by the screeching of an eagle. It resounded three times.

'The guards of the Kiowa,' said Sam. 'They are sitting on the trees. This is the agreed sign if they spotted the Apache

91

on the savannah. Come with me! I'm curious if your eyes work well in the dark too.'

He stood up. I grabbed my gun to follow him.

'Leave your gun,' said Sam. 'In general you shouldn't part with your weapons, but this one is an exceptional situation. The Apache are watching us. They should see that we are only collecting wood, and have no other interest.'

We went out to the main clearance, quite far from the camp. We stopped at bushes, and broke off twigs.

'Can you see anyone, Sam?' I whispered.

'No,' he answered.

'Me neither.'

We stared in the dark in vain because we could not see anything suspicious. Later Winnetou told me that at that time he was fifty steps from me behind a bush, and he watched all our movements.

Sharp eyes are not enough for this job, experience is also needed. Today I would be able to recognise the watching man in the dark, if from nothing else, then from the buzzing of the mosquitoes above him.

We carried the wood to the middle of the peninsula. Now the others helped in breaking up the twigs, and soon we had a large pile of dry wood. We lit it, and the fire cast its light everywhere. "How stupid, inexperienced these men are," the Apache could think, "they light up the path for the enemy!"

We sat around the fire, and calmly dined as if we had nothing to fear. We placed our weapons in the shadow of the bushes, so that they would be to hand.

Sam slipped away. He returned an hour later, that is, three hours from sunset, so noiselessly like a shadow.

'They've sent two men forward,' he whispered. 'One goes on the right edge of the clearance, the other on the left. They steal from bush to bush, but I noticed them.'

He sat down with us, and started to tell us some story. He was not whispering, but talked louder than necessary. We understood his intention, and laughed heartily as if it was some funny story.

We knew that the scouts would be followed by the main group, and then the attack would start. Sam made a funnel of his two hands, and emitted a noise that sounded like a bullfrog. He gave the signal for the Kiowa that the moment was approaching. The sound could not raise any suspicion as we were next to water, and there were many frogs around.

The Kiowa were very impatient. Already before they had received the signal, they had lined up at the edge of the forest. They jumped over the creek, and penetrated the peninsula. Like snakes, they crawled ahead noiselessly, always in the shadows. Within a quarter of an hour there were two hundred Indians on the peninsula, but they hid so well that nobody could see them.

The time passed, but there was still no attack. Could the Apache have figured out our plan? Or, were they following the Indian custom, and they wanted to wait until there was silence in the camp, and attack when we would be sleeping?

'Don't put more wood on the fire,' whispered Sam, 'and make sure that the wood is far enough so that it could not be fanned too quickly.'

We pulled the remaining wood aside, and waited until the fire collapsed. In the meantime we continued the role playing to ease the suspicion of the Apache, if they had any. True, there were two hundred Kiowa around us, but if the battle started, nobody knew who would survive. Still we behaved calmly, pretending that we were already half asleep after the good work and dinner. Fear was visible only on Rattler. He pulled aside, and he pretended that he had already fallen asleep. His turning and twisting showed, however, that the terror had grabbed his heart.

We did not feel sorry for him. Four of us sat next to each other. Sam told us stories, and Parker, Stone, and I listened to him laughing.

When we were all convinced that the attack would not happen until we lay down, Sam stood up, stretched himself and said while yawning, 'I walked about quite a bit today, I'm a tired and sleepy. Shouldn't we go to bed?'

'It's about time. The fire is going out too,' I answered.

'Good night.'

'Good night,' said Stone and Parker.

Then Sam and I pulled back from the fire, and stretched out by a dark bush. Stone and Parker soon followed us, and lay down next to us on the grass.

'Sam,' I whispered quietly, 'if we want to save the life of the two chiefs, have to strike first.'

'Right,' whispered Sam, 'we'll crawl to the horses to be the first in the defence.'

'I'll look after Winnetou,' I continued, 'and you three will get his father.'

'Three against one?' asked Sam. 'Right, I don't mind it. We can go.'

I grabbed my gun, and tried to get to the entrance of the peninsula on all fours. Sam noiselessly crawled next to me, and behind us came Stone and Parker. We knew that we would not have to wait long. We also knew that the attack would start, according to Indian customs, with a loud cry. The leader would give the signal, and then a deafening roaring would follow to frighten the enemy. The Kiowa were waiting for this signal as excited as us.

'Hiiiiiih' The cry resounded on such a high and sharp pitch that I shivered. After the marrow-shaking cry such a roar followed as if a thousand devils had raged. The horses nervously neighed, and raised. The Apache got through our horse-barricade in one minute.

Suddenly it all became quiet, and this was probably more horrifying than the cry. The buzzing of a bee could have been heard. The silence was then broken by a short command.

'*Ko!*' I recognised Inchu Chunna's voice.

This short word means "fire". The chief wanted his men to rekindle the campfire. The wood was near the fire. The Apache quickly carried out the order, and in a few minutes the flames rose high, casting light on the middle of the peninsula.

I could see that Inchu Chunna stood by the entrance of the peninsula with Winnetou. A few Apache warriors were around them.

'Uff, uff, uff!' they cried astonished. They saw that there was nobody by the fire. The white men hid like the Kiowa.

Winnetou understood the situation in a moment.

'*Taticha! Taticha!*' he gave the order of retreat with the unperturbed calmness that I came to admire later in many difficult situations.

My heart throbbed hard. I saw that I had to act before the Kiowa rushed out from their hiding places, because then the battle would start, and I would not be able to defend Winnetou. I jumped up. With a lightning speed I pushed the Apache warriors away, and blocked Winnetou's path. For a moment we stared at each other. Winnetou reached for his knife, but I was quicker. I hit him on his temple, and he collapsed silently. At the same time Sam, Will, and Dick jumped on Inchu Chunna.

The Apache warriors roared in their surprise. But their angry cries were drowned by the terrible battle cry of the Kiowa warriors.

What happened after this, I cannot describe precisely. I only saw that Apache warriors surrounded me, and I stood amongst them. I had to use all my strength to shake them off. I fought only with my fist, because I did not want to use my gun. I did not want to kill any of them, not even wound them. I turned around like a spinning wheel, and distributed blows. A bit further away there was an even bigger struggle. Fifty Apache fought against two hundred Kiowa. The battle lasted for only five minutes. But in such situations this feels like hours.

The Apache fought heroically, but the Kiowa's numeric superiority, which the Apache had not expected, quickly, overwhelmed them. Inchu Chunna, the chief, lay on the ground bound, next to him lay Winnetou, unconscious. Both were bound. Not one Apache warrior had escaped, partly because they did not want to abandon their chiefs. Many were wounded, but fewer than the Kiowa. Unfortunately, there were eight dead: five Apache and three Kiowa. This is what I wanted to avoid, but it did not depend on me: because of the valiant resistance of the Apache, the Kiowa used their weapons. I had to be contented with the result that Winnetou and his father were alive.

All the defeated Apache warriors were tied up. They resisted in vain. There were four enemies for each Apache warrior, and if account for the whites, then five. Each prisoner was held by three or four warriors until another Kiowa tied him up.

They carried away the dead bodies, and lay them next to each other. The wounded Kiowa were looked after by their people, and we, the whites, helped the wounded Apache. They looked at us very gloomily, and some did not want us to treat their wounds. They would rather have bled to death in their pride, than accept the help of their enemies. Fortunately, most wounds were not very serious.

When we finished, I asked old Sam where the prisoners should spend the night, because I would have liked to help their situation as much as it was possible.

However Tangua, the chief of the Kiowa, bellowed at me, 'These dogs are my prisoners, and I decide what would happen to them!'

'And what's that?' I asked.

'At other times we would judge them in our village, but there's no time now. They will be put on the stake here.'

'All of them?'

'All.'

'It's not just!' I cried.

'What are you saying?'

'The prisoner belongs to the one who captured him! You can do whatever you want with those Apache whom you captured, but we will judge those whom we captured!'

'Uff, uff! You speak cleverly! So, you want to keep Inchu Chunna and Winnetou?'

'Naturally.'

'Look here!' replied Tangua in a threatening voice. He pulled his knife, and stabbed it in the ground. 'If you dare to touch them,' he added, while his eyes were flashing, 'I'll stab the knife in your heart as deep as in the ground. Haw, I have spoken!'

It was a serious threat, but I was not frightened. I would have returned the words with the same passion if Sam Hawkins had not lifted his finger to warn me to be quiet.

The bound Apache were around the fire. It would have been the easiest to leave them there, as it was easy to keep an eye on them, but Tangua wanted to show that he gave the orders, and thus he commanded that each prisoner should be tied to a tree.

It was carried out in a very brutal way. The Kiowa did not spare their prisoners, just the opposite, they wanted to cause them the biggest pain. However, the faces of the Apache did not even twitch. They had been trained from childhood to cope with any pain without a visible or audible response. The Kiowa treated the two chiefs the roughest. They tightened the bondages so cruelly that the blood seeped from the prisoners' skin.

It was inconceivable that any of the prisoners could release himself from the bondage and escape. Still Tangua set up guards around the camp.

We had fanned our camp fire by the entrance of the peninsula, and then lay down. We arranged ourselves in such a way that the Kiowa would not have any room around us, because it would have made the rescuing of the prisoners difficult, if not impossible. Fortunately they did not want to join us. They had been unfriendly from the first moment, and my latest quarrel with their chief made them even more annoyed. Their cold and contemptuous glances did not promise much good. We all thought that we would be lucky if we could escape from our "allies".

They made several fires on the clearance, and settled down. It was suspicious that now they were talking in their own language, and not in the Indian-English mixed language that they normally used in the company of the palefaces. They knew that they were the masters of the situation, and behaved accordingly.

We had to wait until they fell asleep. We pretended that were already nodding off. Sam whispered to me that it would be good to sleep a bit, because we would have a hard night. He stretched out near the fire, and in the next moment he was snoring. I was so excited that I believed it could not happen to me, yet the sleepiness overcame me, and Sam had to wake me up. At that time I did not know how to establish the time from the stars, but it had to be around midnight. The whites were sleeping, and the fire had gone out.

The Kiowa fed only one fire. Parker, Stone, Hawkins, and I were awake.

'First of all,' whispered Sam, 'let's decide who will rescue them. Two men are enough. I'll be one.'

'And I'll be the other,' I answered quietly, but decidedly.

'Just reflect! It's extremely dangerous!'

'I don't care.'

'I can see that you're brave, but you have to think! We cannot risk the success, which is not sure anyway, with your inexperience. It's better if I take Dick Stone.'

'Never! If you don't trust me, let's have a trial!'

'How?'

'Firstly, we have to find out if Tangua is asleep,' I replied.

'It's very important, isn't it?'

'Well, yes.'

'Then I'll sneak up to him, and check it. If I can do that I passed the trial, and I can go with you.'

'Right, I agree. But be very careful. If Tangua notices you, he'll be very suspicious. Even if he doesn't say a word, as soon as Winnetou escapes, you'll be accused that you helped him. Use all the trees and bushes as a cover. Avoid the places that are lit by the fire.'

'I'll go in the dark,' I replied.

'There are at least thirty Kiowa awake, not to mention the guards. If you can manage this, then I'd say, you would become an accomplished Westerner from the greenhorn with time, hehehe!'

I pushed my knife and revolver deep into my belt so not to lose them, and then crept away from the fire. Today I can understand how irresponsible I was then. My actions were irresponsible, because instead of sneaking up to Tangua, I decided that I would try to solve a much more difficult task.

I mentioned how warmly I felt about Winnetou. I had barely talked to him, yet I loved him like a brother. I could not let Dick Stone save his life! This was my task! I headed towards Winnetou. With this I risked not only my life, but my companions' life. If I had been caught, they would have been killed too. But I was not considering this because of my youthful impulsion; I only thought of Winnetou.

Approaching someone in stealth is a difficult task. I had read about it many times, and since arriving to the prairie, I had practised it. Sam was my teacher in this too. Then I did not have the skills that I have now, but still I did not have any doubt about my abilities.

I lay down, and crawled into the bushes. I was fifty steps from the place where Inchu Chunna and Winnetou stood, tied to a tree. I should have made this distance by relying only on my palms and the tip of my boots without my body touching the ground. For this, one needs such a strength that requires long practice. As I did not have it, I advanced on all fours. Before putting down my hand anywhere, I first felt the ground to make sure that there were no twigs that could have cracked under my weight, and thus betray me. When I crawled among the bushes, I did not only pushed the branches away, but I also carefully twisted them together because then I could slip through easier. This required a lot of time, nevertheless I still advanced.

The prisoners were tied to the trees on the two sides of the peninsula. The chiefs were on my left side, the others on my right. Five steps from the chiefs a Kiowa guard sat facing them. This made my task extremely difficult. How could I distract the guard's attention for a short time?

I was only half way to them, and it had taken half an hour. Twenty-five steps in half an hour! I spotted something yellow. I crawled there, and it was a small hollow with sand in it. In the rain the hollow was filled with water, and the sand had remained there after the water evaporated. I quickly filled one of my pockets with the sand, and then continued my advance. After another half an hour I got behind Winnetou and his father. I was about four steps from them. The trees, to which they were tied, could not cover me, because they were not thick enough. Fortunately there was a big bush near the trees. A bit further there was a gooseberry bush that I also considered in my plan.

First I crawled behind Winnetou, and stayed motionless for a few minutes to watch the guard. He must have been tired, because his eyes were closing, and he opened them with a great effort. It was promising for my plan.

Firstly I had to find out how Winnetou was tied. Slowly, and carefully I felt around the tree, and touched Winnetou's leg. He must have felt it, and I feared that he might betray me with a motion. But he was much more careful, and did not lose his self-control. I now knew that his legs were tied together by his ankle, and then to the tree with a belt. I needed two quick motions with the knife to release his legs.

Then I looked up. In the light of the camp fire I saw that his arms were twisted back on the two sides of the tree, and then tied together. There one cut would be enough.

I suddenly realised something that I had not considered earlier. When I cut Winnetou's shackles, he might escape immediately, which would have put me in the greatest danger. I was thinking hard how to avoid this, but I could not find any solution. I had to accept the risk. If Winnetou ran away, then I would try to escape too.

How badly I judged Winnetou! I did so, because I barely knew him. Later, when we talked about these events, he told me what he had thought then: he felt that somebody touched his leg, and he believed that an Apache warrior was risking his life to rescue him. Although the attacking

100

warriors were captured, it was not impossible that a scout from the main group found his way to the peninsula. By then Winnetou was sure of his rescue, and calmly waited for the invisible hand to cut the shackles. He did not want to move, partly because he would not have escaped without his father, and also because he did not want to bring danger on his rescuer either.

I cut the belts by Winnetou's ankles first, but I had a problem with the belt that tied his hands. Even if I could reach it, I would have to be very careful not to injure Winnetou's hand. If I stood up to cut the belt, the guard would have noticed me. Thus I had to distract his attention, and this is why I brought the sand. I dived in my pocket, took some sand, and I threw it on the gooseberry bush. This made some noise. The guard turned, and looked at the bush, then he turned back. The second handful of sand, however, made him suspicious as a snake could have made this noise. He stood up, and walked over to the bush. With this he turned his back to me. Fast like lightning, I stood up, and cut through the belt. My glance fell at Winnetou's thick hair. With my left hand I held a curl of his hair, and I cut it off.

Then I jumped on the ground.

Why did I cut off the curl of his hair? I wanted some evidence that could show at some point in the future that I had rescued Winnetou. Fortunately Winnetou remained motionless, and he stood like a statue. I twisted his curl around my finger, and put it in my pocket.

Now I crawled behind Inchu Chunna, and found that he had been tied exactly in the same way as his son. When I touched him, he remained motionless too. First I cut the belt by his ankles. I distracted the guard's attention in the same way as earlier, and released the chief's hands too.

Then I suddenly remembered that it would be better if I took the belts. The Kiowa then would not know how their prisoners were liberated. If they found the belts, they could see how they were cut, and thus they could suspect us. First I collected the cut belts by Inchu Chunna, then crawled to

Winnetou, and put those belts also in my pocket. I now could start my way back.

I had to hurry. When the two chiefs disappeared, the guard would raise the alarm, and I must not be found nearby. First I crawled deep into the bush where I was under cover even when I stood up. With great care I straightened up, and crept towards Sam. I made the distance quicker in this way. When I got near my friends, I lay down again, and crawled to them. Sam was relieved when he saw me.

'We were very anxious for you,' he whispered. 'Do you know how long you had been away? For almost two hours!'

'Yes, I thought so,' I replied. 'Half an hour there, half an hour back, and I was near Tangua for an hour.'

'What were you doing there for so long?'

'Watched if he was asleep.'

'Did you hear this, Dick? Will? He needed a whole hour to establish if the Kiowa rouge was asleep or awake! He's a greenhorn, an incorrigible greenhorn!' He turned to me and asked, 'Tell me, was there any tree bark around there?'

'There was,' I replied. 'Why?'

'Why? Because if you had thrown it towards Tangua, and he moved, it would have meant that he was awake. If not, then he was asleep. Didn't it come to your mind? Did you rather watch him for an hour, hehehe?'

'You are right. But I passed the trial.'

During this discussion I watched the two Apache chiefs nervously. I was surprised that they were still standing there as if they were still tied to the tree.

They could have sneaked away. There was a simple reason for their behaviour. They could not know which was released first. They were waiting for some signal patiently. When the tired guard closed his eyes for a moment, Winnetou slightly lifted his hand to give a signal to his father. His father returned the signal, and now they both knew that they were free. After the signal they could act: they disappeared at the same time as if the ground swallowed them.

102

'True, you passed the test admitted Sam unwillingly, 'you managed to sneak up to Tangua, but ...'

'Nothing "but". We'll go for Winnetou together.'

'That will be a more difficult job. Can't you see the guard opposite them?'

'Of course, I can.'

'It will be harder to deal with his alertness than you can imagine. You are really not at that level yet. I don't know if I can do it. Look there! It's almost impossible to approach them even if ... Good Lord! What's that?'

While he talked to me, he kept on watching the two Apache chiefs, but they disappeared in that moment. This is why Sam broke off so suddenly. Even his mouth remained open in shock.

I pretended that I had not seen anything, and asked Sam innocently, 'What happened? Why don't you continue, Sam?'

'I don't understand it!' he said. 'Maybe my eyes are playing up?' He rubbed his eyes twice, and then whispered excitedly, 'Yes, I'm right! Dick! Will! Look where Winnetou and Inchu Chunna stood!'

They turned their heads, and could hardly suppress the exclamation of surprise.

By then the guard had also noticed the disappearance of the prisoners. He jumped up. He looked at the two empty trees shocked, then roared to wake up the sleeping men. The guard shouted something in the Kiowa language. This created an indescribable noise and turmoil. Everybody rushed towards the trees, even the whites. I followed them as I had to behave as if I had not known anything. On the way I turned my pocket, in which the sand was, inside out.

Unfortunately I could rescue only Winnetou and Inchu Chunna. If only I could have saved some or all the Apache! But it would have been a true madness to attempt it.

More than two hundred men swirled around the trees where the prisoners had stood a few minutes earlier. The Kiowa were raging, and their roaring told me what they would do with me if they suspected me.

103

Finally Tangua ordered silence, and gave his commands. Half of his men went to search the area, which was not promising in the dark. Otherwise Tangua was beyond sanity in his anger. He hit the face of the guard, tore off his medicine bag, and trampled on it. With this, the unfortunate guard was deprived from his honour.

The medicine bag has nothing to do with medicines. The Indians took the word "medicine" from the white men, but gave it a different meaning. They attributed the effects of the medicines of the palefaces to secrets, and magic. This is why they called all magic and secrets medicine. The medicine bag was the same that we call amulet or talisman.

Every warrior had a medicine bag. A young man, before being admitted to the rank of the warriors, retired to loneliness, did not eat, did not drink, and thought only of his plans, desires, and hopes of life. From the abstinence and reflections he became weak and heady. If in this state or in his dream he saw an object or a phenomenon, he considered it as his "medicine" for his life. He also obtained the object, for example, the leg of a rabbit or the wing of a bat. He took this to the magic man of his tribe who processed it. From then on, the young man carried it in his medicine bag. All Indians considered his medicine bag the most important treasure, and if a warrior lost it, he lost his honour. From that moment he would be considered as dead by his tribe, and could only recover his honour, thus his membership in the tribe, if he carried out some heroic deed.

The unfortunate guard, without a word of protest, put his rifle on his back, and disappeared into the darkness.

Tangua glanced at me accidentally, and got even angrier. He stepped up to me, pushed his face into mine, and shouted at me, 'You wanted these two prisoners! Then rush after the mangy dogs, and catch them!'

It was not advisable to argue with him, thus I wanted to retreat silently, but he grabbed my arm, and roared in my ear, 'Did you hear my order? Bring them back!'

I shook him off, and replied, 'You don't command me!'

'This is a Kiowa camp!' he shouted. 'Thus, I command everybody here.'

I took out the tin box from my pocket, and pushed it under his nose.

'Do you want me to blow you up? Do you know what's in it? The white powder that is stronger than any medicine!'

Tangua jumped back.

'Uff, uff!' he exclaimed. 'Get out of my sight with your medicine! You are the same dog as the Apache!'

In other circumstances I would not have let this insult go unanswered, but it was cleverer to be quiet now. With my companions I returned to our place, where everybody was discussing the events excitedly. They were making guesses how the two Apache chiefs had escaped. They all talked over each other, but I remained quiet. I did not even tell Sam, Dick, and Will that I had done it.

I have carried Winnetou's curl of with me ever since.

TWO DUELS

THE KIOWA were our allies, but their behaviour filled us with anxiety. Because of this, when we settled down to rest again, we decided that we would have our own guards during the night. Of course, the Indians noticed it, and they were indignant. From then on they became even more unfriendly.

At dawn our guard woke us. We saw that the Kiowa were busy. They wanted to go after the escapees, which would have been meaningless in the darkness of the night. They found the tracks of the two Apache chiefs, and followed them. They arrived to a clearance where the Apache had tied their horses before they attacked us. The two escapees got on their horses, and rode away. They left the remaining horses behind.

When we learnt this, Sam put on a crafty countenance, and asked me, 'What do you think, why did they leave the horses behind?'

'It's not difficult to answer this question.'

'Really?' asked Sam mocking me. 'One needs experience to answer my question, and you are a greenhorn.'

'But I also have experience that I have drawn from the books.' I replied, and, without letting him enter his usual banter, I continued, 'There could be two reasons. They may return with the necessary reinforcement to save the other prisoners. If they were successful, they would get back their horses. But let's assume that the Kiowa won't wait for them, but return to their village. Then they can put their prisoners on the horses, and carry them. Without the horses, they would massacre them.'

'Hm! Maybe. It's not a bad argument at all. But I can imagine a third scenario. The Kiowa could kill the prisoners even if they have the horses.'

'No chance!' I replied vehemently. 'I won't allow this to happen without doing something against it.'

'You are determined, hehehe! The greenhorn challenges two hundred Kiowa, and forces them to accept his will!'

'Not alone, but with my friends,' I replied. 'I expect Sam Hawkins, Dick Stone, and Will Parker to be on my side. They cannot accept the massacre of the prisoners!'

'We are grateful for the amount of trust you have in us. We won't let you down, that's for sure,' said Sam. 'But do you have some plan? Something like: Old Shatterhand knocks out two hundred Kiowa one after the other?'

'I'm not so stupid! But we can devise some trick.'

'Great! You're a terribly clever fellow. I would like to see you shy once. But I can tell you that no trick will work here.'

'I can see that you want to force me to act alone!' I replied indignantly.

'Not at all! But you must reflect on the situation before you do something! It's not my style to knock down a thick wall by ramming my head against it. I can tell you that the wall is harder.'

'If I could get Tangua,' I was musing aloud, 'and put my knife to his heart, I could force him to spare the prisoners for the time being. The weapon has to be a knife for him.'

Sam was frightened at first, then became anxious, but finally he started to nod.

'Look … this is impossible … very risky … but not stupid! I couldn't have devised a better plan. Probably yours could be tried. You can count on us!'

At this point Bancroft came to tell me to continue my work. He was right. We could not lose time. With the other three surveyors I started the measurements, and, by noon, we advanced a good deal.

Later Sam was looking for me. He came very close, and whispered to me, 'There's trouble. The Kiowa are preparing to kill the prisoners.'

'Then we cannot waste time. Where's Tangua?'

'Among his warriors.'

I looked around. The Kiowa allowed us to do our work, but followed us. They settled at the side of a little forest at about three hundred steps from us. Rattler was also there with his men. Half way between us and the forest there were

107

some bushes. This was good for my plan, because the bushes blocked the Kiowa's view. From where they were sitting, they could not see what was happening on our side.

'We should lure Tangua here,' I told Sam.

'Yes, but how?'

'Tell him that I have something important to report to him, but I cannot leave my work. Then he might come over.'

'And if he brings some of his men?'

'Fortunately Stone and Parker are also here. They can handle them. Get belts ready to tie them up. We have to act quickly, and noiselessly.'

'It's mad, but damn it, let's do it! I have no intention of dying, so I hope we can get away with it,' said Sam decidedly.

'I'm going for Tangua.'

My colleagues worked a bit further away, so they could not hear us. I did not have any intention to tell them my plan. They would have betrayed me. They were more afraid for their life than that of the prisoners'.

I looked at Dick and Will questioningly. 'What do you think, gentlemen? Crazy plan, isn't it?'

'It is, Sir!' answered Dick. 'But we aren't scoundrels who let our friends down. It's a great prank, and we want to be in it, don't we, Will?'

'Yes' nodded Will Parker. 'It'll be a great fun when four men take on two hundred Indians. But look, Sir, they are coming.'

I turned to the bush. I saw that Sam was approaching with Tangua, and, unfortunately, with three Kiowa warriors.

'One warrior for each of us,' I whispered. 'I will deal with the chief, you take care of the others. Squeeze their throat enough, so that they couldn't scream. But wait until I start.'

With slow steps I headed towards Tangua. Stone and Parker walked behind me. I made it sure that we would meet by the bush.

Tangua looked at me gloomily. 'Don't you know that I'm the chief of the Kiowa?' he asked.

'Of course, I know!' I replied.

'Then you should have come to me, even if you have a lot of work to do. But I know that you're a newcomer, and you don't know our customs. What do you want? Speak briefly, because I'm busy.'

'What are you busy with?'

'You'll know it when the Apache dogs howl in their pain. We'll punish them soon.'

'Why is it is urgent? I thought you would return to your village, and torture the prisoners there so that the women and children could see it too.'

'You are right. We wanted to do that. But we are on the warpath. We cannot turn back to our village. We have to kill them now.'

'Please, don't do that!' I said.

'Don't interfere with my affairs!' he snapped at me.

'I only asked.'

'You don't think that for a paleface's request I would change what I decided?'

'Had you killed them in the battle, I wouldn't say a word. But we were in the battle with you, and without us you wouldn't have the prisoners, admit it!'

Tangua straightened up, and replied contemptuously, 'Admit? You paleface dog! How dare a toad stand in the way of a grizzly?'

He spat, and went to turn. My fist immediately hit his head, and he collapsed. But he had a hard skull, and he did not lose his consciousness completely. He tried to get up. I leant forward, and measured another blow at his temple. When I straightened up, I saw that Hawkins was kneeling on a Kiowa warrior, and held his throat. Stone and Parker had overcome the second warrior, but the third ran away shouting.

'Why did you let him get away?' I asked.

'It's silly,' said Parker, 'Stone and I jumped on the same man, and by the time we realised it, the third ran away.'

'Doesn't matter,' Sam consoled him. 'The difference is that the dance will start earlier.'

We tied up Tangua. The surveyors had watched it with great terror in their eyes. Bancroft ran to us, and screamed, 'What were you thinking! What have you done? We will all be dead!'

'You will be, if you don't join us quickly,' replied Sam.

'Call your men! We will protect you.'

'Protect us? That's …'

'Shut up!' interrupted the little man. 'We know exactly what we want. If you don't act fast, you are lost! Be quick!'

We snatched up the three bound Indians, and carried them to the open prairie, where we stopped, and laid them down. Bancroft and the three surveyors followed us. We chose the place because we could see well from there if someone was approaching.

'Who should talk to them when they come?' I asked.

'Leave it to me,' answered Sam, 'just make it sure that you raise your knife above the chief, as if you wanted to stab him, at the right moment.'

He had not even finished his sentence when we already heard the angry roar of the Kiowa. In a few minutes they reached the bush. Each wanted to be the first, but they could get through the bush only one by one, which was very advantageous for us.

Sam walked towards them bravely, and by lifting his two hands he indicated to them to stop where they were. He also shouted something, but he had to repeat it several times until they finally stopped. Now it was possible for Sam to talk to them. He explained something, and pointed towards us repeatedly. I told Stone and Parker to lift the unconscious chief, and hold him while I pointed my knife at him. The Kiowa were screaming in their fright.

Sam continued to talk, and then I saw that one of the Kiowa warriors stepped forward, and with Sam Hawkins he approached in slow, ceremonial steps. He had to be some deputy chief.

Sam pointed at the three prisoners. 'You can see that I told you the truth. We are in control.'

110

The Kiowa's eyes did not move from the chief. His face darkened.

'He's dead,' he said in a mourning voice.

'He isn't. He will regain his consciousness. Sit down and wait for it. Then we'll hold a council. But if anyone raises a weapon on us, the knife will stab through Tangua's heart.'

'You raised your hands against your friends!' protested the Kiowa.

'Friends? You?'

'We smoked the peace pipe with you!'

'That's true, but you cannot be trusted. Or is it a Kiowa custom to insult their friends? Your chief insulted Old Shatterhand, thus we can't consider you to be our brothers.'

We put Tangua on the ground. He soon opened his eyes, and looked at us one by one as if he had not known where he was. Then he completely recovered, and cried out, 'Uff, uff! Old Shatterhand knocked me out … you even tied me up! Take these belts off me! This is an order!'

'You didn't listen to my request earlier. So, I don't listen to your order,' I said.

Tangua's eyes flashed hatred.

'I'll trample on you!' he hissed.

'Hold your tongue!' I said. 'First you called me a white dog, and a toad, this is why I knocked you out. You cannot insult Old Shatterhand unpunished.'

'My warriors will tear you to pieces!'

'But you will get to the happy hunting grounds first. If they move just one finger, I'll stab you. Haw, I have spoken.'

He understood that he was in my power. There was a long pause. Tangua's eyes moved wildly from one place to another like that of a trapped beast's. Finally, he regained his self-control, and asked me, 'What do you want from me?'

'Only that you don't kill the Apache prisoners.'

'None of your business.'

'It's true,' I agreed. 'Later you can do whatever you want with them. But as long as we are here with you, they cannot be harmed.'

111

There was another long silence. Tangua's painted face twitched. Expressions of anger, hatred, fear, and cruel joy alternated on it. Then he began to speak in a calm voice. 'Right, but only if you accept my conditions.'

'What do you mean?'

'First, I have to tell you that I'm not afraid of your knife. If you killed me, you'd survive me only by five minutes, because my warriors would tear you to pieces. Still, I promise that the prisoners won't be harmed, but only if you fight for them.'

'With whom?'

'A Kiowa warrior whom I will choose.'

'With what weapon?'

'Only with knives. If he kills you, the prisoners will die too. If you kill him, the prisoners can live.'

I suspected that he wanted to get out of the situation with a trick. Obviously he had a warrior, who was a master at knife-duel. Still, I did not hesitate.

'Right, I accept you conditions,' I said.

'I can't allow this,' protested Sam frightened. 'Have you ever had a knife-duel?'

'Never in my life,' I answered.

'But your opponent will be someone who has exercised it since his childhood. And even if you won, what then? You can't trust their promises!'

'We will smoke the oath pipe.'

Dick and Will also tried to dissuade me, but it was in vain. I saw that we could not maintain this tense situation anyway. The most I could do was to clarify the conditions. We agreed that we would draw a big 8 shape in the dust. I would stand in one circle, my opponent in the other. As long as the duel lasted, neither of us could step out of his circle. There would be no mercy, one of us must die.

Tangua and I confirmed the agreement by smoking the oath pipe, and then we released him, and the other two warriors. They returned to their people after telling us that the duel would start shortly.

Soon the Kiowa approached. All, but the guards, came to watch the duel. They almost completely surrounded us, and left only a small part of the circumference of the circle for the white men.

For Tangua's signal a huge warrior stepped forward. He put down all his weapons except his knife. Then he undressed to his waist. He was a real giant. When we saw his muscles, we all got a bit downhearted.

'It was very thoughtless to go into this,' murmured Sam to himself.

Tangua announced, 'This is Metan-akva, the strongest warrior of the Kiowa. I ordered him to fight a duel with the strongest paleface, Old Shatterhand.'

'What a giant!' I said surprised.

'And he must be a master of the knife,' said Sam shaking his head. 'Metan-akva means Lightning Knife.'

'I'm ready.' I answered.

'Show me your pulse,' said Sam. I offered my wrist, and he counted my pulse. 'This is miraculous!' he cried out. 'It's sixty-eight. Perfectly normal. Aren't you a bit excited, Sir?'

'That's the last thing I need,' I replied, 'because in such a situation calmness is the most important. I know that it will be hard, but I undertook it, and I will do what I can.'

We exchanged these few words whispering to each other, while I also undressed to my belt. It was not a condition, but I did not want them to accuse me with gaining advantage that my clothing protected me somewhat. I gave my gun and revolver to Sam, who was more excited than I was. In crisis situations I always wanted to remain cold. If one is calm, and trusts his victory, he has more chance to stand his ground, and win.

With the handle of a tomahawk the Indians had marked the circles in the sand, and then Tangua called us to take our place. Metan-akva measured me up with a despising look, and remarked mockingly, 'And this paleface thinks he is strong? He's shaking like a leaf! He doesn't even dare to stand in the circle!'

He had not yet finished the sentence when I jumped in the south circle. I had two reasons for doing this. Firstly, I wanted to immediately contradict my opponent's mocking words. Secondly, I grabbed the opportunity to take the south circle, because, in this way, the Sun was behind me, while my opponent had to face it. It was not completely fair play, but my opponent mocked me, and also he falsely claimed that I was trembling. This was a punishment. It was also a duel for life or death, thus it would have been stupid not to employ a little bit of a trick. Killing someone, taking away his life, is horrible, but I knew that my life was also in danger, and I was determined not to surrender it cheaply. The duel seemed to be uneven. Although I was a good fencer, I had never fought with a knife before.

'Look! He dared to enter!' laughed Metan-akva. 'The Great Spirit confused his mind. My knife will finish him off quickly!'

It was customary with the Indians to show off like this. I had to return it in kind, otherwise the Kiowa would have considered me a coward.

'Enough of tongue-fighting! You really should be called Avat-ya, Loudmouth,' I shouted at him. 'Take you place if you aren't afraid!'

With a leap he was in the middle of the other circle, and bared his teeth.

'Avat-ya? Am I afraid?' he roared. 'You blown up toad! Did you hear him, Kiowa warriors? Just watch how I'll stab this dog!'

'Avat-ya!' I shouted back. 'Show me what you can do!'

'This paleface dog dared to insult me again! You will see how happy the vultures will be when they feast on his intestines!'

He meant these words as contempt and threat, but he also made a big mistake. He involuntarily told me how he wanted to use his knife. He mentioned my intestines. So surely, his plan was that he would stab upwards, rather than aiming at my heart.

We were so close to each other that I could have touched him with my knife. He eyed me up, while in his hanging hand he held his knife upwards. The direction, in which he wanted to stab, was certain now. The important thing was to recognise the time precisely. I knew that the eyes of the attacker flashes, even twitches, at such a moment. I half closed my eyes, but watched him even more attentively.

'Start it, you dog!' he shouted at me.

'Do something, you coward!' I answered.

I hoped that from this insult his blood would be up, and he would act. I was right. His pupils opened, and in the next moment the knife flashed in his hand. He stabbed forward and upwards. Had I not expected this move, I would have been finished. But I was fully prepared, and stabbed my knife deep into his upper arm.

'You mangy dog.' he roared jerking his hand back. The knife fell out of his hand. My arm swung again, and in the next moment, I did not know how, I thrust my knife in his heart. It was such a precise stab that a spray of his warm blood splashed on my body. The giant tottered, and then fell onto the ground dead.

The Indians broke out in angry shouts. Tangua stepped forward, felt the wound of the dead, then cast a murderous look at me. In this look there was not only threat, but also a stubborn anger, fear, and respectful surprise.

'Who's the victor?' I asked him.

'You!' he answered, and clinched his fist. He was about to go, but after the first step he turned around, and hissed to me: 'You're the son of the Evil Spirit! But our magic man will sort you out!'

'I'm not afraid of your threats. But it's important to me that you keep your promise!'

'What promise?'

'That you won't kill the prisoners.'

'Tangua, the great chief of the Kiowa, always keeps his words,' he said haughtily.

'So, we'll cut their shackles off.'

'Yes, when the time comes ...'

'What do you mean?' I asked suspecting something bad. 'You promised that they would be unharmed.'

'Nobody will harm them,' he replied. 'But they may die of thirst and hunger. We won't give them food or drink. I didn't promise that I would feed and water them.'

The anger swelled in me so much that I almost jumped on him, but fortunately Sam embraced me, and squeezed my hand in his joy that I was still alive.

'My dear boy,' he shouted enthusiastically, 'this is the happiest day of my life! You had never seen a bison before, and you killed two bulls. You had never caught a mustang before, and yet you caught a mule. You stabbed a grizzly to death, and you fought a knife duel victoriously!'

Dick and Will also congratulated me for my unexpected victory. Stone added, 'He's not a greenhorn now!'

'Then what?'

'A journey man.'

'No,' said Sam, 'he's a greenhorn because otherwise he wouldn't have dared to take up the duel.'

'How do you feel, Sir?' asked Will.

'Not the best,' I answered, and glanced at the dead man on the ground. I quickly turned my head away.

'You don't have a feeling of guilt, do you?' asked Sam. 'You killed him in self-defence, didn't you? If you were a second late ... Good Lord ... What's this?' he exclaimed. 'The Apache are here!'

A hair-raising scream resounded in the forest, followed by the battle cry of the Apache: "Hiiih". Inchu Chunna and Winnetou returned much quicker than anybody had expected. The Apache warriors attacked the Kiowa camp like a tornado. We had not yet recovered from our surprise, when the battle was already raging around us.

Four of us pulled aside, and did not participate in the battle. The engineer, and the three surveyors pulled their revolvers, but they were mowed over immediately. The number of the Apache warriors kept on increasing. Some

116

had gotten behind our back, and charged at us from that direction. Sam shouted in vain to them that we were their friends. They attacked us with knives and tomahawks, so we had to defend ourselves. We knocked out some Apache with the butt of our rifles, and we gained some air.

'Quickly,' shouted Sam, 'to the bushes!'

He had already jumped, and Dick Stone, and Will Parker followed him without hesitation. I wanted to join them, but I saw that Inchu Chunna was rushing at me.

The Apache chief had first released the prisoners, and then he had entered the battle. He was chasing the fleeing Kiowa, and this was how he arrived to the clearance.

'The land grabber!' he pointed at me, and lifted his silver gun to strike at me. I tried to explain that I was not, and had never been his enemy, but he did not listen. I threw away my gun, and grabbed his throat with my left hand, while I measured a blow with my right on his temple.

The silver gun fell out of his hand, and he crashed on the ground. I heard a victorious cry behind me.

'The Apache chief's scalp is mine!'

I turned around. Tangua stood behind me. Only God knows where he had hid before, and how he had got there so suddenly. He had already thrown away his gun, and with knife in his hand he jumped to the unconscious Apache chief to scalp him.

'Go away!' I shouted at him, and grabbed his arm.

'Are you here, you dog?' he hissed. 'Beat it quickly or I'll trample on you!'

I did not have time to pull the knife, thus I grabbed his throat, and squeezed it so much that he tottered. However, before he lost his consciousness, he had stabbed me on my left wrist. I leant forward to check if Inchu Chunna was alive. From my wound the blood dripped on his face. He lay on the ground motionless, but he was alive. I wanted to lift his head, but I heard some noise, and turned around half way. This motion saved my life, because exactly at that moment my shoulder was hit by the butt of a rifle. Had I not

117

turned, it would have smashed my skull. I saw that the blow was delivered by Winnetou. My shoulder ached, and my arm was lame. Winnetou threw his gun away, pulled his knife, and jumped on me. At the same time he stabbed at my chest. It was a deadly thrust that aimed at my heart.

As I mentioned, I kept my papers in a tin box in the left pocket of my shirt. Winnetou's knife hit this box, slipped, and entered in my mouth under my chin. The knife pierced my tongue. Winnetou pulled back the knife immediately, and lifted it for another thrust. With all my strength I grabbed his wrist, and squeezed hard enough that made him drop his knife. I grabbed the back of his neck, and we started to wrestle. It was a terrible fight. Because of my loss of blood, and my wounds I did not have much hope to overcome his steely muscles, and his snake-like suppleness. But I knew that I was fighting for my life.

I would have liked to ask him; to persuade him, but my mouth was filled with blood, and because of my pierced tongue I could only stutter. With a desperate attempt I threw Winnetou off. He fell on the ground head first, and I was on his back immediately. His fingers searched for his knife, but I was already holding his neck. Hoarse sounds were coming from his throat. I was afraid of strangling him, thus I released my grip so that he could breath. He tried to shake me off, thus I had to make him unconscious with a few blows. It was the first time in his life that somebody had defeated him. I had knocked him out once, but it was not a real victory as there had not been any struggle. I had never wanted to hurt him, and my heart ached that it was the second time that I had to fight with him.

I took a deep breath, but I had to be very careful not to swallow blood. I had to keep my mouth open. I was about to get on my feet when an Apache warriors charged at me roaring. One of the warriors hit me with the butt of his rifle, and I was knocked out.

It was evening already when I regained consciousness. I thought I woke up from a nightmare. I dreamt that I was

118

stuck between the wheel of a water mill and the wall of the mill. I heard a constant buzz, and running water. All my limbs were aching, especially one of my arms, and shoulder. It took a few minutes until I could differentiate between the dream and reality. The buzzing was in my head, and not the sound of a waterwheel mill. It was not the splashing of the water, but the blood that seeped from my mouth. I was then completely awake, and I was groaning, and gurgling.

'He's moving!' I heard Sam's voice. 'Thank God!'

'Yes, he's alive,' said Dick Stone.

'He opened his eyes. He's alive!' This was Will Parker.

Indeed, I opened my eyes. What reached my conscious first was not encouraging. I was still at the same place where I was hit on my head. Around me there were at least twenty campfires, and many Apache warriors swarmed around them. There were at least five hundred of them, many injured. I saw many dead too in two groups. They carried the fallen Apache to one place, and the Kiowa were piled up at some distance. The latter lost thirty men, the Apache eleven. All the Kiowa warriors were captured. Among the prisoners I recognised Tangua.

My eyes turned to the other side. There was a white man there. He was hog-tied: his body was bent into a ring, and then his hands and legs were tied together. The man was Rattler. They tied him in such a cruel way so that he would suffer already. I had no reason for feeling sorry for him, but he was groaning so badly that it was painful to hear. None of his mates survived. They were shot dead in the first minutes of the battle. They spared him only to torture him later for the murder of Klekih-Petra.

My hands and legs were tied. On my left Parker, and Stone were sitting. They were tied exactly in the same way. On my right Sam was stooping. Only his legs, and his right hand were tied. His left hand was left free so that he could look after me. I learnt the reason for this later.

'The most important is that you have come back, my boy!' he said, and caressed my face. 'What happened to you?'

I wanted to answer, but could not, because my mouth was full of blood.

'Just spit it out!' encouraged me Sam.

I felt so weak that I could not even lift my head. I was only able to groan a few words one by one. 'I knocked out Inchu Chunna ... Winnetou too ... He stabbed me in my mouth ... Then, from behind ... I was hit ...'

During this conversation my mouth was bleeding, and only now I noticed that I was lying in a pool of blood.

'Damn it,' exclaimed Sam, 'so this is how it ended! We three jumped in the bush to wait for the outcome of the battle there. We believed that you did the same. When at the end I climbed out, I saw that the Apache were around Inchu Chunna and Winnetou, who were recovering just then. Then I saw you on the ground. For my cry Will and Dick also climbed out, and we wanted to hurry to you to help you if we could, but the Apache immediately charged, and they captured us. I told Inchu Chunna that we are the friend of Apache, but he just laughed in my face. He allowed only Winnetou's request to leave one of my hands untied. I bandaged the wound on your neck, otherwise you would have bled to death. How far did the knife enter?'

'He ... stabbed ... through my tongue,' I stuttered.

'Good Lord! Very dangerous! It comes with traumatic fever, and that's too much even for a bear. I can imagine the buzzing in your head. But it's a smaller problem, and it will go. But the pierced tongue is much more serious. The damned thing is that you cannot bandage it.'

I could not hear more as I lost my consciousness again.

When I came back, it seemed to me that the world was moving around me or I moved. I heard hoofs, and when I opened my eyes, to my surprise, I saw that I was lying on a bear skin. I recognised it. It was the skin of the grizzly that I had killed. The Apache had made a kind of hammock of it: tied it between two horses, and laid me on it. This is how they transported me. I was deep in the fur, and saw only the sky, and the heads of the two horses. The hot rays of the Sun flooded me, my heart throbbed fast, and the blood in my veins pulsed wildly. My mouth was swollen, and it was full of coagulated blood. I wanted to spit it out, but I could not move my tongue.

'Water! Water!' I begged crying, because I suffered from a horrific thirst. But I only believed that I could speak: not a word came out of my mouth. "I'm finished," I thought. My head fell back, and I surrendered myself to my fate.

In the next moment I was fighting with Indians, galloped on perched prairies, chased bison, wrestled with bears, then I swam, swam, swam in the infinite sea, and the waves lapped over my head … This was the traumatic fever that deprived me of my consciousness for a very long time. I was not wrestling with bears, but with death. Sometimes I heard Sam's voice. It came from somewhere far, from the other side of an abyss. Sometimes as if two dark, velvety eyes rested on me, and I recognised Winnetou's eyes. Then I died, I was put in a coffin, and I was buried. I clearly heard the sound of the earth falling on my coffin. Then I lay in the ground for a long time, for an eternity. Finally, the lid of my coffin rose. It floated above my head for a while, and then it disappeared. I saw the sky, and the four sides of the grave collapsed. Was it true? Was it possible? Or was it only a mirage? With a great effort I lifted my hand, and felt my forehead.

'Hurrah! He awoke! He awoke from death!' exclaimed Sam exuberantly.

I tried to turn my head towards the voice. I managed it.

'Look! He can move his head even!' I could hear Sam's dizzy voice.

He bent over me, and his face gleamed with joy. It was a miracle that I could recognise him as his face was covered with a thick beard.

'Can you see me, my dear friend? Can you recognise me?' he asked excitedly.

I wanted to answer, but I could not. I was still too weak, and my tongue was heavy like lead. But I nodded.

121

'Can you hear me?' asked Sam.

I nodded again.

'Come! Look!' screamed Sam.

His face disappeared, and two other heads filled my view: Stone's and Parker's. The good lads almost cried in their happiness. They started to talk, but Sam pushed them aside. 'I'm the first!' he said. 'Let me there!'

He held both of my hands, and gently squeezed them. Then he pointed at the clearance in his beard that was his mouth, and asked, 'Are you hungry, Sir? Thirsty, Sir? What do you think, would you be able to eat or drink?'

I shook my head, because I had no inclination for either of them. I felt so weak suddenly that I would not have been able to drink a drop of water.

'No? Really no? Do you know how long have you been lying here?'

I only stared at him.

'For three weeks, my friend, for three weeks! Just imagine! You probably haven't got a clue what happened to you since you were wounded. First you had traumatic fever, then you fell in tetany. The Apache already wanted to bury you, but I couldn't believe that you were dead. I begged Winnetou to allow me to look after you. So, you can thank everything to Winnetou, Sir! I'm going to him, and report that you are alive!'

I closed my eyes, and continued lying there in silence. It was not a grave, or a coffin, but some wonderful, peaceful relaxation. I wished I could be in this state forever. Then I heard steps. A hand touched me, and lifted my arm.

'Are you sure that your eyes didn't cheat you?' I heard Winnetou's voice asking Sam. 'Has Selkih-Lata really regained his consciousness?'

I knew that he was talking about me. Selkih-Lata in the language of the Apache meant the same as Old Shatterhand in English.

'He opened his eyes! He even nodded!' The good Sam was pushing his argument.

'Then it's a miracle! It would have been better for him if he had remained dead,' said Winnetou. 'He has returned to life only to die again.'

'You speak like this about the best friend of the Apache people,' said Sam clapping his hands, 'who is also Winnetou's faithful friend!'

'And this is why he knocked me out twice,' commented Winnetou contemptuously.

'He had to do it in both occasions,' Sam tried to drive his point home. 'Firstly to save your life, because otherwise the Kiowa would have killed you in the battle. For the second time it was self-defence. We four didn't want to fight against the Apache, and agreed that we would surrender.'

'Your tongue lies, Sam Hawkins,' said Winnetou coldly. 'You are not better than the Kiowa dogs. If you had been our friends, you would not have sneaked up on us to hear our plans, and you would have warned us about the Kiowa's plans. Do you think I'm so stupid that you can mislead me with your feeble lies?'

'I don't lie!' said Sam. He was really indignant. 'When Old Shatterhand recovers, he can also tell you the truth.'

'All palefaces are mean and liars. I have known only one in whose heart truth lived. He was Klekih-Petra, and you killed him! Old Shatterhand raised trust in me in the first moment. I saw his strength and bravery. His eyes were open as if his heart was honest. But I became disappointed in him. He joined the thieves, who wanted to steal our land. He joined my enemies in the battle. His face lies, his eyes lie, his heart is a liar too!'

I wanted to look at him, but my eyelids did not obey. My body felt heavy like lead. But when I heard his harsh words, I opened my eyes with a great struggle. He stood next to me in a light hunting dress. He did not have any weapons on him. In his hand there was a book. I could read the gilded letters of the title: "Hiawatha". I looked at him amazed. This young Apache warrior was reading Longfellow's famous epoch! It was astonishing.

Winnetou noticed that I opened my eyes. He looked at my eyes silently for a long time, and then asked: 'Can you speak?'

I shook my head.

'Do you have big pains?'

I shook my head again.

'Still, you must die!' said Winnetou. 'One shouldn't lie before dying. Tell me honestly, you four really had good intentions towards us?'

I nodded twice with a great effort.

'I can't believe this!' exclaimed Winnetou. 'If you had admitted the truth, I could have asked my father to pardon you, but now … We will look after you very carefully so that you would be healthy and strong again to be able to endure the tortures for long. A sick, weak man dies very quickly, which is not a punishment.'

I closed my eyes. His stubbornness was so insulting that my pride would have made me silent even if I had the strength to speak. As if Sam had read my mind, he started to argue again.

'We gave you irrefutable evidence of our friendship,' he said. 'The Kiowa wanted to kill their prisoners, but Old Shatterhand challenged them. This is why he fought a knife-duel with Metan-akva. He risked his life for the Apache prisoners!'

'This is not true either!' interrupted Winnetou.

'Ask Tangua, the chief of the Kiowa.'

'I did, because somebody mentioned it.'

'And what did he say?'

'That Metan-akva fell in the battle, when we attacked the Kiowa. It wasn't Selkih-Lata who killed him!'

'That is the ultimate villainy!' exclaimed Sam. 'And a damned lie! Tangua knows that we were on your side, and this is his revenge!'

'Tangua swore for the Great Spirit that his words were true, and I would rather believe him then you,' replied Winnetou. 'But I'll tell you something that I just told Old

Shatterhand. Klekih-Petra taught me about peace. Had you been honest, I would have asked Inchu Chunna to pardon you, and he always listens to my requests. But you did not. I don't want blood. This is why we allowed the captured Kiowa to pay for what they did to us with horses, blankets, and weapons. Klekih-Petra was my friend, and my teacher. I cannot let his death go unavenged. The Great Spirit gave me his murderer. He'll die by torture, but you will too, because you are just as wicked as he is.'

It was a long speech from the quiet Winnetou. Even later I rarely heard him speaking for such a length, apart from exceptional situations. It seemed that our fate affected him more than he admitted.

'It's a cruel speech, Winnetou!' replied Sam quietly, and bowed his head.

'Shut up!' cried Winnetou. 'I have been too soft towards you! Selkih-Lata is better, thus he doesn't need you, so you shouldn't be here. Follow me!'

'Don't do this to me, Winnetou, please!' begged Sam. 'I want to stay with him, don't separate me from him!'

'What you want is immaterial. You'll have to do what I'm ordering. Or should I get my warriors to tie you up, and carry you out?'

'And when can I see my friend again?'

'On the last day. When you all die.'

'Then let me say good-bye to him!'

Winnetou turned away. Sam grabbed my hands, and held them for a long time. Parker and Stone said good-bye to me in the same way.

For Winnetou's signal a few Apache warriors came in. They took away Sam, Will, and Dick. I was left alone. Later they came back, moved me onto a blanket, and I was carried. I did not have the strength to open my eyes. I felt the swinging of the blanket, then I fell asleep.

I do not know how long I slept. The sleep that brings recovery is often very long, and very deep. When I awoke, I could easily open my eyes, and I was not as weak as before. I could even move my tongue, and it was not difficult to put my finger in my mouth, and clear out the coagulated blood.

For my surprise I found myself in a square room. The walls were made of stone. The light came from the entrance that did not have a door. My bed was in the back corner. It was made of the skins of many grey bears layered on top of each other, and I was covered with a rich, beautiful Indian blanket. In the opposite corner, by the entrance, two Indian women sat, an older and a younger, probably with a dual role of nursing and guarding me. The older one was as ugly as most old Indian women are, who have overworked themselves during their life. The squaws carried out the most difficult jobs, while the men were warring and hunting, but otherwise they were idle.

The younger woman was pretty, very pretty. If she had worn European clothing, she would have been admired even in an aristocratic house. She wore a long, light blue dress with a completely closed neck. Her belt was made of the skin of a rattlesnake. She did not wear any jewellery. Her hair was wonderful, braided in two strong, bluish-black locks which reached her waist. It looked like Winnetou's hair, and her countenance also reminded me to Winnetou. She had the same velvety, black eyes that were partly covered by the long eyelashes as if they hid a secret. Her cheek bones were not high, and her face was round and full. Many European girls would have envied the playful dimples of her chin. She talked to the old woman quietly so that they would not wake me up, and when she smiled a perfect line of teeth became visible in her well-arched mouth. Her nose was more Greek than Indian, and her skin gleamed as if her light bronze colour had been sprayed with silver. This girl was about eighteen years old. I was convinced that she was Winnetou's younger sister.

The two squaws were embroidering a white-tanned belt.

I sat up on my bed, yes, I simply sat up without any effort, although, before my sleep, I had been so weak that I could barely open my eyes.

126

The older woman heard the noise of my movement, glanced towards me, and cried out: 'Uff! *Aguan inta-hinta*!'

In this case the "uff" expressed surprise, while the "aguan inta-hinta" meant: "look how fresh and lively he is". The girl looked up from her work, and seeing that I was sitting, she hurried to me.

'Have you woken?' she asked me in quite good English, which surprised me. 'Do you have any request?'

I opened my mouth to answer, but closed it immediately, because I remembered that I could not speak. Could I not? But if I could sit up, maybe I could speak too. I tried, and answered, 'I have requests, more than one.'

I was happy that I could hear my own voice. Naturally it sounded strange because it was difficult to press out the words: there were sharp pains deep inside my mouth. Yet, I could speak again after such a long silence.

'Talk quietly or with signs,' she said. 'Nsho-chih can hear that speaking hurts you.'

'Nsho-chih is you? Is it your name?' I asked.

'Yes.'

'You should thank the person, who gave you this name. It really suits you, because you are beautiful like a spring day, when the first flowers of the year open.'

I knew that Nsho-chih meant "Beautiful Day" in the language of the Apache, maybe this encouraged me to make this compliment. The girl blushed slightly, and reminded me to what she had asked.

'You said you had more than one request.'

'First tell me if you are here because of me.'

'I was told to nurse you.'

'Who ordered you?'

'My brother, Winnetou.'

'When I first saw you I thought that the brave, young warrior is your brother, you look so much like him.'

'Still you wanted to kill him!'

It was a half-statement, and a half-question. She looked in my eyes searchingly as if she wanted to read my soul.

'I didn't want to kill him,' I said.

'He doesn't believe you, and he thinks you are his enemy. You defeated him twice. Nobody could beat him before.'

'Yes, twice. The first time to save his life. The second time he wanted to kill me. I liked him already when I first met him.'

She lifted her eyes at me for a whole minute again, and said finally: 'But he doesn't believe you, and I'm his sister. Do you have pains in your mouth?'

'Not now.'

'Can you swallow?'

'I can try. Can you give me some water? I'm thirsty.'

'You'll get water in a minute and you can wash.'

She left the room with the old woman. I looked after her musing. So, Winnetou considered me an enemy, and it did not matter how hard I tried to show that I was his friend. Yet, I was nursed by his sister. What did it mean? Maybe I would learn the solution to this puzzle later.

The two squaws soon returned. There was a clay cup in the young girl's hand. It was the type that pueblo Indians made. It was full of fresh water. She thought I could not hold it alone, and so she held the cup to my lips. Swallowing was very difficult, because it caused a sharp pain, but I overcame this. With short sips and long pauses I drank the whole cup.

It was so refreshing! Nsho-chih probably could read it from my face, because she said, 'I can see that you liked it. I could bring something else to you later. You are surely very hungry too. Do you want to wash?'

'If it was possible!'

'Try it!'

The old woman brought a gourd filled with water. Nsho-chih put it down next to my bed, and gave me a kind of towel made of raffia. I tried to wash myself, but I failed, I did not have enough strength. Thus she dipped the corner of the towel in the water, and patiently washed my face, hand, arms, and shoulders.

She quietly asked, 'Have you always been so lean?'

I? Lean? I had not thought of this. Of course! The fever and the wound that had caused tetany! It could have killed me! For a very long time I had not eaten and had not drunk. Naturally, all these exhausted my body. I touched my face, and said, 'I've always had a good weight.'

'Then look at yourself in the water.'

I looked in the gourd, and immediately recoiled in my shock. From the water a spectre looked back at me; I was a skeleton.

'It's a miracle that I'm still alive!' I sighed.

'Yes, Winnetou said the same. The Great Spirit gave you a strong body. You survived even the five days on the road.'

'Five days? Where are we?'

'In our pueblo, by the Pecos River.'

'And the Apache warriors have also come here?'

'Yes, they live near the pueblo.'

'And are the Kiowa prisoners here also?'

'Yes. They would have deserved death. Other tribes would have executed them. But Klekih-Petra taught us to avoid wars among the red men. When the Kiowa paid for their crimes against us, they can and must leave.'

'And my three friends? Do you know where they are?'

'Yes, in a room like this, but it's dark. They sit in the dark tied up.'

'Without food and water?' I asked.

'No, they are well kept. They will be strong to endure the torture. If they die right away, it is not a punishment.'

'Will they die on the torture pole?'

'Yes, they will.'

'Me too?'

'You too,' she answered calmly, without any sympathy in her voice. Was it possible that this beautiful girl was so cold hearted?

'I would like to talk to them,' I said.

'Winnetou forbade it.' she replied.

'Can't I see them, even from the distance, just once?'

'You can't.'

'Can't I send a message to them?'

'You can't.'

'At least that much that I feel better?'

She did not reject my request immediately, and after a short reflection she said, 'I'll ask Winnetou to allow this.'

'Won't Winnetou visit me?'

'He doesn't want to see you. I can take a message to him.'

'No, thank you. I am also proud. If Winnetou doesn't want to talk to me, I don't want to talk to him.'

'You can see him on the day of your death. Now, I have to go. If you need something, you can give the signal with this. Then someone will come in.'

She gave me a small clay whistle, and then left with the old woman.

The talking made me tired. My tongue ached, and I felt a sharp stab at every word. I closed my tired eyes, and fell asleep again.

A few hours later I awoke feeling terribly thirsty and hungry. I blew the little whistle. For the signal the old woman, who probably sat by the entrance, immediately put her head in, and said something. I did not understand her words, but I knew that she had asked what I wanted. With signs I explained to her that I wanted to drink and eat. For this she disappeared, and soon Nsho-chih arrived with a clay dish, and a spoon in her hand.

She knelt down by me, and fed me like a child. It was a strong broth in which they mixed maize flour. The Indians ground maize between two stones, but this flour was so fine as if it was made with a grinder. Maybe Klekih-Petra had bought a grinder to them.

Eating and swallowing were more painful than drinking or speaking. After every spoonful I had to rest. My eyes were wet from the great exertion.

Nsho-chih noticed it, and when I had the last spoonful, she remarked, 'You're still very weak, but your heart is strong. You are a hero! It is really bad that you weren't born as an Apache, only a mendacious paleface.'

'I'm not a liar,' I said, 'and not all white men are liars.'

'I've known only one paleface who had a true heart,' said Nsho-chih. 'We all loved Klekih-Petra, and you killed him. You'll die on the day when we bury him.'

'You haven't yet buried him?' I asked astonished.

'We closed his body in a strong coffin to which the air cannot enter,' she explained. 'You'll see it, when the time comes. Rest now.'

My lethargic mood had gone. I wanted to live again, and insisted on being alive, even if the situation looked hopeless. Hopeless? Why? I only had to convince Winnetou that his judgement was wrong. I had the proof: his hair! I had not had the strength to show it to him yet. In fact I did not really want to do this, because I wanted him to come to the recognition of his mistake by himself. But if he continued to be stubborn ...

This is how far I got in my thinking, when I was suddenly seized by fear. What if I did not have the box with the curl of hair anymore? Indians normally took everything from their prisoners. Surely they had emptied my pockets while I lay unconsciously.

I wore the same clothing in which I had been captured. A lot had happened since then, and it can be imagined what state my clothing was in, but at least I had it. I dived in my pockets excitedly. For my joy and surprise I found all my belongings in my pockets. It seemed that they had taken only my weapons. I pulled out the tin box. I breathed freely. My documents, notes were there, and also Winnetou's hair. I carefully put the box back to my pocket, and stretched out on the bear skins relieved. I could sleep calmly now.

I awoke in the evening. Nsho-chih brought a bowl of broth and water again. I could eat without help. While eating, I asked a number of questions. There were some that she answered without hesitation, but also a few for which she lifted her hand in a forbidding manner.

'I'm glad that nothing was taken away from me,' I said.

'It was Winnetou's order,' she answered.

'Why?'

'I don't know. But there is something else I want to tell you. You'll be even happier for that.'

'I'm curious.'

'I visited the palefaces whom were captured with you. I wanted to tell them that you were better. One of them, whose name is Sam Hawkins, asked me if he could send to you something.'

'The good Sam! What did he send to me?'

'A present. He made it. He worked on it for three weeks, when he looked after you. I asked Winnetou if I could give it to you. He allowed it. Here it is.'

She gave me a necklace that Sam made of the teeth, and claws of the grey bear that I had killed. He even put the tip of the bear's ears on the lace.

'He told me that you killed the grizzly. You are a brave, and strong warrior as you dared to attack it with a knife only,' said Nsho-chih.

I turned the necklace in my hand a few times silently. I felt touched.

'How could he make this? He needed a knife, and other tools! Did you not take his belongings either?'

'The others couldn't keep their belongings,' answered Nsho-chih, 'but he told Winnetou that he wanted to make a present for you, and Winnetou allowed it. He ordered that he should get the tools that he needed. It's a nice necklace. Put it on as you won't be able to wear it for very long.'

'Because I have to die?'

'Yes.'

She leant over me, and put the lace on my neck herself. From that time I always wore it when I was on the prairie.

'Thank you,' I said to the Indian girl, 'but you're wrong that I won't be able wear it for very long.'

'Don't let fake hopes overcome you,' she remarked a bit saddened. 'The council of the elders has decided already that you have to die.'

'And if I could prove that I'm innocent?'

'Do, Selkih-Lata! I'd be very happy if you could prove that you aren't a lying, paleface traitor, and you aren't Winnetou's enemy.'

She turned around, and ran out of the room.

When the evening arrived, the old woman came in with a night-light in her hand. She arranged my bed, and took the bowl, and the spoon.

On that night I slept better than any other time, and awoke refreshed. I had meals six times every day, but unfortunately it was always the same. I could not protest as I knew that the broth, and the maize flour were nutritious, and were easy to digest. I had to wait for meat in my meals until I could chew, not only swallow.

My condition improved day by day. The skeleton that I had seen in the water, regained its muscles. The swell in my mouth reduced, and then completely disappeared. Nsho-chih looked after me, but she became more and more silent. I noticed that she glanced at me in secret, and in her eyes there was sadness. Had she started to feel sorry for me? It seemed that I had been wrong when I thought that she was heartless. I asked if I could get out of the room to enjoy the fresh air. She told me that it was impossible. There were two guards at the entrance, and I was not allowed to leave the room. Only because of my weakness I had not been bound, but it still could happen.

I started to think again. So far I had hopes because of the curl of hair, but I could be disappointed in my hopes. In such circumstances I had to rely only on my own strength.

I had to get stronger, but how?

I lay on the bear skins only in the night, during the day I walked up and down in the room or stooped. I told Nsho-chih that I could not sit so low when eating, as it was alien to me. I asked if I could get a larger stone on which I could sit. She took my request to her brother, and for Winnetou's order they brought two big stones into my room, or rather into my prison. When I was left alone, I started to lift these stones. In two weeks' time the results of the weightlifting started to show. At the end of the third week, my muscles regained their strength.

I had been a prisoner for six weeks, but I had not heard that the Kiowa prisoners had been released, even though it meant the feeding of two hundred men. Surely, the Kiowa were bargaining. "The longer they try it, the larger would be the price," I thought.

It was late autumn now. On a nice and sunny morning Nsho-chih brought me my breakfast, and while I was eating, she sat down. Her eyes twinkled strangely, and finally a teardrop rolled down on her face.

'Are you crying?' I asked her. 'What happened that made you so sad?'

'Nothing happened,' she said, 'but today the Kiowa are leaving. Their messengers arrived last night. They brought everything that we demanded.'

'And are you sad because of this? I think you should be happy instead.'

'You don't know what you are saying, because you don't know what will happen. Our warriors will celebrate the leaving of the Kiowa by tying you, and your companions, to the torture stakes.'

I had heard this threat many times, but I had not taken it seriously. Now I was shocked. So this was the decisive day, maybe the last day of my life! By calmly eating my breakfast I pretended indifference. After eating the last spoonful of it, I gave the bowl to Nsho-chih. She took it, and left. However, at the entrance she turned around suddenly, and returned to me. She stretched out her hand to me

'This is the last time I can talk to you, and I have to say good-bye to you. You are a great warrior, and be strong whatever tortures you have to endure. Nsho-chih's heart aches that you have to die. But it would be worse to her if you died cowardly.'

She wiped away her tears, and ran out. I went after her to see her once more, but as soon as I reached the entrance the two guards raised their guns at me. They would have shot me dead had I made one more step. I withdrew to my prison. I could not think of any way of escaping as I did not know the area. Still, I tried to remember everything that I had heard and read about the pueblo.

Pueblo is an ancient way of building accommodations. The pueblo-Indians chose the high bank of rivers, or the cliffs of a canyon. They utilise the characteristics of the terrain, and they raise high stone walls among the gaps of the cliffs. These reached the height of many storeys. Every storey was smaller than the one below, and there was a terrace in front of the room, which was also the ceiling of the storey below. Thus the ground floor was the largest, and every storey above was smaller and smaller. It looked like a pyramid made of cells or a house of cards. There were no staircases in the pueblo. The next level could be reached only by a ladder from outside. If an enemy approached, the ladders were pulled up, so only the enemy with siege ladders could get in. But still, the enemy would have to siege every floor exposed to the weapons of the warriors on the floor above.

I was in such a building on the eighth or ninth floor judging from what I had seen when I had put my head out. No, I could not attempt an escape. I lay down and waited.

The waiting was painful as it lasted for hours. Finally at noon there was the sound of steps. Winnetou entered the room with five Apache warriors. I sat up.

He cast a long, searching look at me, and asked, 'Has Old Shatterhand recovered?'

'Not quite,' I answered.

'But you can speak, as I can hear.'

'Yes.'

'And run?'

'I believe so.'

'Can you also swim?'

'Maybe … a bit …' I answered carefully.

'That's good, because you'll need it. I sent a message to you when you could see me again, have you forgotten it?'

135

'No, on the day of my death.'

'That's right. And the day has arrived. Stand up! My warriors will tie you up.'

Resistance would have been futile. I was faced with six well-trained warriors. Even if I could have knocked out one or two, I would not have achieved anything, only my situation would have become more difficult. I offered my hands, and I was happy that they were tied at the front and not at the back. They also tied my legs, but only loosely, thus I could step slowly in small steps, but I was unable to jump or run. They led me out to the terrace.

There was a ladder at the edge. It was not a real ladder, but a strong, thick pole. They cut grooves in it, and these substituted for the steps of a ladder. First three Indians descended, then I, and two Apache warriors followed me. It was difficult to get down with my tied legs. This is how we progressed from floor to floor. On every terrace women and children gathered, and stared at me, but they were quiet. Soon they followed us. Finally many hundred curious people joined the procession. They would become the audience of the show in which, unfortunately, I was to become the star.

The pueblo was built in a ravine that led to the broad valley of the Pecos River. The Pecos River is not a very deep river, especially not in the autumn, but in parts it was still deep. The landscape was hemmed in by forests and bushes, but at the entrance of the ravine there was a big, grassy clearance which continued on the other side of the river. It was a good pasture. There were no trees on it apart from one big cedar that was quite far on the opposite bank.

On the nearside of the river there was some buzzing. First I caught sight of our wagon that the Apache brought as a loot. Behind it there were the horses that the Kiowa brought as ransom. The Apache pitched tents to show off the weapons that were also part of the ransom.

While approaching our wagon, I recognised Sam, Dick, and Will; all tied up. They were tied to poles not far from the wagon. There were four such poles there. The fourth was empty. They tied me to that one. Sam was the closest to me, then Stone, and then Parker. Not too far from us they piled up lots of dried wood. Their plan was probably that they would burn us after torturing.

My companions looked well. It was clear that they were not starved. Their faces were gloomy, and lightened up a bit only when they saw me. The poles were close enough to each other, thus we could understand each other's words well.

'Welcome, my friend,' said Sam. 'What a sad meeting. I can't even be happy for you being so much recovered. I doubt that we can survive the day. Especially as, after they torture us, they will burn our bodies.'

'Do you consider the situation so bad?' I asked. 'I think I have an idea.'

'And when did it come to you?'

'On the night when Winnetou and his father escaped.'

'It doesn't seem to be working today. Anyway, how do you call your idea?'

'A curl of hair.'

'A curl of hair?' he repeated astonished.

'You have no faith in me.'

'Because it sounds like drivel. Did a girl once pay you with her braid, and now you want to give it to the Apache as a ransom?'

'No, it's not a girl's curl, but that of a boy.'

He looked at me as if he doubted my sanity. He shook his head and said, 'Listen, Sir, something is wrong in your head. Perhaps the wound left something behind. I can't see how a bunch of hair could help us on the torture stake.'

'It's a greenhorn's idea, I admit,' I replied. 'We just have to be patient to see whether it works or not. And, of course, I'll try it before they start the torture.'

'And why do you think you can do that?'

'Because I want to swim,' I even managed to smile a bit especially because Sam looked at me even more sadly. 'And since I'll swim, they have to untie me. Winnetou told me that I will swim.'

137

'Oho! I can see it now.' Sam's eyes twinkled a little. 'You think they'll make us fight for our life. You must know that they will make it as difficult as possible. But still, we would have more chance to survive than on these poles. And if I must, I'd rather die in a battle than tied up.'

During this conversation I saw that Winnetou and his father were talking to Tangua by the Kiowa's tents.

The Apache formed a large half-circle around the poles. I did not know if it was ordered, or they followed an ancient custom, but in the first row there were the children, then the women and girls, then the adolescent boys, and finally the adult warriors. In the middle of the second row I saw Nsho-chih, and I noticed that she did not move her eyes from me. Then Inchu Chunna stepped in front of the rows, and started to speak.

'My Apache brothers, I'm talking to you, and the sons of the Kiowa tribe can also hear my words.'

He paused, and when he saw that everybody was paying attention, he continued.

'The Great Spirit gave this land to us. Our fathers and grandfathers lived here happily. Then the palefaces came over the Great Water, and put their boots on our land. In the beginning there were few of them, and we received them amicably. But more and more came, and they became wickeder and wickeder. They built large cities, and burnt the forests. They killed the bison and the mustangs. The red children of the Great Spirit couldn't find their food. They retreated to the forests, but the whites pursued them even there. On the prairies, where our mustangs had grazed, now the Fire Mustang runs, and it brings many palefaces in large carts, and they all want to rob and murder.'

'Haw, haw!' resounded from everywhere.

'Every year, when the bison migrate, a group of our warriors go hunting. In the forest, where nobody had been last year, we found palefaces. They started to build a path for the Fire Mustang. We told them that this land was our property, and thus they could not build anything without our agreement. They laughed at us, and continued with their work. They also killed our beloved teacher, Klekih-Petra, who had never hurt anybody, and was always for peace.'

'Haw, haw!' they all agreed.

'We brought the body of our murdered teacher, and we have not buried him until today, the day of the revenge. We captured the murderer, and also four palefaces who belonged to the land grabbers. They deny their sin. Klekih-Petra taught us to be just and good. Because of his teaching we won't carry out the punishment without hearing them, if my Apache brothers agree.'

He paused, and then turned to us.

'You heard me. You must tell us the truth and you must answer all my questions. Did you belong to the white men who were measuring the land for the Fire Mustang?'

'We did. Three of us did not measure anything. We were there as scouts,' answered Sam. 'Old Shatt ...'

'Enough!' shouted the chief. 'Don't play with words! Answer to the question. You betrayed yourself with your first words. Tell me, who owns the land that you surveyed? You do or we?'

'You.'

'Do you know what the punishment of the horse thief is according to the law of the prairie?'

'Death,' answered Sam.

'What is worth more: a horse or a country?'

Sam remained quiet.

'Speak or I'll get you whipped!' shouted the chief at him.

'Don't threaten me!' replied the little brave man really angrily. 'You cannot force Sam Hawkins to anything.'

'Calm down, Sam, don't entice them!' I asked him.

'So, dog, what's your answer?' continued Inchu Chunna.

'What's worth more: the land or the horse?'

'The land of course,' said Sam shrugging his shoulder.

'A land thief deserves a hundred death, but had this been your only crime, we would have simply shot you dead. But you committed a more serious crime for which you deserve the torture. You took side with Kiowa, and wanted to entrap us. Our sixteen warriors died because of you, not to mention the wounded.'

'We had to ally ourselves with Kiowa, because of you.'

'Was there no other way?'

'No.'

'You lie again. You could have left our land as I ordered. Why didn't you do that?'

'Because we hadn't finished our work then.'

'So, you wanted to continue your land grabbing. Your friend, whom you call Old Shatterhand, did not recoil from attacking me, and knocking out Winnetou twice. Is it true?'

'Old Shatterhand only wanted a good outcome,' replied Sam. 'From the first minute he was the friend of the Apache, and wanted to save Winnetou's life. If he had not knocked him out, then …'

'Shut up, you rascal,' interrupted Inchu Chunna. 'He's responsible for our imprisonment by the Kiowa. We were tied to the trees until execution! But the Great Spirit sent an invisible helper to our rescue. You didn't want to rescue us, but wanted our death. Is it true?'

'No!' said Sam stubbornly.

'Do you dare to deny it? I'll prove that you lie! Here's Tangua, the chief of the Kiowa. I asked him to be a witness. Did these palefaces want to help us?'

'Never!' cried Tangua with gleeful joy. 'They enticed us against you. They chewed my ear that we shouldn't pardon any Apache, but kill them all! Especially this one, who boasts about the strength of his fist, pushed for it,' Tangua pointed at me.

'Rabid lie!' I shouted indignantly.

'How dare you speak?' hissed Tangua at me. 'I'll smash your skull.'

'Hit, if you don't feel ashamed for hitting someone who cannot defend himself! Are you talking about investigation and justice? What investigation is it, when you don't even allow one to finish his sentence? What justice is it, when

140

your questions suggest guilt, even if the person is innocent? I can only spit for such a judgement! Start the torture that you've already decided! But you won't hear a single woe from us!'

'Uff, uff!' A female voice cried with great appreciation. I did not have to turn my head to know who it was, because I recognised Nsho-chih's voice.

'Uff, uff, uff!' others shouted too. The Indians respected courage the most, even in their enemies. I felt this, so I continued even more determined.

'When I met Inchu Chunna and Winnetou for the first time, my heart told me that these were brave, and just people who must be liked, and appreciated. I was wrong. The lies of a nobody were enough to mislead them, and they cannot hear then the truth.'

'I'll beat you to death, you dog!' shouted Tangua raging. He picked up his gun, and turned it to hit me with the butt.

Winnetou, however, stepped in.

'You will stay calm,' he said to the Kiowa chief, 'Old Shatterhand spoke daringly, but maybe he was right in one or another thing. Inchu Chunna, the chief of the Apache, has not finished the investigation. Only he can speak, and those he addresses.'

Tangua had to retreat.

Inchu Chunna came very close to me, and looked in my eyes. 'Why did you knock me out?'

'You attacked me, I only defended myself,' I replied 'I could have shot you dead if I wanted your death, but I didn't want to kill you. This is when Tangua rushed there to scalp you. You were unconscious, and I protected you from him.'

'The mangy coyote is lying!' roared Tangua.

'Is it really a lie?' asked him Winnetou.

'Yes. Hopefully you don't doubt my words, Winnetou, my brother?'

'When I arrived to the scene, you lay motionless, and so did my father. That's the truth. Old Shatterhand may now proceed!'

'This is when Winnetou hurried to help Inchu Chunna,' I said. 'His knife stabbed through my tongue, otherwise I would have explained to him everything. Somebody hit my head from behind, and I lost my consciousness. This is how you captured me.'

'Why did you intervene in the war of two Indian tribes?' asked Inchu Chunna.

'To avoid bloodshed,' I replied. 'Tangua wanted to kill the Apache prisoners. I prevented it.'

'He's lying,' crowed Tangua, 'all his words are lies. He has always wanted war, and never peace! His fist is strong, because the Bad Spirit lives in him! This is why he can knock out everyone!'

'I hit only to avoid bloodshed,' I answered. 'I have never killed anyone with my fist, only knock them out, if it was necessary. But with you, I will settle the bill differently, when I have a weapon in my hand!'

'Settle the bill with me?' laughed Tangua. 'You won't live that long. We'll burn you, and disperse your ashes in the wind! But fine, I promise, I'll fight with you if you have the chance.'

'Old Shatterhand is very bold when he thinks he'll be free again,' said the chief of the Apache. 'He may want to consider that he provided no evidence to us. Do you have anything else to say?'

'Not now. Maybe later.'

'Say it now because later you won't be able to speak!'

'No, not now. If I want to say it later, you will hear it, because Old Shatterhand's words cannot be disregarded. I'm silent now because I'm curious to hear your verdict.'

Inchu Chunna turned away.

'The time of judgement has arrived. The brave warriors whom I chose must join me to make the judgement.'

For his signal a few old warriors stepped forward. They held a council with the three chiefs. From the distance I saw that Tangua was animated. Obviously he tried everything to make the judgement the most severe.

While they held the council, I had the opportunity to talk to my companions.

'I wonder what will come out of it,' I asked Sam.

'Nothing good,' answered Sam.

'I say that everything could turn out good.'

'Then think of me after your death, Sir,' said Sam, 'and then you will recognise that I was right, hehehe!'

This little man never lost his strange humour, not even in the most difficult circumstances. He could not have hopes anymore, still he laughed, and made us laugh.

The council was finished. The old warriors returned to their place.

Inchu Chunna stepped in the middle, and started to speak, 'Apache and Kiowa warriors, listen to my words. The council of the elders have decided that these four palefaces first would be hunted in the water, then they would have to fight each other, and finally they would be burnt. But the youngest of them, the one whom they call Old Shatterhand, defended himself bravely, and his judges haven't forgotten his words. Thus we decided to change their punishment. We will turn to the Great Spirit to decide if they were guilty or innocent.'

He paused for increasing the tension in the audience.

Sam asked me: 'Do you know what would happen, Sir?'

'I think so,' I answered.

'Some kind of judgement of God, like in the old times in Europe,' said Sam. 'But let's listen!'

The chief of the Apache continued, 'The duel of two men will show the will of the Great Spirit. The paleface, who seems to be the noblest of them, Old Shatterhand, will fight with the leader of the Apache, Inchu Chunna.'

'Uff, uff, uff!' roared the sound of astonishment from all directions.

Inchu Chunna offered further explanations.

'Inchu Chunna's and Winnetou's names were blemished by the fist of this paleface. One of us would have to fight him. Winnetou had to give way to me, because I'm older, and

143

I'm also the high chief of the Apache. My victory will cleanse his name too.'

Inchu Chunna continued, 'Old Shatterhand will jump in the water, without weapons. He will have to swim across the river. I will swim after him with a tomahawk in my hand. If he can swim through the river, and get to the big tree on the other side alive, he won, thus he, and his companions will be free, and can leave to go wherever they want. But if I kill him either in the water or on the other bank before he reaches the big tree, then his companions must die too. We won't torture them, but will shoot them dead. Those who understood what I said, and agree with the judgement, should express their agreement.'

'Haw!' they shouted in agreement.

We recovered from our surprise, But Sam did not like the idea. 'I knew that there would be some trick in it. That you were chosen because you are the noblest! No! It's because you are a greenhorn! They should have sent me in the water, I can swim like a trout!'

'Don't worry about this, old man!' I encouraged him. 'I know something about the water too. He won't catch me!'

'But he will have the tomahawk! It's good not only in fighting, but also for throwing. These reds are so skilled that they can cut off the tip of a finger from a hundred steps.'

'I know, dear Sam. But I trust my luck, especially as I will add a little bit of trick.'

'You tell me about this trick only to console me,' waved Sam to express his despair.

'No, I mean it,' I replied. 'I have an excellent plan.'

'Yes?'

'You'll see it! Until then: if you see that I drowned, you can rub your hands happily.'

'I don't understand it at all, but I'm sure you are mad,' Sam shook his head.

I did not have time to explain because Inchu Chunna talked to me, 'Old Shatterhand, listen to me. We'll cut off your bondage. But don't think you can escape!'

144

'I've no intention! I wouldn't let my companions down!'

They cut my bondage. I stooped down a few times, and moved my hands up and down to refresh my circulation, and then I said, 'I'm proud that I have an opponent like the famous chief of the Apache. It's really a shame that I'm a bad swimmer. I got into trouble in small brooks, let alone such a broad river!'

'Uff, uff! I'm disappointed,' said Inchu Chunna, 'because it's not a glory to defeat a bad swimmer, especially as I'm one of the best in the tribe.'

'Who gets in the water first?' I asked stupidly.

'You.'

'And when do you throw the tomahawk?'

'When I feel like,' he answered contemptuously.

'So maybe when I'm swimming?'

'Maybe.'

I put on an even more care-burdened face. 'So, you can kill me when you want. Can I do the same?' I asked.

'If you don't kill me, you'll never get to the tree,' he replied, and it showed it on his face that he thought that I was so frightened that I lost my ability to think.

'And if I kill you, will it be alright?' I continued asking.

'You can kill me if you can,' he laughed, 'then you are all free. Let's start!'

I undressed to my belt, and also took off my boots. Inchu Chunna headed to the bank.

'One more question,' I said before I followed him. 'Do we get our property back, if we are free?'

He gave a short, impatient laugh, for he considered this question almost crazy, and replied haughtily, 'Yes, all your belongings. Everything.'

'Even the horses, and the guns?'

He snapped at me angrily, 'All! I have said it! Have you got no ears? As if a toad wants to compete with an eagle in flying, and asks the eagle what he would get if it defeated the eagle! If you swim just as stupidly as you speak now, I should have given you an old squaw as an opponent!'

The warriors, the women and the children gave way to us. As I passed by Nsho-chih, she cast a look at me as if she had said good-bye forever. They all followed me, and settled at the bank to watch the promising show.

It was a dangerous game for me. Had I swam directly over the river or up and down, Inchu Chunna's experienced, and strong hand would have thrown the tomahawk into my neck. There was only one way to avoid it: if I swam under water, and I was experienced in that. But it was not enough. At some point I had to put my head to the surface to take air. I had to arrange it so that he would not see me doing that. I looked along the bank in both directions if there was any opportunity. I was pleasantly surprised because the terrain was advantageous for me.

We stood at the middle of a clearance. On my left hand side, upstream, at about one hundred steps from me, there was a forest by the river bend. On my right, downstream, the edge of the forest was at four hundred steps.

Thus, I thought, if I dived, and nobody saw me coming up, everybody would believe that the water carried me downstream. Thus I would have to swim upstream even if it was difficult. I could do this, but how would I get air? I cast another look to the left. I noticed a little cavity just above the water level that I could reach while swimming under water. There the river washed into the bank, and thus the bank stuck out over the water. Even further, at about the same distance, there was driftwood gathering along the bank. I could use this for hiding too. "I'm lucky," I thought happily. The only thing left was to further reinforce Inchu Chunna's mistaken belief that I was a bad swimmer.

The Apache chief undressed, and put his tomahawk in his belt. He began to urge me, 'We can start, jump in!'

'Isn't it very deep?' I asked hesitating.

There was an infinite contempt on the chief's face. He signalled to one of the warriors to bring his spear. He put it in the water, and it could not reach the riverbed. I was very happy for this, but showed an even more anxious face.

146

'Now, you really know everything,' said Inchu Chunna impatiently. 'Let's start!'

What did Nsho-chih think of me? For a second I glanced back. Tangua was uproarious. Winnetou was wrinkling his forehead angrily. Nsho-chih was standing next to him, and downcast her eyes. She was ashamed for me.

'Now what?' growled Inchu Chunna at me. 'You should be afraid of me, not of the water. If you don't jump right now, I'll kill you right here!'

With a big sigh I jumped in the water. Inchu Chunna, as I learnt later, wanted to give me some advantage to get to the other side, and kill me there, but because of my pretended cowardice, he jumped in right after me to kill me as soon as I emerged.

I dived. The comedy was over. I swam against the current hard. I reached the overhanging bank, and lifted my head out of the water just to my lips. Nobody could see me from the bank, only from the river. But the chief, who was in the river, was looking for me in the opposite direction. I took another deep breath, and swam further underwater. I got to the driftwood, and there I could come up to the surface for air again. The branches covered my head, and I could look around safely.

There was only the third phase now: to the beginning of the forest. I climbed out of the water there, and ran along the bend of the river. The bushes covered me. I calmed my breathing, and looked back with a smile.

Inchu Chunna was still swimming about looking for me. He was waiting for when I would appear. He did not understand it. Did Sam Hawkins understand it? Did he know what I had meant when I had told him to rub his hand joyously if I drowned?

After the bend I jumped in the water again, and crossed it. Now I was on the bank of the river where the big tree was. From behind the bushes I could see that many Indians jumped in the water, and raked it with their spears to find my body. I could have walked to the tree if I wanted, but my plan was to give a lesson to Inchu Chunna, and prove to him that I did not want to kill him.

I entered the water, and lay on my back. I swam along the bank to the point opposite of the audience.

I climbed out of the river again, and shouted loudly, 'Sam Hawkins! We won! We won!'

The Indians spotted me only now. Their response was an indescribable howl. As if a thousand devils had roared, and stumped in anger. But they could not prevent me running towards the big tree. Inchu Chunna was still in the middle of the river; too far to throw his tomahawk towards me. But he was swimming hard to reach the other bank.

The tree was about three hundred steps from the bank. At half way I stopped, and I waited for Inchu Chunna. He approached panting, but he had not thrown his tomahawk yet. He knew that as long as I faced him, I could avoid a flying weapon. He could hit me only if I turned my back to him. "Well," I thought, "I'll do this favour to you!"

I started off towards the big tree again, but after twenty steps I stopped suddenly, and quickly turned around. What did I see? Exactly what I expected. Inchu Chunna was just throwing his tomahawk. In the last moment I jumped aside, the tomahawk flew near my head, and hit the ground well behind me. This was what I wanted. I ran there, picked up the weapon, and instead of the tree, I approached the chief.

He was raging in anger, and wanted to jump at me, but I swung the tomahawk threateningly.

'Stop, or I'll smash your skull with your own hatchet!'

He did not come closer, but he clinched his hand in a fist in his helpless anger.

'How did you get here? With the help of the Bad Spirit?'

'No! It was the Good Spirit who looked after me. Don't come closer, because if you attack me, the tomahawk will split your head, and I would really regret ...'

He completely lost his self-control. He leapt forward, and wanted to jump on me. I avoided it, and he crashed on the ground from the acceleration of the jump. In the next moment I knelt on him, grabbed him by his throat with my left hand, and with my right I raised the tomahawk high. 'Surrender!' I yelled at him.

'Never!'

'Then I'll smash your head!

'Kill me, dog,' he panted.

'No, I won't kill Winnetou's father. But I'll make you harmless. You forced me to do so.'

I hit his head with the flat end of the tomahawk. On the other side everybody thought that I had killed him. This rising roar was even more terrible than the previous. I tied up the chief with his own belt, and then I pulled him to the big tree, where I laid him on the ground. I had to make this unnecessary journey to meet the conditions. Leaving the chief by the tree, I rushed back to the river. On the other side a number of warriors jumped in the water led by Winnetou.

If these reached the bank, I could have ended up badly, thus I shouted to them, 'Back! Inchu Chunna is alive! He only lost his consciousness. But if you don't turn back right away, I'll kill him. Only Winnetou should cross. I want to talk to him.'

They did not listen, but Winnetou shouted a few words to them. They obeyed him, and they swam back. Winnetou came to the bank alone.

When he climbed out of the water, I told him, 'Don't worry, your father is fine.'

'Didn't you kill him?'

'Not at all. But I had to make him harmless.'

'But you could have killed him,' said Winnetou surprised.

'I don't like killing my enemies, let alone Winnetou's father. Here's his tomahawk, I give it to you.'

He took the tomahawk, and then he looked at me for a long time. His glance became gradually softer.

'What kind of a man are you, Old Shatterhand?' he asked at the end. 'I can't understand you.'

'You will, once you know me better.'

'You give me the weapon, and you give yourself over to my decision?'

'Winnetou is just, and he won't break his word.'

His eyes gleamed. He stretched out his hand to me while saying, 'You are right. You are free, and so are the other palefaces, except for Klekih-Petra's murderer. But let's see my father! Your hand can kill even if you don't want to.'

We both hurried to the big tree, and we untied the chief together. Winnetou leant over, and examined him.

'He's alive! His head will be buzzing for some time when he recovers. I'll send some men to carry him over the river. You, my brother, should also come with me.'

This was the first time he called me "brother". No matter many times I heard this kind, warm word from him later, he always meant it seriously.

We swam across the river. The Apache were waiting for us excitedly. Seeing that we were swimming next to each other in peace, they were at first surprised, and then started to understand what had happened.

Arriving to the bank, Winnetou grabbed my hand, and announced loudly, 'Old Shatterhand is the winner. He and his three companions are free.'

'Uff, uff, uff!' shouted the Apache.

Winnetou led me directly to the stakes. My friends greeted me bursting with joy.

'There are miracles!' cried Sam. 'How did you do this?'

'Long live Old Shatterhand!' cried Will and Dick.

Winnetou pulled out his knife, and gave it to me.

'You should release them. Their joy will be double if they can thank you for their freedom.'

A minute later six arms embraced me so enthusiastically that I was afraid of being strangled.

'When I saw that you disappeared under the water, I felt my heart broke,' said Sam. 'You frightened me, Sir!'

'Because you didn't listen to what I told you,' I replied. 'Can't you remember? "If you can see that I drowned, you can rub your hands happily." This was what I told you.'

'You told him?' asked Winnetou. 'Then the whole thing was a trick!'

'It was,' I admitted honestly.

'You are strong like the grey bear, but crafty like the prairie fox, my brother,' said Winnetou. 'I'm not envious of your enemies.'

'Still you were my enemy.'

'I was, but now I'm your friend.'

'So do you believe me more now than Tangua?'

He looked in my eyes for a long time. 'Your eyes are clear, and there are no signs of dishonesty in them. I believe you.'

I dressed up, and took the tin box from my pocket. 'And now I prove it to you that I have always been your friend,' I said. 'You, my brother, may know what this is.'

I took the curl of hair from my box, and gave it to him.

Winnetou stepped back in his surprise.

'My hair!' he exclaimed. 'How did you get it?'

'Inchu Chunna spoke about when the Kiowa tied him, and you to the trees, and the Great Spirit sent an invisible helper for their rescue. That was me.'

'You? You? So was it you who cut the shackles? It's you whom we can thank for our freedom and life!' he cried out completely confused.

It took a very long time until he completely regained his composure. Then he took my hand, and led me to the place where his sister was watching us from the distance.

'Nsho-chih,' said Winnetou, 'this is the brave warrior who rescued me and my father from the Kiowa. I just learnt it, he had not spoken about it before.'

The pretty Indian girl offered her hand to me, and said only, 'Forgive me …'

Instead of thanking what I had done for her family, she apologised. I understood her. She felt that she had been unjust to me. She had considered me wicked, coward, and useless even in the last half an hour. I squeezed her hand gently, and asked, 'Do you trust me now, Nsho-chih?'

'I will never again doubt you, my white brother.'

Tangua stood nearby, and looked at the ground gloomily.

I asked him, 'What do you, chief of the Kiowa, say now?'

'I've nothing to say to you,' he said.

'But I have something to tell you. Have you forgotten what I told you this afternoon?'

'I don't remember your mutterings.'

'I told you that I would settle the account with you when I have a weapon in my hand again.'

'I've nothing to do with you,' he growled.

'But you said that you would accept the challenge. Have you also forgotten that you called me a mangy dog? That you slandered me, and you wanted me to be dead, that you wanted my demise? You have done enough wicked things against me. I could kill you, and nobody would interfere. But I'm offering you an honest duel.'

'You are just a grain of sand, and I'm the chief of the Kiowa. I would fight a duel only with a chief.'

'I am a chief!'

'Prove it!'

'I'll prove it by hanging you on the first tree if you refuse to give me satisfaction.'

Threatening an Indian with hanging is an insult, as it is considered to be the most shameful death. Not surprisingly, Tangua immediately pulled his knife, and shouted, 'Dog, I will stab you!'

'You may, but in an honourable duel, man against man, and knife against knife.'

'I have nothing to do with you!'

'But I have with you! When I was tied up, and could not defend myself, you slandered me!'

Winnetou stepped between us and said, 'My brother Old Shatterhand is right. Tangua promised that he would fight with Old Shatterhand. Tangua also slandered him, and he has to take up the challenge. If he refuses, he is a coward. The duel has to happen right away, because nobody should say that the Apache warriors had a coward as their guest. So, what will the chief of the Kiowa do?'

152

Tangua was in the corner. Before he answered, he looked around. There were almost four times as many Apache than Kiowa, and they were on Apache land. In reality the Kiowa were half prisoners.

'I'll think about it,' he replied evasively.

'For a warrior there's no need to think about anything, if he's called a coward,' said Winnetou.

For this remark Tangua straightened up, and shouted, 'Tangua a coward? Who dares to say that? I'll stab him!'

'I will say it,' said Winnetou proudly, and calmly, 'if you don't accept Old Shatterhand's challenge.'

'I'm willing to fight him right now.'

'Then we have to decide the weapon.'

'Who will decide?'

Winnetou said, 'Old Shatterhand, because it was you, who insulted him.'

'But I'm a chief, and he hasn't proven that he is one.'

I started to have enough of it.

'Tangua can choose,' I said. 'It doesn't matter to me with what weapon I defeat him.'

'Do you think I would be so stupid to fight with you only with fist?' asked Tangua. 'I know your fist, I won't give you such an advantage.'

'Then knife?' I asked.

'No! I saw how you finished off Lightning Knife. You won't stab me like him. And also you won't hit me with the tomahawk as you hit Inchu Chunna.'

'Then?'

'Guns! My bullet will hit your lying heart.'

'Right. We will have a gun duel. But everybody can see who the liar is. You said that I had stabbed Lightning Knife. Earlier you stated that he had died in the battle. Now everybody can see what your words are worth!'

'Bring the guns!' roared Tangua raging. 'Let me silence this yapping dog forever!'

Winnetou sent somebody to the pueblo for my gun and the ammunition. When they had been taken from me, he had ordered that they should be preserved. Had he been thinking then that he would give them back to me?

'You can set the conditions, my white brother' said Winnetou turning to me.

'Doesn't matter to me,' I said. 'Tangua can name them.'

'Two hundred steps, and as many shots as needed until one dies,' stated Tangua.

'Right,' nodded Winnetou. 'I'll make sure that there won't be any cheating. You'll shoot in turns. I'll stand with a gun in my hand. The one who doesn't wait for his turn will get a bullet in his head. Who will shoot first?'

'I, of course,' cried the Kiowa chief.

Winnetou shook his head.

'Chief Tangua wants all the advantages. In my opinion Old Shatterhand has the right for the first shot.'

'I won't insist on it,' I answered. 'He can shoot first, then I, and that's it.'

'Not "that's it",' said Tangua. 'We will shoot until one of us collapses.'

'I said the same thing. My first shot will stretch you out.'

'Boaster!'

'You deserve to be shot dead,' I said, 'but I pardon you. It will be enough punishment for you to remain crippled for a whole life. My bullet will destroy your right knee!'

'What a boaster!' mocked Tangua. 'This paleface, whom his companions call greenhorn, wants to hit my knee from two hundred steps!'

I did not respond.

'Let's measure the two hundred steps,' said Winnetou.

They brought my bear slayer gun. I examined it, there was nothing wrong with it. Both barrels were loaded. For the sake of safety I shot the bullets in the air.

Sam approached me, and asked, 'I heard that you want to hit his knee only. Does this make sense?'

'I only want to give him a lesson.'

'I'd regret if he could get away so lightly. He's mean, and will remain our enemy forever. It's imprudent.'

154

'He is mean, that's true,' I answered, 'but the white men aren't innocent in it.'

'If I were you, I'd aim at his head or heart. You'll see he will do that.'

'But he'll fail. His gun is worthless.'

We stood at our places. I was calm as always in these situations, but Tangua was cursing, and even shook his fist towards me. Winnetou, who stood on the side, halfway between us, had enough of it, and warned him, 'The chief of the Kiowa should listen to me. I'll count to three, then he can shoot. Whoever shoots before "three" will regret it.'

The Indians lined up in two rows on the right and the left. There was a big enough space between the two rows. They were very quiet now.

'The turn of the chief of the Kiowa is the first one,' said Winnetou. 'One ... two ... Three!'

I stood motionless opposite my enemy. He lifted his gun to his shoulder already for Winnetou's first word, aimed carefully, and pulled the trigger. The bullet whistled by my ear. There was no other noise.

'Now Old Shatterhand's turn comes!' cried Winnetou. 'One ... Two ...'

'Just a moment!' I interrupted. 'I turned my chest to him, but the Kiowa chief shows me only his side!'

'Who can object to that?' asked Tangua. 'It's not one of the conditions.'

'It's true,' I agreed. 'The Kiowa chief can stand as he wants. He turns his narrower side to me believing that it gives him some advantage. He is mistaken. I'm only saying it as a warning. I promised that I would hit his right knee. It would have been, but now, if he shows me only his side, I would have to destroy both of his knees. This is the only difference. He can stand as he wishes.'

'Stop shooting with your words, use your gun!' shouted Tangua mockingly.

'It's Old Shatterhand's turn now,' repeated Winnetou. 'One ... two ... three!'

My gun went off. Tangua cried out, dropped his gun, swung his two arms and then fell on the ground.

'Uff, uff, uff!' I could hear from every direction. The Indians ran to see his wounds. I also approached, and the crowd opened me a path.

'He shot his knee! Both knees!' I could hear.

When I arrived, Tangua jerked on the ground whining. Winnetou knelt by him, and examined his wounds.

He turned to me, and announced. 'The path of the bullet was as you had described, my white brother. It smashed both knees of the Kiowa chief. Tangua won't be able to mount a horse again. It could be good; maybe he won't want to steal other tribes' horses.

The wounded man caught sight of me, and flooded me with his curses.

Instead of a reply, I only said to him, 'You can thank your trouble to yourself.'

He did not dare to whine loudly in spite of his pains, because the Indians considered it a shame to express pain.

He bit his lips, and clinched his fist.

'How will I go home now?' he murmured. 'I'll have to stay with the Apache.'

Winnetou heard it, and shook his head.

'You cannot stay,' he said. 'There's no room here for horse thieves. You caused the death of many of our warriors. We didn't kill you because we were contented with the compensation. You cannot ask more than this. But we won't accept any Kiowa in this pueblo.'

'I can't mount a horse.'

'Old Shatterhand's wound was more serious, yet he made the journey all the way here. You have to leave today. If we find a Kiowa tomorrow, there won't be a pardon. Haw, I have spoken.'

Winnetou took my arm, and led me out of the crowd. His father, with the support of two warriors, was just arriving then. Winnetou hurried to him, and I was looking for my friends.

'At last we can speak in private!' cried Sam. 'Tell me, what ring were you showing to Winnetou?'

'It wasn't a ring, but his hair. I cut it off when I sneaked up to release him, and his father.'

'Sneaked up to them! Damn it! This is why they could disappear then! And you didn't tell us at all!'

'I don't like boasting.'

'Damn it! How did you do it?'

'Only,' I answered smiling, 'as it could be expected from a greenhorn.'

'You are mean! Definitely mean! I can imagine how you laughed at us! But you were right I have to say. Respect to such a greenhorn! At least there's someone who can rescue me, if everything is breaking!'

'I did this time, dear Sam, didn't I?'

'You did! Once you will become the most famous man of the West, hehehe!'

It would have continued in the same manner, but then Winnetou was approaching us with his father and sister.

Inchu Chunna looked in my eyes for a long time, and then said, 'I know now everything … Winnetou told me everything. Please don't have a grudge against me. You are a brave warrior, and a clever one too. You'll defeat all your enemies. Do you want to smoke the peace pipe with me?'

'With joy,' I said. 'I'd like to be your friend and brother.'

'Then come with me and my daughter to the pueblo. You'll get a new room; one that's right for you.'

Inchu Chunna and Nsho-chih came on my two sides, and we started off towards the pueblo. My three companions followed us. We now climbed up to the pueblo, which had been our prison for many weeks, as free men.

"BEAUTIFUL DAY"

ONLY WHEN I returned to the pueblo could I see how huge this building was. I was led to the third floor. The nicest rooms of the building were there. This was where Inchu Chunna lived with his son and daughter, and this is where we four got our accommodation.

I got a nice, big room. It did not have any window, and received the light only through the entrance, but it was tall and broad, and the Sun shone in.

I had not even looked around when Beautiful Day came in. She gave me a beautifully crafted calumet with tobacco. I filled the pipe and lit it.

'My father gives you this calumet as a present,' said Nsho-chih. 'He gained the clay from the sacred mine, and I crafted its head. Nobody's lips have touched it, and when you smoke it, think of us.'

'I don't know how to thank your goodwill,' I replied, 'as I don't deserve it.'

'You do! You saved my father's and my brother's life several times. We took you to our heart, and we consider you to be a brother, as if you were born an Apache.'

'It's a great honour to me that such brave warriors accept me as one of theirs. This is a beautiful pipe! Your work is artistic, Nsho-chih.'

She blushed for my compliment,

'I know that the daughters and wives of the palefaces are much more light-handed than I am,' she said. 'I'll bring you something else.'

She left, and then returned with my revolvers. She also brought the ammunition, my knife, and everything else that were not in my pockets. I thanked her, and told her that nothing was missing.

'Will my companions get back their belongings too?'

'Yes, everything. I believe they have already got them. Inchu Chunna is with them right now.'

'And our horses?'

'You will get them back. And Sam Hawkins will get back his mule, Mary.'

'You even know its name?'

'Yes, he talked a lot about it. And also about his old gun, Liddy. He's an amusing man, but he's a good hunter too.'

'And a faithful friend,' I said. 'But I would like to ask something. Promise that you'll answer honestly.'

'Nsho-chih never lies,' she answered proudly.

'Have you taken everything from the Kiowa?'

'Naturally.'

'And from my companions?'

'From them too.'

'Then why didn't you search my pockets?'

'My brother, Winnetou, ordered not to.'

'But he thought I was his enemy!'

'His heart ached that he couldn't consider you anything else, even more …'

Nsho-chih became quiet suddenly.

'I know what you wanted to say, Nsho-chih. Not only did he consider me an enemy, because we can respect even our enemies if they deserve it, but Winnetou considered me a mean, lying man, didn't he?'

'You said so.'

'I hope he can see that he was wrong. Let me ask one more question. What will happen to Rattler?'

'He's being tied to the torture stake by the river.'

'And I wasn't told!'

'Winnetou thought that you probably did not want to see and hear it.'

'Possibly. What will the tortures be?'

'The most serious ones,' answered the girl. 'He's the most debased paleface we have ever met. He killed the White Father, Winnetou's teacher, the teacher of the whole Apache tribe, whom we loved and respected, without any reason.'

'This is inhuman!'

'He deserves it!'

'Could you watch it?'

'I will watch it.'

'You, a young girl?'

For a while she looked at the ground, then she lifted her eyes to me, and asked, 'Are you surprised?'

'Yes. It's not for women.'

'Do the women of the white men think like this?'

'Naturally.'

'You aren't saying the truth. Or you are mistaken. If a criminal is beheaded among the white men, the paleface squaws watch it, don't they?'

'That was a long time ago. Not anymore.'

'I've heard many things about your squaws. They are not as gentle-hearted as you said. They don't like when they suffer, but others' suffering doesn't move them, be it a person or an animal. They keep birds in a cage in their houses. Do you know how much a bird suffers when it's deprived of its freedom? Winnetou has been in your towns. Aren't race horses ridden to death? Are there no dogfights? I am a young, inexperienced girl, and the white men may call me a savage, but I can tell you many things that your delicate squaws do without any feeling. I would feel horrified in their place. Count the many thousands of delicate, beautiful white women who have tortured their slaves to death! Those who stood with smiling lips when black servants were whipped! And here we have a criminal, a murderer. He ought to die, he deserves it. I want to be there, and you judge me for this! Is it really wrong of me that I want to see his death? And if it was wrong, who is to blame that we are forced to repay cruelty with hardness?'

So far I had known Nsho-chih only as a gentle, quiet, pretty young girl, but now she spoke passionately. Her face was flaming, and her eyes were flashing. Involuntarily I thought that she was even more beautiful like this.

'Maybe you are right,' I said. 'Go, if you want to. But I'll be there, if your father and brother don't prevent me.'

'They won't be happy, but still, they won't prevent you. You're a free man now, you can do what you want.'

She left, and a little later I stepped out onto the terrace. Sam stood there, and smoked his pipe.

'Did you hear what they are preparing?' I asked.

'Nothing special,' he replied. 'They're executing Rattler in the Indian way.'

'But he's still a human!' I exclaimed indignantly.

'He doesn't deserve to be called a human,' he said. 'He's closer to the beasts. Who knows how many murders he has committed? Klekih-Petra didn't do anything against him, still he murdered him.'

'He was drunk.'

'So what? I'm angry whenever I hear this! This is not a mitigating circumstance, but it makes the sin even bigger. Would you let him go, Sir?'

'No, not at all,' I said. 'But I think a bullet in his head would be enough.'

'Don't you think of speaking for him!' Sam warned me. 'The Indians have the right to judge him according to their laws, and Rattler caused an unrepairable damage to them by killing their teacher. Are you going down to the river?'

'Yes.'

'Then I'll join you, and I will also call Dick and Will.'

The four of us went to the valley of the Pecos River. The Kiowa had gone. Our wagon was still there. The Apache formed a circle around the wagon, and they were waiting. I caught sight of Inchu Chunna and Winnetou in the middle of the circle.

Soon Winnetou spotted me, and he hurried to me.

'Why didn't my white brother stay in the pueblo?'

'I heard that Rattler was about to be executed.'

'Yes,' said Winnetou.

'Where is he? I can't see him.'

'In the wagon, next to his victim.'

'What will his death be?'

'What he deserves.'

'I don't want to argue for his life,' I said, 'I only ask you to finish him quickly.'

161

Winnetou's face darkened.

'It's good that only I heard your request,' he replied. 'My warriors would despise you for this, and your request would have hurt them.'

'Tangua committed an offence, but you forgave him.'

'Tangua regretted what he did,' said Winnetou.

'And if Rattler regretted?'

'Never! And he offended you too. But if he apologises to you, I'll shorten his sufferings, because you saved my life, and my father's life. You can talk to him in a minute. Look!'

They lifted the canvass of the wagon. They took out a long, coffin-like box. A man was tied to it.

'The coffin,' said Sam, who had come closer. 'They built it from trunks of trees, and then covered them with wet skins. When the skins dried, they shrunk, and this made the coffin airtight.'

On the bank, a few hundred steps from us, there was a lonely rock. Around the rock there were big stones. They carried the coffin there. They put the coffin down, and propped it up on the rock. Rattler was now in a standing position. The Indians lined up around the rock in a half circle. There was a deep silence. Inchu Chunna stepped into the middle of the circle, and started to speak. In the flowery language of the Indians he remembered the achievements of Klekih-Petra. Then he pointed at Rattler, and stated that the punishment for his crime was slow death.

Rattler's hands were tied behind the coffin. His mouth was gagged. When I reached the scene, Inchu Chunna took the gagging from Rattler's mouth, and said, 'Selkih-Lata wants to talk to the murderer. He can.'

Rattler could see that I was free, and that I was friendly with the Apache. I thought he would beg me to plead his case with the Apache. But he had no intention to bow to me, just the opposite.

As soon as the gagging was taken from his mouth, he growled at me, 'What do you want from me? Go away! I've nothing to say to you!'

'Look, Mr Rattler,' I told him patiently, 'you are at the threshold of death. This cannot be changed, but …'

'Stop barking, you dog!' he hissed, and he wanted to spit on me, but he could not turn his head because of the bondage.

'Even if you must die,' I continued, 'it does matter how you die. Winnetou promised that you would have a quick death with one condition.'

I expected him to hook on the opportunity, and ask me what the condition was. But he did not ask anything. He started to swear obscenely. I interrupted him.

'The condition is that you apologise to me,' I said.

'Apologise to you, you dog? I would rather bite off my tongue, and suffer all the tortures of the red bastards. Go to hell!' he yelled.

'Think it over, Rattler!' I warned him for the last time.

'Are you still here? I would smack you if I wasn't tied up!'

Inchu Chunna's face showed his disgust with the man. He took my arm, and pulled me aside.

'Your intervention was in vain,' he said. 'He's a vile man, and his debasement is infinite!'

I still tried to excuse him.

'I have to say, he's brave,' I said.

'This is not bravery,' commented Sam contemptuously, 'only blinding anger.'

'What is he angry about?'

'About you, my friend. He thinks you're to blame that he has fallen into the hands of the reds. He hasn't seen us since the day when we were captured, and now he sees you and us free. The reds are friendly towards us, while he has to die. For him this is, of course, a good enough reason to think that we caused his sufferings. But you will see: when the torture starts, he will whistle quite differently.'

The horrible event started. As I had never seen such a thing before, I decided to stay as long as I could cope with it.

For Inchu Chunna's order a few young warriors stepped forward. They had knives in their hands. They stood about fifteen steps from Rattler. They threw the knives at him, but they made sure that they would not hit him. The first knife hit the coffin on the right of Rattler's leg, the other on the left. They continued until they marked out Rattler's two legs.

So far Rattler had showed indifference, but now the knives flew higher and higher. I could see that they wanted to frame Rattler's body with their knives.

Once it was done, they pulled out their knives from the coffin. This was only a prelude in which the young warriors could show what they had learnt. They had acquired the skill of aiming, and throwing knives. For the chief's signal they returned to their place, and sat down.

Now the older warriors came. They threw from thirty steps. When the first warrior took his place, Inchu Chunna pointed at Rattler's right upper arm, and said, 'There!'

The knife flew, and hit precisely. This was now serious. Rattler felt the pain, and he let out a howl. The second knife went through the same muscle of the other arm, and the howling doubled. The third and fourth flew to his thighs as the chief designated. I haven't seen any blood as Rattler was not stripped naked, and the warriors made it sure that the wounds would not be serious as it would have shortened the punishment.

Apparently Rattler had not believed that the Apache would carry out their threat. But now he whined so loudly that it was bad to listen to. The audience expressed their contempt with mocking shouts.

An Indian would have behaved very differently at the torture stake. He would not have shown his fear or pain. He would have pretended that he did not feel anything, and would have poured scorn on his opponents. Whining or begging for mercy was despised. The warriors declined to deal with such a coward because it was shameful to them.

Women and children finished off such prisoners.

Rattler screamed my name several times. Inchu Chunna told me, 'You may go to this man, my brother, and ask him why he screams. The knives have not yet done any harm.'

'Come, Sir, come,' cried Rattler. 'I need to talk to you!'

I went to the coffin, and asked him, 'What do you want from me now?'

'Please pull the knives out of my arms and legs! Who can endure so many wounds?'

'I cannot do that! Did you really believe that you will be pardoned? You killed a man!'

'I cannot help what I did. You know that I was drunk!'

'The fact remains. And you were warned. This is the consequence of ignoring the advice. Still, if you apologise to me, you'll die quickly, without torture.'

'Dying quickly? But I want to live!'

'That's impossible.'

He screamed at the top of his voice, and then began such a wailing and crying that I could not stand anymore, and moved away.

'Stay with me, Sir, or they will start it again!' he shouted after me.

Inchu Chunna growled at him, 'Stop it, you skunk! I believe our warriors won't want to make their knives dirty with your blood.'

He turned to the warriors and asked, 'Who wants to take revenge on this cowardly murderer?'

Nobody stepped forward.

'Haw!' said the chief. 'It's not appropriate for an Apache warrior to kill such a whining toad. He cannot be buried with Klekih-Petra either. How could a toad and a swan arrive to the eternal hunting grounds at the same time? Cut his belts!'

Two boys jumped forward for his signal, and cut him off from the coffin. Neither was more than ten years old. They tied the murderer's hand on his back. Rattler did not dare to resist. 'Push him in the water!' came the next order. 'If he reaches the other bank, he can run wherever he wants.'

Rattler ejected a short cry in his joy. The two boys led him to the river, and pushed him in the water. He did not have enough self-respect to jump in by himself. He first dived, but soon came to the surface. He turned on his back, and tried to swim to the other bank. It was not easy with tied hands, but not impossible. As his legs were free, he could push himself forward.

I was surprised. Surely, the Apache would not allow him to reach the other bank? I did not want this. He deserved death. If he was free, who knows what further crimes he would commit! The boys stood on the bank motionlessly. They followed the murderer with their eyes.

'Shoot him in his head!' ordered Inchu Chunna.

The boys ran to a pile where the warriors had left their weapons. Each grabbed a gun, and hurried back to the bank. It was clear that they knew how to handle guns. They considered it a sport. They had not yet shot. They wanted to make their task more difficult. Rattler almost reached the other bank, when both boys pulled the trigger, and they yelled the Apache war cry in their adolescent voice. Both hit Rattler's head. The swimming man immediately immersed.

The Indians usually followed the death of their enemies with cries of victory, but at this time there was not a single sound. They did not even care to check if the body of the coward was thrown up by the water, or he was only wounded, and survived.

Inchu Chunna came to me, and said, 'This paleface was not afraid to commit any kind of villainy, but when it was about his skin, he was crying like a child.'

'Yes,' I answered, 'but you must remember that there are evil and good people in all skin colours.'

'You misunderstand me,' said the chief. 'I don't want to insult you. No peoples are better or worse than the others. I agree with you. But it was not what I wanted to talk to you about. We will bury Klekih-Petra now. He talked to you the last person in his life. What did he tell you? I ask it, because nobody understood it.'

'He spoke to me in his mother tongue. He asked me to love Winnetou like my brother. To be his faithful friend, and look after him. I promised that I would do that.'

'You have fulfilled your promise.'

'Can I be present at the funeral?'

'I wanted to ask you to attend it,' said Inchu Chunna. 'Come with me.'

Under Winnetou's supervision they had already dug the grave by the rock. A strange ceremony started, and it lasted for about an hour.

I listened to the monotonous mourning songs, which were occasionally interrupted by the loud cries of the old women, with bowed head. In the crowd a strange figure appeared. His face and body were completely covered by his long, loose, hooded robe on which there were all kinds of shapes. He was the magic man of the tribe. With strange motions he jumped, and danced around the coffin.

A bit later I caught sight of Nsho-chih. She brought two nicely burnt clay cups from the pueblo. She filled them with water from the river. When she arrived, she put them on the coffin. Inchu Chunna lifted his hand for which the mourning song stopped. The magic man stooped down on the ground. The chief went to the coffin, and in a ringing, ceremonial voice he started to speak.

'The Sun rises in the East, and it sets in the West. The forests become green in the spring, and in the autumn they prepare for a long winter sleep. Isn't it the same with men?'

'Haw!' rambled the answer around.

'The man rises like the Sun in the beginning of his life, and at the end of his journey he goes to the grave. The man's life has spring, summer, autumn, and winter. The Great Spirit ordered this, and we have to accept it. But if the sky becomes dark already in the afternoon, if the frost freezes the foliage already in the autumn, if the life of the man breaks too early, we have to ask: why it happened?'

Then he related Klekih-Petra's death in details. He was killed without reason, his murderer attacked him like a predator. He remained faithful to the Apache people, on whose rising he was constantly working, until his death. But the Great Spirit led another paleface to the scene at that

167

moment, a paleface who was just as honest as he was. He promised to the dying man that he would continue his work, and he would become a faithful friend of Winnetou. He was a brave warrior, not like other palefaces whose aim was to rob the Indians. Selkih-Lata wanted the Indian people to live in peace with other tribes, even with the palefaces.'

'This is why,' said Inchu Chunna, 'we consider him Klekih-Petra's successor. I decided that I would adopt him as my son, and he would become Winnetou's brother, if you also want it.'

'Haw! Haw! Haw!' the stormy agreement resounded.

For Inchu Chunna's signal I stood by the coffin, while Winnetou stood opposite me on the other side. We both rolled up our shirt sleeves on our left arm. Inchu Chunna made a little wound on Winnetou's arm with his knife, and then captured some of the sipping blood in one of the cups. He did the same with my arm and blood for the other cup.

'From today, you are brothers, and you should look after each other as it's right for good brothers to do. To confirm it, drink each other's blood.'

We drank the water from the cups at the same time. The water of the Pecos River was refreshing, and one could not taste the few drops of blood.

Inchu Chunna squeezed my hand and said, 'You aren't only my son, but a son and warrior of the Apache people. We expect many more brave, and just deeds from you. Your fame will reach other Indian tribes, and everyone will respect you as the chief of the Apache.'

Enthusiastic cries confirmed this statement. On the basis of the blood contract they elected me as a chief. The greatest chief, of course, was Inchu Chunna, but they recognised me as an equal to Winnetou. Their trust and their friendship was touching. I was affected by the ceremony, still I smiled at my chieftainship. Not much earlier I had been a poor private tutor in St Louis, then I had become a surveyor, and now I was a junior chief of the Apache. It was a wonderful career, I should say!

The coffin was lowered in the pit, and was covered with soil. They placed the big stones on the top so that the grave could stand out from the ground for a long time. Further mourning songs were sung, and then the funeral was over.

We returned to the pueblo, where a lunch, similar to our wake, followed. The warriors and their families sat down in smaller or bigger groups. I was invited to Inchu Chunna's own room.

The chief lived in the best room of the third floor. It was a very simply furnished, big room, however, its walls were decorated with an exceptional Indian weapon collection. Nsho-chih served us. She had cooked also the food and was an expert in making Native American dishes. The lunch was consumed in silence as everybody was in their thoughts.

I felt it was right to say good-bye to the host, and return to my room. Winnetou followed me, and stopped me on the terrace.

'Are you going to bed, my white brother,' he asked, 'or would you like to have a walk with me?'

'A little walk would be good to me.'

Our path led to the bank of the river. I asked Winnetou if the whole tribe lived in the pueblo. He explained that the pueblo could accommodate only a small part of the tribe. Only the chiefs and leading warriors lived there with their families. It was the centre of the life of the tribe, but most of the Apache lived in nearby villages. He also explained that the Apache tribe had many, many branches, the Llanero, the Jicarilla, the Tonto, the Chiricahua, the Pinaleño, the Gila, the Lipan, the Mimbreño, the Copper Mine Apache, and others, but they all obeyed Inchu Chunna. Even the Navajo, though they did not belong to the Apache, often followed Inchu Chunna's orders.

'From today I belong to the Apache tribe,' I said, 'and I'm proud of this. What will happen to my companions?'

'We cannot adopt them, because it's possible only in exceptional situations,' replied Winnetou. 'But don't worry about your good companions. We consider them to be our friends and allies. We will smoke the peace pipe with them tomorrow.'

'It's not our custom,' I said smiling. 'The white men think a handshake is enough.'

'I know,' said Winnetou with despise. 'The whites are all brothers, except that they wage war among each other, just like the red men. They keep on talking about love, but their behaviour is different.'

I had to agree with him.

Then Winnetou suddenly asked me, 'Why did you leave your homeland, my white brother?'

The Indians are more discreet to raise a question like this. He could do it because he had become my brother. It was understandable that he wanted to know everything about me. Still he had to have a more serious reason to ask this.

'To make my fortune. This was my goal,' I replied.

'What do you call "fortune"? Money?'

'Yes,' I answered a little ashamed.

Winnetou, who so far had held my arm, now let it go. There was an uncomfortable silence. I looked at his face in secret. There was disappointment on it.

'Is money so important for your people?' he asked after the pause.

'Yes, everything turns around money,' I admitted.

'Is it … why you joined the land-grabbers?' he asked with long pauses as if every word had caused him pain.

'In our world everybody says that happiness is about money,' I explained.

'And you believe this? It's a mistake! Gold made the Indians unhappy. The gold brought the palefaces who chase us out from our ancient lands. It's the gold that causes the demise of the Indian tribes. Don't tell me that gold is the happiness.'

'I didn't mean this,' I said. 'I know that health, wisdom, honesty, and friendship are worth more.'

'Haw!' cried Winnetou. 'I'm happy that this is how you think. But then why did you mention money?'

I explained to him that the game, the fruit did not belong to everyone in my society, and most people lived on working for other people for which they received money. If one did not earn money, he could die of hunger. This was why I left my homeland, crossed the ocean, and became a surveyor.

'Did you get much money for it?' he asked.

'I only got some advance payment, clothing, and the equipment,' I replied. 'I would have got the rest when the work was done.'

'And if it's not done?'

'Then, I don't know.'

Winnetou was quiet for a long time, then said, 'I'm sorry that we caused you a loss with our action. Was there a lot of work left to do?'

'We would have finished it in a few days.'

'Uff! Had I known you then as I do now, we would have attacked the Kiowa only a week later.'

'When we finished the … the land-grabbing?' I asked slightly insulted.

'I just said it,' he remarked. 'In fact you didn't start the land theft, you only measured, and drew maps. The land-theft starts when the paleface workers come, and build the path of the Fire Mustang. But it won't happen!'

Suddenly I remembered something.

'What happened to our tools?' I asked.

'My men wanted to break them up, but I didn't allow it,' said Winnetou. 'I didn't go to the school of the whites, but I know that such tools are very valuable. This is why I ordered that they should be preserved. They will be returned to you.'

'I'm glad, but I won't do surveying anymore.'

'Then you lose your money that you have earned with your work so far.'

'Not really. I made a copy of the drawings. They are all here,' I hit at the tin box in my pocket.

'Uff, uff!' exclaimed Winnetou.

It expressed joy, but also the surprise of my carefulness and cleverness.

We returned to the pueblo. For a long time I had not slept so well as that night. On the following day Hawkins, Stone and Parker were the centre of the events. In a great celebration the Apache smoked the peace pipe with them. As always, there were long speeches. To these Sam responded in his own clownish way. To my big surprise, the Indians understood his jokes well, and laughed aloud. In the evening I hosted my companions in my own room. We killed the time with joyous, teasing talk until midnight.

On the following day the scouts, whom were sent after the Kiowa, returned. They followed the Kiowa for some distance, and now they reported that they had not found anything suspicious. The whole Kiowa group returned to their village, and it seemed that they did not plan anything malicious.

The time of idyllic peace had arrived. We enjoyed the hospitality of the Apache thoroughly, and also allowed ourselves a well-deserved rest. Sam's only occupation was to ride to the forest on his Mary every morning so that the mule would not forget what she already knew, and also to improve on this.

I was not resting on the bear skins for long. Winnetou decided that he would train me as an Indian. We rode out every morning, and often returned only in the evening. All day I had to exercise what a good hunter and warrior must know. Winnetou showed me how to approach the enemy without being noticed, and find out their plans. Sometimes he separated from me, and gave me the task to find him. With excellent skills he erased his tracks, and I really had to push myself to find him. How many times he hid in the bushes or stood in the water of the Pecos River up to his chin, hiding in the branches of the bushes on the bank! He watched me smiling as I passed by him without noticing him. He warned me of my mistakes, and showed to me how I should act, and what I should not do. It was an excellent practical education, and he enjoyed teaching me so much that I learnt with joy from him.

He never praised me, but not a word left his lips that could have been considered as a reproach. He was a master in everything that the Indian life demanded, but he was also a master of teaching.

Sometimes I returned from our journey so tired that I could not move. On the day following such a journey, it was easier, because Winnetou gave me language lessons. He wanted me to learn the language of the Apache of which I had known something, but only small. In fact, I had three teachers because in my language education Inchu Chunna and Nsho-chih participated too. Nsho-chih taught me the dialect of the Mescalero, Inchu Chunna of the Llanero, and Winnetou of the Navajo. Fortunately for me, the languages of the different Apache tribes, and their vocabulary were similar, thus I could progress quickly.

Sometimes Nsho-chih accompanied us on our journeys. She was clearly happy when I solved my task.

One day we were deep in the forest when Winnetou told me to separate from them, and be back in a quarter of an hour. They would not be there, and my task would be to find Nsho-chih, who would hide in the meantime. I walked about, and returned to the place at the agreed time.

The tracks of Winnetou and Nsho-chih started from there, and it was easy to find, and follow them. Suddenly I lost the track of the Indian girl. I knew that she had a very light walk, but the ground was so soft that even the lightest footprint had to be visible. I leant forward, strained my eyes in vain, because I could not find a single bent grass. The ground was not only soft, but thick and sensitive moss covered it. I could find Winnetou's tracks, but not that of his sister's, and my task was to find her. Winnetou must have been near, and watched the mistakes that I made.

I examined the ground again in a great circle, but I could not find anything that could have helped. I could not understand it. Nobody could have left from there without leaving a footprint on the moss. It was enough if she touched it with her moccasin, however light was her step. Touching?

173

That was it! What if Nsho-chih's feet did not touch the moss-covered ground? I examined Winnetou's footprints for the third time. I noticed that from a certain point they became deeper. Could he have taken his sister in his arms and carried her? He had said that the task would be difficult. But once I recognised the clue, it was not difficult.

I assumed that his feet's impression were deeper because of Nsho-chih's weight. Now the only thing was to find the tracks of the slim Indian girl. Of course, I had to look for it not on the ground, but in the air.

When Winnetou walked alone, his two arms were free, and thus he could turn away the branches of the bushes. When he carried the girl, he could not make it sure that no branches were broken off, thus when following his tracks, I did not watch the path, but the bushes, and the branches. Nsho-chih had not thought of pushing the branches away from her, and I found broken branches, and torn leaves here and there. All these confirmed my assumption.

The footprints led to a clearance. I could have simply crossed this clearance, however, I wanted to surprise them. Therefore I went around the clearance, of course with necessary care, and also noiselessly in the cover of the bushes. When I got to the other end of the clearance I examined the ground. I could not see Winnetou's footprints. So he did not go further, and he was hiding with his sister nearby. I lay down on the ground, and crawled forward in a large semi-circle. I could not find footprints anywhere. So, they must have been in the bushes at the edge of the clearance where the tracks ended. I crawled very carefully. After one more noiseless motion I spotted them. They were stooping in a bush with their back to me, which was quite natural as they expected my approach from the opposite direction. They whispered to each other, I could hear their words, but I could not understand them.

I was contented that I could surprise them, and thus I crawled closer. I was so close to them that I could have touched them. Then I heard Winnetou's voice.

'Should I go for him?' he asked.

'Not yet,' answered Nsho-chih. 'He may yet find us.'

'You are wrong, sister. The task is too hard. His eyes would find all the tracks, but this time he would have to follow my thinking, and he hasn't yet learnt that.'

'Let's wait a bit,' whispered Nsho-chih.

'Yes, he would have to find out my thought,' repeated Winnetou, 'and yours. And the wish of all of us.'

"What wish?" I thought, "I would do anything for them!"

'Couldn't we ask him?' whispered the girl.

'No,' stated Winnetou decidedly.

'Why? I'm the daughter of the greatest Apache chief!'

'Exactly for this reason. Every Apache warrior or even a paleface would be happy if he could lead such a girl, as Nsho-chih, to his tent. But Old Shatterhand is different.'

'How do you know this, Winnetou, if you haven't asked Old Shatterhand?'

'I know it, because I know him. If he chose a squaw, it wouldn't be an Indian girl, whatever beautiful she was.'

'Maybe he has already chosen a paleface girl?'

'I don't think so. But if he chooses somebody, she must be outstanding.'

'And aren't I such?'

'You are, but only among the Indian girls. You have learnt everything that an Indian girl must know. But you don't know the life and customs of the palefaces. You have to learn a lot to be the first among them too.'

Nsho-chih bowed her head, and stayed silent. Winnetou caressed her face, and continued, 'I know that it's painful what I'm saying, but Winnetou doesn't lie, not even for gentleness. Your desire cannot be fulfilled, except if …'

Nsho-chih tossed up her head. 'So, is there a way?'

'Maybe. If you went to the town of the palefaces.'

'What for?'

'To learn everything that the girls of the palefaces study. Everything that's necessary for Old Shatterhand to consider you as the right partner.'

'Then I'll go there as soon as it's possible! Talk to our father, Winnetou! Ask him to let me go there. Because if he doesn't agree, then I ...'

I could not hear anything else, because I withdrew into the thicket. I was deeply ashamed for my eavesdropping. They should never know this! I must disappear without being noticed. The smallest noise could have betrayed that I had heard their secret. And then I could not stay among them even for a moment.

I crawled back so carefully as if my life depended on it. When I reached the appropriate distance, I stood up, and quickly went around the clearance. I breathed freely only when I stood where the track led to the clearance. Now I stepped forward, and shouted, 'Are you here, Winnetou?'

Nobody responded.

'I know that you are here,' I continued. 'You are hiding among the bushes. I spotted you!'

Then the twigs cracked, and Winnetou appeared, but he was alone.

'Have you found Nsho-chih, my white brother?' he asked.

'I know where she is,' I answered.

'Where?'

'Where her track led to.'

'You couldn't see her track.'

'I could. Not on the ground, but higher. The broken branches showed where you carried her.'

'How come you started to watch the branches?'

'Because of your footprints,' I answered. 'They had a deeper impression from a certain point, and from this I found out everything. Should I show you where she is?'

I did not have to, because Nsho-chih stepped out of the bushes, and in a joyous voice she addressed her brother, 'You see, he found me! I was right, wasn't I?'

'Yes, sister, you were right,' answered Winnetou. 'Now I can believe that Old Shatterhand can follow not only the tracks, but the thoughts too. He knows everything, there's nothing more for him to learn.'

'I don't deserve the praise of my brother Winnetou,' I responded. 'I can learn a lot from you.'

This was the first time that Winnetou praised my skills, and I was happier for this than the praises I had got from my teachers in the school.

In the evening Winnetou visited me in my room, and brought a beautiful Indian hunting jacket made of leather that had been tanned to white. It was decorated with red embroidery.

'Nsho-chih made this for you. Your old clothing is not appropriate for Old Shatterhand.'

He was right. My clothing was over-worn even in the eyes of the Indians. In the cities I would have been taken for a tramp. But could I accept a present from Nsho-chih?

Winnetou found out my thought, and asked me, 'Is it forbidden for a white man to accept a present from a squaw?'

'Yes,' I replied, 'except if she is his squaw or a relative.

'You are my brother, so Nsho-chih is your relative. And anyway, this is my present, only my sister prepared it.'

On the following morning I tried the jacket on. It fit me as if it was made to measure by the best New York tailor. I praised Nsho-chih's skills. She listened to my words happily.

At noon I was the chief's guest. After lunch Winnetou and his sister retired, and I remained alone with Inchu Chunna. We talked about all kinds of things. It seemed that he wanted to test me.

He told me that he had seen Sam Hawkins walking with a young Apache widow, Kliuna-ai, or Moon in the language of the Apache, several times. Although it did not come to a marriage, what was my opinion of such a marriage? Did I think it was wrong?

'Not at all,' I replied. 'If they love and understand each other, they can be very happy.'

'Would you choose a white or an Indian girl for squaw?'

As I did not want to hurt him, I gave him an evasive answer. 'One cannot know it in advance. The heart decides this. If my heart talked to me, I would not care what nation that girl belongs to. The Great Spirit created all men equal. Those who match would find each other sooner or later.'

'Uff! Just as you said. You, Old Shatterhand, always say the right thing.'

With this the subject was finished, and I had avoided the trap. I considered Nsho-chih a very kind girl, and wished her everything good. She deserved to be the wife of the bravest, most honest Apache warrior. But I had not come to the West to have an Indian wife. And I was not considering a white wife either: marriage was simply not a part of my plans.

After lunch Inchu Chunna led me to the first floor, where I had never been. This was the storage floor. In one of the rooms they kept treasures. In one of the corners of this room I spotted the tools with which I had worked.

'Check if the tools aren't broken, and all are here,' said the Apache chief.

Apart from some small, easily repairable faults, the tools were working, and it seemed that all were there.

'At the time when we took them from you, we considered you an enemy,' said Inchu Chunna. 'But now we know that you have always been our friend, thus we give you back your belongings. What do you want to do with them?'

'They aren't my property, I got them only for work,' I answered. 'I would like to give them back to the people who entrusted them to me.'

'Where do they live?'

'In St Louis.'

'I know the name of that town, and I know where it is. Winnetou has been there, and he talked about this town. So, you want to go there? Do you want to leave us?'

'When the time comes,' I replied, 'not right now.'

'I would regret if you left. We thought you would stay with us forever like Klekih-Petra. And you are Winnetou's brother, aren't you?'

'And I will remain that,' I answered, 'but the brothers don't always live in the same place. They could have their own goals, and they have to depart from each other.'

178

'But not forever,' said Inchu Chunna.

'I will return to you,' I replied.

'I'm glad. Whenever you come, you'll be received with joy. But I regret that you talk about other goals. Wouldn't you be happy with us?'

'I don't know. I don't know your life well enough. It is like when two birds rest on the branches of a bush. One finds its food and stays, while the other flies away.'

'You would get everything here that you need.'

'I know. But I don't only mean physical necessities.'

'I see,' nodded the chief. 'Sometimes Klekih-Petra was also sad, because he longed for something that he couldn't find with us even though he loved us. I don't want to hold you back. Go if you feel that you have to go. But please, return as soon as you can.'

'I feel that I will return.'

'In the town where you are going, you cannot live on hunting. I know that you'll need money. Winnetou told me that for the wicked work that you started, you would have been given a lot of money. We prevented you from finishing it, thus we owe you compensation. Do you want gold as a compensation?' I noticed that at this point he looked at me searchingly as if he wanted to read my thoughts.

'You don't owe me anything,' I answered. 'You didn't take anything from me, and I cannot demand gold from you.'

This was also an evasive answer. I knew that the Indians despised the white men for their greed for gold. I had never been greedy. I considered money only a tool, but I needed it.

'I don't have gold here,' continued Inchu Chunna, 'but I can get you some if you want.'

Other people would have jumped on this offer, and then would have got nothing! This was what I had read from the searching look of the chief.

Thus I said, 'Thank you, but don't bother. Easily gotten money doesn't bring me joy. I want the money for which I worked honestly. If I return to the town, I will find some work. Don't worry about me, I won't starve.'

The tension on the chief's face eased visibly.

He offered his hand, and he said, 'Your words show that you won't disappoint us, Old Shatterhand. The golden dust for which the palefaces push, and murder brings disaster to everyone. But I'll make sure that you won't go to the town empty handed.'

'No!' I said resolutely. 'I told you that I wouldn't accept gold from you.'

'Then we arrange that you could finish your work so you could get the money for it. We'll ride back to the place, where we interrupted your work, and you can finish it.'

I looked at him surprised. I remembered his passionate anger when he had learnt that we were working on building the railways.

'I don't understand,' I said. 'You threatened us with death for building the Fire Mustang's path.'

'Because you did it without my permission,' answered the chief. 'But I let you draw and measure. Winnetou says it won't hurt us.'

'He is wrong. From the drawings and the measurements there will be railway. If the whites decide that they would take over this land, you cannot hold them back: there will be so many of them. Sooner or later the Fire Mustang will rush through the Apache land.'

'You are right,' nodded the chief, and his face became gloomy. 'First a few come, like your group did. We can chase them away. Then more and more come, and our struggle is hopeless then. But it also means that your work doesn't change anything. I discussed it with Winnetou. I'll go with you with thirty warriors. We will defend you, and supply you with food until you are ready. Then we will accompany you to the river, to the point from where the great steam-canoe leaves for St Louis. I will accompany you on your journey.'

'Did I understand you right, my brother?' I asked with wide open eyes. 'Are you going to the palefaces' town?'

'I am, and I'm taking my son, and my daughter too.'

'Nsho-chih? To St Louis?'

'Yes. She would like to know the life of the palefaces. She wants to learn. She will stay there until she will be like a white squaw.'

Apparently my face did not show too much enthusiasm about this plan, because Inchu Chunna asked, 'Don't you like the plan, my white brother? Tell me honestly!'

'I don't have any objections,' I said. 'Just the opposite, because then I could be longer with those people whom I have come to love.'

'Haw!' he nodded contented. 'Will Nsho-chih find people there who can give her accommodation, and also teach her?'

'Of course, I will arrange it. But you, the great chief of the Apache, know that the palefaces interpret hospitality differently from the Apache.'

'I know. If we make friendship with a paleface, he would get everything he needs, and we wouldn't ask anything in exchange. If we go to the palefaces, we have to pay for everything. Even more, we have to pay a double price, and we get the worst of everything. But Nsho-chih will pay for what she needs.'

'Unfortunately, you are right about the whites. But don't worry. You generously allowed me to finish my work, and when I get my money, you will be my guests.'

'Uff! What do you think of Inchu Chunna and Winnetou, the chiefs of the Apache, my brother? If we go to the town of the palefaces, we won't accept even a glass of water as a present. We'll pay for everything with gold. The red men know the mountains where gold can be found. If I see that Nsho-chih would have to stay for several years, I'll leave enough gold with her. When do you want to return to the town?'

'When you think it's appropriate, chief.'

'I think soon, because it's already the end of autumn. We don't need much time to get ready. We can leave tomorrow morning.'

'Right,' I said, 'only tell me what to take, and how many horses we need, and ...'

'Winnetou has arranged everything,' interrupted the chief, 'and you don't have to care about it.'

We returned to the third floor. I said good night to the chief, and headed to my room. Sam was waiting for me on the terrace.

'Big news,' he told me, and he was rubbing his hands, 'we are leaving soon.'

'I know,' I said. 'I just heard it from Inchu Chunna.'

'And I thought I would surprise you with the news. It seems I'm late again.'

'Who told you?'

'I went for a walk to the river, and met Winnetou on the bank. He was choosing the horses for the journey. I asked him what for, and he told me. I'm happy for this. And you?'

'Me too. I don't want to grow old in this pueblo.'

'Have you heard that Nsho-chih will also come?'

'Of course.'

'Interesting! It's none of my business, just remarkable. I'm curious what would come out of this. Maybe they want her to become your Kliuna-ai ...'

'I don't know what you mean,' I replied, 'but let's have some rest, because we'll have a long journey tomorrow.'

The life was the same as at other times. Nothing showed that the leaders of the tribe were about to go on a long journey. Nsho-chih was just as calm, and prepared the food as in any other day. This young Indian girl had a long, and maybe dangerous journey in front of her. She wanted to enter a world whose customs and laws she did not know. She would meet the often praised greatness and richness of the white civilisation. Still she carried on with her tasks quietly, and she did not bother anyone with her questions.

I got ready quickly too. Packing the tools was the only trouble. Winnetou sent five or six soft woollen blankets to me, and I wrapped the more delicate tools in these.

The calmness of the Apache affected me too. After going to bed I immediately fell asleep, and awoke only when Sam Hawkins came in. It was a cool autumn dawn. The sky was cloudy, and gloomy. We quickly had our breakfast, and left the pueblo. Not only the thirty warriors, but everybody from the pueblo accompanied us to the river where another ceremony was to be held. We were waiting for the magic man who had to let us know if our journey was to be lucky.

Our wagon still stood in its old place, but in the past few weeks the magic man had appropriated it. He put up the canvass so that nobody could look into the cart. The people formed a half-circle around the cart, and waited for the ceremony. I should call this ceremony a comedy, because our wagon now looked like a circus coach. For a while nothing happened, and then sounds came from the wagon as if dogs and cats were fighting.

I stood between Winnetou and his sister and I mused. Now I could really see the similarity between the two. The girl wore men's clothing that was identical to her brother's. She brushed her hair in the same way as her brother. There was a knife and a revolver in her belt, and the medicine bag hung from it. She had a gun on her back. Her dress was decorated with fringes and embroidery. Her appearance was quite militaristic, yet girlish. Everybody admired her.

The noise from the wagon resounded again. It seemed that my face showed that I was unimpressed with the event, because Winnetou remarked, 'You don't know this ceremony, my brother, and you probably smile at it to yourself. What you can hear from the wagon is the struggle between the good and bad spirits.'

The noise became roaring which occasionally alternated with softer sounds, when the magic man could see more encouraging signals in the future. He suddenly jumped out of the cart, and rushed around in a circle like a mad man.

Then he slowed down, and started a strange dance that he accompanied with some monotonous songs. I looked at him with reservations because he wore a horrible mask, and from his clothing the strangest objects hung. Finally he stopped, stooped and now rested his head on his knee. He stooped there for a long time motionless.

Then he suddenly jumped up, and announced his vision. 'Listen to my words, sons and daughters of the Apache. The Good Spirit showed me the future. Inchu Chunna and Winnetou, the chiefs of the Apache, are going on a long journey. Old Shatterhand, our new white chief, also goes with them. They go with warriors. They go with Nsho-chih, the most beautiful flower of our tribe, who will visit the big town of the palefaces. The Good Spirit will protect her from all troubles. She will happily return with her father, brother, and the brave Apache warriors. There is only one person who won't return, and whom we see today for the last time.'

He bowed his head, and he remained silent for a long time showing as if there was some deep sadness in his heart.

'Uff, uff, uff!' the Indians cried out curiously, but nobody dared to ask the magic man whom he meant. He only stood there with his head bowed, motionless.

Sam had run out of patience, and shouted at him, 'Who won't come back? Why don't you name him?'

The magic man lifted his head, opened his arms, and looked at the little paleface with reproach.

'It would have been better had you not asked it. I didn't want to name him. But this curious paleface forces me. Old Shatterhand is the one whom we won't see anymore. Death will catch up with him. Those who travel with him should keep their distance from him, because he brings trouble on everyone. This is what the Great Spirit showed me. Haw, I have spoken!'

After these words he quickly climbed back into the wagon, and disappeared behind the canvass. Everybody looked at me with frightened, and sympathetic glances. I was a marked man who had to be avoided.

'What happened to this bloke?' asked Sam angrily. 'What a stupidity! How could it come to his mind?'

'We should really ask what goes on in his mind,' I replied. 'He is against us. He has never talked to me, and I repaid him with the same coins. He's probably fearful that the chief comes under our influence, and he wants to prevent it.'

'I'll go over, and hit his face!' raged Hawkins.

'Don't do anything stupid, my friend! This situation is rather delicate.'

Inchu Chunna and Winnetou were shocked. They just stared at the ground for a while. Even if they did not believe the magic man, they knew well the effects of his words. We were taking thirty warriors. If they believed that I brought bad luck, they would snarl at me.

Inchu Chunna held my hand, lifted it and said, 'Apache brothers and sisters, listen to my words. Our brother, who talked to the Great Spirit, showed us the future many times. What he said often happened. But not always. We have experienced his mistakes. During the big drought he wanted to make rain, but the rain did not come. When we went on the warpath against the Comanche he predicted a rich loot. We won, but the loot was three old guns, and a few wretched horses. Two years ago, when we went to hunt, he said that we would kill many bison. But we met so few of them that we barely brought any meat back, and we almost starved during the following winter. He could be mistaken again. My advice is: let's wait and see.'

At this moment the little Sam Hawkins jumped out of the row, and cried out, 'We don't have to wait. There's a way to find out if the magic man was correct or mistaken.'

'What's the way, my white brother?' asked the chief.

'I tell you. We, the whites, also have magic men who can read the future. I haven't yet told you, I'm one of them!'

'Uff, uff!' cried the Apache surprised.

'You can't see it on me, can you?' continued Sam. 'I don't like telling the future, hehehe! But I'll do so this time. Could some of my Apache brothers come with their tomahawks, and dig a narrow, but deep hole in the ground?'

'Do you want to look in the depth of the Earth, my white brother?' asked Inchu Chunna.

'Yes, because one can read the future either from the stars or from the depth of the Earth. It's morning now, and there are no stars. Thus I have to ask the Earth.'

185

Some Indians were already digging the ground with their tomahawks.

'What is this silliness, Sam?' I whispered to him. 'You'll make trouble.'

'Why? What this worm did wasn't silly? He can and I can't? Relax, Sir, I know what I'm doing.'

His self-confident face just increased my anxiety. I knew Sam. He liked jokes, especially in difficult situations. I wanted to warn him, but he ran over to the Indians to show them how deep they should dig. When the hole was ready, he took off his shabby leather coat, then buttoned it up, and erected it above the hole. It stood as if it was made of tin.

'My Apache brothers!' cried Sam. 'Watch me! For my command the ground will open, and I can look in the depth of the Earth. I will tell you faithfully what I saw!'

He put on a serious face, and with slow steps he went around the coat three times, while swinging his arms around. "He's like a windmill," I thought anxiously. Finally he screeched, and pushed his head in the coat. I watched this childish comedy nervously, but the Indians followed it with tense attention. Sam stood there for five minutes, then he pulled his head back, unbuttoned the coat, put it on, and finally said, 'My Apache brothers should now fill in the hole, because I cannot say anything whilst it's open.'

They carried out his command. Sam then continued, 'Your magic man was mistaken. In the ground I saw the opposite of what he said. I heard gunshots, thus the group will be attacked. The last shot came from Old Shatterhand's gun, so he survived, he did not die. He was the victor of the battle. Nobody could be hurt who's near him. Haw, I have spoken!'

It was visible on the faces of the Indians that they had believed Sam's words. They glanced towards the wagon. They expected their magic man to come out, and argue with the little paleface. But the magic man did not appear.

Sam Hawkins came to me, and he asked, 'Well, Sir, how did I perform?'

'Like a real flash man.'

'Yes, it's true. But the important thing is that I achieved what I wanted.'

Winnetou's look was very telling, but he did not say a word. However, his father remarked, 'You are a clever man, my white brother. You deprived our magic man's dark vision from its strength.'

The order was given for the departure. They led out the horses. There were many pack horses too because, apart from my tools, we also took food, and other necessities. The Indians normally accompanied the leaving warriors for a while. However, this time Inchu Chunna forbade it. The thirty warriors did not even say good-bye to their family.

The order of the column developed spontaneously. Inchu Chunna rode in the front with his son and daughter, I rode behind them with my three friends, and then the warriors who also led the pack horses.

Nsho-chih sat on the horse in the men's way. She was an excellent rider. If someone saw her, and did not know her, he would have taken her for Winnetou's younger brother. In three days we arrived to the place where the Apache attacked the Kiowa. On the fourth day we reached the site where we had stopped the work. There we made camp.

After the battle the Apache did not bury the dead whites and the Kiowa; they had left the bodies on the field. The vultures and predators had done their job. The bones lay scattered, most were completely white, but some were festooned with rotting meat residues. It was a task for me, Sam, Dick, and Will to collect these remains, and place them in a mass grave. As expected, the Apaches warriors did not participate in this.

After this I immediately started my work. I had to hurry as winter was coming. The nights were so cold that we had to keep the fire going all night. Winnetou helped me in everything, but Nsho-chih even more. The pretty Indian girl was able to read my thoughts. When I spoke, she listened so attentively as if she wanted to learn from every word.

In a few days I completed the remaining work, and we started the second phase of our journey.

After a few hours' ride the forest thinned. I appreciated this, because it was advantageous if one could see far, and notice if someone was approaching. Indeed, four white riders were coming from the opposite direction. They also caught sight of us. They stopped to discuss the situation. The appearance of a large Indian group obviously made them anxious, especially as they could not know what tribe the Indians belonged to. But when they saw that there were white men among the Indians, they probably calmed because they started to ride towards us again. We saw that they were dressed like cowboys. They had guns, revolvers, and knives. When they were twenty steps from us, they stopped again.

One of the riders, holding his gun ready, addressed us, 'Good morning gentlemen! Is it necessary to keep my finger on the trigger of my gun?'

'Good morning!' replied Sam. 'You can put away the guns. We don't have vile intentions. Where are you coming from?'

'From the good old Mississippi.'

'And where are you going?

'To New Mexico. We heard that they are looking for cowboys, and that the wages are good there. And you?'

'We are going to St Louis.'

'Your Indian friends too?'

'Only their leader, Inchu Chunna, the chief of the Apache, with his son and daughter. They want to see St Louis.'

'Interesting! An Indian chief's daughter in St Louis! Quite unusual, isn't it? And would you tell me your names?'

'Why not? They are honest names, and we don't have to be ashamed of them. I'm Sam Hawkins, and these are my friends, Dick Stone and Will Parker. And this gentleman is Old Shatterhand, who kills grizzlies with his knife. And who are you?'

'I've heard Sam Hawkins's name, but not the others',' said the stranger. 'My name is Santer. Of course, I'm not a famous hunter like you, only a simple cowboy.'

He named his three companions, and then had some more questions about our journey. Then they said good-bye, and rode on. When they were at some distance, Winnetou turned to Sam. 'You spoke more than necessary and wise, my white brother. You shouldn't have been so open.'

'Why? I always answer politely to polite questions.'

'I don't trust the palefaces' politeness. These were so polite because we have eight times as many men. I'm not at all happy that they know who we are. Did you look at the man whom you talked to? I didn't like his eyes.'

'I didn't see anything suspicious in them,' Sam shrugged his shoulder. 'Anyway they rode to the opposite direction. We won't see them again.'

'I would like to know what they are doing. My brothers should ride forward slowly. I will go, and follow these palefaces with Old Shatterhand for a while. I want to know if they have really gone.'

This is what happened. Two of us turned around, and went after the four strangers. I have to admit that I did not like Santer, and his companions did not fill me with trust either. I could not say what was suspicious about them. I asked Winnetou what he was thinking.

'They could be robbers or thieves,' he answered. 'But even if they were determined robbers, they wouldn't dare to attack more than thirty people. But it's possible that they only pretended that they had left, and they try to follow us. Maybe they watch out if one of us breaks off from the main group, and try attack him.'

'We don't know who would be their target.'

'The one whom they suspect to carry the gold.'

'Gold? Why would they think of gold?'

'They could figure it out. Sam Hawkins light-heartedly told them that we were chiefs, and that we were heading to St Louis. That would be enough for them.'

'You are right, my brother,' I said and nodded gloomily. 'Sam Hawkins likes gossiping.'

'Of course, whatever their plan is against us, they won't achieve anything, because we didn't bring gold with us. We'll go for it only tomorrow, when we are closer to the forests. Nobody knows the place apart from my father and I. It's such a bonanza that one just has to bend down for the nuggets.'

'Is it on our way?' I asked.

'Of course. This is why we came this way. The mountain is full of nuggets. For convenience let's call it Nuggets' Hill. We will be near the place by the evening.'

I was careful not to show my surprise. How strange these people were! They knew of an unbelievable treasure, and they did not utilise it. They did not mine it, did not hoard it, but continued with their undemanding life style. White men would not have been able to do the same!

We advanced extremely carefully so that Santer would not notice that we were following him. We used every bush, and every hollow as a cover. In a quarter of an hour we spotted them. They were riding in steps, and talked in good humour.

'It seems that they don't have malicious intentions,' said Winnetou.

We turned our horses reassured, and soon caught up with our companions.

In the evening we camped by a spring after the chief had carefully scouted the area. The spring had crystal clear water, and the lush grass offered good pasture for our horses. Because trees and bushes surrounded the clearance we could lit a camp fire. Inchu Chunna set up two guards, and then we sat down by the fire, and ate our usual dinner of dried meat.

The bushes protected us from the cold wind.

After dinner Inchu Chunna told us that we would leave later than usual on the following day, at around midday. Sam asked why. The chief replied with surprising honesty.

'It's secret, but I'll tell you, my white brothers, if you promise that you won't follow it up.'

Naturally, we promised, and he continued, 'In the town we will need money. So tomorrow morning I will go with my son and daughter to collect enough nuggets, and will return only at midday.'

'Is there a bonanza nearby?' asked Sam surprised.

'Yes,' replied Inchu Chunna, 'but nobody knows about it, not even our warriors. My father showed it to me. It's a sacred secret that is told by the father to the son. There are no others to whom I would show the place, and if somebody followed us, I would kill him.'

'Including us?' asked Sam.

'You too. I trust you, but if you disappointed me, you would deserve death.'

On one side of the fire Inchu Chunna, Winnetou, Nsho-chih, and I sat with our back to the bushes. On the other side Sam rested with his friends facing the bush. During the conversation Sam cried out suddenly, jerked his gun to his shoulder, and shot at the bush. The shot created commotion. The Indians jumped up, and asked Sam why he had shot.

'I saw eyes flashing in the bush behind Inchu Chunna,' explained Sam.

The Indians grabbed torches, and searched the bushes, but they could not find anything.

'Maybe,' said Inchu Chunna, 'the flickering light of the campfire cheated Sam Hawkins's eyes, or the wind turned the leaves, and their bottom side was lighter than the top, and that flashed.

'In any case,' said Winnetou, 'You shouldn't have shot. It was a mistake.'

'Why?' flared up Sam.

'Because if it was only the leaves of the bush, the shot was unnecessary. It could have been a friendly scout. But if there was an enemy in the bush, it was wrong to show that we were suspicious. It was impossible to hit him like this.'

'I don't normally miss the target,' said Sam.

'Everyone would miss the target in such a situation,' said the chief. 'The man can see that I aimed at him, thus he could jump aside or on the ground, and could disappear in the dark thicket.'

'What would you have done, my brother?' asked Sam.

'I would have shot from my knee, or I would have gone around to get behind the man.'

"Shooting from the knee" is the most difficult shot. I had heard about it, but I could not yet do it. Winnetou taught me, much later, how to master it.

I explain it briefly. Let's assume that I am sitting by a camp fire, my gun is loaded, and it is next to me. I notice a pair of eyes in the bush. I cannot see the face of the enemy because of the darkness. Even to spot his eyes requires training. Thus, I cannot see anything else, but the flashing eyes. It is about my life, thus I have to kill the man. I have to hit exactly between the two eyes. If I lifted the gun to my shoulder, and aimed, the enemy would escape. Thus I have to aim at him without raising his suspicion. I pull up my right leg, as I sit or lie, until my knee is at the same level as my eye. My eye, my knee, and the target is in one line. Now I stretch out for my gun, lay it on my thigh, and pull the trigger. I could say that I aimed with my knee even before I held my gun. One of a hundred marksmen can do this.

For the time being we could not do anything. Winnetou doubled the guards, and we all lay down to sleep. I had nightmares. I wrestled with Santer, but he slipped out of my hands, and escaped.

For breakfast we had dried meat, and porridge made with cold water. After breakfast Inchu Chunna left with his son, and his daughter. I kept on thinking of Santer, and I was anxious for my friends. I asked the chief to allow me to accompany them for a while, but he refused.

'You shouldn't worry, my brother,' said Winnetou, 'but to assure you, I'll scout around again. We know that you don't strive for gold, but if you come only for a short distance with us, you would imagine the bonanza, and you would get the fever of getting the gold. Thus we ask you not to come with us, not because of mistrust, but because of love.'

So I could follow them only with my eyes. Soon they disappeared in the thicket. As they went on foot, the place, where the gold was could not be very far.

I lay down on the ground, and lit my nice calumet, and I was musing. However, I could not regain my calm. I soon stood up, got my gun, and went for a walk. Maybe I could find a game, and stalk it to make time go faster. Inchu Chunna left to the South, thus I went to the North because I wanted to avoid even the slightest suspicion that I was about to follow them.

After fifteen minutes' walk, to my surprise, I found footprints. Three people passed there. I found the prints of two large, two medium-sized, and two small moccasins. The footprints were fresh, so obviously Inchu Chunna and his children left them. Thus they left to the South, and then turned to the North to keep their direction secret.

In such circumstances I could not continue towards the North, but I did not want to return to the camp either, thus I turned to the East.

After another fifteen minutes I found footprints again. I examined them. Four men, who had worn boots with spurs, left them. I immediately thought of Santer.

The tracks turned to the North, that is, to the direction in which the Apache had gone. Following the tracks I arrived to a thicket from which an unusually tall oak tree rose. I entered the bush, and found four horses tied to the tree.

The ground showed that the four men spent the night there. So, they had turned back, and had bad intentions. Sam had not been mistaken. Somebody had been watching us in the previous night.

I examined the oak tree thoroughly. I found scratches on the bark, probably from a spur. One of these men climbed up on the tree, and from there he could see our fire. Then they had sent somebody to eavesdrop. Suddenly a thought flashed through my mind. Good Lord! What had we talked about just before Sam shot? About the gold, the bonanza. The man in the bush could have heard it. They could have learnt Inchu Chunna's plan. At dawn they had climbed up again on the oak tree, and had watched as the three Apache had left the camp. Winnetou, Nsho-chih, and Inchu Chunna were in a great danger! I had to hurry after them to help them. I did not even have time to go to the camp. I untied one of the horses, and led it out of the thicket. I jumped on it, and rode after the robbers.

While I was following the track of the four men, I made a plan in case I lost the tracks. Winnetou had called the place Nuggets' Hill. Therefore, it was a hill of some height. To the North I saw several high points covered by thick forests. One of them had to be the place.

The horse that I took was an old nag, and it did not want to gallop. I broke off a strong branch of a bush, and urged the nag with it. It started to run a bit faster. The tracks led between two hills. Soon I got to the entrance of a gorge. The ground was rocky, and there were no tracks. I had to get off to decide which way I would have to go.

After a long examination I found some footprints to the right. I got on the horse again, and rode into the gorge. The path in the gorge was ascending and narrowing. It was difficult to continue on horseback, so I jumped off, tied the horse to a tree, and rushed forward on foot.

I arrived to a forest, and ran among the trees. I could not see footprints anymore, but I trusted my good luck and my instincts. It seemed that the forest thinned in the distance. Probably there was a clearance there, thus I headed there. I was still in the forest when I heard some gunshots. In the next moment a roar resounded through the air. My back shivered because I recognised the death cry of the Apache.

I was not running anymore, but leapt like a panther. Two more gunshots rang out right after each other. It had to be Winnetou's gun. So he was still alive. Three more leaps, and I was at the clearance. I stopped by the last tree because the scene paralysed me.

The clearance was small. In the middle, Inchu Chunna and Nsho-chih lay on the ground. I could not see if they were alive. Not far from them there was a rock. Winnetou knelt behind it. I could see that he was loading his gun. On my left there were two men among the trees ready to shoot if Winnetou stepped out from behind the rock. On my right a third robber stole forward among the trees to get behind Winnetou. The fourth lay dead a few steps from me. A bullet had hit his head.

At that moment the two men were the most dangerous. I took my bear slayer gun, and killed both. Then, without loading my gun, I rushed after the third. Hearing my two shots, he turned back. He saw that I was fast approaching, and he aimed at me. His gun went off, but I jumped aside just at the right moment. He swore in his anger, and fled to the forest. I followed him. When he turned back to look, I recognised him immediately. It was Santer! "I must catch him!" I thought. I rushed after him, but he disappeared among the trees.

After a short consideration I turned back because it was possible that Winnetou was also wounded, and therefore he needed my help.

When I arrived back to the clearance Winnetou was kneeling by his father and sister. He was examining their wounds. The pain distorted his face. He caught sight of me, and stood up. I will never forget his countenance. His face was ravaged by mad anger and grief.

'Can you see, my brother, what happened? The most beautiful daughter of the Apache won't go to the palefaces' town. She's still alive, but she won't open her eyes again.'

I was suffocating, I could not speak, and I could not ask. What could I have asked? What was important, and could not be helped, was in front of me. They lay in a pool of blood: Inchu Chunna with a bullet in his head, Nsho-chih with bullet in her heart. The Apache chief was dead, but his daughter was still alive. Her breathing was rattled, and her nice bronze colour was turning to paler and paler. Her round

195

face became sunken, and the approaching death had already marked her countenance.

She moved, and turned her face towards her father. She opened her eyes slowly. She could see that her father was in a pool of blood, and she got frightened, but her face was so tired that her feeling was barely visible on it. She seemed to be thinking, and then she recognised what had happened. She moved her hand to her heart. She felt the sipping blood, and sighed deeply.

'Nsho-chih! My dear sister!' cried Winnetou in such a voice that my heart squeezed.

Nsho-chih lifted her eyes to her brother. 'Winnetou … my dear … brother …,' she whispered. 'Revenge me!'

Her glance fell on me, and on her trembling lips a joyous smile fleeted.

'Old Shatterhand …,' she breathed, 'are … you here? … If I die, then …'

She could not finish her sentence. Death closed her lips. I felt as if my heart broke. We both knelt by her, but I jumped up, and gasping for air, I cried out so loud, deep from my lungs, that the forest echoed.

Winnetou also stood up, slowly, very slowly, as if some heavy weight had been put on him. He embraced me with both arms, and said, 'Both are dead! The greatest, and noblest chief of the Apache, and Nsho-chih, my dear sister, who gave her heart to you. She saw you the last, and she died with your name on her lips. Don't ever forget her!'

'I won't,' I said.

His face suddenly changed, and his voice became angry like a thunder. 'Did you hear her last wish?'

'I did.'

'She asked me to revenge her horrible death. You know who killed her. The palefaces against whom she hasn't done anything. This is how it has been and will be until Indians live. Whether they love you or hate you, the end is the same. Wherever palefaces go there is the devastation of the Indians. We were going to a white town peacefully. Nsho-chih wanted to know it. She wanted to study, because she hoped it would be easier for her to gain your heart. She wanted to become a white squaw to be right for you. She paid with her life for this. Now all Apache look at Winnetou to see how he revenges the death of his father and sister. The grief and the anger will sweep all the Apache villages. My revenge will be such that all palefaces will remember it. Listen to my oath, my brother. I swear to the Great Sprit, and all my brave ancestors who have moved to the happy hunting grounds that from today, with this weapon that fell out of my father's hand, I will, to every palefaces ...'

'Don't finish it, Winnetou!' I begged him. 'Wait! Wait with the oath!'

'What for?'

'For such a sacred oath a calmer soul is needed.'

'Enough!' His eyes were flashing. 'Do you want to hold me back from what my most sacred duty is?'

'Don't misunderstand me, my dear brother! My soul is just as upset as yours. I also want the revenge! Three have been punished. The fourth escaped. Now we have to catch the fourth.'

'It's not only them,' shouted Winnetou. 'The fourth was a son of the palefaces too. All palefaces are responsible for his doing! And I will make them accountable! I, Winnetou, the high chief of the Apache!'

I could vividly imagine that he would gather all the Indian tribes, and lead them to the battle against the cruel land grabbers. He stood in front of me with flaming face and proudly, and I felt that, in spite of his young age, he could unite the Indians. Then blood would deluge the waters of the American continent. Such a war would start in which hundreds of thousands would die. The Indians would lose at the end, as the superiority would overwhelm them, but they would make their enemies pay for their death!

I grabbed Winnetou's hand, and said, 'You do what you feel right, but hear my first, and perhaps my last appeal to you! Maybe this is the last time we see each other. But look at this dear creature, who died with my name on her lips as you said. Her heart was full of love. In the name of this love I ask you to postpone your oath to the day when we bury the great chief and his daughter.'

He looked at me seriously for a long time. Finally his face eased, and he said, 'You have a great power over hearts, Old Shatterhand. You found the only word that could make me reconsider what I wanted to say. Nsho-chih would have certainly accepted your request. For her I'll do the same. I'll wait until the sad day. Then I'll decide whether the water of the Mississippi and its tributaries run to the sea flooding with blood. Haw, I have spoken!'

"Thank God," I thought with a sigh, "for the time being I could divert a disaster." I squeezed Winnetou's hand, and said, 'You will see my brother, that there's no forgiveness in my heart towards the murderer. We have to catch Santer. We have no time to lose.'

'My hands are tied,' he replied, and his face became hard again. 'The customs of my people demand me to stay with my dear deceased until we bury them.'

'When will it be?'

'The council of the elders will decide whether their grave should be here, where they died, or in the pueblo, where they lived. There will be quite a few days until this decision is made.'

'And the murderer will escape in the meantime!'

'No! It cannot happen! You should tell me my brother, how you got here.'

Now that he had to act, he was calm and cold again. I reported to him about all the events. As I was finishing, we heard a rattling sound from where one of the bandits lay. We ran over there. One of my bullets went through one of the bandit's heart, and he was dead. But the other had a wound like that of Nsho-chih's. It was mortal, but he was still alive.

I leant over him, and shouted, 'Pull yourself together! Can you recognise me?'

He opened his eyes, and looked at me with cloudy eyes.

'Where's … is … Santer?' he mumbled.

'He escaped,' I replied, because I did not want to lie to a dying man even if he was a murderer.

'Where to?'

'I don't know. But I want you to help me. Answer! At the threshold of death you could ease your sin. Where has Santer come from?'

'I … don't know.'

'Is Santer his real name?'

'He has … many … many names.'

'Where were you heading to?'

'Where … the money … is … the loot …'

'What loot?'

'Nuggets.'

'So you turned back to rob us?'

'Yes.'

'Did you scout us by our camp fire?' He nodded.

'Who was it?'

'Santer.'

'So he was the one. Where did he lead you then?'

'Nuggets' Hill,' he sighed.

His eyes closed. Winnetou turned to me.

'You ask him in vain my brother, because he won't say anything. He's dead. Everything is clear. They wanted to find the place of the treasure; this is why they followed us. But they were late. We were already coming back when we met them. They shot at us from behind the trees. My father and sister immediately fell, but I was only grazed by a bullet. I shot at one of the bandits. I missed him, because he jumped behind a tree. But my second bullet killed his accomplice. I tried to find cover behind the cliff, but I wouldn't have survived if you had not arrived on time. Two bandits were behind the trees, and the third wanted to get behind me. That third was Santer, and unfortunately he escaped.'

'We can't accept this!' I said.

'It's your task to catch him. Hurry back to our camp. Take ten warriors with you. Send the rest to me.'

'It will be done, Winnetou!' I replied.

He offered me his hand, and I squeezed it. Then I leant over the two dear bodies once more, and said good-bye to them. After this I hurried away. I turned back at the edge of the clearance. Winnetou had already covered the head of the two dead, and started to sing the grief song of the Apache in a heart breaking voice. My heart was full of pain, but I had to go on my way quickly.

My first thought was that Santer would have gone back to the place where they had left the horses, as he would have needed one to escape. If I was quick enough, I could catch him there. I rushed through the gorge. Arriving to the entrance I had a terrible disappointment. The horse that I tied there had gone. Santer obviously found it, and escaped on this horse. I searched for his tracks in vain. The ground of the gorge and its entrance was covered with small pebbles that the waters carried there in the spring. Although I could not hope anymore that Santer would return to the oak tree, I wanted to ascertain it, and it did not mean loss of time as my way to our camp passed by that point. I ran as never before in my life.

I had always been a good runner, but now it was such a distance that I had to use my strength as well. I made it sure that my breathing remained regular. In addition, I did what I had learnt from Winnetou: during my run I put my weight on one leg for a while, and when that got tired, on the other. At last I arrived to the oak tree, where Santer had spent the night with his accomplices. The three horses were still there. I untied them, got on one of them, and led the other two by their reins. I arrived to our camp by noon.

Sam addressed me surprised. 'What does it mean, Sir? You left on foot, and now return with three horses? Have you become a horse thief?'

I could not joke with him. With a loud shout I called the Apache, and informed them about the sad news. I also told them, 'My Apache brothers can see who was right, their magic man or Sam Hawkins. Inchu Chunna and Nsho-Chih separated from me, and they are dead. But Winnetou is alive.'

They received my words with a deep shock. They could not believe it, but when I described the tragedy to them, there was such a roar that could have been heard from a mile away. The Apache were raging, they shook their weapons, and it was difficult to take back the word. Had they got Santer in their hands, they would have torn him into small pieces.

'Listen to me, Apache brothers!' I shouted as loud as I could. 'Listen to Winnetou's orders!'

When they became quieter, I told them their task. I immediately selected the ten warriors whom I wanted to take, and explained the way to the clearance to the others. They left immediately.

'How will we start?' asked Sam.

'It would take a very long time to search the forest,' I replied, 'as it seems that here one hill follows the other.'

'That's right!' interrupted Sam. 'I've been here, I know this area quite well. There is a chain of hills towards the North, and then it becomes a prairie again.'

'Prairie? This is excellent. Then he cannot hide! There we will catch sight of him.'

'I think so too,' nodded Sam, and with his two hands he made a motion as if he was grabbing Santer's neck.

'Then I know what we will do,' I said. 'We will split into two groups by the chain of the hills. The ten Apache will go to the left, we will go to the right, and we'll meet on the prairie. Does it sound right?'

'Excellent,' answered Sam. 'I'll explain it to the Apache.'

In a few minutes we started off. The Apache understood the plan, and rode to the left of the hill, while we galloped on the opposite side.

When we arrived to the oak tree I stopped, and jumped off my horse. I leant forward searching for the track of the horse on which I rode to the gorge. I took a pencil and paper, and drew the print of its hooves exactly.

'What are you doing, Sir?' he asked, and stared at me. 'Are you taking the measurement of a hoof?'

'Indeed, Sam!' I said. 'What do you think? Which horse's hoof is it?'

'Hell knows!' shrugged Sam his shoulder.

'I'll tell you: the horse on which Santer is fleeing from us. You'll see how useful this drawing will be!'

We continued our way by the leg of that accursed hill on our right. I kept on watching the ground looking for tracks.

Two hours later we found the track of a rider.

I compared the prints to my drawing, and ascertained that Santer had passed there less than two hours earlier.

'One can learn from this greenhorn,' mumbled Sam.

We had to wait for the Apache, and it took three quarters of an hour unfortunately, but it could not be helped. They had travelled on a much more difficult terrain. I sent one back to Winnetou to report that we were on Santer's track.

The days were shorter in this season, and the night fell early. We had to find a good place to spend the night. It was a painful loss of time, but it was meaningless to continue our journey in the dark, when we could not see the ground.

Santer's task was easier. He did not have to watch for the track, and could continue his fleeing all night to get as far as he could, because he must have known that he was pursued. By the morning he would have some gain on us, but, sooner or later, he also would have to rest somewhere, if for nothing else, because of his horse. Thus, overall, we would not lose too much time.

We left the fateful Nuggets' Hill behind us. Soon we got to a place of high grass. We dismounted and let the horses graze. At night, we lay down, wrapped in blankets, and tried to sleep. It took a long time for me to fall asleep. The terrible picture of Santer's two victims stayed in my mind constantly. I also felt responsible for Nsho-Chih's death.

The cool dawn woke us up early. The Sun had not yet risen when we were already on our horses. We rode for hours. Occasionally we saw the track of the fleeing Santer.

'This rascal rides in such a straight line as if he had a destination,' I remarked.

'He wants to save his skin,' opined Sam.

'He must know that we would catch up with him,' I said encouragingly.

'Except if he tricks us,' remarked Sam disheartened.

'What do you mean, old man?'

'I have to say, there's something,' he said. 'It's possible that he wants to find refuge with the Kiowa.'

'And they will scalp him,' I replied without conviction.

'It's unlikely,' said Sam, 'because if he tells them that he killed the Apache chief, they would receive him with joy. We have to catch him as soon as possible.'

We arrived to the point where Santer had had a longer break at midday. We recognised the place where his horse had lay down in the grass. Surely Santer and his horse had arrived deadly tired. I assumed that we had closed the gap since the evening by half an hour. The track turned now. Santer was probably heading to the Red River.

We were not on a real prairie. Although there were no hills, the ground was uneven, scattered with hillocks. This area was called the Rolling Prairie, or the Rolling Plains.

In the afternoon we arrived to a forest again. At this point the track was not more than half an hour old, yet I was not happy with the situation. On the open prairie one could see far, while among the trees a trap might be laid. But fortunately it was not a real forest, only smaller or bigger groups of trees that interrupted the monotony of the grassland. The ground declined, and we soon recognised that we were heading to a creek. It was a very broad, but dry river bed. In this season there was no water in it at all. From the declination of the bed we could see that we were on the left bank of the creek.

The Sun was going down on the horizon. I was annoyed because of the lack success. I galloped forward as I believed that we could catch Santer before the full darkness. Judging from the track on the ground, he was heading directly to the river. By the last trees I stopped to wait for my companions. This was my luck. Had I made a few more steps forward, we could have got into a big trouble. While waiting for the others, I stood up in the saddle, and peered at the other bank of the creek. Then I saw something that made me withdraw.

Below me, hardly five hundred steps from my position, Indians crowded on the other bank. They were erecting poles in the ground, and stretched out belts among these to dry meat on them. Had I gone a bit forward, they would have noticed me. I got off the horse, and signalled to my companions to be careful.

'Kiowa,' said one of the Apache.

'Kiowa,' agreed Sam as soon as he arrived next to me, and peered out. 'This is what I suspected. This rogue Santer is in cahoots with the devil. He slipped out of our hand in the last minute.'

'Not a very strong group,' I remarked.

'Much bigger than you think, Sir,' replied Sam. 'There are more of them to the right. They probably returned from a successful hunt, and stopped here to preserve the meat in their own way.'

In such circumstances we had to be very cautious. We decided that we would retreat to a small wood, and settle there. We agreed that we would hide there for the time being, and make a plan about how to proceed the following morning. I took Sam aside, and asked him what he thought of the situation.

'It's dark,' he said, 'but I'll use this darkness.'

'What do you mean?' I asked.

'I won't wait till the dawn, but I'll slip through the creek tonight. Maybe I can catch Santer.'

'A rather brave thought.'

'He who dares, wins,' said Sam shrugging his shoulders. 'I'm surprised that you have become so cautious, Sir. It's not right for a man who attacked a grizzly with a knife! The Kiowa feel completely safe here. If Santer is with them, he would have told them everything, and they would expect us

204

to arrive only tomorrow. Don't forget that we made a four-day journey in two days.'

On the other bank fires were lit. The Kiowa made large campfires, and the flames rose high.

'Can you see the fires, Sir?' said Sam. 'The Kiowa don't suspect anything.'

However, I considered these large fires suspicious. The Indians were more careful with the fire. Why did they make fires like these that could be seen from the distance? Did they want to lure us there? Did they want to entrap us?

The Apache warriors skilfully hid for the night. I sat down with my three friends in the middle of the last group of trees. Later I went to the last trees, where I spotted the Kiowa. There was only one big blueberry bush between me and the bank. I sat down to think. The train of my thoughts was interrupted by some noise. As if the branches of the blueberry bush had cracked. Maybe some little animal was moving there? Or a man?

"I have to check it out," I thought. However, I did not get up to go to the bush. Just the opposite. I lay down, and crawled to the other side of the bush in a big arc. I arrived there just in time.

An Indian was crawling out of the bush. His legs were already visible. A moment later only his neck and head was in the thorny bush. At the moment when he pulled out his head I seized his neck, and squeezed it. At the same time I jumped on him, and hit him twice or thrice at his temple. The Indian lost his consciousness for a while.

I stood up calmly, and walked back to my companions. They were talking about me.

'Where's Old Shatterhand?' asked Will Parker. 'He was here just before.'

'He's gone,' replied Sam. 'Where can he be? He may even do something really stupid!'

'He hasn't done anything stupid so far!' said Dick.

'But he may want to scout the Kiowa. That's too much for him considering these camp fires!'

'You're mistaken, Sam. You thought I'd gone, but I'm here,' I said quietly.

'Where have you been, Sir?' asked Sam.

'Come, I'll show you.'

'Huh! This was a good job,' admired Sam looking at the knocked out Kiowa. 'How did he get here?'

'Now, that's a greenhorn question,' I replied. 'It's not too difficult to figure it out. But you can see that they expect us. This is why they sent this scout.'

'We will tie him up, and gag him, and then they can wait for news about us for a very long time,' said Sam, and he tied up, and gagged the Kiowa. Then we pulled the prisoner well into the bush.

In the following quarter of an hour I did everything to dissuade Sam from his plan, but he was stubborn. He was determined to scout the camp of the Kiowa, and, if it was possible, catch Santer. He imagined that he could catch the man alive. What a glory it would have been if he could give Santer to Winnetou alive! He was completely obsessed on that day, and not only I, but also the Apache, Will, and Dick had recognised the change.

My argument failed, and Sam left. He did not take his old Liddy. After half an hour I followed him, and I also left my bear slayer gun in the grass.

I knew that Sam would go directly to the creek, and cross the dried out bed. I did not follow his example, but made a detour on the bank, and crossed the creek downstream beyond the light of the camp fires. Then I crawled towards the camp of the Kiowa. I counted eight fires. This had made me think because I was sure they did not need so many fires. There were about fifty Indians around the fires, and on the bank. The bank was not as barren here as on the other side. There were many trees, and at a point there were so many that they formed a small forest. While watching the camp I noticed that all the Kiowa held their gun on their lap, ready to shoot. It would have been a disaster if we had tried the crossing. We would have been entrapped.

206

I would have liked to listen to the conversation of one of the groups, especially if there was a chief among them. As I was watching them, I caught sight of Santer in one of the groups. He was with four Indians. None of them wore an eagle feather, but they obviously belonged to the leading warriors, and the eldest must have been their leader. I contemplated the way in which I could approach them.

The eight campfires created dark and half-dark shadows. The shadows followed the movement of the flames: they fluttered, and their movement made the inside of the little woods mysterious.

To my surprise the Kiowa were not whispering but talked quiet loudly. Maybe it was also a part of their plan. I managed to get fifteen steps to Santer.

Santer was talking. He was loud, and he boasted. He said that he had almost found the treasure of the Apache, only he had been too late, and he had met the Apache chief when he had been on his way back. In his anger, he said, he had shot the chief and his daughter.

'We've heard this,' said the eldest Indian.

'I'm telling you again to remember that the gold is still there,' said Santer. 'Let's find it together.'

'That will be difficult,' said the Indian. 'Such places can be hidden cleverly. For us Winnetou is the important. But we cannot attack him by the graves. The Great Spirit would punish us. We will either have to catch him on the way home or, with Old Shatterhand, if he decides to join him.'

'He sent a small group after me,' said Santer. 'Surely Old Shatterhand, the white dog, leads them.'

'I hope he will enter our trap,' said the Indian. 'We will know his plans. My scout will return soon. I also put four guards on the bank, and I'm expecting their report.'

My heart throbbed hard when I heard this. So there were guards on the bank. Sam rushed directly into their arms. If only I knew what had happened to him!

Then the sound of some big commotion resounded from the bank. The leader of the group jumped up, and listened attentively. Four Kiowa warriors appeared. They brought a white man with them. The white man was struggling with his arms and legs, but he could not escape. They had not tied him yet, but four knives pointed at him threateningly. A moment later I recognised him. It was Sam Hawkins. I did not need to think, I made up my mind immediately. I had to intervene even if it cost my life.

'Sam Hawkins!' shouted Santer joyously. 'Good evening! You surely did not think we would see each other so soon!'

'Murderer! Rascal!' yelled the brave man, and grabbed Santer by the throat. 'It's too early for you to be happy! I'll kill you, don't worry.'

The Kiowa jerked him back. It was a tumultuous scene, and I wanted to exploit it. I pulled both of my revolvers, and with a few leaps I was among them.

'Old Shatterhand!' cried Santer, and fled.

I sent two bullets after him, but I could not hit him. I quickly shot all the bullets from both of my revolvers. I grabbed Sam's arm, and shouted at him, 'Follow me!'

My sudden appearance surprised the Kiowa so much that they had become paralysed for a few minutes. This was my only hope. I turned around, and through the groves I ran towards the place where I crossed the river.

'It was about time,' said Sam when we reached the river bed, 'I was in the hands of ...'

'Shut up now! Follow me!

I rushed like a mad man in the belief that Sam Hawkins was running after me. Soon a hellish noise broke out behind me. Guns popped, Kiowa bellowed, but the shadow covered me, and I disappeared from their view. When the noise became distant, and I thought that I had run far enough from their camp, I stopped, and looked back.

'Sam!' I said in a suppressed voice. There was no answer. 'Sam, where are you?' I asked louder.

There was still no answer. Where could this obstinate man be? Was he injured? Did he fall over in the mud? I would have to go back for him, I thought, but first I loaded my revolvers. After a few steps I recognised that I could not do anything for him. For a few minutes I continued peering in the darkness, then I returned to my companions through the dried out river bed.

They received me as excited as if they had been in deadly danger and not I. My disappearance made them nervous, then came the shooting that had resounded all the way to them. In a few words I told them what had happened, and also about my failure. I could not even be really angry for Sam's stubbornness as I reported to them. The only thing in my mind was how we could help him. We held council with the Apache. Their view was that we had to wait. Thirteen of us could not attack the Kiowa because it would have been suicidal, but after midnight, when everything would become quiet, we might be able to surprise them.

We sat down, waited, and listened.

The quietness of the night was broken by the sound of hatchet blows. The Kiowa were probably cutting down trees with their tomahawks. Were they planning to feed the fires till the morning? Were they suspicious? If they were, and if they expected us to attack them during the night, we had no chance of success.

The noise of the hatchets died down. There was a great silence. We were waiting. When the stars finally appeared at midnight, we tied our horses, and examined the Kiowa prisoner's bondage to assure that he would not be able to escape. We gagged him even more. Then we headed towards the river bed with a detour as I had done earlier.

When we crossed the dried out river bed, we lay down on the ground, and listened. There was nothing suspicious, so we carefully climbed up onto the high bank. We carried on stealing closer and closer. There were no guards, but we really only understood the situation when we reached the edge of the woods. There was nobody by the fires; the Kiowa had gone.

'They got away,' said Parker surprised, 'but why did they feed the fires again?'

'That was part of the trick,' I replied. 'They wanted us to believe that they would spend the night here. They wanted to gain some time on us.'

'Surely they were not afraid of us? They knew that they have more men, than we have.'

'Strange, indeed,' I nodded, 'they must have a plan.'

'Maybe they returned to their village, and took Sam to torture him there. They have an advantage of ten hours on us, so they can be sure that we won't be able to catch them before they reach their village. Probably they want us to follow them,' mused Stone aloud.

'Everything is possible,' I said, 'but I suspect something else. Maybe Santer convinced the Kiowa to search for the treasure of the Apache chiefs, and they went there. Or even more likely: they want to capture Winnetou. That would be the biggest prize for them. In either case they are heading to Nuggets' Hill. Thus we have to go there too, and as quickly as we can.'

Everybody agreed with me, so we returned to our horses. We tied the prisoner on Sam's mule, and then headed to Nuggets' Hill.

As this time we did not have to follow Santer's track, we could shorten our journey, and we were in the valley that led to the place of the double murder at early afternoon on the following day.

Soon we met an Apache guard. We gave our horses to him, and continued the journey on foot. At the edge of the clearance we found another guard, who let us approach the clearance without asking or saying anything.

On the clearance we could see some tree trunks and many large stones that the Apache had gathered. We knew what it meant: the preparations for the funeral of the chief and his daughter had been made for the following day.

On one side of the clearance they built a hut, and this is where they guarded the two bodies. Winnetou was also in the hut. Our arrival was reported to him, and he appeared. I looked at him shocked. Winnetou had always been very serious, and a smile rarely appeared on his face. I had probably never heard him laughing aloud. But this time his seriousness was stubborn grimness. As if his face had become stone. Only his eyes flashed feverishly. All his motions were slow as if he was recovering from a serious illness. He came to me, and we shook hands. He looked into my eyes deeply.

'Have you caught up with the murderer?' he asked.

'I caught up with him, but he escaped.'

I had not committed any error, still I downcast my eyes. I was ashamed for reporting on my failure. Winnetou also looked at the ground. How much I would have liked to look into his soul!

After a long pause he asked quietly, 'Have you completely lost his track?'

'No,' I answered, 'I have all the reasons to assume that the wretched murderer will come here.'

'Old Shatterhand must tell me everything in detail.'

He sat down on a stone. I sat next to him, and told him everything honestly and precisely.

He nodded, offered his hand, and said,

'You should forgive me my brother for reproaching you in my mind just before. You did everything that you could. You couldn't have done anything more. Sam Hawkins got into trouble because of his carelessness. I forgive him, and we will try to rescue him. Your conclusion, my brother, is correct. I also think that the Kiowa will come here. But we will use their plan for our advantage. We will bury Inchu Chunna and Nsho-chih tomorrow. Do you want to be there, my white brother?'

'If you allow me, Winnetou' I answered.

'I don't only allow it, I would like to ask you. Many, many palefaces can thank their lives to you, Old Shatterhand, because I was ready for a terrible revenge. But your words are like the rays of the Sun, they melted the hard ice around my heart. Be my father instead of my father, and my brother instead of my sister. This is what I ask you, Charlie.'

Tears filled my eyes. In his great grief he expected support from me. He felt that I was the only person who was close to him. He knew my first name, but this was the first time in his life when he called me Charlie.

I cannot and I don't want to report about the funeral in details. Even today, if I remember that day, my heart throbs heavily because of the pain, and I fear that the pen would fall out of my hand.

Enough to say that Inchu Chunna was buried with his horse, his weapons, and his medicine bag. They rolled heavy stones on the grave. They put Nsho-chih to a tree in sitting position, covered her with soil, and then put stones around it. They kept on putting the stones on the grave until they reached the branches. In this way the grave became a strong pyramid from which the huge crown of the tree stood out.

I visited the place many times with Winnetou. We always found the graves untouched.

RESCUING SAM

I KNEW that Winnetou's grief and sadness was infinite. Still, after the funeral, he seemed to be a changed man. He did not turn inward, he was not hesitant, but he turned to the tasks of the day. In this he followed the Indian traditions. From his childhood he was trained to keep his emotions hidden. Moreover, he was now a main chief, and his warriors were threatened by a hostile attack. He had to focus on this. He took my arm, and led me to the edge of the clearance.

'I would like to discuss our tasks with my brother,' he said. 'I hope you will agree on my battle plan.'

'Have you got a plan already, Winnetou?' I asked him.

'I want to outwit these Kiowa. They gave refuge to the murderer. They must die. All of them!'

His face had a menacing, resolute look as he said these words. I understood that the Kiowa were our enemies, but they had not played a part in the murder of Inchu Chunna and his daughter. How could I persuade Winnetou to change his mind without offending him?

I ascertained that we were alone, then I told him, 'I'm sorry to hear that my brother Winnetou makes the mistake that leads to the destruction of the red peoples.'

'What mistake do you mean, Old Shatterhand?'

'That the Indians wage war against each other instead of supporting each other against their common enemy. Allow me to speak sincerely to you! What do you think who are smarter and more cunning, the red or the white men?'

'The palefaces, this is the truth. The whites have more knowledge than we have. You are superior compared to us in many things.'

'Yes, we are. But you are not an ordinary Indian warrior. The Great Spirit has given you gifts which rarely occur among men, and, therefore, you should think differently than other Indians. Your mind is sharp, and your gaze reaches far, far further than that of other warriors'. Your constant wars are a form of suicide. And now you want to participate in this suicide! Inchu Chunna and Nsho-chih were murdered by the white men, and one of them has fled to the Kiowa. He persuaded them to attack you, thus we have to fight with them. But it doesn't justify shooting the Kiowa like mad dogs.'

He listened to me quietly, and when I finished, he said, 'You are a sincere friend of all red men, Old Shatterhand, and you are right when you speak of the suicide. I'm going to do what you want. I will capture the Kiowa, but then release them, and just keep the murderer.'

He led me further into the forest and pointed to South-east. 'Can you remember the place where the gorge starts, my brother?' he asked. 'A very long valley opens from there leading to the North, to the great prairie. We call it the Long Valley. The attack of the Kiowa could be expected from there. We left our horses in the southern corner of the valley, and tied them to the trees there. We couldn't bring them here, because the gorge is too steep. It would have exhausted the animals.'

'I see,' I nodded.

'Not far from the entrance of the gorge, there is a canyon to the South. We all move to that canyon.'

'Are we retreating?' I asked surprised. 'Are we avoiding the battle? Do you think, my brother Winnetou, that we don't have enough men to face the Kiowa?'

His eyes flashed angrily, but he only said, 'Do you know me, Charlie, as someone who retreats from the enemy? The canyon will be a trap for the Kiowa.'

'How?'

'You'll see when we are there.'

In a quarter of an hour we all went to the horses. A young warrior guarded them. Winnetou looked towards the other end of the Long Valley frowning.

'They will come from that direction,' he said. 'This is the only route for a larger group. They'll be here tomorrow, or maybe even tonight. And Santer will be with them,' he added in a dark tone.

'How do you know that they haven't arrived yet?'

He pointed to the next hilltop. A very high tree grew out of the forest there. It was the highest point in the chain of hills overlooking the plains.

'You don't know it, my brother,' he explained, 'that I sent a warrior up there. As soon as he sees them coming, he will descend to report to me.'

'Good. He's still there. And when the Kiowa arrive, they may bring my friend Sam too,' I said hopefully.

'I don't think so, Charlie. He was probably sent to the large village of the Kiowa by the Red River with a few warriors. Only a smaller band would come so much to the North. They had to send a message to the chief, and may even ask help. But I'll destroy their plan!'

He led me to the entrance of the southern canyon.

'Listen to my plan,' he said. 'This canyon is almost a mile long. If we could make the Kiowa believe that we retreated in this way, they would follow us; there's no doubt about that. But at the other end of the canyon we will receive them with bullets. They will have to surrender, otherwise none of them would survive.'

'And if they ran back?'

'It will be your task to prevent them from leaving the canyon at this end. I give you the ten Apache warriors who were with you at the dried out creek. With them and your friends you hide here, and as soon as the Kiowa enter the canyon, you'll block the entrance. In this way they will be between two fires. Even if there were five times as many Kiowa as our number, it wouldn't help them.'

'The plan is excellent,' I said. 'So, I'll stay with ten-some people here.'

'No,' replied Winnetou. 'You'll come with us. We all go along the canyon. I want you to know the area. At the other end we will split to two groups. You will return here with the smaller group on a different path, not through the canyon. I'll show you the way. Then you will know the vicinity of the canyon, and you can choose the best position.'

'Everything will be as you ordered,' I answered with the due respect to the commander.

It was a short way to the entrance of the canyon, and we rode there as Winnetou ordered. In the front of the canyon he turned the horses around a few times. He wanted to make sure that we left enough tracks behind. In the canyon we led the horses by the reins.

It was a frightening place. On the right and left steep cliffs rose to somewhere high, and the rays of the Sun barely reached the narrow path. If the Kiowa were so careless to follow us here, they would not come out alive unless they surrendered. The canyon was very winding, which made the journey difficult. It took us more than half an hour to get through.

The scout from the tree arrived, and reported that the Kiowa were approaching from the prairie.

Will, Dick, and I with the ten Apache warriors crossed the forest, and with a big detour we reached the northern entrance of the canyon. Winnetou had urged us to hurry, as there was only an hour left until sunset. With my group I hid in the forest. The Apache lay on the ground silently. Parker and Stone whispered to each other. I pulled away from them a bit, and peered into the twilight.

My friends became quiet. Soft wind shivered the leaves of the trees. The air was filled with a monotonous whir as if the trees were panting. This noise could not be confused with anything else.

Suddenly I thought I heard another sound. Was there a small rodent in the bushes? I was listening intensely. It seemed that I saw as if somebody or something stole among the bushes. I jumped up, and tried to catch him. I grabbed something, and a piece of cloth remained in my right hand.

'Hell!' I heard a frightened, stifled voice, but then the shadow disappeared. I listened for a long time, but could not hear anything. I almost thought that I had imagined the events, but I heard the swearing so clearly that it could not imagined. It was likely that a scout was in the bushes, a white man, perhaps Santer himself, as the Kiowa had no other paleface with them. I had to go after him.

I went in the forest to the North because if the man was a Kiowa scout, he had to head that way. I ran for about ten minutes after the invisible ghost. Once it seemed to me that I heard the crackling of wood.

'Stop or I shoot!' I shouted in the darkness, and shot twice. I did not consider if it was right to shoot. It could not be a big mistake because if he was a Kiowa scout, he already knew that we were here. I returned to my companions.

'Even better,' said Parker, when I told them the strange adventure. 'Then the Kiowa will come here, and everything will happen as Winnetou planned.'

I did not have the patience to wait idly. I decided that I would go out scouting. I hurried along the Long Valley, always in the shadow of the trees. I was not far from the prairie, when I heard neighing, for which I quickly retreated to the forest. In a few minutes I ascertained that the Kiowa were camping nearby. Probably they wanted to spend the night at the edge of the prairie, but considered the entrance of the valley safer as they could hide among the trees. They obviously sent Santer out scouting. Now they were waiting for his return.

"I can do what he did," I thought. "If he could sneak up on us, I can get close to the Kiowa." It would have been valuable to listen to their conversation. They did not make fires, but this was my advantage too as the darkness covered me. Soon I could discern the shapes in the darkness. The Kiowa hammered poles into the ground, and tied their horses to these poles. If they were attacked, it would be easier for them to jump on the horses there, than getting them out of the forest first. The Indians stood or lay at the edge of the forest. At about fifty steps from me, a tall Indian stood in the middle of a small group. I could hear his voice, although I did not understand what he was saying. He had to be the leader of the group, and I wanted to eavesdrop on his commands.

I examined the area, and recognised that it was possible. The edge of the valley was rocky, and there were large stones on the ground. I moved from one stone to another, and finally got to two huge rock sheets. One was about three or four feet high; the other much taller and smooth like a table. From the smaller rock I climbed on the larger, and lay down. I had an excellent place, I could hear everything, but nobody could see me. The only problem was that I did not know the Kiowa language. I was envious of Winnetou who knew many Indian languages. Later I also learnt a few, but it took me a long time until I recognised the importance of knowing languages. I had been on the rock sheet for about ten minutes, when the signal of a guard resounded, and soon voices hit my ears.

'It's me, Santer. Are you camping in the valley?'

'Yes. My white brother can continue to the valley. Our warriors are there.'

Now I could understand their words, because Santer talked in the language of the frontiers, a mixture of English and Indian words, that everybody understood in the West. The conversation continued in the same language when the leader of the Kiowa called Santer.

'You have been away for a long time, my white brother. There had to be a reason.'

'More important than you would think. How long have you been here?'

'About the time that the palefaces call one hour.'

'Wouldn't it have been better to stay on the prairie?'

'We can hide here better. Did you find out something?'

'Old Shatterhand is near,' answered Santer.

'Then we will capture him, and we will take him home. He destroyed our chief's knee. We will get a reward for him. He will be tied to the torture stake with the other paleface.'

'What will happen to Winnetou?' asked Santer.

'We will catch him tonight. We will attack him and his men while he's sleeping.'

'You are wrong. They know that we are coming.'

218

'How do you know?'

'I listened to their conversation. They want to entrap us in a canyon at the southern end of the valley.'

'This is where you heard them?'

'No. At the forest clearance where he buried his father and sister. I climbed up there through the canyon, because I knew that the Apache would be distracted by the funeral.'

'You were very brave, my white brother. It was a difficult, and dangerous journey.'

'I wanted to know their plans. It's about my skin.'

'What else did you hear?'

'Winnetou split his group into two. He waits for us at the other end of the canyon, and Old Shatterhand on this side. He's already there.'

'How do you know?'

'He almost caught me. A piece of my coat remained in his hand. He even shot at me. But he couldn't hit me in the dark.'

'Uff!' the Kiowa admired him.

'I can imagine how angry he was!' boasted Santer. Anger was not the dominant feeling in me then. I was glad that my scouting was successful, while he did not learn anything by our camp.

'What's your advice?' asked the Kiowa.

'We won't go to the canyon, but find Old Shatterhand's camp, catch him or kill him.'

'But then Winnetou will hear the shooting, and he will be able to slip away.'

'True,' said Santer. 'What's your plan?'

'We'll avoid them, and ride back to our village. We won't erase our tracks. They will come after us. Tangua will send us warriors in the meantime. There will be so many of us that we can easily defeat the Apache.'

'And if they don't follow us? If Winnetou sees through the trick?'

'Even if he does, he will follow us,' opined the Kiowa. 'He's driven by the revenge. He knows that you are with us, and he wants to get you to torture you to death.'

'This is what I want to avoid,' replied Santer. 'I have two enemies, I would like to finish off at least one of them. Old Shatterhand is near. We could attack him tonight.'

'I told you that we can't. The shots would be heard at the other end of the canyon.'

'It can be done without noise,' said Santer. 'I know that the Kiowa warriors can crawl so noiselessly like a snake. After midnight we could surprise him. We will use only our knives. If we do it well, it will be without a single cry. Then in the morning we get Winnetou.'

'Uff, uff!' cried the others. They liked Santer's proposal.

It was time to get away. While the Kiowa leader hurried to his men to give orders, I slipped off from the stone sheet, and crawled back to the forest. In a few minutes I was already running uphill fast to my companions in the light of the stars.

'Who is it?' asked Stone, when he heard my footsteps.

'It's me, Dick,' I replied panting. 'We have to hurry. We cannot stay here for a minute more.' I told them everything in a few words.

'Where should we go to?' they asked.

'To Winnetou, naturally.'

Our Apache understood that the situation had changed, and they did not hesitate. We followed the same path as in the afternoon, just to the opposite direction, and in the dark. It was not a pleasant journey. Two Apache warriors went in front, and felt the trees to push away the dangerous branches. Then the next two held onto these warriors. By forming a column like this we could get out of the forest without trouble, and then we could advance quicker.

Winnetou had not expected any hostile attack from this direction, but as a precaution, he had put a guard up there too. The guard was surprised by our arrival, and reported it immediately to Winnetou.

'What happened?' asked the chief.

'The Kiowa won't walk into our trap,' I replied. 'Santer heard our conversation by the tombs. But I sneaked into the

Kiowa's camp, and I heard what he discussed with the leader of the Kiowa.'

'Tell me everything in detail, my white brother!' ordered Winnetou.

He listened to my report attentively, and asked, 'And in such circumstances you decided on a retreat, my brother?'

'I could do three things. First: staying in my place as I was ordered, and wait for further commands. But then my brother Winnetou would have been in danger. The second: go against the Kiowa group, and attack them. It would have been suicidal. The third, what I did: hurry here to help Winnetou with my friends, and the ten Apache warriors. If the Kiowa attack us tomorrow morning, we still won't have enough men, as they will come from both directions.'

'You did the right thing,' said Winnetou. 'But I don't believe in a morning attack. The Kiowa aren't stupid. It's better for them if they force us to a battle in their own territory. Thus they will ride back home. They know that I would follow them.'

'Do you know the largest village of the Kiowa, Winnetou? Do you know where it is?'

'Of course, like my own pueblo! It's over the Canadian River, at the northern branch of the Red River, where the Salt Fork Red River enters it.'

'Is it to the South-east from us?'

'Yes.'

'So they will expect us from the North-west. But we can approach them from the opposite direction.'

'My brother reads my thoughts,' said Winnetou. 'With a detour we could surprise them. We will attack them from the South-east. The question is, when should we leave?'

'We are tired, that's true, but I would rather go now.'

'So would I, but it's better if we wait until the morning. If we left now, we would be ahead of them. It's better if they are ahead. And I would like to know their plans for sure. They could still attack us tomorrow morning. They may believe that we have fled. Let's stay here for the night.'

'Then we need a good hiding place,' I said.

'I know such a place,' answered Winnetou.

Half a mile from the exit of the canyon there was a small valley. It was covered by a thicket. Winnetou led us there. The horses were also hidden there.

It was a cold night, but because of my tiredness I slept deeply. I got my horse to lie down, and then I lay next to him. His body warmed me. He was as quiet as possible, and woke me up only at dawn. We watched the exit of the canyon for another hour, but the Kiowa did not appear. Winnetou's assumption was correct, and by then they had to be well ahead of us. With appropriate care we started off to the South. After two hours' riding we found very visible tracks on the ground. A large group had passed there.

'They didn't try to hide their tracks,' I told Winnetou.

'And they did everything to make them more visible,' added Winnetou. 'The Kiowa wanted to be too clever.'

The horses of the ten Apache warriors were tired, and our supplies were also short, thus we could not advance as quickly as we wanted. Fortunately in the late afternoon we found the tracks of a small bison herd. These animals probably lagged behind the large herds that migrated to the South. We followed them, and hunted two cows. Now we had enough food for at least for a week.

In the following day we crossed the Canadian River, and continued our journey towards the Red River. With short breaks we reached the Salt Fork Red River. We were on the Kiowa's land now, and we had to be more careful. We went around the large Kiowa village built at the confluence of the two rivers. We crossed the Salt Fork Red River, then the Red River, and thus we were now behind the village. With this we could approach it from the opposite direction from where they expected us. We carefully erased our tracks everywhere, and for the same reason we even rode some distance in the shallow water of the river.

At an appropriate place we stopped, and our group hid carefully. Only two of us continued: Winnetou and I. We felt it was necessary to scout the area. We lost time with it, but we were rewarded for our caution.

We were still far from the Kiowa village, when a kind of caravan approached us. There was a rider in the front of the column, followed by about ten or twelve well-packed mules, and finally another rider. We could not yet see the faces of the riders, but from their clothing we knew that they were white men.

When they spotted us, they stopped. It would have been suspicious if we avoided them, and I wanted to talk to them anyway. They were coming from the direction of the Kiowa village, and thus it was possible that we could have learnt something useful from them.

'What do you think, my brother, who are these people?' asked Winnetou.

'I think they are peddlers, who made exchanges with the Kiowa. They cannot harm us, but it's better if we don't tell them who we are.'

'Right. What do we tell them then?'

'I'm a subordinate officer of the Indian Agency,' I said smiling. 'I was sent to negotiate with the Kiowa, but I don't understand their language. You are an Indian interpreter, my brother. Of course, not an Apache, but a Pawnee.'

'Very good,' nodded Winnetou. 'You will talk to these two palefaces, my brother.'

I rode towards them. As customary in the West, they held their guns ready to shoot.

'You can put your guns away, gentlemen!' I shouted to them. 'We don't have bad intentions.'

'We don't have either,' one of them replied, 'but don't be surprised if we found you suspicious.'

'Suspicious? Why?'

'A white gentleman in the company of a redskin is rare, isn't it? At first I was sure that we should be very careful with you.'

'In any case, I thank you for your honesty,' I replied. 'But look at me again. Do I look like a bandit?'

'I can't say that,' he smiled in a friendlier manner. 'You have an honest face. But you would oblige me if you told me where you have come from, and where are you going to.'

'Your curiosity is understandable. We have no reason to keep it a secret from you. We came from Wichita, and we look for a Kiowa chief.'

'What's his name?'

'I heard that his name is Tangua.'

'Yes, there is a large Kiowa Indian village between the two rivers. Tangua lives there,' answered the peddler, 'but I advise you not to visit him.'

'Why?'

'He loves scalping, and he's in a really bad mood now.'

'How do you know?'

'We are coming from his village. He told us that he would tie all white men, whom he could capture, to the torture stake. Even Indians, if they are not Kiowa.'

'Are you then black?' I asked innocently.

'What do you mean?'

'If he's angry with all white men, and Indians too, and he didn't harm you, then you are surely black.'

'Leave the stupid jokes out of this!' he exclaimed. 'He received us kindly as we are old acquaintances, and we have visited his village a number of times. The Kiowa appreciate the traders, especially the honest traders. In general, they are cheated by others, but they cannot have a complaint about us, thus they are kind to us. They are happy when we visit them. They need our wares.'

'I work for the Indian Agency.'

'For the Agency? Listen, this is much worse! Don't take me wrong, but I tell you that the reds are talking pretty badly about the Agency, because … because …'

He hesitated to continue, and so I finished his sentence. 'Because they have been so often deceived by the Agency.

You are right. I admit this.'

'It's interesting to hear that from you that the agents are thieves,' he laughed. 'The Kiowa are quite angry because of

224

the last delivery. If it's your intention to be tortured to death, then just continue, and they will help you with this.'

'I hope not. If the Kiowa don't like what happened to them, then the joy will be bigger, when I tell them that we recognise the errors made, and also that there will be a compensation. They will also get what they are entitled to.'

'What a rarity!' he exclaimed in amazement. 'In this case, they will do nothing to you of course. But who's this Indian with you?'

'My interpreter,' I answered. 'He's a Pawnee, but he understands the language of the Kiowa.'

'Then Tangua may forgive him that he's not a Kiowa.'

'Why is this Tangua so angry?'

'He told us why. He said that the Apache had invaded his territory, and had stolen several hundreds of their horses. He had naturally followed them, but because the Apache had three or four times more warriors than he had, he was beaten. It was not only because of the numerical superiority, but because some white men supported the Apache. One of these people made him a cripple later. His name is Old Shatterhand, because he can knock out anyone. But it won't help him.'

'Why is that? Because of the revenge of the Kiowa?'

'Of course! Tangua is raging, and he swore that he won't rest until he captures this Old Shatterhand, and Winnetou.'

'Winnetou? Who is that?'

'A young Apache chief who is somewhere around here two days' ride away. A number of Kiowa rode out to lure them in their village.'

'Will they be so stupid to fall in the trap?'

'Tangua is quite certain. I would probably have stayed a few days at Tangua's, but to watch a white man being tortured to death, that's not my taste.'

'But he hasn't caught them yet.'

'No, not yet, but he caught the man's companion. I tried to intervene in his interest, but Tangua became so angry that I had to abandon it.'

'Have you seen the prisoner?'

'Of course! He's a kind little man with lively, small eyes. He's a very jolly fellow; he's still laughing, though he must know what awaits for him.'

'Did you talk to him?'

'Just a few words. I asked if he had any request. He said that he loved custard, and if I could bring a large pot of it from St Louis. Have you heard such a thing? I told him that I was surprised that he had such a good mood. "Don't be anxious for me!" he said. He's hoping that his friend would rescue him. Otherwise they don't treat him badly, but there's a white adventurist, called Santer, he tries to make his life bitter.'

'Santer? Who's he?'

'I don't know. A repulsive bloke. A Kiowa group brought him, but he's not a prisoner. Tangua doesn't particularly like him, but considers him as his guest. Well, more or less.'

'Does he live in the chief's tent?'

'No. Tangua gave him a tent, a big one, at the edge of the village. It seems that Santer isn't good enough to get a tent near the chief.'

'Do you know the name of the white prisoner?'

'His name is Sam Hawkins. Strange little man, but I heard that he's a famous hunter. I regret that I couldn't help him. You could also try though. Maybe you'll have more luck.'

'Where do they keep the prisoner?'

'They took him to an island.'

'Is there an island there?'

'More than one. The one where they took the prisoner is by the confluence, not far from the village.'

'Is Santer's tent the last one?' I asked.

'No. The fourth or fifth from the end of the village. But don't visit him. He is a villain. It's better if you don't have anything to do with him. I have to go now. Take care, young man! I hope you'll get back home safe.'

I would have liked to get more information, but it was not possible unless I told them honestly who we were, but I could not risk it. I also saw on Winnetou's face that he was becoming impatient. He had already started off.

After I had said good-bye to the traders, and had caught up with Winnetou, he told me in a reproaching voice, 'You asked too much, my brother. You could see that these palefaces are the Kiowa's friends!'

'I learnt important things from them,' I answered. 'How far are we going?'

'Until the traders can't see us. Then we will return to our camp. We will wait until the evening there, and then we two will steal into the village.'

The two traders with their pack mules walked slowly. We were lucky that we had met them.

When we had lost sight of them we turned, and carefully went back to our group. Dick Stone and Will Parker listened to my report happily. They said that our scouting had been very fruitful. They were especially happy that Sam was well, considering the circumstances, and that he had not lost his humour. They begged us to let them join in the evening, but Winnetou did not want to hear of it.

'Only two of us can go,' he said. 'At the moment it's only about scouting. We can rescue Sam Hawkins only tomorrow. Then I will need my white brothers' help.'

He examined our hiding place, and shook his head.

'We cannot stay here unnoticed until the evening,' he said. 'We have to find a much better place. I know that there are some smaller and larger islands upstream in the river. We will choose one, where there are trees and bushes. We can hide there better.'

We rode along the bank of the river towards the village. Soon we found an island that was just right for our purpose. The water was very deep and fast there, still we swam over with our horses. Winnetou had been right. The bushes of the island offered an excellent cover.

I lay down among the bushes, and decided that I would sleep as I knew that during the night I would not be able to do so. Winnetou thought the same. He also wanted to gather strength for the task. A few hours' sleep refreshed us. He and I awoke almost at the same time. It was getting dark. We partly undressed, and left our weapons behind apart from our knives. Then we jumped in the river, and swam to the other bank. This was the Salt Fork, where the Kiowa felt completely secure. They would not have imagined that any enemy would enter this part of their hunting grounds. We slowly and carefully stole towards the village.

The village was nothing else, but a long line of leather tents as it was December. These Indians used canvass tents only in the summer.

There was a fire in front of each tent. This is where the inhabitants of the tents sat, and prepared their dinner.

We were shivering in our wet clothing.

The largest tent stood in the middle of the village. At its entrance there were spears. They were decorated with eagle feathers and other trophies, as well as medicine bags. There was a wonderful fire by this tent. Tangua sat there with three Indian boys. The oldest was about eighteen years old, the other two much younger.

'Tangua's three sons,' whispered Winnetou. 'The oldest is his favourite. They say that he will become a good warrior. He's the best runner of the tribe, this is why he's called Pida, which means Deer.'

Women were working around the tents, but they did not sit by the fire. Indian women and girls could not eat with the head of the family, and his sons. They could sit down only later, and they had to be contented with what the men left. However, all work, including the hardest ones, were their tasks. The men had no other task, but to fight, and to hunt.

There were several islands in the river here. I turned all of my attention to these islands. It was already dark, and the sky was covered by grey clouds. Fortunately, I could observe the islands, because the fires gave enough light. I saw three islands near the bank.

'What do you think, Winnetou, on which island do they keep Hawkins?' I asked.

'I think, on the middle one,' replied Winnetou, 'because that's the closest to the village.'

'Indeed, the trader said the same thing,' I nodded.

'There's the end of the village,' continued Winnetou. 'Santer lives there in the fourth or fifth tent. Now we have to part. You, my white brother, are concerned about rescuing Sam Hawkins, while for me Santer is much more important. Each should focus on his task.'

'And where will we meet again?'

'Here, where we separate.'

'Right, if everything goes well. But if either of us is spotted, he may not be able to return here. We should agree on a meeting place that is further away from the village.'

Winnetou was thinking for a couple of minutes, and then answered, 'Your task is more difficult because you'll have to swim to the island, and the guards could easily spot you. I have to go behind the tents, where it's easier to hide. If you get into trouble, I'll come to your help. If there's no problem, go back to the island where our camp is. Of course with a detour, so that they couldn't find us.'

'But in the morning they'll find my tracks.'

'Don't worry. There'll be a rain during the night, and it will wash away our tracks.'

'Good. If you get into trouble, I won't let you down either.'

'I know that, my brother. But it won't happen unless there's an unfortunate twist. Look! In the front of the fifth tent there's no fire. Santer is probably sleeping there. It won't be too difficult to get him.'

In the next moment he disappeared. I considered how to get to the island without being noticed. If I simply swam over, they could easily spot me. If I swam under water, there would be a danger when I put my head out. It could happen just by the guard. No, it would be better if first I swam to the neighbouring island that looked deserted. It was just about twenty yards from the middle island.

I carefully stole along the bank until I was opposite the island. I carefully entered the water, and swam under water.

I got across without a problem. When I put my head out, I breathed deeply, and looked around. Then I saw something that made me change my plan.

On the bank, from where I swam, many boats were tied to branches of trees and bushes. I passed them by, but did not notice them as I was watching the island. Now that I could see them from the island, I recognised that along the boats I could approach the middle island. I did not hesitate. I dived again, and swam back to the bank, and then swam from boat to boat until I got opposite the middle island. I held onto the sixth boat. I stood in the cold water. Only my head was out of it. From there I could see the middle island well.

It was covered with small bushes; only two tall trees rose from them. I could not see Sam or his Kiowa guards. I was about to swim over, when I heard some noise from behind my back. I looked up. A tall, young Indian man headed towards the water. It was Pida, the son of the Kiowa chief. He jumped in one of the canoes, fortunately not the one that covered me. He untied it and rowed over to the middle island. At this point I could not yet swim after him, and I had to wait.

Soon I heard a conversation from the island, and for my joy I recognised Sam's voice. I did not understand what he was saying, but in the next moment I heard a different voice, probably Pida's.

'My father, Tangua, won't wait any longer,' he said. 'He wants to know!'

'He wants it in vain, I won't tell you!' answered Sam.

'Then you will endure triple torture.'

'I don't care with your threats! You won't get anything from me. I don't know where Old Shatterhand is, and even if I knew, I wouldn't tell you.'

'Surely you don't expect him to rescue you?'

'I don't need him! I can escape without his help.'

'Are you mad? You are tied to a tree, and four guards watch you day and night! How can you imagine that you can escape from here?'

'I won't tell you!' answered Sam. 'Tell your father not to challenge Old Shatterhand. He tried it once and ...'

He became quiet suddenly. His attention was caught with the same thing as mine. From the village a loud noise resounded: thumping of feet, and yelling. "He's running there! Catch him!" they shouted. It seemed to me that they shouted Winnetou's name. I turned my head towards the village in shock.

The noise of the angry shouting increased. It sounded that they had spotted Winnetou, but they could not catch him. Whatever happened, it nullified my plans. I saw that the son of the chief stood up on the island, and was looking towards the bank. In the next moment he jumped in his canoe, and ordered the guards, 'Hold your guard, and shoot this paleface dead if someone tries to rescue him!'

He grabbed the oars, and rowed quickly towards the bank. My plan was to rescue Sam during the night if I had the smallest chance, but now I could not attempt it. Even if I attacked the guards with my knife, they would have had enough time to kill Sam Hawkins. My attack would have only hastened his death.

Then I had an idea. Winnetou had said that Pida was the chief's favourite. If I captured him, Tangua would exchange him even for a thousand Hawkins. It was a brave idea, but I could not even think it over if it was possible. My mind was focused on catching Pida.

The situation was advantageous. Winnetou was running to the left, to the confluence of the two rivers. The camp of our group was to the right, but Winnetou rushed to the opposite direction to mislead his pursuers. The shouting came from the left, and the four guards turned that way too. Nobody looked to my direction.

The son of the chief reached the bank, and wanted to tie his canoe. As soon as he bent down I rose from the water next to him. I knocked him out with one blow, threw him in the canoe, and jumped in after him. I grabbed the oar, and rowed against the flow of the water right along the bank with all my strength. The audacious trick worked. Nobody in the village noticed what had happened, and the guards were still looking to the opposite direction.

My intention was to get out of the light of the fires. As soon as I was far enough from the village, I rowed to the bank, and got out of the boat. I picked up the unconscious Kiowa, and laid him in the grass. I cut off the belt from the canoe, and tied up my prisoner. I kicked the boat away from the bank, and the water took it.

I put the bound Pida on my back, and then started off towards our hiding place. It became difficult when he recovered because of his resistance. I had to put my knife to his heart many times to force him to obedience.

Winnetou's forecast was precise. It started to rain, and soon it rained so hard that I had to find cover under the foliage of an old tree, especially because in the rain and darkness I could not find the place on the bank that was opposite our island. I decided that I would wait until the end of the rain, or even until the dawn under this tree.

I put Pida on the ground.

'Who are you?' he asked grinding his teeth. 'How dare you to raise your hand at me, you paleface dog? My father is Tangua, the great chief of the Kiowa!'

'I know,' I nodded.

'He'll beat you to death like a rabid dog tomorrow!'

'I don't think so,' I replied, 'because he cannot walk.'

'But he'll send warriors to find me!'

'Then the warriors will end up as your father when he challenged me.'

'Uff! Have you met him?'

'Yes.'

'When?'

'When I destroyed his knees.'

'Uff, uff! You are then the famous Old Shatterhand!'

'You should have known earlier because I knocked you out with one blow. And who else would have dared to enter your village but Winnetou and Old Shatterhand?'

'Then I'm finished. But I'll die without a woe.'

'We won't kill you. We aren't murderers like you. If your father gives over the two palefaces who are in your village, we'll let you go.'

'Santer and Hawkins?'

'Yes.'

'My father will certainly agree as I'm worth more than ten men like Hawkins, and ten times ten men like Santer! When will you talk to him?'

'Tomorrow. Now be quiet.'

The waiting tried my patience. The rain did not stop, and the morning was still far. Only one thing consoled me that I could not become wetter. I started to do some gymnastics to warm up my limbs. I felt sorry for Pida who was tied up under the tree, but then I thought that he was more trained than I was, and he could endure it.

My desires about the morning were fulfilled at the same time: the dawn arrived, and the rain stopped. Heavy, thick fog descended, but I could recognise the outlines of our island just opposite me. I shouted over.

I could hear Winnetou's reply, 'Is that you, my brother Old Shatterhand?'

'Yes, it is.'

'Come over! Why are you shouting?'

'I have a prisoner. Send somebody over here with some strong belts. He has to be a good swimmer.'

'I'm coming.'

Soon I saw his face between the fog and water. What a joy it was. The Kiowa could not catch him.

When he arrived to the bank, and saw the young Indian, he exclaimed in his surprise, 'Uff! Pida, the son of the chief! Where did you catch him?'

'On the bank opposite Hawkins's island.'

'Have you seen Hawkins?'

'No, I heard only his voice as he was talking to this Deer. I couldn't rescue Hawkins, because they spotted you. There was a big turmoil, and I had to escape.'

'Yes, it almost ended up badly. I was by Santer's tent, when some Kiowa approached. They stopped there talking. One caught sight of me, and raised the alarm. He was only four steps from me, and the light of the fire fell on me. I jumped up, and ran towards the river to mislead them. I couldn't see Santer.'

'You will see him soon,' I said. 'I caught Pida to offer him in exchange of Santer and Hawkins.'

'Uff! Very good. You action was dare-devil, my brother, and yet you could not have made a wiser decision.'

When I encouraged Winnetou that he would be able to see Santer shortly, I would not have thought that it would happen so soon.

We tied Pida to ourselves. His legs were free, but his hands were bound to ours. Three of us jumped in the river at the same time. Pida's head and shoulder was between us, but he could help us by swimming with his feet. He did not resist. He was obediently kicking the water in the rhythm appropriate for our swimming.

The fog covered the water so much that we could not see further than two yards. However, sound spreads in fog better. We barely started to swim, when Winnetou warned, 'Let's swim quieter. I can hear something.'

'What?'

'The sound of an oar. Listen!'

We stopped swimming, and moved our hands and legs only to stay on the surface. Winnetou was right. A boat was approaching fast.

I thought we should dive, and glanced at Winnetou. He immediately understood my questioning look.

'I want to see who it is. It's enough if we bow our head.'

Pida watched as excitedly as us. He could have cried for help, but he did not do that. He knew that I would have immediately pushed his head under water.

The rowing sound came from very close now. A canoe appeared from the fog. There was only one man in it.

Winnetou cried out, 'Santer! He wants to escape!'

He usually retained his calm even in the most dangerous circumstances, but seeing his deadly enemy, he jumped towards the boat without thinking. However, he was tied to Pida. He pulled his knife, and cut the belt.

Santer heard Winnetou's cry and stared at us. 'Hell!' he cried in his frightened surprise. 'This is …'

He bit his word. Instead of fright there was gloat on his face. He recognised that our situation was bad. He threw the oar into the canoe, picked up his gun, and yelled victoriously, 'You'll die dogs!'

Fortunately he pulled the trigger in the moment when Winnetou kicked himself from us. All three of us got about a yard from the point at which Santer aimed. The bullet whistled amongst us.

Winnetou did not swim: he was flying. He had his knife between his teeth, he jumped with huge leaps like a deer on the surface towards his hated enemy. He was like a flat stone that children make bounce on the water. There was one more bullet in Santer's gun.

He aimed at Winnetou, and shouted mockingly, 'Just come, you damned Injun! I'll send you to hell directly!'

He thought he had won. But the mocking grin froze on his lips, when Winnetou dived to reach the canoe under water, and to knock it over. If he could do that, Santer would fall in the water, and his gun could not have helped him. If they started to wrestle in the water, the skilled Indian would finish him off in moments.

Santer recognised it; he dropped his gun, and grabbed the oars. He moved the canoe just in time, because Winnetou's head appeared where the boat had been. Santer, with a few strong pulls got far enough away from his angry pursuer, and he shouted mockingly, 'You won't catch me! And I put away this bullet for you for our next meeting!'

Winnetou was as fast as possible, but it was useless. The canoe glided so fast that nobody could have caught it.

I am sure that this dramatic scene did not last for more than two minutes. The fog swallowed Santer. A few Apache warriors jumped in the water for the gunshot sound to support Winnetou. I shouted to them to help me to take Pida to the island.

When we arrived to the island, Winnetou immediately gave the order, 'My Apache brothers, get ready! We'll catch the murderer!'

I had never seen him so out of his mind as then.

'What will happen with Hawkins?' I asked.

'It's your task,' he answered. 'You stay here, and we'll go after Santer! My father's and sister's murderer must not escape from us!'

'Where and when will we meet?'

'Where and when? The wish of a man doesn't move even a leaf. Everything depends on the will of the Great Spirit. What do you think, why did Santer try to escape?'

'He learnt that we were here.'

'And also that Pida was in our hand, and he knew that Tangua would give everything for him.'

'Why didn't he escape on horseback?'

'So that he wouldn't leave tracks! He didn't expect us to meet him in the water. But we will cut through the bend of the river, and will overtake him.'

'That's not good, Winnetou, because he can disembark anywhere, and flee on foot. We don't even know which bank he's heading to.'

'You are right, brother. We have to follow the bend of the river, and I have to split my group into two.'

'I would like to ride with you,' I sighed, 'but I cannot let Hawkins down.'

'No, you can't! Winnetou has never asked you to abandon your responsibilities. If the Good Spirit wills, we will meet soon. When you finish, ride to the confluence of the North Fork Red River and this river. I'll leave one of my men there. You will learn from him where we could meet.'

'And if I don't meet anyone there?'

'Then you'll know that I didn't capture Santer, but I will continue to chase him even to the end of the world.'

236

'And what should I do then?'

'Ride with your friends to St Louis, and visit there those palefaces who want to build the path for the Fire Mustang. Arrange with them what you have to. I'll try to leave you a message in St Louis. If I can't, you are always welcome in our pueblo by the Pecos River. You can find me there, or they will let you know where I am.'

In the meantime the Apache warriors mounted their horses. Winnetou shook hands with Dick Stone and Will Parker, and then turned to me again.

'You know, my brother, how happily we started our journey. But this journey caused Inchu Chunna's and Nsho-chih's death. When you return to us again, you won't be able to see the beautiful face of the Apache girl. She wanted to go to the palefaces' town, but moved to the country of the spirits. The revenge will separate us now, but love will bring us together. Don't spend too much time in the towns of the palefaces, come back to us as quickly as you can. Will you promise me this, Charlie?'

'You know what I promised to Klekih-Petra before his death. I'll be faithful to you, and my word.'

'Then the Good Spirit should lead your steps, and guard you from troubles. Haw, I have spoken!'

He squeezed my hand, and jumped on his horse to swim through the river. His warriors split into two groups. One followed Winnetou, the other hurried to the other side of the river. I looked after Winetou until he disappeared in the fog. My heart had never been so sad.

Stone and Parker looked at me touched.

'Don't get disheartened, Sir!' Stone consoled me. 'We will ride after them once we have rescued Sam. Let's begin! How do we want to start?'

'What do you think, Dick?' I asked. 'You are cleverer, and more experienced than I am.'

My praise obviously felt good to him. He brushed his beard with his hand, and said, 'We have another prisoner. It's good that we brought him with us. We'll send him to

Tangua, and send our demands with him. What do you think, Will?

'Hm,' hummed Parker, and said. 'Nothing can be more foolish than this.'

'What do you mean?' asked Stone angrily. 'What's your plan, smart boy?'

'We go somewhere far from here. We settle on the open prairie, where we could see if somebody comes. We'll send the Kiowa prisoner to Tangua, and let him know that he should send Sam with two warriors. If more come, we get away, and take Pida with us. Won't it be better, Sir?'

'I think we shouldn't send anyone to Tangua.'

'I don't understand it.'

'I will go.' I said.

'No, Sir! No way! We cannot let you risk your life!'

'Tangua knows if he harms me, you would kill Pida.'

'Wouldn't it better if I went to Tangua?'

'I know that you're a brave man. But it's more effective if I talk to Tangua.'

'He is the angriest with you. If he sees you, he will rage in his anger.'

'This is why I'll go. I'll let him rage. He should see that I'm not afraid of him.'

'If you think so, Sir ... And where should we wait for you? Here on the island? Or should we find a better place?'

'There's no better place.'

'Well! But woe to the prisoners if something bad falls on you in the village! When are you leaving?'

'In the evening.'

'Only in the evening? Won't that be too late? Then the exchange of prisoners will happen only tomorrow noon. How will we catch up with Winnetou?'

'If we hurry too much, we won't ever catch up with him.'

'Are you serious?'

'The most serious. Tangua would happily give over Sam to get back his son, but as soon as he gets him back, his thoughts will be about revenge. The exchange of prisoners

238

will have to take place in the same evening. Then we ride away, and we get as far during the night where they cannot catch up with us. Also by the evening Tangua will be more anxious, so he will accept all of our demands.'

'That's true, he'll be softer,' said Parker. 'But what happens if they find us in the meantime?'

'On this island? Never. They'll find Winnetou's tracks on the bank, they will follow him. Listen!'

We heard noises from the bank. The fog had started to dissolve, so we could see what was happening there. Several Kiowa were bending over the prints of the hooves, and were discussing them. Then they hurried back towards their village.

'They go back to inform Tangua,' said Dick Stone. 'You'll see that he sends riders to follow the tracks.'

His prediction was confirmed two hours later. A strong group of riders arrived from the village, and then, following the tracks, turned to the prairie. We were not afraid that they would catch our friends. The Apache had several hours' advantage, and galloped at least as fast as the Kiowa. Our prisoners could not see anything. They were lying bound in the bushes. They could not hear our conversations either as we were whispering.

For our joy, the Sun rose in the morning, and we could dry our clothing. We enjoyed the blessed, warm sunshine. We hoped that nothing would happen until the evening, and we would be successful.

The Sun reached its zenith when we saw a dark object on the water. The waves of the river swirled it towards our island. Soon it hooked up in the branches of the bushes of the island. It was a boat with an oar in it. The cut off belt showed that it was the same canoe in which I took Pida to the other bank. I was happy for this, because I knew that in the evening I could make good use of it. I would not have to swim through the river, and shiver in my wet clothing.

When it was twilight, I pushed the canoe in the water, and rowed towards the village. Stone and Parker looked after me with hope. I told them that there would be a reason for anxiety only if I did not return by the following morning.

When I got close to the village, I rowed to the bank, and tied up the canoe, on which I fixed a new belt, to a bush. There were fires by the tents just as the day before, and the women were busy preparing the dinner. I thought that they would guard the village more this time, but there was no sign of it. The Kiowa found the tracks of the Apache, and sent out riders after them, thus they felt safe.

Tangua sat in the front of his tent, but only his two younger sons were next to him. He sat there with bowed head, and stared gloomily in the fire.

There was nobody near who could have seen me. I lay down by the bush on the bank, and crawled behind the tent. I could hear the monotonous grieving song. Tangua was grieving for his favourite son according to the Indian customs. I went around the tent, and suddenly I stood in front of the chief.

'Why is Tangua grieving?' I asked him. 'A brave warrior should never give up hope. Grieving suits old squaws only.'

My sudden appearance frightened him so much that he was paralysed. He wanted to say something, but not a sound came out of his throat. Then he wanted to jump up, but his destroyed knees did not allow it. He just stared at me with goggling eyes as if he saw a spectre.

'Old ... Old ... Shatt ... Shatter ...' he stuttered finally.

'Uff! Is it you? How did you get here?'

'I came because I wanted to talk to you.'

'Old Shatterhand!' he shouted when he finally recovered sufficiently to pronounce my name.

His two young sons escaped to the tent hearing the feared name.

'Old Shatterhand!' repeated Tangua in a shaky voice. It was shaky not because of fear, but because of anger.

Turning his head to the other tents he yelled some order which resulted in a turmoil. In the next moment I was surrounded by armed Kiowa. They pointed their spears at me, and they were bellowing. I grabbed my knife, and cried in Tangua's ear, 'Pida sent me! If you touch me, he'll die!'

Tangua immediately understood the meaning of my words. He lifted his hand, and ordered silence. The warriors became quiet, but they drew a tighter ring around me. Angry looks were devouring me.

I calmly sat down next to Tangua, who, shocked by my audacious act, stared at me with eyes flaming with anger.

'Listen to my words, Tangua!' I told him. 'You are my enemy, I know. It's not my fault. You hate me, but I'm not afraid of you. You can see, I came to you. I have an important thing to discuss with you. Pida is in our hands. My friends are guarding him. If I don't return to them on time, Pida will die.'

The nearby Kiowa stared at me silently, and they stood motionlessly. They did not show what they thought. The chief's eyes flashed, but he controlled himself too. He understood that if he had not bridled his anger, his son would pay for it with his life.

'How did you capture him?' he asked grinding his teeth.

'He visited Sam on the island. I was there too. When he wanted to row back, I knocked him out, and took him.'

'Uff! Old Shatterhand is the favourite of the Bad Spirit, and he helped him. Where's my son?'

'In a secure place, but I won't tell you where. Pida will tell you. You can see that I don't want to kill him. We have another Kiowa warrior, whom we captured earlier. I'll release both prisoners if you give us Sam in exchange.'

'I will, I will! Just bring Pida, and the other warrior!'

'To here? What do you think? I know you, Tangua, I know how much your words are worth! I give two prisoners for one, what else do you want? But forget about all tricks!'

'Prove that you have Pida!'

'I don't prove anything! Old Shatterhand always tells the truth. I want to see Sam Hawkins. I'm sure he's not on the island anymore. Order your men to bring him here. I want to talk to him.'

'Why?'

'I will ask how you treated him. My conditions depend on his answers.'

'Then wait a bit. I have to discuss this with my elder warriors. Go a bit further away! There, to the next tent! Soon you'll learn our decision.'

'Right, but hurry. If I don't return on time, Pida will take the punishment. Do you know what they will do to him? They'll hang him!'

Tangua clinched his fist, but did not say a word.

I went to the next tent, and sat down. Naturally I was surrounded by warriors. Tangua called the elders, and he started to discuss the affair with them. Time to time they glanced towards me, and their look was filled with hatred. But I also saw that my calm and bravery impressed them.

Soon the chief sent a warrior to a tent, and he led Sam Hawkins out. I jumped up and hurried to him.

As soon as he noticed me, he joyously cried out, 'Old Shatterhand! Welcome, greenhorn! I knew that you wouldn't let me down!'

He stretched out his bound hands as a greeting.

'Well, yes,' I replied. 'The greenhorn came to rescue his master who got into trouble because of his stubbornness.'

'I fully deserve the reproach, Sir, but let's leave it for the time being. Tell me if my mule, Mary, is still with you?'

'Yes, she is with my pinto.'

'And Liddy?'

'Your shabby gun? We brought that too.'

'Then it's excellent. Let's go.'

'Patience, dear Sam. It seems to me that you think that everything is so easy.'

'For you, Sir, it is,' smarmed Sam, 'because with your fist you can knock out a whole army if necessary.'

'I'm glad that your mood is so good. It seems you didn't have a bad time here.'

'They didn't hurt me, and they gave me enough food.'

'But first they took your belongings, didn't they?'

'In this respect they did a thorough job, hehehe,' he answered grinning.

I turned towards the council.

'I wonder how long they want to discuss it,' I murmured impatiently. 'I have to interrupt.'

I went to them, and told them that I could not wait any longer. They had to make the decision if they wanted Pida alive. They understood this, but there was a long bargaining about the exchange of prisoners. I did not retreat from my demands, and they had to accept my conditions. We agreed that four armed warriors would accompany us by boats, and I would take them to the place where I would give up the prisoners. If others followed us in secret, Pida would die.

I slightly overplayed my hand, when I demanded to take Sam right away, because it would have allowed me to trick them. But Old Shatterhand's name was such by then that they could not doubt my words. Of course, I did not tell them where we would row to, and reiterated that they should not try to follow us.

Sam, as soon as his belts were cut off, lifted his arms to the sky, and cried out happily, 'At long last, I'm free again! My gratitude and thanks to you, Sir! My legs will never run to the left if yours run to the right!'

When we started off there was such a threatening noise that I involuntarily grabbed the handle of my knife. The anger of the Kiowa was infinite when they saw that I left without harm, and I also took their prisoner.

'Go, just go!' hissed Tangua. 'You don't have to be afraid until I get Pida back! But then there's no mercy! Woe to you if we catch you again.'

I ignored his threats, and walked between the lines of the Kiowa with Sam and the four warriors behind us. We got into the canoes in pairs, obviously I was with Sam. We rowed in the front, and the other two boats followed us. The Kiowa on the bank broke out in ear-piercing yelling for the first pull of the oars. It had accompanied us until the darkness swallowed our boats.

While I rowed, I told Sam what had happened since we had been separated at the dried out creek. He regretted that Winnetou was not with us. We arrived to the island safely. The two faithful friends received us jubilantly.

We gave up our two prisoners to the four Kiowa. They got in the canoe silently and ashamed. We waited until they disappeared on the dark water of the river, and then we did not waste a moment more. We got on our horses, and rode to the other side of the island to swim to the bank. Sam knew the area well, which was particularly useful, because we had a hard journey for the night in front of us. We would have to gallop for hours so that they could not catch us on the following day.

When Sam was mounting his Mary, he shook his fist towards the village, and said, 'Now they are discussing what to do. But they won't catch me anymore, that's for sure. I had enough of the hospitality of the Kiowa! Not least because I had to be rescued by a greenhorn, hehehe!'

VOLUME II

I BECAME A DETECTIVE

WE ARRIVED to the confluence of the North Fork Red River and the Red River. I looked around excitedly in the hope that an Apache warrior would wait for us to give us news about Winnetou. We found footprints, but these did not suggest anything good. Following the tracks we soon found the body of the two traders, those whom we had met near the Kiowa village. I later learnt from Winnetou that Santer had killed them.

Santer rowed so fast that he arrived to this point at the same time as the trader and his helper, even though these had left Tangua's village much earlier. Santer failed to get Winnetou's treasure, the desired nuggets. He left the Kiowa destitute, but when he spotted the two traders, he immediately decided that he would rob them. He probably shot the two unsuspecting men from a hiding place, and then drove away their well-packed mules. Winnetou read this from the tracks when he arrived there.

The murderer risked a lot. Driving the packed animals through the savannah was a big task for one man. He also had to hurry as he knew he was pursued, and did not have time to erase his tracks. Unfortunately, the weather changed, and many days' of rain washed away the tracks. Winnetou had to rely on guessing rather than on his sharp eyes to make a decision. He correctly assumed that Santer was hurrying to the nearest white settlement to sell the loot.

Winnetou lost time, but eventually found Santer's tracks again. Santer had been to the Gaters' trading post, where he sold everything, and bought a good horse on which he rode to the East. At this point Winnetou parted with his warriors, who would have made the pursuing of the bandit more difficult. He sent them home to the pueblo, and continued the chase alone. He had enough gold on him to get his supplies even in a town.

I did not forget Winnetou's command for the case if I could not get news about him at the North Fork. We turned our horses to the North, and rode towards St Louis quickly through Arkansas, that is, in the shortest way. My heart ached that I could not be with my good friend, but I also knew that only one thought worked in him: the revenge.

It was dark when we arrived to St Louis. We were very tired. The first thing to for me do was, of course, to visit Mr Henry. When entering his workshop, I saw that he was leaning over his work bench. He was so deeply involved in his work that he did not notice even the creaking of the door.

'Good evening, Mr Henry,' I greeted him as if I had seen him only the day before. 'How's life?'

The old man stared at me, and then exclaimed: 'You? ... Is it really you? The tutor ... the surveyor ... the famous Old Shatterhand?'

In the next moment he embraced, and kissed me.

I waited until he recovered a bit from his surprise and joy, and asked, 'Old Shatterhand! Tell me, how do you know this name?'

'How? Everybody knows it! The whole town speaks about it! Mr White, the engineer, brought the first news. He talked about you with great appreciation. But it's nothing compared to what I heard from Winnetou.'

'What? Winnetou has been here?'

'Naturally.'

'When?'

'Three days ago. You must have talked a lot about me, and my guns, and as he was here, he visited me. I heard about the bison hunting, the grizzly hunting, everything! Even that you were elected as an honorary chief.'

In another situation I would have happily listened to all his words, but now only one thing interested me: what he knew of Winnetou. It took me several attempts to interrupt his hugging, and the flowing of his words. When finally I succeeded I learnt that Winnetou had not found Santer in the town of St Louis. Apparently he had headed towards New Orleans and, naturally, Winnetou had followed this lead. He had left a message for me that I should hurry after him, and he hoped that we would meet there.

I could not go after him right away, because first I had to sort out my official affairs. Thus early the following morning I was sitting in the same engineering office where, without my knowledge, I had been examined. Hawkins, Stone, and Parker came with me. Of course, old Mr Henry joined us. In the office I gave my report. I also learnt there that nobody had survived from the team, except the four of us.

Sam tried everything to squeeze out some special bonus for me, but it was in vain. Our wages were immediately paid, but not a dollar more, even though I gave them my drawings and the notes that I had prepared. The gentlemen employed five surveyors, and four were lost. They refused to consider the fact that the work was completed only because I worked for the other four. Sam made a rather strongly worded speech about it, but his only achievement was that we were ushered out of the office. He, Dick, and Will laughed at each other, but I left the office disappointed. Still, the substantial sum of money that was paid to me consoled me to some degree.

Now I wanted to find Winnetou. He left the address of a hotel in New Orleans with Mr Henry. Out of politeness I asked my companions if they wanted to join me. They answered that they wanted to rest a bit in St Louis, and I could not reproach them for this. I bought some necessary things, such as clothing, underwear, and other things. I changed from my Indian clothing to these, and I was ready to travel. What I did not want to take with me, including the heavy bear slayer gun, I left with Mr Henry. I left my pinto in Saint Louis too. I was convinced that I would soon return.

But everything happened differently because I did not account for the political situation. We were in the middle of the Civil War. By then Admiral Farragut had destroyed the fleet of the Southern states, and occupied New Orleans. Travel on the Mississippi became free all the way, and I believed that I would easily get from St Louis to New Orleans. But there were all kinds of obstacles. The ship was held up a number of times, and by the time I arrived to New

247

Orleans, Winnetou had gone. He left a message for me in the hotel, telling me that he was travelling to Vicksburg in his pursuit of Santer. His plans were uncertain, and there was no reason for me to follow him. Maybe at a later time he would have an opportunity to contact Mr Henry.

What could I do? After a long consideration, I decided to travel home. I suffered from home sickness, and I also knew that the financial situation of my relatives was not the best. I had money, and I could help them. I enquired at the port, and I found a small boat that was heading to Cuba. From there I could continue either directly to Germany or at least to New York. I bought the ticket, and an hour later I was on the deck. It occurred to me to leave the money with a bank, and take only the banker's draft with me, but which banker could be trusted in New Orleans? In any case, I was also in a hurry as the ship was ready for departure, so I took my money in my purse.

We left the port. The sky was cloudy, and a cold wind blew, but nobody had a bad premonition. The passengers were happy that they could leave war-stricken New Orleans behind. After dinner everybody went to bed, and slept peacefully. At midnight I awoke for the wild swings of the ship, and the roaring of the sea. A hurricane had arrived. The rushing, swirling wind whipped up the waves. The waves rocked the ship so much that I fell on the ground. The cabin, which I shared with three other passengers, collapsed on us with a huge crushing noise. I did not think of my possessions, because every moment counted, and finding my coat and wallet in the dark and turmoil would have taken some time. I tottered through the ruins of the cabin to the deck. I could barely stand on my feet.

It was a dark night, and I could not see anything. The hurricane threw me on the deck, and a huge wave washed over me. I heard screaming and shouting, but the roar of the storm overpowered the human voices. Suddenly there were many lightning strikes, one after the other, and for a moment they lit up the night. It seemed that behind the waves I saw a coastline. The ship stuck between cliffs. The waves lifted it then smashed it to the cliffs again and again. The lifeboats had been washed away by the waves. I knew that the ship was lost, and I could only escape by swimming. In the light of another lightning I saw humans rolling on the deck holding on chains and ropes so that they would not be washed away. "Bad idea," I thought, because I knew that only the waves can save anyone.

Another huge wave was rushing towards us. It was as high as a many-storey house. It had a greenish fluorescent light, and when it hit the ship, it fell on the deck. The energy of the wave squeezed and cracked, maybe even split the boat. I immediately let the beam, that I was holding, go. I felt as if some horrible force lifted me high, twisted me, and then threw me in the depth. I was in a vortex. I did not do anything, because I knew it would have been in vain. If the wave carried me to the coast, I would need all my strength so that it could not take me back out to the sea.

I was the prisoner of the vortex for two minutes at the most, but it felt like hours. Then a huge wave took me high again. It simply spat me between two cliffs, where the sea was calmer. "Don't let it catch me again!" I prayed as I tried to keep myself on the surface. Luckily, in the light of the lightning I could see the coast, and so I knew which direction I had to swim. Slowly I moved there, but in the darkness I could not find a place where I could get out of the sea safely. As a result I banged my head on a cliff. Fortunately I had enough strength to climb up on this cliff, but then I lost consciousness. When I recovered, the storm was still raging. My head ached, but I did not care. I was more interested in the question of where I was: on the beach or on an outer cliff. I could not move at all, because the cliff was smooth and slippery, and I could hardly hold myself. Then the storm suddenly had gone. The rain stopped, and the stars appeared in the sky.

The light of the stars was enough for me to see that I was on the beach. Behind me white waves hit the cliffs, but on the other side there was ground. I saw trees in the distance, and I tottered there. Some trees coped with the storm, but others were torn out of the ground. Behind the trees I saw blinking lights. "Humans must live there," I thought with hopes, and as quickly as I could, I hurried to that direction.

I arrived to small houses. They were also damaged by the storm; one of them had lost its roof. People approached me, and looked at me as if they had seen a ghost. The sea roared so much behind me that we had to shout, otherwise we would not have been able to understand each other. They were fishermen. The storm drove our ship to the Dry Tortugas, near Florida, at the beginning of the shipping route to Cuba. Fort Jefferson, where Confederate prisoners of war were held, was on the island where I had ended up.

The fishermen were very generous to me. They offered me the most necessary clothing as I wore only what one would wear in bed.

The good fishermen searched the coast to help others who might have got to the beach. By the morning they had found sixteen people, but they could revive only three of them. When the dawn arrived I saw that the beach was full of the debris of the completely broken up ship. Only its front piece was still stuck on the cliffs.

I was a castaway in the true sense of the word as I had nothing at all, even my clothing had come from charity. The money for which I had good plans was on the bottom of the sea. Although I regretted the loss, my heart was not broken. I consoled myself that I was still alive. Of so many people only four of us survived the storm, thus I had to be happy for my own life.

The commander of the fort was also generous. He put me on a ship that stopped at the island on the way to New York. He paid for my ticket, and wished me good luck. This is how I arrived to New York for the second time in my life, again with an empty pocket, much poorer than at the first time. However, I was not downhearted, and I was ready to start everything from the beginning.

I could have gone to St Louis, where Mr Henry would have supported me, but I felt already too indebted to him. Still I would have visited him, if Winnetou had been there, but as he was pursuing Santer, it was very unlikely. I decided that I would try to get on my feet alone, thus I had to find employment in New York.

My luck did not let me down. I accidentally met Mr Josh Tailor, the director of the then famous Tailor Detective Agency. I asked him if he had any job for me. He was very reluctant, but when he heard how I had stood my ground in difficult circumstances, he gave me some very difficult cases in which I proved my skills. After this, he started to offer me better cases for which the reward was higher.

One day he called me to his office, and introduced me to an elderly gentleman who was sitting there with a care-burdened face. I learnt that his name was Ohlert, and he was the owner of the reputable Ohlert Bank. He turned to us because of a private affair. It was a family problem that also threatened his business interests.

His only son, William, who was twenty-five years old, and for a while had a job in the bank, had become more and more careless about his responsibilities. William thought he had the skills and talent to become a poet. As some of his poems were published in some New York newspapers, his decision to become a poet was reinforced. He decided that he would write a tragedy about a poet who lost his mind. He started to study mental illnesses, and gradually found more and more symptoms in himself. He thought he was insane, just like his hero in his tragedy.

The banker had heard about a doctor who ran a private hospital for similar patients. This doctor had gained the elder Ohlert's confidence by talking about being an assistant to famous doctors. The banker had become very hopeful when his introverted son had begun to trust the doctor, and they had become friends. Then one day William Ohlert had disappeared with the doctor. The banker only then on making enquiries learnt that the doctor was a quack.

The young Ohlert had a lot of money on him. A few days later the elder Ohlert received a telegram from Cincinnati. A banker, with whom he had a close business relationship, informed him that William had visited him, and took 5,000 dollars at the cost of his father for "bringing his bride from Louisville".

Obviously the son was completely under the influence of the doctor who was ready to squeeze money out of this. William knew all the business partners of his father, and could get as much money from them as he wanted. Thus capturing the "doctor" was also a business interest.

'What's the name of this doctor?' asked Tailor.

'Gibson,' answered the banker.

My boss looked at me, and I nodded. We had heard this name from another case. He was a confidence trickster who operated in Mexico and the United States. We had a photo of him. We showed the photo to the banker, who immediately recognised his son's doctor. Tailor gave me this case. Since Gibson knew me, I even took some props to disguise myself if necessary, and I left New York on the same day.

In Cincinnati I visited the banker, and I learnt from him that young Ohlert had taken money there. He was accompanied by Gibson. From there they went to Louisville, where I learnt that the two bought tickets to St Louis. Of course I followed them, but I could find their tracks again only after some time. It was Mr. Henry who helped, because, it goes without saying, I went to see him. He was quite surprised to see me as a detective, and made me promise that I would give up my position once I solved the case, and return to the Wild West. The prototype of his new repeating rifle was almost ready.

Ohlert and Gibson took a steamer to New Orleans on the Mississippi, and I followed them. So far William Ohlert collected money at every city and town they had passed through. In New Orleans, however, I could warn the elder Ohlert's business partners in time, and asked them to immediately send for me if William and Gibson called.

The southern character of New Orleans was obvious, especially in the old quarter. The dirty, narrow alleyways gave excellent hiding places to those who had the reason to hide. The windows of the houses and the balconies almost disappeared behind the ivy that covered the walls. In the crowd every skin colour was common from black to white. On every street corner street musicians played on some instruments. Men bellowed, and women screamed. An angry seaman jerked a Chinese peddler's braided hair in one corner, and at another two black men were fighting in the ring of a laughing audience. At another place two porters argued. They threw off their packs, and started fighting. A third wanted to separate them, and he received the blows that the two meant for each other.

There were more peaceful quarters too, where in the depth of the gardens clean little houses hid. In the gardens roses, hollies, and oleanders pleased the eyes, but there were also fig, peach, orange, and lemon trees. At the edges of the noisy, busy town one could live there in peace.

The port was the noisiest, and also the most busking place. Smaller and larger barges as well as ships were anchored there. Hundreds of porters carried the huge bales of cotton, the barrels, and the sacks of flour. Whole mountains of cotton bales were waiting to be transported to various parts of the world.

I wandered around in the town in the hope that I would accidentally catch sight of the Ohlert and Gibson. At noon the heat became unbearable. I was on the busiest street of the city, called Cannon Street, when the coat of arms of a bar stopped me. As I was terribly thirsty and hot, I went in for a drink, and some rest.

The huge bar was full of guests. I saw only one empty chair in the corner by a little table. Somebody sat on the chair opposite the entrance. His appearance was not too trustworthy, probably this was the reason why the other chair remained free. I went there, and asked politely if I could sit down. The man looked at me with searching and slightly mocking eyes, and said abruptly, 'Have you got money, young man?'

'Of course,' I answered.

'So, you can pay for your beer. Then why do you ask permission from me to sit down? If I see a free chair, I take it. If someone protested against it, I would make him regret it. One should insist on his rights. Learn this well, greenhorn.'

I was called greenhorn again! I got red, and responded indignantly, 'I might be a greenhorn, but even an old fox should be polite, you know!'

'Just calm down, young man!' he said smiling. 'I didn't mean any harm with my remark, and your anger will not take you anywhere. Old Death is not someone, who could be shaken out from his equanimity with threats.'

Old Death! Fate brought me together with this man: the oldest, and the most famous hunter! How many times had I heard about him by campfires! His name was known even in the far away cities. If only a tenth or twentieth was true of those things that were said about him, it would have made him the bravest, the most experienced hunter, warrior, and scout west of the Mississippi. He had spent a long life in the West; he had coped with all dangers, and yet he had never been wounded. This is why the superstitious people thought he was bulletproof.

Old Death was of course a nom de guerre. Nobody knew his real name, but his war name fitted well.

He was a tall, lean man: he was skin and bone in fact. He sat with his shoulders dropping forward. His cheekbones stuck out of his sunken face. He looked like a combination of a skeleton and a skull! There was not a single hair on his head, and his Adam's apple stuck out horribly. His huge hands were also emaciated; the bones in his long fingers almost rattled. His blue eyes were sunken, but strangely they gleamed youngish.

His clothing was also strange. As if his colourful shirt, tight jacket, and breeches had shrunk together with his body. His shapeless boots were made of s single sheet of horse skin. He wore such huge spurs that I had never seen before. The wheels of the spurs were made of Mexican silver peso coins.

But the most interesting was that next to his legs there was a completely equipped saddle. His gun was put to the wall. It was the so-called Kentucky gun, a long barrel, front loading gun, a rarity by then. Of course, he had other weapons too. In his belt there was a huge Bowie knife, and two revolvers. The belt was decorated by palm-sized scalps, obviously the scalps of Indians that he had removed from the head of the original owners after killing them.

The waiter brought the beer. I lifted it to my lips greedily, but Old Death grabbed my arm.

'Just slowly, young man,' he said. 'Let's click glasses first, as they do in Europe.'

'Yes, with friends.'

'Well, I'm an honest and simple man, not a thief, a trickster or a mole. You aren't either of these, I can see that.'

This sounded friendlier, and I was happy to clink my glass to his.

'Thank you for the trust that you have in me without knowing me. I consider it to be a great honour that I can talk to you. I haven't been around long, still I know who Old Death is.'

'So, you've heard of me. This is good, then I don't have to talk about myself. But you ... what are you doing here? Why did you come?

'As many other men, to make my fortune,' I answered.

'Haha!' he laughed. 'On the other side of the ocean they think that dollars fall from the sky, and we only have to keep our pocket open under this rain. The few to whom it has happened are written about by the newspapers. The rest disappear without a trace. I don't want to dishearten you, but I'm afraid, you won't do better either.'

'Why do you think so?'

'First of all, because you have too honest a face. Your hair is perfect; the Indians would love it. Then I looked at your clothing. Clean, ironed, fine. Do you want to catch the tail of the fortune pig with gloved hand?'

'I bought the clothing in New York. I didn't know then what my task would be here.'

'What's your task, if I may ask?'

With his cold blue eyes he looked at me in such a way that I could not lie.

'I came here under the commission of a banker.'

'A banker? Of course! It's visible on you that you are an educated man who knows finance.'

'It's not about finance. I cannot tell you more. I hope I don't hurt you with this.'

'Not at all! You don't have to tell your secrets to the first curious man. And anyway, I know it already.'

'And what's that?'

'You are looking for someone, aren't you?'

'I don't deny it.'

'You would make a mistake if you did. So, you are looking for someone. This is why you run up and down on the streets, and visit the bars. I wouldn't be Old Death if I couldn't figure that out. Do you know what you are?'

'You said it: a greenhorn.'

'I didn't want to insult you. Let's say it more delicately: a trainee detective. Are you?'

'Maybe, continue the guessing.'

'The person whom you seek is a criminal. I don't know if it's a family member or connected to a family member, but there's a criminal element.'

'You have a strong fantasy, Sir,' I said, and I was already regretting what I had told him.

'One needs fantasy in life. But you're wrong if you think that I want to question you. And you are making a mistake by not listening to me. Anyway, I have to leave. Good bye, young man.'

'We may meet again.'

'Everything is possible, though it's unlikely. I'm going to Mexico through Texas.'

He took his hat from the hook. It was a kind of small sombrero, not bigger than a cartwheel. He threw his saddle on his shoulder, grabbed his gun, and walked out of the bar. I followed him with my eyes. I saw that men looked after him on the street smiling.

I would have liked to be angry with him, but I could not be really. His words were harsh, but his voice sounded well-intentioned. I liked him despite his ugliness, but I thought that it would have been imprudent, and also reckless to initiate him in my plans, although he might have been able to give a good hint to me. The word "greenhorn" did not bother me, Sam Hawkins had made me get used to it. I also did not feel like telling him that I had been in the West before.

I put my elbow on my table, and resting my head on my hand I dived in my thoughts. The old man was right, it would be difficult to find Gibson in this big port town.

Then the door opened. I turned my head in that direction involuntarily, and I caught sight of Gibson!

"Fortune favours me," I thought, "or, what is more likely, it's the most popular bar in town, and almost everybody visits it daily."

Gibson stopped by the door, and looked at the guests one by one. I quickly turned my back to the door. Old Death's seat was still free. I hoped Gibson would sit down there. I already imagined his face when he would see me.

But he did not come in. The door banged again, and when I looked again I saw that Gibson turned around, and hurried away. In a second I put my hat on my head, threw a coin on the table, and rushed out. Gibson tried to disappear in the crowd on the street. I hurried after him, and caught sight of him by a cross street. He turned there, but first he looked back, and lifted his hat mockingly. By the time I got there, he had disappeared.

The cross road led to a small square. On one side of the square there was a block of flats, while on the other there were villas at the end with pretty gardens. I spotted a little barber shop by the first house on the right hand side. There was a black man leaning on a table there. Obviously, he had been standing there for some time. I asked him if had seen a gentleman hurrying. His mouth opened to a wide smile, and he flashed his big, yellow teeth at me.

'Yes, Sir,' he answered, 'I saw him. He was in a hurry. He rushed in that villa over there.'

He pointed at a gate at the front of a garden. I ran there, and pushed down the handle. It was locked. I was pulling the bell until somebody came out. It was a young black servant.

'First I have to ask the Master. I cannot let you in without his permission!' he said after my enquiries.

He went away, and I had to wait there for ten minutes on tenterhooks. Finally he returned.

'I was told that I'm not allowed to let you in. I was instructed that the door must stay locked. If you jump over the fence, you will be shot.'

I was helpless. Should I break through the gate? They may arrest me for trespassing. I left angrily. As I crossed the square, a boy ran to me with a piece of paper.

'Sir! Sir!' he shouted. 'Wait! Ten cents for this paper that was sent to you.'

'By whom?'

'A gentleman who came out from that house,' he said and he pointed at the house opposite to the one that I was sent earlier.

I took the paper. It was a page from a notebook. The following was written on it by pencil:

Dear Mr Sniffer
You surely didn't come to New Orleans for me! If you have any brain, you forget your dream that you can capture me. I advise you not to interfere with my business. Return to New York, and pass on my greetings to Mr Ohlert, who surely won't forget me. And I suppose you will always remember our near encounter.
Gibson

I crumpled the letter angrily. I looked around. The boy had disappeared, and so had the black man who had been by the barber shop earlier. They were all in cahoots against me.

Gibson's insolence upset me the most. He had time to mock me, and I could not even inform the police about him.

My instinct told me that Gibson was already packing to leave New Orleans quickly. Although it was unlikely that I could find him, I wandered around the town, visited the bars and inns, all possible places without success.

I went to bed deadly tired. I fell asleep quickly, but I had nightmares. I was fighting with Gibson, but he slipped out of my hands; he pulled a revolver, and shot me dead! I awoke for the bang. It was not a revolver, but I knocked down the reading lamp from the table as I was turning and twisting in the bed. I sat up sweating.

In the morning I started the search again. I went to the same big bar as the day earlier. It was quite empty now. I sat down by a table, ordered food and drink, and picked up a newspaper that had been left on the table. As I flicked through it, my eyes were caught by a long poem. "The most horrible night" was its title. Under the poem, instead of the name of the poet, there were only two letters. W. O. These were William Ohlert's initials!

Now I read the poem carefully. The content suggested that it was probably written by the unfortunate young man. It was about the horrors of nights. The first part was about a stormy winter night. If one was in a house, he could listen to the whistling of the wind calmly. The night of an old man, who was fearful of death, was more horrible, because he could not fall asleep. But, according to the poem, the most horrible was the night of the ghosts, when one was afraid of losing his mind, by which such darkness falls on him that would not dissolve by the arrival of the dawn.

The poem was not a masterpiece, but I was captivated by its honesty. It was like a cry for help, including my help. I overcame my emotions quickly: I had to act. I checked the office address of the newspaper, and hurried there. I learnt that the poem was delivered by hand, and the author requested an immediate publication. Since they had troubles with filling in the paper, they had immediately put the poem in the newspaper. I was told that the young man was decent, and he kept on repeating that he had written the poem with the blood of his anxious heart. He had to give his address, which was a hotel in the newer part of the city.

It was easy to find the hotel. Its owner was a pleasant looking lady of about fifty years of age.

I started the conversation by telling her that I wanted to talk to Mr Ohlert.

'Why?' she asked carefully, and by this I knew that I was at the right place.

'Because of the poem. It was excellent. I'm an editor of the newspaper, I brought his fee, and we would like more poems from him, and also some information about him.'

'He's a fine, quiet, educated young man, and also rich, but he doesn't speak to anyone and, apart from the day when he took the poem to you, he doesn't go out. Nothing interests him. The shopping and other affairs were arranged by his secretary.'

'Really, he has a secretary?'

'Of course, Mr Clinton.'

'Mr Clinton?'

'Yes, yes. He's also a fine gentleman. I had the most contact with him. He was the one who paid the bill. It seems that he manages Mr Ohlert's money.'

'I see,' I nodded. 'But his behaviour ... I mean, is there ... some secret?'

'I cannot talk about this, though Mr Clinton told me everything. My best guests often honour me with their trust.'

'I'm not surprised by this, Madame,' I said flatteringly. 'I would really like to know more about this secret, but then if confidentiality ...'

'Well, you published the poem, and I can see that you are interested in the story of the poor man, and newspapers are very powerful and ... and the gentlemen have left, so I can speak to you about it.'

'Is it some unhappy love?'

'Oh, Sir!' sighed the lady. 'When I was young, I had a great love ... But it caused only bitterness instead of happiness. Exactly the same as in the life of the young man.'

'You too, Madame? This is very interesting! If I wasn't afraid of opening old wounds, I would ask you ...'

I was punished for my hypocritical interest, because I had to listen to the history of love of the lady. The son of a rich French settler courted her, but the cold hearted father did not want their marriage to happen, and sent his son to Paris to forget, and he did forget.

'Now, you can understand, Sir,' finished the lady, 'why I have so much sympathy for Mr Ohlert.'

'How? Maybe he too ...'

'The young couple decided to marry in Mexico, and start a new life there. The poor girl had already gone to Veracruz. Mr Ohlert had important things to arrange, and this is why he stayed here for some days. In the meantime, he was in constant fear that his father would send somebody after him, a detective, and this man would force him to return. Apparently this man has arrived, so Ohlert and Clinton had to leave in haste. They couldn't travel to Veracruz directly, so they got on the Dolphin that left for Quintana. There they'll find another ship that takes them to Veracruz.'

'Maybe I could catch William at the port,' I said jumping up from my chair.

'You don't have to hurry, Sir. Our servant took their luggage to the port, and waited until the Dolphin had left.

He waved off our guests.'

I had heard enough, and hurried to the port.

My enquiries there were not very fruitful. There were many ships to leave for Quintana, but only in a few days' time. Finally I found a sailing ship that took goods to Galveston. They had finished the loading, and it was ready to sail in the afternoon. "Let's go then to Galveston," I thought, "and from there I can get to Quintana somehow." An hour later I was on the ship, and by the afternoon we were crossing the waves of the Gulf of Mexico.

In Galveston, another disappointment awaited me. I could not find a ship that would take me to Quintana. I had to make a compromise, and boarded a ship that left for Matagorda, by the estuary of the Colorado River, which was well beyond Quintana. I was convinced that I would find a ship there that would take me back to Quintana.

At this time Mexico was in turmoil, and the excitement spread to its North-eastern neighbour, Texas. The hero of Mexico was Benito Juárez, an Indian descent, who had been elected as president. He introduced many reforms, and in this the French found a pretext for an intervention. Napoleon III sent an army against him. The French army took the capital of Mexico. Following Napoleon's instructions, the leaders of the Catholic Party invited Archduke Maximilian Habsburg to the throne as the Emperor of Mexico. The government of the United States supported Juárez, and called on Napoleon to withdraw his troops. By 1866 this request could not be ignored, because the United States had recovered from the Civil War, and in Europe, Napoleon's main ally, Austria, was defeated at Sadowa. Napoleon, facing this situation, had to give in, and his army left Mexico. With this Emperor Maximilian's downfall was sealed.

During these time political affiliations and views had become a common subject of conversations. Everybody was talking about Juárez. He was popular in Texas, but many Texan hated him because Washington supported him. In the Civil War Texas was on the side of the slave states, thus there was still resentment after the victory of the North. Thus, there was turmoil in both Texas and Mexico, and one, strangers in particular, had to be alert.

Our ship entered the gulf of Matagorda, and anchored behind the long and flat peninsula that separated the small bay from the Gulf of Mexico. I saw several sailing ships and a steam boat there. Because of the shallow water they were anchored far from the port. On a boat I was transported to the port, where I enquired about transport to Quintana. It was as if a bucket of cold water had been poured on me, when I learnt that the next schooner would leave only two days later. I was very annoyed, because then Gibson would have had four days' lead on me, which was enough for him to disappear. I could only console myself with the thought that I had done everything I could. I took a room in an inn, and got my luggage from the ship.

Matagorda was an unimportant town then, and there were fewer ships in its port than in Galveston's port. Its shores were flatlands, and although they were not swampy, it was easy to catch a disease there. I was not happy at all that I had to spend time there.

The inn was third class, although the owner called it a "hotel". My room was small like a cabin, and my bed was so short that I had to choose whether my head or my legs should hang down from it.

Once I had sorted out my belongings, I went for a walk to look around in Matagorda. As I was heading to the stairs, I passed by an open door on the corridor. I glanced in the room. It looked exactly like mine. On the floor there was a saddle, and by the window a Kentucky gun stood. Was Old Death my neighbour? It was possible as he had said that he would go across Texas.

He was more surprised than I was, when we spotted each other in the street.

'Look! It's my good greenhorn!' he exclaimed joyously. 'What wind has blown you here?'

'The same as you,' I answered.

'Where did you set up your abode?'

'In Uncle Sam's Hotel.'

'Huh, I'm staying there too!'

'I know, I saw your coat of arms: the saddle!'

'You laugh at me, don't you? But it's not silliness, you know. You can get a good horse everywhere, but a good saddle is rare. This is why I carry my good, well-shaped saddle at all time. But, let's have a drink for our reunion!'

He took my arm, and we went to a bar. There were no other guests. We sat down, and ordered three bottles of beer: I ordered one, and Old Death two. I offered him a cigar, but he shook his head, and took a pressed roll of tobacco from his pocket. He cut a slice of it, and began to chew.

'This is the real stuff! I learnt it from the seamen,' he said, as he enjoyed chewing the tobacco.

I told him that I wanted to get to Quintana, but ended up in Matagorda, and that I would have to stay there until the following day.

'The same here,' he laughed. 'I wanted to get to Austin upstream on the Colorado River, and then over land to the Rio Grande. I thought that in this season the rain raised the flow of the Colorado River sufficiently for the flat bottom boats to get to Austin.'

'I heard in the port that driftwood obstructs the shipping on the river.'

'Yes, but only at one point, about eight miles from the estuary. Because of the driftwood the river broke up into many branches. Thus the boat turns back there. I decided to walk that eight miles. I took my saddle, and then walked. I just arrived, when the boat, with horrible whistling, left upstream.'

'So we are fellow sufferers.'

'No, I'm not, because I don't chase anyone, so it doesn't matter if I arrive a week later to Austin. Why I'm annoyed is that one of the passengers, the ugliest person I have seen in my life, unlike me, caught the ship, and laughed at me again mockingly, while I stood on the bank with my saddle!'

'Again? Have you met him before?'

'Yes. I had a quarrel with him. He was on the Dolphin from New Orleans to here.'

'On the Dolphin? That's interesting!'

'Whenever he saw me on the deck he made fun of my appearance, and always grinned. Finally I asked him what he had found so amusing. "I've never seen such a skeleton in my life," he answered impertinently. For this remark he got a slap on the face. He pulled a revolver, but the Captain intervened. He threatened him with arrest if he did not change his behaviour. Then the man went away, and stopped bothering me. Only I felt sorry for his friend.

The quarrel upset him so much that it was difficult to calm him. He behaved like some mentally ill person.'

'Mentally ill?' I cried out. 'Do you know his name?'

'The Captain called him Mr Ohlert.'

'And the other ... What was his name?'

'Clinton if I remember correctly,' answered Old Death.

I jumped up from my seat.

'Damn it!' I swore. 'And you were with those two on the same ship!'

Old Death looked at me surprised.

'What happened to you?' he asked. 'You jumped up like a rocket! What does it have to do with you?'

'What? Those are the two whom I have been pursuing!'

'Hm ...' hummed Old Death, 'you see, had you been honest with me last previously, you would have gone further.'

'I couldn't do that. But I don't understand. They wanted to travel to Quintana, and not to Matagorda.'

'They probably just said that to mislead their pursuers. If you want to be clever, my friend, you should tell me all you know. Then I may be able to help you.'

I took the two photos from my case, and showed them to him. He recognised them immediately.

'They're the ones,' he nodded, 'I'm sure.'

I told him everything. He listened attentively, and then he asked, 'What do you think, is the young William Ohlert really mentally ill?'

'I don't think so,' I answered. 'Probably just a man with a monomania, who is completely under the influence of that trickster. Clinton, or rather Gibson, if that's his real name, exploits the situation, and fleeces the poor young man.'

265

'He may fail,' Old Death consoled me.

'Are you sure they were going to Austin? Won't they disembark on the way?'

'I don't think so. I heard when Ohlert told the Captain that they were going to Austin. If the other had said it, I would have thought it was another trick. But it was Ohlert. We'll go after them with tomorrow's ship.'

'When will we get to Austin?'

'With the current water level, in two days.'

'That's long time!'

'Don't forget that they are delayed too. The ship can go aground easily, and then it takes time until it can start to move again.'

'If I only knew what Gibson's plans are! Where is he taking Ohlert to, and why?'

'He must have some plan, that's for sure,' replied Old Death. 'He already fleeced a lot of money from him, and he could leave him. But apparently he wants to squeeze out even more money from him. I'm really interested in the case, and as our path, at least for a while, is the same, I'm at your disposal.'

We shook hands, and I thanked him for his help. We drank our beer, and ordered a second. The waiter was putting the bottles on our table, when we heard some big noise outside: thumping of feet, shouting, and barking. The door was swung open, and six men entered. They must have visited other bars as none of them were sober. All had rough faces, and strong bodies. They had guns, knives, revolvers, and all of them had a slave whip in their hand. Each of them had a huge dog on a leash. These dogs were especially trained for catching escaping black slaves in the Southern states.

They cast challenging looks at us as they passed by our table. They sat down in another corner, put their feet on the table, and started yelling, and banging for the waiter's attention. The innkeeper himself went to them, and asked for their order.

'Beer!' bellowed one of them, whose broad head, low forehead, and thick neck reminded me to a bison.

'Yes, Sir!' answered the innkeeper humbly, and hurried for the beers.

Involuntarily I turned my head towards the loud man. He noticed it. There was nothing insulting in my look, but it seemed that he wanted to quarrel, because he shouted over, 'What are you gazing at? Haven't you seen a whip? Did you come from the North?' he asked menacingly

I turned away without answering.

'Look out,' whispered Old Death to me. 'These are very dangerous thugs. All are slave overseers, who were fired after the abolition of slavery as their masters went bankrupt. Now they have formed gangs. The best is not to look at them. We'll finish our beer quickly, and then leave.'

The thug did not like our whispering. 'What are you whispering about, old bone?' he shouted over. 'If you are talking about us, open your mouth so we can hear it too!'

Old Death drank up his beer, and did not say a word. Soon the gang also got their beer. It was good beer, but the thugs were rowdy, and one of them poured it on the floor.

'Don't pour it on the floor! I can see that those two like it,' said the thug, 'I'll give them mine to make them happy!'

He stood up, made a few steps towards us, and splashed his beer towards us. A few drops hit Old Death's face. He calmly wiped the beer off with his sleeve, and remained quiet. However, most of the beer ended up on me. It was dripping from my face. I could not control myself. My face went red, and I protested, 'Make jokes with your mates! We didn't say a word to you! Leave us alone!'

'Do you think it was a bad joke?' he asked. 'And what do you say if I repeat it again?'

'I advise you against it!' I answered angrily.

'Then let's test it!!' he exclaimed. 'Innkeeper! Bring me another beer!'

His gang cheered, and waited for the amusement. It was clear that he would repeat the insult.

'It's unfortunate that you lost your self-control,' said Old Death shaking his head. 'It would have been better to remain quiet.'

'I didn't want them to think that we were cowards!' I said stubbornly.

'It's not a question of bravery. There are six of them, and they are well-armed. A treacherous bullet can kill even the bravest. Not to mention the dogs.'

The thugs tied their dogs to the legs of the table, and the dogs growled at us from there. I moved onto another seat so that at least my back would be covered.

'Look, he wants to defend himself!' laughed the rogue. 'If he makes one more move, I'll let Pluto loose on him!'

He untied the dog, and kept it on its leash. We had time to get away, but I did not feel like doing that. Firstly, it was unlikely that they would let us leave in peace. Secondly, I would have felt ashamed for escaping from such a debased gang. "Only their mouth is big," I thought, "if they met a brave man, they would become quieter immediately." Just in case, I dived into my pocket, and cocked my revolver. If it came to wrestling, I didn't have any reason to be afraid, but I was more doubtful about the dogs. I had experiences with dogs trained for attacking people, and I knew that I could defend myself only if one dog attacks me.

The innkeeper brought the beers.

While he was putting down the glasses, he turned to the rowdy group, 'Enjoy it gentlemen! I'm very happy for your custom, but please leave those two gentlemen alone, they are also my guests.'

'Shut up!' barked one of them at him. 'Why are you interfering? I'll cool your zeal a bit!'

He splashed his beer in the face of the barman, who did not dare to protest, and hurried away.

'Now comes the big boy,' shouted the thug, 'let's make him dance a bit.'

He held the leash in his left hand, and with his right he tried to splash his beer on me. I avoided it in time, and was about to jump on the insolent man with my clinched fist, but he was quicker.

'Pluto! Catch!' he ordered his dog, pointed at me, and released the leash.

I had just enough time to retreat to the wall. The huge animal jumped like a tiger. It was about five steps from me, but covered the distance with one leap. I knew that it would try to grab me by my throat. In the last moment I jumped aside, and the dog, because of its speed, could not stop, and hit its head on the wall. I grabbed its two hind legs, swung it, and hit its head to the wall so hard that I broke its skull.

A terrible noise broke out. The dogs were barking, and tore their leashes. The men were swearing, and the owner of the dead dog wanted to jump on me. At this moment Old Death stood up. His revolvers were pointed at the gang.

'Stop!' he shouted in a thunderous voice. 'It's enough, boys! If anyone comes any closer, or tries to grab his gun, he will be shot in the head. You made an error. Do you know who I am? I'm Old Death, the path finder. You may have heard about me. And my friend is a harder man than you imagined. Just sit down, and drink your beer in quiet. For the first suspicious motion I'll shoot.'

The warning was to one of the men, who put his hand in his pocket, obviously for his revolver. He pulled his hand back. Now I also had my revolver in my hand. We had eighteen bullets between us; enough to keep the gang under control. My friend had really changed. His bent back was straight, his eyes flashed, and on his face so much energy and determination glowed that contradicted his age. It was amusing to see how the gang recoiled. They murmured something, but they sat back. The owner of the dead dog did not dare to check the body of the animal, because he would have to come near me.

We were still standing with revolvers in our hand, when the door opened, and a new guest arrived. It was an Indian.

His white-tanned deer-leather shirt was decorated with red embroidery. His leggings were made of the same leather.

There were fringes along the seams. His clothing was clean. He wore moccasins on his disproportionately small feet. Pears and porcupine quills were sewn on the moccasins. On his neck his medicine bag, an artistically shaped calumet, and a triple necklace made of the claws of the grey bear hung. A fine blanket was wrapped around his waist as a belt. There was a knife and two revolvers in this belt. In his right hand he held a double-barrel gun whose wooden parts were decorated with silver nails. His long, thick, bluish-black hair was twisted in a helmet-like bun. Rattlesnake skin held it together. He did not wear any eagle feathers or any other symbols of office, but everybody had to know that the young man must have been a chief, and also a famous warrior. His serious, masculine, smooth face was almost Roman, his cheek bones did not stick out, and it seemed as if his light-brown skin had been gilded with bronze.

It was Winnetou, the chief of the Apache, my friend, and blood brother.

For a moment he stopped, and glanced around the room. Then he sat down by a neighbouring table, as far from the gang as it was possible.

I almost rose to greet him, but he turned his head away, and ignored me, although he surely recognised me. He must have had a reason for this, and because of this I also tried to show an indifferent face.

It was visible that he understood the situation. His eyes narrowed as he, now with contempt, looked at the gang. His light smile showed that he had seen as we put our revolvers in our pockets.

His presence was so powerful that the bar became silent. The barman peeped in to check the situation. He saw that he had no reason to be anxious, he went to his new guest.

'A glass of beer, please,' said the Apache with a ringing voice, and in excellent English.

The gang took notice of this. They started to whisper among themselves, and cast dark glances at Winnetou. They wanted to quarrel with him.

Winnetou got his beer. He raised it to the light to look at it, and then drank it with joy.

'This was good,' he said to the innkeeper. 'Your beer is excellent. The Great Spirit taught the white men many things, and brewing is not the least among them.'

'You wouldn't believe that this man was an Indian!' I said pretending that I did not know Winnetou.

'And an excellent one.' nodded Old Death.

'Do you know him?'

'I haven't met him, but it's easy to recognise him from his carriage, clothing, and especially from his gun. This is the famous silver gun that always hits the target. You, Sir, have the honour to see the most famous chief of North America. His name is often mentioned by campfires, villages, blockhouses, even in the palace of the governor. He's intelligent, just, proud, brave, and a faithful friend, supporter of everyone who needs help, be it a white man or a redskin. He's an Indian gentleman, the most famous hero of the West.'

'Tell me, where did he learn such good English, and excellent manners?'

'He's been in the Eastern cities many times. And he had a white teacher, a European scholar, who was captured by the Apache, but he was treated well, and so he stayed with them, and became their advisor, and Winnetou's teacher. However, his philanthropy did not penetrate the Indians, and he gradually became neglected.'

We talked very softly, but still, Winnetou could hear it from five steps away as he replied, 'Old Death is wrong. My people received the white teacher, who came to us, kindly and surrounded him with love, and he wasn't neglected. He taught Winnetou to differentiate between truth and lie, innocence and crime, humanity and villainy. He liked to be with us, and never wanted to return to the white men. We built a mausoleum over his grave after his tragic death. His soul is now delighted by the smile of the Good Spirit on the eternal hunting grounds. His student, Winnetou, will once

271

meet him there, and there they will not encounter the hatred that separates people.'

Old Death's eyes beamed because Winnetou addressed him by his name, and asked, 'Do you know me, Sir?'

'I haven't had a chance to meet you, but as soon as I saw you, I recognised you,' replied Winnetou. 'Old Death's fame has reached us too.'

While saying these words his face remained motionless. He turned away, and apparently was lost in his thoughts. However, I knew that from under his eyelashes he watched what was happening in the bar.

Now the gang stopped whispering. They nudged and looked at each other which suggested that they had come to a decision. They did not know this Indian, they had no reason for being angry with him, but they wanted to take revenge on someone for their earlier failure. As they despised the red men, Winnetou was the right target for them. They did not think that we would intervene as, according to the then customs of bar brawls, strangers had no right to intervene. One stood up, and walked towards the Indian with challenging steps. I took out my revolver, and put it on the table.

'Unnecessary,' whispered Old Death, 'Winnetou is able to deal with them with one hand tied behind his back.'

The leader of the gang stopped by the Indian, put his hand on his hips, and said, 'What are you doing here in Matagorda, redskin? We don't like savages around here!'

Winnetou did not even look at him. He had a sip of beer, clicked with his tongue, and put the glass on the table.

'Did you hear what I said, you damned redskin?' roared the thug. 'I want to know what you are doing here! Are you Juárez's spy? The reds are all for Juárez as he's one of you. But we support Emperor Maximilian, and hang all Indians that we can catch. We will hang you, if you don't praise Emperor Maximilian right now!'

The Apache chief still did not say a word. Not a muscle twitched on his face.

'Are you deaf, you dog? Answer or you'll be taught of manners,' shouted the thug with foaming anger, as he put his fist on the shoulder of the Indian.

For this Winnetou's supple body rose like lightening.

'Back!' he cried in a commanding voice. 'I don't mind if a coyote howls, but I don't let it touch me.'

'Coyote?' roared the thug. 'This insult demands revenge.'

He pulled his revolver, but what happened then, he had not expected. Winnetou knocked the weapon out of his hand, picked up the man by his waist, and threw him to the window. The window broke, and the man flew out to the street.

These events happened faster than the reading of it. The crashing glass, the barking of the dogs, and the angry yelling created such a noise that it almost suppressed Winnetou's voice as he went closer to the gang, pointed at the window, and asked, 'Anyone else wants to fly? Just come!'

One of the dogs tried to charge at him, but Winnetou kicked it so hard that it hid under the table whining. The slave overseers withdrew, and became quiet even though Winnetou had no weapon in his hand. His bravery was enough to make them stop. He was like a lion tamer, whose presence makes the lions recoil.

The door was kicked in, and the thug entered. His face and hands were bleeding. He had a knife in his hand, and he jumped on the Indian. Winnetou stepped aside, grabbed the man's wrist with one hand, and his belt with the other, then he lifted him, and threw him on the floor so hard that the man lost his consciousness. None of his mates dared to rise to help him. Winnetou calmly, as if nothing had happened, finished his beer. Then he beckoned to the innkeeper who hid behind the door by the bar. He took out a bag from his belt, picked a piece of gold from it, and gave it to the innkeeper.

'For the beer and the broken window,' he said. 'As you can see the savage pays. Hopefully, these civilised gentlemen will also pay you. They don't want to be near a redskin.

273

Winnetou, the chief of the Apache, leaves not because he's afraid of them, but because he wants clear air. Their skin is white, but their soul is dirty and disgusting.'

He picked up his silver gun, and stepped out of the door without casting a look at those present in the bar.

The shocked gang slowly recovered from the surprise. Their curiosity was stronger than their anger. Not caring with their unconscious companion, they surrounded the innkeeper to see what the Indian had given him.

'A nugget,' said the innkeeper, and showed the hazelnut size gold piece. 'It's worth at least twelve dollars. He paid generously for that worn out window. He had a whole bag of these nuggets.'

'It's awful that a redskin can have so much gold,' said one of the slave overseers gloomily.

The nugget went from hand to hand, they tried to put a value on it. We used the opportunity: we paid, and left.

'What do you think of this Apache, Sir?' asked Old Death in the street. 'I don't think that there is another Indian like him. These thugs flutter, like sparrows when they see a hawk. I'm curious why he is in this town. His horse must be somewhere, because the Apache are always with horses. By the way, you weren't bad at all the way you handled that dog. You were brave and skilful. You won't be a greenhorn for very long. What should we do? Should we go back to the inn? An old trapper like me doesn't like being in a room. Should we look around, or do you want to play cards?'

'No. I have never liked cards, and I hope I won't come to like it in the future either.'

'You are right, young man, but here in Texas everybody plays some gambling game. It's even worse in Mexico. The men, women, the young, and the old all play either cards or dice, and the knife easily slips in the hand there. Then let's have a lunch somewhere, and walk. Then we can go to bed early. We will need our strength for tomorrow.

'Tomorrow we will board the ship to Austin.'

'Well, this is our plan, but we may not go that far.'

'Why?'

'If Gibson gets out earlier, we have to do the same.'

'How will we know?'

'We will enquire. The ship goes slowly on the Colorado River. It spends at least half an hour in every port. And it could happen that it cannot go further. Then we will take our luggage, and find accommodation.'

'Then I can carry my suitcase!' I remarked peeved, but also laughing at my own exclamation.

'You have a suitcase! Wow! What an antediluvian habit! I barely have anything apart from my saddle. And what do you carry in that suitcase?'

'Clothing, underwear, toiletries …'

'Come on! All unnecessary. One wears a shirt until it keeps, and then buys another one. Toiletries? Don't take it wrong, but hair and nail brushes, pomade, moustache wax, and the like just defile a man. Do you want to catch Gibson with a hair brush and creams?'

He looked me up and down from head to feet, and pulled his lips mockingly, and added, 'There aren't many theatres around here to impress the ladies! I thought you were going to Mexico? Because I'm quite sure that Gibson's heading there.'

'You could be right, but then why didn't he take a boat directly to a Mexican port? Why this detour?'

'Firstly, he had to flee New Orleans quickly. He got on the first boat as he didn't have time to choose. Secondly, all the Mexican ports are controlled by the French army. Maybe Gibson has to avoid them. No, my friend! He goes overland to Rio Grande, of course, on horseback. He will cross the border river, and then he will disappear into Mexico. The situation is very confused there, and the hands of the law can't reach him. But your nice clothing will be just rags by the time you reach the Rio Grande!'

'So what should I do?' I asked.

I knew he was right, even though his mocking was a bit too sharp for my taste.

'I tell you, young man. You sell your suitcase, and all the gentlemen's equipment to a trader, and buy a trapper suit instead which is more appropriate for your current goal. I hope you have some money.' I nodded.

'To hell with all the unnecessary stuff. You'll buy a horse, because without it you are like a fish out of water. Along the river you can buy only a bad horse at a high price. We'll buy one from a farmer further away from the river. But we'll buy the saddle here.'

'Woe to me! Then will I go about like you, with a saddle on my back?'

'So what? It's nobody's business. I'd even carry a bed on my back to stretch out comfortably in the forest! And if somebody laughed at me, I'd box him between his ears so that he saw stars. The only shame is if one commits some debased thing or stupidity. I'm sure that Gibson and Ohlert will also get on a horse to progress. So decide quickly.'

But he did not give me time to decide. After ten steps he pushed me into a shop that advertised itself by a board:

STORE FOR ALL THINGS

The scene that followed was stupefying. I felt I was a schoolboy, and Old Death acted as my father in some department store. He also led the negotiations. He told the shopkeeper what we wanted to sell, and what we wanted to buy. The shopkeeper was contented, and sent his assistant with us to carry my belongings to the store. Once it had been done, the shopkeeper valued the items one by one, and added them up. It was an appropriate price which I immediately spent.

Old Death chose the following items for me: black leather breeches, high boots with spurs, a red cotton shirt, a vest of the same colour with big pockets, black scarf, unpainted deerskin jacket, a broad leather belt with pockets, a bag for ammunition, and another for gun powder, a pipe, tobacco, a compass, and a dozen other things. I changed my socks to cloth, my hat to a huge sombrero. I also bought a poncho, a lasso, a Bowie knife, flint, a saddle, and reins. Then came the gun. Old Death did not like new style things. He chose one of the outdated guns with expertise, and then tried it behind the house.

'This is good,' he said contentedly. 'One would think that it's a broomstick, but it was made by a good gunsmith, and it had good owners. We don't need bullets. We'll buy lead, and we'll make the bullets. It's more reliable.'

'But let's buy some handkerchiefs too!' I proposed.

'I don't mind,' replied Old Death with such a disdain that clearly showed that he considered them an unnecessary luxury.

I could not laugh now as I was also walking back to the inn with a saddle on my back next to Old Death. He looked at me with appreciation. He probably found the whole thing, and my appearance amusing. I have to admit though, he helped me carry my new belongings.

After arriving to the inn, my old friend lay down, but I went out to find Winnetou. I was happy that I had seen him in the bar, even though I could not show it. I needed great self-control not to jump on his neck. He pretended that he did not know me. He had to have his own reasons for this, and I had to accommodate it.

I was sure that he wanted to talk to me just as much as I did to him, and he was waiting for me somewhere, where we could talk in private. He surely followed us to the hotel, but he did not come in.

I knew his habits, and it was not difficult to find him. I turned onto an alleyway that lead to a meadow. He was standing there, a few hundred steps from me, leaning on a tree. He spotted me, but he did not greet me. Instead of this, he walked across the meadow towards a nearby forest. I followed him. He waited for me in the forest, and his face glowed with joy.

'Charlie! My brother! How happy I am that I can see you. The meadow cannot be as happy for the rising Sun after the night as I am for you!'

We embraced each other, and I said, 'The meadow knows that the Sun would rise, but I couldn't have hoped that we would meet here. I'm happy to hear your voice again, my brother.'

'How did you get here, Charlie?'

'I undertook a difficult task, and I want to accomplish it with honour.'

'Can you tell me what it is about, my white brother? If not, then at least tell me what happened to you since we got separated by the Red River.'

'I have no secret from you, Winnetou,' I replied.

He took my arm, and led me even deeper into the forest. We sat down on the trunk of a fallen tree, and I told him everything. He listened to me, and when I finished, he nodded sadly.

'You see, my brother,' he said, 'I allowed you to complete the surveying, because you wanted money. You got it, but the hurricane took it. Had you stayed with us, you wouldn't have needed money. But it was good that you didn't wait for me in St Louis as I wouldn't have gone there.'

'Have you caught Santer, the murderer?'

'Unfortunately I haven't. The Bad Spirit took him in his protection, and the Good Spirit wanted me to postpone my revenge. The murderer joined the Confederate Army, and disappeared among the thousands. But he hasn't escaped forever! I returned to the Pecos River as I urgently had to visit the Apache tribes to hold them back from what they had decided to do while I was away. They wanted to participate in the war of the palefaces in Mexico, but I didn't allow them. Have you heard of Juárez, the red president?'

'Quite a lot.'

'What do you think, who is right, he or Napoleon?'

'Juárez.'

'I agree. Please don't ask me, I can't tell you why I'm in Matagorda. I promised Juárez in El Paso del Norte that I would keep it a secret. I suppose you will continue to chase the two palefaces whom you have followed to here.'

'I have to.'

'I know. And I have responsibilities and these could be more important than yours. I'll travel to La Grange by boat, and then to Rio Grande del Norte through Fort Inge.'

'Then we'll go on the same boat! I'm happy that I'll meet you again tomorrow.'

'Don't recognise me!'

'Why?'

'I don't want you to be involved in my affair. This is why I behaved as if I didn't know you. But I also didn't recognise you because of Old Death. Does he know that you're Old Shatterhand?'

'Maybe he doesn't even know the name.'

'Of course, he does! Old Death knows more than you think. And you cannot know that while you have been to the East, your fame spread in the West. I saw that Old Death thinks you are greenhorn. He'll be surprised when he knows who you are. Let's wait for that; I don't want to spoil your amusement, my brother. So, we won't talk on the boat. Once you save the young Ohlert from Gibson, you will come to us, and then we can talk. You will come to us, won't you?'

'Definitely.'

'There are a couple of palefaces who are waiting for me here, I have to visit them now.'

He stood up, and I didn't ask anything, as I didn't want to query his secrets. We shook hands, and separated again. I hoped it would not be for long.

On the following morning Old Death and I hired two mules, and rode on them to the place where the steam boat waited for the passengers. The boat was a very flat bottom one built according to the American fashion, and there were many passengers on the deck already. We walked up onto the ship bent under our saddles. On the deck we were received with mock laughter.

'Just look!' somebody shouted. 'Give way to the two-legged mules. And lead them to the stables. Such beasts shouldn't be among gentlemen.'

The voice was familiar. The best places of the first class, which were protected by a glass ceiling, were occupied by yesterday's gang. They spread out as if the boat was theirs. Their leaders wanted a quarrel, this is why he had insulted us again. I glanced at Old Death, but he was walking calmly as if he had not heard the words. Thus I did not say a word either, and we sat down opposite the gang after pushing our saddles under our chairs.

Old Death stretched out, and then took out his revolver. He cocked it, and put it on the table. I followed his example.

The gang was whispering amongst themselves, but they were not loud now. Their dogs were next to them; one fewer than yesterday. Their leader stared at us with eyes glowing full of hate. He sat slightly bent, it seemed that the flight through the window injured him, as there were marks on his face caused by the glass.

The conductor collected the fares, and asked how far we were travelling. Old Death bought the tickets to Columbus, thinking that Gibson could have disembarked there. If he had not, we could still buy tickets to travel further.

The second whistling resounded when a new passenger arrived: Winnetou. He rode up on the ship on a wonderful black stallion, and dismounted only when he was on the ship. Then he led his horse to the front deck, where there were boxes for passengers who brought their horses. He did not look left nor right. He sat down on the railing of the ship near his horse. The gang watched him, coughed, and cleared their throat to attract his attention, but it was useless. Winnetou sat indifferently resting his hand on his silver gun.

The third whistle cut into the quietness of the air. They waited for one or two more minutes, and then the wheel started to roll, and the boat started off.

The journey was smooth. The time passed calmly until Wharton where one passenger left, but a group embarked. Old Death went to the port for a few minutes to talk to the guard. He was enquiring about Gibson. He learnt that nobody, corresponding to our description, disembarked. We got the same answer in Columbus, where we bought tickets to La Grange. The journey from Matagorda to Columbus would have required fifty hours of walking. The ship really made travelling easier. It was now about lunchtime, but Winnetou had stood up only once since the departure, and only to feed his horse.

It seemed that the gang forgot about us. They were more interested in the new passengers. They wanted to talk to them, but they got only short answers. They were boasting about their solidarity with the Southern States, and their deeds against the North. They asked everyone if they hated the North, and scolded those who were not enthusiastic enough for the rights of the slave master landowners. They threw words like "Damned Republican", "Nigger-friend", "Yankee batman", but all they achieved was that people pulled away from them. Probably this was the reason why they had left us alone. They could see that the majority of the passengers were not their sympathisers.

However, in Columbus many of the quieter passengers disembarked, and much louder ones embarked. Among them was a drunken group of fifteen or twenty men who staggered onto the boat. They were received by the gang with loud greetings. With their arrival the quieter passengers became a minority. They were pushing about and in, lay down on the benches, not caring whether other passengers had places to sit. The Captain considered it unnecessary to tell them off. As long as they were not interfering with his work, he wanted to avoid any uncomfortable situation.

Most of the South supporters went to the bar, and soon a terrible noise and shouting came from there. They broke bottles, sang, and yelled. A few minutes later a black man ran to the Captain. He was the waiter of the bar, and told the Captain that he was whipped, and the gang threatened him to hang him.

There was now real anxiety on the Captain's face. Once he set the steering properly, he headed towards the bar. The conductor stopped him on his way just where we sat.

'Captain,' said the conductor, 'we have to do something. They are preparing for something evil. I tell you, let's put the Indian on the bank, because they want to hang him. They had a quarrel with him yesterday. And there are two white passengers of whom they say are Juárez's spies. They want to lynch them too.'

'This is serious! Who are those two white passengers?'

'We are,' I said, and stood up.

'You? For God sake, I'll eat this boat for breakfast if you are Juárez's spies.'

'Well, we aren't!'

'You know what? I'll steer the boat to the bank, where you can quickly disembark, and you will be safe.'

'But we won't disembark! We have some urgent business upstream.'

'Then I don't know what to do. Wait a bit!'

He went to Winnetou, and talked to him. The Indian listened to him politely, and then shook his head. The Captain came back, and said annoyed, 'He won't disembark either! These reds are a stubborn lot!'

'Then all the three will be finished,' said the conductor. 'We don't have enough men to help them.'

The Captain stared at the ground thinking hard, then a sudden, broad smiled flooded his benevolent face. He hit his forehead showing that he had a good idea.

'No problem!' he said. 'We will trick them. But you have to help me. Do what I tell you! Hide your guns under the bench, next to your saddles. Don't use your weapons!'

'Should we wait calmly until they lynch us?' exclaimed Old Death angrily.

'I didn't say that. I need some time, but I'll intervene at the right moment. They'll be cooled down so quickly that they'll remember it for a very long time! Trust me!'

'What's your plan?'

'I don't have time to explain. The rascals are coming!'

It was true, the gang was coming up from the bar. The Captain turned away from us, and gave his orders to the conductor quietly. The conductor hurried to the mate, and informed him. A few minutes later I saw that he walked about among the passengers, and whispered something to the more reliable ones. I saw that these passengers moved to one of the corners of the front deck in one group. The gang immediately surrounded us.

'He's the one!' shouted the thug, and pointed at me. 'He's a spy of the North who supports Juárez. He was dressed as a gentleman yesterday, today as a trapper. Why does he disguise himself, I ask! He must have a reason. Yesterday he killed my dog, and threatened me with a gun.'

'Spy! Let's hang him! Down with all the Yankees who bankrupted us.'

'Down with Juárez, and everybody who supports him!'

'What is this noise?' shouted the Captain from the bridge. 'Quiet, gentlemen! Leave the passengers alone!'

'It's none of your business,' somebody cried. 'Supporting spies is not your responsibility!'

'It's my responsibility to ensure that paying passengers travel in peace! It doesn't matter if he's an abolitionist or a secessionist. Whoever breaks the peace, I'll put him on the bank, and he can swim to Austin!'

They laughed at him mockingly, some even neighed. We were so tightly surrounded that we could not even move. With beastly yelling they were pushing both of us towards the chimney whose rings were appropriate for hanging someone. Old Death was about to pull his revolver, but the Captain gave the signal not to.

'Whom should we hang first?' asked a loud voice, 'these two or the Indian?'

'Let's start with the Injun,' roared my thug. 'Let's bring him here!'

Two men rushed to the front, where Winnetou sat. We could not see anything, because the crowd blocked our view. Suddenly we heard screams. Winnetou knocked one of them out, and threw the other into the river. Then he jumped on the iron box that surrounded the wheel, and the barrel of his gun appeared. The gang was yelling so loudly that my ear began to ache. Everybody ran to the edge of the boat. For the Captain's order a lifeboat was let down onto the water, and a member of the crew started to row to the man. The swimmer grabbed the side of the lifeboat.

Old Death and I remained alone. The gang seemed to forget about us. We saw that the mate and the rest of the crew was looking at the captain as if waiting for a command.

The captain called me over, and said, 'I'll make them bathe now. Just watch it!'

In the next moment the engine stopped. The river swirled the boat to the right bank. There was a shallow bank there. The captain signalled to the mate, the mate nodded smiling, and stirred the boat right there. We heard a creaking noise followed by a strong shaking. Everybody lost his balance on the deck, some even fell over. The boat ran aground.

The informed passengers started to scream as if they were fearful for their life. Their excitement spread to the gang. They really believed that there was a major problem. One member of the crew came up to the bridge, and reported in a frightened voice, 'Captain! There's water in the boat! In five minutes we will sink!'

'Swim for your life!' shouted the Captain. The water is shallow here!'

He rushed down from the bridge, took off his coat and vest, threw off his cap, pulled off his shoes, and jumped over into the water. The water did not reach his neck.

'Jump! Jump!' he shouted. 'There's still time! If the ship sinks, the vortex will swallow everyone.'

Nobody noticed that it was the Captain who left the ship first. The gang was frightened. While pushing each other, they jumped into the water, and then quickly waded to the bank. They did not see that the Captain swam to the other side of the boat, and climbed on board. The ship was free from the gang. The yelling that had demanded lynching was replaced by joyous laughter.

Once the first men reached the bank, the captain gave the order to restart the engine. There was no damage to the strong-built boat, and it began its journey again. The captain swung his coat like a flag, and he cried over to the bank, 'Enjoy it, gentleman! If you still want lynching, hang each other. I'll leave your belongings in La Grange, you will find them there!'

His teasing words made the thugs rage. They demanded the Captain return to them, and take them on board again. They threatened him that they would report him to the authorities, and even with lynching. Some even shot after the ship. They shook their fists in their helpless anger, and yelled, 'You will regret this, you dog! We'll wait for your return, and hang you on the chimney of your own boat!'

The Captain only laughed, 'You'll be hanged first! I will attend your funeral!'

The boat went at full speed to make up the delay.

THE MEMBERS OF THE KU-KLUX-KLAN

THE ORIGINS of the name of the infamous Ku-Klux-Klan is unclear. However, for its members the name was irrelevant. They were only interested in its goal.

The secret society was founded in Tennessee in around 1865, and spread quickly to Carolina, Georgia, Alabama, Mississippi, Louisiana, and other states, including Texas. It comprised of the bitterest enemies of the North: the slave overseers, who lost their job after the abolition of slavery. The organisation was widely supported by the landlords of the South, whose huge cotton fields had been cultivated by black slaves. The victory of the North bankrupted them, and finished their lazy, luxurious lifestyle. Unsurprisingly, they could not accept this, and tried to create uncertainty and rebellion by all means. For many years they carried on their vile actions without punishment.

Members of the Ku-Klux-Klan, the Klansmen, had to take an oath that they would obey their leaders, and keep the secrets of the association. They took the latter one very seriously, and they punished its breach with death. They held regular meetings in secret in which they agreed on their next crime. They were ready to carry out the most debased ones. Attacks on houses, robbery, and arson was just as common as lynching and murder. They left their meeting places on horseback, and wore a kind of blanket-like robe around their bodies, and a hood on their head so that they would not be recognised. Their primary targets were the black people, but they also attacked those whites who spoke out against their crimes.

It was enough for the Klansmen if someone was suspected of being a Republican, or a progressive. He was sentenced to death in a secret meeting, and then he was murdered.

The towns, whole counties, were under such a terror that a few years later the Governor of South Carolina had to ask for Federal help from President Grant. The President put the question to the congress which brought in a stern law against the Ku-Klux-Klan, and it was passed. However, the law was, ineffective. They murdered a priest during mass as he was praying for the soul of one of the victims of the Ku-Klux-Klan, when a figure with a hood appeared, and shot the priest in the head. By the time the flock recovered from their fright, the assassin had disappeared.

Judges and other brave people who stood up against them were also murdered.

It was already dark when our boat arrived to La Grange and the Captain announced that he would leave only in the morning, because the low water level made travelling on the river dangerous in the dark. Passengers had to leave the boat, and find accommodation. Winnetou had left the boat before us, and soon disappeared behind the nearby houses.

Old Death approached the duty officer of the port and enquired.

'Could you tell me, Sir, when did the previous boat from Matagorda arrive? And maybe you could also tell me if somebody disembarked here.'

'The last boat arrived the day before yesterday at the same time as today. All passengers disembarked because the boat was anchored here.'

'And were you here when the boat left in the morning?'

'Naturally, I'm here for every arrival and departure.'

Old Death continued, 'We are seeking our two friends who travelled on the previous boat, and we don't know if they stayed here or continued their journey.'

'Hm! It's not easy. There were many passengers, and in the morning mist it's difficult to recognise the faces. But as far as I know they all embarked except for two. One was called Clinton, if I remember his name correctly.

'Clinton! Excellent! He's our friend! Do you know where they found accommodation?'

'I think with Señor Cortesio, because his men carried their luggage.'

'Does he have an inn?'

'No! He's a gentleman of Spanish origin, who has many businesses. General agency as they say. I think he smuggles weapons to Mexico.'

'You said "a gentleman".'

The officer shrugged his shoulder.

'Nowadays everybody is a gentleman even if he carries the saddle of his horse.'

This was a rude remark, but not meant to be insulting, so Old Death did not care; just the opposite, he continued the enquiry in a light tone.

'Tell me, Sir, is there an inn in this wonderful town, where we could have accommodation for the night?'

'There's one inn, more like a bar. But since you asked so many questions, it's very likely that the other passengers were quicker, and took the few available beds.'

'This is quite bad,' nodded Old Death still ignoring the teasing. 'But maybe there is a private house here that would accept us.'

'I don't know. I cannot help you, because our house is to small. But there's a blacksmith, Mr Lange, from Missouri. He has a big house, and he may take you in for the night. I would take you there, but I haven't finished my work yet.'

'Where's the house?'

'You won't find Mr Lange at home now. He's in the bar at this hour, as it's customary around here. Tell him that I sent you. Just go on this road until you see a light on the left hand side. That's the bar.'

We thanked him for the help, gave him a tip, and walked towards the bar. It was easy to find it, not only because of the light, but also because of the noise through the open windows.

The coat of arm was some animal. First I thought it was a huge turtle, then I saw that it had wings and only two legs. Now I could read its name: "Hawk's Inn".

When we entered the bar, there was such a thick tobacco smoke that our eyes ached. The guests must have had good lungs considering that not only could they breathe in such a thick smoke, and apparently enjoyed themselves, but also they had to yell, because nobody talked, everybody was shouting even if they were talking to the man closest to them. When our eyes adjusted to the smoke, we noticed that there was a small lounge next to the main bar, probably for "better customers".

Since the main bar was very crowded, and we considered ourselves to be "better customers", we headed to the lounge.

There were only two free chairs in this room, and we occupied them without hesitation after putting our saddles in the corner.

There was only one long table in the lounge. The men around it were drinking beer, and were talking. When we sat down, they cast a look at us, pulled their chairs closer to each other, and by this they separated themselves from us. From the way they talked I knew that they suddenly changed the subject of their conversation.

'Don't worry, gentlemen,' said Old Death. 'You can talk about anything. We are honest people, and I can see that you are too.'

Two men sat next to us, a younger and an older, and from their faces I thought that they were father and son.

'I don't know you, Sir,' replied the older after some observation, 'but you look very much like someone my son has talked a lot of.'

'What's his name?'

'Old Death.'

'Who's that?' Old Death showed a silly face.

'Have you never heard this name? The most famous path finder in the country. An excellent man. My son, Will, can thank his life to him.'

Old Death looked at Will, and asked, 'How did it happen? Where and when? I have always been interested in such stories.'

'In 1862, in Arkansas, before the battle of Pea Ridge,' answered the father. 'It would be difficult to explain it to someone, who doesn't know the then situation.'

'Why wouldn't I know it? I've been in Arkansas at that time, and if I remember correctly, near the Pea Ridge.'

'Really? Then can I ask whom did you support? Even today, especially here, it is useful to know the political affiliation of the person sitting by the same table.'

'Don't worry, Sir, I assume that you don't support the slave masters, and we agree on this. To me all men are equal, providing that they are honest. And rascals can be found mainly on the other side. So, how was this story?'

'Arkansas didn't want to leave the Union. Most people were against slavery, and hated the boasting landlords, and the soulless slave overseers. But the rabble, and I include the landlords here, won, and they terrorised the rest. As a result, eventually Arkansas left the Union. However, many people slipped over to the North, and fought on their side against the slave masters. At that time we lived in Missouri, in Poplar Bluff. My son joined the army as a volunteer. He was sent over the border with his platoon to scout around. The Southerners captured them.'

'That's serious,' remarked Old Death, 'We all know how cruel the Southerners were with their prisoners of war. Only about a fifth survived. How did your son do it?'

'His life depended on chance both in the battle and in captivity. Don't you think that they surrendered easily. The good lads, after running out of ammunition, fought with knives and the butt of their guns, and inflicted losses on the enemy. But they were inferior in numbers. Their resistance made the Southerners so angry that they decided that they would execute the prisoners. This is when Old Death appeared, and saved them.'

'How? With his own troops?'

'No! Alone! With infinite boldness.'

'Come on! This is interesting. Tell me, how did he do it!' enquired Old Death.

'He crawled in the camp of the Southerners like an Indian. A sudden rain also helped him, because it put out the fires. The battalion camped on a farm. The officers were accommodated in the house, the soldiers settled wherever they could. The prisoners, there were about twenty of them, were locked up in a sugar press. They were told that that was their last night. Four soldiers guarded the house, one in each corner. After the change of the guards, the prisoners heard a strange noise from above, but it was different from the sound of the rain. Suddenly a gap opened on the roof. It became bigger and bigger, and the rain fell freely in the sugar press. Soon a hand let down a ladder made of a young tree, whose branches were cut and they could step on the remaining stumps. The prisoners climbed up to the roof, and from there to the ground. The four guards lay in the grass as if they were sleeping. But this was an eternal sleep. Old Death's knife killed them one by one, without any noise. The prisoners took the weapons of the guards, and with Old Death's lead they slipped out of the camp to the road. This was when they learnt that it was Old Death who had rescued them risking his own life. They managed to cross the border to Missouri, and they all arrived home safely.'

'Did Old Death go with them?' asked Old Death.

'No, because he said, he had important things to do, and disappeared into the dark rainy night. But Will had talked to him before that, and remembers him well. He was a terribly lean and tall man, his sunken face was like a skull. I tell you that he looked like you.'

'It happens,' nodded Old Death. 'I'm glad that you told me this interesting story. However, if you used to live in Missouri, then you surely know the blacksmith, who also came from Missouri. His name is Mr Lange. We would like to talk to him.'

The other opened his eyes wide.

'With him? What do you want from him?'

'I was told by the duty officer at the port that we wouldn't get accommodation in this inn, and he advised me to look for a Mr Lange, and tell him, that he sent us.'

The man examined us thoroughly once more, and then said, 'You're lucky, because I'm Mr Lange. I think, you are

291

an honest man, and hopefully you won't disappoint me. Who's you companion who hasn't yet said a word?'

'He just came over from Europe to make his fortune.'

'Oh! Another one who thinks that gold grows on trees here! Well, I hope you'll succeed, and I welcome you. You can both sleep in my house.'

'Thank you for your trust, Mr Lange,' said Old Death. 'But to reassure you completely, I would like to ask a few questions from your son. Tell me, Will, what did you talk about with that tall man who looks like me?'

Will started to speak animatedly. 'What happened was that Old Death was at the front, and I was right behind him. It was difficult to keep up with him, because my wound ached. Before I was captured, a bullet had grazed my arm. It wasn't deep, but I couldn't bandage it, it bled, and my shirt stuck to the wound. We were crossing a thicket. Old Death bent the branches away, and a back-swinging branch hit my wound. It hurt, and I cried out for which Old Death ...'

'Turned around, and he told you: "Be quiet, you ass!"' interrupted Old Death.

'Yes ... How do you know?' asked Will surprised.

Old Death, ignored Will's question, and continued. 'And you told him that your wound was aching, and might even swell, and hopefully it wouldn't inflame. His advice was to soak your arm in water, then the shirt would not stick in the wound so much, and also that you should bandage it with plantain, because it soothes, and prevents gangrene.'

'Yes, word for word!' exclaimed the young man. 'How do you know?'

'You still don't know, young man? Because I gave you these good advices! You were surprised how similar I looked. Of course, I'm four years older now.'

'Oh! You!' exclaimed Will.

He jumped up from his seat, and opened his arms to embrace Old Death, but his father pushed him aside, and back to his seat. 'Wait a bit! If it's about embracing, I'm the first, because it's my right and responsibility to embrace my son's rescuer. But we'll postpone it, because I don't want to attract too much attention. So, stay on your seat. Excuse me, Sir,' he now turned to Old Death. 'I have all the reasons for this. You don't know the situation here. As if all the devils of hell had been released. Don't think that I'm afraid, I'm fearful for you. And so I don't want people to know that you are here. Everybody knows how heroically you fought against the slave masters, how you led the Northern troops through forests and swamps to the rear of the Southern Army, and how much damage you caused them. The slave masters hate you so much that they would be happy to hang you on the first tree without hesitation.'

'I know Mr Lange, but I don't care,' replied Old Death calmly. 'I don't long for the noose; I have been threatened with it many times; yet I'm still alive. A gang wanted to hang me on the chimney of the boat today.'

Then he related our lucky escape. Lange listened to it, but he shook his head, and remarked, 'The Captain acted honourably, but he risked his life. He will have to stay here in La Grange till the morning, but these tramps could arrive already during the night, and their first thought will be revenge. You can't ignore that.'

'I have dealt in my life with more dangerous men,' said Old Death as he waved contemptuously.

'Don't be so self-confident, Sir! La Grange has become a real hotspot. From the whole county the rascals come here; strangers whom we have never seen before. The situation is becoming worse and worse. I can tell you that I won't stay here for very long, because I don't want to live in constant excitement and fear. I'm a widower, my daughter lives in Mexico with her husband. I don't have anybody else but my son. A few days ago I sold my house to a gentleman who paid in cash. I have to arrange a few more things, and then we'll move to Mexico.'

'Did I hear you right?' asked Old Death in surprise. 'You want to go to Mexico? But it's just as dangerous in Mexico; there's war there!'

'Mexico is big and where I want to go, there is peace. It's true that Juárez had to flee to El Paso, to the border with New Mexico, but he gathered an army, and now they are pushing the French back to the South. The days of the conquerors are counted. The Mexican patriots will sweep the French out. It will be poor Maximilian, who was made Emperor against his will, who will pay for this. I heard that he's a good man, and he was forced into this ugly adventure. But that's his problem, he should have stayed home. The war is now around the capital. In the North it's quite calm. I'm going to Chihuahua, where my daughter and son-in-law live. My son-in-law is well off, he used to be the principal manager of a man called Davis, but now he owns his own silver mine. He wrote to me in his last letter that the silver prince was born, and he shouts rather loudly for his grandfather. Why should I stay here? A grandfather should be near his grandson, shouldn't he?'

'Yes, ideally,' nodded Old Death.

'If you are going that way, you could come with us, Sir,' continued Mr Lange. 'I would consider it very fortunate if I could make this long journey in Old Death's company.'

'Well, I may hold you to that,' said Old Death.

'Let's shake hands then!' exclaimed the father, who was also a grandfather.

'Just slow down a bit!' laughed Old Death. 'It's not sure yet. I'm going to Mexico too, but we have a little affair here. We don't know what way we have to go.'

'If you are really going to Mexico, Sir, I'll wait or I'll go with you. A little diversion doesn't matter really. It's not important to me if I arrive to Chihuahua next week or in a fortnight. And also, you are an experienced Westerner, and a famous path finder. If I travel with you, I surely can cross the border, which is quite a challenge currently. Can I ask you what your affair is?'

'I have to find a Señor Cortesio. Do you know him?'

'Of course! It's a small town, everybody knows everyone well. And Señor Cortesio is the one who bought my house.'

'First of all, I would like to know if he's a reliable man or a rascal.'

'Not a rascal at all. It's none of my business how he earns his money, but he pays for everything, and he doesn't cheat. He probably has contacts in Mexico. I've seen in the nights that mules, with heavy burdens, leave his yard, and also that many people visit his house in secret, and then leave for the Rio Grande. It's said that he works for Juárez, and sends weapons and men who want to fight the French. For such an enterprise one has to be brave. Señor Cortesio probably follows his political conviction, but it's also a good business.'

'Where does he live? I'd like to talk to him tonight if it's possible.'

'Nothing is easier, I arranged a meeting with him in his house tonight at 10 pm, but it has become unnecessary. I'll lead you to his house.'

'When did you agree on this meeting?'

'Yesterday, in his house.'

'Did he have a guest or a business partner there then?' enquired Old Death.

'Yes, two men, an older and a younger.'

'Did you hear their names accidentally?'

'I did because I was there for a whole hour. The younger's name was Ohlert, the other was Gavilano. Cortesio and Gavilano mentioned the times that they had spent together in the capital of Mexico.'

'Gavilano? I haven't heard this name. However, he must be Gibson. What do you think, young man?'

'Could be,' I replied, 'he has had so many pseudo-names that one cannot keep a list of them.'

I took out the photos, and showed them to Mr Lange, who immediately recognised them.

'Yes, they were the ones, Sir,' he said. 'This lean Creole is Gavilano, and the other is Ohlert who spoke so strangely that I could not make head nor tail of it. He kept on talking about people whom I've never heard of in my life. He spoke of a Moor called Othello, a young woman called Joan, who was a shepherd girl in Orleans, then became a soldier, and helped the French king to defeat the English, and a queen called Mary Stuart, who was apparently beheaded. I think Ohlert didn't have his full faculty.'

Old Death and I looked at each other. We were sure that Gibson was there with his unfortunate victim.

'Do you know, Mr Lange, if they are still in La Grange?' I asked excitedly.

'No, I know that they left the town already yesterday morning. Señor Cortesio led them to Hopkins's farm, and from there they continued their journey to the Rio Grande.'

'Annoying!' exclaimed Old Death. 'We'll hurry after them tonight if it's feasible. Tell me, Mr Lange, from whom could we buy two good horses?'

'Only from Señor Cortesio. He always has many horses in his stables for those whom he recruits for Juárez's army. But I'd like to dissuade you from the night riding, because you don't know the terrain well enough.'

'We'll see. I have to talk to Cortesio first of all. It's almost ten o'clock, he is probably at home now. Please, show us where he lives.'

'Right, we can go if you want.'

We started to gather our belongings, when the noise of horse hooves came from the street, and a few minutes later new guests entered the bar.

It was not a pleasant surprise, when I recognised that they were members of the gang whom the Captain had put on the bank with his trick. It seemed that many in the bar knew them, because they were greeted loudly. From the questions and answers I understood that they had been expected earlier.

For the time being they were busy with greeting each other, and they did not have time for anything else. This was good as I did not want to attract their attention. We sat back to see how the situation would develop. If we crossed the bar, they could block our way, and find a way to quarrel with us. When Lange learnt of the gang, he opened the door just enough so that we could hear their conversation, but they could not see us. We also swapped places with his friends, thus we had our back to the door.

'It'll be better like this,' said Lange, 'because after a few glasses of brandy it's impossible to control them. Not to mention that they think you are spies, and they wanted to hang you.'

'Very nice,' said Old Death, 'but I don't feel like sitting here until they leave. I don't have time, because I want to talk to Cortesio.'

'This is true,' Lange scratched his head, 'but we have to leave without being noticed.'

'I cannot see another door here,' said Old Death, 'only through the main room.'

'And this?' asked Lange, and pointed at the window.

'Ridiculous!' exclaimed Old Death. 'I won't flee through the window like some thief! That would make me laughable! They would think that I'm afraid of them.'

'It's not cowardice if one does what common sense dictates,' replied Lange. 'Apart from their large numeric superiority, they are also extremely angry because of the events on the boat, and they would surely attack us. I'm saying it not because I'm afraid. I'm a blacksmith, and my fist is like a hammer. But they have firearms, and bullets that can defeat even the bravest. Listen to me, Sir, and let's go through the window. Think of their faces if they come in, and cannot find us.'

I agreed, and I was happy when Old Death gave in too.

'Let's do it,' he said, 'let's climb out of the window. Can you hear how they are shouting? I think they are telling the others what happened on the boat.'

We could not resist eavesdropping. First, they cursed the Captain, and kept on swearing that they would settle the account with him in the morning.

'And how did you get here so quickly?' somebody asked.

'We found a farm where we borrowed two horses.'

'He had to be a generous farmer,' somebody laughed.

297

'We didn't ask him,' replied the other. 'Then we visited another farm, and in an hour we were all on horseback.'

'You're good lads! Let's have a drink for this!'

'But apart from the Captain, we must settle the account with the two Northern spies. They must be here, because the boat is still here. They don't have horses, only saddles. Just imagine, two men, an old and a young, both carrying their saddles on their back!'

'Saddles?' many exclaimed. 'Two men came in with their saddles on their arms. They went to the saloon and ...'

'Gentlemen,' said Lange, 'this is the last moment. Quick to the window! We will throw the saddles after you.'

Without hesitation I opened the window, and jumped out. Old Death followed me. Lange gave us our guns and saddles, and then he and his son followed us.

We were not on the street, but at the back wall of the house, in a small yard. We just had to jump over the fence to be outside. When we looked back, the others from the saloon were also climbing out of the window. They did not want to face the thugs either, and followed our example.

'They cannot catch us now,' sighed Will relieved.

'I'm embarrassed that I fled,' murmured Old Death. 'I can almost hear their mocking laughter.'

'We will see who laughs the last,' said the elder Lange.

'Give us the saddles, let's share the burden!'

We started off. Soon we turned into a small street, where two houses stood opposite each other. The larger one was completely dark, from the smaller one some light spread into the darkness of the street through the blinds.

'Señor Cortesio is at home,' said Lange. 'I'm not going in, I don't want to interfere with your affairs. Just knock. The servant is still up, and he will let you in. Our house, or rather it's now Señor Cortesio's, is on the left. We still live there. When you have finished with him, come over. We'll have made dinner by then.'

We departed. For our knock the door opened slightly, and a voice asked, 'Who is it?'

'Two friends,' answered Old Death. 'We want to speak to Señor Cortesio.'

'What do you want from him?'

'It's a business affair. Mr Lange sent us.'

'If it's Mr Lange, then I inform the Señor. Wait a bit.'

Soon he returned, and let us in. He was a tall, strong, young black man.

'Please enter, Señor Cortesio expects you.'

From the hall, through a door, we entered a small room that was furnished as an office. In the middle of the room there was a desk with a few chairs. From the desk a tall, slim man turned to us. His lively, black eyes, brownish skin, and long nose immediately showed that he was a Mexican Spaniard.

He greeted us politely, and asked, 'I was informed that Mr Lange sent you. How can I help you, Señores? Is it business?'

'You can call it that. We'll see if it's business, or simply asking for information,' replied Old Death. Before knocking on the door of Cortesio's house he had asked me to leave the negotiations to him.

'Please,' said the host, and pushed a cigar box to us. The Mexicans conduct negotiations while smoking a cigar. As I liked cigars, I took one, squeezed it, and lit it. Old Death was not impressed as he preferred tobacco in a stronger form.

'Señor Cortesio,' started Old Death, 'our intention is to ride to Mexico, and join Juárez. Careful people don't do such a thing without studying the situation. We have to know if we would be welcomed by them. Our friend suggested that we should talk to you.'

The Mexican did not give an answer immediately, but first examined us carefully. I saw that he was contented with me as he needed young and strong men. However, Old Death's appearance got him thinking. The old man's lean face and body, his bent carriage did not encourage him.

'I'm an old soldier,' remarked Old Death as if he was replying to an unspoken question, 'I fought with General

Thomas and General Grant against Jefferson. I can state without immodesty that I did an important service to the North on a rough terrain.'

'This is all very nice, Señor,' said the Spaniard, 'But if you forgive my honesty, I'm afraid that the difficult Mexican terrain would be too much for you now.'

'Hm! Nobody has said this to Old Death!' replied my old friend smiling.

The name had a magic effect. Señor Cortesio, who was sitting by the table, jumped up, and exclaimed, 'Old Death? Are you Old Death? The most famous hunter and scout! I'm honoured that I can shake hands with you. Of course, I can see that the description that I have heard matches exactly! Legends are said about you.'

'People like exaggeration,' replied Old Death modestly. 'The truth is that since I've been conscious … yes, since I've been conscious, I've always followed my values, and I'm not afraid of my own shadow.'

'And not even of the numerical superiority of the enemy, I know. I don't have to tell you that my activities are secret. My work requires caution. But I can talk to you honestly. I'm happy for your request, and you deserve an officer rank over there. I'll arrange that. As to your friend …'

'As for my companion,' interrupted Old Death, 'even if he was first only a private, he'll have a higher rank soon. His name is Miller. He served under Sheridan, and gained the rank of a lieutenant in the famous flank march on the Missionary Ridge. You surely know what a daring raid it was! Miller was the special favourite of Sheridan. He was a widely celebrated cavalry officer at the Battle of Five Forks. He'll be a good acquisition for you,'

I was embarrassed because of his praise and his fluent lies that I had not expected, but before I could say a word, Señor Cortesio tapped me on my shoulder, and said, 'Right, you'll be an officer too. I've heard of your devil daring exploits! I will also give you a small advance payment immediately.'

'Unnecessary, Señor,' I said quickly, because I did not want to take the hustling so far as to take money from him.

'Why, Señores?' asked the host. 'The wise saying that war needs money is not my invention, but it's true.'

'We have everything,' I insisted, 'we only need two good horses. We have the saddles.'

'Good! Then you will get two very good horses from me. You can choose them in the morning. Have you found accommodation?'

'Yes, we will be Mr Lange's guests.'

'I'm glad because I'm short of space, so ...'

'We understand it,' I said.

'There are some formalities, filling in forms and so forth. Should we do it tomorrow or right now?'

'If possible, now,' stated Old Death. 'What is it about?'

'Nothing really. Since you travel on your own funds, you can take the oath when you arrive to the troops. I give you only identification papers, and a letter of recommendation that ensures your officer status. You're right, Señor, the best is to do it now. We live in times when one doesn't know what the next hour would bring. So, I'll need a quarter of an hour. The cigars are on the table, and I'll bring some wine for you. You haven't tasted such a wine! Unfortunately, I have only one bottle left. But for you, gentlemen ...'

He brought the wine in with the glasses, and put it on the table, then he went to the desk. Old Death made funny faces indicating to me that everything had worked well, and he felt fine. He filled the glasses, and drank his wine in one gulp. I drank mine much slower, and let him have three quarters of the bottle.

By the time the bottle of wine was finished, which was less than a quarter of an hour, Señor Cortesio was ready too. Before closing the letters of recommendation, he read them out, and we were very contented with both the content and the style. Then he took two forms printed on thick paper, and entered our names and other information. These were Mexican passports. To my surprise, Juárez's signature was on them. But I was even more surprised when Cortesio took out two more passports, and filled them in.

'These are French passports,' he said smiling. 'Don't ask me how I got the signature of the little Napoleon's general. I rarely give these passports to the men. But Old Death and his friend deserve an exceptional service.'

Old Death had not yet mentioned the real reason of our visit, which made me a little anxious, but I kept my promise, and I did not intervene. At this point he felt that the time was right for him to enquire, 'When did the last group leave?'

'The last one? Yesterday. More than thirty volunteers, I took them to Hopkins's farm. There were two gentlemen among them, who also received an exceptional treatment. They travelled to Mexico on private business.'

'Do you help private people over the border?' asked Old Death surprised.

'No, of course not, smuggling people over the border would create inconvenience,' protested Señor Cortesio. 'I don't do such things! But one of the two gentlemen is my acquaintance from Mexico, and I couldn't refuse his request. Probably you'll meet them as you will get such good horses that you will catch the transport before the Rio Grande.'

'Where will they cross the river?' asked Old Death in an indifferent tone.

'They are heading to the Eagle Pass, but as it's a busy area, they cannot show up there. Thus they cross the caravan path from San Antonio between the Nueces River and the Rio Grande. They will pass by Fort Inge, and cross the Rio Grande by a ford. Only our guides know this ford. Then they go through Baya, Cruses, San Vicente, and San Carlos to Chihuahua.'

My ears were aching from the town names. In contrast, Old Death was nodding as if he was greeting his old friends, and he repeated the names to remember the route well.

'If our horses will be as excellent as you said, we will catch up with them,' he said affirmatively 'especially if their horses are only mediocre. The only question is will they let us join them.'

'They will,' Señor Cortesio assured him, but Old Death was still anxious.

'And what will the two gentlemen, who are travelling on private business, say?'

'They'll have nothing to say,' said Cortesio forcefully. 'They should be happy that they could make the dangerous journey under the protection of my group. They won't think of protesting. Pass my greetings to them. As I said, one of them, Gavilano, is my old acquaintance. He was born in Mexico, likes drinks, and we had some pleasant evenings in the capital. He introduced me to his sister. She's an excellent singer, and an adorable dancer. They called her Felisa Perillo. I have to say she was very beautiful, and she has attracted many men!'

'Is Gavilano also handsome?'

'I cannot say that at all! You see, the girl is his half-sister. We spent some time together, then one day she suddenly disappeared. Gavilano said that she lived near Chihuahua, and now he wants to visit her.'

'And what does he do?' enquired Old Death.

'He's a poet!'

Because of Old Death's bewildered and contemptuous look Cortesio hurried to add, 'He doesn't need to earn money from his poems as he has property, and he's well off. But due to some cabal that was organised against him, he had to leave the city and the country. Now he's taking this Yankee, who wants to know Mexico, and also wants to be introduced to poetry. They want to open a theatre in the capital.'

'I wish them all the luck. But tell me, Señor Cortesio, how did Gavilano know that you live in La Grange? Did you correspond?'

'Not at all. It was accidental. I was at the port when the boat arrived. We recognised each other, and, of course, I invited him to my house. I learnt that they wanted to go to

Austin by the boat, and cross the border from there. But we live in dangerous times, so I offered them that they could join my transport. I don't have to say that they accepted my offer very willingly and gratefully. It's really not safe nowadays to travel alone or in pairs. The robbery is common, they burn down houses, murder innocent men in their own homes. The sheriff is helpless. The felons disappear after their crimes.'

'Probably the Ku-Klux-Klan.'

'No doubt. They found two bodies in Hallettsville the day before yesterday. There was a note on one of the bodies: "Yankee dogs!" Yesterday in Shelby they whipped a whole family half-dead because one of the sons served in General Grant's army. This morning they found a black hood near Lyons. Two white lizard-looking shapes were sewn on it.'

'The hood of the Klansmen!' exclaimed Old Death.

'Yes, they cover their faces with black hoods decorated with white shapes, and they often wear a white robe. Every shape is a symbol so that they can recognise each other, because they don't tell their names even to each other. Fortunately, I haven't met them.'

'One day in Hallettsville, then Lyons. They are getting closer to La Grange. They could be watching your house, Señor Cortesio,' said Old Death.

'You're right,' replied the Spaniard. 'I'll put the bolt on all doors and windows, and I will make sure that my gun is near my hand.'

'Good. This is the only language they understand. They don't deserve mercy, because they don't give mercy to anyone. Have we finished for today?' asked Old Death.

'Yes, señores. I'm glad that I met you.'

We shook hands, and left. In the street I nudged my old friend. 'You did it very well! But why did you have to hustle?'

'Because I wanted him to want us.'

'You would have accepted his money if I hadn't refused it.'

'Yes, why not?'

'Because we don't want to join Juárez's army.'

'Who knows what the future brings? But I'm glad that we didn't accept the advance. We are freer, and also we got the passports. It was a fruitful visit. We now know Gibson's path. Where's the blacksmith's house? Oh, this is it. Let's knock.'

However, we did not have to knock, because Lange waited for us behind the door. He immediately led us to the room that had three windows, all covered with thick rugs.

'Don't be surprised by the precautions, gentlemen,' said Lange, 'and I would like it if we talked quietly. It wouldn't be good if the Klansmen knew that you were here.'

'Have you seen the rascals?'

'Only their scouts. While you were with Señor Cortesio, I heard suspicious noises from the side of the house that looks to the inn. I opened the door very slightly, and peeped out. I saw three men, all with hoods.'

'Then they were Klansmen indeed,' nodded Old Death.

'No doubt. Two stopped by the door, and the third looked in at the window. Soon he returned, and reported that he saw a young man, probably the blacksmith's son, and also that the blacksmith was probably in the kitchen making the dinner because the table was laid. They agreed that they would wait until we would eat, go to bed, and then they would attack. Then they disappeared. I'm afraid our night won't be very peaceful.'

'Fortunately we are here,' said Old Death. 'And where's your son?'

'He has slipped out of the house to get help. We have some reliable friends. You saw two of them in the inn.'

'I hope they come without the hooded lot noticing them.'

'You can be sure, Sir, that they know this. But let's have dinner. It's simple, but I give it with good heart.'

The dinner consisted of excellent ham, good bread, and beer. While we were eating, a quiet bark came from near.

'This is our signal,' said Lange. 'This means that our friends have arrived.'

He went out to open the door, and soon returned with his son and five men. They were all well-armed. I could see that

305

they were men whom we needed. They did not say much, but they were ready to act. There was an old man among them, who kept on glancing at Old Death.

'Excuse me, Sir,' he said finally. 'I think we have met.'

'Quite possible,' said the path finder. 'I have my age, and I have been to many places in my life.'

'Don't you remember me?' asked the old man.

Old Death carefully looked at the man, and replied, 'You are familiar, but I don't know from where.'

'But I remember,' said the old man. 'We met in California, in Frisco's Chinatown. It was about twenty years ago. It was an opium den, where they also gambled. I lost all my money, almost a thousand dollars. I had only one note left, but I didn't want to risk it, because I wanted to buy opium with it, and then shoot myself. Then you sat down next to me and ...'

'Yes, I remember now!' interrupted Old Death. 'The rest is unimportant.'

'It is important, Sir, let me finish it. You saved my life. You said that you will play for me on a joint account, and you won back almost all my money. Then you pulled me aside to a corner, and talked to me until I promised that I wouldn't touch cards and opium. I gave my word of honour, and I haven't regretted it. Today I'm a well off man, and I can thank everything to you. Let me repay you!'

'You surely don't want to offer me money?' growled Old Death. 'Forget it, and stop this profuse gratitude! Two devils held you in their clutches, the opium and the card. If you managed to escape, it wasn't because of me, but because of your will power. You are a man who could overcome your addictions. If I ... but it's enough, let's not talk about it anymore.'

His bitter voice caught my attention. I remembered what he mentioned to me in New Orleans that his mother had put him on the right path to happiness, but he left it. Could he have been a prisoner of these two cursed addictions? He probably broke with the cards, but as to the opium ... his lean figure could be explained with this. Even if he had broken with this horrible poison, it must have been a terrible struggle, and it could still be visible on him. I looked at him now differently. I had always felt respect towards him, but now also a good deal of pity. Who knows what an athletic body he had once, and his intellect also lifted him above the average. He was destined for great things, and he became an aged adventurer. His nickname to which he gained honour, made me shiver. Old Death, a man who was a friend of death in many senses. His last words, "let's not talk about it anymore", were saddening. Our host's remark woke me up from my musing.

'You are right, Sir. Let's focus on the third devil, the Ku-Klux-Klan, because this is the danger of the moment. They will surely attack tonight. Let's be prepared for them. What should we do? Has anyone got a good idea?'

Nobody spoke up, because everybody looked at Old Death, the experienced fighter, and all were waiting for his plan and advice.

Old Death understood it, grimaced as usual, and said, 'If everybody is silent, then it won't be immodest if I spoke. First, I'd like to know if the back door has a bolt or a lock.'

'Only a lock,' replied Lange.'

'Good, that's a start. But they probably know it too, so they'll try a skeleton key. The question then is, how should we receive them?'

'With a gun, of course,' answered Lange, 'we'll shoot whoever comes to the door.'

'That's no good,' said Old Death shaking his head. 'I'd rather let them in. Imagine the joy of capturing the whole gang.' The blacksmith looked at him astonished.

'Don't you like my plan, Sir?' asked Old Death.

'You can't carry it out, Sir. They aren't stupid to simply walk in the trap.'

'But I'd like to try it,' Old Death was stubborn. 'Firstly, because I want to avoid the spilling of blood if possible. Secondly, if we can capture them, we would stop their affray in La Grange. What would you achieve if you shot three or four rascals? You'd only have the revenge of the Ku-Klux-Klan. We have to sort them out for once and for all.'

'This is a dangerous plan.'

'The situation is dangerous. But this is the only one that my friend and I would support, and participate in. We have to be brave. The important thing is that we act effectively. I'll go out for scouting.'

'The rascals surely left a guard somewhere near the house. What will happen if he notices you?' asked Lange anxiously.

'I'll make sure that he doesn't. Have you got a chalk? Draw the plan of the house on the table so that I could fully understand it. Then let me out through the back door, and wait for my return. I won't knock, only scratch on the door with my nails. This will be my signal. If there's a knock, don't open the door.

Lange took a chalk, and quickly drew up the plan of the house on the table. Old Death studied it thoroughly, then nodded grinning. He started off to the back door, but then turned back, and looked at me musingly.

'I'd like to take you with me,' he said. 'Have you tried to sneak up to someone, like the Indians?'

I remembered my conversation with Winnetou, when we had agreed that I would keep my incognito.

'I haven't,' I replied.

'Then you'll have the opportunity to learn it tonight. Follow me!'

'Isn't it too risky?' asked Lange. 'If he's inexperienced, he can end up in trouble, and if he does, so do we.'

'He'll be careful,' replied Old Death. 'Of course, if the task was to sneak up on an Indian, I wouldn't take him. But these rascals aren't Indians. Only their mouth is big. They cannot compete even with a simple hunter. There are no hunters among them. A real Westerner wouldn't mix with such a riff-raff. Let's go, young man! But leave your sombrero here. Follow me all the time, and do what I do.'

Lange opened the back door, let us out, and then locked it again. Outside Old Death stooped down, and I followed his example. His eyes were searching in the darkness. He even sniffed in the air.

'I think there isn't anyone here,' he whispered to me. 'But I'll check it just in case. Tell me, have you tried to imitate the crickets when you were a child? You know, you put a blade of grass between your thumbs and ...'

'I know,' I replied.

'Stay here. Tear a blade of grass, and wait for me motionless. If something happens, imitate the cricket, and I'll come back.'

He went on all four, and disappeared in the darkness of the night. He returned ten minutes later, as he suddenly appeared next to me. 'Nobody is on this side,' he whispered. 'But there could be someone on the other side. Let's crawl there, but carefully! Don't go on your belly like a snake, but on your fingers and toes like a lizard. Also make sure you feel the ground before you move forward so you wouldn't crack a twig. Let's go!'

Old Death moved like a lizard in front of me, and I followed him. After a short while he turned his head. 'They are here,' he whispered, 'two of them. Let's get closer.'

We continued our crawling. I spotted a little tent by the fence. Later I recognise that it was not a tent, but poles and beams piled up in a pyramid shape. Two men sat by it.

Old Death slipped back to me, and whispered in my ear, 'We have to get behind them to eavesdrop. I go from the right, and you go from the left. When you are there, put your face on the ground so your eyes wouldn't show in the dark. Understood?'

'Fine,' I replied.

'If they spot us, we have to kill them, but in silence.'

'With a knife?' I whispered.

'No,' he replied. 'I don't think you have the skills. But I can see that you are strong. So, I'll catch one by his throat, and you the other. Forward!'

309

I got behind the pile. I was only a yard from the two men. There I lay down, and put my two hands by my ears to hear their whispering better, and also to cover my face.

'I'm really angry with the captain of the ship,' said the one who was closest to me. 'He deserves to be hanged, but we won't hang him. You know, Locksmith, if we want to get Texas on our side, we mustn't challenge the shipmen.'

'You know this better than I do, boss,' said the other. 'Unfortunately, it seems that the Injun has escaped. But I want the two spies. They are still here; we can catch them.'

'This is why I left Snail in the inn. He may learn where they are hiding. Then there is the blacksmith and his son. The son was an officer in the North's army, and his father knew this. They both deserve the noose, but we will hang only the younger. Then give a good beating to the father: no flesh will remain on his back. Then we will throw him in the john. Are you sure that you can open the door?'

'This is why I'm a locksmith. There's no lock that I can't open with this bent piece of iron.'

'Good. We just have to wait until they go to sleep. I know our men are impatient behind the stable. They don't like waiting for so long under the elderberry bushes.'

'We should check what's going on in the house. They might have gone to bed.'

'You are right, Locksmith, I'll go, and check it.'

The boss stood up, and tiptoed to the house. The other took out a master key from his pocket, and examined it. Somebody carefully tugged my leg. I slipped back, and lay next to Old Death. We both heard the conversation.

'We will finish them now,' whispered Old Death. 'When you hear my voice, jump on the boss. He should survive but shouldn't cry for help. Grab his throat with both hands, pull him down, and kneel on him. Hold him until I come.'

He disappeared, and I crawled back to my place. The boss returned, and sat down next to Locksmith.

'We have to wait,' he said with an annoyed ring in his voice. 'The blacksmith is still awake.'

'Damn it!' swore Locksmith. 'But it's just a question of time. When we have finished with them, let's find that tall skeleton. I want him! If I knew where he was!'

'Here!' I heard Old Death's voice. Without hesitation I jumped up, and caught the boss's throat from behind. He did not have time to cry out. In less than half a minute he was on the ground, and I was on him. In another half a minute Old Death appeared, and with the butt of his revolver he hit the temple of the boss.

'You did this quite well, my good friend,' said the old man complimenting me, 'You may even become a Westerner one day. Now pick him up, and let's go back to the house.'

We hurried to the back door, Old Death scratched the wood with his nails, and the door opened.

'What's this?' asked Lange, who could only see that we were carrying something.

'We'll see,' replied Old Death. 'Lock the door.'

The company in the room was really surprised when we put down the two Klansmen on the floor.

'Wow!' exclaimed the blacksmith. 'Two Klansmen! Are they dead?'

'I hope not,' answered Old Death. 'You see I was right when I took this young man with me. He captured the boss of the gang.'

'Is this the boss? Excellent! And where is the gang? And why did you bring them here?'

'Can't you figure it out? We will undress them, and I and my friend will put on their outfit. Then we'll lure the gang here from behind the stable.'

'And if they recognise the trap?'

'Just trust us!'

Old Death quickly told them what we had heard, and explained his plan. I would play the role of Locksmith, and he would be the boss.

'They'll consider it natural that we will be whispering,' he added, 'and whispering voices cannot be identified.'

'And what's our task?' asked Lange.

'For the time being: slip out to the garden, and bring in some strong sticks or rods. We will need them. Then put out all the lights, and hide in the house.'

While Lange and his son went out to the garden, we undressed the two captured men. One had the figure of a sword made of white linen sewn on his hood, the other's symbol was a key. While we were pulling off the robe of the boss, he somewhat recovered, and immediately moved his right hand to his pocket for his revolver. However, we had already removed all of his weapons. Old Death quickly pushed the boss's head on the floor, and pointed his knife at the Klansman's chest.

'Just calm down, boy! One sound or motion, and the steel will enter your heart!'

The boss was a man of about thirty years of age, and his dark-brown skin and haughty countenance suggested that he was probably one of the defeated landlords of the South. He involuntarily felt his aching temple, and asked in a whining voice, 'Where am I? What do you want from me?'

'You'll learn it in a moment,' replied Old Death, 'only we'll tie you up first.'

'Tie me up? Me? Never!' protested the boss, and tried to get up again.

'Do you want to die?' hissed the old man. 'Do you know who I am? Old Death! You surely have heard this name. You can imagine how much I love the slave masters, and the Ku-Klux-Klan!'

'Old Death?' stuttered the boss in his fright. 'Then I'm surely lost!'

'Not yet. We aren't murderers like you. If you surrender, and help us in making your gang surrender too, we'll pardon you. But if there's a fight, the river will carry as many dead bodies as many as you are. I hope you recognise this, and do what I tell you. And we also want you to leave Texas, and not to re-enter. Your affray is finished here. I'll bring your men in soon. Make sure you do everything so that they surrender if you value your life.'

312

Then we tied and gagged him with a handkerchief. In the meantime his accomplice also regained consciousness, and he had to endure the same treatment. Finally we carried the two thugs to the sleeping chamber. We lay them on the bed, tied them to it, and covered them with a blanket.

'Like this,' laughed Old Death. 'The comedy is about to begin. It would be a joy to see the faces of the bandits when they see their boss. I'd like to watch them.'

'It's easy,' replied Lange, who had returned with his son, and brought sticks. 'The ceiling of the chamber is a layer of boards. We can take up one of them.'

'Excellent,' nodded Old Death. 'But first we will change our outfit.'

I put on Locksmith's robe. I found a number of skeleton keys in one of the pockets.

'I'm afraid you can't handle these tools,' Old Death turned to me. 'Bring the real key, just in case. Leave your gun behind, the knife and the revolver will be enough. When the birds are lured into the cage, we'll fix the doors and the windows with these sticks.'

We slipped out of the back door, and I closed it behind me. Old Death remained by the house, while I started off towards the stable. I did not have to care with quietness as my aim was that they would hear my arrival. Behind the stable I almost stumbled on a stooping figure.

'Stop!' he said. 'Is that you, Locksmith?' I was glad that he recognised me so instantly.

'Of course!' I whispered. 'Don't shout!'

'At last! What's the news?'

'You can come, but quietly.'

'I'll inform the lieutenant. Just wait a bit.'

"Great!" I thought, "they have a lieutenant. A military organisation!" I did not have to wait more than a minute.

'Have they gone to bed?' asked the man whispering. 'They made us wait, didn't they?'

'They had drunk a whole bottle of brandy before they went to bed,' I said barely audibly.

313

'Even better,' he said. 'It makes our job easier. It's past midnight now. Soon the other group will start their job at Cortesio's house.'

A group of men in black hoods appeared behind him. I waved to them to follow me. Arriving to the house, Old Death stepped forward in the outfit of the boss.

'Come on, Locksmith, unlock the door!' he ordered.

I went to the door with the real key in my hand, but for a few moments I pretended that I was struggling with the lock. Finally I opened the door, and stepped aside. Old Death did the same on the other side. We let the men go ahead. The last one was the lieutenant.

'Should we light the lamps?' he asked.

'Only yours for the time being,' ordered Old Death.

We followed the gang. I closed the door but did not lock it. The lieutenant took out a small lamp from his pocket, and lit it. I could see that his symbol was a knife. We counted fifteen bandits. Each had a different symbol: cross, crescent moon, star, snake, toad, cogwheel, scissors, bird, and some other animals.

'Shouldn't we put up a guard by the door, just in case?' asked the lieutenant.

'What for?' replied Old Death, 'it's enough if we lock it.' I turned the key, but left it in the lock.

'Let's go!' said Old Death, and he took the lamp from the lieutenant. He pointed at the door of the bed chamber. 'There! Quickly, but noiselessly! We can lit the lamps once we are inside.'

This is how he wanted to make sure that they would not recognise the two "sleeping" men too early. There was barely enough room for so many people in the chamber, but Old Death pushed them in. Once it had been done, he quickly slammed the door behind them, and I locked it.

'Bring the sticks!'

With the sticks we secured the door, and now not even the strength of an elephant could have pushed it open. It was all done very quickly.

I rushed up to the attic for our men. 'Come down!' I whispered. 'They are in the trap.'

The men hurried down.

'Three men to the window!' shouted Old Death. 'Fix the blinds with the sticks! If somebody gets through, shoot him in the head!'

A roar resounded from the bed chamber. The bandits recognised that they were duped. They had lit the lamps, and after removing the blanket, they could see who were lying on the bed. They were raging, they swore, yelled, and banged on the door with their fists.

'You will pay for this,' bellowed the lieutenant. 'Open it, or we'll smash up the whole house!'

'Break the door!' shouted somebody else.

But the door was too strong for them. We could hear that they were trying the window.

'Off from the window!' cried somebody outside loudly. 'If anyone opens it, he will be shot dead!'

Old Death banged on the door with his fist. 'Shut up!' he shouted. 'The boss will tell you what you have to do!'

He leant to me, and whispered, 'Let's go up to the attic. Hold the lamp, and bring our guns!'

In the attic we found the place where the board was loosened. We threw off our hoods, lifted the board, and looked down to the chamber.

The Klansmen stood next to each other around the two prisoners, whom they had already released from the bondage and the gags. The boss was explaining something to them keenly, and we could see that their accomplices did not like what they had heard.

'Surrendering to a few people?' asked the lieutenant. 'How many men do they have?'

'Enough to shoot all of you!' cried Old Death from the attic, and pushed the barrel of his gun in the opening.

All the eyes turned to the ceiling. At the same moment gunfire resounded from outside. Old Death immediately understood what it meant, and how he could utilise it.

'Can you hear it?' he continued. 'Your accomplices are warmly welcomed by Cortesio. The whole of La Grange is against you, and they wish you went to hell! We don't need the Ku-Klux-Klan! You are finished. We have more men than you. In the other room there are twelve men, by the window six, and here in the attic another six. You might have heard of me, I'm Old Death! I give you ten minutes. If you put down your weapons, we'll pardon you. If not, then you will die! These are my last word. Think!'

He pushed back the board, and whispered to me.

'Let's hurry downstairs, and help the Spaniard!'

We took two men from the house, and also two from the window, where now one guard was enough. Thus our relief team consisted of six men.

We saw a few hooded men at the front of the house. Four or five similarly dressed figures rushed from behind the house, and cried in a frightened voice, 'They are shooting there as well! We couldn't get in!'

We threw ourselves on the ground, and crawled forward. We heard more shots. One of the men by the fence swore loudly, 'Damned Spaniard! He was alert. He'll wake up the whole town. Let's break the door in before half the town comes here!'

'Gentlemen,' I whispered to the others, 'We haven't got time to lose! Let's use the butts of our rifles!'

'Now!' they responded, and we attacked.

The gang was dispersed, except for four bandits who remained on the ground wounded. We disarmed them while Old Death went to the door, and knocked.

'Who is it?' came a voice from behind the door.

'Old Death, my dear Sir. It's safe now. You can let us in.'

The door opened a little. Cortesio recognised us in spite of our robes.

'Those who escaped from us fled,' said Old Death. 'Was it you who shot?'

'I from here, and my servant at the back. Fortunately you warned us. You were right.'

316

'Come to Lange's house, because we had visitors there too. We still have to sort out fifteen rascals. Your servant should run from house to house to wake up the people.'

'Right!' replied Cortesio. 'He will go first to the sheriff's house, because we'll need him. I will follow you soon.'

In the little street two men with guns hurried towards us. They came because of the gunfire. We told them what had happened, and they immediately joined us. Even if there were people in La Grange who disagreed with the abolition of slavery, they had enough of the abomination of the Ku-Klux-Klan. We took the four injured bandits, and carried them over to Lange's house. Nothing had happened there. Those in the bed chamber were very quiet. Soon Cortesio arrived with a number of citizens. There were so many that some had to wait outside. The noise could not escape the attention of the prisoners, and they must have understood that their situation was hopeless. Old Death and I went to the attic again. When we lifted the board we saw a scene that made us contented. Grim despair ruled in the chamber. The bandits leant against the walls with bowed head. Some even collapsed on the floor.

'The ten minutes have gone!' shouted Old Death to them. 'What's your decision?'

He did not get a response, but one of the bandits swore.

'So, no response? Right. Then we start shooting.'

We both aimed. Surprisingly, none of the bandits dared to turn their revolver at us. They were only brave when they attacked defenceless people.

Old Death whispered in my ear, 'I don't want to kill anyone, but we have to sober them up. You aim at the lieutenant's hand, and I'll manicure the boss's hand.'

Our shots went off at the same time, and both were precise. Their two leaders cried out because of their pain, and their accomplices yelled. Of course, our people also heard the shots. They thought that a fight had started, and now they shot through the window and the door. Many bandits were wounded, and all jumped on the floor hoping for same safety. They howled as if they were on the torture stake. The boss knelt down to wrap the blanket around his bleeding hand.

He then shouted to us, 'Stop it! We surrender.'

'Good,' replied Old Death, 'then everyone should put their weapons on the bed, and we will let you out one by one. If we find weapons on anyone, we will shoot him dead. Can you hear the noise? Hundreds of people are outside. Only by surrendering can you be helped.'

The gang's situation was really hopeless; they could not escape; they did not want to fight. Following Old Death's order, they threw their knives and revolvers on the bed.

'Right!' shouted the old man. 'Now wait a bit until I arrange the opening of the door.'

He sent me downstairs to pass on his command. I went downstairs whistling whilst not expecting the unpleasant situation that I would get into. The room was full of people. I forgot to take off my disguise, and as soon as they saw me, they thought I was one of the bandits. They grabbed me, and started to hit me. I protested in vain, because they did not listen to me. I had to be happy that I could slip out of the door. A strong man hurried after me, and put his huge, bony hand on my shoulder.

'Don't rush, my friend!' he shouted. 'I have a different plan for you. Can you see that tree? Beautiful tree with excellent branches! I'll hang you on that!'

'Leave me alone! I'm not a Klansman! What do you want from me?'

'Wonderful branches!' he replied. 'Very strong! Don't worry, they won't break because of your weight.'

He grabbed me by my throat with one of his hands, and with the other he kept on boxing my side. I feared that he would break my ribs.

'I'm Mr Lange's friend, for God's sake. Ask him, if you don't believe me!'

'Great branches! It'll be a joy to swing on it! And we produce excellent ropes here in La Grange!' he replied, and now he hit my stomach for a change. I could not hold back my anger, and I hit his nose.

He let me go, and I was about to hurry back to the house, when some people arrived to the yard, and without a word they started to hit me. The big-handed man yelled, 'Hang him up! Don't waste time! Look what he did to me! I haven't got many teeth left, and this wretched bandit knocked out my only two front teeth!'

His nose and mouth bled, and if he had wanted to hang me earlier, probably he would have wanted to torture me on a stake now. Fortunately Lange heard the shouting, and he came out.

'What do you want from him?' he asked recognising the situation. 'He has never been a Klansman! Just the opposite. We can thank him and his friend that we and Cortesio are alive, and our houses still stand.'

'To him?' asked the big-handed man in an unbelieving voice. 'I should thank him too?'

He pulled out a handkerchief from his pocket, and wiped away his blood. His nose looked like onion. Now everybody was laughing at him. However, I did not feel like laughing. I was touching my arm and side angrily, because I was sure that I was full of blue and green bruises from his fingers.

'Are you mad?' I yelled at him. 'Charging at me like a wild boar!'

He could not reply, and showed me on his hand his "only two front teeth".

I told the men quickly what had happened. Lange got ropes, and held them ready at the door of the bed chamber.

'Now let them out one by one,' I said. 'As soon as somebody steps out, tie him up. Somebody should go for the sheriff! Cortesio has sent his servant for him, and he should be here already.'

'The sheriff?' opened Lange his eyes wide. 'But he's here! You knocked out his teeth!'

'Damn it!' I said. 'So, you are the highest official of the county, responsible for law and order, and you wanted to act

319

as Judge Lynch! Not surprising then that the Ku-Klux-Klan is so strong in this county!

He was clearly embarrassed, and he could only stutter, 'I'm sorry, Sir, but you have such a criminal face ...'

'Thank you humbly,' I replied acidly. 'Yours looks pitiful! Now, let's show these good people of La Grange how you can handle the Klansmen, and not by lynching.' He regained his composure.

'Then let's begin the official procedure. Two men stand on the right and left of the door with a gun.'

In the meantime Cortesio also arrived, and joined the capturing of the Ku-Klux-Klan gang. We removed the sticks from the door.

'Gentlemen, you can come out,' I said, but none of them wanted to start. Because of this I called the boss and the lieutenant to step forward. They had already bandaged their hands, and with them a further three or four wounded men came forward. In the attic Old Death, grinning, encouraged the gang. As soon as someone stepped out, his hands were tied behind his back, and he was led out to the front of the house. We did not allow them to take off their hoods, except their two leaders, so that they could not disappear. In the crowd there was also a surgeon, who bandaged the wounded although they did not deserve this humane treatment. When all the Klansmen were out, we had to decide what to do with them. Although La Grange had a jail, there was not enough room for nineteen prisoners.

'Take them to the ball room!' ordered the sheriff. 'We will sort them out, but we will keep to the legal procedure. There will be a jury for making the judgement.'

The decision spread quickly through the town. Many started off to the inn to secure a good place in the ball room. The bandits were led there, and the sheriff made it sure that they were not harmed on the way. Of course, curses were flying at them. In the large yard of the inn there was a big building. This was the ball room. There was a platform for the musicians. The prisoners were lined up there. Now the hoods were removed. There was not a single familiar face among them. They all came here from another area.

They appointed the jury, the persecutor, and the legal representative of the gang. The latter did not want to take on this task, but the sheriff insisted on the formalities. The two Langes, Cortesio, and the five men who had arrived to Lange's house first, my old friend, and I became witnesses.

The jury sat down, and the case started. The weapons of the gang were put on the desk in front of the jury, thus the court had the *corpus delicti*. Old Death examined the guns, and stated that they were all loaded.

First the persecutor spoke. Using colourful words he described the danger that threatened the town. He pointed out that the accused not only threatened the public order, the basis of peaceful work, but they were also prepared for murdering citizens of the town. Therefore, he asked for capital punishment. His speech attracted a number of "Bravo!", and he thanked them by bowing to the audience.

Then it was the turn of defence followed. He started with the statement that he was ready to hang the accused with his own hand. But then he took his task more seriously. He said that the whole proceeding was invalid, because first the identity of the accused should have been established.

'We don't care,' said the sheriff stopping him. 'The noose is enough! We won't waste ink and paper on them!'

The defence abandoned this line, and only referred to the fact that the accused had not carried out the planned crimes, because the famous guest of the town, Old Death and his companion prevented it. Thus he asked for some lenience: executing only every second bandit.

The jury declared the men guilty, after which the sheriff, said, 'But we won't execute any of them.' The accused were relieved, but then the sheriff continued, 'We will confiscate their weapons, and everything that we find in their pockets. This will be the main punishment. As a supplementary punishment their hair, moustache, and beard, if they have, will be sheared off and we'll do this immediately.'

'Hear! Hear!' exclaimed the audience, and in a moment scissors, razors, and even shears appeared.

'I also propose,' continued the sheriff, 'that we put the shamed and disarmed gang on the boat that arrived from Austin at eleven o'clock, and leaves for Matagorda at dawn. The sheriff of Matagorda will make it sure that the gang is removed from Texas. They will be sent back to where they came from.'

'Hear! Hear!' cried the audience again, and the jury was in agreement.

'This is not all,' continued the sheriff for whom I had felt more sympathy as his speech matched my values. 'We will auction the weapons and other confiscated things, and use the money found on the bandits for a charitable purpose.' He paused for a moment for a theatrical effect. 'Yes, charitable. We will spend the whole sum on beer, brandy and whiskey that we will consume tonight in this dance hall. It's so late now that it isn't worth to go to bed. We'll organise a ball, and then we'll go together to the port to bid farewell to the members of the Ku-Klux-Klan with music and songs. And from this speech you can see we have a lot to do till dawn. Members of the Jury! Do you agree with my proposals?'

The audience applauded, only the accused looked sad.

'Does the defence have anything to say to this?' asked the sheriff.

'The sentence is just, lenient, and appropriate, and I support it,' said the defence. 'I would only like to add that I charge two dollars per accused for my work, that is, thirty-nine dollars. I offer this for the ball. This is my contribution for the rent of the hall, and the cost of lighting. I propose an entrance fee to pay for the musicians. Every gentleman should pay fifteen cents. Ladies, of course, come free.'

They applauded his words too. I could not believe what I was hearing. Were all court cases conducted like this in La Grange? I glanced at Old Death, who sat next to me, and I could see that he enjoyed it. He was laughing aloud, and slapped his knees. In any case he was right. Even though the proceedings were a comedy, the important thing was that the gang got a harsh lesson, and they would not come to La Grange again.

The citizens immediately started the execution of the sentence. The bandits were searched, and their belongings were confiscated. Apart from some rings, necklaces and watches, they collected almost three thousand dollars in cash. Then they took out the tools, and sheared the hair of the bandits mercilessly. They coped with it with downcast eyes, and did not dare to protest in any form. Once this was completed, the auction started. The weapons were all sold.

In the meantime many had hurried home to change, and the women prepared for the ball. Of course, this created a lot of noise and movement. The musicians had also arrived: a violinist, a clarinettist, a trumpeter, and one man with a bassoon. This wonderful orchestra settled in the corner as their stage was still occupied, and started the tuning. This gave an indication of the frightening musical experience that we would experience later. I would have liked to slip away, but Old Death plainly refused. Also the sheriff approached us, and said that the citizens of La Grange would consider it an insult if we did not attend the ball, moreover, it was our task to open the first round of dancing. He embraced me so familiarly as if I had never knocked out his "only two front teeth". He organised a separate table for us, and put it in the best place, that is, next to the orchestra. Or maybe this was his revenge for his teeth. He settled by this table with his big wife and his extremely lean, but pretty daughter. The girl was probably a connoisseur of literature as she carried a poetry book. Right after the introduction, she asked Old Death, 'What's your view of Pierre-Jean de Beranger?'

'Well, Miss, I have never met the gentleman, and if he said that he knows me, he's a liar,' said the old scout.

After this reply the thirty years old girl became silent.

The first round of the dance was announced. Old Death offered his arm to the sheriff's wife, and I took the dreamy girl to the dance.

I do not want to describe the ball in detail. The huge drinking party, in which the ladies also took part although with a bit more moderation than the men. But I cannot keep quiet about an embarrassing thing that completely upset my plans. Old Death enjoyed the dance so much that he wanted to outdo the youth, and in one turn he made too strong a swing. I did not know if he stumbled or lost his balance, but he crashed on the ground pulling down his partner with him. The lady survived it as nature had padded her excellently, but Old Death hit himself so much that he barely could get up.

There was plenty of drink, and it was free, thus the whole company was rather merry, except for those who guarded the prisoners. However, at dawn, just before the departure of the ship, they all got up, and started off to the port. The musicians led the way, then the members of the jury, followed by the Klansmen in their infamous uniform with their hands tied behind their back under the guard of armed men. Finally the citizens of the town.

Only the devil knows how the whole town learnt the news, but they were all there, and all brought some tools with which they could make a noise, including pots, lids and stokers. The musicians played the Yankee Doodle.

After the last line an unbelievable noise broke out. There is no word that could describe the whistling, screaming, yelling that was produced. It was completely mad. Then like a mourning crowd they walked slowly to the port, and gave the prisoners to the Captain, who assured the sheriff that they would not escape from his boat. Then, when the boat departed, the music restarted, and this is how the town said good-bye to the effectively punished gang. Old Death took my arm, and with the two Langes we walked back to the scene of our heroic deed.

We lay down with the plan that we would sleep for half an hour. However, it became much longer. When I awoke, Old Death was sitting on the bed. He was feeling his thigh and hip. For my complete shock he announced that he would not be able to ride on that day. The younger Lange brought the surgeon, who examined the old man, and said that his leg was strained.

'You'll have to rest for at least a week,' he said.

This made me so angry that I would have liked to slap his face.

'I'll try to put it back,' he said, and assured us that we would hear when the two bones clicked together. Then he started to jerk Old Death's leg with full strength. I put my hands on my ears so that I would not hear his cries because I knew how painful such an intervention was. However, for my surprise Old Death did not even groan. It obviously was not painful. I pushed the surgeon aside. There was a huge bruise, whose edges were yellow, on Old Death's thigh. It was clear that he had had a bruise.

'You must spread mustard on it or some spirit' I said; and then added, 'That damned Gibson has his luck! Now, he'll get away!'

'Don't worry,' said Old Death, 'an old bloodhound like me won't leave the trail until he catches the game.'

'But he gains so much time ...'

'We will make it up, Sir,' the old man assured me. 'Keep your chin up. I'm really ashamed for my silly accident, but I'll make it up.'

Although his promise did not calm me, I had to accept it. I could not continue the journey or rather the chase, alone. At lunch Lange told us that he would like to join us with his son if we accepted them.

'I can assure you that we won't be burden on you,' he said. 'We both know horses and guns.'

Naturally we agreed. A bit later Cortesio came over, and asked if we wanted to see the two horses that he had to offer. Old Death, in spite of his pain, hobbled with us to the stable. He wanted to look at the horses.

'This young man,' he pointed at me, 'insists he is a good rider, and I believe him, but judging a horse requires more experience. I have to take the responsibility for this.'

He thoroughly examined the horses in the stable, and watched their movement. The two horses that Cortesio offered looked nicer than the others, but Old Death did not like them. He chose two old, fox coloured horses.

'Are you sure about choosing these two nags?' asked Cortesio surprised.

'I do, if you don't mind it, señor,' replied the old man. 'These two are mustangs, but they have not been treated appropriately. They are more enduring than the other two horses. So, we would take two foxes if you don't mind, Sir.'

'As you wish, Sir,' replied the Spaniard shrugging his shoulder as we were already taking the two "nags".

ON THIS SIDE OF THE BORDER

A WEEK later five riders rode in Medina county, in the South-western corner of Texas: one black man, and four white men. The whites rode in pairs, the black man rode behind them.

The first pair wore almost identical leather jackets, but the one that belonged to the older rider, who was very lean, was more worn that that of the younger's. Their fox horses neighed happily, which showed that they were feeling well, and homely on the infinite prairies.

The second pair were visibly relatives, son and father. Their woollen clothing were identical. Both wore a felt hat with a wide brim. Their weapons consisted of revolvers, double-barrelled guns and knives.

The black man wore a dark blue calico suit, and a hat. In his hand he carried a long, double-barrelled gun, and there was a machete in his belt.

Of course, the riders were I, Old Death, Lange and his son. The young black man was Señor Cortesio's servant.

Old Death recovered from his injuries only after three full days. He was ashamed because, while being wounded in a battle is a glory, being injured in dance is ridiculous. These injuries, whose marks were still visible on his thigh, had to be more painful than I thought, otherwise Old Death would not have delayed our departure for so long.

When Cortesio had learnt that Lange and his son would join us, he asked if we could take his black servant, Sam. We could not refuse, especially when we learnt that Cortesio had got an important despatch from Washington, and as a result, he had to send an important letter to Chihuahua. He needed an answer, thus he could not trust it to anyone else, but Sam, the intelligent and reliable black servant. He had made the journey across the Mexican border many times. He was an excellent rider, and he told me that when he was really young, he was a cowboy with a huge herd.

Old Death considered it a complete waste of time to follow Gibson's track. We knew what way the group had

327

gone, and where they wanted to cross the border. We followed the shortest way to the Eagle Pass. Gibson gained a big advantage, but Old Death reassured me, by saying that the group had to avoid attention, thus they had to take detours, while we could follow the shortest way, and thus we could catch up with them.

In six days we made two hundred miles, and our two horses coped very well. Nobody else but Old Death could have expected this from them. On the prairie they became younger. The clear air, the fresh grass, and the quick riding changed them.

We passed San Antonio and Castroville. We crossed the northern edge of Medina county that was rich in streams and springs, but now we were riding in an area, where the water became a treasure. We were approaching the desert of Texas. It was the worst between the Rio Grande and the Nueces River. We first headed to the Leona River, a major tributary of the Frio River, then to the confluence of the Nueces River and the Turkey Creek. In the distance we could see Fort Inge on the hillside. The group that we followed could not go in any other way than this, but it was unlikely that they would have visited the fort, where the officers hated Juárez.

This prairie was excellent for galloping. Our horses almost flew over the flat, short grass prairie. Our direction was South-west. Suddenly we caught sight of a black spot coming apparently very slowly from the North-west.

Old Death was the first to notice it. He pointed to the horizon, and exclaimed, 'Look there! What could it be?'

'Hm,' hummed Lange putting his hand over his eyes, 'maybe some grazing animal.'

'An animal,' smiled Old Death mockingly, 'and grazing too? Wonderful! I'm afraid, my friend you need to study a lot. True, it takes years until your eyes can adjust to the perspectives of the prairie. That dot is about two miles from here. From such a distance you wouldn't even notice an elephant. And don't forget that from a distance movement appears to be slower. I would bet against any sum that that point is approaching us very fast.'

'Impossible,' Lange shook his head.

'Let's hear Sam's opinion. What do you think, Sam? I noticed that you have good eyesight.'

The black man had been quiet until now, but now he immediately said, 'Riders, Sir. Four or five, maybe even six.'

'I think so too. Could they be Indians?'

'No, Sir. Indians wouldn't come so openly. If they saw a white rider, they would first hide in a bush, watch him, and only then would they ride towards him.'

'You're right, Sam! Your senses are excellent!' Sam smiled as he appreciated Old Death's appraisal.

'If they are white riders, and they come to us, maybe we should wait for them,' opined Lange.

'Not at all,' replied the old man. 'They can see that we are riding, thus they are coming to us diagonally. Let's go forward, we don't have any time to waste. They are probably scouts from Fort Inge. If so, I'm not happy.'

'Why?'

'Because then something is wrong. But we will learn it.'

We continued our journey. After a while the black dot broke up to six smaller ones, and soon we could see that they were uniformed soldiers. Two minutes later they caught up with us, and they ordered us to stop. A sergeant rode up to us with five dragoons.

'Why are you in such a hurry?' he asked in a rough voice when he stopped his horse. 'Couldn't you see that we were coming?'

'We did,' answered my old friend calmly, 'but it's not a reason for interrupting our journey.'

'But we must know who you are.'

'We are travellers, and we are heading to South-west.'

'Don't' joke with me,' brayed the sergeant.

'I didn't intend to joke,' said Old Death, 'but I don't feel like being questioned. We are on the open prairie, and not in some school, where pupils are obliged to answer.'

329

'We are armed, and we can force you to stop. I have an order to check everybody's identity.'

'That's different, but still you should be polite. You can only ask, and not order. We are free people, and we aren't obliged to answer anyone. And if somebody was insisting on ordering me, I would just simply walk through his body.'

'We will see!' said the sergeant as his hand moved for his revolver.

Old Death's eyes flashed. His horse, by the pressure of his thighs, rose. The sergeant pulled back his horse.

'I'll tell you something, boy,' continued Old Death in a harsh tone. 'Firstly I'm at least twice as old as you are, thus you should show more respect. It also means that I have more experience than you. I also have weapons, and, believe me, I can handle them better than you. If you think that our knives are made of marzipan, our guns of sugar, and our bullets of chocolate, you may find that this mixture of candies would affect you rather badly. You say that you're carrying out orders. That's fine. Just don't imagine that you are a general, and I'm some tramp.'

The sergeant looked embarrassed. 'I only want your name,' he said, 'If you have nothing to hide, you can name yourself. We're close to the border, and there are rabble around here.

'Are you saying that we are rabble?' roared Old Death.

'I can't say if you are or not. I need to know your names, and the purpose of your journey. There are too many scoundrels who are heading to Mexico to join the army of that damned Juárez.'

'Are you then with the French?' asked Old Death.

'Of course, and I hope you are too.'

'I'm with the honest people against the rascals. I don't have anything to hide. We come from La Grange.'

'So from Texas. All good, honest, and real Texans are against Washington. We are like-minded people'

'Well, instead of five names, I give you only one, mine. I'm an old hunter known as Old Death.'

330

The effect of the name was visible. The sergeant leant ahead on the saddle, and just starred at the old man. The dragoons looked at each other, and then cast friendly looks at Old Death.

'Old Death!' exclaimed the sergeant while knitting his eyebrows. 'You're the famous path finder ... the spy of the Northerners?'

'Check your tongue!' bellowed the old man. 'I served the North with all the skills and strength, because I agreed with their policies, and I had always been repulsed by how the blacks were treated in the Southern states. But a spy is something different. It's an insult that requires revenge. Old Death is not afraid of five or six dragoons, not even of twenty! I'm curious what the commander of Fort Inge would say when he learns how you talked to me.'

The sergeant became even more confused than earlier. He knew that he would have to report on his return, and he could not hide that he had met such a famous hunter. His duty would have been to ask for his advice, and also what he had seen on his way.

'I respect your uniform,' continued Old Death, 'and in my own way I'm a soldier too. Who's the commander?'

'Major Webster.'

'The one who was captain in Fort Ripley?'

'The same.'

'Then pass on my respect to him. We know each other. I have competed with him in target shooting many times at Fort Ripley. You can give me your notebook, and I'll write a few lines for him. He'll have a good laugh when he learns that you called me a spy.'

The sergeant blushed. He swallowed, and began again on a friendlier tone.

'I was only joking! I had no intention of insulting a famous man like Old Death!'

'This sounds better! I can see that our conversation starts only now. How are you with cigars in the fort?'

'Bad. We have run out of tobacco.'

'Soldiers without tobacco are only half soldiers. My friend has plenty. He will offer you some.'

The sergeant and his men cast longing looks at me. I pulled out a handful of cigars, and distributed them. I even gave them light. On the face of the sergeant there was heavenly happiness after the first puff.

'Thank you,' he nodded, 'let's take this as a peace pipe. The smell of these cigars makes peace between anything.'

'So cigars can break hostility between the Northerners and Southerners?' laughed Old Death. 'You aren't a bad guy.'

'No, I'm not,' he said. 'Tell me, have you met Indians?'

'Why do you ask?'

'I have my reasons. These damned reds dug up the war hatchet again.'

'Bad enough,' shook Old Death his head. 'What tribes?'

'The Apache and the Comanche.'

'Uh! We are just between the hunting grounds of the two tribes. At the end we will pay the bill.'

'This is why I'm telling you. We did everything we could. We asked for reinforcement and supplies, and we send out scouts every day.'

'How did it happen?'

'It's all because of Juárez! You probably heard that he had to abandon the capital city, and he ran all the way to El Paso. The French followed him. He would have to cross the border had Washington not helped him. But they did. Juárez is an Indian, but most tribes are against him.'

'Including the Apache?'

'No, the Apache wanted to stay neutral, because of their young, and famous chief, Winnetou. But Bazain's agents have managed to raise the Comanche against Juárez.'

'Mexico has nothing to do with the Comanche. Their villages are on this side of the Rio Grande. Does it matter to them who rules Mexico? It was only a pretext for them for robbery!'

'This is none of my business,' said the sergeant. 'The Comanche are the enemies of the Apache. The Comanche attacked an Apache village, shot and captured many people, and their belongings. As to the captured male prisoners ... Well, you know ... Torture stake and alike.'

'Shame!' Old Death was indignant. 'The French will have to bear all the moral responsibility for this. And I suppose the Apache have revenged it?'

'They are too coward for that.'

'What? This is the first time I've heard that the Apache are cowards. Why do you think so?

'They started peace negotiations with the Comanche in our fort.'

'Why there?'

'Because they considered it a neutral territory.'

'They were right. Who were there?'

'Five Comanche chiefs with twenty warriors.'

'And how many Apache?'

'Three.'

'And you call it cowardice? Three against twenty-five? If you knew the Indians, you would know that it was a heroic deed. What was the outcome of the negotiations?'

'The Indians couldn't agree on anything, and quarrelled. Finally the Comanche jumped on the Apache, stabbed two to death; the third managed to get on his horse, and escaped. The Comanche chased after him, but could not catch him.'

'And all these happened in an American fort, on neutral territory, in the Major's presence! Perfidious Comanche! It's not surprising that the Apache dug up the hatchet. As two of their envoys were murdered in a white fort, they have all the reason to be angry with the palefaces. What can we expect from the Comanche?'

'Before they left the fort, the chiefs said that they would fight only against the Apache, and that they consider the palefaces their friends.'

'When did all this happen?'

'On Monday.'

'Today is Friday, so four days ago. How long did the Comanche stay in the fort after the Apache had escaped?'

'Not more than an hour.'

'They shouldn't have been allowed to leave! They broke the law of the prairie. They also committed treason against the United States! I don't really understand the Major that he didn't arrest them.'

'The Major wasn't in the fort. He rode out in the morning for hunting, and did not return till the evening.'

'So that he wouldn't see, and wouldn't hear anything! I know this! If the Apache learn that you let the murderers go, it's woe to all whites!'

'The Apache should be happy that the Comanche left so quickly,' said the sergeant. 'because otherwise they would have killed the Apache chief who arrived a bit later.'

'Another Apache chief?' asked Old Death surprised. 'Ah, yes, I know. It was four days ago. He's got an excellent horse, and he rode much faster than us. It had to be him!'

'Whom are you talking about?'

'Winnetou.'

'Yes, it was him. As soon as the Comanche left to the West, from the East an Apache rider arrived to buy lead, ammunition, and gunpowder. There was no eagle feather in his hair, and we did not recognise him. He turned to the officer on duty and ...'

'What did he say?' interrupted Old Death curiously.

'Only this: "Many palefaces will regret this!". Then he stepped out of the store, and got on his horse. The officer on duty went after him to admire his wonderful black horse. Then the Indian said: "I'm more honest than you are. I tell you openly that we are now enemies. The Apache were in their villages in peace. The Comanche attacked them, stole the women, children, horses, and tents, killed many of our warriors, and took the rest as prisoners. But the elders of the Apache tribe have always listened to the voice of the Great Spirit, thus we didn't dig up the war hatchet, but sent three men for negotiations. These were murdered, and you let it happen. Much blood will flow because of this, and it will be your fault!"'

'I can recognise his words! He was perfectly right!' cried Old Death. 'What did the officer on duty say?'

'He asked the Indian his name. When he heard that it was Winnetou, he ordered the gate to be closed, and the Apache chief arrested. He had the right to do so, as the Indian declared war, and he was not protected by any truce. But he only laughed at the officer, made his horse leap among us, and then the horse jumped over the fence. A dragoon squad rode after him, but it was too late.'

'You see! Who else has visited the fort?'

'A lone rider, the day before yesterday. In the evening. He said he was on the way to Sabinas. I was the guard. I asked his name, he said it was Clinton.'

'Clinton! Listen!' said Old Death, and then he described Gibson to the sergeant. I took out the photo, and the sergeant immediately recognised him.

'This man lied to you,' said Old Death. 'He wasn't going to Sabinas, he only wanted to sniff around, while his squad hid somewhere in the distance.'

'It's possible.'

'Well, there's nothing more to discuss! Report to the Major that you met me. As he's your superior, you don't have to tell him my opinion about his conduct. So long, sergeant! So long, boys!'

He turned his horse, rode away, and we followed him. The dragoons were heading back to the fort. We were riding in silence. Old Death was musing. On the West the Sun was setting. We wanted to be by the Leona River by the evening, but we did not know how far it was. Soon a sharp line to the South appeared in the horizon. The barren, sandy ground changed to grassland again. The sharp line was the foliage of a row of trees.

Old Death slowed down, pointed to that direction, and remarked, 'Where trees are, there is water. It will be the Leona River. We'll spend the night there.'

Finally we arrived to the trees. The two banks of the river were covered by thickets. The bed of the river was

335

broad but shallow. However, the banks were high, because in springtime this river carried much water. It would have been difficult to descend on the steep slope at that point, thus we rode upstream to find a better ford. Old Death was in the front. When his horse put its hoof in the water, Old Death stopped the horse, got off, and examined the stones gleaming in the water.

'I thought so,' he murmured. 'Somebody crossed here.'

We also dismounted, and looked at the palm-sized prints that led to the river.

'Is it a track of a rider?' asked Lange.

'No,' replied Old Death, 'let's hear Sam's opinion!'

The black man came forward, and he examined the river bed. 'Two riders crossed here, Sir,' he said.

'How do you know that they were riders, and not just mustangs?'

'Mustangs don't have horseshoes,' answered Sam. 'And these prints are deep, thus the horse carried weight. The mustangs would have stopped here to drink, and would have left more tracks. These horses went in a straight line, so they obeyed to reins.'

'You're right, Sam' nodded the old man in agreement. 'I couldn't have summarised it better! They were in a hurry, and watered their horses only on the other bank. Why were they hurrying? Well, let's see.'

While we talked, our horses drank the water greedily. When they finished, we mounted them again, and waded through the river. It was so shallow that the water did not reach our boots.

As soon as we got to the other bank, Old Death, whose attention missed nothing, exclaimed, 'Now I understand it! Can you see that elm tree? Its bark was cut off to a man's height. And look at these sticks pushed in the ground!'

He pointed to the bank. There were two rows of sticks. They were as thick and long as a pencil.

'Why?' mused Old Death aloud. 'How are they related to the elm tree? Have you seen how fishermen make their net?

The riders stretched the bark on these sticks to make a bandage of it. It cools the wound, and when it dries out, it becomes so tight that it holds better than plaster. So one of the two riders was wounded, and he was bandaged here.'

I was mesmerised by his ability of observation.

'This is not all,' continued the old man. 'Just look in the water. Two horses rolled in it. Indians' horses do it often. The blankets were removed from them, and they rolled in the water to cool down, and also to refresh. They are only allowed to do this if they are tired, but there is still a long way to go. So what's the conclusion from this, gentlemen?'

'I'll try,' I replied, 'but please don't laugh at me if I say something stupid.'

'I won't! I consider you as my student, and I cannot expect you to know as much as I, an experienced, seasoned pathfinder, does.'

'As these were Indian horses, I assume that their masters were also Indians. Consider what happened in the fort! One Apache was wounded, but escaped. Winnetou followed him, and, as he has an excellent horse, caught up with him.'

'Agreed,' nodded Old Death. 'Continue!'

'Winnetou's most important task is to warn the Apache of the danger. This is why he hurried so much. He stopped here only to look after his companion's wounds.'

'Logical,' nodded the old man again. 'It seems that they were heading to the Rio Grande. I hope we'll find their tracks again. Let's camp somewhere here, and we'll continue our journey tomorrow at dawn.'

Soon he found an appropriate place; a small clearance surrounded by thick bushes. There was lush grass there, so our horses could feed well. We lay down, and took out our provisions. I asked if I should make a small fire.

'I've waited for this question, Sir,' replied Old Death with a mocking smile. 'You probably read many books by Cooper and others, and in those books there is always a campfire for the dinner. It's really poetic, but I would rather avoid it as the Comanche would smell the smoke of such a fire from as far as two miles away.'

'Aren't you exaggerating, Sir?'

'You can't imagine how good their noses are, and if they can't smell it, their horses can. Many white men paid with their life because of the snorting of the trained Indian mustangs.'

'The Comanche cannot be here yet,' I said.

'You are wrong. This area is their hunting ground, and sometimes they go to Mexico too. I'm afraid it'll be very hard for Winnetou to reach the Rio Grande.'

'Are you then with the Apache, Sir?' I asked.

'In my heart, yes. Firstly, because they were attacked treacherously. Also, Winnetou made a great impression on me. But it wouldn't be very clever to be open about my sympathies. As they are on the warpath, we have to keep the appearance of neutrality, otherwise we won't get to Mexico.'

'Do you think that the Comanche would prevent us?'

'I hope not. I have been in their villages several times, and I've never been their enemy. One of their most famous chiefs, Oyo Koltsa, White Beaver, is a good friend of mine. Once I rescued him, and he promised eternal friendship for this. It happened by the Red River, where the Chickasaw Indians captured him, and they were about to scalp him when I intervened. This friendship could be useful if we find that the Comanche are hostile to us. We have to be alert. I suggest that one of us should be on guard during the night. We'll decide it by drawing straws.'

He tore five blades of grass of different lengths, and held them out to us. Whoever drew the shortest one was to be the first guard. I pulled the longest one, which meant that I could rest the longest time without interruption. As long as we were awake, we did not need guards, and for the time being we did not want to go to sleep. We were smoking cigars, and talked. Old Death entertained us with the stories of his adventures, and they were so exciting that we forgot about sleepiness. I took my watch out of my pocket, and was surprised to see that it was already eleven o'clock. Old Death suddenly stopped talking, and was watching tensely. One of our horses snorted strangely. I also noticed it.

'Hm,' hummed the old man. 'Wasn't I right to choose these "nags" from Cortesio's stable? They are at home on the prairie, and they had good masters. This one is suspicious of something. Don't stare, gentlemen, because the bush is dark, and you cannot see anything, while your glowing eyes can tell the enemy that we are here. Downcast your eyes! I'll look around. Can you hear it? Again! Don't move.'

The snorting of the horse was repeated, and one of the horses stomped with its hoof as if it wanted to escape. We became quiet.

'Why don't you talk?' asked Old Death. 'If somebody is spying on us, he shouldn't recognise that we have become suspicious. Just talk! It doesn't matter what about!'

Sam said very quietly, 'I know where the enemy is. I can see his eyes. On the right, under the hawthorn bush. At the very bottom two dots are glowing.'

'Excellent,' whispered the old man. 'I'll go behind him. Talk loudly, it will suppress the noise of my steps too.'

Lange asked something, and I answered loudly. For a while we argued, then laughed to give the impression of being carefree. Will and Sam also intervened, and for ten minutes we talked nonsense. The comedy was interrupted by Old Death's voice, 'Enough, you'll lose your voice. I've done my job. I'm bringing the result.'

Soon we heard his heavy steps from the hawthorn bush. He appeared panting, because he carried something on his back that he put it down on the ground in the front of us.

'There!' he said. 'It was easy.'

'An Indian,' I exclaimed. 'Are there are more around?'

'There could be, but it's unlikely. We'll make some light. There's some dried wood there, I'll bring it here. Look after our guest!'

'He doesn't move. Is he dead?'

339

'No, he's unconscious. I tied his hands with his own belt. By the time he recovers, I'll be here.'

He broke off the branches of a dead tree; brought it over, and we chopped it up with our knives. We had matches, so we soon had a small fire. The wood was so dry that there was barely any smoke.

I looked at the prisoner. He was a young Indian who wore simple moccasins, and the usual dress. His hair was long and parted. His face was painted yellow with black lines across it. Old Death had already taken his weapons, and everything that was in his belt. He did not have a gun, only a knife, a bow and arrows. He lay motionless.

'A warrior, who hasn't yet achieved anything or lost his honour,' remarked Old Death. 'There is no scalp on his belt nor human hair is sewn in the fringes of his trousers. He doesn't have a medicine bag either. It seems to me that he lost his name as the Indians say. Probably he came on this scouting mission to regain it. Look, he's starting to move. He'll recover in a minute.'

The prisoner stretched out his legs, and breathed deeply. When he noticed that his hands were bound, he trembled in fright. He opened his eyes, and he wanted to jump up, but fell back. He looked at us with glowing eyes. When his eyes turned to Old Death, he exclaimed, 'Kosha Pehveh!'

His words meant Old Death in the Comanche language.

'Yes, I am.' nodded Old Death. 'Do you know me?'

'The Comanche warriors have not forgotten the great white hunter, who visited them.'

'Yes, I can now recognise the colours of the Comanche on your face! What's your name?'

'I lost my name. I went on the warpath to regain it. But I was caught, and brought shame on my tribe. I only ask you to kill me. I will die with songs, and without a woe, on the torture stake.'

'We can't fulfil your request, because we are Christians, and we are your friends. In the dark I couldn't see that you were Comanche, otherwise I wouldn't have knocked you out

340

as we are the friends of the Comanche. You will live, and you will achieve heroic deeds to regain your name. You are free!'

He cut off the bond. I thought the Indian would jump up happily, but he did not move.

'The Comanche must die,' he said. 'Stab me!'

'I don't feel like, and I have no reason to. Tell me why should I kill you?'

'Because you captured me. The Comanche warriors will say that it's not enough that I lost my name and my medicine bag, I'm so clumsy that even palefaces could capture me. I'm blind, deaf, and thus I cannot be a warrior.'

He spoke in such a sad voice that I felt sorry for him. I didn't understand all his words because he spoke Comanche mixed with English words, but I could still follow it.

'No shame happened,' I said quickly, before Old Death could reply. 'Being captured by such a famous paleface like Kosha Pehveh is not shameful. And nobody will know it. We will keep our tongue.'

'Can Kosha Pehveh promise this?' asked the Indian.

'Of course!' replied the old man. 'We will say that we met, and we talked. You knew that I was a friend of the Comanche, and you recognised me right away.'

'Your words console me, my white brother. I won't have to die, and I can return to my tribe. I'll always be grateful to my white brothers.'

Now he sat up, and breathed deeply. Although I could not read his face because of the thick paint, I knew that he was relieved. I left the leading role in the talk to my experienced, old friend.

'You can see that we are your friends, my brother' said Old Death. 'I hope he will answer honestly to my questions.'

'Ask! I will speak the truth.'

'Did you come alone, my brother, to kill an enemy or a great prey to regain your name? Or did you leave your village with many warriors?'

'With many warriors. As many as many water drops are in a river.'

341

'Have all the Comanche warriors left their tents to step on the warpath?'

'Almost all.'

'Against whom?'

'The Apache dogs. The bad smell of the Apache coyotes bothered our noses. We will wipe them off the Earth.'

'Was it the advice of the council of the elders?'

'They decided on the war. The magic man asked the advice of the Good Spirit, and he got an encouraging answer. From the Comanche villages to the Great River, that the palefaces call Rio Grande, the ground resounds under the feet of our warriors. The Sun has set four times since the war started.'

'Where does your group stay?'

'Upstream along the river. They sent out scouts, and I was permitted to scout too. I came downstream, and smelt your horses. I crawled here to see how many you were, when Kosha Pehveh killed me for a short time.'

'Forget it. I said that we won't mention this anymore. How many warriors camp upstream?'

'Ten times ten.'

'Who leads them?'

'Avat Vila, the young chief.'

'Avat Vila? Great Bear? I haven't heard his name.'

'He got his name recently, when he killed a grey bear in the mountains, and brought home the fur and the claws. His father is Oyo Koltsa, the chief, whom the palefaces call White Beaver.'

'I know him well. He's my friend.'

'I know. I saw you in his tent. His son will receive you as a friend too.'

'How far are they?'

'Half of the time that the palefaces call an hour.'

'Then let's visit them. I ask you, my younger brother, to lead us to the Comanche camp.'

Five minutes later we were on our horses. The young Comanche first led us to the open space, and then headed upstream. In twenty minutes several figures appeared in the darkness. They were the guards of the camp. Our guide exchanged a few words with them, then disappeared, and we waited. Soon he returned, and led us to the camp. The sky was cloudy, and there was no star in the sky. It was impossible to see anything. Our guide stopped us.

'Stop here, my white brothers. The Comanche warriors don't light a fire when they are on warpath, but we don't have to be afraid of enemies here, and we will make a fire in a minute.'

He disappeared again, and in a few minutes I saw a small flash of sparks, about the size of the head of a pin. 'Punk,' remarked Old Death.

'Punk,' I repeated, 'what is it?'

'The fire-making tool of the prairie. Two pieces of wood, one is flat, and the other one is a stick. There is a hollow in the flat one, and it's filled with dry tinder that they take from old, dried out trees. This is the best tinder in the world. They put the stick in the hollow, and turn it with two hands very quickly. It's like a vertical rolling pin. It warms up, and sets the tinder alight. It's done already!'

A small flame lit up, and started to devour the dried leaves. The flame was kept small, because the Indians did not like fires whose light could be seen from the distance. They put dry branches around the fire like spokes. If they wanted higher flames, they pushed the branches in, if they wanted smaller, they pulled them out.

Now I could see that we were surrounded by Indians. Very few had guns; most had spears, bows with arrows, and tomahawk. When the fire subsided somewhat, we were told to dismount, and our horses were led away. We were in the hands of the Comanche, as without horses, there was no way to escape. They did not take our weapons, but there was five of us against a hundred.

By the fire there was one warrior. His hair was braided, and an eagle feather stood out from it. I could not guess his age because of the thick layer of paint on his face. There

343

were two scalps on his belt. His medicine bag and calumet hung from his neck. He had a very outdated gun, at least twenty or thirty years old. He looked at us one by one.

'Look at how he plays the great chief,' whispered Old Death. 'I'll show him that we are chiefs too. Let's sit down opposite him.'

He sat down, without hesitation we all followed his example, except Sam. The Comanche, unlike many other tribes, were slave holders, and Sam would have risked his life had he sat down.

'Uff!' cried out the Indian angrily, and said something else that I could not understand.

'Do you know the language of the palefaces?' asked Old Death in a quiet voice.

'Avat Vila understands your language, but does not speak it, because he doesn't want to,' said the young chief.

'I ask you to make an exception.'

'Why?'

'Only because my companions don't understand the language of the Comanche.'

'But they are on our land, and in our camp, so they have to speak our language; this is what the courtesy requires from them.'

'But if they don't understand your language, how could they speak it? You ask something impossible. And don't forget that they are the guests of the Comanche, so the courtesy requires you to give way. You say you can speak English. I would believe it if I could hear it!'

'Uff!' exclaimed the Indian angrily, then continued in broken English. 'Now you can hear that I spoke the truth. If you don't believe it, you insult me, and I'll kill you. How dare you sit down next to me?'

'We have the right, because we are chiefs too.'

'What chiefs?'

'I'm the chief of the pathfinders.'

'And this?'

'He's the chief of the blacksmiths.'

344

'And he?' pointed the Indian at Will.

'He's the blacksmith's son, who can make beautiful swords and sharp tomahawks that can cut a skull into two.'

The Indian nodded with appreciation. Finally he pointed at me, and asked, 'And who is he?'

'He came over the Great Water from his country, where he belongs to the greatest chiefs. He came over to know about the Comanche. When he returns home, he will tell everything about you.'

The chief looked at me, and then remarked doubtfully, 'Is he really so clever? His hair is not yet grey.'

'In his country the youth are as clever as the elder here.'

'Then the Great Spirit must like that country very much. But the Comanche warriors don't need his wisdom. They know themselves what is good for them. If he was really so clever, he should know that he shouldn't have crossed our warpath. When the Comanche are on the warpath, they don't allow palefaces nearby.'

'Your envoys promised in Fort Inge that you won't harm the white men, because you fight only against the Apache.'

'I don't care what they said. I'm saying what I want.'

'How dare you speak to me like this!' exclaimed Old Death angrily. 'Who are you? What makes you think that you can speak to Kosha Pehveh like this? You didn't even tell us your name.'

The young chief was almost paralysed by such bravery.

'Do you want me to tie you to the torture stake?' he hissed at Old Death, when he regained his composure.

'You will rethink that,' replied Old Death. 'Why aren't you answering my question?'

'I'm Avat Vila, the chief of the Comanche. I got this name when I killed a grey bear alone!'

'I was a child, when I killed the first grizzly, and since then so many that I could cover myself with their claws.'

'Then look at the scalps on my belt!'

'I could decorate a whole band of warriors with the scalps of the men whom I have killed.'

'My father is Oyo Koltsa, the great chief!'

'Now this means more to me. White Beaver is my good friend, and I smoked the peace pipe with him. I'm sorry that you are so different!'

'What are you saying? Do you think that the young Comanche chief is a sheep that any dogs can bark at?'

'Did you call me a dog?' shouted Old Death. 'I'm sending you to the eternal hunting grounds!

'There are a hundred warriors here!' said the chief, pointing around.

'Yes, but we are sitting here, and I can easily shoot you. Look, I have two revolvers, each with six bullets. My friends have the same, thus we have sixty bullets. And we have other weapons. By the time we are overcome, half of your warriors will be dead. So you have to decide if we are your friends or your enemies.'

Nobody had ever talked to the chief like this before. Five men against a hundred! It was incomprehensible to him.

'I have to discuss it with my warriors.'

'You? The chief? I cannot believe it, but I must, because you said it. But we are chiefs who can do whatever we want. So we are getting on our horses, and we are leaving.'

The old man jumped up with his revolvers in his hands. We joined him.

Great Bear clenched his fist. Contradictory emotions waved through his face. He knew the power of the revolver, and also knew that any hasty action could cost a lot of lives. He also had to think of his father, who smoked the peace pipe with Kosha Pehveh, and that he could make his son accountable for any stupid actions. The Indians were not forced to join a war party, but if they did, they were under military discipline. If one made a mistake, and it was a big enough one, either his own father would have killed him, or he would have been expelled from the tribe until he redeemed himself. This is what the young chief was thinking about. How could he look his father in the eyes if he denied the rights of the guests from his old friend?

Old Death knew all these things. He was standing calmly, but kept his fingers on the triggers of the revolvers.

'You can see that I'm not afraid of you,' he told Great Bear. 'It depends on you if there is a war between us. But my first bullet will kill you. And your father won't grieve for you, because he'll say that he didn't have a warrior son, only a hasty boy.'

The young chief untied his calumet.

'You say that you are my father's friend,' he replied in a different tone. 'So I'll smoke the peace pipe with you too.'

'You are young, but wise,' nodded Old Death, and sat down again. We followed his example.

Great Bear filled his pipe with kinnikinnick. He made a short speech in which he assured us of his friendship, and blew the smoke to the sky, the ground, and also to the four cardinal points of the compass. He passed the pipe to Old Death. The old man also made a speech, and repeated the ceremony. One by one we did the same, except for Sam, but the oath covered him too. Nobody tried to stop him, when Old Death asked him to bring some cigars from his saddle. Only the chief was given a cigar as his warriors could not receive the same present as him. Great Bear knew the cigar, and when he lit it, joy spread on his face.

'Have you met the Apache dogs on the way?' he asked.

'No,' replied Old Death. He did not lie, because he only saw their tracks, but he did not want to betray Winnetou.

'His chief passed here with a wounded companion,' said Great Bear. 'He wants to get to Mexico, but the Comanche warriors will catch him by the Great River, no matter wherever he wants to cross. In particular, we watch the Eagle Pass.'

Old Death glanced at me, but he did not show how unpleasant the news was to him.

'Where are you going?' asked Great Bear.

'We are following a paleface to settle an account with him. He is probably going to Mexico. But as I'm here I would like to visit White Beaver, the great chief. Where is he?'

347

'If you ride to Turkey Creek, you will arrive to a great desert. In this desert the warriors of White Beaver watch whoever arrives to the ford from the Eagle Pass.'

'Excellent! This is our planned route too!'

'Then I suggest that you spend the night with us, my white brothers. You rest, and you can leave tomorrow morning.'

We had to accept the friendly offer. Great Bear stood up, and led us to a huge tree, whose branches hung down deep, and formed a tent. He had our saddles and blankets brought to us. Since smoking the peace pipe he had become a changed man. When we were left alone, we checked our belongings. Nothing was missing. We put the saddles under our heads, and wrapped ourselves in the blankets.

'Good night!' said Old Death, closing his eyes, and soon he was sleeping.

"Good night," easy to say, but I could not fall asleep for a while because of my anxiety for Winnetou. It seemed that the main aim of the Comanche was to capture him. I was lying there, and I could not see any way to protect, or at least warn, my Indian brother. I was tossing and turning half sleeping all night. I rose at the first rays of the Sun. I woke my companions, and we started to get ready. By then the Indians were up as well. I could look at them properly now. I shivered at the look of their painted faces. Their clothing was ragged, but they were all strong, healthy, and tall.

Great Bear asked us if we wanted something to eat. We politely refused the offer saying that we had provisions although it was nothing but a piece of ham. Great Bear wanted to give us a Comanche warrior to lead us to White Beaver. Old Death dissuaded him by saying that it would have been an insult to give a guide to an experienced warrior like himself. He assured Great Bear that we would find the great chief. We filled our bags with water, and accepted some hey for our horses. We said good-bye, and started off. My watch showed four o'clock.

In the beginning of our journey we rode in steps so that the horses could warm up. The ground was still grassy, but slowly it became more and more barren. By the time the trees of the river bank disappeared behind us, there was only sand.

'We have to hurry a bit,' said Old Death, 'because we have to utilise the morning. We will ride to the West for a while, so the Sun will shine on our back. However, in the afternoon it will shine in our eyes. It will be very tiring.'

'Won't we lose our way on this monotonous plain?' I asked as a "greenhorn".

'You not serious, are you?' laughed Old Death. 'We will use the Sun. Our next target is Turkey Creek. It's about sixteen miles from here, but I hope we can get there in two hours.'

We stopped talking, and started to gallop. We did not make any unnecessary movements so that we would not tire our horses. Occasionally we changed from galloping to steps to help the animals.

There was a dark stripe on the horizon, and we could see trees and bushes.

'Check your watch, Sir!' said Old Death. 'We started off two hours and five minutes ago.'

I looked at my watch. His estimate was precise.

'It's only a question of practice,' replied Old Death to my appreciating glance. 'I can tell you the time even in the night. We have arrived to Turkey Creek.'

There was barely any water in the Turkey Creek, but we could refill our water bags. The horses quickly ate the hay that we brought, as there was no grass on the ground for grazing. We let them drink from Will Lange's big sombrero that substituted for a pale. After half an hour's rest we continued to Elm Creek.

The Sun reached the zenith, and its rays were burning. The hot sand was so deep that the horses almost waded in it, which was very tiring for them. At around half past two we had another break, and watered the horses from the water bags. We did not drink as Old Death considered the thirst of the horses more important than ours.

'In any case,' he remarked smiling, 'we are over the most difficult part. I thought we would reach Elm Creek only in the evening, but we'll be there just after five o'clock.'

I noticed that our direction changed, when Old Death said, 'I'm surprised that we haven't seen the tracks of the Comanche. They have wasted a lot of time to find the two Apache. They could have crossed the Rio Grande instead, and could have surprised the Apache villages.'

'It still can happen,' remarked Lange, 'if they can catch Winnetou, and there's nobody to warn them.'

'I wish I knew what happened to Winnetou,' I sighed. 'It would be horrible if the Comanche caught him.'

'It would be horrible,' agreed Old Death. 'They wouldn't kill him, but would take him to one of their village, feed him well, but only because then he could be tortured longer. It would be a great glory for them if they could watch the death of the famous Apache chief. But hopefully it won't happen. Now we are turning to the South to get to the house of an old friend of mine. We will be able to rest and sleep there.'

'Will he welcome us too?'

'Of course! Otherwise I wouldn't call him a friend. He's a rich landowner, and the offspring of an old Spanish family. One of his ancestors became a knight, thus he is entitled use the title of caballero. This is why his estate is called Estanzia del Caballero. You should call him Caballero Atanasio.'

We were impatient, and tried to make the horses gallop, but it was not possible. Their legs sank into the sand almost to their knees. Slowly we got out of the desert, and reached the edge of a prairie, where there was plenty of green grass. *Vaqueros*, that is cowboys, rode with cattle and flock. Our horses started to run at once. For our joy trees appeared, and soon a white building emerged from the green background.

'This is Estanzia del Caballero,' said Old Death. 'It's a very strange house: it was built in the style of the pueblo Indians. It's a fort really, and appropriate for this area.'

When we got closer, we could see the details of the house. It was surrounded by an almost four-yard high, thick wall, which was surrounded by a deep trench. A broad, strong gate was cut into the wall, and a bridge led to this gate. It looked as if the house was built of cubes put on top of each other. We could not see the ground floor because of the wall. The first floor was built further inward from the ground floor, thus there was a terrace in the front of it. It was covered with canvass. There were no windows. Above the first floor there was another, smaller cube, again with a terrace. It was also covered with canvass. Thus every floor was smaller than the lower. There were portholes around the wall on every floor, probably these substituted for the windows.

'A real fort,' said Old Death smiling. 'When we are in, you will be surprised even more. I would like to see an Indian chief who could besiege this house!'

We rode to the gate through the bridge. There was a peeping hole on the gate, and a bell as big as a skull. Old Death pulled it. Its sound was so strong that it probably reached half a mile.

Soon a nose and lips of an Indian appeared in the hole. We were asked in Spanish, 'Who are you?'

'A friend of the Caballero,' replied Old Death. 'Is Señor Atanasio at home?'

The nose and lips disappeared, and two black eyes became visible. Finally we could hear the owner of the nose, lips, and eyes, 'What a joy! Señor Death! Of course, I let you in, Señores. I'll announce you.'

Bolts creaked, a padlock clicked, and the gate opened. We rode in. Behind the gate a fat Indian stood in a white dress. He was one of the *indios fideles*, that is, a Christian Indian, who accepted civilisation, unlike the *indios bravos*, the wild Indians. He closed, and locked the gate, bowed, and then headed towards the house, where he pulled a wire.

'We have enough time to ride around the house,' said Old Death. 'Let's go, and look around.'

Now we could observe the ground floor. There were lines of portholes on all sides. The yard was quite large and grassy. We could not see any door or windows. When we arrived back to the front of the house, the white dressed Indian was there.

'How will we get in the house?' asked Lange.

'You'll see,' replied Old Death.

A man leant forward from the terrace on the first floor to check who were on the ground. When he saw the Indian servant, he retreated, and soon an iron staircase descended. We climbed up on it. We believed that there would be a door on the first floor, but we were wrong. A servant leant forward from the second floor, and lowered a staircase like the previous one. This terrace was covered by tin covered by sand. In the middle we saw an opening. This was the entrance to the inside staircase.

'This is how the Indians built the pueblos for hundreds of years,' explained Old Death. 'It's difficult to get to the yard. Even if the enemy manages it, he is again in front of a wall that doesn't have a door. In peace one could stand on his horse, and pull himself up. But in war, it's not advisable, because from the first floor, and especially from the second, it's a child game to keep the yard and the wall under fire. Señor Atanasio employs about twenty men: *peons*, that is, farm hands, *vaqueros*, servants. All have guns, and are sharpshooters. If there are twenty such brave men on this floor, the attackers would lose a hundred men by the time they get in. This type of house is very useful here, and our haciendero can boast with a number of defeated sieges.'

One could see for a distance from the second floor. The Elm Creek ran just behind the house. It had clear water, and irrigated the banks. It was very appealing, and I had the desire to swim in it.

The servant led us down on the stairs, and we arrived to a long and narrow corridor. The light came from two portholes at the two ends. There were doors on both sides, and at the back another staircase led to the ground floor.

Thus to get into the house, one first had to climb up two floors outside, and then two floors down in the house. It was quite uncomfortable, but perfectly reasonable in this area. The servant disappeared behind the door. When he returned a few minutes later, he announced to us that the caballero was waiting for us. Old Death warned us in advance, 'Don't be surprised if Atanasio receives us ceremoniously. The Spanish pay a lot of attention to etiquette, and the caballero is a pure Spaniard. Had I arrived alone, he would have met me much earlier. But he receives strangers in a formal way. Don't smile if he puts on a uniform. When he was younger, he was a captain in the Mexican cavalry, and sometimes he likes putting on his old uniform. However, he's a very good man, and friend.'

The servant opened the door. We entered a pleasantly cool room. The furniture once must have been expensive, but now quite worn. Through three portholes dim light entered. In the middle of the room a tall, lean man stood. His hair and moustache were white like snow. He wore a pair of trousers decorated with a broad, gilded stripe. His mirror-bright boots had spurs that were bigger than the silver Thaler coin. He wore a blue dinner jacket with much gilding. The epaulettes were decorated as such as if they indicated a general, and not a captain. He had a huge sword, and in his left hand he held a triangular hat covered with more gilding, and two feather bunches. To me it looked like some carnival outfit, but when I looked in the old, serious face of our host, and also into his still bright, friendly eyes, I did not have any inclination to smirk at him.

When we entered he saluted us, pulled himself straight, and addressed us, 'Good afternoon, gentlemen! Welcome! Enjoy your stay in my house.'

We bowed, and it was Old Death, who answered on our behalf, 'Thank you caballero! Thank you captain! As we were around here, I wanted to give the honour to my friends to meet an old and brave fighter of Mexico's independence. Let me introduce them to you.'

353

For the flattering words a broad smile appeared on the caballero's face. He nodded, and said, 'I'm glad to shake hands with your friends.'

Old Death introduced us one by one, the caballero shook hands with us, including Sam, then offered us seats. Old Death asked about the Señora and the Señorita, for which the host opened a door, and the two ladies entered. The Señora still had some of her beauty, and her eyes were open, while the Señorita, their granddaughter, was an extremely attractive young girl. Both were dressed in black silk. Old Death shook hands with the elderly lady, the Langes were bowing clumsily, and Sam was smiling at the appearance of the ladies.

I stepped up to the lady of the house, held her hand with the tip of my fingers, and breathed a kiss on it. The lady rewarded my politeness by offering her face for a *beso de cortesia*. The Señorita did the same.

After this we sat down again. Their first question was, of course, the purpose of our travel. We told them everything honestly, including our encounter with the Comanche. They listened attentively, but I also noticed that the host exchanged looks with his wife. Then he asked if we could give a better description of the two men whom we followed. I took out the photos. After a single look the Señora exclaimed, 'They are, aren't they, for sure!'

'No doubt,' nodded the caballero. 'These men stayed here last night.'

'When did they leave?' I asked excitedly.

'They arrived late in the night, deadly tired. One of my *vaqueros* met them, and brought them to the house. They slept till about noon. They left about three hours ago.'

'Excellent!' said Old Death. 'Then tomorrow we will definitely catch up with them.'

'They were heading to the Rio Grande, and wanted to cross it by the Eagle Pass. I had to send a few *vaqueros* after them, they will tell you exactly which way they went.'

'Why did you have to send your men after them?'

'Because these people returned my hospitality with ungratefulness. On the way they met my horse herd, sent away the *vaquero* with some excuse, and stole six horses.'

'The rascals! But I'm not surprised,' said Old Death. 'Did they talk about their plans?'

'Not at all. One was very talkative and funny, the other very quiet. It didn't occur to me to be suspicious. They asked me to show them around the house, which I did. I even showed them the wounded Indian, who found refuge in my house.'

'Wounded Indian? How did he come here?'

'It's an interesting story about the same Indian whom you talked about.' smiled the caballero with some superiority. 'The one who represented the Apache in Fort Inge, but then the Comanche tried to kill. His name is Inda Nisho, the oldest chief of the Apache.'

'The Good Man! He really deserves his name,' exclaimed Old Death. 'The cleverest Indian chief who always wanted peace. I'd like to see him!'

'I'll lead you to him. He was half dead when he arrived. You have to know that the famous Winnetou likes me, and always visits me when he comes around this area. On the way he met Inda Nisho, who was shot in his arm and his thigh. Winnetou tied his wounds by the Leona River, and then rode on. But the old man was suffering from traumatic fever, and also the Comanche were everywhere. Winnetou brought the wounded man here, I don't understand how he could do it; only Winnetou is capable of achieving this. But Inda Nisho was running out of his strength; he had lost a lot of blood, and he's over seventy years of age.'

'Unbelievable! Sitting on the horse from Fort Inge to here wounded! It's more than hundred and sixty miles! Only an Indian can cope with this at his age. Please continue.'

'They arrived after sunset, and pulled the bell. I went to the gate, and for my surprise it was Winnetou. He told me everything, and asked me to protect the wounded until he could send someone for him. He had to cross the Rio Grande

355

to warn the Apache tribes of the danger and the treachery. I gave him my two best *vaqueros*.'

'Have they returned?'

'Yes, Winnetou crossed the river. They didn't cross at the ford, but downstream, where the water is very quick. It's very dangerous to swim across the river there, but they succeeded. The *vaqueros* accompanied him until he was far enough from the Comanche. So he was able to warn his tribe. But let's now go to the old chief if you want.'

We stood up, greeted the ladies, and went to the ground floor. There was a similar corridor there as on the floor above. We entered the last door on the left.

The old chief lay in a pleasantly cool room. His fever had abated, but he was still so weak that he could hardly speak. His face was sunken. There was no doctor, but the caballero said that Winnetou knew the treatment of wounds. He put herbs on Inda Nisho's wounds, and told them not to loosen the bandage. Once the traumatic fever had gone, the life of the chief was not in danger, even though the loss of blood made him weak.

When we left the room, I mentioned to our host that I would like to swim in the river.

'Then you don't have to go upstairs,' he replied. 'I'll let you out through the back yard.'

'I thought there was no door in this building.'

'There is, but it's a secret one. It's an emergency exit if the hostile Indians enter the house. You'll see it.'

There was a cupboard by the wall. Our host pushed it aside, and I could see the narrow passage that led to the yard. Shrubs completely hid it on the other side. The caballero led me out, and pointed at the wall opposite where similar shrubs were planted.

'You can get through there. This is the shortest way to the river. Very few know about it. If you wait a bit, I'll send a more comfortable dress for you.'

At this moment the bell tolled. The host hurried there, and I followed him. Five riders stood by the gate. These strong men were the *vaqueros* who had been sent after the horse thieves.

'Well?' asked the haciendero, 'have you caught them?'

'No,' answered one of them, 'even though we got very close to them. When they crossed the Elm Creek, they had only a quarter of an hour advantage on us. But then we found new tracks: tracks of many horses. We understood that the thieves met the Comanche. We carefully followed the tracks, and caught sight of them. There were at least five hundred Comanche there, so we had to retreat.'

'You done well. Where did they go?'

'To the Rio Grande.'

'So away from here. Good,' said the master. 'You may go.'

Señor Atanasio walked back to the house. I was not as calm. If Gibson told the Comanche that Inda Nisho was in this house, unpleasant surprises could happen to us.

Soon a *peon* came with a white suit on his arm. He led me to the river, and said, 'Just leave your clothing with me, Señor. After swimming put this white suit on, it's much more appropriate here.'

As soon as he left me alone, I jumped in the river. After the hot day it was a joy to swim in the deep river. I swam for about half an hour, then dried myself a bit, and dressed. I accidentally glanced at the other side of the river. Among the trees I could see as far as the bend of the river. For my shock I saw a long line of Indian riders.

I quickly rushed to the gate, pulled the bell. The *peon* who took my clothing let me in.

'Quickly to the caballero!' I said panting. 'Indian riders are coming in a gallop towards the house.'

'How many?'

'At least fifty!'

When the *peon* heard the number, he became calm.

'Only fifty?' he said, 'Then there's no problem. We can easily manage them. But I have to let the *vaqueros* know and you, señor, hurry to the caballero! Don't forget to lock the gate, and to pull the ladder up.'

Señor Atanasio was also calm.

'What tribe do they belong to?' he asked.

'I don't know, I couldn't recognise the colours from such a distance.'

'Maybe they are Apache whom Winnetou sent for the wounded chief,' said the caballero. 'But even if they are Comanche, it's not a problem. They are probably scouts. They'll ask if we saw the Apache, and then leave.'

'We have to prepare for the worst,' said Old Death.

'All my men know what they have to do in such a situation,' replied the caballero. 'Look, the *peon* is already riding to inform the *vaqueros*. Two will stay with the animals, while the rest will march against the Indians. Their lasso is a dangerous weapon, and it's worth more than the bows or the guns of the Indians have. Fortunately you are here too. There are eight servants in the house. So, we have fourteen men to defend the house. That's more than enough.'

Old Death shook his head, and said, 'They don't want to attack the house, they came for the wounded man.'

'They cannot suspect that he's here.'

'They don't suspect, but they know it. Gibson told them to get their support.'

'I didn't think of that. Do you think they will try to force me to surrender the wounded chief?'

'Yes. Will you?'

'Never,' stated the caballero. 'Winnetou entrusted to me the Good Man, and I won't let him down. I won't let them in the house.'

'We can defend against fifty warriors, but if they bring five hundred, we are lost.'

'We are in God's hand,' he replied. 'I made a promise to Winnetou, and I'll stand by my words in all circumstances.'

'It's worthy of you, señor! You can rely on our help. I know the chief of the Comanche, maybe I can soften him a bit. Did you show the secret door to Gibson too?'

'No, señor.'

'Good. If the Comanche don't know of this door, they cannot get in the house. Let's bring the guns.'

While I was out, they arranged rooms for us, and took our belongings there. My room was on the front side of the house. A porthole let in the light. My gun was hanging on the wall. When I lifted it down, and peeped out, I could see the Indians. They would be by the gate very soon. Instead of their usual yelling, they approached in a mean quietness. I felt that it was even more threatening. I could recognise the colours on their faces; they were Comanche indeed. All had spears, bows and arrows, but only their leader had a gun. I saw that some riders were pulling some long thing. First I thought that these were tent poles, but I soon recognised that I was wrong. When they got to the gate I lost sight of them, because the tall wall covered them. I hurried out of my room to inform the others. In the corridor I bumped into Old Death, who also rushed out of his room.

'Look out,' he shouted. 'They cut down young trees to use them as ladders! They are climbing over the wall. Let's go up to the top floor!'

We could not be quick enough, because the servants, who lived on the ground floor, were also moving up on the stairs. In addition the caballero also stepped out with the ladies, and all the three asked many anxious questions. Two important minutes had been lost because of this.

By the time we got up to the top floor, the first Indian was already at the edge of the terrace, and behind him the second, third, and fourth. Although we had guns in our hands, but without shooting at the Indians, they were useless, but, for the time being, we wanted to avoid bloodshed.

'Let's aim at them!' cried Old Death. 'If they come any closer, we are shooting!'

There were now twenty-five Comanche at the edge of the terrace with their bows ready. They left their spears on the ground as these would have obstructed them in climbing. They surprised us, but for the time being they did not dare to approach. The caballero stepped forward, and shouted at them in the mixed language that was commonly used at the frontiers.

'What do want here, my Indian brothers? How dare you enter my house without my permission?'

Their leader stepped forward, and answered, 'The Comanche warriors came because you are our enemy! You won't see tomorrow's sunrise!'

'I'm not an enemy of the Comanche. All Indians are my brothers, irrespective of the tribe.'

'You are lying, paleface! You hid the old Apache chief in your house. Whoever supports the Apache are our enemy, and will be killed!'

'Carramba! Do you want to tell me whom I can take in my house, and whom I cannot? Who's the master of this house, I or you?'

'We occupied your house, so we are the masters! Give up the Apache! Or do you dare to deny that you have him?'

'I don't deny anything! Only those lie who are afraid! I'm not a coward and I tell you ...'

'Stop!' whispered Old Death decidedly. 'For God's sake, Señor, think of what you are saying!'

'Should I lie then?' whispered the caballero.

'Of course! I hate lies too, but this is an exceptional situation. Which is the bigger sin: lying or suicide?'

'We aren't yet there!' flared up the caballero.

'Let me do the talking,' whispered Old Death, and he pulled back our host.

Now he stepped forward, and shouted to the Comanche, 'Why are you insulting the master of the house without a reason? How do you know that there's an Apache chief in the house?'

'We know it,' said the Comanche leader stubbornly.

'Then you know more than we do.'

'You're lying.'

'If you say this again, you'll die! Can you see these guns? They'll go off at my command!'

'Who are you that you dare to speak to me?' asked the Indian, and then he added in a despising tone, 'You aren't the master of the house!'

'And who are you?' replied Old Death. 'You aren't a chief, because you don't have an eagle feather in your hair. You cannot be a leading warrior, because otherwise you'd know whom you are speaking to. I'm a chief among the palefaces. I smoked the peace pipe with Oyo Koltsa, the great chief of the Comanche, and even with Avat Vila yesterday. I'm Kosha Pehveh, who has always been the friend of the Comanche.' A small murmur ran through the rows of the Indians. Their curious look showed what an impression the name made on them. The leader of the group had a short discussion with other warriors, turned to us, and spoke in a more moderate tone, 'The Comanche warriors know who Kosha Pehveh is. They know that he's a famous chief, and a great warrior. But if he's a friend of the Comanche, why doesn't he give over the Apache chief?'

'Just because he's not here!' stated Old Death decidedly, without moving his eyelids.

'A paleface told us that he is here.'

'What was the name of the paleface?'

'His name is not for a Comanche's tongue. Ta-hie-ha-ho or something like this.'

'Maybe Gavilano?'

'Yes, perhaps.'

'Then the Comanche made a mistake. I know that man. His heart is mean, and his tongue lies all the time. The Comanche warriors will regret that they protect him.'

'You are wrong. The paleface said the truth. We know that the Inda Nisho was wounded in his arms and legs. Winnetou found him on the prairie; he took him after treating his wounds. Then he brought him here, and then he rode away. Maybe he had crossed the Avat-Hona, that the palefaces call Rio Grande, but we'll catch him, and he'll die on the torture stake. I even know where they hid the wounded man in this house.'

'Tell me if you know!'

'Two stairs down, where there is a narrow corridor with many doors. One has to turn to the left, and enter the last door. Inda Nisho lies there, because he's weak.'

'The paleface lied. There's no Apache there.'

'Then why don't you let me to check it?'

'Because only the master of the house can allow it. You didn't ask his permission to enter.'

'Your words show that the Apache chief is here. White Beaver ordered us to take the Apache to him, and we will.'

'Don't you believe Old Death? Do you want to enter with force? Then try it! On the stairs one man is enough to shoot anyone who dares to approach. I'm the friend of the Comanche, and I don't like shedding blood. I advise you to go back to the front of the gate, toll the bell, and then ask permission to enter. This is the right way! Then you may be received in a friendly way.'

'Your advice is bad, Kosha Pehveh,' answered the Indian. 'We won't move from here until you let us in. Meanwhile we'll send a messenger to the main group, and we will have so many warriors that you will have to speak differently.'

'You're wrong,' argued Old Death in a friendly tone, but stubbornly. 'My bullet will kill your messenger as soon as he steps out from behind the wall. We can defend this entrance against ten times ten warriors if necessary. I'm a friend of the Comanche, but I won't give in to force.'

His determination made the Indian think. After a short hesitation he asked, 'If we toll the bell, will you let us in?'

'I have to ask the master of the house,' he replied. 'Wait in peace, you'll get an answer.'

Holding his gun ready he retreated, and there he held a quiet council with us.

'It's a damned situation!' he said scratching his ear. 'If we resist openly, they can finish us off. We can't hide the wounded man anywhere because they will search the whole house.'

'Then let's hide him outside the house,' I proposed.

'Are you mad, Sir?' he asked in an irritated voice. 'How do you imagine it?'

'Have you forgotten the two secret gates? They open to the backyard, and the Comanche are at the front. I'll take the wounded man to the river, and hide him in the bushes.'

'This is a good idea,' nodded the old man. 'It didn't come to my mind. We could take him out there ... if the Comanche haven't put guards up there too.'

'I don't think so. They have fifty warriors at the most, some are needed for guarding the horses; they don't have surplus men.'

'Right. Try it, Sir. With the help of one of the *peons* you may succeed. We'll make it sure here that they don't become suspicious by standing next to each other very closely, so they won't notice that two men have gone. When you have left the house, the ladies will push back the cupboard to its place.'

'Then I have another idea. Why don't the ladies move to the room of the wounded man? When the Indians see that women live there, all their suspicion will go. They wouldn't think that an Indian slept there.

'Excellent,' said Atanasio. 'It's enough if they put down some blankets, and take the hammocks over. There are hooks for them in every room. The ladies will rest there, and they will wait until everything is over. For the Apache the best place is where you swam. The branches of the flowering petunia bushes lean over the water, and we have a boat under that. Lay the Apache in the boat, and nobody will see him. Take Petro, and we'll wait until you return. We won't let the Indians in until then.'

With the *peon* called Petro I hurried to the room where the ladies retreated waiting for the developments of the siege. They were excited and anxious. When I informed them of the situation, they immediately helped. They carried the blankets, and the hammocks to the room. We wrapped up the old Indian chief in blankets.

When he learnt that the Comanche were looking for him, he said in a weak voice, 'Inda Nisho has seen many winters, and his days are numbered. Why should the good palefaces put their lives in danger for him? Give Inda Nisho over to the Comanche, or kill him right now. This is my last request.'

I shook my head decidedly, and then carried him out of the room. We pushed the cupboard aside, and we got to the back wall.

Nobody had noticed anything. Behind the wall there were thick bushes, which hid us well. But we had to get to the river through open ground.

I peeped out, and for my big disappointment I spotted a Comanche, who sat on the ground. His spear was next to him, while his bow and quiver were on his knee. His task was to watch the back of the house, which made our plan impossible.

'We have to go back to the house, Señor,' said the *peon*, when I pointed out the Comanche guard to him. 'We may be able to kill him, but it would be useless as the others would take a revenge.'

'I don't want to kill him. But maybe I can distract him, or pull him away from his place.'

'I don't think so. A guard won't leave his post until he's replaced.'

'Still, I have an idea, and it may succeed. Stay here, I'll show myself. If he sees me, I'll pretend to be frightened, and I'll run away. He'll chase me surely.'

'Or he will send an arrow.'

'I have to risk that.'

'Don't do that, señor! The Comanche are as sure with their bows as we are with our guns. If you try to escape, you'll have to turn your back to him, and then you won't see when he sends the arrow.'

'I'll jump in the river, and escape towards the other bank. I'll swim on my back, and I can watch him then. If he shoots, I'll dive. Then he will think that I'm planning something against his comrades, and he'll jump in the river to follow me. I'll attack him on the other bank. Don't leave your hiding place until I return. I saw the petunia bushes when I swam. I'll go for the boat, and bring it here.'

The *peon* tried to dissuade me from my dare-devil plan, but I did not listen to him as I could not see any other solution. So that the guard would not know our hiding place, I stole along the wall in the bushes, and then stepped out suddenly as if I had just turned by the corner of the house.

The Comanche immediately spotted me, turned to me, and jumped up. As much as I could, I tried to hide my face so that he would not be able to recognise me later. He shouted at me to stop, but as I did not obey, he picked up his bow and one arrow. Before he could shoot, I reached the bushes on the bank with a few leaps, and jumped in the river. With strong strokes I swam towards the other bank on my back. In a few minutes he broke through the shrubs, spotted me, and aimed. The bow hummed, and I dived. When I came to the surface again, I saw him watching the water to see where I would turn up. He noticed me, but he did not have any more arrows, because he left his quiver at his guarding place. He threw his bow on the ground, and jumped in the water. This was what I wanted. To lure him further, I pretended to be a bad swimmer: I kicked about, and allowed him to get closer to me. Then I dived, and swam downstream with all my strength. When I came to the surface, I was already very close to the other bank, while the Comanche was looking for me in the distance. Now I could climb out of the water. I rushed along the river with great leaps. I noticed a thick, old oak tree that was just right for my plan. I rushed by it at a distance of five steps, then changed my direction, and with a detour I returned to it. I hid behind the tree. The Indian lost sight of me, thus he had to watch my tracks to be able to follow me. When he passed by the oak tree, the roles were reversed, as I started to follow him. He was panting so loudly that he could not hear my quiet steps. At the right time I jumped on him, and he fell on the ground headlong. By the time he lifted his head, I was kneeling on his back. I delivered two blows, and he was out.

365

Not too far from this place, there was a fallen plantain tree trunk. Half of its foliage and its dead branches hanged over the bank and into the river. I recognised that if I entered the river there, I would not leave traces. I stepped on the trunk, ran along it, and then jumped in the water. The petunia bushes were on the other side. I swam there, untied the boat, and rowed to the place where we wanted to put the wounded man. I tied the boat to a root.

We had to act very quickly. With the *peon* I carried the wounded man to the boat, made a nest of blankets, and then I rowed with the boat to the petunia bushes. I tied the boat, and then crawled back towards the house. By the wall I quickly undressed, and twisted my clothing to dry it. I also tried to find out whether the knocked out Comanche had recovered, but I could not see him from my position. Finally we returned to the house through the hidden door.

The whole adventure took less than a quarter of an hour. I got a new suit from the Señora, and changed. If somebody had seen me, he would not have thought that I had been in the water a few minutes earlier.

The ladies settled in the hammocks, and I hurried up to the terrace with the *peon*. Naturally we did not forget our weapons. The negotiations were still going on. Old Death cleverly extended it by arguing that the search would be an insult to the host. I whispered to him that the wounded man was safe. From then on he became more accommodating in the negotiations. Finally he said that five Comanche could enter the house.

'Why only five?' asked the Indian. 'None of our warriors are worse than the others! Or are you afraid of theft?'

'Fine!' said Old Death. 'As you wish. All of you can come in, but without weapons. Put your weapons down where you are standing!'

The Comanche discussed the request, and accepted it. They put down their bows and quivers at the edge of the terrace, and then entered the house. The *vaqueros* were getting ready outside. I saw that they lined up not far from

366

the gate with guns and lassos in their hands, and they were waiting for the signal of their master.

We also made our safety arrangements: two men stayed on the terrace, while everybody else was positioned along the corridors to intervene if it was necessary. I stood by the room where the wounded man had been resting earlier. The Comanche were heading straight there.

Old Death opened the door. As the Indians were sure that they would find Good Man there, they recoiled when they saw the ladies. The ladies were reading books in the hammocks.

'Uff!' exclaimed their leader, disappointed. 'But this is the room of the squaws.'

'Of course!' laughed Old Death. 'You surely don't believe that the wounded Apache is here? Search the room!'

The Comanche's eyes flitted around the walls, and then he said, 'A Comanche warrior wouldn't step in the room of the women. I can see that there isn't anyone else here.'

'Then search the other rooms!'

The search took a whole hour. As they could not find any trace of the wounded man, the Comanche returned to the "squaws' room". The ladies had to leave, and the Comanche searched the room very thoroughly. They even lifted the blankets to see if there was a hollow under the floor. At the end their leader had to admit that we were not hiding any Apache in the house.

'I told you, but you didn't believe me,' shrugged Old Death. 'You would rather believe to the liar paleface than me, an old friend of the Comanche. I'll visit Oyo Koltsa, and I will complain to him.'

'You want to talk to the great chief, my white brother? Then you can come with us.'

'My horse is tired, I can go only tomorrow, while you are leaving now.'

'No, we stay too. It's sunset already, and we don't like riding in the night. We could leave tomorrow together.'

'Very good, but I have four companions.'

367

'They are also welcome. Would you allow us, my white brothers, to stay near the house during the night?'

'I have no objections,' said the caballero. 'I said that I'm a friend of all Indians, who approach us with peaceful intentions. And to show this to you, I'm offering you a fat ox. Make a fire, and roast it.'

The generous offer made the Comanche contented, and now they felt that their earlier threatening behaviour was unjust. Of course, Old Death's name and reputation also contributed to this change. They did not touch anything in the house, and left it in order. We lowered the stairs, and opened the gate. The caballero ordered one of the *vaqueros* to slaughter an ox for the Indians.

The horses of the Comanche stood by the gate. Three warriors guarded them. There were some guards behind the house, and they were now called back. One of them was the Comanche whom I lured to the other side of the river. He had not yet had the opportunity to report. He went to the leader in his wet clothing, and talked to him. He kept on glancing at me. I could not read from his facial expression because of the painting, but judging from his voice, he was rather angry.

He pointed at me a number of times, and finally the leader stepped up to me.

'This young paleface swam across the river just before. Why did he knock out the guard?'

I pretended that I could not understand his words. Old Death hurried to my help, and asked what it was about.

When he heard it, he laughed.

'My Comanche brothers cannot differentiate between the palefaces,' he said, 'maybe he wasn't even a white man.'

'He was a paleface!' insisted the guard. 'I know that it was him,' he pointed at me again. 'I could see his face when he swam on his back. He wore the same clothing as now!'

'Don't tell me!' mocked Old Death. 'He was dressed when he was swimming! But your clothing is wet, and his is dry.'

'Maybe he put on dry ones when he entered the house!'

368

'Where? How? Your warriors stood by the gate, they would have noticed him. And we lowered the ladders only now. Did he climb up on the wall? No! He could not possibly leave the house!'

They looked at each other confused, and finally even the guard believed that he was mistaken. The caballero then remarked that there were horse thieves around, and they had stolen some of his horses. Could it be that a tramp attacked the guard? He added that searching the area for the attacker would benefit him. The leader of the group was inclined to do the search, but it was already getting dark, thus it was meaningless to send out scouts.

The crafty Old Death took me by my arm for a walk. First we walked up and down along the river, then further to the petunia bushes.

The old man stopped there, looked around, and as if he was talking to me, said quietly, 'Kosha Pehveh is here with the young paleface who brought you here. Can you recognise my voice?'

'Yes,' we heard the weak voice.

'The Comanche will leave tomorrow morning. Will my brother survive the night here?'

'Definitely. There's a good breeze from the river, and it refreshes me. Will you be here for long?'

'No. We will go with the Comanche.'

'Why do you join our enemies, Kosha Pehveh?'

'We are pursuing two men. They found refuge with the Comanche.'

'Will you meet Apache warriors?'

'That could happen,' replied Old Death.

'I would like to give a totem to the young paleface who risked his life for me. If he is among the Apache, they will treat him well if he shows my totem. Kosha Pehveh is an experienced warrior. When it's dark, you can steal here. I'd like you to bring me a piece of white leather and a knife. During the night I'll make the totem, and you can come for it before dawn.'

369

'It will be done,' said Old Death, and asked, 'Do you need anything else?'

'Nothing. May the Good Spirit guard the path of Kosha Pehveh and his young friend.'

We walked back to the house. Nobody noticed that we stopped for a minute by the petunia bushes. Old Death remarked, 'It's rare that a white man gets the totem of an Indian chief. You are lucky, Sir. The totem of Good Man can help you a lot.'

'Are you really taking the leather and the knife? It's very risky. If the Comanche notice it, we are finished!'

'Trust me, young man! I know very well what I can risk and what I cannot.'

Nothing disturbed our night.

At dawn Old Death woke me, and gave me a square piece of leather that was tanned to white. I looked at it, but I could not see anything on it, apart from some scratches on the smooth side.

'Is it a totem?' I asked. 'I can't see anything on it.'

'You can't see the writing, because Good Man didn't have paint. But if you give it to an Apache, he will paint the scratches, and the symbols will be visible. But for goodness sake, make it sure that the Comanche don't find it on you! Now get dressed as we have to leave soon.'

The front of the house was busy. The Comanche had finished their breakfast. It was the leftover from the dinner. They led their horses to the river to water them, fortunately far from the place where the old chief was hidden. Soon the caballero came down with the ladies, who were now not afraid of the Comanche at all.

When the *vaqueros* led our horses out, our host, the caballero, shook his head.

'This is not a good enough horse for you, Señor,' he told Old Death. 'You know the value of a good horse. I don't care how Lange, his son, and the black man go, but I'd like to give you and your young friend, who did such a great service to us yesterday, two really good horses.'

We accepted his present, and he ordered his *vaquero* to bring us two mustangs. We said good-bye to our host and the ladies, and left with the Comanche.

The Sun had not yet risen on the horizon, when we had already crossed Elm Creek, and galloped to the West. Our group of five rode in the front with the leader of the Comanche. I felt uncomfortable, and turned back several times fearful of a spear being thrown into my back or an arrow being shot at me. I did not trust these poorly dressed warriors with their painted faces, who were riding on lean, long-haired, yet enduring horses. However, Old Death's behaviour calmed me. He started to talk to their leader, and learnt a few things. The main group did not stop when they sent out the fifty warriors to capture Good Man. They had been ordered that after accomplishing their task, they should ride to the Rio Grande, and try to catch up with the main group of the Comanche. White Beaver learnt from Gibson that Winnetou had crossed the border, and was gathering the warriors of the Apache villages in Mexico. The Comanche had to hurry if they wanted to surprise the Apache. I also wanted to hurry as I hoped that I would still find Gibson with the Comanche.

In two hours we arrived to the place from where the fifty warriors had been sent to the hacienda. We were not far from the Eagle Pass. Fort Duncan was also near, and the Comanche wanted to avoid the fort. After another two hours' riding the ground became more grassy: we were probably near the river.

The Comanche leader was relieved that they could get there without being noticed. We slowed down, and rode in step among ash trees and elm trees. The track of the main group led straight to the ford. The Rio Grande was very broad there, but shallow with sand banks sticking out of the water. Many signs suggested that the main group spent the previous night at this place. Probably they left at dawn, but they could not advance quickly. They were now on hostile territory, thus they had to send out scouts to all directions.

We could see from the marking sticks that they had crossed the river with great care. These sticks had been pushed in the riverbed by the scouts so that the main group could avoid the vortexes.

We also crossed the river, and continued our journey between the Rio Grande and the Bolsón de Mapimi. The latter is a stone desert, a completely barren plateau covered with eroded stones.

I admired the endurance of the small Indian horses. It was late afternoon, and the mustangs were still riding hard, while the horses of the two Langes and Sam barely could keep up with them. We were grateful for the horses that the caballero gave us in exchange of our nags.

At a point, which we reached at sunset, the tracks of the main group suddenly turned to the South-west. Why? Our little group stopped. Old Death dismounted, examined the ground, and then summarised his findings.

'The main group stopped here as you can see from the broader track. Two riders arrived from the North, and joined the Comanche. Maybe this is why they stopped. But I'm sure that these two riders brought important news, and this made White Beaver change his direction.'

Whatever had happened, we had to turn to the Southwest to follow the tracks. Suddenly my horse neighed, and started to run. It probably smelt water. Indeed in a few minutes we arrived to a river. It was a joy for the men and the animals after such a long, forced gallop.

We found a place for camping, and set up the guards. We watered the horses, and everybody rested. Old Death thought that we were by the Rio Escondido that enters the Rio Grande not far from Fort Duncan.

'I cannot understand why White Beaver changed the direction,' he frowned. 'Do you know where we are?'

'Near the Bolsón de Mapimi.'

'Yes, and we won't enjoy it. The worst possible terrain. But it's a smaller problem. I'm more anxious because there are Apache settlements to all directions. In the North,

372

between Rio Grande and the Pecos River there are many Apache villages. There are many Apache bands among the mountains of Mapimi, and also to the South-west. I'm afraid the Comanche are in a trap.'

'And we too?'

'We'll survive it as we didn't do anything against the Apache, and hopefully they won't be hostile to us. In the worst case, we'll show Good Man's totem to them. But the Comanche won't have a great future.'

'Why don't you warn their leader?'

'I did, but he said that I shouldn't interfere.'

'Quite rude.'

'Yes, and also stupid. Anyway, it cannot be helped. We have crossed the border, but whether we can get back is hidden in the future.'

NEAR THE MAPIMI

IN THE BEGINNING I had hoped that I could catch Gibson in the United States. Now I had to go after him to Mexico, and moreover, to the most dangerous part of Mexico. Gibson apparently was heading to Chihuahua through the Mapimi desert. It was not a pleasant thought that I would have to continue to chase him on such a terrain, not to mention that we arrived to the border rather tired, which was visible even on the trained Comanche. We had ridden a good distance at a high speed from the Estanzia del Caballero. The Indians lived on dried meat, but we still had some food that the caballero had packed for us.

The ground was ascending to the South as we stumbled among barren rocks. The tracks showed that the main group also advanced very slowly here. Above us vultures were circling. They had followed us for hours waiting to see if they could come down on a dead horse or human.

In the early hours of the afternoon a dark strip appeared on the horizon, and the horses started to pick up speed. They smelt water. Old Death's face brightened.

'I think we are near the Sabinas River. Where there is water,' he said, 'there is grass and forest, and maybe even game. Let's spur our horses to gallop! The more they strain themselves now, the sooner they get their rest.'

The tracks of the main group turned to the East into a long, narrow gorge. After the gorge we arrived to a green valley with a brook in the middle of it. We jumped off the saddle, and watered the horses. Although the Comanche wanted to push on, their horses also needed water. We then continued the journey from the valley into another gorge. We could ride only in a single file in the canyon. The walls of the canyon were tall rock. They were so tall that they seemed to reach the sky.

At sunset we wanted to stop to camp, but the leader of the Comanche thought differently. He was very inpatient, and wanted to catch up with the main group during the night.

Soon we heard a shout for which our guide responded with a joyous cry. Old Death rode forward, and later he returned with the news that the main group was camping there.

'They didn't dare to advance before scouting the area, and their scouts, whom they sent out at noon, haven't yet returned. I learnt that much. We'll see the campfires soon.'

'Surely, they cannot be so light-headed to make fires?' I said surprised.

'Maybe the terrain allows it there,' said Old Death.

We left the canyon, and spotted about ten little fires. The Indians knew how to keep the flames down.

We were at the entrance of a large, round valley. As far as we could see, it was surrounded by high, steep rock walls. Probably this is why the Comanche chose this place.

Our guides rode directly to the camp, but we were ordered to wait until they came for us. We had to wait a long time until a Comanche came to lead us to the chief, who was sitting at the middle fire with two elder warriors.

The long hair of the chief was grey. He wore it in a bun and he had three eagle feathers in it. He wore moccasins and a pair of black trousers. The colour of his vest was slightly lighter. His double-barrelled gun was next to his leg. There was an outdated pistol in his belt. He had a knife and a piece of meat in his hand, but when he saw us, he immediately put them aside. The whole place was smelling of roast horse meat. Near the fire, where the chief sat, a small stream murmured.

As soon as we dismounted, five or six warriors took our horses, and led them away. As Old Death accepted this, I did not protest. I noticed some white faces among the warriors. The chief stood up, and the two elder warriors followed his example.

'Your arrival, Kosha Pehveh, is a pleasant surprise,' he said in the mixed language of the frontiers. By this time I could understand it. The chief offered his hand according to the custom of the white men. 'I'm happy that you are here, and you'll fight against the Apache dogs with us.'

Old Death used the same flowery language. 'The Good Spirit leads his white and red children on surprising paths. I'm very happy when I meet a good friend, a great warrior, like Oyo Koltsa, who is not only brave, but also faithful. Are you ready to smoke the peace pipe with my friends, great chief of the Comanche?'

'Your friends are my friends,' said White Beaver. 'They can sit down, and smoke the peace pipe with the chief of the Comanche.'

Old Death sat down next to the fire, and we followed his example. Only Sam pulled aside, and sat down in the grass. The Indians stood silently and motionlessly like so many statues. Behind them there were some white men, but I could not differentiate their faces, because the light of the fire was not bright enough. White Beaver took his pipe, and filled it with tobacco. The ceremony was the same as the one we had performed with his son. Now we did not have to be afraid of the hostility of the Comanche.

While we had been waiting outside the camp, our guide had reported on the events at the hacienda. White Beaver asked Old Death to tell him what had happened. My old friend made his report in a way that helped to dissolve the suspicion towards us, and also towards Señor Atanasio.

White Beaver was musing for a few minutes, and then he said, 'I have to believe your words, my white brother. But I also have to believe the words of the paleface who is with us. He has no reason to lie to me, and he knows that if he did, he would die. It seems to me that you were misled, my white brother.'

He spoke politely, but very perceptively. Old Death saw that he had to be careful. White Beaver might even send back some men to search the house again.

'Old Death's eyes are sharp, and cannot be misled. It's you, Oyo Koltsa, who was misled by the lies of that paleface!'

'I smoked the peace pipe with him!' exclaimed the chief.

'You offered him your calumet?' Old Death showed surprise. 'I'm really sorry that I arrived only now, because I would have intervened. That paleface doesn't deserve such an honour!'

'Why?'

'You'll see later. But tell me first, do you like Juárez?'

White Beaver made a dismissing movement with his hand, and responded, 'Juárez is an estranged Indian. He lives in a stone house, and lives like the white men. I hate him, and despise him. The Comanche warriors offered their services to Napoleon, who gave us weapons, horses, and blankets, and also gave us the Apache. The palefaces who are here are also Napoleon's friends.'

'This is the lie with which they misled you! They came to join Juárez's army. Do you know whom the Great White Father in Washington supports?'

'Juárez.'

'That's right. They recruit soldiers for Juárez, and they send them over the border in secret. In La Grange there is a Mexican Spaniard, whose name is Cortesio. We visited him when we were there, and these two men on my right are his neighbours. He told us that he was recruiting soldiers for Juárez. The palefaces who are with you came from him. You are Juárez's enemy, and you smoked the peace pipe with Juárez's soldiers! It's not your fault, you were misled.'

The eyes of the chief were flashing. He wanted to stand up, but Old Death held him back.

'Let me finish, because now comes the most interesting part! These palefaces visited the house of Señor Atanasio, who is a friend of Napoleon. There was an old French officer in the house as a guest. He was afraid that these palefaces, who were Juárez's soldiers, would take the opportunity to capture a French officer, and would kill him. He didn't have much time, so Atanasio suggested that the French officer should pretend to be ill, and lie down. They painted his face so that he would look like an Indian. When the palefaces asked who the ill person was, Atanasio answered that he was Good Man, the old chief of the Apache.'

'Why him?' asked White Beaver, surprised.

377

'Firstly because the French officer looked like Good Man a bit because of his age, grey hair, and lean body. Atanasio knew that the Apache support Juárez, and that the palefaces were on Juárez's side, so he knew that they wouldn't harm an Apache chief.'

'I can see that now! This señor must be a very clever man! And where is this French officer now? When my warriors searched the house, they couldn't find him.'

'Once he rested, he continued his journey. He had to carry out an important commission. But now you can see what sort of people you smoked the peace pipe with!'

'By the time the Sun rises, they'll be punished,' nodded White Beaver.

'They deserve it,' continued Old Death, 'but there are two among them with whom I want to settle an account.'

'Why?'

'They are my old enemies, and I've been pursuing them for a long time.'

I was mesmerised by Old Death's inventiveness. His was the right answer. If he had started a long tale, he would not have achieved anything. The two words of "old enemies" were sufficient.

'Good, then I give them to you as a present, you can do with them what you want, once they aren't protected by the smoke of the calumet,' said White Beaver. 'But I'd like to hear what they say if you interrogate them.'

'Call their leader, I'll talk to him.'

For Oyo Koltsa's command a Comanche warrior went to the leader of the whites, told him something, and then led him to the chief. He was a black haired, black bearded, marital looking man.

'What do you want from me?' he asked, and cast a hatred-filled look at me.

Obviously Gibson had spoken to him about us as had recognised me. I was happy that I did not have to conduct the talk, because I would not have known what to say. I also suspected that Old Death had not yet dissolved White

378

Beaver's suspicions completely, so I was curious how he would do it.

My crafty old friend looked into the Mexican man's eyes friendlily, and greeted him in the same manner, 'Good evening, Señor! I brought greeting to you from La Grange, from Señor Cortesio.'

'Do you know him?' asked the Mexican unsuspecting, and not recognising that he was walking into the trap.

'Of course!' replied Old Death. 'An old friend of mine. You and I almost met in his house, but unfortunately you left a day earlier. However, Cortesio described your route to us, so we could follow you. But then, at a certain point, you diverted from the planned route.'

'Yes, because we met our Comanche friends,' replied the Mexican almost in an excusing manner.

'Your friends?' said Old Death surprised. 'I thought you were the enemies of the Comanche!'

The Mexican was clearly confused. He cleared his throat to give a signal to Old Death to be more careful, but the old man pretended as if had heard nothing.

'But you took the oath for Juárez!' he said with a naïve astonishment. 'Don't you know that the Comanche are on the side of the French?'

At last the Mexican recollected himself, and exclaimed indignantly, 'I don't know what you are saying, Sir! We are also on the side of the French!'

'Are they recruiting volunteers in the United States?'

'Yes, for Napoleon's army.'

'Really? So Señor Cortesio works for Napoleon?'

'Of course, who else for?'

'I thought for Juárez.'

'Come on, what do you mean?'

'Thank you, you can go.'

Anger distorted the face of the bearded Mexican. How dare this old man talk to him like this!

'Don't send me anywhere,' he flared up. 'I'm an officer, if you didn't know!'

'Of Juárez?' asked Old Death suddenly.

'Of course! ... No, not at all. Of Napoleon! You have confused me completely.'

'I'm very surprised that an officer so easily gives himself away!' snapped Old Death at him. 'We have finished. Go back to your place!'

The officer still wanted to say something, but for the commanding motion of the chief he thought better of it.

'What do you think, my brother?' asked Old Death turning to the chief. 'Do you believe now that these palefaces came from Cortesio?'

'Yes, his face showed it, and he admitted it,' answered White Beaver. 'But maybe this Cortesio really recruits for Napoleon?'

'I can prove the opposite,' said Old Death. 'Look at this!'

He took out the passport that he had received from Cortesio, and showed it to White Beaver.

'When we learnt that the men, whom we were pursuing, wanted to cross the border with Cortesio's help,' continued Old Death, 'we also visited Cortesio. Of course, we told him that we wanted to join Juárez. For this he gave us horses, and told us the route of the group, so we could catch up with them. He even gave us a passport, and look, Juárez's signature is on it!'

The chief took the passport, examined it, and then said, 'Oyo Koltsa has heard that the palefaces can talk on paper. He doesn't know their symbols, but he can see Juárez's totem. Among my warriors there's a half-cast, who lived with the palefaces when he was a child, and can make papers talk. I'll call him.'

A minute later a young warrior arrived. For the chief's command he took the passport, knelt down by the fire, and he started to read it, and translated it at the same time. I did not understand it, but Old Death's face became brighter and brighter. When the Indian finished the reading, he gave the passport back to the chief, and left with the pride that he could accomplish such a difficult task.

'My friend has the same type of passport,' said Old Death pointing at me. 'Do you want to see that too?'

'Unnecessary, I know everything now,' replied White Beaver, and gave the passport back to Old Death. 'These palefaces lied to me, and I'll punish them. I'll call the leading warriors for council.'

'Do you need me?'

'No. You, my white brother opened my eyes, the rest is the Comanche warriors' task.'

'Can I ask you something?'

'What do you want to know, Kosha Pehveh?'

'I don't understand why the Comanche diverted from their original path. I saw when the track turned to a new direction suddenly.'

'Because we learnt that Winnetou gathered a large army, and he was marching to the Conchos River. Thus the Apache villages around here remained unguarded, and we decided that we would raid them. We would get such a rich loot as never before.'

'Winnetou at the River Conchos? Why would Winnetou be there? Whom did you learn this from? The two Indians who joined the Comanche?'

'How do you know it? Did you see their tracks?'

'I did. What kind of Indians are they?'

'They belong to the Topia tribe. Father and son.'

'Can I talk to them?'

'My white brother can do what he wants.'

'Can I also talk to the palefaces?'

'As you wish.'

'Then I'd also like to scout around the camp. We are on the enemy's land, and I would like to be sure that nothing threatens our safety.'

'You can do that, but it's unnecessary. I chose the place, set up guards, and sent out scouts. You can be sure that I have accounted for everything.' He stood up, and left for the council in ceremonial steps. The two old warriors, who so far had been sitting in silence, followed his example.

Old Death took me by my arm, and walked with me where Gibson and William Ohlert sat by a fire with the other whites. For our approach the officer stood up, and came two steps closer.

'What was the purpose of that interrogation that you conducted just before?'

'You will learn it from the Comanche, and therefore I don't have to answer you. As far as I'm concerned, you are horse thieves. And don't you ever use such a tone with me, because the Comanche are with me against you. I just have to give a signal, and you are finished.'

He turned around proudly, but stayed, because he knew that I also wanted to speak. The young Ohlert's appearance shocked me. His clothing was ragged, his hair was unkempt, and his face was pale and sunken. There was a piece of paper on his knee, and sometimes he wrote a word on it with a pencil, then he stared at the ground as if he did not know where he was. I addressed the bandit who turned him into such a puppet.

'At last I have caught up with you Gibson!' I shouted at him. 'And hopefully we'll stay together now!'

'Are you talking to me?' he asked, and laughed straight in my face.

'Naturally.'

'It's not so natural as you mentioned some Gibson.'

'Should I have said a different name?'

'Yes, probably. I'm not Gibson.'

'Haven't we met in New Orleans?'

'I don't know what you mean. I've never been Gibson.'

'So you had so many names that you have forgotten it,' I replied mockingly. 'In New Orleans you were Clinton, in La Grange Gavilano.'

'Gavilano? That's my name. And what do you want from me? Leave me alone! I've nothing to do with you.'

'You will though! Because now I won't lose sight of you until you are put on trial! I will just tie you on a horse, and take you to the court!'

382

He pulled a revolver on me, but Old Death knocked the revolver from his hand. Then he took my arm again, and pulled me aside.

'What was this for?' he asked. 'We can deal with him later. We have more urgent things to do.'

He led me to a campfire, where two Indians, a younger and an older, sat some distance from the others. Old Death went to them, and he asked, 'Have you come from the mountains of the Topia's land, my brothers? Are you Topia warriors, who are the friends of the Comanche?'

'Yes, we are,' replied the older Indian. 'Our tomahawks have always helped the Comanche.'

'Then how is it that you came from the North, where the Apache live, and not from the North-eastern mountains where the villages of the Topia are?'

The Indian was thrown off by Old Death's question. He answered only after a short pause.

'Because we dug up the war hatchet against the Apache, and first we rode to the North to learn their plans.'

'And did you learn something?'

'Very important things. In one of the Apache villages we saw Winnetou, the greatest chief of the Apache. He was marching to the Conchos River. So, the Apache villages are not protected here, and it would be easy to attack them. We were hurrying back to our village with the news, when we met the Comanche warriors.'

Old Death remained silent for a while; but he looked at the two Indians strangely, searchingly. Finally he asked in a sharp voice, 'Are the Topia honest people?'

For this question the younger Indian's eyes flashed, while the older was searching for words. Finally he replied, 'Do you have any reason to doubt our honesty, Old Death?'

'It's not my intention to offend you. But tell me, why aren't you with your Comanche friends, and why are you sitting near the palefaces? Don't you feel comfortable with the Comanche warriors? Or did they just want information from you, but they don't want to be with you?'

The last question was an insult. The Topia almost lost his self-control, but then he regained his calm.

'We sit where we want to,' he said stubbornly. 'We sat with the Comanche earlier, but then we moved closer to the palefaces, because we wanted to learn from them about other lands. I don't understand your questions, and I don't understand your thoughts, my white brother.'

Old Death leant over the elder Topia, looked in his eyes, and said in a stifled voice, 'You know my thoughts very well! You have seen enough winters to know them!'

'No, I don't,' replied the Topia scornfully. 'Tell me!'

'Did you smoke the calumet with the Comanche?'

'We did.'

'So you are under the obligation that you would do only what is advantageous for the Comanche.'

'Do you mean that we are acting differently?'

The eyes of the two men engaged as if they were fencing with their looks. Finally Old Death replied, 'I can see that you know what my thoughts are. I can see it in your eyes that you understood me, and my thoughts. And you know that if I had said them, you wouldn't see the next sunrise!'

'Uff!' exclaimed the Indian. He jumped up, and pulled his knife. His son also stood up, and grabbed his tomahawk.

'Be quiet!' whispered Old Death with a strong emphasis. 'Kosha Pehveh is a good friend of all Indians, irrespective of the tribe.'

'What are you saying?' hissed the Indian. 'Don't you believe that we are Topia warriors?'

'I kept my thoughts to myself, because we want to be your friends. Your actions and words show that you have forgotten that there are five hundred Comanche here!'

The hand of the elder Indian flinched. He held the knife even tighter as if he was ready to stab.

'Speak then!' he said. 'What do you think of us?'

Old Death put his hand on the wrist of the Indian, leant even closer, and whispered in his ear, 'Nothing bad ... only that you are Apache.'

'You're a liar, you dog!' shouted the Indian; released his wrist from Old Death's hand, and lifted his hand to stab. I was about to jump on him, when Old Death said gently, 'Do you want to kill Winnetou's friend?'

I don't know if the words or Old Death's eyes affected the Indian, but the muscles in the lifted arm visible eased.

He put his knife back to his belt, and he whispered to Old Death's ear, 'Keep quiet!'

The two Indians sat back to their place, and they stared at the ground so indifferently and calmly as if nothing had happened. The quick events filled me with surprise, and I did not understand many things. What made my old friend suspect the two Indians? Were they really Apache? They must have been brave to undertake such a dare-devil task. It seemed that they trusted us, because they did not even look up, when we continued our walk.

At this point there was some commotion. The chief had finished his talk to the elder warriors, and returned to the central fire. His warriors immediately gathered around them in several circles. I could see that whites were pushing there too. Only William Ohlert remained at his place, and stared at the pencil he was still holding in his hand. The two Topia had not stood up either. They sat with the same indifferent faces as earlier. White Beaver started to speak slowly, emphasising every word.

'A small group of palefaces arrived, and they asked us to permit them to join the Comanche warriors. They said that they were the friends of the Comanche. We granted their request, and we smoked the peace pipe with them. But today we learnt that they lied. Oyo Koltsa has thought over everything that count for and against them. Then he held council with the most experienced warriors. We have decided that the palefaces don't deserve our friendship. From this moment they are our enemies.'

The chief paused. The bearded officer jumped in.

'It's a slander!' he cried. 'The four whites and the black man have confused the mind of the chief. Their words are lies! Before you make a judgement, listen to us too! I'm an officer, a chief among the whites. I have to be involved in a council which is about us!'

'Who allowed you to speak?' asked the chief in a stern voice, and he lifted his chin proudly. 'If Oyo Koltsa speaks, then everybody else must be quiet. You said that we hadn't listened to you. This is not true! Old Death put questions to you. Your answers showed that you were Juárez's soldiers. Old Death is a brave and honest warrior, and I've known him for many winters. I would rather believe him than you. You demand to be included in our council. We didn't allow that even to Old Death. The Comanche don't need your advice. They know what they have to do, what is right ...'

'I smoked the calumet with you,' interrupted the officer. 'If you treat us as enemies ...'

'Shut up, you dog!' thundered White Beaver. 'There's an insulting word on your tongue, and in your stupid anger you forget that we could easily push those words down in your throat! There are five hundred warriors here to do so! You smoked the peace pipe with me, but you gained this with deception. Yet, the Comanche warriors respect the will of the Great Spirit. As long as you are under the protection of the calumet, we won't touch you. The sacred clay of which the calumet is made is red. The rising Sun is also red, when it sheds its light on the sky. The council breaks the alliance with you. The calumet will protect you until the Sun rises. The night is the time for resting. You are our guest until dawn, but you may not leave the camp. When the Sun rises, you can leave. We won't chase you for the time that the palefaces call five minutes. You can take everything that belongs to you. But after the five minutes we'll ride after you, then you'll die, and all your property will belong to us. And something else. The two men, whom Old Death has chosen won't go with you. From the morning they will be Old Death's prisoners, and he can do with them whatever the great white hunter wants. Oyo Koltsa, the high chief of the Comanche, has spoken.'

'What?' shouted Gibson, 'that I will be a prisoner of this old man? Never!'

'Shut up, for God's sake,' the officer warned him. 'I know the reds, the chief won't change his words! The night is long. A lot can happen till dawn.'

Gibson and his companions sat down by the fire again. The Comanche warriors, however, did not go back to where they had rested earlier. They put out the fires, and then settled around Gibson and his company in four circles.

Old Death took me by my arm.

'Can't Gibson escape during the night?' I asked.

'Impossible,' he replied. 'Four rings surround them, and the Comanche left the fire of the whites on so that they could watch them.'

'Wouldn't it be better if I tied up Gibson right now?'

'Don't even think of it! He's under the protection of the calumet. The Comanche would intervene. But at dawn we can cook him, roast him, and eat him if we wanted. Except if something happens ...'

'What do you mean?'

'I don't know. I think the two Apache, who say that they are Topia, are up to something.'

'Are they really Apache?'

'You can hang me if they aren't. Firstly, I don't believe that Winnetou went to the Conchos River. What for? I also think that the two Topia warriors' faces are also suspicious. The Topia are civilised Indians, and thus they are more well-fed than what the faces of these two suggest. Their dialect is also suspect. And they also betrayed themselves with some of their words.'

'Why?'

'Can't you remember how he spoke of Winnetou? He said "the greatest chief of the Apache". Someone who hates Winnetou wouldn't speak about him with such a respect.'

'These are serious arguments. If they are really Apache, I'm really impressed by their bravery.'

'Winnetou knows his people.'

'Do you think he sent them?'

'Obviously. If you remember, Señor Atanasio told us where Winnetou crossed the Rio Grande. It's impossible that he would have reached the Conchos River with a big army so quickly. The whole thing was about luring the Comanche to the Mapimi, where the Apache villages are supposedly defenceless. I think he's gathering his army here, and he will launch a surprise attack on the Comanche, because they feel secure, thus they are less cautious.'

'Damn it! Then we are in trouble! Those two Apache think we are their enemies.'

'I don't think so. They know that I could have informed the Comanche, and they would have been killed. But I didn't do that.'

'Shouldn't we inform the Comanche?'

'This is a very delicate question. The Comanche support Napoleon, and attacked the Apache villages treacherously at peacetime. They deserve punishment by the law of the prairie. On the other hand we smoked the peace pipe with them, thus we cannot betray them.'

'Even though I wish Winnetou's victory.'

'Me too, but we cannot help him. The best would be to leave during the night, and take Gibson and the unfortunate young man. But we cannot do that either.'

'We have to wait till dawn,' I nodded.

'If, by then, we aren't on the happy hunting grounds with the Comanche and the Apache,' said Old Death. 'Do you think that the situation is so dangerous?'

'I do. Firstly, the Apache villages are very close, and Winnetou cannot wait until the Comanche attack the women, children, and the elderly. And this Mexican officer also spoke strangely. Didn't you hear when he told Gibson that a lot could happen till the dawn? But let's scout around a bit. It seems that I've been in this valley before, and I hope I can find my way easily.'

We found that we were in a round valley. Its radius was not more than a five-minute walk. The entrances to it were narrow, otherwise it was surrounded by steep cliffs that seemed to be unscalable. We walked around, and passed the two strong guard groups that were at the entrances.

'A damned situation!' murmured the old man. 'It's a trap. I can't see any other way to escape from here than when the fox chews off its trapped leg.'

'Can't we persuade White Beaver to break camp, and find a new place?' I asked.

Old Death shook his head.

'Not without telling him that he has two Apache in his camp, and we won't do that.'

'Maybe you see the situation too dark. The guard is quite strong considering the narrow entrances,' I opined.

'Yes, ten people on each side. But let's not forget that our opponent is Winnetou. Let's return to the others.'

On the way back we met the chief. We recognised him, even in the darkness because of his eagle feathers. He came to us, and asked, 'Are you convinced that we are safe?'

'No,' answered Old Death. 'This valley is a trap.'

'You are wrong, my white brother. It's not a trap, but rather like a fort. The enemies cannot come in.'

'True, not through the entrance, because it's narrow enough to be defended by ten warriors. But the enemy could come down on the cliffs.'

'It's too steep. We arrived at daylight, and we examined it. Nobody could climb up on the cliff.'

'I believe that, but maybe it's easier to descend. And I also know that Winnetou can climb like a chamois.'

'Winnetou is far from here,' replied the chief, 'I know that from the two Topia.'

'Maybe they were mistaken because they confused Winnetou with another Apache. If it is true that Winnetou was at Fort Inge, he couldn't have gone with his gathered warriors beyond the Rio Conchos. There wasn't enough time for such a long journey.'

The chief bowed his thoughtful head. He seemed to have come to the same conclusion, because he said, 'Yes, the time was too short for such a long journey. I'll ask the two Topia warriors again.'

White Beaver went to the campfire, and we followed him. The whites glared at us malevolently. Lange, his son, and Sam sat a bit aside. William Ohlert was writing on his paper. He was deaf and blind to everything.

The two supposed Topia looked up only when the chief addressed them, 'Are you, my brothers certain that …'

He became quiet. From the height of the cliffs two noises resounded. First the frightened chirping of a small bird, followed by the hooting of an owl. White Beaver listened attentively, and so did Old Death. I could see that Gibson leant over the fire, and was playing with a branch. He pushed it in the fire, and stirred the embers with it. The fire flared up for a moment, and then collapsed again. Gibson wanted to stir the fire again. I could see that his companions became excited too. Old Death jumped there immediately, and tore the branch from Gibson's hand.

'Stop it right now!' he brayed at him.

'Why?' flared up Gibson. 'Can't I even stir the fire?'

'Do you take me for some idiot? You responded to the hooting! Was it the agreed signal?'

'What signal? Are you completely mad?'

'Yes! If you dare to touch the fire, I'll shoot you dead!'

'Damned old ass!' hissed Gibson. He turned around, and addressed his companions, 'How much longer do we allow this, gentlemen?'

He wanted to pull his revolver, but Old Death was quicker, and he stood in front of Gibson with two pulled revolvers. In a flash we joined him: I, the two Langes, and Sam. The chief ordered, 'Arrows up!'

The Comanche jumped up, and at least two dozen arrows pointed at Gibson and his companions.

'Here you are,' laughed Old Death partly bitterly, partly contemptuously, 'this is what the rascals do under the protection of the calumet! I say that they should have been disarmed.'

The chirping, and the hooting resounded again from the height. Gibson's hand moved as if he wanted to pick up a branch to push it in the fire, but he did not dare.

The chief repeated his question to the Topia. 'Are you certain that Winnetou is beyond the Conchos River?'

'Yes, we are,' replied the elder of the two.

After some further questioning to which the Topia men answered promptly, White Beaver said, 'Your explanations have satisfied the chief of the Comanche.'

He then turned to Old Death, 'You may want to join me now, my white brothers!'

Old Death indicated to the two Lange and Sam that they should come with us.

'Why did you call all your companions, my brother?' asked the Comanche chief.

'To be together at the moment of danger,' answered Old Death briefly.

'I can't see any danger.'

'Didn't you hear the hooting of the owl? It wasn't an owl; it was a man.'

'Oyo Koltsa knows all animals' sounds. Man cannot hoot like this.'

'Winnetou can imitate any animal sound so well that it would mislead its mate,' replied Old Death. 'Please don't be overconfident! What do you think, why this rascal stirred the fire? It was an agreed signal.'

'He couldn't agree with anyone because he couldn't leave the camp.'

'Then he got a message. He didn't do it accidentally.'

'Do you think then that we have a traitor among us? Impossible. But even if we have, this is not a problem. The guards can protect the entrances, and they cannot come down on the cliffs.'

'And if they come down on nets? Anything can hap … just listen!'

The hooting resounded again, but this time not from the height, but from somewhere near.

'I told you it was a bird!' waved White Beaver.

'Hell! Not a bird! The Apache are in here!'

From the entrance of the valley a sharp, shivering cry resounded. It was a death cry. In the next moment the polyphonic war cry of the Apache waved through the air. If one hears this cry, he will never forget it.

At the same time the whites jumped up.

'Let's kill the dogs!' shouted the bearded officer, and pointed at us. 'We'll take our revenge!'

'Let's beat them to death,' rasped Gibson.

Fortunately we were in the dark, thus we did not offer a good target. So, instead of wasting their time with shooting, they decided to attack us with the butt of their guns. They obviously had agreed on everything in advance, because their actions were so quick, similar, and measured. We were not more than thirty steps from them, but this distance gave enough time for Old Death to shout to us, 'Wasn't I right? Aim! We'll give them what they deserve!'

Six guns received the attackers as White Beaver joined us too. The shots popped, those from double-barrel guns, twice. I did not have time to count the hits, I could only see that the bodies swayed, and dead or injured men fell on the ground. The Comanche also entered the battle, and many arrows flew through the air. This is when I noticed that Gibson, who enticed his companions so industriously, did not join them. He stood by the fire, and he was pulling the arm of the young Ohlert, who was still sitting on the ground, and did not want to get to his feet. I could not watch it any longer because the war cries came from near: the Apache entered the camp.

In the dark they could not see how many enemies they had. They broke through the lines of the Comanche, but the real battle started only then. Guns popped, arrows and spears swirled, and knives flashed. It felt as if yelling devils were jumping about, and wrestled at the entrance of the hell. From the turmoil an Apache warrior appeared leaving his companions behind. He had a revolver in his left hand,

392

and a tomahawk in his right. Each of his shot stretched a Comanche, while his hatchet opened skulls. He did not wear an eagle feather, and his face was not painted, yet he was terrifying. White Beaver recognised this warrior at the same time as me.

'Winnetou! At last! I will have your scalp!' cried White Beaver, and jumped in the battle.

The fighters blocked our view of the duel.

'I can see that the Comanche outnumber the Apache,' remarked Old Death. 'The Apache fight in vain, they'll be overpowered.'

I had the same thought, and I wanted to hurry to help Winnetou, but Old Death held me back by grabbing my arm.

'Don't do anything stupid!' he shouted. 'We smoked the peace pipe with the Comanche, we cannot fight against them! You don't have to be afraid for Winnetou, he knows what to do.'

As if he had wanted to confirm Old Death's statement, I heard Winnetou's voice.

'We were misled! Retreat quickly. Quickly!'

The only remaining fire was put out, but I could see the retreating Apache even in the darkness. It was obvious that Winnetou recognised that he had to yield to the numeric superiority. I did not understand why he had not scouted the enemy before attacking them. Soon, however, I learnt the reason for his uncharacteristic hastiness.

The Comanche wanted to pursue the defeated enemy, but the Apache carried out the retreat masterly. They shot a volley fire at the Comanche. In the midst of the noise I heard the sound of the silver gun, that famous gun that Winnetou inherited from his father. For White Beaver's command they lit a fire again. When it flared up, he sought us, and said, 'The Apache escaped. But tomorrow morning we'll ride after them, and kill them all.'

'The dawn is far away,' replied Old Death.

'What do you mean, my white brother?'

'I told you that this valley is a trap.'

'We repulsed them,' said White Beaver proudly. 'Only the darkness protects them.'

'Then why are you shooting? If you run out of arrows, there are enough birch trees to make new shafts, but you can't make the heads here. Be careful with the ammunition. And where are the ten warriors who guarded the entrance?'

'They are here, because the fight enticed them.'

'Send them back! Secure the path of retreat!'

'Unnecessary! The Apache fled to the opposite direction.'

'You should guard both entrances.'

The Comanche chief agreed, although not because he was convinced, but because he did not want to insult the great paleface warrior. Soon it became clear that Old Death's anxiety was not unfounded. As soon as the ten warriors took their post, we heard the popping of guns. In a few minutes two guards ran back, and they reported that there was such a volley fire by the entrance that only two of them had survived.

'Was I wrong?' asked Old Death. 'Both sides of the trap are closed.'

'What can I do?' asked White Beaver dispirited.

'Save your strength,' answered the old man. 'Put twenty or thirty men to the two entrances, and the rest should have a good night's rest, because hard struggles will await us in the morning.'

The chief now listened to the advice. Then he counted the dead and the wounded. When it came to the whites, he found that most of them had died, but ten men, among them Gibson and Ohlert, had disappeared.

'Damn it!' I exclaimed bitterly. 'They fled to the Apache!'

'Of course,' nodded Old Death, 'and those welcomed them as they helped the two Topia warriors, that is, the Apache spies.'

'So we can give up on Gibson.'

'Why? The Apache know me, and anyway we have the totem of Good Man. I'll persuade them to give us the two.'

'And if they leave in the meantime?'

'I don't think so. They can flee only through the Mapimi, and it's a bad terrain. They will reconsider it a hundred times if they try to attempt it ... What's going on there?'

About twenty Comanche had gathered at a place from where the sounds of whining was coming. We approached, and saw a wounded white man who had been taken for dead earlier. A spear had spiked him from behind, probably a Comanche did it when the Apache attack started. Old Death knelt down to the man, who suffered horrible pains.

'Man,' said Old Death, 'you have ten minutes left of your life. Make your soul light, and don't go to the other world with lies. Did you conspire with the Apache?'

'We did,' responded the dying man.

'Did you know that there would be an attack tonight?'

'Yes, the Topia told us.'

'And did they tell Gibson to give the signal?'

'They agreed that he would flare the fire as many times as many hundred Comanche were here. If Winnetou had known that there were five hundred of them, he would have postponed the attack until tomorrow. He had only a hundred warriors. He'll get reinforcements in the morning.'

'I thought so,' nodded Old Death. 'They cut off the path in both ways. There will be a massacre here tomorrow!'

'We'll defend ourselves to the last drop of our blood,' exclaimed White Beaver. 'However, this traitor will be a dog hounded by wolves in the eternal hunting grounds!' He stabbed the man in his heart.

'That was a completely unnecessary murder!' cried Old Death angrily.

'I killed him so he would be my slave in the other world. And we won't wait till the morning. We'll break out during the night.'

He had a council with his elder warriors. Old Death had to participate in it too. They were arguing very quietly. Although I could not understand them, I could see that Old Death was passionately arguing for something, but the Comanche were not listening.

395

At the end he jumped up, and I could hear his voice, 'You're running to your destruction. I've been right, and I'll be right again! I don't care what you do, I'll stay here with my friends.'

'So are you a coward to fight with us?' asked one of the subordinate chiefs.

Old Death clinched his fist, but overcame his emotion, and answered calmly.

'First you should show your own bravery before you question others' determination. I'm Old Death, and it's enough to say this.'

He turned around, came over, and sat down with us. The Comanche leaders continued the discussion, and it seemed that they had made a decision. At this moment a voice resounded behind the Comanche who stood around the campfire.

'Look here, White Beaver! My gun is impatient to be introduced to you.'

All eyes looked to the direction of the voice. Winnetou stood at the bottom of the rock wall with his gun in his shoulder. The two barrels of the gun flashed. White Beaver, and one of his deputies crashed to the ground dead.

'All treacherous men will die like this!' we could hear Winnetou's voice, but could not see him.

It all happened so quickly that the Comanche did not have time to act. By the time they jumped up, and rushed where Winnetou had stood, he had gone.

Old Death leant over the two chiefs. Both were dead.

'What a dare-devil act!' exclaimed Lange. 'This Apache is a real devil!'

'Just wait,' laughed Old Death, 'the real thing will come only now!' As soon as he finished his sentence, we heard yelling from the entrance of the valley.

'Just as I said,' cried the old man. 'He punished not only the chief, but he also lured his warriors out of the valley!'

We heard the sharp sound of a revolver three times, five times, eight times in quick succession.

'Winnetou's revolver,' said Old Death smiling. 'The Comanche probably surrounded him, but they cannot get close to him.'

He was shrugging his shoulders indifferently, or even bored, as if he was sitting in a theatre watching a play that he had seen several times. In reality he had seen such scenes many times, and often he had played the main role. He was nodding as if he knew the end of the scene.

The Comanche soon returned. They had been shooting at Winnetou, but they missed their target. However, they brought back some dead and injured warriors. They were yelling in their grief, and danced around their dead.

'It would be cleverer if they were quiet, and put out the fire,' remarked Old Death.

'What was the decision of the council?' I asked.

'That they try to break out to the West.'

'This is stupid! They will immediately encounter the Apache who are coming to help Winnetou.'

'It won't happen, because they won't be able to break through, or if they can, Winnetou would attack them from the rear, thus they would be in the crossfire.'

'What's their hope then?'

'They think that they still have numeric superiority, and they are also awaiting the Great Bear, the son of the fallen White Beaver, whom we met. They have the burning desire for revenge. I advised them to wait with the breakthrough till the morning, but I was shouted down. Who cares! But what's this noise? Just listen!'

We listened in vain, because the grieving yells of the Comanche overpowered all other noise. 'Mad!' hummed Old Death. 'They help Winnetou with their shouting. I think the Apache are felling trees to block the entrances of the valley. I heard the crushing of falling trees just before. If so, then none of the Comanche will escape. Well, it serves them right for their treacherous attack at peacetime.'

Finally the Comanche became quiet. One of the chiefs lined up the warriors.

'It seems that they'll start it,' said Old Death. 'It's time that we looked after our horses, otherwise they may take them. Mr Lange, take your son and Sam, and bring our horses here. We two will stay here because I think there will be a little quarrel.'

As soon as our friends left, the new chief approached us with slow steps. He stood in front of us, and said, 'The palefaces are sitting here, while the Comanche warriors are on their horses. Why aren't you getting ready?'

'We don't know what you decided.'

'We are leaving this valley.'

'If you can,' added Old Death.

'You are a croaker, Kosha Pehveh! The Comanche warriors will roll over whoever wants to block their way.'

'Good luck. We are staying.'

'Are you not our friend, Kosha Pehveh? Didn't you smoke the peace pipe with us? Don't you want to come with us? The palefaces are brave warriors. It would be right if they led us!'

Old Death stood up, and laughed in the chief's face. 'You are really crafty,' he said. 'You want us ride in front, make the path for you, and die for you! This is what you want? We are friends of the Comanche, but we don't obey you. You said that we are brave warriors. It's true. But we won't take part in a fight whose outcome we know in advance.'

'So the palefaces won't take side with the Comanche?'

'No. We are the guests of the Comanche, and not their allies. Since when is it a custom to send the guests to fight?' The new chief was at first confused, then he flared up in anger. 'Do you want to join the Apache?'

'But you are rolling over them, how could we join them?'

'If you don't join us, you won't get back your horses!' said the chief.

'I've already arranged it,' said the old man. 'Look, they are here!'

Our friends were arriving. They led the horses by the reins. The Comanche was wrinkling his forehead.

'I can see that the palefaces are prepared for treason,' he said. 'I'll order my warriors to tie you up.'

A strange grin appeared on Old Death's face. This was the grin that indicated that he was about to give a lesson to someone who was unjust to him. He looked around. There was no Comanche warrior nearby apart from the new chief. He whispered to me, 'When I knock out this rascal, jump on the horses. We will all ride to the left entrance, as the Comanche are at the right one.'

'What are you whispering about?' brayed the chief at Old Death. 'I want to hear what you said!'

'You will know it. So, do you think that we are your prisoners? You want to force me to do something I don't want to do? Look!' he pulled his revolver, and aimed it at the Comanche's chest. 'One motion or a loud word, and you'll die! Your warriors are far! We aren't your prisoners, but you are ours!'

The face of the Indian flinched. Even under his war paint it could be seen. He glanced towards his men, but he did not dare cry out.

'Don't expect help from them!' continued Old Death. 'By the time they arrive, you are dead. Just think! It's not enough to you that the Apache surrounded you, but you also start a fight with us! Don't you have enough enemies?'

The Indian was silent for a few minutes, then changed his tone completely.

'You misunderstood me, my white brother,' he said. 'I didn't mean this.'

'Then say what you think. I'll listen.'

'Put your gun away! Let's be good friends,' said the Comanche in a coaxing voice.

'I want that too,' said Old Death, 'but first prove that you mean your words honestly.'

'Isn't my word enough?'

'No, not your word.'

'Then what can I do?'

'Give me you calumet.'

'I can't!'

'But I want it and more! Give me your medicine bag too!'

'Uff, uff!' he exclaimed. 'I cannot part with that!'

'Don't worry, you'll get it back when we leave you.'

'An Indian warrior doesn't separate from his medicine bag for a moment!'

'I know your customs. But if I have your calumet and your medicine bag, then I will be you, and therefore you cannot attack me, because if you kill me, I'll take your place in the eternal hunting grounds, and therefore you cannot get there!'

'I know,' said the Comanche in a whining voice.

'Then give them to me!'

'I won't!' cried the Comanche in despair.

'Then I'll kill you, scalp you, and you will be my dog on the happy hunting grounds! Is it better? Listen! I will lift my arm three times. After then I'll shoot you.'

The Comanche's eye goggled in his fright. Old Death lifted his left arm while he aimed at the Indian with his right. He waited a bit, and then lifted his arm again. When his arm moved for the third time, the Indian said in a begging tone, 'Wait! Will you really give it back to me?'

'I will. Kosha Pehveh never lies.'

The Comanche moved his hand to his neck, but the old man brayed at him, 'No! My friend will untie it!'

The Comanche dropped his hands. I stepped up to him, untied both the calumet and the medicine bag, and gave them to Old Death. He put them in his pocket, and then put away his revolver.

'Right,' he said, 'now we are good friends. You can go wherever you want, we stay here.'

The Comanche chief was raging. He grabbed his knife, but did not dare to pull it.

'Nothing bad can fall on the palefaces now,' he hissed, 'but when I get my calumet and medicine bag back, I'll take my revenge! You'll die on the torture stake!' Old Death did not even listen to him.

'We are safe,' he said, 'but let's not ignore the necessary caution. Let's not stay by the fire, but go to the other end of the valley, and wait for the developments there. Follow me!'

We grabbed the reins of the horses, and followed him. We tied our horses to a tree, and sat down by the cliff.

'How quiet it is now!' remarked Lange.

'Just wait,' replied Old Death. 'It'll soon start.'

In five minutes yelling came from the other entrance. 'Only the Comanche are yelling,' said the old man. 'The Apache are quiet, and they act.' Two shots resounded.

'It was Winnetou's silver gun,' nodded Old Death. 'I bet he stopped the Comanche.'

After a while a sharp cry pierced our ears, 'Ivi-vi-vi-vi!'

'The Apache's victory cry,' said Sam. 'They beat back the Comanche.'

We saw the retreating riders by the campfire. It was a tumultuous scene. They carried the wounded and the dead to the fire. The grieving song resounded in the valley again. When they stopped, their leaders held council that lasted for about half an hour. Old Death was convinced that they would seek our advice.

Indeed an old warrior looked for us. He spotted us, and came to our group, 'The palefaces should come to us!'

'What for?' asked Old Death.

'The chief allows you to participate in the council.'

'He allows? How graceful! But we want to sleep.'

The Comanche's tone was initially demanding, but then he was almost begging us to fulfil his mission.

'You know what?' said Old Death. 'If he wants to talk to me, he can come here.'

'He can't. He's a chief.'

'I'm a chief too, and greater and older than he is. I don't even know his name!'

'Still he can't ... his arm is wounded.'

'I didn't want him to come on his hands,' laughed Old Death. 'He can move his legs, can't he? So, if he wants to talk to me, he can, although he may not like what I want to tell him. And he should come alone! I don't have any intention of participating in a big council.'

Finally the Comanche agreed to take the message, and he returned to the fire. For a long time nothing happened. Then we saw that somebody rose by the fire, and came towards us with slow steps.

'Look! He has already put White Beaver's eagle feathers in his hair,' said Old Death. 'He has tied up his arm. It seems that he was really wounded.'

The Indian stopped by us, and waited. He obviously wanted us to address him. Old Death, however, stared at the ground indifferently, and we followed his example. Finally the Comanche broke the silence, 'You asked me, my white brother, to come here …,' he started.

'I didn't ask anything!' interrupted Old Death. 'I was told you wanted to talk to me. I don't even know your name!'

'I'm Quick Deer,' said the new chief proudly. 'Everybody knows this name on the prairies!'

'I've been everywhere on the prairies, but I have never heard your name, but I allow you to sit down here.'

Quick Deer hesitated as he was deeply insulted, but after a short musing he recognised that he had to give way. He sat down on the grass, and said, 'You are an experienced warrior, Kosha Pehveh, and we need your advice.'

'Why? Did you fail with the breakout?'

'The Apache blocked the entrance with trunks of trees, stones, and shrubs. What should we do now?'

'Yes, and you didn't hear any of this because of your yelling. Why should I say anything? You haven't listened to me so far!'

'It'll be different now. Please, speak!'

'How many warriors have the Comanche lost?'

'Ten times ten. And many horses,' admitted Quick Deer. 'But we still have more men than the Apache have.'

'But their situation is better! They blocked you in, while they can move freely. Winnetou will receive reinforcements by the morning. You are finished!'

'Can't you see any hope, my white brother?'

'I can see only one possibility, otherwise you won't escape from this valley. Start peace negotiations with the Apache.'

'Never! We won't ask for mercy, and we know that they won't give us anyway. They are thirsty for our blood.'

'I'm not surprised!' Old Death's sharp reply came immediately. 'They have all the right reasons for this! You attacked their villages at peacetime, you stole their belongings, killed the warriors, tortured the prisoners, and took their children and women. It was an outrage that cannot be revenged hard enough!'

This was a very honest statement, and Quick Deer could not answer anything. He stared at the ground silently and he was almost paralysed.

'Uff!' he said finally. 'Are you talking to the chief of the Comanche like this?'

'I would say the same even if you were the Great Spirit! What did the Apache do to you that you murdered them like this? How dare you attack their envoys? Why?'

'Because they are our enemies,' growled the Comanche.

'It's not true! The Apache want to live in peace. You dug up the hatchet. You know your guilt, this is why you want to fight now to the bitter end. Your only luck is that your fate is in Winnetou's hands. He is the only chief who wants peace, and does not long for revenge.'

'We won't ask for mercy from anyone,' stated Quick Deer firmly again.

'Then do what you want. It doesn't matter to me.'

'Your words show that you are the friend of the Apache,' said the Comanche gloomily. 'We can't use your advice. I ask only one thing. Don't forget your promise that you'll give back what is mine.'

'Old Death always keeps his words,' said the old man. 'That's it, we are finished with each other.'

'Uff!' exclaimed the Comanche. His eyes glowed with anger and hatred.

He returned to the camp fire.

'He still believes that they outnumber the Apache,' Old Death shook his head as he turned to me, 'even though Winnetou is worth a hundred warriors. He has very few peers among the Indians, and even fewer among the whites. I don't want to talk about myself, because I don't like boasting. But there's Old Firehand, the great hunter, you might have heard about him. And there's somebody else who just arrived from Europe, but already legends are talked about him.'

'Who's that?'

'I don't know his real name, but they call him Old Shatterhand. A great man: strong, brave and crafty. His mind and heart are in the right place. I'd like to know him.'

I suddenly heard a quiet noise. Somebody whispered next to me, 'Uff! Is it Old Death? I'm glad!'

My old friend almost pulled his knife.

'Who crept up here?'

'You don't need your knife, my white brother, or do you want to stab Winnetou?'

'Winnetou? Then I'm not surprised that you could creep up on us.'

The Apache chief came even closer. He ignored me.

'The Apache warriors didn't know that Old Death was here, otherwise we would already have talked to you!'

'You made a mistake with coming here, my brother,' said Old Death quietly. Bypassing the guards was too dangerous! You risked your life.'

'I didn't bypass the guards,' replied Winnetou. 'I came in a different way. This valley belongs to the Apache, and I know it like the back of my hand. Its cliffs can be climbed. At three-man's height the Apache cut a narrow path that goes around the valley. One can go up and down with a lasso. This is why we lured the Comanche here. They will all die.'

'Won't you step back from shedding so much blood?'

'I heard what you said to the Comanche new chief, and I could also hear that you agreed with us. I have to revenge what they did against us, because they don't admit their guilt, and they don't want peace. You should come over to us with your friends.'

'When?'

'Now. Soon six hundred Apache warriors will arrive. They have guns, and when they shoot at the Comanche, your life won't be safe.'

'And how will we get out?'

'Is Old Death asking me this? You will find you way. Wait for ten minutes, and break through to the right hand side entrance of the valley. I'll be there by then.'

In the next moment he had disappeared.

'What do you think?' asked Old Death.

'Not an everyday man!' opined Lange.

'I agree. If he had been born a white man, he would have become a military leader. And it would be woe to the whites if Winnetou decided to unite the Indian tribes to regain their lands. Fortunately he wants peace. He knows that the fate of his people is sealed, but he closed this terrible thing in his heart, and he only wants that the end of this fate would happen as late as possible.'

It was quiet in the valley. The Comanche leaders were still discussing their options. After ten minutes Old Death mounted his horse.

'Do what I do!' he said.

We rode to the fire in step. The Comanche looked at us surprised, but let us pass. When we got near the fire, Quick Deer jumped up.

'What do you want here?' he brayed at us. 'The council is still on.'

'I brought back what is yours!' shouted Old Death, and threw the calumet and the medicine bag to him. 'You said that when you get them back, we would be your enemies! But we won't wait for your revenge!'

He spurred his horse, and it jumped over the fire. Sam was the first to follow him, he simply waded through the council, and we followed them. By the time the Comanche had recovered from their surprise, we had already arrived to the entrance of the valley, and waded through the guards too as they did not expect any attack from behind. We galloped forward ignoring the mad yelling of the Comanche.

'Stop! Here's Winnetou!' resounded from the darkness.

Winnetou and two Apache warriors emerged from the background, and led us through the barricade. The gorge widened at this point, and we could see a small campfire. Two Apache sat there, and they were roasting some meat. As we arrived they stood up, and left. Further away we saw many horses. The whole place looked like a well organised military camp. The movements of the Apache were so precise as if they had been through military training.

We dismounted, and our guides took away our horses.

'You can sit down here, if you want to sit down, my white brothers,' said Winnetou. 'I've arranged an excellent bison roast for you. Eat until I come back.'

'Do we have to wait long?'

'I don't think so. I have something to do. The Comanche are probably raging, and they may commit the error of chasing you. I have to sober them up.'

He went back towards the entrance of the valley. Old Death sat down by the fire comfortably, took out his knife, and tasted the roast. It was excellent. As we had not eaten anything for some time, we started to eat the big piece of meat, and soon we consumed all of it. By then Winnetou returned. He glanced at me, and I understood the question in his eyes. He wanted to know if I was ready to discard my incognito. I stood up from the fire, offered my hands, and said, 'I'm happy to see my beloved brother, Winnetou, and also that I didn't have to go to the Pecos River for this.' We embraced each other.

'What does this mean?' asked Old Death surprised. 'Do you know each other?'

'Old Shatterhand is not only my closest friend, but also my blood brother,' replied Winnetou.

'Old ... Shat ... ter ... hand!' stuttered the old man, and showed such a face that made me laugh. He scolded me angrily, 'You dare to do this to me, you hypocrite! Showing yourself as a greenhorn, and laughing in secret that I was taken up the garden path!'

We left him alone with his astonishment.

Winnetou started to tell me, 'You know that I had to ride to Fort Inge and there I ...'

'I know what happened, Winnetou!' I interrupted. 'Tell me first, where the ten palefaces are who came from the Comanche to you?'

'They rode to Chihuahua, to Juárez.'

'Terrible!' I exclaimed in despair.

'Why?'

'Because among them were the two men, whom I have pursued since New Orleans.'

'Uff, uff! The two? I didn't know this! They said that they had an appointment in Chihuahua, and they had lost a lot of time with the Comanche. Winnetou is on Juárez's side, thus I gave them support. They got rested horses, food, and guides. The guides are the two supposed Topia, who know the route through the Mapimi well.'

'Even this! Rested horses, food and guides! The damned Gibson was in my hand, and now he disappears again!'

Winnetou mused for a minute, and then he said, 'I made a big mistake, even if I didn't know about it. But I'll repair it. I have completed my task that I mentioned in La Grange. Once I finished with these Comanche, I'll join you on your journey to Chihuahua. If nothing happens, we will catch up with them in two days.'

An Apache hurried to us, and reported, 'The Comanche dogs put out the campfire, they will attack again.'

'They'll be beaten back again,' replied Winnetou. 'If you come with me, my white brothers, I'll show you a place from where you can watch the battle.'

Of course, we stood up. Winnetou led us back almost to the barricade. There he gave a lasso to Old Death. The lasso hung down from the cliff; it must have been attached to something somewhere in the height.

407

'Climb up on it to about the height of two men,' said Winnetou. 'Among the bushes you'll find the narrow path that I talked about. I have to join my warriors.'

'Hm,' hummed Old Death. 'Climbing up on such a lasso. Am I a monkey or what? But let's try!'

Considering his age, he climbed up quickly, and the rest of us followed him. A tree grew out of the rock wall almost horizontally, and the lasso was fixed on this. By the roots of the tree there were some bushes that hid the entry to the path. Feeling the path with our hands, we groped forward, and then stopped in a hollow where there was enough room for all of us.

'There's some movement down there,' said Old Death. 'I can't see or hear them, but I can smell it. The smell of the horses is much stronger when they are in motion. They are passing just under us to the entrance of the valley.'

At that moment a sharp cry hit our ear, '*Na-ho!*' This meant now in the language of the Apache. At the same time two shots popped. Winnetou's silver gun opened the battle. Yelling followed, guns went off, and tomahawks and spears hit each other. The excited neighing of the horses, and the yelling of the Comanche was soon overpowered by the victory cry of the Apache, 'Ivi-vi-vi-vi!'

'The situation of the Comanche is hopeless,' said Old Death. 'Crowding in a small place means high losses. All the bullets, arrows and spears of the Apache hit. The breakout attempt will collapse soon.'

In five minutes the Comanche retreated. The Apache did not chase after them. It was unnecessary as the Comanche could not go anywhere.

When everything became calm, we descended. Winnetou waited for us, and led us back to the campfire.

'The Comanche will try now on the other side,' he said, 'but my warriors are ready there too. Nobody will leave this trap alive.'

He suddenly leant ahead attentively. Then he jumped up, and stood in the front of the fire so that he would be well lit.

'What happened?' I asked.

'I heard the hooves of a horse from somewhere. It was a lone rider; he must be looking for me. I stood up so that he could see me.'

We did not hear any noise, but Winnetou's hearing was just as perfect as his other senses. In a few minutes a rider appeared, and dismounted. He hurried to Winnetou, and stood there until the chief addressed him.

'What news did you bring?' asked Winnetou.

'Our group is approaching,' the messenger reported. 'For Winnetou's call all warriors joined.'

'How far are they from here?'

'They'll arrive at dawn.'

'Good. Take your horse to the herd, and rest.'

The warrior turned around, and left. His behaviour was militaristic, but not submissive.

Winnetou returned to us, and started to question me. I had to tell him everything that had happened in La Grange, at the Estanzia del Caballero, and since then. Winnetou listened to me attentively, and interrupted my report only rarely with some questions. This is how we passed the time. We did not even recognise when the sky became a shade lighter. Then Winnetou lifted his hand, pointed to the West, and said, 'My white brothers will now see how punctual the Apache warriors are.'

We all stared in the indicated direction. From the grey fog a rider's contours appeared, then the second, the third, and then a long, long line of riders. Their leader spotted Winnetou, and rode to him. He was also a chief as he wore two eagle feathers in his hair. A few minutes later the whole group stood there in files of five, like the best trained European cavalry battalion. They rode the horses without saddle, and instead of the reins and bridle, they only had a piece of rope. Yet the discipline was perfect. Most of them had guns, the rest had bows, spears, and tomahawk. The leader reported to Winnetou, and they exchanged a few words. Then they gave orders. The warriors dismounted.

Some men led away the horses, while the rest climbed up on the lasso, and disappeared from our view. It happened so quickly and noiselessly as if they had agreed in advance. Winnetou stood by the fire like a statue, and he followed the movements of his warriors only with his eyes calmly but attentively. When the last Apache climbed up on the lasso, he sat back with us, and said, 'You can see, my white brothers, that the life of the Comanche is in my hands.'

'I hope that Winnetou won't shed so much blood.'

'And don't the Comanche deserve it?' snapped Winnetou. 'They attacked our villages in peacetime in the North of the Rio Grande, and now they wanted to do the same with the Apache villages in Mexico! Don't the palefaces revenge the murder and robbery?'

'Not every Comanche warrior participated in the murder and robbery,' said Old Death.

'But they didn't protest! Those, who don't stand up for justice, who don't do anything to help the innocent victims, are just as guilty as those who committed the villainy.'

'But if they return the property they stole, you can be generous, and forgive them!'

'I know this word! You talk like a Christian who always demands from us to follow just the opposite of what he does! Have the Christians showed us mercy at all? You came here, and took our land. If you find any of us in the forest hunting, you put us in a dark building, to a jail. But do you do the same to the whites? Where are our prairies and savannahs? Where are the herds of horses, bison, and other animals that used to belong to the Indians? Many of you came, and stole from us everything that we used to live on. You took one patch of land after the other without any right. And if the Indians defended their property, you called them murderers, and you killed not only him, but his family too! You want me to forgive my enemies, when we have done no harm to them! Why didn't you give us mercy? If we defend ourselves, it is our duty, but you punish us with complete destruction. You say that the Indians are savages who cannot be educated, and they must vanish from the Earth. Your behaviour doesn't show that you are educated! This is my answer to your request. I know that you don't like it, but you would say the same thing in my place. Haw, I've spoken!'

He looked away from us, and stared into the distance. He was upset, and wanted to regain his self-control. Soon he turned back to us, and said to Old Death, "It was a long speech, but you will agree with me, my white brother, because you are a just man. However, you are right, I don't want to see the spilling of so much blood. I hoped that the Comanche would send an envoy to me. Since they haven't, I don't have to show mercy, but I'll send a messenger to them.'

'That makes me very happy," cried Old Death. 'It would make me despair if all these people here died without an attempt to rescue them from their own choice. Have you got somebody who can conduct the negotiations with the Comanche? Because if you don't, I'm ready to go to them, and talk to their chief. What are your conditions?'

Winnetou thought for a long time.

Finally he lifted his head, and said, 'You are a great man, Old Death, my white brother! I'm admiring your heart and your bravery.'

'What do you demand from them?"

'To give back everything that they stole. Then pay five horses for every Apache they killed, and ten horses for each who were tortured.'

'Very generous conditions,' responded Old Death.

'And the Comanche chiefs must meet the Apache chiefs, and agree on a long peace that would last thirty summers and winters.'

'And where would this council take place?'

'In this valley. They can send a few men to their villages to bring everything that we demand from them. The rest must stay. They have to surrender, and they will be our prisoners until we smoke the peace pipe.'

'It's a generous offer, Winnetou. It makes it possible to avoid the massacre. I'm going to them now.'

Old Death cut off a branch of a tree with foliage as a signal that he was an envoy, but just in case, he also took his gun. It was still very risky, but Old Death was a man who did not know fear. Lifting the branch high he started off to the barricade. Winnetou accompanied him for a while, and then returned to us.

He beckoned us to follow him. We went to the herd. The group that had just arrived brought many extra horses, and Winnetou was examining them. He chose five excellent animals, and he gave them to us.

'You got one of my own horses, Charlie,' he told me, 'but your friends will also be contented.'

We did not stop admiring the wonderful animals.

After forty-five minutes Old Death returned. I saw that his mission failed. There was disappointment on his face.

'I know what you want to say, my white brother,' said Winnetou as he turned to him. 'The Comanche don't want to listen to the clever words.'

'Unfortunately, they don't,' replied Old Death. 'But at least I tried everything to change their mind.'

'Are they blind? Are they deaf?' asked Winnetou with a strange emphasis. 'What do they hope?'

'They still hope that they can break out.'

'Did you tell them, my white brother, that another five hundred warriors arrived this morning?'

'I started with that, but they didn't believe me. They laughed at me.'

'Then they must die!' cried Winnetou.

'Terrible!' sighed Old Death.

'So you still cannot accept what is unavoidable? Yes, it will be a terrible massacre. I only have to raise my hand, and the guns will go off. But I'll make one more attempt for Old Death's favour. Follow me to the barricade, my brothers, to make a proper judgement.'

We accompanied him. Winnetou climbed up on the lasso, and started off on the path. He was not hiding, but showed himself to the enemy.

When he reached the middle of the path he stopped, and shouted down to the valley, 'Comanche! I want to talk to you! Listen to me!'

His words were followed with a deep silence. Winnetou repeated his offer, and called the Comanche to surrender.

'Look here!' he said, and lifted his arm.

At this moment the warriors stooping on the path stood up. They formed a long chain that stretched along the entire valley. Winnetou wanted to inform the Comanche that they were surrounded, and their resistance was meaningless. But the effect of this show of power was different from what we had all expected. I could see only that Winnetou had jumped on the ground. At the same time a gun went off in the valley.

'This is Quick Deer's answer,' said Old Death. 'He shot at Winnetou for the second time. Fortunately the Apache saw it, and jumped on the ground. But look!'

Winnetou appeared, and fired with the silver gun. The Comanche yelled.

'He shot the chief dead,' said Old Death, who was in the position where he could see more.

Winnetou lifted his arm again, but now higher with his palm facing the ground. The long line of the Apache aimed. At least four hundred guns went off at the same time.

'Let's go back, gentlemen,' said Old Death. 'This is not for my old eyes even if the Comanche deserved it.'

While returning to our horses we heard one more volley, and then the blood curling battle cry of the Apache. A few minutes later Winnetou joined us. His face was serious, almost sad.

'There will be a big grieving in the Comanche tents,' he said gloomily. 'None of their warriors will return. It was the will of the Great Spirit to revenge our dead. I couldn't do anything else, but I don't want to be by this death-valley anymore. My warriors will do what they have to, and I will ride with you.'

Even though we hurried, it had still taken half an hour until we were ready. Winnetou selected ten warriors, all

413

excellent riders, and we headed towards the Bolsón de Mapimi. I did not look back, and I was happy to leave the terrible death-valley behind.

The Mapimi is so huge that it occupies a large part of two Mexican provinces, Chihuahua and Coahuila. The easiest access is from the North, as the plateau is surrounded by steep limestone mountains from the other directions. Many narrow canyons cut through the ground, and there are many sandy hillocks. My first thought was that there was no water, grass or trees here, but then I had to recognise that I was wrong as we saw many lakes in this limestone desert. While in the summer many dry out, the evaporation provides enough humidity for plants to exist.

The first phase of our journey led to such a lake, the Laguna de Santa Maria. It was about ten miles from our departure point. After a sleepless night it was a long travel, especially as we rode mostly in the canyons. From the morning till the evening we barely could see the Sun. Sometimes we had to go to the right, then to the left, and this completely confused us, so we often thought that we were riding in the opposite direction to ours.

It was sunset when we arrived to the lake. The ground was sandy, and although there were no trees, we were happy for the thick bushes. In the narrow, gloomy canyons we were cold, and now, at least, we could enjoy the heat. The ground, heated by the Sun from the morning to the evening, was hot like an oven, but by midnight it cooled down, and at dawn such a fresh wind rose that we had to roll ourselves in our blankets tightly.

We continued our journey in the early morning heading to the West, but because of the canyons, we had to travel through detours. It was quite difficult to descend to such a canyon, and it was even more difficult to get out of it. Sometimes we had to grope in the labyrinth of canyons until we found a path that led out of the gorge. Pebbles covered the ground of the canyons which exhausted the horses. There were places where we had to go on narrow paths on the side of the canyon. Above us we could see the ribbon of the flaming sky, while below us the depth opened. Vultures followed us in flocks, and when we rested, they settled near us. Their ugly, croaked screams showed their impatience of waiting for when one of us would fall to the bottom of the canyon, and they could devour the body. This was also the hope of the bony, lean jackals. These hid in the shadows.

At noon we left the canyons, and started to ride on a plateau covered with thin grass. We soon found the tracks of about ten riders. Winnetou was sure that these were left by Gibson and his company. There were two types of hoof prints, because the two Indian guides rode on unshod horses. The group had about six hours advantage on us.

In the late afternoon we found new tracks. These came from the South. About twenty or thirty riders rode in a file, which suggested that these were Indians.

'What kind of Indians could these have been? Surely they can't be Apache,' opined Old Death. 'I don't expect anything good from them.'

'You are right, my white brother,' said Winnetou. 'There are no Apache around here. It can only be a hostile band. We have to be alert.'

Soon we found the place where the two groups had met. They obviously had stopped, negotiated there, and then had ridden together. This was the point where the two Apache had left the group.

The thin grass became stronger, and there were some bushes. Soon we arrived to a small stream which was rare on this barren land. The group that we followed obviously had stopped there, and had watered their horses. The stream ran to the North-west.

Old Death was looking to that direction. When we asked what he saw, he said, 'I can see two dots in the distance. Could they be coyotes? But why are they sitting there? They must have smelt us, but then why didn't they run away? They are normally cowards!'

'Silence!' said Winnetou. 'I can hear something.'

We stood motionless and quietly, and listened. Soon we could hear a sound from the direction of the two dots. It was muffled, but it sounded like cries for help.

'It's a man's voice! He's crying for help!' exclaimed Old Death. 'Let's hurry there!'

We got on our horses, and in a few minutes we saw that the two dots first moved, and then disappeared. Indeed two prairie wolves had sat at the bank of the stream, they had watched something, and then they had run away because of our arrival. A man sat in the stream. Only his head was out of the water, his eyes, ears, nose and lips were covered by mosquitoes. He did not have a hat on his head. He must have been in a terrible pain.

'Help, Señores! For God's sake, save me! I can't bear it anymore!' cried the human head sticking out the water.

Naturally we jumped off the horses, and hurried there.

'What happened to you?' asked Old Death in Spanish as the man started in this language. 'How did you get in the water? Why don't you climb out? The water is not more than three feet deep!'

'I can't move. I'm dug in the bed.'

'Hell! Who did it to you?'

'Indians and whites.'

'We have to rescue this poor man. Come on, gentlemen! We don't have tools, so we have to do it by hand!'

'My spade is in the creek, behind my back. They buried it,' said the human head.

'Do you have a spade? How comes?'

'I'm a *gambusino*, that is, a prospector! We always have a pickaxe and a spade.'

We found the spade, and then started to work. The bed of the stream was sandy, so it was not difficult to dig the man out. We understood that they pushed a spear behind the man into the river bed, and they tied his neck to it. It was so tight that he could not move his head. His mouth was two inches from the water, but he could not drink. They rubbed his face with fresh meat to attract the mosquitoes, and these

416

would torture him even more. His hands were also tied behind his back. When we finally could lift him out, and untie him, he fainted. He was in a terrible state. He was naked, and his body showed the marks of a beating.

The unfortunate man soon regained his consciousness. We took him to the place where we had noticed the two dots, because we wanted to camp there during the night. We gave him food, and I cut up my spare shirt to use it as bandage.

Now he could speak.

'I'm a *gambusino*,' he started. 'I'm employed by a mine owner, whose bonanza is about two day's ride from here. It is in the mountains. I have a colleague, a Yankee, his name is Harton and ...'

'Harton?' interrupted Old Death. 'What's his first name?'

'Fred.'

'Do you know where he was born, and how old he is?'

'In New York, and he could be around sixty.'

'Has he got a family?'

'His wife has died, and his son lives in Frisco. Why? Do you know him?'

Old Death behaved very strangely. He put his questions in a very excited voice. His eyes were flaring, his sunken face was red. He was now trying to regain his control, and replied in a calmer voice, 'Yes, I met him once. I thought he was well off. Has he talked about it?'

'Many times. He came from a rich family, and he became a trader. His business developed well, but he had a debased brother, who, like a leech, sucked his blood.'

'Did he mention his brother's name?'

'Yes, his name was Henry Harton.'

'I'd like to meet your colleague.'

'There's not much hope for that. I don't think he's alive. The rascals, who buried me in the stream, took Fred Harton with them.'

Old Death made a motion as if he wanted to jump up, but he overcame his emotions with a great effort.

'How ... has ... it ... happened?' he stuttered.

417

'I just wanted to tell you when you interrupted me. So, his brother stole all his money, and Fred Harton was made bankrupt. He didn't complain about it, I just deduced it from his words. He still talked about this debased brother with love. When he lost his fortune, he joined the prospectors. He tried it, but he didn't have any luck. He became a *vaquero*, and finally my boss employed him. He helped me in searching for nuggets, but he wasn't really good in it to be honest.'

'Then why didn't he stop it?'

'It's not easy, señor! Many millions of people are doing things that aren't for them. It's rare that somebody finds work that suits him the most. Interestingly, his cheating brother apparently became a gold prospector, and it's said that he was lucky. Maybe Fred has become a prospector because of this. Maybe he hoped that he would meet his brother in Mexico.'

'Strange story!' waved Old Death. 'This debased brother once is a leech on his sibling, then a successful prospector. This is a big contradiction.'

'Whatever you think, señor. That's for sure, however, that I met him in Chihuahua, and I recommended him to my boss. He got a job. We became friends, which is rare among *gambusinos*. We worked together to find silver.'

'What's your boss's name?'

'Davis.'

'Hang on! Can you speak English?'

'Just as well as Spanish.'

'Then let's talk in English, because these two people here may well be very interested in your boss.'

'Why?'

Old Death summarised the conversation for the two Langes. Although Davis is a common name, in combination with the silver mines, it was likely that this Davis was the boss of Lange's son-in-law.

'What's the name of your son-in-law?'

'Ulman!'

'Yes, he's the mining manager. And he'll probably become a co-owner soon.'

'My only daughter is his wife. Agnes! The sister of this lad,' Lange pointed at William.

'We call her Señora Inez. A very kind lady. I've talked to her many times.'

'I can hardly wait to meet her!' sighed Lange.

'You can meet her earlier than you'd think. You don't have to travel to Chihuahua. Señor Ulman cares about nothing but the new bonanza. He owns it now. Davis gave the capital to start the exploitation as soon as possible, and they established a joint company. It will be a truly huge business.'

'Can you hear this, Will?' asked Lange. 'What a luck!'

'I wasn't lucky though,' said the prospector. 'Three days ago we left the camp to cross Mapimi, and search around here. We hoped that we would find something, because we suspected that these mountains contain silver, maybe even gold. We arrived to this stream last night. We were very tired, and fell asleep. When we woke up, a group of riders surrounded us. They were whites and Indians.'

'What kind of Indians?' asked Winnetou.

'Chinarra. Forty Chinarra and ten whites.'

'A wild band!' said Old Death. 'Yet, I'm surprised that they attacked you. I thought they were in peace with the palefaces.'

'One cannot be sure,' replied the *gambusino*. 'They are neither friends nor enemies. They don't wage war against the whites, but I have to say, I wasn't happy when I saw them. One cannot be sure, as I said.'

'What did they want?'

'Obviously robbing us. Señor Ulman gave us excellent equipment. Each of us had two horses, modern weapons, ammunition, food, tools, everything needed for spending a couple of weeks on this barren land.'

'And these things attracted them,' nodded Old Death. 'What did they say?'

419

'They asked who we were, and what we were doing here. We told them the truth, and they pretended to be extremely angry. They said that the whole Mapimi was theirs, and also everything that was in the stones, and under the ground. They demanded from us, as a punishment, to hand over the horses, and the equipment.'

'And you did.'

'I didn't. Harton, however, was more considerate, and immediately gave them everything, emptied his pockets even. I was raging. I picked up my gun, which was complete madness against fifty people. They immediately jumped on me, beat me up, and took everything, even my clothing. The white riders didn't help me at all. Just the opposite, they questioned me. I reproached them for their inhumanity, for which they whipped me with their lasso. Harton learnt from my example, and answered all their questions. He told them about Señor Ulman's bonanza, the findings, and the work that had been done. They were interested in it, and they asked where the bonanza was. I shouted at him to stop talking, and he did. Because of this the anger of the whites turned against me again, they tied me up, and dug me in the river bed. They beat Harton until he gave them all the information. But it seems that they were suspicious that he wanted to mislead them, because they took him, and promised the most torturous death if he did not lead them to the bonanza by tomorrow evening.'

In the past weeks I had many opportunities to watch my old friend. But I had never seen the expression that this time dominated his face. His lips were firmly pressed together, his forehead was wrinkled, and there was the flame of dark, merciless determination in his eyes. He was like a murderer at the moment of the murder.

'Do you think they have ridden directly to the bonanza?' he asked in a hoarse voice.

'Definitely. They decided to attack it. There would be a rich loot for them there. Ammunition, food and many other things, not to mention the already unearthed silver.'

'The rascals!' cried out Old Death. 'The Chinarra will get the guns and ammunition, the whites anything that can be sold. How far is the bonanza?'

'They'll arrive there by tomorrow evening except if Harton pulls himself together.'

'What do you mean? What can he do?'

'Well, it would be honourable to lead them the long way around. I hoped that somebody would rescue me. I would have asked him to ride to the bonanza, and inform Señor Ulman of the danger.'

Old Death was frowning, and said, 'I'd ride after them right now, but it's dark soon, and I can't follow their tracks. But you probably know which way they went.'

The Spaniard warned him not to ride after them during the night. Old Death eventually accepted that he would have to wait until dawn.

'Then we will go together,' he said. 'There are sixteen of us against forty Chinarra and ten white bandits. We don't have any reason to be afraid. What weapons did the Chinarra have?'

'I saw only bows and spears, but they now have our guns and revolvers,' answered the *gambusino*.

'That doesn't matter, because they don't know how to use them. I'd like to know where the bonanza is. I assume that it's near some water, thus near a canyon or a gorge; a place difficult to find. Am I right?'

'Just imagine a deep ravine surrounded with a forest,' replied the *gambusino*. 'It's about two miles long, so it's more of a valley than a ravine. In the middle it becomes broad, but the cliffs are very steep on both sides. The cliffs are full of silver deposits, but they also contain copper and lead. The forest reaches the edge of the cliff, and some bushes and trees grow from the cliff. At the end of the valley there's a strong spring. So strong that it becomes a stream right away. The valley has only one entrance, and the stream exits there. It's s so narrow that between the water and the cliff only three men or two horses can pass.'

'Very advantageous,' nodded Old Death. 'It would be easy to defend such a place.'

'Nature created this,' said the prospector. 'There's also a man-made entrance, but only a few people know it. The mining is in the middle of the valley. As a result, just to get out of the valley takes more than half an hour. This is why Señor Ulman made a secret exit in the middle of the valley. There is a point where the cliff descends in steps. For my boss's order they felled huge trees at the edge of the cliff, and let them down on ropes to the steps. On every step a tree leans on the cliff, and these trees cover the steps with their branches and foliage. Only those who know about it can find these steps.'

'This is something! Although I bet I could find the steps immediately! The stumps of the trees would tell me a lot.'

'You only think that, Sir! The trees were not cut down, but were lifted out of the ground with their roots, and the resulting holes were filled in. Thirty men held the ropes to let down the trees.'

'Has he got so many workers?'

'Currently about forty.'

'Well, then he doesn't have to be afraid of the attack. And how did he organise the contact with the rest of the world?'

'There is a mule caravan every fortnight that brings the supply, and transports the silver from the mine.'

'And the guarding of the entrance?'

'There is a guard at the entrance of the valley during the night. And we have a hunter who constantly scouts around the area to supply the workers with fresh meat. If he sees something suspicious, he immediately reports it.'

'Did you build barracks?'

'My boss lives in a big tent, and there is an even bigger one for storage. There are huts around the tents in a half-circle. This is where the workers sleep.'

'If enemies arrive there, they would notice the tents!'

'Señor Ulman thought of that too. Branches and foliage cover the tents and the huts.'

'How are you with weapons?'

'Fine. Every worker has a double-barrelled gun and, of course, knife and revolver.'

'Excellent! Then the Chinarra and the bandits will be received appropriately. Of course, we have to overtake them to warn Señor Ulman. We'll leave tomorrow morning, and ride hard. Let's rest until then.'

Old Death had told me many times of the importance of resting, but I could not fall asleep. Old Death was also twisting and turning next to me, although other times he only had to close his eyes, and he was sleeping. I could hear as he was sighing, and murmuring incomprehensible words. Something was on his soul. When the *gambusino* mentioned his colleague, he behaved as if he had known him. It had to something serious, because he had become too upset.

I had lay for three hours half-sleeping, when I noticed that the old man stood up, and went towards the stream. I waited for a quarter of an hour then another one, but Old Death did not return. Because of this, I also got up, and went after him. In ten minutes I spotted him. He stood at the bank of the stream with his back towards me, and stared at the moon. I did not want to creep up on him, but the grass suppressed the noise of my steps, and probably he was also deep in his thought. I was only a step away from him, when he suddenly turned, and pulled his revolver.

'Who's there?' he growled. 'Who is in the dark? I'll shoot!' He suddenly stopped, because he recognised me. 'Is that you?' he continued. 'Why aren't you sleeping?'

'Because I keep on thinking about Gibson.'

'I'm not surprised, but tomorrow we will catch him, you can be sure. You will have achieved what you wanted, and we part because I'll stay in the mining camp.'

'There? Why?'

'Just because ...'

'I'm sorry, I don't want to peep into your secrets. I heard your sighing, and I thought that maybe I could help you. Excuse me, Sir.'

I turned around and was about to return to my place, but he caught my arm.

'Don't be so sensitive, Sir!' he said. 'I thank you for caring for me. I have to admit that my heart is heavy, and I would like to lighten it. But it is something that it's very difficult to talk about.'

We were walking slowly along the stream.

The old man suddenly stopped, and asked me, 'Tell me, what do you think of me? What kind of a man am I? You and I have been together for some time. What's your view of Old Death's character?'

'Very good, open-hearted, honest man,' I replied. 'I think of you with the greatest respect, Sir!'

'Hm! Tell me, have you sinned in your life?'

'A lot,' I replied. 'I made my parents and teachers angry, I climbed over the neighbour's fence, and raided his orchard. If I had an argument with my friends in the school, I beat them up, and so forth.'

'Don't make jokes about it! I mean serious sins, the ones that the law persecutes.'

'Then my soul is clean.'

'You see, this is it! I'm not jealous by nature, but for this one I envy you.'

He sighed, and I had to recognise the weight on his soul. I did not want to interrogate him, so I did not say anything.

He soon continued, 'There's an invisible judge in us, who cannot be misled with lies. He's silent, yet he talks, we can hear him day and night as he makes judgements on us.'

'Why have such dark thoughts come to you, Sir?'

Instead of an answer, he asked me, 'Did you hear what the *gambusino* said about the brother of that Harton? What do you think of that man?'

The problem started to become clear to me, and thus I said only, 'A reckless man.'

'Reckless? That's not an excuse! Such reckless men are the most dangerous, because they are often sympathetic, but they bring danger to everyone. They start as loose men, and then they end up as criminals. There's no stoppage on the slope. If you knew what this Henry Harton did, what I did!'

'Are you ... Henry Harton?'

'Yes. I wish I could say that this is my honest name! Can you remember when in New Orleans I commented on my mother? I don't want to go into details. My mother spoilt me, and when she died I thought it would remain the same: I would get everything immediately, without work and effort. I spent my inheritance in a year, while my younger brother, who got the same amount, opened a shop, and developed it. He worked hard. I did not feel like taking a job, thus I became a gold prospector. I got into an environment, where my bad instincts overcame me. I dug the soil for months without results. I starved, and lived in poverty. When I was lucky, I put the found nugget on a dice or cards, because I wanted to become rich quickly. I also became addicted to opium. Before that I had been an athletic giant, but the opium destroyed my body quickly. I was ragged and ill, when I arrived to San Francisco, where my brother lived with his wife and son. Fred felt sorry for me; he dressed me up, gave me food, and offered me the job of manager with a salary on which I could have easily lived. I wish he had not helped me! I'm ashamed of telling you how I repaid his goodwill.'

He became silent, and now I could hear how heavily he breathed as he was fighting with his memories.

'The devil of gambling caught me again,' he continued. 'Frisco is a port, full of gambling dens. I spent all my free time in these, and soon my working time too. I kept on losing. I took smaller, then larger sums of cash from the shop. I hid the missing money with forged receipts; I could forge the signatures of our business partners very well. Finally I couldn't hide my theft, and I fled. My brother had to pay, and he went bankrupt. He fell into poverty. His wife fell ill with her heart because of her sadness, and died in a heart attack. Fred disappeared with his son. I learnt all this years later when I dared to return to San Francisco again. The news shocked me so much that I made the resolution to

425

break with cards. I stopped smoking opium, and only I'm only eating it with my chewing tobacco. I started with a large dose, and now it's only a minuscule piece. It took a huge effort, but I didn't break my resolution. Only one desire has kept me alive: to find Fred, and compensate him at least partially for what I did against him. I returned to the gold prospectors, but now I lived very differently from them. I wandered in California and Mexico, and I was lucky. I lived on cents, and put aside every dollar for Fred.'

He sat down on the grass, rested his elbows on his knees, and buried his face in his hands. I stood next to him, I could not say a word, and I did not dare to disturb him in his dark thoughts. When he lifted his head, he looked at me as if he had never seen me before.

'Ah, is it you? Of course! Are you still with me? Aren't you horrified by me?'

'No, Sir,' I replied. 'I have no right to judge a person who has repented his sins as much as you, and suffered for it to this extent. But remember that chance has now put you on the track of the person whom you have sought for so long. You will see your brother tomorrow, and Mr Harton will surely forgive you.'

'Yes, yes! The joy made me mad, and stirred the dark memories of the past … I forgot about tomorrow. Tomorrow I will finish the past!'

'These are the right thoughts, Sir. Just forward, always forward!' I exclaimed because at least I could say something consoling to him.

'I'd like to tell you something else,' said Old Death. 'As you know, I have carried my old saddle everywhere, and I don't part with it even if I don't have a horse. You probably considered it eccentric, but the saddle is not silly. I told you the secret of my life. Now I'll tell you the secret of the saddle. If you cut its inside, you will find things that I gathered for my younger brother. If something befalls me, and I have premonitions right now, everything that's in it belongs to Fred Harton. Will you remember it? Promise it!'

'I give my word.'

'Thank you. I trust you, and your promise is important to me. Now, go to sleep. I'll stay here, because a lot of things have to be clarified in my soul. Go, young man, to sleep. You can do that as your conscience is clear. Good night, Sir, we will meet at dawn.'

I walked back to the camp slowly, and lay down, but it took me a long time till I could fall asleep, as I was very much affected by everything Old Death told me. Finally I fell asleep. In my exhaustion I felt that I had slept only a few minutes when people started to move around me. It was dawn, and everybody was getting ready. Old Death was urging the departure. The *gambusino* stated that only his back was aching, and he was strong enough for the journey. We gave him two blankets. He wrapped one around his waist like a skirt, while he put the other on his shoulders. We put him behind one of the Apache warriors, and started off.

We had to go through canyons again, from one gorge to another till midday. Then we got to a better terrain. We could gallop on a grassy plateaux for hours following the tracks. Suddenly the *gambusino* lifted his hand, and stopped our group.

'We won't follow the tracks now,' he said. 'Here Harton followed my advice, and took the bandits on a detour. But we turn to the right, to the direction of the bonanza.'

'Well,' said Old Death, 'you know the way, so lead us!' On the West a bluish fog closed the horizon.

'They are mountains,' said the *gambusino*, 'and behind them is the mining settlement.'

It took two more hours of galloping until we could see the mountains clearly. We had a short rest, ate something, and then continued the journey. The landscape became greener, there were bushes, more and more of them. Both humans and animals felt that we were approaching to our destination.

It was about time, because the sunset was approaching. My heart throbbed when I spotted the first tree. It stood lonely in the middle of the prairie with branches torn by the wind. We looked at it as the first sign of forests. Soon more and more trees appeared, and soon we got to the woods. The ground was ascending, and after we crossed the woods we got to a ridge. On the ground, in the thin grass, to our surprise, we saw tracks, it was a whole path.

'A large group passed here,' said Old Death. 'There were at least forty riders.'

'Could the Chinarra overcome us?' asked the *gambusino* anxiously.

'I'm afraid so,' replied Old Death grimly.

Winnetou jumped off his horse, and followed the tracks on foot for a while. Then he announced, 'Ten palefaces and four times as many Indians. They were here an hour ago.'

'Then they haven't started the attack,' I said, 'because they would send out scouts first, and it takes time.'

'They don't need it. They know everything from Harton.'

'As far as I know the Indians attack just before dawn.'

'We can't build on this,' said Old Death impatiently. 'They are led by white bandits, and they wouldn't care with the Indian customs. Let's not waste time!'

We spurred our horses, and almost flew. We did not follow the tracks, but headed to a different direction. Harton had enough brain and bravery not to lead the bandits and the Chinarra to the entrance, but to the other end of the valley, while we took a shortcut. Unfortunately it became dark earlier than we thought, and we also had to cross a thick forest on the other side of the ridge. The *gambusino* tumbled in the front, and we had to rely on his knowledge of the terrain, and the instincts of our horses. Of course, we dismounted, and advanced with revolvers our in hand, ready to shoot as we could have bumped into Indians at any time. Finally we could hear the running of the stream.

'We are at the entrance,' said the Spanish. 'Look out! The water is on the left. Let's go after each other. Feel the cliff with your right hand.'

'Where's the guard?' asked Old Death.

'He hasn't yet taken his position. It happens only when the workers go to sleep.'

'Very economical! A mine that is not guarded! I can't see the path in this darkness.'

'Just straight forward. The ground is smooth. We'll get to the tents without a problem.'

We walked carefully and slowly, and led the horses by the reins. Now I was in the front, behind me Old Death, and then the *gambusino*. It seemed to me suddenly that a shadow passed in front of me. I warned my companions. We stopped, and listened, but it was perfectly quiet.

'One can imagine things in the dark,' asserted the *gambusino*. 'We just got to the secret stairs.'

'Then somebody came from there,' I argued.

'Then it is a friend. There's no reason for anxiety! But I think you are mistaken, señor.'

Soon we saw a light in front of us. It was the light of a lamp from one of the tents. A bit later we could hear voices too. We picked up speed.

'Wait for the others,' said Old Death to the prospector, 'and I'll inform Señor Ulman of our arrival.'

Those in the tent must have heard our footsteps, and especially our horses, but the tent remained closed.

'Let's enter the tent, Sir,' said the old man to me. 'It'll be a pleasant surprise.'

He went straight to the tent entrance.

'They are here!' exclaimed a voice. 'Don't let them in!'

The sentence had not been finished when a gun popped. I could see that the old man grabbed the canvass of the tent with both hands. From the tent some guns pointed towards us. Old Death tottered, and then collapsed on the ground.

'My premonitions ... my brother ... forgive me ... the saddle ...' he groaned.

'Mr Ulman! For God's sake, don't shoot!' I shouted. 'We are your friends. Your father-in-law and brother-in-law are with us!'

'What are you saying?'

'We came to defend you from the Chinarra! Let me in!'

'Wait! Hold fire! Right, come in, but only you!'

I entered the tent. I saw twenty people there with guns in their hands. From the top of the tent three lamps hung.

A young man came forward, and turned to another one, who looked much older, partly because of his torn clothing, and exhausted face.

'Was he one of them, Harton?' asked the young man.

'No, señor.'

'Poppycock!' I cried. 'Stop this interrogation. The enemy may arrive at any moment! What Harton are you talking to? Is he the one who was captured by the Chinarra?'

'Yes, but he escaped. He arrived two minutes ago.'

'So, it was you slipped by us, Mr Harton? I warned my companions, but they didn't believe me. Who shot?'

'I did,' said one of the miners.

'Thank God!' I sighed because I was afraid that it had been a fratricide. 'You killed an innocent man. The one to whom you can thank your escape from danger.'

This is when Lange entered the tent with his son, and the *gambusino*. The joyous surprise then happened, the one that Old Death had mentioned, but he could not see.

People were running from the huts to the tent, which created a big noise and turmoil. I had to order silence. Only after this I leant over my old friend. Old Death was dead, the bullet hit his heart. With Sam's help I lifted him, and laid him on the ground in the tent. The faithful Sam cried. Two women stepped out from a separated section of the tent. One was a nurse with a little boy on her arm. The other was Lange's daughter, and she embraced her father.

In these circumstances I had to take over the command. First I asked Harton about his escape.

He quickly reported, 'I led them in a detour to arrive here as late as possible. I led them to the end of the valley to search for the entrance if they wanted. They settled in the forest, and the chiefs went to scout the area. I was left tied up near the horses. Slowly I freed my hand, and then my

430

legs. At the right moment I slipped away, and got down to the valley on the secret stairs. I saw you, but in the dark I though the Chinarra found the entrance. I slipped past you, and hurried to the tent to warn Señor Ulman. Fortunately most of the men were awake, and were in the tent. We were determined that we would fight, and would receive the first man with a bullet.'

'It wasn't a good plan, I have to tell you,' it burst out of me bitterly. 'You don't yet suspect what a tragedy you caused. But enough of it now. Let's prepare for the defence. We have no time to lose!'

I quickly made the most important arrangements. We led the horses to the end of the valley. The Apache and the armed miners were positioned behind the tent. This is where we took Old Death's body to. We placed a barrel of oil, and a bottle of petrol by the stream. We removed the top of the barrel, and put a man there with the order that for a signal he should pour the petrol on the oil, light it, and push the barrel into the stream. I wanted the burning oil to spread on the stream's surface, and light up the whole valley.

Fifty men were ready to receive the enemy, who had lost their numeric superiority, and also in terms of weapons, were much weaker than us. Some men were put by the entrance to report to us the approach of the enemy in time. We loosened the back of the tent so that we could exit the tent in that way too.

Only five of us remained in the tent: I, Ulman, Winnetou, Lange, and his son. We had been waiting for about ten minutes, when one of the guards reported that two whites wanted to talk to Señor Ulman. Winnetou, the two Langes, and I pulled back to the separate section of the tent, and peered from there to see how Ulman was receiving the visitors.

Gibson and William Ohlert entered the tent. It seemed that there was some motion in the dark behind them. Ulman greeted them politely, and offered them seats. Gibson

431

introduced himself as Gavilano. He said that they were geographers, and they had come to the area for surveying. They had made their camp in the forest, when they had met a *gambusino* called Harton, who had told them that there was a mining settlement nearby, where they could get better accommodation. As his colleague was ill, they had asked Harton to lead them here, and he hoped that Señor Ulman would take them for one night.

I could not listen to this stupid tale any more. I stepped out. Gibson, when he caught sight of me jumped up, and on his face a mixture of his shock and extreme fright reflected.

'And your Chinarra, Gibson?' I thundered at him. 'Are they also ill, and want accommodation for the night?'

Ohlert was just staring at the ground, and ignored what was happening around him. Gibson, however, was raging.

'Rascal!' he yelled. 'Are you following me everywhere?'

He grabbed the barrel of his rifle, and lifted it to hit my head. I jumped on him, and pushed him partially aside, but the rifle was in full swing already, and it hit Ohlert's skull. The young man crashed on the ground. In the next moment several miners entered the tent. They aimed at Gibson whom I held with my two hands.

'Don't shoot!' I cried as I wanted to capture him alive, but it was too late. A gun went off, and Gibson fell on the ground from my hands with a bullet in his head.

'Never mind, señor! This is the custom here! He got what he deserved,' said the miner who shot him dead.

The shot must have been the signal, because an Indian battle cry resounded near the tent. The Chinarra with the white bandits had already entered the settlement, and thought that they would finish everyone off.

Ulman rushed out, and the others followed him. The guns crashed, men yelled and swore. Only I remained in the tent. I leant over Ohlert to see if he could be helped. His pulse was still throbbing. This reassured me, and for the time being I did not care about him, but rushed out to participate in the battle.

The burning oil on the stream had high flames, and cast light over the whole valley. The battle was over, I was not needed. The attackers did not expect such a reception. Many of them died, while the rest ran to the exit of the valley, but they were still pursued.

Ulman stood by the tent, and kept on shooting. Almost all his bullets hit the target. I went up to him, and advised him to send Harton with some miners to the place where the enemy had tied their horses. It would have been good to get their horses, and the escapees too. Ulman accepted my advice, and gave the orders.

A few minutes after the first shot the valley was free of the enemy.

The miners, who were sent out to capture the horses, were successful, and now they were combing the area. Only Harton returned. He had no idea who was our only loss, the man, who died of friendly fire. I took his arm, and walked to the end of the valley with him, away from the light. I sat down with him, and told him everything that I had to. It was one of the most difficult moments in my life. Harton cried like a child. His sobbing grabbed my heart, and made my grief over the loss of a good friend almost unbearable. He had always thought of his brother with love. He had long forgiven what his brother had committed against him. I had to tell him everything that had happened from my first meeting with Henry to his death. And when I finished he begged me not to leave him, but accept him as a friend in place of his unfortunate brother.

In the morning we took Old Death's saddle, and opened it. We found a leather case in it. It was thin, but contained a fortune. There were a number of banker's drafts in his brother's name and a precise description and map of a mine in Sonora. It was an extremely rich bonanza. Old Death found it during his wanderings. He left it to his brother. Fred Harton was a rich man now.

Ohlert had not regained his consciousness, but he was alive. It was my responsibility to stay with him until he fully recovered. I did not mind it as I could rest after the tiring events of the previous days.

Old Death's funeral affected me deeply, and I had to have the strength to support his brother. After the funeral Fred Harton quit his job, and travelled to Chihuahua. When he left, he begged me to accompany him to Sonora, and help him find the bonanza. I could not commit myself at that time, and told him that I would give him the final answer in Chihuahua.

Winnetou decided to stay with me for the time being, and sent the ten Apache warriors home to their village. Ulman gave presents to them. Sam travelled with Harton to carry out his master's instructions. I do not know if he returned to Cortesio after that.

Two months later I was sitting in Father Benito's room in the abbey of Buono Pastor in Chihuahua. The father was the most famous doctor in North-Mexico. It was a good decision to take William there, because his condition started to improve. The miracle was not done by the father, but by the hard butt of the gun that knocked Ohlert out from his monomania. As his wound improved, his mind became clearer too. He became just as full of life as his father whom he now longed for. I made it sure that it could happen. I sent a detailed report to Ohlert, who immediately responded, and informed me that he would come to Mexico as he wanted to take his son home. I wrote to Mr Tailor too with my notice. I had the desire to travel to North-west Mexico, to Sonora, with Harton, where I would have new adventures. Only one thought ached in me: the brave, great, and kind old warrior, who helped me in so many things, from whom I had learnt so much, the unforgettable Old Death, could not ride with me.

OLD FIREHAND

I COULD write a lot about the adventures in Sonora, but as Winnetou did not come with us, and this book is about him, I skip these events. It is enough to say that after much struggle, and many dangers we found Old Death's bonanza, and it was rich. Fred Harton, as a fee for my services, offered shares in it. However, I had no intention of settling in Sonora to exploit the bonanza, so I sold my shares to Harton, and I got more than enough money to compensate for the loss of the shipwreck. I rode to the Pecos River to visit the pueblo of the Apache. I was received with brotherly love, but I did not achieve my goal, because Winnetou was not there. He had gone on a long journey. He had gone on visiting the dispersed Apache villages to discuss the future of the Apache people.

They asked me to wait for him in the pueblo. It would have meant waiting for half a year, and I was restless. With a big detour, through Colorado and Kansas, I decided to return to St Louis. On the way I met Emery Bothwell, an educated, brave, enterprising English gentleman, whom I met again in Africa. I describe this in another book.

My visit to St Louis took to my fatherly friend, Mr Henry, of course. From him I learnt that the fame of my adventures were well known in the southern states, and everybody was talking about Old Shatterhand in St Louis.

'You have become a great man, since I last saw you, my dear son!' said Mr Henry. 'They never stop praising your character; your bravery and graciousness with which you are merciful even with your worst enemy. If you continue like this, you'll surpass even Old Firehand, though he's twice as old as you. I also have something to boast about. Look!'

He unlocked his gun cabinet, and took out a rifle. It was, the first working Henry rifle. He took me to his shooting range to try it as he was interested in my opinion. I praised it, but I repeated what I had told him earlier, that the more perfect it would become, the more trouble it would cause to the life of humans and animals.

'I know, I have heard it from you,' he replied. 'I decided that I would make only a few of them. This is the first of them, and I give it to you as a present. It'll be useful for you in the Wild West.'

'But I'm not going there right now!'

'Then …?'

'First back to Europe, and from there to Africa.'

'To Africa?' he asked, surprised. 'What will you do there?'

'I promised Mr Bothwell that I would meet him in Algiers. His relatives live there.'

'And then?'

'We plan a little excursion to the Sahara.'

'And then the lions or the hippos will eat you!'

'There are no lions in the Sahara, because they cannot live without water, and the hippos don't eat meat.'

'And how will you talk to them?'

'To the hippos?'

'No, the humans.'

'I speak good French.'

'And to the Bedouin?'

'If you don't mind, I can speak some Arabic too.'

'You know a lot! But knowledge is not enough for such a journey, you need money too!'

'I have money too from the bonanza, from Mr Ohlert, and from the Tailor Detective Agency!' I stated proudly.

'Well, then I don't know what to say to hold you back.'

'It's a waste of time, Mr Henry.'

'I know! You are stubborn like … a hippo! Go, go, I don't want to see you!'

He put the rifle in my hand, and pushed me out of the house. I knew he was angry because he was afraid that he would never see me again. I heard how angrily he locked the bolt inside. But by the time I was on the street, he put his head out of the window, and asked, 'But you'll come in the evening, won't you?'

'Naturally,' I replied.

'You'll have an excellent dinner! Steamed beef stew!'

436

'I look forward to it!' I replied smiling, and waved to him.

In the evening he made me promise that I would return within half a year.

'I promise that six months from today I will knock on your door,' I announced.

Exactly six months later I visited him, and reported on my journey in Africa. He was happy to hear how useful the rifle was in the fights against the robbers. He told me that Winnetou had visited him, and when he had learnt when I would return, he had left a message for me that he would be hunting by the ephemeral Saint Simon River, and if I wanted to meet him, I would find him there.

I departed immediately. After three weeks' riding I found the Apache camp. Winnetou was joyous to see me. I showed him the Henry rifle, and he admired it sufficiently, but he did not want to try it. He said that such a gun had a soul, and it would be offended if I allowed anyone to handle it.

'You were given a wonderful present by Mr Henry,' he said. 'But I would also like to give you a present, Charlie.'

Winnetou's present was a beautiful, raven-black stallion that he had trained for me. Its best attribute was his speed. He almost flew, so I called it Swallow.

At that time an argument broke out between the Navajo and the Nijora tribes. Winnetou decided that after hunting he would visit these tribes, and facilitate a peace between them. He wanted me to accompany him, but something prevented us from carrying out our plan. We met a small group of white riders that carried gold from California. They were frightened, when the Apache suddenly surrounded them, but they became assured when they heard Winnetou's and Old Shatterhand's name. I could see the honour attached to these two names. They asked me to accompany them to Fort Scott for an appropriate fee, because then the gold would definitely reach its destination. I did not want to undertake it at first, but Winnetou persuaded me. It would make him proud if I could carry out this task, he told me. He suggested that I should ride from Fort Scott to the North, to

437

the Sand and Gravel Prairie, east of the Missouri River. He wanted to visit his old friend, Old Firehand there, and he would have liked to introduce me to the great man. Thus, I accompanied the group, and the gold arrived to Fort Scott. We were attacked a number of times, and I could thank my life only to the Henry rifle and Swallow.

I rode to the North alone. I crossed the Kansas River, then the River Platte in the hunting grounds of the Sioux. Winnetou had mentioned to me that my journey will take me across a recently found oilfield owned by a man called Forster. By the oilfield there was a settlement, and it had a store. I could buy anything I needed there.

By my calculations I could not be far from this place. I knew that the settlement was called New Venango, and it was surrounded by steep cliffs. The prairie is cut through by such gorges in which is a small river or stream which is very shallow or dry during the summer.

I rode slowly on the plain that was full of sunflowers, but I could not see any gorge. Swallow was tired, and I was also exhausted by the long journey. I hardly could wait to arrive to a settlement where I could rest, and buy ammunition, because my stock was very low. However, I could not see any sign of hope of these things. I was about to give up my objectives, when Swallow lifted his head, and made the noise with which a mustang signals that a living creature was nearby. With a motion I stopped him, and looked around.

I did not have to search for long. From the right hand side I noticed two riders in the distance. They also spotted me, and galloped towards me. The distance was still too big, so I took out my telescope, and with surprise I concluded that one of the riders was only a teenage boy, a rarity in this area. "Look at that," I thought, "A child in the middle of the prairie, dressed like a trapper. And who is the man?" I continued my musings. "Is he the 'ghost of the prairie', who, according to the Indians, rides on a flaming horse during the night, and puts on all kinds of shapes during the day to take humans to destruction? And was the child a victim?"

As the outfit of the approaching riders was excellent, I cast a look at my own that was quite worn by my journey. My moccasin seemed to be hungry as the sole had clearly got bored by the uppers, and wanted to separate from it. My leather trousers were shiny and certain stains showed that I cleaned my hands from bison dripping or the fat of raccoon by wiping them on my trousers rather than a serviette. My leather shirt, which protected me against the weather, both from cold and heat, in a self-sacrificing way, now made me look like a scarecrow. The worst was my favourite beaver-fur hat, because it became too big, lost all its hair, and here and there burn marks indicated the occasions when I had been too close to the campfire.

I consoled myself by the fact that I was not in the foyer of a theatre, but somewhere between the Black Hills and the Rocky Mountains. I did not have much time to think about my appearance, because the two riders caught up with me. The boy lifted his whip as a greeting, and addressed me in a ringing voice, 'Good morning, Sir! Do you have a problem that you're standing here hesitatingly?'

'Greetings, little Sir! No problem at all. Only I buttoned up my armour so that the arrows of searching eyes would not wound me.'

'Is it forbidden to look at you?'

'I let it happen, but only on a mutual basis.'

'Then lift your visor, armoured knight, and examine me.'

'Thank you. I can already see that you are perfect little gentleman. I'm afraid I look like a beggar. But it's the fault of the branches, because they made me ragged on the way. I'm looking for a house number, but I can't find it'

'I'll show you the way,' the boy laughed then he rode his horse in steps and finally started to gallop.

Swallow, as if he knew that it was a competition, started to gallop too and in minutes he left behind the young rider, who suddenly stopped his horse, and when I turned back to him, he cried out, 'You have an excellent horse! Sell it to me. I'll give any price for it.'

439

'I wouldn't sell this horse for all the treasures of the world!' I replied, and stroked Swallow's neck. 'This mustang has saved me in many difficult situations, and I can thank my life to it.'

'Indian training,' he nodded with expertise. 'Where did you get it?'

'I got it as a present from Winnetou, an Apache chief.'

'From Winnetou?' he asked astonished. 'The most famous chief from Sonora to Columbia! And I thought I had met a Sunday hunter who has never seen an Indian in his life. Now I can see that your clothing carries the marks of the forest, your horse is also excellent, only your gun is strange.'

'Not strange, but unusual. It's from St Louis, where, as you may know, they make excellent guns.'

'And what do you think of mine?' he asked, and pulled out an old, rusty pistol.

'I'm sorry, but this pistol looks as if it had been made before Pocahontas was born.'

'I don't think they made such things then!' the young man laughed.

'I'm only joking!' I replied. 'I have seen Indians who could always hit the target with the shabbiest guns.'

'And you?' he asked, 'can you do this?'

He turned his horse, rode around me very quickly, and then he shot. I felt a little hit on my barren beaver-fur hat, and the sunflower that I had just put on it, flew away. This unexpected circus attraction made me angry, and instead of appraisal, I remarked in a dry voice, 'For rudeness it's quite good, for aiming, it's quiet ordinary.'

'What does he say?' asked a voice behind me. I turned around, and I saw the companion of the teenager. He just reached us on his well-fed, heavy horse. 'The head of such a prairie-wanderer isn't worth as much as the bullet that flies by his head!'

He was a haggard man, his neck was long and thin, his countenance sharp, his eyes stern, and his thin lips bent downwards. For some reason I did not retort to his rudeness.

The boy turned his horse around, and asked, 'Are you going to New Venango, Sir?'

'Yes.'

'And you came from the savannah?'

'As you can see.'

'But you aren't blood and flesh Westerner, are you?'

'It depends what you mean by this. I wasn't born here, that's for sure. And you?'

'My father came from Europe, from Germany, but I was born here, in America. My mother was an Indian woman, an Assiniboine.'

'I see,' I nodded, because I did not want to show my surprise. I would have liked to ask him many things, but I felt it would have been insensitive to enquire further. Half Indian! His skin was a shade darker than the white. From what he said, it seemed that his mother was dead, and his father brought him up.

'Look!' he said. 'Can you see the smoke there?'

'Oh, this is the cliff that I looked for in vain. Then in the valley I will find New Venango. Do you know Emery Forster, the oil man?'

'Of course, I know him! He's the father-in-law of my brother. My brother lives in Omaha with his wife, I'm just returning from visiting them, and now I'm Mr Forster's guest. What do you want from him?'

'I came to buy things, and I also heard that he owns everything here, and such a man interests me. And as I'm here, I'd like to meet him.

'But you know him!'

'I? I have never seen him.'

'He's riding next to you. He didn't introduce himself, but you didn't tell him your name. On the prairie the etiquette is not adhered to.'

'You are wrong,' I replied without casting a look at the bad mannered money-bag, who rode on my other side. 'The prairie has its own rules. For example, people are judged according to their character and not by their fortune. Here

441

those men attract the respect, who keep their stance even in the most difficult circumstances. In the prairie or in the forest money doesn't mean much.'

The boy's eyes flashed, and I saw that deep in his heart he agreed with me, but, maybe because of his relative, he argued with me, 'But the trappers work for money!'

'The hunter needs ammunition, gunpowder, and many other things. And he has to buy them,' I replied. 'But he doesn't work for money. He wouldn't exchange his freedom for anything else.'

In the meantime we arrived to the edge of the cliff, and I could see the houses of New Venango in the valley. There was a river in the bottom of the valley, and also a large oil derrick, and all kinds of barrels. The houses were huts made of blank wood except for two houses. One was the factory with the stores, while the other building was a pretty house surrounded by a little garden.

'There's the store,' the boy pointed at a large blockhouse. 'It's also an inn and everything else. But be careful, because the path is narrow and steep!'

He jumped off his saddle, and I followed his example.

'Lead your horse by the reins,' he advised me.

'Unnecessary,' I answered. 'Swallow will nicely follow me. Just go ahead.'

He walked with calm and sure steps on the steep path leading his horse by the reins. I stayed behind him, and my good mustang faithfully followed me. Forster stumbled at the back leading his broad horse clumsily. When arriving to the valley I wanted to say good-bye to them believing that they were heading to the pretty house, while my path led to the store on the right.

'Don't say good-bye yet,' said Forster suddenly. 'We will accompany you to the store. I want to talk to you. Come, Harry!' he added turning to the boy.

I did not ask what he wanted from me, only shrugged my shoulder, and headed to the store. On the door it was written with chalk: "Store & Hotel". Forster grabbed Swallow's reins. 'I like this horse too,' he said. 'I'll give you a hundred dollars for it.'

'I said that it's not for sale,' I replied.

'Two hundred.'

I shook my head.

'Three hundred!'

'Forget it! You aren't rich enough to buy my horse! Do you think that a prairie hunter would part with his horse?'

'I'll give you my horse too!'

'Thank you! I would be ashamed to sit on such a nag!'

'You want to buy from me, don't you? Choose whatever you want, and that will also be paid for. I have made you an offer that could buy me ten mustangs for the same price.'

'Yes, ten. But not like this. Deal with a horse trader, but leave me alone.'

'What do you think, Harry?' he turned to the boy again. 'His toes are out of his ragged shoes, but he doesn't want three hundred dollars!'

'Choose your words better, Mr Forster, because you'll end up badly!' I burst out.

'What? Are you threatening me? Do you think you are on the savannah, where every tramp can do whatever they want? Here, in New Venango, I'm the God, and everybody does what I order! I ask you for the last time: do you sell me your horse or not?'

Instead of an answer I stepped up to tear the reins from his hand, but suddenly he pushed me in my chest so hard that I tottered, and in the next moment he jumped on the saddle of my mustang.

'I'll show you, you nobody, that Emery Forster is the master here! The mustang is mine whether you like it or not! You can take my horse, and in the store they will give you the money! Come, Harry, we have finished here!'

Harry did not follow him immediately. Only when he saw that I did not do anything for protecting my property, he put on an infinitely contemptuous look on his face.

'Tell me,' he asked, 'do you know what a coyote is?'

443

'Of course,' I replied indifferently.

'So, what?'

'Prairie wolf. The most cowardly animal in the world that is afraid of even a barking dog.'

'You know it well. I'm not surprised, because you are also a coyote!'

He whipped his horse, and with a few jumps he caught up with God of New Venango, Emery Forster.

His last word would have been a serious insult if it had come from an adult, but I could not take it badly from a boy. As to Forster, I was only smiling at him, I had no intention of letting him have my mustang. "He can feed him," I thought, "I'll go for him in the night". It would have been enough to whistle to Swallow, and he would have thrown off the strange rider, and return to me.

A few men stood about, and had heard my argument with Forster. One came up to me, and asked, 'Do you want to stay in New Venango for some time?'

'I doubt it,' I replied.

'Then it was the right thing that you gave way,' he said. 'It's not advisable to start an argument with Mr Forster.'

'Who is the owner of this shop?' I asked.

'I am,' he replied, 'but Mr Forster has shares in it. I heard what he promised to you. Come in, choose what you want, and you won't have to pay. I'll put in on Mr Forster's account.'

'I have nothing to do with that horse thief,' I answered. 'I'll pay for what I buy.'

He looked at me astonished, but as he glanced at the golden coins that I was taking from my belt, his countenance changed, and he said, 'As you wish, Sir. Come in!'

I chose a nice, new trapper suit with everything that belonged to it. I bought enough ammunition and food that would last for a week. He asked a very high price for everything, but after bargaining he reduced his prices. I packed everything in a bag, put it on my shoulder, and left the store.

In the meantime it became evening, and the valley was dark. I started off to the villa with the intention of giving Forster a good lesson on his sovereign rights. The path led along the river. I recognised then the smell of oil that dominated the whole valley was much stronger along the river. I leant over the river, and sniffed. I was right, there was a lot of oil on the surface. I did not understand it, but thought that probably too much oil had come up suddenly, and they had to pour it in the river.

I passed by the factory. It was deserted. The path turned, and I caught sight of Forster's villa. The veranda was lit by several lights and I could see a small party there. I did not go to the gate, but went around the house first. There was a small garden in the back, surrounded by a low stone wall. Next to the wall was my mustang, tied to a tree. The well trained animal greeted me with a short snort, but it did not move. I was glad to see that the saddle was still on him. Swallow would not have allowed it, and, of course, he would not have allowed that the hand of a stranger led him to a stable. Probably they tried, but failed with it, and this is why he was in the garden.

I silently jumped over the wall, caressed him, and hung my bag on the saddle. I untied him, and was about to jump on him, when I heard a quiet conversation.

So far I had seen only three sides of the house, now I stared to the fourth side. The voices came from there. In the semi-dark I saw two chairs. In one of them Harry, in the other Forster found comfort, and they talked.

'I don't like this, uncle,' said Harry. 'I think, you haven't thought it through properly.'

'You don't understand it, Harry,' replied Forster. 'Oil is a great treasure, and more and more will be needed. But at the moment there's an overproduction.'

'And is it a problem?' asked Harry.

'Of course! Prices depend on the demand and the supply. This is what we discussed in the town with the owners of the oilfields last week. We cannot increase the demand, thus we have to reduce supply so that prices would not drop. We decided that for a month we will reduce the stocks. I let out the production of the largest well into the river. I cannot do anything else with it. All my barrels are full. When the prices go up, I'll put my stock on the market, and will make a fortune in the oil-hungry East. It was my proposal, and they accepted it. I'm proud of it.'

'Is it fair? Wasting the presents of nature?'

'Fair? The oil is mine, I can do with it whatever I want. This is business, don't you understand?'

'I hope it won't end up badly!'

'Trust me, Harry! You are too young to interfere with it.'

He would have continued, but then there was a huge explosion that shook the air and the ground under my feet like an earthquake. I looked around frightened, and at the top end of the valley, where the large oil derrick stood, I saw a huge flame column that shot up to fifty feet high. At the highest point it shot flames everywhere. I could also smell the sharp, hot smell of the gas. It felt as if the air had become liquid fire. I knew this phenomenon, because I had experienced it once in the Kanawha valley, when the fire devastated everything. I rushed to the veranda, where frightened faces looked at me.

'Put out the lamps! Quickly!' I shouted. 'The well blew up, and the gases have caught fire! The valley can go up in flames!'

They just stared at me, and they did not understand me or they could not recover from the paralysis of their fright. I jumped from lamp to lamp to put them out, but then I recognised that the lamp was still on in the store building.

The fire spread at an extreme rate, and reached the river.

'Flee!' I yelled. 'Up to the mountain! Run!'

I could not care with them anymore. I rushed to Harry, simply picked him up, and in the next moment he was on Swallow in front of me. He did not understand the danger, and stubbornly resisted, also because he was angry that I just picked him up. I held both of his arms, and Swallow,

446

following his instincts, began to run. He jumped over the stone fence, and galloped upstream.

The best would have been to climb up to the edge of the cliff where I had first caught sight of New Venango's houses, but the fire had already reached there. The path was free only downstream, but there the valley was so narrow that it was filled by the water of the river.

I looked around helplessly.

'Is there a path out of the valley?' I asked Harry.

'No! And let me go!' he shouted. 'I don't need your help! I can look after myself!'

'Enough of this!' I yelled at him. 'Stop it!'

I felt that fingers moved about my belt, and in the next moment something flashed in Harry's hand: he had pulled out my Bowie knife, and aimed it at my side.

'If you don't let me go, I'll stab you!' he shouted.

I did not have time to argue with him, thus with my right hand I twisted the knife out of his hand, and with my left I pressed him so closely to myself that he could not move.

The danger heightened minute by minute. The fire had reached the storage, and the barrels blew up. The oil from these increased the strength of the fire-storm. The air was so dry and hot that I felt as if my lungs were burning. I had to gather all my strength not to faint. I could not faint, I had to save my own, and the boy's life.

'Forward, Swallow, forward, Swal ...'

I could not speak anymore, but Swallow did not need encouragement. The excellent mustang almost flew. I could see that on the near side of the river we would die. We were approaching the gorge where there was no room even for a greyhound, thus we had to get across.

For the pressure of my thighs the clever and obedient horse jumped in the water. I felt a new strength, and my pulse throbbed normal again, but Swallow disappeared. So I had to swim across the river. Swallow was quicker than the fire that was coming downstream. Still, I could see that the fire would catch us at any minute. The boy had fainted, but

447

his rigid arms held me. I had never swam so desperately. My heart was squeezed by the fear. Where was my mustang? Where was the dear, faithful Swallow? Then I heard his snorting. Although the other bank was close, I did not have the strength to climb up. I was paralysed. Then suddenly I was on the saddle again, and the wonderful mustang jumped on the bank. We made it! Swallow galloped forward, away from the flaming hell.

I did not know where we were galloping to, but I did not care. My eyes ached, I felt my brain was burning, my tongue wanted to push out between my dry lips, and my body was like burnt sponge which was about to become ash. The horse jumped over rocks and passages, sometimes like a tiger, sometimes like a snake. I held his neck with my right hand, and with my left I held the boy. One more jump, a large, frightful leap, and we were over the cliff on the open prairie. Swallow stopped, I slipped off the saddle, and then crashed on the ground.

Swallow was also exhausted, it trembled all over, and I felt that I would faint. The excitement and efforts were too much. Still I got up; went to him, and embraced my faithful mustang. I kissed my horse more passionately than anyone had ever kissed his lover.

'Swallow, dear Swallow! You saved our life!' I whispered.

The bottom of the sky was red like blood, and the mist of the river mixed with the smoke. How many had survived? I could not think about that, because I had to look after Harry, who lay on the ground. He was pale and motionless. He was so lifeless that I thought he was dead. Had I saved him from the fire so that he would drown?

His wet clothing stuck to his body. I started to rub him, lifted his arms, I did everything that I knew of first aid. I worked without a result for a long time, but then there was a little tremor in his body, and I felt that his heart started to throb, and he was breathing. When he recovered, he opened his eyes, and stared at me.

'What happened? Where I am?' he asked.

'We have escaped from death by fire,' I replied.

'Death by fire ... yes ... God ... Is it true? The valley ... and Forster?'

'I don't know,' I answered. 'I'm afraid ...'

He jumped up suddenly. He interrupted me passionately, 'You don't know! You are a coward! I told you, a coyote that runs away from the barking dog! You could have saved all of them, but cared only for your own life!'

'And yours, Harry.'

'I wouldn't have left them there! I would have tried to help them! You took me by force, and left the rest to their fate! I can't stay here, I must go back to help them!'

He wanted to run away, but I grabbed his hand.

'Stay! You can't help anyone! You're going to your death!'

'Leave me alone! I've nothing to do with you! I despise you, and hate you, you coward!'

He tore himself from my hand, and ran away. I felt that a small object remained in my hand. I looked at it. It was a small golden ring that slipped off from his finger when he pulled his hand away.

I hurried after him, but he had already disappeared. He was unjust, but I could not be angry with him. I understood his youthful passion. The sudden catastrophe also deprived him from the faculty of judgement. I returned to my horse, and sat down. I decided that I would stay there, rest, and after then I would continue my journey. All my nerves were heightened, and when I looked down to the valley, where the oil was still burning, I believed that I saw the burning hell from which I had miraculously escaped. My old clothing was burnt and peeled off in pieces from my body. I took out the one I bought in the store. It was wet, but remained intact.

Swallow also lay down. There was plenty of grass, but he did not want to graze. It was not only tiredness, but also the excitement that had exhausted him both physically and psychologically. I would have liked to sleep, but I could not. My heart ached when I thought of the many unfortunate people who died in the settlement. During the night I got up a number of times, and looked down in the valley. The fire had reduced, but it was still frightening. In the place of the oil derrick a fire column rose, and it would continue to burn until the oil is burnt, because it was impossible to put it out. In the morning the fire subsided further. The villa, the store, the factory had all burnt down. I could not even see the ruins of the huts where the workers had lived. The whole valley was black, like a huge frying pan that was left on the fire.

I could see only one house on the other side of the river at the highest point that the fire could not reach. There were some people in front of the house, among them Harry. The brave boy probably went down on the path, and swam through. I started off towards the house. Harry noticed my approach, and pointed at me, obviously calling the others' attention to me. A man hurried in the house, and returned with a gun. He ran down to the river, and waited for where I would appear.

'Hallo!' he shouted. 'What are you doing here? You have no business here! Go if you don't want a bullet in your head!'

'I want to help you!'

'We don't need your help!'

'Send Harry here, I want to talk to him. I have to give him something.'

'Harry doesn't want to talk to you. Go away from here! You probably lit the oil well as a revenge, you coward!'

The stupid accusation shocked me so much that I could not answer.

'Ah! So you are silent! Bad conscience! Arsonist!'

He lifted his gun. The indignation burst out of me, 'Man! The well blew up because of negligence, and the lamps!'

'Very good! Are you going or should I shoot you?'

'Would I have saved the boy if I was an arsonist?'

'You could have saved all of them if you had not ran away! But they all burnt to death! Here's your reward!'

He shot at me. I did not move, and this was my luck, because his aiming was bad. I would have liked to show him how to shoot properly, but the scene made me so bitter that without a word I turned around, and climbed up on the path. Then I jumped on my horse, and galloped away. I did not want to see the cursed place, where I saved a boy's life, and I got such a thank you.

A few days later I arrived to the Gravel Prairie, where I had to wait for a whole week until Winnetou arrived. I was not starving, because there was enough game, and I was not bored, because the Sioux crossed the prairie, and I had to be careful to avoid them. When Winnetou finally arrived, I told him about this, and he agreed that we could not stay there.

I was happy that I would soon meet Old Firehand, the famous hunter, from whom I could learn a lot. The journey to him was not less dangerous. Already on the following day we found suspicious tracks. They were left by an Indian warrior, who was probably a scout. I carefully examined the ground. I found the place where the Indian had tied his horse. The horse grazed the grass in a half circle, and his master lay next to him. Probably he played with his arrows, and one of them broke in his hand. He threw them away carelessly. I examined the arrow. It was a war arrow, and not a hunting one.

'They are on the warpath,' I said. 'This scout was an inexperienced, young warrior, otherwise he wouldn't have left the arrow here. His footprint is also smaller than that of an adult warrior's.'

He had been there not much earlier, because the tracks were fresh, and the grass had not yet straightened. We followed the track for hours, but then the evening arrived. We decided that we would spend the night there, and would continue to follow the tracks in the morning. Before I jumped off the horse, I took out my telescope to look around.

This prairie was like a frozen sea; the hillocks followed each other like waves. We stood on the top of such a hillock, and we could see far into the distance.

Through the telescope I could see a straight line that stretched from the East to the West. I gave the telescope to Winnetou, and showed him where to look.

'Uff!' he exclaimed after a short time, and looked at me questioningly.

'Do you know, my brother, what path is that?' I asked. ''They aren't the tracks of the bison or Indians.'

'I know,' he nodded, 'it's the path of the Fire Mustang.'

He lifted the telescope to his eyes again, and watched the tracks with great interest. Suddenly he jumped off his horse, and quickly pulled it downhill. I knew that he had a reason for this, so I followed his example without hesitation.

'There are men behind the path of the Fire Mustang. They are Indians. I didn't see them, but I saw one of their horses.'

He left the hillock quickly, because the Indians could have spotted us even though the distance was considerable. Indeed, in my wanderings in the West, I had seen telescopes in Indians' hands.

'What do you think, what is their intention?' I asked. 'To destroy the path of the Fire Mustang,' he replied.

'I agree. I'll sneak up there,' I said. 'I have to find out their plans.'

I took my telescope from him, and told him to wait for me there, and then advanced with great care. I used every advantage of the terrain, and I crawled close enough to watch the Indians. There were about thirty of them, equipped with bows, but some had guns. They all wore war paint. They had more horses than men, which reinforced our suspicion that they wanted to attack the train, and they wanted to transport their loot onto the surplus horses.

I felt that I had heard somebody breathing behind me. I pulled my knife, and turned quickly. Winnetou lay behind me. He did not have the patience to wait by the horses.

'Uff!' he exclaimed to express his surprise. 'You are very brave, my brother, that you came so close to them. These are Ponca, and there sits Parranoh, the white chief.'

'White chief?' I looked at him astonished.

'Have you not heard of Parranoh, the bloodthirsty chief of the Arapaho, my brother? Nobody knows where he has

452

come from, but he's a frightening warrior, and the Arapaho adopted him. When the old chief moved to the eternal hunting grounds, Parranoh got the calumet of the chief, and he collected many scalps. Then the Wicked Spirit made him blind, and he treated his warrior like slaves, and he had to flee. Now he lives with the Ponca, and leads them on raids.'

'Have you met him, my brother?'

'Winnetou fought with him with tomahawk, but the white chief is deceitful, he doesn't fight honestly.'

'What do you expect from a traitor? He wants to stop the Fire Mustang to murder and rob his white brothers!'

'What do you want to do?'

'I'll ride to the Fire Mustang, and I will warn my white brothers.'

Winnetou nodded. At those times it often happened that white or Indian robbers derailed the train. In this book, I will relate several such cases.

It was so dark now that I could not watch the Ponca, but I had to know what they were doing, thus I asked Winnetou to return to the horses, and wait for me there, because I wanted to get closer to the enemy.

'Right,' said Winnetou. 'If you get into trouble, my brother, imitate the voice of the prairie hen, then I'll come to help you.'

He retreated, and I crawled closer. I was very careful, and it took me a long time to get to the position where I wanted to be. I climbed over the tracks, and approached the place where I had spotted the Ponca earlier. Now I could see what they were doing. They carried big, heavy stones, and put them on the track.

I had to act, but I did not know where I was, what time the train would arrive and from which direction, but I assumed that it was from the cities of the East. I had to hurry to warn them. First I returned to Winnetou. I told him my plan, and then we galloped to the East along the tracks. While the sky was cloudy, so there was no moonlight, fortunately it was easy to follow the railway tracks.

After a quarter of an hour we stopped. The only question was how to warn the train. I wanted to make a fire, but Winnetou disagreed, because on the prairie the fire could be seen not only by the train driver, but also by the Ponca. Thus we continued our ride.

After another quarter of an hour we were far enough from the Ponca. We tied our horses to a bush. I tore up a lot of dry grass, and twisted them into a torch. I put gunpowder on it, and with this easily ignitable torch I calmly waited for the train. We put a blanket on the ground, lay down, and waited for the train.

Time passed very slowly. Finally a small twinkling dot appeared somewhere very far in the darkness, but it became bigger and brighter. Then we heard a noise that became stronger and stronger, and finally it was like the sound of a thunder from afar.

The moment of action arrived. We could see the light of the huge lamp of the engine. I took my revolver, and I shot into the torch. It immediately lit, and I started to wave with it. With my other hand I indicated to the train driver to stop.

He immediately noticed the signal. We heard a sharp whistle, and then the sound of the brakes. In the next moment the train passed us by, but at slower pace. Ignoring the passengers leaning out of the windows, I jumped at the front of the engine, and put my blanket on the lamp.

'Put out all the lights,' I shouted

The train became dark immediately. The crew of Pacific Railways had experienced many things, and knew that in certain situations they had to act quickly.

'Damn it!' swore the train driver. 'What happened? Why did you stop us?'

'There are Indians ahead of us!' I shouted to him. 'They want to derail the train!'

'Hell! Then you are the bravest men on this cursed land!'

He jumped off, and squeezed my hand so hard that I could see more stars than those in the sky. There were not many passengers on the train, but now they were around us.

'What's up? What happened? Why did we stop?' they asked excitedly.

With a few words I explained the situation, and it made them even more excited.

'Quiet, gentlemen!' said the train driver. 'Let's keep our cool! This is a very good opportunity to deter the Indians from attacking any train in the future. Do you know, Sir, how many there are?'

'The Ponca? About thirty,' I answered.

'We have fewer men, but our weapons are better! Who's there in the dark! Oh my God! A redskin!'

He pulled his knife, and wanted to jump on Winnetou, who was behind me.

'Calm down, my friend!' I grabbed the train driver's arm. 'This is my hunting companion, who will help us.'

'That's different. Then he can come. What's his name?'

'His name is Winnetou.'

'Winnetou?' exclaimed a voice in the background, and a man broke his way through the crowd. 'Is Winnetou here, the chief of the Apache?'

In the dark I could see that he was a real giant. He wore a simple hunting suit, but his appearance immediately triggered respect in an inexplicable way. He stood in front of Winnetou, opened his two arms, and he cried with joy,

'Can't Winnetou recognise his old friend's voice?'

'Uff!' cried Winnetou with the same happiness. 'Can Winnetou forget Old Firehand, the greatest white hunter even if so many moons have gone since he saw you last?'

'I'm happy that fortune brought us together again, my dear young brother!'

'Old Firehand?' I exclaimed. The crowd stepped back, and they stared at the famous hero of the Wild West, of whose deeds had passed from mouth to mouth.

'Old Firehand?' repeated the train driver. 'Why didn't you name yourself, Sir, when you got on the train? We would have been very proud that we have such a famous passenger. You would have been given the best seat!'

'Thank you, Sir, but I had a comfortable journey. Let's not waste the time! Let's agree what we have to do!'

Every eye looked at Old Firehand as everybody assumed that he was the commander. I also reported to him on what I had seen and experienced.

'So, you are Winnetou's friend?' he asked after he had listened to my report. 'Although I don't like making new friendships, those whom Winnetou respects with his friendship, I'm happy to shake hands with too.'

'He's more than my friend; he is my blood brother,' said Winnetou.

'So?' said Old Firehand, and he stepped closer to me to see me better. 'So he is ...'

'Yes, Old Shatterhand, the man who knocks out any of his enemies with one blow,' said Winnetou.

'Old Shatterhand! Old Shatterhand!' came from all directions. People came closer.

'I won't forget this night in my life!' cried the train driver. 'Old Firehand, Old Shatterhand and Winnetou! The three Invincibles of the West! What a meeting! Now we are safe. Gentlemen, tell us what we have to do, and we will obey.'

'Nothing at all,' waved Old Firehand. 'Thirty bandits. We'll shoot them dead.'

'They are humans, Sir!' I remarked.

'Bestial humans,' he replied. 'But I've heard of you. They say that you are merciful even to the worst bandit. My view is very different. If you had my experiences, you wouldn't be so merciful. This gang is led by Parranoh, the traitor of the whites, many times murderer. Even if I tore him to pieces, it wouldn't be enough punishment to him!'

'Haw!' cried Winnetou. He must have had a serious reason for being so blood thirsty on this occasion.

'You are right, Sir,' nodded the train driver. 'There's no room for mercy here. Tell us what to do.'

'The crew should stay on the train, this is their duty. The other gentlemen may come with us if they want to. We will teach the Ponca that it's not advisable to attack a train. In

456

the dark we'll sneak up on them, and finish them off. As they don't expect us, they'll lose their head after the first shots. When we have overpowered them, we'll make a fire, and the engine can start, but only slowly, because we have to remove the stones from the rails. Who will come with me?'

'I! I! I!' came from every side as none of the passengers wanted to be left out of the adventure.

'Then bring your guns, and follow me. We don't have time to lose, because the gang knows when the train should arrive, and if it's late, they could get suspicious.'

We started off. Winnetou and I were in the front. There was a deep silence in the land, and we also tried to remain quiet. Nothing showed in the night that soon the calm of the endless prairie would be replaced by the noise of a battle.

For some distance we hurried along the tracks without any caution, but then we had to stoop down, and continue the advance on all fours. Meanwhile the moon appeared among the clouds, and one could see quiet far. This light made our approach more difficult, but it also helped us as we could not bump into the enemy unexpectedly knowing the place where they waited.

Time to time we stopped, and I looked ahead. On one of these occasions I spotted a dark figure on a small hillock on the left. The contours were very visible on the horizon. The Ponca had set up a guard, but fortunately he looked not only towards the approaching train, but in all directions, otherwise he would have easily noticed us.

We advanced even more carefully now. Soon we spotted the whole group of the Ponca. They were hiding in the grass. A bit further we could see the horses that made our task more difficult, because they could smell us. Now I could see how the Ponca wanted to derail the train. They put huge stones on the tracks, and I could imagine the fate of the passengers and crew, had they succeeded. This thought made me shiver.

The most urgent task was to deal with the guard. Only Winnetou could carry out this difficult task. The guard stood alone in the moonlight, and he could see anyone who approached him. And even if someone could have got close enough to him, he had to be finished with one leap, with one blow so that he would not have time to cry out. Winnetou passed by me, and soon I was astonished to see that the guard had disappeared as if the ground had swallowed him. In the next moment he stood there again in his place. It was only a flash, but I easily understood what happened. It was Winnetou who stood in the place of the Ponca. He got behind him, pulled him off by his leg, and stabbed him. Then he stood up. It was all over in a moment.

The Indians know a lot that we, the whites, cannot ever understand. However, what Winnetou had just carried out, was such a masterpiece that it would have surprised even the Indians.

Old Firehand had not yet given the signal for the attack, when a gunshot resounded behind us. One of the passengers accidentally fired.

We had to jump up, and start the attack before the right time. The Ponca also jumped up, and rushed to their horses yelling. They wanted to reach a place where they would have had an advantage against us.

'Look out!' cried Old Firehand. 'Shoot at the horses only! Then we'll sort out the bandits!'

Our volley resounded. There was confusion among the Ponca. A few horses collapsed burying their riders. Many Ponca had managed to get out of the crowd, but I shot them with my Henry rifle.

Old Firehand and Winnetou, lifting their tomahawks, entered the battle immediately. I did not expect much from the other whites, and soon the proof of my judgement was visible. They industriously shot with their revolvers, but they did not hit anyone, and if a Ponca approached, they retreated immediately, or simply ran away.

When I discharged my last bullet, I put aside my guns, and grabbing my tomahawk I hurried to help Old Firehand and Winnetou. In reality only three of us fought the Ponca.

I knew Winnetou's way of fighting, so I did not watch him on this occasion. I was more interested in Old Firehand, who reminded me of the giants of the fairy tales or the heroes of the legends of whom I had read in my childhood. He stood in the crowd with legs apart, turning his tomahawk distributing blows. Whoever he hit was dead. His long hair flew in the wind, and his face showed the calmness of the victor.

I spotted Parranoh among the Ponca, and rushed there, but he avoided me. By doing so though, he had to face Winnetou. He stepped back, but Winnetou leapt forward, and shouted at him, 'Parranoh, stop! You, chief of the Arapaho, are a coward! May the vultures feed on your eyes, may the soil drink you blood, you dog! Your scalp will decorate my belt!'

He threw his tomahawk away, and drew his knife. He grabbed the white chief by the throat, but somebody held him back from the deadly stab. The contemptuous words attracted Old Firehand's attention, who turned there, saw Parranoh's face, the face that he hated with all his nerves and cells, the one whom he searched in vain for years, and now faced with accidentally.

'Tim Finnetey!' he yelled, and pushed the Ponca warriors out of his way. He grabbed Winnetou's arm, and said, 'Give him to me, brother, this rascal is mine!'

Parranoh was momentarily paralysed when he was called by his real name, but when he saw Old Firehand's face distorted by the desire for revenge, he turned around quickly, and ran away. Seeing this, I pushed away the Ponca whom I was fighting, and rushed after Parranoh. This was the first time I had seen this man, and I had no reason for taking a revenge on him, in spite of his planned attack on the railways. But I heard Winnetou's and Old Firehand's words, and I knew that he was their deadly enemy.

My friends also joined the chase. I immediately saw that the white chief was an excellent runner as the distance between us increased. Firehand was a master in everything that the West demanded, but in his age he could not compete with younger runners. Not even Winnetou could keep up with me.

Parranoh, as I saw, had made the mistake of not being economical with his strength. He did not run right and left as an Indian would do, but rushed forward, putting all his strength in it, because he wanted to disappear from our view. I, even if I got behind, was careful with my breathing, and reserved some of my energy. My two companions fell more and more behind, and I could not hear their panting. Winnetou's shout came from quite a distance.

'Stop Old Firehand! My young white brother will soon trample on the Arapaho toad. His feet are like the storm, they can catch up with anyone.'

Whatever pleasing comparison this was, I had not got any closer to Parranoh. Then suddenly I noticed that he started to slow down. Now I put all my effort into the running, and soon I could hear his panting. Apart from my two empty revolvers, I had no other weapon but my Bowie knife, and I pulled it from my belt. I had thrown away my tomahawk earlier as it had obstructed me in the running.

Parranoh jumped aside suddenly so that I would rush past by him, and he could attack me from behind. Of course, I saw through his trick immediately, and I changed direction too. The result was that we bumped into each other with full momentum, and my knife penetrated his body to the handle.

The collision was so strong that we both crashed on the ground. I quickly got up as I could not be sure if he was mortally wounded. Seeing that he did not move, I had a deep breath, and pulled my knife out of his body.

He was not the only enemy whom I had killed so far having received and given wounds in the American prairies and forests. Still, I stood there with a bad conscience, when from behind me I heard running steps. I looked up, and saw Winnetou.

'You are quick like an arrow, my white brother, and your hand doesn't shake when you stab,' he said.

'Where's Old Firehand?' I asked.

'He's strong like a bear at the first snow, but the weight of his years was on his feet,' he replied. 'Don't you want to decorate your belt with the scalp of the Arapaho chief?'

'No, Winnetou, I give it to you.'

He quickly leant ahead, and with three cuts he took the scalp of his enemy. He must have hated this Tim Finnetey so much as he wanted his scalp so badly. I turned away so I would not see as he put the scalp on his belt. At this moment I noticed that six Ponca headed towards us. They obviously wanted to gather their men.

Winnetou's sharp eyes even saw that the Ponca were on foot, and that they led their horses by the rein so that they could jump on them at any moment. As our horses were far away, we could have been in danger. Therefore, Winnetou lay down, and crawled away from the path of the Ponca. I followed his example. His aim was to make a big detour, and get behind the Ponca. I considered it an excellent plan, because if we were lucky we could even get the Ponca's horses.

We were quite far from the battlefield, and here the Ponca did not expect any unpleasant surprise. We heard their cries when they caught sight of the man on the ground. They let their horses go, and they rushed there. Then they started to yell.

This was the right moment. We jumped on two of the horses, and took the rest by the reins. We returned to our group with the scalp of the white chief and six horses.

I could imagine the faces of these Ponca when they recognised that we had tricked them. Even the always serious Winnetou smiled when I told him my thoughts, but the smile did not last long. His eyes were looking for Old Firehand, but he could not see him anywhere. He was anxious that he had bumped into a group of the escaping Ponca that was strong enough to finish off one man.

This made me anxious too, because the battle was over, and Old Firehand should have already returned by then.

461

The passengers, who had very little part in the battle, had collected the dead Indians. There were no wounded warriors around, because the Ponca had taken them. We removed the stones from the railway track, and made a big campfire that had to be visible from the train. The train arrived soon. The joy of the crew was great when they heard of our victory.

The passengers described the battle to them so vividly as if they had participated in it seriously. Winnetou and I took our weapons, and left to search for Old Firehand.

'I hope we will find you here when we return,' I told the train driver, 'But if you cannot wait, it's not a problem. Keep to the rules.'

The train driver assured me that he would enter our heroic deeds in his report, but I felt it was not necessary.

The pale moonlight was not strong enough to see far, thus we relied more on our ears than our eyes, even though the noise of the railwaymen's work did not help. When we were far enough from the track, and the silence of the night surrounded us, we stopped time to time to listen, but we could not hear anything. We were about to turn back to check if Old Firehand had returned, when we heard some faint shouts from the distance.

'It's him,' said Winnetou. 'It can't be the escaping Ponca, as they wouldn't want us to know where they are.'

'I agree,' I replied. 'Let's hurry there.'

'Yes, and quickly,' said Winnetou. 'He is in trouble as he cries for help.'

We started to run, but to two different directions, thus we immediately stopped.

'Why are you running to the East?' asked Winnetou. 'It came from the North.'

'You are wrong, Winnetou. It's from the East. Listen!'

We listened again. The shout was repeated, but I still heard it from the East, while Winnetou from the North.

'Then each of us should go after his ears,' I proposed. 'You should run to the North, my brother, and I to the East. Then we will definitely find him.'

This is what we did. Soon I knew that I was right as I heard the cries louder and louder. In a few minutes I spotted a desperately fighting group of people.

'I'm coming, Old Firehand! Hold on!' I yelled as I ran even faster.

Old Firehand was wounded, and was fighting on his knees. He had knocked out three Indians already, but the other three were still attacking him, and he was in a very tight situation. I was still fifty steps from him, and I was afraid of being late with my help. So I stopped, and lifted my already recharged gun.

It was risky to shoot in the moonlight, as I could have hit Old Firehand, especially as I was panting, and my heart was throbbing hard, but there was nothing else to do. I shot three times in quick succession, and the three Indians crashed to the ground.

'Thank God! You arrived in the last moment!' exclaimed Old Firehand when I got there.

'Are you injured, Sir?' I asked. 'I hope it's not serious.'

'I'm sure it's not life threatening. Two tomahawk hits on my leg. The rascals couldn't get me, so they aimed at my legs that I would collapse.'

'Such wounds cause a lot of loss of blood,' I said. 'Let me, Sir, examine your wounds.'

'Go ahead! I have to say, you are a sharp shooter! In such a situation three hits! Only Old Shatterhand can do this, nobody else!' he said, and then continued, 'I saw that you were chasing Tim Finnetey, but I couldn't keep up with you, because an arrow hit my leg. I was looking for your tracks, when these six Ponca appeared as if they had grown from the ground. Obviously they saw me from the distance, jumped on the ground, hid, and waited until I arrived. I did not have any other weapons, but my knife, and my two fists, because I had to throw away the rest while running. They hit my leg with their tomahawk. I stabbed three of them, but the other three would have easily overcome me if you hadn't arrived. Thank you, Old Shatterhand, I won't forget this!'

While he talked, I examined his wounds. They had to be very painful, but fortunately they were not dangerous. In the meantime Winnetou found us, and helped me in bandaging the wounded hunter. He admitted with some unease that his hearing misled him. We left the six dead Ponca there, and returned to the railway track. It took a long time, because Old Firehand could barely walk, and for some distance the two of us carried him. By the time we arrived to the track, the train had gone. We found the looted horses next to ours. It was very useful, because it helped with transporting Old Firehand, although first he had to rest for a week. He knew a place that was good for camping. It was about half a day's ride. We made this little journey safely. We found water and a forest, that is, everything we needed for a longer rest.

IN THE FORT

WHEN OLD Firehand had regained his strength, and was able to sit on the horse, we started off. Three quarters of our journey led through the territories of hostile Indian tribes, but we successfully crossed these.

Although we had not been able to shoot food for days, we had enough provision, because we caught animals with traps. One evening I was sitting with Old Firehand by the little campfire, while Winnetou was out scouting. When he returned, Old Firehand said to him, 'You are surely tired, my brother. You can sit down now with us.'

'The Apache warrior is always alert,' said Winnetou. 'The night is like a woman, you can't trust it.'

He then disappeared among the trees again. It would have been best if I lay down, and slept a few hours, but I did not feel like. I had always liked the quiet talk next to the campfire under the starry night, and this is what I longed for at this time. I did not know what an unforgettable conversation would follow.

'I'm afraid Winnetou is a woman-hater,' I remarked.

Old Firehand took out his favourite pipe, comfortably filled it, lit it, and only then replied, 'Do you think so? I think you are wrong.'

'He has never talked about a squaw.'

'Maybe,' nodded the great hunter, 'But there was once a squaw for whom he would have given his life.'

'Then why didn't he lead this girl to his tent?'

'Because the girl loved somebody else.'

'And Winnetou gave up on her for another man?'

'Yes. Because the man was his best friend.'

'Best friend? What's his name?'

'They know him now as Old Firehand,' he replied quietly.

I looked at him surprised. I would not have thought that such a love drama, which is an everyday occurrence in the town, could happen in the Wild West. I was very curious, but of course I didn't dare to question Old Firehand.

After a while he looked at me, and continued, 'It's unnecessary to stir up the past, Sir. I don't know why I mentioned it to you, such a young man. It seems I like you.'

'Thank you, Sir,' I answered, 'I don't think I'm obtrusive or insensitive.'

'I don't think that either. How could I when you saved my life? Although I'm a little bit annoyed. I would have liked to settle the account with Tim Finnetey, but damn it, you were quicker!'

His eyes flashed angrily, he clenched his fist. What could he have done to Old Firehand that made the hunter raging even at the thought.

I have to admit, different feelings struggled in me. On the one hand I regretted that I raised such a subject with my remark that made this excellent man lose his control. On the other hand I was very curious as it was about men who were very close to me. I was also a little hurt that Winnetou had a secret that he did not share with me. Old Firehand was musing, and I was thinking about the events of the previous few days, and about my plans.

I was happy that Old Firehand's wounds healed well, and our journey had been undisturbed. We had ridden through the territories of the Arapaho and the Pawnee, and crossed the quick waters of the Keya Paha River two days earlier. In a few days we expected to reach the White Earth River that the Indians called Mankizita Wakpa, where the fort was that Old Firehand called his home. I heard that several excellent trappers worked for him, and stayed in his house. I decided that I would join them for a while. Then if I had enough of it, I would continue my travel through Dakota to the Great Lakes, where I had never been, and would have liked to visit.

Old Firehand was still quiet. Occasionally I leant forward to stir the fire. In one such motion the ring on my finger twinkled in the light of the fire. Although the object was small, Old Firehand noticed it. He suddenly sat up. There was a deep shock on his face.

'What ring is it, Sir?' he cried at me. 'How did you get it?'

'A memory,' I replied. 'The memory of the most horrible hour of my life.'

'Show it to me, let me see it from close!'

I pulled it off from my finger, and gave it to him. He took it eagerly, but as soon as he looked at it, his voice snapped again, 'Where did you get it? From whom?'

'From a kind boy in New Venango, but he was not too kind to me.'

'New Venango?' he asked with uncontrolled excitement in his voice. 'Did you visit Forster? Did you see Harry? What horrible hour do you speak about? Was there a catastrophe?'

'I could thank only my good Swallow that I wasn't burnt alive,' I replied, and stretched out for the ring.

'Leave it!' he shouted at me, and pushed my hand away. 'I have to know how you got this ring! Nobody has a more sacred right to it than I do!'

'Calm down, Sir. If somebody else talked to me in such a tone, I would resent it, but I'll give you all the information.'

'I say the same: if I saw this ring on somebody else's finger, I would ask the information with my gun! So speak!'

I thought he knew Forster and Harry, but I could not understand what happened to him. I did not want to increase his excitement, so I told him everything.

He rested himself on his elbow, looked in my face, and listened to my words with great attention. When I got to the moment when I had lifted Harry on my horse against his will, Old Firehand jumped up, and interrupted me, 'You did the right thing! This was the only way to save him! But I'm still too anxious. Continue, please, continue!'

I continued in a shaky voice, because the memory of the shocking event filled me with excitement too. Old Firehand came closer and closer as if in this way he could catch the words quicker. His eyes were wide open, and they did not move from me. He leant forward as if he was on Swallow's back, and jumped in the burning river, and climbed up on the steep cliff. He did not notice that he had grabbed my arm, and squeezed it like a drowning man. He breathed

467

deeply, and groaned aloud when he understood the events of those terrible moments.

'Thank God!' he sighed with relief when he learnt that I had reached the top of the cliff, where Harry was safe. 'This was terrible! I was trembling as I listened to you, and only the thought calmed me that you surely saved his life, otherwise he wouldn't have given you this ring.'

'But he didn't give it to me! It slipped off from his finger, when he jerked his hand away from mine. Maybe he did not even notice it.'

'Then why did you keep the ring?'

'I wanted to give it back to him, but he ran away. In the morning I tried again, but I failed. Only one family survived and I went there ...'

'And?'

'They received me with a gun. They shot at me before I could say anything. I had to retreat quickly.'

'Yes, that's him! I can recognise Harry! Wild, unbridled, impatient! He hates nothing more than cowardice. And what happened to Forster?'

'The flame-sea destroyed everything. As far as I know only those few people survived, and, of course, Harry too. But Forester ...'

'He was punished. He could thank it to his own stupidity and greed.'

'Did you know Forster, Sir?'

'I've been in New Venango a few times. He was a greedy money-bag.'

'Did you meet Harry in his house?'

'Harry?' smiled Old Firehand. 'No, I've known him from earlier times. From Omaha, where his brother lives, and maybe from somewhere else.'

'Tell me about him, I'm very interested.'

'At another time. Your report shook me so much that I cannot talk right now. Didn't he tell you what he was doing in Venango?'

'He said he was just travelling through.'

'Good. And is he definitely through all dangers?'

'Definitely.'

'Did you see him shooting?'

'Excellent shooter. In all, an excellent boy.'

'I'm happy that you think this. His father is a famous hunter, who fought a lot against the Indians, and all his bullets hit the target. So, he taught his son about guns too, but also that he should use it only for good purpose.'

'Must be an interesting man. Where is he?

'Here and there, but I tell you I know him well. Maybe I'll introduce him to you.'

'I'd be happy for that.'

'Well, we'll see! Anyway, you deserve his father's thanks for what you did for Harry.'

'Oh, I didn't meant that!'

'I know, because I know you well already. Here's your ring, I give it back to you. Once you'll know what it means that I give the ring back to you. But we talked so much that it's time for replacing Winnetou. You can go to sleep, I will be the guard.'

'I should be, Sir.'

'No, sleep! You did enough service to me already! I want you to be strong tomorrow. I hope we can make two days' journey in one day.'

I went to bed with a strange feeling. I did not know what to think of this conversation. I had many assumptions, but none seemed to be likely. Winnetou had long returned, and slept next to me, while I was still tossing and turning. When I finally fell asleep, I remembered Old Firehand's words when he had said "You did enough service to me already!"

When I woke in the morning, the fire was lit, but nobody was there. I knew that my companions could not be far, because the water was boiling in the little tin cauldron over the fire, and I saw our flour bag, and the piece of roasted meat from the night before.

I climbed out of my blanket, and hurried to the stream to wash myself. I found my two friends there in conversation,

469

which they immediately stopped when they caught sight of me. Did they talk about me?

Soon we started off on a path that ran parallel with the Missouri, at about twenty miles from the great river, and led to the White Earth River.

It was a cold morning. Since in the last section of our journey we had not exhausted our horses, and had looked after them during the rests, they almost flew on the green prairie now.

I noticed a strange change in my friends' behaviours. They had been friendly with me, but now they talked to me almost with respect. Old Firehand's eyes sometimes rested on me, and there was a loving care in his look. Winnetou talked to me like a brother to a brother, but I also saw the close friendship between him and Old Firehand. Thus the harmony was perfect among us. This made the journey very pleasant.

At noon we rested, but Old Firehand, following his usual caution, went on a small scouting. I took out our provisions, and made a fire, while Winnetou sat down on the grass.

'You are brave like a lynx, but also silent like a rock, my brother' remarked Winnetou.

I did not reply.

'You rode through the oil-fire sea, but you didn't mention it to your friend,' continued the Apache chief.

'The man's tongue,' I answered, 'is sharp and pointed like a knife. It's not for play.'

'You speak wisely, my brother, but it still hurts Winnetou, that you did not tell me this.'

'Did you open your heart to your brother, Winnetou?' I replied.

'Didn't he show you the secrets of the prairie? Did he not show you how to read tracks, throw lasso, cut off the scalp of the enemy, everything that a great warrior must know?'

'You showed to me all these, Winnetou. But you did not speak about Old Firehand, and about the girl, whose memory has not died in your heart!'

'Winnetou loved her, and one must be silent about love. But why didn't you talk about the boy, whom he saved from the fire, my brother?'

'Because I don't like boasting. Do you know the boy?'

'I carried him in my arms,' replied Winnetou. 'I showed him the flowers of the meadows, the trees of the forest, the fish of the rivers, the stars of the sky. I taught him to shoot arrows, ride on the mustang. I gave him the language of the Indian peoples, and finally gave him the gun whose bullet killed the daughter of the Assiniboine, Ribbana.'

I looked at him surprised. Something started to emerge in my mind, something that I did not dare to put in words, especially because Old Firehand had just returned, and we sat down for our lunch. However, I kept on musing about Winnetou's words. From this it came that Harry's father must have been Old Firehand! But on the other hand Old Firehand had talked about Harry's father as somebody whom I would have to be introduced to.

After lunch we continued our journey. Our horses, as if they felt that we were approaching to our destination, happily rode ahead. We were also surprised how much distance we made in half a day. By sunset the ground started to rise. This was the mountain range that separated us from the White Earth River. However, we did not have to climb up, because we arrived to a gorge that cut through the mountain, and led to the river.

'Stop!' came from behind the bushes, and the barrel of a gun pointed at us. 'Password?'

'Brave!'

'And?'

'Silent!' replied Old Firehand for which the branches parted, and a man stepped out. His appearance filled me with joy and surprise.

From under the broad rimmed, shapeless, colourless old hat lively, small black eyes gleamed at me. On his round face, grown all over by a forest of hair, a broad smile spread as soon as he noticed me. His leather jacket was so big that the little man was almost lost in it. He looked like a young child dressing up in his grandfather's clothing.

'Are you mad, Sam?' asked Old Firehand laughing. 'Are you asking the password from me too?'

'From everybody,' he replied. 'Let's keep to the rules and regulations. Welcome, Sir, master of the Rock Fort! Welcome Winnetou, the great chief of the Apache, and Old Shatterhand, my dear student, who surpassed his master, hehehe!'

I grabbed both of his hands, and squeezed them.

'I'm very happy, dear Sam, for this surprise! Didn't you talk to Old Firehand about me? Didn't you tell him that we are good friends?'

'Of course, I did. Many times!'

'And he has never mentioned that you were here.'

'I meant it as a pleasant surprise,' smiled Old Firehand.

'There are others of your acquaintances in the fort.'

'Dick Stone and Will Parker? I know that they are always with Sam Hawkins.'

'Yes, we are together,' nodded Sam.

'Who's at home?' asked Old Firehand.

'Three went for meat, Bill Bulcher, Stone and Harris,' replied Sam. 'The rest are at home. The young gentleman has also arrived.'

'I'm happy for that. Have you seen Indians?'

'Not one. Although my Liddy,' he patted his gun, 'would have wanted to marry them.'

'And the traps?'

'We had a very good harvest, hehehe! You'll see, Sir. The water is low at the gate.'

We rode further, while Sam Hawkins retreated to his hiding place in the bushes. From his words I understood that we had arrived to Old Firehand's fort, and he was on guard duty, but when I looked to either the right or left or forward, I could not see any gate.

Soon I noticed a very narrow gap in the cliff to the left. Its entrance was covered by thick blackberry branches. The bottom of this opening was covered by a stream, whose perfectly translucent, clear water entered the White Earth River further down. One could go into the opening only through the water of the stream. As it had a rock bed, no footprint would have been left. Old Firehand turned to the left, and simply waded into the stream. We followed him. Now I understood what Sam Hawkins had meant with the low water in the gate.

The gorge became narrower and narrower, and it seemed that it closed. For my surprise Old Firehand continued his riding, and then he suddenly disappeared. Then Winnetou was swallowed by the cliff. When I arrived to this point I could see that the hanging ivy was not covering the cliff, but there was another opening that was like the entrance of a tunnel.

I followed the two riders for a long time in the dark, twisting tunnel, until some light appeared again, and I arrived to another gorge which was just as narrow and gate-like as the first one. When I went through this, I held back my horse. I was astonished by the surroundings.

I stood in a huge, almost perfectly round yard. This yard was built by nature. It was surrounded by high, steep cliffs, but its middle was grassy and there were even trees and bushes. Horses and mules grazed, dogs chased each other on the huge yard. These dogs were partly strong, big animals that the Indians used for carrying burden, and some small mongrels that could be overfed, and whose meat was highly appreciated by the Indians.

'This is my fort,' said Old Firehand proudly. 'I feel as secure here as on Abraham's bosom. It's quite difficult to get here, isn't it?'

'And there's no other entrance?' I asked.

'Not even a ferret could enter through the other gaps,' replied Old Firehand. 'And it's impossible to descend from the rocks. Even if the Indians were in this area, in these mountains, I'm sure they wouldn't think that the cliffs enclosed such a pleasant valley here.'

'And how did you find it?' I enquired.

'Accidentally. I followed a raccoon through the tunnel, and went through the opening that was not covered by the ivy then. This is how I came into this beautiful yard, and, naturally, I took ownership of it.'

'Alone?'

'In the beginning I stayed here alone. How many times I found safety here from the redskins who chased me! Later I brought fellow hunters here, and we collected furs together. They liked it here. It's easy to overcome the vicissitudes of the winter here.'

His words were interrupted by a sharp whistle for which men came forward from the bushes. Their faces and clothing showed that their home was the forest and the prairie.

We rode to the middle of the large yard, and these men surrounded Old Firehand. They greeted him with such a joy, whose honesty was not in doubt.

In this turmoil Winnetou jumped off from his horse, took his saddle, and let his horse free to graze as it wanted. He put the saddle and the blankets on his shoulders and then ignoring the curious glances, he moved to his night place.

Old Firehand had so many responsibilities now that he could not look after us, so I followed Winnetou's example. I took the saddle off my mustang, and let it go to the pasture to graze. Then I went for a walk to look around.

At the edge of the yard, behind the bushes, I found openings in the steep wall. These openings were covered with animal skins. They had to be caves or chambers for the hunters, and for the provisions. Judging from the number of chambers, I concluded that in the winter there were many more hunters than now, because during the nice autumn weeks they preferred the forest.

In my walk I spotted a hut high on a cliff. It was like a terrace. "One can see the whole valley well from there," I thought, and decided that I would climb up. Although there was no path, the footprints showed in which way it was easiest to approach it. I had not reached the point, when a slim figure appeared in the narrow doorway of the hut, stopped at the edge of the cliff, and raising his hand above his eyes he watched the evening movements in the yard. He wore a checked shirt, leather trousers with fringes along the edges, and Indian moccasins decorated with glass beads and hedgehog spikes.

On hearing my approach, he turned around, and I immediately recognised him.

'Harry, can it be you?' I exclaimed partly surprised, partly with joy in spite of his unfriendly behaviour to me earlier.

'If it wasn't possible, then we couldn't have met. The right question is, how did you get here?' he told me haughtily.

'Who allowed you to enter our fort?'

His hostile voice shocked me so much that I did not answer him. I turned around without a word, and returned to the yard. But now I knew for sure that he was Old Firehand's son. After his last words there was no doubt. The night fell slowly. In the middle of the yard they made a huge fire, and this is where all the habitants of the fort gathered. They were laughing, and joking. They told each other their stories. I listened to them from a distance. Soon Harry appeared, and I saw that he walked among the hunters, and talked to them like a full-right adult.

I then decided to find my horse. The sky was clear, and the thousands of stars smiled at the Earth.

Near the stream I heard a quiet, joyous neighing. Swallow recognised me in the dark, and rubbed his nose to my shoulder. Since he broke through the fire and water so bravely, I considered him a friend. I stroked his clever head with love.

I heard the quiet noise of steps, and suddenly Harry appeared from the dark.

'Excuse me for this,' he said hesitantly, ' but I brought something to Swallow. I haven't forgotten that I can thank him for my life.'

I gave way to him and turned around to leave. I wanted to continue my walk, when Harry stepped up to me.

'I'm really sorry that I insulted you, Sir,' he said, and looked in my eyes openly.

'Insulted?' I replied. 'You are too young to consider your words as insults. But I have to say I expected a different behaviour from you.'

'Then forgive my ungratefulness,' said Harry hard.

'I don't expect any kind of gratefulness from anyone.' I stated decidedly.

'I know,' he said, 'I also recognised that I completely misjudged you. And I also learnt that you saved not only my life, but my father's too. I won't forget it.'

'It isn't worth the words,' I shrugged my shoulder. 'Every Western hunter would do it for his companions. There are many, even more exceptional deeds. You will understand this when you are older.'

'So far I have been unjust to you, but now you do the same to me,' said Harry.

'Right,' I replied, 'then let's forget the whole thing!'

'Thank you!' said the boy. 'Then please follow me, I want to show you your sleeping chamber. I advise you to have some rest right away, because we get up early tomorrow.'

'Why?

'I set up my traps at Bee Fork and I would like to check them. My father would like you to accompany me.'

He led me to one of the chambers, pulled aside the curtain, and with punk, the firelighter of the prairie, he lit a deer-tallow candle.

'This is your room, Sir,' he said. 'These chambers are good against rheumatism, because we are in the mountains, and the air is humid, but there's no wind. Good night!'

I offered my hand to him, he accepted it, and nodded in a friendly way.

Once I was alone, I looked around in the little chamber. It was not a natural cave, but the work of human hands. The floor and the wall were covered by tanned hides, and in the back there was a simple bed made of cherry tree branches. It was made comfortable by real Navajo blankets.

Wooden wedges hammered in the gaps of the wall served as a wardrobe. Harry had given me his own chamber. I must have been very tired, for I am one, who spends his nights in the infinite, open prairie, under the starry or cloudy sky, could not feel well in a small, airless prison that millions of civilised people call house, as soon as I lay on the bed I fell asleep. It was probably because of the quietness of the chamber that I could not wake myself at dawn. Thus I awoke only when a not particularly gentle hand shook my shoulder.

'Isn't it enough of the horizontal stretching, Sir!' croaked somebody. 'It's time for vertical stretching!'

I opened my eyes. Sam Hawkins was standing there with a gun, and full trapper equipment.

'I'll be ready in a minute, dear Sam.'

'Good. The little Sir is already ready.'

'Are you also coming with us, Sam?'

'Somebody has to carry the equipment, don't you agree? Although Sam Hawkins could be useful in other ways too.'

In three minutes I was by the gate, where Harry was waiting for me. Sam put some traps on his back, and started off. 'Are we leaving the horses here?'

'We do,' said Sam.

'Then I have to check Swallow.'

'Unnecessary. The little Sir has checked on him if I'm not mistaken.'

Harry nodded. So, he had visited my mustang in the very early dawn. I was happy for this, because I could see that there was real peace between us now. I was about to ask him about his father, when he appeared with Winnetou, and another hunter. He greeted us kindly, and he wished us a good journey.

First we waded through the stream, and then followed the running of the water, that is, to the opposite direction in which we had arrived. We did not stop until we reached the confluence of the stream and the White Earth River.

The bank of the river was covered with thick bushes. In the network of vines we could carry on by using our knives. Sam was always at the front. His small, black eyes constantly scanned the environment, and nothing escaped his attention. He slipped under branches of the wild vine,.

'Follow me, Sir!' he told me. 'This is where the path of the beaver start.'

Behind the green curtain a well-trodden path led to the bank of the river.

'Look out!' whispered Harry. 'Make sure that their guard doesn't get suspicious.'

We slipped forward to the bend of the river in silence. There I could watch the life of a large beaver colony. The four-legged workers worked hard on reinforcing a dam. It stretched deep into the river, and was so broad that with appropriate care a man could have walked on it. On the other side the beavers chewed through thin trunks but so cleverly that the trees could only fall in the water. Other beavers moved the trunks to the right place. There the bricklayer beavers, using their broad, flat tails as a spatula, spread fatty earth and mud on the trunks, and tied them together with branches of bushes and vines.

As I watched the work of the industrious animals, I spotted a fat individual which sat on the dam, and looked into all directions. Obviously this was the guard. Suddenly it lifted its ears, turned several times around, cried out, and disappeared under the water. In the next moment all the beavers jumped in the water with a big splash. It would have been a humorous scene, but we had a different opinion. The animals could not see us, they must have stopped their work because they spotted Indians.

We lay on the ground, and from under the branches of the pine trees we watched. Soon two Indians appeared from the reed, and came towards us on the bank. One had a few traps on his shoulder, the other carried a lot of pelts.

'Rascals!' hissed Sam. 'They are robbing our traps! My Liddy will teach you some moral!'

He lifted his gun, but I stopped him. These were Ponca, and their faces were painted. They were on warpath.

'Only with knife, Sam,' I whispered. 'I'll sort out one, and you the other!'

The two Indians were with their backs to us examining the footprints on the ground. I put my gun down, and, with my knife between my teeth, I crawled forward carefully. At the edge of the bush I jumped up, and in the next moment one of the Indians, with my knife between his ribs, collapsed noiselessly. Sam did the same with the other.

'We have to get rid of the bodies,' I said.

'Yes, but not in the water, but among the reed!' With Harry's help we carried them to the reed.

'I suggest,' said Sam, 'that you two hurry back to the fort to warn our friends. I will follow the tracks of these two Ponca, maybe I could learn something important.'

Harry did not want to hear this plan, and he insisted that he and I would go on scouting, while Sam would return to the fort to report to Old Firehand. Harry was a brave and skilful little fellow. He moved forward as noiselessly and carefully as an experienced hunter. We had followed the tracks for an hour, when we got to another beaver colony.

'Here were the traps that the two Ponca stole,' said Harry. 'Bee Fork, where we wanted to go, is not far, but we have to follow these tracks leading to the forest.'

We could advance quicker in the forest. The wet moss showed the footprints well. Soon we arrived to a clearance, where we could see the tracks of four Indians. They had arrived there together, and split on this clearance. Two of them had headed to Bee Fork. These were the two Ponca whom we had killed. But the other two had gone directly to the direction of the Rock Fort.

'What should we do?' asked Harry. 'These tracks lead to our camp. Should we follow them, or continue on our way in the forest to find out where they had come from?'

'I'm for the latter,' I replied. 'If the two Ponca approached the gate, the guard will manage them. Meanwhile we could learn some important things, for example, where the Ponca's camp is, how many there are, and what was their plan.'

'I agree! Forward then!'

The forest was cut through by a number of brooks. In the spring, with the melting of the snow, a large amount of water rushed down to the valley in these brooks. At one of these brooks, we smelt a burning smell, and soon we could see a thin smoke column that fluttered above the foliage of the trees. It was the characteristic fire of the Indians. I remembered Winnetou's remark when he said that the pale faces made so big fires that they could not get close to it, and warm themselves. The Indians were cleverer. They did not throw a whole piece of wood in the fire, but only its end. A regulated fire gives enough heat, but it produces less smoke.

I waved to Harry to hide in a bush, and wait for me there, until I had investigated the source of the smoke.

I advanced from tree to tree. When I arrived to a brook I almost cried out in my surprise, because there were so many Indians sitting or lying in a hollow in the ground. There was a guard at each end of the hollow. Fortunately I hid behind a huge oak tree whose thick trunk covered me.

I tried to count the Indians, and by doing so, I looked at each of them. At one moment my heart missed a throb, and with an involuntary motion I rubbed my eyes. Next to the fire sat Parranoh, or as Old Firehand called him, Tim Finnetey! It could not be a mistake, because I saw his face the night when I stabbed him. One thing surprised me. The man by the fire had thick, black hair, while Winnetou had scalped Parranoh. I would have liked to get closer to look at him better, but it was not possible. The guard was staring at the oak tree behind which I hid. It was time to retreat.

I found Harry, and only told him that I had found a bigger group, thus we had to return to Rock Fort. We turned back, and without trouble we reached the clearance where the tracks separated. From there we chose the shortest way home. Meanwhile I was musing if I really had seen Parranoh by the fire. Did the Ponca arrive here accidentally. or had they followed us? Judging everything I came to the conclusion that it was the same group that had failed at the railways. After we had dispersed them, they had gathered again, gained more warriors, and had followed us to take revenge. But why had they not attacked us? Why had they allowed us to pass through their land?

Probably they had heard about the existence of the hunting camp but they did not know where it was, and thus they let us lead them here hoping that they would finish us all off, and get a rich loot.

We were not far from the gate, when in a bush I suddenly spotted a pile of traps, next to it a pair of crooked legs, with feet in huge moccasins, soon a coat and a hat. It was Sam.

I decided that I would surprise him I sneaked up behind him. I grabbed his Liddy, and aimed it at him. In his surprise seeing his own gun directed at him, his mouth opened.

'Sam,' I whispered, 'if you don't close your mouth, I'll put all these traps in it.'

'Good point, Sir,' he replied. 'You frightened me, but I'm relieved that you aren't a redskin, because ...'

'Why are you sleeping here?' I interrupted him.

'Sleeping? Not at all!' he said very self-consciously.

We learnt from him that the two Ponca whose tracks we found at the clearance had almost found the gate, but for our good luck, and for their bad, Sam Hawkins noticed them, and sent them to the eternal hunting grounds.

'You did it very well, Sam,' I said appreciatively. 'You can't imagine what a great danger you have prevented.'

In a few words I told him everything that I had seen. Sam whistled.

'The danger is really big, Sir!' he remarked scratching his head. 'We killed all the four scouts. This is good and bad. It's good, because they failed, but bad, because the Ponca will inevitably attack. Let's hurry to Old Firehand.'

The guard on the gate was Will Parker. He received me with great joy, but I did not have time to talk to him. I could hardly wait to report to Old Firehand.

481

Old Firehand listened to my report calmly, but when I started to speak about Parranoh, he exclaimed excitedly, 'Are you sure, Sir? Was it really him?'

'I'm sure but he has a long, black hair ...'

'The hair doesn't matter,' said Old Firehand. 'Think of Sam Hawkins, who also survived when he was scalped! Probably his wound wasn't mortal, the Ponca found him, and took care of him. While I was recovering, so was he, and he replaced his scalp with a taupe. Now I will be able to settle the bill with him! Are you tired?'

'I can't say I am,' I replied.

'Would you come with me?'

'Happily. But it's a bit dangerous. The Ponca are waiting for the return of their scouts in vain, and if they are looking for them, they can easily capture us.'

'I don't care! I can't miss Tim Finnetey for the second time. I'll also take Dick Stone.'

For his call Dick Stone immediately picked up his gun, and joined us.

'Harry, you will join Will Parker!' instructed Old Firehand. 'Bill Bulcher! With some men you will hide our cache, so that the redskins, even if they broke in, wouldn't find them!'

Harry begged to be taken, but his father refused to hear his pleading.

When we arrived to the forest, I remembered Winnetou. I had not seen him since dawn, and was a bit anxious about him. What if he had met the Ponca, and got into trouble? Suddenly a bush cracked near us. I grabbed my knife, but I let it go relieved, when the branches opened, and the young chief of the Apache was in front of us.

'Winnetou will join his white brothers who are going against Parranoh and the Ponca,' he stated without any introductory words.

We looked at him surprised. He clearly knew everything, and probably had learnt it earlier than we did.

'Have you seen the Ponca, my brother?' I asked.

'Winnetou didn't forget his brother, Old Shatterhand, and Harry, Ribbana's son. He followed them so that he could help them if necessary. He also saw Parranoh, who borrowed the scalp of an Osage Indian. His hair is a lie, and all his thoughts are deceit. Winnetou will kill him today.'

'No Winnetou!' protested Old Firehand. 'He is mine!'

'Winnetou has given him to you. If he slips out of your hand for the second time ...'

I could not hear the end of the sentence, because I just noticed a burning pair of eyes in the bush nearby. With one jump I threw myself on the peeping man.

It was him, the rascal of whom we had just talked. When I recognised him, I grabbed him by his throat. From the nearby bushes many Indians jumped out to help Parranoh. Meanwhile my friends came to my aid, and fought the attacking Ponca.

The white chief crushed to the ground, and defended himself desperately. I knelt on his chest; squeezed his throat with my right hand, and with my left I twisted his knife out of his hand. He tried to push me away. His eyes goggled in the effort. His taupe slipped off his head, and on his scalped skull the veins swelled. His mouth was foaming in his anger, and the villainous ugliness of his face became almost frightening. My fingers dug further into his neck, his head fell back, his body became limp, and finally he lost his consciousness.

I rose, and looked around. The scene was unforgettable. None of the fighters used firearms as they were afraid that their enemies would hear it. All fought with knives and tomahawks. Winnetou just stabbed a Ponca, and did not need my help. Old Firehand had overcome an Indian, but the other made a deep wound on his arm, and he was a major danger. I jumped there, and with the Indian's own tomahawk, that he had dropped in the fight, I cut the Ponca's skull into two. Then I hurried to help Dick Stone because a strong Ponca knelt on him. I knocked off his knife in the last moment. Dick sorted out the rest.

Old Firehand only now saw Parranoh.

'Tom Fin ... So he was here too! Who defeated him?' he asked, looking around.

'Old Shatterhand,' replied Winnetou smiling. The Good Spirit gave him the strength of the bison. But this was only a scouting group. If the main group arrives, we will be defeated. We should hurry back to the fort.'

'You are right,' nodded Dick Stone. 'We would lose against the main group. Let's return.'

'Right,' said Old Firehand, 'but first bandage my wound, and then let's remove the traces of the battle as much as it's possible.'

He lifted his arm. It was bleeding profusely. Winnetou quickly tore off a strip from Old Firehand's shirt sleeve, and skilfully bandaged the wound.

In the meantime I saw that one of the three Indians who had attacked Dick, had stabbed him in his side. Fortunately, it was not a dangerous wound, and I was able to remove the knife from his side.

'And the prisoner?' asked Old Firehand pointing at the still unconscious Parranoh.

'We will carry him home,' I said. I hope he won't recover in the meantime.

'I won't carry this dog!' protested Dick Stone. 'I have a better idea!'

He cut down a few thick branches, and made a kind of sled from it. He tied the unconscious bandit on it, and said, 'We will pull him home. If it's not comfortable enough for him, it's his problem.'

We had to agree that it was the cleverest solution. The only disadvantage was that it left too visible a track.

The following morning I got up early. There was deep silence in the camp, all that could be heard was now birds starting their morning song. I climbed up to the cliff where I had first met Harry in this camp. I was thinking hard, as the night before a returning hunter brought some unpleasant news. On his way he had found the other camp of the Ponca.

They had their horses there. It seemed that they had come with a much stronger group than we thought. In the afternoon and the evening we made arrangements for defending the place against an attack. We prepared the ammunition, and agreed on the tasks of each man if we were attacked. While we were busy with these things, we did not have time to decide on the fate of the prisoner. Parranoh was tied up, and he was guarded in one of the chambers. He could not escape from there. The train of my thoughts arrived to the conclusion that the following days, and maybe hours, would decide the fate of the camp.

While I was evaluating our situation, I heard someone approaching. I looked up, and saw Harry.

'Good morning, Sir!' he said. 'I can see that you got up as early as I did.'

'Good morning, Harry!' I said returning the salutation. 'Being vigilant is a virtue in such a dangerous situation.'

'You are not afraid of the Ponca, are you?'

'I know that you don't mean these words seriously. But you shouldn't forget that we have only thirteen men in the camp, and the enemy has a multiple numeric superiority.'

'You consider the situation too gloomily. Thirteen men like us equal a hundred Ponca. They flee when they encounter brave men.'

Although my mood was quite dark, I had to smile at his self-esteem as he counted himself among the warriors.

'Maybe we are braver,' I answered, 'but the Ponca are craftier. They surely found their fallen warriors during the night, and they also know that we have Parranoh. They'll do everything to rescue him.'

'Then let them come!' exclaimed Harry. 'I hope many will die here!'

I looked at him astonished. He understood my look and continued, 'Do you think I'm cruel, Sir? Do you think it doesn't suit my age? There are feelings that affect equally irrespective of age. Had we got to Bee Fork yesterday, you could have seen the grave that I cannot forget. The dearest being, whom nobody can substitute, is in that grave. She was killed with this pistol.'

He pulled the weapon from his belt. It was the one I had seen in New Venango.

'You are an excellent marksman, Sir,' he continued, 'but this gun is so bad that you won't be able to hit a hickory tree from ten steps. You can imagine how much I exercised until I learnt to use it. I took the oath that I would revenge everyone who had anything to do with my mother's death, the murderer and his allies, and I would do it with this gun.'

'Did you get this gun from Winnetou?'

'Yes, did he tell you that?'

'He mentioned it.'

'Then I tell you the rest!' exclaimed Harry, as he sat down next to me.

He stared at the ground for a long time, and I did the same because I did not want to disturb him in his painful memories. Finally he lifted his head and started to speak.

'My father was a forester in Germany. He lived happily with his wife and his son until he had to flee his homeland because of political disturbances. His wife died during the journey. He stepped on the shore of a strange country with his son, my half-brother, where he had to start a new life. He did not have any money and friends. He knew only the forest, and thus did the only thing he could: he became a hunter. He left his son with a wealthy family. This is how he became a Westerner.

A few years passed with dangerous adventures that made his name famous. During his travels he got to the land of the Assiniboine Indians. This is where he first met Winnetou, who came from the Colorado River to mine some sacred clay at the Northern Mississippi for the calumet of his tribe. Both were the guests of Tah-sha-tunga, and they met Ribbana, the chief's daughter in his tent. She was beautiful like the dawn, and fresh like the rose of the mountains. No other girl of the tribe could tan leather so soft, and embroider them so prettily as she. When she went for water to the stream or for twigs to the forest, everybody admired her slim body, carriage, and her hair that reached her ankle. She was the favourite of the Good Spirit, the pride of the Assiniboine. The bravest warriors competed for her, but she had already given her heart to the paleface hunter, although he was much older than her. Winnetou was the youngest of those who courted her, almost a boy. The white hunter's heart opened for Ribbana, he followed her everywhere, and talked to her as to a paleface girl. Winnetou watched them from the distance, and one evening he went to the white hunter, and told him, "You are different from other palefaces, who constantly lie, my white brother. Your lips always tell the truth, and there's no meanness in your eyes. Do you allow Winnetou to speak to you honestly?"

My father responded, "You have always been honest with me, my young brother. Your arms are strong, your heart is brave, and your thoughts are clear like the water of the mountain stream. I'm proud of your friendship. Talk, Winnetou, I'm listening."

"Do you love Ribbana, Tah-sha-tunga's daughter?"

"I love her more than the forest, the stars of the sky, my own life!"

"And will you be kind to her, when you take her to your home? Will you look after her, and protect her from the storms of life?"

"I'll carry her on my hand, I will watch all her desires, and I will protect her from all dangers."

"Then Winnetou will leave with a sad heart. His path will be dark, there won't be stars above his head. When he saw Ribbana for the first time, he believed that his life will be bright. But her eyes fell on you, my white brother, and she speaks your name. Winnetou will return to the Pecos River alone, and won't think again to lead a squaw to his tent. When he returns from bison hunting, a woman or a child won't wait for him. But every year, at the time when the elk appears among the mountains, he will come here, and will see if Ribbana, Ta-sha-tunga's daughter, is happy!"

He returned a year later. Ribbana received him happily with a baby on her arm. The baby was me. Winnetou lifted me, embraced me, kissed me, and blessed me. "Winnetou will be the tree, under whose strong branches little birds, like you, can find protection. May storm come or rain fall, Winnetou will protect you! May your life be joyous, and may you be the joy of your father, Winnetou's paleface brother!"

The years passed. I played with the children of the tribe, but I also participated in hunting, and exercised fighting. My father happily observed my development, but sometimes he was sad, because he wanted to see his other son too. His desire became so strong that finally he went to the East, and took me too. I met my half-brother, and I loved him. A new world opened up for me, the civilised life of the white men. My father left me there, and returned alone to the land of the Assiniboine. A few months later, I became homesick. I did not have the desire or patience for anything, I just longed for my homeland. However, I had to wait for my father's next visit, and then we started off for the West.

Our arrival was terrible. The village was empty, it was burned down. After a long search we found a wampum that Tah-sha-tunga had left behind so that we would know what happened.

Tim Finnetey was a white hunter. He had visited the Assiniboine several times, and he used to court Ribbana. However, the tribe chased him away, because he was a thief and tried to steal the pelts of the tribe. With vengeance in his heart he moved to the Blackfeet, and tried to entice them against the Assiniboine.

These listened to him, and attacked the village when the men went out hunting. They pillaged the village, murdered the children and the elderly, and took the young girls and the women. When the warriors returned, they immediately pursued the robbers. This had happened a few days before our arrival, thus we immediately followed them.

It's difficult to speak about the rest. On the way we met Winnetou. When he heard the terrible news from my father, he immediately turned his horse, and joined us. I will never forget the faces of the two friends: darkened by sadness, anger, and the thirst for revenge. They followed the tracks with torturing impatience.

We caught up with our warriors at Bee Fork. They were hiding in the forest, and waited for the night to attack the Blackfeet who were camping at the bank of the river. They left me behind with the guards of the horses, but I could not stay, and as soon as the attack started, I crawled to the edge of the forest. The first gunshot went off when I arrived. A terrible struggle started against the numerically superior enemy. The raging noise of the battle died down only at dawn. I was lying in the wet grass, and prayed for the victory of justice. In the depth of the valley I saw desperately fighting figures in the grey dawn, and I could hear the groaning of the wounded. I rushed back to the guards, but they weren't there, and neither were the horses. I felt a terrible fear because I could hear the victory cries of the enemy. I knew that my people had been defeated. I hid in the forest all day, and when it became dark again, I went to the battlefield. There was a deep silence, and the moon lit the dead bodies. Some bad premonition forced me to examine the bodies one by one, and suddenly I found my mother among them. She was lying dead in a pool of blood. A bullet had hit her heart. Her arms embraced her younger sister whose head was crushed by a blow. The pain deprived me from my consciousness, and I fell on the ground next to her.

I don't know how long I lay there. When I opened my eyes, it was morning, but it could have been a morning of a later day. I could hear some noise. I turned, and there, for my joy in my grieving, I recognised my father, and Winnetou. Both were in a terrible state. Their clothing was ragged, and they had many wounds, but they were alive. They were overcome, and were tied up, but they escaped.'

Harry took a deep breath, and stared in the distance. After a long silence he turned to me and asked, 'Tell me, Sir, is your mother still alive?'

'She is.'

'And what would you do, Sir, if you learnt that somebody murdered her?'

'I would leave the punishment to the law.'

'Yes, but when the law is weak or far, like here in the West, you must take the law in your own hands.'

'No. Punishment and revenge are two different things. Punishment is demanded by the moral law, the law of justice that is in our heart. This is a clear, noble passion, a desire that can go blunt for a while, but cannot be exterminated from the humanity. Revenge, however, is an ugly and a repulsive feeling that reduces man to an animal.'

'Only those can speak like this who don't have Indian blood in their veins!' cried Harry. 'You can call murderers animals, and they deserve no mercy. When Winnetou saw our dear dead, he made an Indian oath of revenge against Finnetey.'

'Was he the murderer?'

'Without doubt. There was a moment of the battle when the surprised Blackfeet thought that the attackers would sweep them away. The rascal Finnetey aimed at my mother with his pistol. Winnetou saw it, and jumped on him. He even took his pistol, but it was too late. The inhuman crime had happened, and nothing could undo it. Winnetou would have killed the murderer, but five enemies attacked him. They overpowered him, and tied him up, and they were celebrating that they captured Winnetou. They mocked him, and cursed him. They left the pistol with him as part of the taunting. He later gave it to me. I always have it with me, even if I'm in the towns.

'Harry!' I exclaimed, 'I have to say that ...'

Harry interrupted me with a motion of his hand, 'I know what you want to say, I have heard it many times. And I also tried to tell myself! But I'm the son of the forest and the prairie, these pulse in my veins!'

The way he spoke was against all my values, and thus his words were repugnant to me, yet I understood him well. I knew that he would never forget the tragic night, and the passion of revenge could not be eased by anything else, but by its satisfaction. The law of justice was in him as well, but a stricter one: life for life. This was not an experience for a child, and probably this is why he behaved and talked like an adult. I could not condemn him for what he said and I felt sorry for his very short childhood.

A sharp whistle resounded from the yard. Harry jumped up, and said, 'My father is calling the men. We have to go down too. It's time to judge the prisoner.'

I stood up, and grabbed his hand. 'I'd like to ask you something, Harry. Promise me that you would fulfil it.'

'Willingly if you don't ask something that is impossible.'

'Leave the revenge to the adults.'

'I knew that this is what you meant. I have imagined the moment of facing my mother's murderer a thousand times. I have imagined how I would repay him for what he did against me, and my dearest. This has been the goal of my life, the meaning of my daily struggles, and sufferings and now I should give it up for your sentimental request? Never!'

'It's not only about my request, Harry!'

'I can't, even if I wanted!' he said impatiently. 'Let's go!'

I parted with him, because I wanted to visit my mustang as I had not seen him on that day. After this I joined the others. The men surrounded a tree to which Parranoh was tied, and they discussed the mode of execution.

'I wouldn't spend a bullet on him,' said Sam Hawkins. 'I believe if my Liddy could speak, she would protest against making her do such a dirty job.'

'You're right,' nodded Dick Stone, 'Let's hang him, and that's it. Am I right Sir?'

'Only partially,' replied Old Firehand. 'I wouldn't like if his body stained our nice yard. He committed his most vile crime at Bee Fork. He should be executed there.'

'Excuse me, Sir,' complained Dick Stone, 'then I carried him here in vain! Let's not waste time with him. Hang him, and then we can bury him outside.'

491

'What's the view of Winnetou, the chief of the Apache?' asked Old Firehand.

'Winnetou has the scalp of the Arapaho dog, he doesn't care with the rest. He is yours, my white brother, and you can do with him whatever you wish.'

'And what's your view?' asked Old Firehand as he turned to me.

'I ask you kill him quickly, and as soon as it's possible. None of us is afraid of the Ponca, but why should we take an unnecessary risk? This bandit isn't worth that much.'

'Then you should stay, Sir, and go to sleep!' said Harry mockingly. 'I also say that the punishment should be where the murder happened. This is the least that we owe to our dearest deceased.'

The prisoner stood motionlessly, and he did not show what pain the belts that cut into his flesh caused to him. He heard that they discussed his fate, but stared at the ground indifferently. The years, the crimes, and the vices engraved deep wrinkles in his rough and cruel face. His red, scalped skull made the whole head even more repulsive. I turned away with disgust.

The discussion had finally come to an end. The hunters accepted Old Firehand's and Harry's proposal. While they were preparing for the journey, Old Firehand came to me, and put his hand on my shoulder.

'If you don't want to make mistakes,' he said, 'don't use the measure of the so-called civilisation on everything!'

'I don't have the right to criticise your procedures, Sir,' I replied, 'but if you don't mind, I don't want to participate in the execution.'

'I don't mind that you stay, because then I know that the security of our camp is in the right hands.'

'When will your return?'

'It's difficult to say,' he said. 'It depends on the situation by Bee Fork. Good-bye! Keep your eyes open!'

They untied the prisoner from the tree, gagged him, and started off. Winnetou joined them.

Only a few hunters stayed for guarding the camp, among them Dick Stone. I went to him, and told him that I would go out scouting.

'Unnecessary, Sir,' asserted Dick. 'The guard is alert, and the young Apache chief scouted in the morning. I suggest that you rest a bit while everything is quiet.'

'What do you mean?'

'The Ponca are not stupid. If their scouts tell them that the camp is half empty, they may want to visit us.'

'You are right, Dick. This is why I'll go out, and scout around the bushes. I won't be away for long.'

I took my Henry rifle, and left our camp. The guard assured me that there could not be a single Indian nearby, but I trusted my eyes more than the words of other people. I penetrated into the thicket, and searched the ground for Indian footprints.

At one place, just the opposite of the entrance of the fort, I noticed a few broken branches. After searching through the ground I concluded that an Indian had lay there, who had tried to carefully erase his tracks before retreating. It was unpleasant, but still a fact: the Ponca had found our camp, and perhaps had even heard our council.

They would then be stupid if they did not attack the camp as it was guarded by only a few people. Then I thought that it would not be the first thing that the Ponca would do. They would more likely to go after Old Firehand and Winnetou to rescue Parranoh. I had to warn them of the danger.

After giving the necessary instructions to the guard, I hurried to the place of the battlefield of the day before. I was right, the Ponca had found their dead, and took them. The tracks showed that many Indians had been there earlier.

Soon I found more footprints. These led to the Bee Fork, the place where Old Firehand had left for an hour earlier. At the quickest pace that carefulness allowed, I followed the tracks. I covered a long distance. Soon I was at the place where our stream entered the White Earth River.

The stream there made an arch around a clearance. In the middle of this clearance there was a small group of balsam fir trees. I saw Parranoh tied to one of them, and near him my friends, who with damned light headedness talked as if they had been in the fort. Probably they were still arguing the mode of execution.

But I also saw something else. In the bushes around the clearance, just opposite me a few Indians were hiding, and watched. It was not difficult to understand their plan. They split into three groups. A few men stayed in the bushes, while the other two went to the left and right and surrounded the clearance. They would attack my friends at the same time.

I could not waste any time. I shot with my rifle. For half a minute this had been the only noise, because both friends and enemies were shocked by the unexpected shot. However, soon as the first surprise had gone, the battle cry of the Ponca resounded, and arrows flew to the clearance from all directions before the Indians charged forward.

I jumped out at the same time to save Harry. I did it just at the right moment. The boy had already lifted the old pistol to kill Parranoh, when a Ponca jumped on him. My fist knocked him out.

The hunters fought bravely, but they were outnumbered. They were all experienced trappers, who had survived many tight situations, but the outcome of the battle was clear, because almost all of them were already wounded from the first shots of the Ponca, while more and more redskins were arriving to the battle.

Some of them rushed to Parranoh, released him, and pushed Winnetou away. He wanted to kill the prisoner in the last minute. The huge, muscular bandit moved his arms and legs to help the restart of the circulation of his blood, and then he grabbed one of the Ponca warrior's tomahawk. He swung it towards Winnetou.

'Come you, dog of the Pimo! Come you mangy coyote! I'll kill you now!' he rasped in mad anger, and ground his teeth.

Winnetou was bleeding from several wounds, but when he heard the bandit using the mocking name of the Apache, he lifted his knife not caring with the tomahawk. At that moment a Ponca jumped on him from behind, and pulled him onto the ground. Old Firehand was surrounded by several enemies, and could not help his friend. I was fighting with three warriors, and far from Winnetou. I saw that the tomahawk flew, but missed.

Standing our ground was meaningless. When I shook off my attackers, I grabbed Harry's arm, and pulled him.

'In the water!' I shouted. 'Everybody! In the water!'

With one jump I got into the water. Everybody, who followed me, did the same. The stream was quite deep here, but also narrow, and with a few strokes we could get to the other bank. We were not yet safe, however. My plan was that I would run towards the White Earth River, cross that, and we would be then safe.

On the left, about a hundred steps from us, there was a group of dark willows. As I looked towards this direction, I saw that Sam Hawkins was running that way. It seemed that his crafty eyes twinkled, and he beckoned us before he disappeared behind the hanging branches. I immediately recognised that his plan was much better than mine, and I followed his example without hesitation.

'And my father?' exclaimed Harry. 'I cannot leave him in this trouble!'

'Hurry!' I urged him, and dragged him by this arm. 'If he couldn't get out of the clearance, we cannot help him!'

Under the cover of the willows we quickly went back to the stream, but much further upstream. The Ponca were running towards the White Earth River, as their plan was to cut off our escape route.

'How stupid they are, hehehe!' laughed Sam contented with his trick. 'Look! They even left their guns behind!'

The Ponca could not have imagined that their defeated enemy could be behind their back. In order to be quicker, they put down their guns and bows in a pile, and left them there. Sam jumped there with comical leaps like a kangaroo. With his knife he cut through the tendons of the bows, and threw the guns in the stream.

'It's not really a waste,' he laughed. 'They are all rusty old guns anyway. But now let's hurry!'

We ran in the shortest way towards our camp, because we knew that not all the Ponca warriors were at the Bee Fork. At half way we heard gunshots from the direction of the fort. We hurried even more because all three of us thought that our companions in the camp were in trouble, and we must help them. The gunshot was repeated. When we arrived to the place where I had found the tracks of the Indian in the morning, we stopped to discuss the situation. We hid behind the bushes, listened, and peered, because we were afraid that Indians were hiding between us and the gate. Suddenly twigs cracked behind us, and we could hear approaching steps.

Ready for everything I grabbed my knife, and waited for the Ponca. My joy was then even bigger when Old Firehand appeared from the bushes, with Winnetou behind him with two hunters. They had escaped. Harry jumped on his father's neck.

'Did you hear the shots?' asked Old Firehand hastily.

'Yes, I'm afraid the Ponca found our camp,' I replied.

'That's true!' said Sam Hawkins. 'But today Bill Bulcher is the guard, and he's good enough to defend the gate alone.'

'Yes,' replied Old Firehand, 'but we need certainty. Also our pursuers will be here soon.'

'And the scattered men?' I interjected.

'You are right. We will need as many men as it's possible. Hopefully some of them will return here.'

'You should wait here,' said Winnetou, 'I'll be back soon.'

He disappeared, and we could not do anything else, but sit down in the bush. The waiting was not a waste of time, because two more men arrived. We were happy for this as now there were nine of us, thus we had a significant strength again.

Finally Winnetou returned. There was a fresh scalp on his belt. He ascertained that the Ponca were around the gate. He had killed one of them. We could not wait any longer in the bush, because they would know from the body that we were behind them. But to get back to the camp we had to remove the rest of the Ponca.

Following Winnetou's advice, we formed a chain, and for his signal we shot a volley of fire. Frightened howls were the responses. The Ponca believed that there were many of us, and ran away. Now we could reach the water gate.

Bill Bulcher stood his place very well. He noticed the approaching Ponca in time, and with his well-aimed shots kept them away from the gate. Later Dick Stone joined him. We shook hands with the two men, and we were about to enter the camp, when there was a noise as if a bison herd was breaking through the bush. We held our guns ready to shoot, when a man appeared with a number of horses. He was dressed in a hunting suit. He was bleeding from several wounds, including a head wound.

'Well!' exclaimed Sam Hawkins, 'It's Will Parker! What are you doing with these horses?'

'I thought the reds would look for me everywhere, except in their own camp. They left two guards with the horses. It was a hellish job to get rid of them, I tell you! They have punctured me in several places. Then I drove their horses to the prairie, chased away the bad ones, and brought here only the good ones.'

'This one is a wonderful horse,' remarked Old Firehand. 'If I was asked, I couldn't decide which one I would have, this or Swallow.'

'Winnetou understands the soul and heart of the horses,' said the Apache chief. 'I would choose Swallow.'

An arrow flew through the air, and hit Sam Hawkins's arm, but it could not penetrate the rock solid coat. The shot was followed by some war cries. Because the entrance was narrow, and we had the horses, we could not escape to the camp. We had to face the Ponca. We rode half way through the thicket, but could not see any Indian. Clearly, they had retreated waiting for reinforcement.

Finally we entered the yard where we could rest a bit.

By the camp fire we discussed the events. Old Firehand thought that there was no major danger. We had enough food and ammunition, the gate could easily be defended, so we did not have to be afraid even of a long siege. Sam Hawkins was of the same opinion. Only Winnetou stared at the fire with knitted eyebrows, and a gloomy face.

'What worried thoughts are flying through your mind, my brother?' I asked him.

'The palefaces' eyes are blinded by their hatred, and their wisdom is blunted by their thirst of revenge. I feel that Parranoh will come, and scalp the white hunters.'

'But they cannot break through the entrance!' I replied.

'You can say these words, my brother, but you should think of the meaning of the words too! How many red men are needed to break through?'

I had to agree with him. Even if it cost them a lot of lives, a large number of Indians could break through.

Old Firehand dismissed the argument by saying, 'Let them come! We will kill them one by one in the gorge.'

After dinner I went to my mustang as I had not seen him since the morning. Swallow was grazing in the depth of the valley beyond the reach of the light of the fire. I stroked the faithful animal, and was about to return to my chamber, when I heard a light noise as if a little piece of stone had fallen off from the cliff.

Swallow also heard this noise, because he lifted his head. I stroked him again to calm him, but his nostrils opened, and he sniffed suspiciously. If it was a small stone, why did it roll down? I decided that I would wait a bit, and listen.

I stood for two minutes motionlessly, when I noticed a shadow on the top of the cliff as it rose, and lifted its arm. Soon a whole row of shadows appeared. They followed the first shadow, who obviously knew a path, and descended on the almost vertical cliff that we had considered unscalable.

Had I brought my gun with me, it would have been simple to take out the leader, and raise the alarm. Without him the others would not have been able to make a step as only the front man knew the cliff, and the places where he could put down his foot. Unfortunately I had only my revolver, which was useless for such a distance. True, if I had wanted to raise the alarm it would have been good, but then I could have said good-bye to my life as I would have been an excellent target for the guns of the Indians above. I had to try something else.

I was sure that the bold leader, who was approaching from rock to rock, was Parranoh. If I could kill him, the attack would fail. The moment appeared advantageous. He had to go around a large, bouldering rock that I could reach from below. If I could get there, Parranoh would walk right into my revolver.

I immediately started to climb. At the same time I could hear gunshots from the gate that were followed by some more. I understood the plan of the Ponca. They pretended to attack the gate to distract us from the real danger. I gathered all my strength, and climbed even faster. I reached the bouldering rock when the stone went loose under my foot, and I fell down. Stones fell on me, and I hit myself so much that I fainted for a few minutes.

When I opened my eyes, the first Ponca had almost arrived to the yard. He was less than ten steps from me. All my limbs ached, but I jumped to my feet, and shot at the approaching shadows. Then I leaped on my mustang, and rode towards the fire. My most urgent task was to save Swallow from the enemy.

The Ponca, seeing that they had been spotted, yelled their battle cry, and rushed after me. I jumped off my horse by the fire, but nobody was there. The hunters, hearing the gunshots, had rushed from their chambers to the gate.

'The Ponca are in the yard! Back to the chambers!'

This was the only possibility. The chambers could be defended against a large number of enemies, because they could have been shot dead one by one. I also ran towards my chamber, but it was too late. The Ponca were attacking those in the yard.

I saw that Old Firehand, Harry and Will Parker were in a tight situation, and I hurried to help them.

'Back! To the cliff!' I shouted at them as I entered the battle. My sudden appearance distracted the Ponca. I hoped that my friends would utilise this opportunity, and retreat to the cliff so that at least their back would be covered.

'I'm also here, if necessary!' I heard a sharp, high-pitch voice, and Sam Hawkins appeared in one of the gaps in the cliff. 'Little Sir, come here! I kept a good place for you!'

Harry jumped there after a short hesitation, and they started shooting wildly. Apparently Harry loaded the guns, and Sam shot, because the gun flashed almost every minute.

But only those two shot, the others had to fight hand to hand, with knife and tomahawk in the light of the campfire, in the noise of battle cries and curses.

Our situation was hopeless. The number of the Ponca in the yard kept on increasing, and we knew that we could not escape towards the gate either, as we could hear gunshots from there too. But we were all determined not to give up our life so easily. I remembered my old parents back in Europe, who would not receive news about their son from America anymore. I quickly chased away the painful thought as I needed all my concentration in this dangerous situation.

If only I had my gun! But I left it in my chamber, and I could not get there now. The problem that I foresaw in the morning had happened! Unfortunately no one listened to me! This raised anger in me, and I pressed my lips together. I hit out with my tomahawk to the left and right desperately. Now the battle noise subsided, and it became more eerie. This is when I suddenly heard the familiar high-pitched voice.

'Good, Sir! Just carry on!'

It was Sam Hawkins who encouraged me from the gap.

Will Parker, who was fighting with the butt of his rifle, heard him, and replied, 'Sam Hawkins! Look here, this how it's done correctly?'

A few steps from me Old Firehand stood with his back against the cliff. He was fighting off the onrushing Ponca. His stance was solid as if his feet had been rooted in the ground. His long grey hair fluttered in the wind. In one hand he had a tomahawk, in the other a knife. He was wounded, but his huge figure stood out from among the attackers.

Then another big figure broke through the crowd of the Ponca. Parranoh spotted Firehand, and rushed towards him with a revolver in his hand.

'Your life is mine!' he yelled. 'Go after your Ribbana!'

As he ran by me, I grabbed his shoulder, and lifted my tomahawk to split his head. Parranoh recognised me, and jumped back quickly like lightning, thus my tomahawk hit only the air.

'Are you here too?' brayed Parranoh at me. 'I'll make sure that you are captured alive!'

Before I could raise my tomahawk again, he shot. Old Firehand pushed both of his hands in the air, made a huge leap forward, and then collapsed silently.

This was then the fate of the great hero, who had always looked in the eyes of death bravely in so many battles! I felt as if the bullet had gone into my heart. I pushed the Indian in the front of me aside, and was about to throw myself on Parranoh, when a dark, slim figure broke through the row of the Ponca warriors.

'Arapaho toad! The chief of the Apache will revenge the death of his white brother!'

'You Pimo dog! I'll tear your tongue out!'

This was all I could hear. The event caught my attention so much that I forgot about my own situation. In the next moment a sling caught my neck, somebody pulled it, and a huge blow hit my neck. I lost my consciousness.

When I recovered, I was in complete quietness and darkness. I could not remember anything until the terrible

501

pain in my neck reminded me to the events. My other wounds ached too, and the ropes with which they tied my hands and legs just increased the pain. I was unable to move.

Then I heard some noise as if somebody was whining.

'Is there somebody here?' I asked.

'If you can call Sam Hawkins somebody,' hummed a voice.

'Is that you, Sam? Where are we?'

'In the cave where we used to keep the furs. Fortunately we hid them the day before yesterday, so at least the bandits won't have it. A little joy, if nothing else, hehehe!'

'And how are the others?'

'Acceptably, Sir. Old Firehand fell, Dick Stone fell, Will Parker fell, should I continue? Bill Bulcher was killed, Harry Corner was killed, everybody was killed, only we two are alive, and probably the Apache chief, and perhaps the little Sir too.'

'When have you seen Harry last?' I asked earnestly.

'When they carried me here. Harry and Winnetou were pushed into the next chamber.'

'How was Winnetou?'

'Like my coat, Sir. Patch on patch, but at least he's alive.'

'How could they catch him alive?'

'Like you and I, Sir. Knocked him out, and tied him up. I don't think it was his intention to survive the battle, and then be roasted on the torture stake.'

'Of course, we cannot think of escaping,' I said gloomily.

'You speak like a greenhorn again! Of course, one can think of many things,' replied Sam Hawkins. 'I, for example, think a lot of my old Liddy, and my revolvers. The jackals took them. And also my pipe though that stinks like a skunk, hehehe. The dogs have them. The only consolation is that they left my knife.'

'Left your knife?' I was astonished.

'Not because of politeness, but because of stupidity. Or because of my wisdom. Sam Hawkins always keeps a knife in the sleeve of his coat.'

'This is excellent, Sam!'

'It would be excellent if I could get to it. But I'm tied up so much that I cannot even wipe my nose.'

'Just wait, let's see what we can do about it.'

I tried to crawl closer, but it was so painful that I had to pause. This was lucky, because the rug that covered the entrance was lifted, and Parranoh entered with a torch in his hand. A Ponca warrior accompanied him.

'I got you, you dog,' he growled at me, and lit my face with his torch. While I did not look at him, I did not pretend that I was unconscious either.

'I got what belongs to me!' I heard his voice. 'Do you know what this is?'

He pushed a scalp in my face. I recognised Parranoh's own scalp that Winnetou cut off. The Apache chief certainly had not told him that I was there, but Parranoh apparently remembered. Perhaps he had seen my face that night. Now he wanted to boast, and enjoy his victory, this is why he visited me.

'You must understand that you'll have to pay for this!' he shouted with joy but also bitterly. 'But you have to wait till the morning! I'll skin you in front of your friends! Your scalp will be the last piece!'

'I wonder how you'll scalp me,' remarked Sam, 'because the Pawnee did my hairdressing some time ago!'

'There's enough skin on you to flay!'

Being satisfied with these threats, the bandit continued, 'Did you believe that Tim Finnetey did not know your camp? Do you know who told me the secret of the valley? He!'

He took out a knife from his pocket, and showed it to Sam, who glanced at the handle of the knife. There were two letters on it: F and O.

Sam exclaimed, 'Fred Owens? I'm not surprised! He was a scoundrel! What was his reward?'

'Don't be envious of him, old man! He thought I would give him his life for the secret. I took his life, and then his scalp! You will enjoy the same, just in reverse. I'll skin you first, and then kill you.'

'Oh, I made my will already. I left my taupe to you in it, hehehe!' laughed Sam.

'Shut up, dog!' brayed Parranoh, and kicked him. Then he left the chamber with the warrior.

We were quiet for a few minutes, and did not move at all. When we were sure that nobody watched us we started to get closer to each other. With tied hand finally I fished out the knife from Sam's sleeve, and cut off his bonds. A few minutes later we were both untied. We got on our feet, and rubbed our numb limbs until they became supple again.

'Let's see what's happening outside' I said.

'You're right, Sir, this is the first task,' nodded Sam.

'The second is that we need weapons. At least you have a knife, but I haven't got anything.'

We peeped out. The Ponca were carrying out Winnetou and Harry from the other chamber. It was light enough to see well, even though it was only dawn. I spotted Swallow near the gate, and next to him Winnetou's strong and enduring mustang.

"If I could get some weapon, the situation would not be hopeless," I thought. However, Sam Hawkins pulled my sleeve.

'Look, Sir!' he whispered.

I followed his look. An old Indian lay there. It seems he had not yet completely awoken, because he was stretching his limbs. There was an old gun next to him. 'What do you think, Sir,' whispered Sam rubbing his hands. 'It's my Liddy! I'm very lucky.'

I could not share his joy very much, because Parranoh attracted all my attention. They carried the two prisoners to him. I saw that he talked to them, but I did not understand what. However, soon he became angrier, and raised his voice, and thus I could hear his last words.

'Can you see those stakes, Pimo dog? One is for you! And this boy will die with you! I'll burn you alive!'

For his signal the two Ponca carried the tied Winnetou and Harry to the middle of the yard. Not far from them they made a fire, and the flames were dancing mysteriously in the grey light of the dawn.

'The fire is also for you!' told Parranoh to his two helpless victims, then he tossed his head up, and walked away.

'We can't lose a moment,' I whispered to Sam. 'You have the man on the right. I'll deal with the other.'

'Good, Sir. Quickly and noiselessly.'

'And at the same time,' I added.

I lifted my hand, and in the next moment we quickly got behind the two Ponca. Sam killed his man with one sure motion, but my task was a bit more difficult because I had to pull the man's knife first. Then we released the prisoners. All this happened in moments, noiselessly and unnoticed.

'Now the weapons!' cried Sam, and picked up his Liddy. He embraced it with such love as if it had been in a living being.

I armed Winnetou and myself with the weapons of the two stabbed Indians. For my surprise Winnetou was not running to the gate, but to the horses. I also recognised that our life could only be saved by speed.

'Swallow!' I cried to my mustang, and in the next minute I was sitting on it, while Winnetou jumped on his own bony horse. I also saw that Hawkins quickly, but slightly clumsily climbed on the mustang of one of the Ponca. Harry bravely aimed for the bay horse that Will Parker captured, but the horse was kicking about.

'Harry! Here!' I shouted at him frightened. By his arm I lifted him on my horse. Sam had already disappeared in the gate, Winnetou rode after him, and Swallow did not need encouragement to follow them.

This was the most exciting moment. By now the Ponca had recovered from their shock. Gunshots resounded behind us, arrows whirled, and the air was filled with wild yelling.

I was the last of the three riders, and it was a miracle that I could get through the gorge. Hawkins disappeared from my vision.

Winnetou looked back to see if I followed them, then he turned to the right, and rode downhill.

We got to a bend, when there was a shot, and I felt that Harry's body jerked. He was hit.

'Swallow, dear Swallow, run!' I cried frightened. My horse responded, and we were galloping at the same mad speed as in New Venango.

I looked back, and saw that Parranoh rode after us on his horse. He was right behind me. He was on that bay horse that Old Firehand had admired a day earlier. The bend covered his companions. Although I only cast a quick glance back, I saw the mad determination on his distorted face that indicated that he wanted to catch up with us at any cost. I had to consider that I had a wounded boy with me, thus I would have been disadvantaged in a fight. Consequently, everything depended on Swallow's speed and endurance.

We were riding along the stream. Swallow kept up with Winnetou's mustang. I did not look back, still I knew that Parranoh was getting closer, because I could the sound of the hooves of his horse had become louder.

'Are you wounded, Harry?' I asked anxiously.

'I am.'

'Seriously?'

The sipping blood from his wound dripped on my hand, thus I kept him tighter so that he would not fall off.

'Can you hold yourself?'

'I hope so.'

I urged my mustang harder. He showed that he deserved the name of Swallow. He flew, and I felt as if his hooves had not touched the ground.

'Just a bit more, Harry. We have half escaped.'

'Put me down. Without me you can escape more easily. I don't want to live.'

'But you must live! You are young, and thus you have the right to live.'

'I'm not interested in life now that my father is dead. If I could have died with him!'

We rode for a while in silence.

'It's all because of me!' cried out the boy suddenly. 'Had I accepted your advice, we would have executed Parranoh immediately in the fort, and my father would be still alive.'

'What happened, happened. Now we have to concentrate on the present.'

'Put me down! You can! Parranoh is lagging a bit.'

'Right, let's try it!'

I was determined that I would face Parranoh, I glanced back. We had long passed the stream, and we were on the plateau. On the left hand side there was a forest, and we rode along that. There was a larger distance between us and Parranoh now because his horse could not keep up with Swallow. He was followed by his Ponca. Some rode alone, some in small groups. Although the distance had increased, they had not given up the chase.

I turned forward, and noticed that Winnetou jumped off from his horse, and was standing behind it. He loaded the gun that I had given him. I also dismounted, and lay the boy in the grass. I wanted to load my gun too, but did not have time, because Parranoh was now close. I stood up, and grabbed a tomahawk. The bandit saw my motion, but he was carried away by the chase, and galloped towards me swinging his tomahawk. Winnetou aimed, and shot. Parranoh's shoulder jerked, and in the same moment my tomahawk hit him. With a bullet in his heart, and split skull he crashed from the saddle onto the ground.

Winnetou turned the body with his foot, and said, 'The Arapaho snake won't hiss at anyone anymore. This is how those end up who dare to call the Apache Pimo. You should take back you weapons from him, my white brother.'

Only now did I see that Parranoh had my rifle, revolver, and tomahawk. I quickly took what belonged to me, and hurried back to Harry, while Winnetou caught the bay horse.

The Ponca were close enough now that they could aim at us, thus we jumped on the horses, and rode away. Suddenly, from the left, we saw that light was gleaming on weapons. A large cavalry group rode out of the forest between us and the Ponca. They then turned, and attacked the Indians.

They were from Fort Berthold. When Winnetou saw that he had reinforcements, he turned his horse, and riding with the dragoons, lifting his tomahawk, he charged at the Ponca.

I used the opportunity, and got off from my horse to examine Harry. With relief I saw that his wound was not dangerous. I cut off a strip from my shirt, and provisionally bandaged the wound to stop the bleeding.

'Can you get on the horse, Harry?' I asked.

The boy smiled, stepped to Parranoh's horse whose reins Winnetou had given me. This was the horse that had not let the boy near in the yard. Now he got on with one jump.

'My wound stopped bleeding, I can hardly feel it,' he said.

'How the Ponca are running! Let's chase them, Sir!'

We changed roles as we chased the Ponca who lost not only their leader, but also their bravery. There was nobody to encourage them to resist or at least to retreat organised. They fled on the path on which they pursued us. It was possible that they would try to find refuge in our camp.

We rode by the dead and wounded Ponca, and well before the gate we caught up with the dragoons. It was important that either we overtook the Ponca or at least arrive to the gate at the same time. I encouraged my Swallow to gallop even faster, and pass the dragoons. Soon I rode next to Winnetou, who, like the angel of death, rode close to the Ponca with his tomahawk held high.

The Ponca rode to the gate in a large arc. The first rider wanted to turn into the gorge, when there was a shot from the bushes, and the Indian fell on the ground dead. Another shot rang out, and a second Ponca crashed on the ground. Their bodies blocked the entrance. The group retreated frightened, and fled towards the valley of the White Earth River. The dragoons went after them.

The two shots surprised not only the Ponca, but they also astonished me. But I did not have to crack my head to find out who gave us such an effective help, because from the

508

bush a well-known, fat-faced, bright-eyed little man stepped out, and said, 'You see Liddy can do her job, if necessary!'

'Sam Hawkins!' I cried joyously. 'I thought that the Earth swallowed you! How did you get here at the right moment?'

'Well, I didn't ride out, because the horse that I chose was an old nag that hurt my thighs,' answered Sam grinning. 'Anyway I saw that all the Ponca were riding after Parranoh, I said good-bye to the mustang, and slipped back to the gate. I thought that the fort was empty, and thus it needed some guarding, hehehe. I then found the best place for the returning Ponca. Their face must have been a picture when I shot the two bandits by the gate, hehehe! But how did the soldiers get here, Sir?'

'I would like to know too! I really don't understand what they are doing at such a deserted place. For sure though, like a miracle they saved our life.'

'Well …' said Sam pouting his lips. 'Old Shatterhand, Winnetou, and Sam Hawkins would have got out of trouble somehow without a miracle. It really bothers me a little that I didn't participate in the chasing of the Ponca. Shouldn't we ride after the dragoons?'

'What for? There are enough of them to give a good lesson to the Indians.' This is what Winnetou thought probably, because I could see that he rode into the fort with Harry. 'Let's go after them,' I said, 'and give the final respect to our great dead man!'

When we crossed the gate, and arrived to the middle of the yard, we could see Winnetou and Harry, at the place of the battle of the previous day, leaning over Old Firehand's body. The sobbing Harry took his father's head on his lap, while Winnetou examined his wound. We had just arrived, when Winnetou exclaimed, 'Uff! He's not dead!'

Winnetou's words electrified us, Harry even screamed. I immediately hurried to help my Apache brother with the resuscitation of the unconscious man. Soon Old Firehand opened his eyes. He recognised Harry, there was a faint smile on his lips, but he could not speak, and after a few minutes he fainted again. I also examined the wound. The bullet entered his lungs from the front, and exited in the back, making a serious wound that caused a large loss of blood. His condition was more serious because of the wounds he had received at the battle by the railways, and he had not yet completely recovered from those. Still, I shared Winnetou's hope. He thought that this very hard man could recover with meticulous care. He bandaged the wound, and I provided him a place that was as comfortable as it was possible in the given situation.

Then we could look after ourselves. All of us had some wounds, and if our mood had not been so sombre, we would have laughed at each other. But we were sombre because although we survived the events, many of our friends paid with their life for not listening to me.

It was noon when the cavalry arrived to our camp. They had completely dispersed the Ponca, and had not lost a man. From their commander we learnt that their arrival was not accidental. They had earlier received a report that the Ponca planned an attack against the train, thus the squad had been sent for a punitive action. Following the tracks of the Ponca they had arrived to the plateau near our camp.

The officer gave three days' rest to his men that they spent in our camp. At the same time he invited us to Fort Berthold where Old Firehand could receive appropriate medical care even if not a better care. Naturally we accepted the invitation.

Sam Hawkins was badly stricken by the death of his two beloved friends, Dick Stone and Will Parker. He made the resolution that, without asking a word, he would kill any Ponca he would meet. I had a different opinion. Parranoh was a white man, and it only reinforced my belief that if an Indian was wicked and cruel it was mainly caused by the palefaces.

THE PEDLAR

SINCE our last adventure three months had passed, but this long time had not been enough to completely recover. Still we did not complain, because our most important hopes were fulfilled. Old Firehand, although his recovery was very slow, was over the danger. He was so weak that he could barely walk, thus we gave up our intention to transport him to Fort Berthold.

Harry's wound was insignificant; Winnetou's were more serious, but they had already healed. My wounds only ached when touched. Old Firehand understood that for the time being he had to return to civilisation. He decided that as soon as he had enough strength, he would visit his elder son in the East, and he would take Harry with him. In such circumstances it would have been unreasonable to leave the furs behind. He could not take them with him, and he could not sell them in the fort. One of the soldiers mentioned that a rich trader had set up business by the Turtle River. He apparently bought everything, and paid in gold. Somebody would have to talk to him, and invite him to see our stock.

When I offered that I would ride there, I was warned that the Oohenonpa band, a subdivision of the Dakota, was roaming the area, and they hated the white men. The trader lived in peace with them, because the Indians needed the trader to provide them with goods they needed. Winnetou decided that he would accompany me, which was especially helpful as he knew the area well.

But how can I find the pedlar? Settlers, who had moved into the area when the Indians were friendlier, could be the source of this information. We rode for four or five hours along the stream without seeing anyone. Finally towards the evening we spotted rye fields, and we arrived to another stream. At the confluence of the stream and the river there was a blockhouse surrounded by a strong wooden fence. We stopped, dismounted, and tied our horses to the fence. We were about to knock, when from one of the porthole-looking narrow windows two gun barrels appeared, and a rough

511

voice shouted at us, 'Stop! This is not a dovecot for you to fly in an out of! Who are you, and what do you want?'

'After three days' riding I expected a friendlier reception, even if you don't know us,' I replied annoyed. 'I'm looking for a pedlar who works in this area.'

'Then find him for yourself!'

'I came from a place where Old Firehand has his camp, if you know his name.'

'I do! One of his companions, Dick Stone has been here.'

'Well, he's dead, and he was my friend.'

'Still! You are with a red. It's very suspicious nowadays!'

'But he's Winnetou, the famous chief of the Apache.'

'Oh!' exclaimed the voice. Both gun barrels disappeared from the window. 'Ask him to show me his gun.' Winnetou held his gun towards the settler.

'Silver nails,' he said contented. 'The famous silver gun. And as far as I can see, you have two guns. Tell me, is the larger one a bear slayer?'

'It is.'

'And the smaller is a Henry rifle, isn't it?'

'I don't deny that.'

'Then I know who you are. I'm opening the door in a moment. Come in, gentlemen. It's a great honour to have Old Shatterhand as a guest.'

In the next moment a strong, bony, and rather old man appeared by the door. His face showed that he must have had a hard youth. He led us to the blockhouse, where his wife and son received us. We learnt that he had two other sons, but they were in the forest.

The house had one room. There were weapons, and hunting trophies on the wall. On the fire something was cooking in a cauldron, and on the shelf above it other dishes were placed. A big box served as a wardrobe. From the ceiling so much smoked meat hung that was sufficient for this five-member family for months. They were about to dine, and, without invitation, they laid the table for us too.

It was a simple, but tasty dinner.

'Don't be offended, gentlemen, that I was suspicious,' said the settler. 'The Oohenonpa attacked a similar blockhouse recently at about a day's ride from here. And as to the whites wandering around here, and most of them are worse than the Sioux. Tell me, what are you doing here?'

'We are looking for a trader,' I replied.

'So you want to make a deal with him?'

'We want to sell a lot of fur to him.'

'For money or for goods?'

'Preferably for money.'

'Then Burton is the only possible trader. He always has money as he trades with the gold prospectors too. He's a rich trader, not a pedlar, who carries his stuff on his back. He works with four or five assistants.'

'Is he honest?'

'Well,' said the settler shrugging his shoulder, 'traders want to make good businesses. They cheat wherever they can. You have to be on your guard with them.'

'Where can I find this Burton?'

'You may learn where he is tonight. One of his assistants, a man called Rollins, visited me yesterday, and asked if I needed anything. From my house he rode to my nearest neighbour upstream, but he said that he would spend the night in my house. Burton has had many disappointments recently.'

'Why?'

'In five or six cases he made a long journey for making a deal, but by the time he got there, the Sioux raided, and burnt down the settlement. They leave him alone, but he wasted his time.'

'Has it happened near?' I asked.

'Near means something else here than in the towns. My nearest neighbour lives nine miles from me.'

'Than you cannot feel too safe either.'

'I'm not afraid of the Indians. I haven't had any trouble with them. It seems to me that they got used to the good old Corner. This is me, you see. My name is Edward Corner. '

'But still, if they attack you? What can four people do?'

'Four? My wife is the fifth. She's brave, and can handle the gun like any man.'

'Yes, but they may come in large numbers!'

'Who cares?' answered the old man. 'I don't have a Henry rifle, but we would wipe the floor with a hundred of them. But listen! It must be Rollins.'

We heard the sound of hooves of a horse. Corner went out, and we heard that he talked to someone. Soon he led in a man, and introduced him to us.

'This is Mr Rollins whom I mentioned to you. He's the first assistant of Mr Burton.' He then turned to the guest, and continued, 'Do you know who these two gentlemen are, Mr Rollins? This is Old Shatterhand, and this is Winnetou, the famous chief of the Apache. They came, because they want to talk to Mr Burton. They have many good pelts, and they want to sell them.'

Mr Rollins was neither young nor old, and his face was not distinctive either. But for some reason I did not like his behaviour. When he heard that he had met such famous people, he should have shown some emotion, joy or surprise, but his face remained completely indifferent. "Who cares," I thought, "there are such men. It's not my business!" Rollins also got his food, but he just fumbled with the meal as if bored. I did not like this either. I was not a glutton, but I liked when people appreciated food, and sat by the table with happy faces. Rollins soon stood up, and went out to look after his horse. I found it natural, however, I was surprised that a quarter of an hour, then half an hour had passed, and he still had not yet returned. Something prompted me to go after him. I went to the front of the house. Rollins's horse stood there, tied to the fence, but I could not see his master anywhere. The Moon was very bright, thus I would have noticed him if he was nearby. Finally I caught sight of the approaching Rollins. When he noticed me he seemed to be surprised, but then he quickly came to me.

'I can see, Mr Rollins, you like moonlight.'

'Why do you think so?'

'Because you were away for so long.'

'Yes I had a walk, but not for the moonlight. It seems I spoilt my stomach. I also wanted to air my head a bit.'

He untied his horse, and led it to the pasture. I followed his example. We went in the house together. "Well, his stomach aches," I thought. "It happens." I tried to shake off the strange suspicion that I felt towards Rollins.

The talk naturally turned to the business. We talked about the price of fur, treatment and quality of fur, and it was clear from his remarks that he knew his trade. In these discussions Winnetou was more active than usual. I asked Rollins when I could talk to Burton.

'It's difficult to say,' said Rollins. 'I never know where my boss is. Normally I organise the deals, and then once a week I meet him at a certain place to report to him. How many days' ride are the furs from here?'

'Three days.'

'Hm! Quite a lot. In six days Mr Burton will be at the place where the Turtle River branches off to South and North. I could check the goods until then. You could tell me how much you want, and I would also value the goods. Then I would report to my boss.'

'I would prefer if Mr Burton looked at them,' I replied.

'Mr Burton's time is more expensive than you believe. He would make such a long journey only if he sees that it was a serious business. Discuss it, and then let me know so that I can plan my time.'

This was reasonable, and we could not turn it down.

'Right,' I said, 'you can join us tomorrow if you want. But then let's not waste time, and let's leave at dawn.'

'Good,' he nodded. 'Let's go to bed early then.'

He stood up from the table, and helped Mrs Corner to make the sleeping places. They lay fur and rugs on the floor.

'Thank you,' I told the woman, 'but don't be bothered with our sleeping places. I'll sleep outside with my friend. The room is smoky, and we prefer the fresh air.'

'What do you mean!' said Rollins. 'Nights are cold here, and the Moon is very bright.'

'We got used to cool nights,' I replied, 'and I cannot forbid the Moon to cast its lights as it wants to.'

Had I reflected immediately, I would have recognise the strangeness with which he wanted to dissuade me from sleeping outside, but by the time I recognised it, it was too late. When we went out, the host remarked, 'For the night I put the bolt on. Should I leave it open tonight?'

'Why?'

'If you have any request …'

'We won't have any. Just lock the door as other times. If I want something, I will tell you through the window.'

'Right, I leave the window open.'

When we stepped out of the house, we could hear that he put the bold on. We went over to the pasture, where our horses lay. I put down my blanket, and lay down. I rested my head on Swallow's neck. The faithful animal coped with my using his neck as a pillow motionlessly. Soon I fell in a deep sleep. I had slept only for an hour, when Swallow moved. I immediately awoke, and knew that something exceptional happened, because Swallow lifted his clever head, and sniffed suspiciously. I jumped up, and hurried to the fence, and bent forward so that nobody could see me from outside. After a few minutes of watching I saw some motion at about two hundred steps from the fence. Men were in the grass, and crawled towards me carefully. I quickly turned around to inform Winnetou, but he was already behind me. He heard my quiet steps in his sleeping.

'Can you see those men, my brother?' I asked.

'I can,' he replied quietly, 'They are Indians. Probably the Oohenonpa, who want to attack the blockhouse. Let's go to the house, and help the old paleface to beat back the attack. But we cannot leave our horses here in the open, otherwise the Oohenonpa will steal them.'

'Then we will take them to the house,' I said. We led the horses to the other side of the house. Winnetou was about to call the settler though the window, when I noticed that the door was open slightly. I waved to Winnetou, and I pulled Swallow in the house. Winnetou followed me with his horse, and locked the door. We moved as quietly as other times, but the settler woke up.

'Who's that? Horses in my house?' he asked, jumping up.

'Calm down, Mr Corner,' I replied. 'It's only us.'

I named ourselves as the fire had gone out, and it was dark in the house.

'How? How did you come in?'

'Through the door.'

'But I locked it!'

'It was open.'

'Damn it! Then I didn't push the bold in the hook. But why did you bring the horses in the house?'

I knew that he had not made a mistake, but I did not want to further upset the old man.

'Because the Oohenonpa want to attack you,' I answered.

My words created a big excitement. Corner had boasted in the evening that he was not afraid of the Indians, but now his teeth almost clattered. Rollins pretended that he was shocked, and complained loudly.

'Quiet!' said Winnetou. 'You can't chase the enemy away with shouting. Let's agree on the method of defence.'

'What should we talk about?' said Corner. 'We'll stand behind the window, and shoot them one by one.'

'I would rather like to avoid the shedding of blood.' stated Winnetou.

'Why? These red dogs must be taught a lesson!'

'Are you calling the Indians red dogs? I'm an Indian too. I know them, they wouldn't attack a paleface without reason, unless another paleface enticed them. Old Firehand was attacked because the Ponca were led by a white men. If the Oohenonpa attack you, it's probably because of a paleface.'

'The house is mine,' flared Corner. 'Whoever comes in my house without my permission, I shoot him like a dog. I have the right to this, haven't I?

'It's better if you don't talk about rights,' said Winnetou. 'The house is yours, it is true. But from whom did you buy the land on which you built it?'

'Bought? I'm not stupid! I occupied it because it suited my needs! According to the Homestead Act!'

'This land has always belonged to the Sioux Tribe. They have nothing to do with the Homestead Act! You came here, stole their land, you call them "red dogs", and want to shoot them all. And you are talking about rights!'

'So what should I do? Should I wait until they kill me?' said the settler more meekly.

'Don't do anything,' replied Winnetou. 'I'll take the affair in my hands with my brother, Old Shatterhand.'

During the conversation I stood by one of the windows, to watch the approach of the Oohenonpa, but I could not see anything.

'Are they coming?' asked Winnetou stepping next to me.

'Not yet.' I answered.

'Do you also want to avoid the spilling of blood?'

'You spoke from my heart, Winnetou. This settler stole their land, but there must be another reason. However, I cannot see any other solution.'

'I can. And if you think it over, you will find it.'

'I know!' I replied. 'We'll capture one of them.'

'Correct! Our thoughts are on the same path. And it will be the one whom is sent as a scout. Let's go to the door.'

We opened the door a bit, just enough to be able to see outside, and then waited patiently for a long time. The lamps were off, and the family remained quiet. Then I heard the approach of the scout, or rather sensed it with that instinct that develops in all Westerners sooner or later. In a few minutes I could see him. He was crawling towards the door. When he was close enough, I suddenly opened the door, and jumped on him.

He tried to defend himself, but I squeezed his throat so much that he could not cry out. I quickly pulled him in the house, and Winnetou locked the door behind us.

'Lamp, Mr Corner!' I said quietly. 'I want to see this man.' The settler lit a candle. It lit the face of the prisoner.

'This is Brown Horse, the chief of the Oohenonpa!' said Winnetou. 'You got a good loot, my brother.'

I released the Indian's throat. He breathed deeply a few times, and then sighed, 'Winnetou, the chief of the Apache!'

'Yes, I am,' replied Winnetou. 'We have met before. But you don't know the paleface who captured you. Did you hear how I called him?'

'Yes, I know who Old Shatterhand is.'

'Then you also know that you cannot escape from him. What do you think, what will happen to you?'

'Nothing. The famous Winnetou will release me.'

'I? Why?'

'Because the Apache and the Oohenonpa are not hostile to each other.'

'But the Ponca attacked us recently.'

'We have nothing to do with them,' said Brown Horse.

'I'm a friend of all red men, but I'm against anyone who is doing wrong whatever his skin-colour is. And don't try to mislead Winnetou. The Ponca belongs to the Great Sioux Tribe as the Oohenonpa. You wanted to attack this settler family in the night. Do you think Old Shatterhand will tolerate this?'

Brown Horse looked at the ground gloomily for some time, and then said, 'Since when do you, Winnetou, the great chief of the Apache, support the palefaces?'

'I support justice,' replied Winnetou.

'Justice? Isn't the land ours? If someone wants to live here, doesn't he have to ask permission from us?'

'You are right. Nobody denies this right. But the question is how you want to exercise your right. Why do you need to burn down this house, and murder the family? Why do you have to become thieves and robbers? If you have honourable aims, why do you come in the night, and secretly? Every warrior must face their enemies bravely. Winnetou would be ashamed to do what Brown Horse wanted to carry out.'

519

The Oohenonpa clinched his hand, but Winnetou's stern look grabbed his eyes, and he only said sulkily, 'All Indian tribes launch the attack during the night.'

'Only if necessary,' replied Winnetou. 'But if you are the master of this land, then command the land grabber. Tell him that you won't let him be on your land. Tell him the day by which he has to leave in peace, giving him enough time until he can get ready. If he doesn't obey, you can then punish him. This is the correct procedure.'

The Oohenonpa stared at the ground again. I saw that he was embarrassed, and did not know what to say. Winnetou smiled, and asked me, 'Brown Horse hopes that I would release him. What do you think, my white brother?'

'Brown Horse miscalculated. He forfeited his life.'

The Oohenonpa looked at me, and asked, 'Do you want to murder me?'

'There's a difference between murder and punishment!'

'Do I deserve to die?'

'You do,' I replied. 'You broke into the home of a paleface. The land belongs to you, but you have to respect the home of the stranger. Anyone is entitled to defend his home here in the West. This is the law of the prairie. Winnetou told you how you should have acted. If we killed you, you couldn't complain. But you know that Winnetou and I want to avoid shedding blood if it was possible. Winnetou can judge you.'

Many feelings were expressed on the Oohenonpa's face: anger, shame, and fear. But I also noticed that he glanced at Rollins as if he was asking for advice or help. It could have been a coincidence, but it seemed that there was an understanding between them.

Indeed, Rollins started to speak, 'It's also customary in the West that one punishes acts that had been carried out, but here nothing has yet happened.'

Winnetou's eyes flashed at the man, and said, 'We know the law of the prairie, and we don't need to be reminded. So, your words are useless. Remember that men are not chatterboxes, but only speak when it's right.'

I was surprised by Winnetou's strong rebuke, but it corresponded to my instincts about Rollins.

Winnetou turned back to Brown Horse. 'You heard what Old Shatterhand said. I completely agree with him; you deserve punishment, but you will be pardoned if you answer my questions honestly. What did you want to do here?'

'Raid the house, and burn it.'

'And the inhabitants?'

'Killing them.'

'Who enticed you against the settler? Who persuaded you to attack him?'

The Oohenonpa chief was hesitating. He clearly wanted to avoid answering this question. Winnetou reminded him about the situation very forcefully, when he repeated the question, and added, 'You forgot about your own life, Brown Horse. If you don't want to lose it, you should answer honestly. Who planned this attack?'

'Would you betray your ally, chief Winnetou?' asked Brown Horse instead of an answer.

'No,' said Winnetou.

'Then you understand that I won't betray mine.'

'I understand it. Anyone who betrays his friend deserves to be beaten to death like a mangy coyote. I don't insist on you naming him. But I have to know if he belongs to the Oohenonpa tribe.'

'No.'

'Other tribe?'

'No.'

'So a paleface.'

'You are not mistaken, Winnetou.'

'Then one more question! Is this paleface here?'

'No, he's away.'

'So Old Shatterhand was right. But before we exercise our clemency I have two requests.'

'What do you want from me, chief of the Apache?'

'Firstly, I want you to break the alliance with the paleface who persuaded you for this attack.'

Brown Horse did not like it, but after some resistance he accepted it. He then asked what the second condition was.

'Tell Corner to buy the land on which his house is, and the land that he cultivates. If you make an agreement with him, don't disturb him. If you cannot agree, then don't kill him, but chase him away.'

Brown Horse was quick to accept this condition, but now Corner argued against it. He referred to the Homestead Act, and said that he would not pay anything. Winnetou warned him sternly, 'We have nothing to do with what you call law. In our eyes, you are a robber and a thief. If you don't make a deal with the Oohenonpa, I won't help you. I will now smoke the peace pipe with the chief of the Oohenonpa to confirm the agreement.'

He said all these in such a voice that made Corner stop putting obstacles in the way. Winnetou filled his calumet, and the two Indians smoked it according to the usual ceremony. Then Winnetou went to the door, opened it, and told Brown Horse, 'My brother is free, and I ask him to lead his warriors home. We don't doubt that he'll fulfil his promise.'

Brown Horse went out. From the window we watched his actions. He stopped in the front of the house in the full moonlight. He put his two fingers in his mouth, and gave a loud whistling signal. For this his warriors hurried forward. Brown Horse loudly, so that we could hear all his words, told his warriors the events of the last quarter of an hour. 'I didn't expect that Winnetou, the chief of the Apache, and Old Shatterhand, the great white hunter, would be in the house. Being captured by such men is not a shame. We agreed that the paleface can buy the land from us or he would have to leave on the day we appoint. I smoked the calumet with Winnetou, and the friendship between us is restored. I ask you to follow me, and return to our tents.'

A few minutes later we also went out, and ascertained that the Oohenonpa warriors had left the area. We did not doubt that Brown Horse would keep his word, thus we led out our horses, and lay down by the fence as earlier. Only Rollins appeared to be suspicious, and said that he would make sure that the Oohenonpa were not staying nearby. Of course, we learnt later that he had a different intention. I did not know what time he returned, but in the morning when we got up, he was there. He sat next to the host on a trunk that was used as bench at the front of the house.

Corner received our greeting in an unfriendly manner, showed a gloomy face, but we did not care. The old man had strange ideas of what was his right, and what was not. I would have liked to ask him what people would say if an Indian set up his tent in a garden in Illinois or Vermont, and stated that from then on it was his. However, I recognised that there was no meaning to have such a discussion.

We finished our breakfast, and thanked Corner for his hospitality. We rode away with Rollins, who behaved as if he was our subordinate. He rode behind us at some distance. This was useful, as, at least, we could talk freely.

However, a few hours later Rollins joined us, and he started to talk about the deal. He enquired about the number and types of pelts, and the price Old Firehand expected. Then he tried to shift the conversation, without drawing our attention, to the route to the place where he could examine the fur, the place of the cache. He did not learn much. Every Western hunter knew that asking about the cache of food, fur, and any other stocks was almost impertinent as no hunter liked to talk about these things. Rollins, seeing that we refused to be drawn into a discussion about the pelts, dropped back again, and followed us from an even bigger distance.

We rode on the same way in which we had arrived, thus we did not need too much orientation. However, the habit that we constantly scanned the environment had become part of our being. At noon we found tracks that attracted our attention probably because somebody attempted to remove them. Following the tracks we arrived to a place where obviously a number of people had rested. The grass had not had enough time to rise. We stopped, jumped off the horses, and examined the tracks. Meanwhile Rollins had also arrived, and participated in the investigation.

'I think they are the tracks of animals,' he said.

Winnetou did not say anything, but I remarked, 'I can see that you don't know much about reading tracks. They were left by humans.'

'Then they would have trampled the grass more,' argued Rollins.

'Why? So that somebody with bad intentions would find them easier?'

'But it's difficult to erase the tracks of the horses,' argued the assistant of the peddler.

Winnetou made an impatient motion, and said, 'Three palefaces were here. They did not have either a horse or a gun. They had sticks in their hands. When they walked, they stepped in each other's footprints, and the last leant back to wipe the tracks. Probably they were afraid of pursuers.'

'Very suspicious!' exclaimed Rollins.

'Not suspicious, but strange,' I replied. 'Three unarmed whites in this dangerous area? Maybe they were attacked, and robbed.'

'Probably this is what happened,' nodded Winnetou. 'These holes show that they leant on the sticks.'

'Do you want to help them, Winnetou?' I asked.

'Winnetou is willing to help anyone who needs his help, be it an Indian or a paleface. But I don't trust these.'

'Why?'

'Because they erased the tracks everywhere, except here, where they camped.'

'Maybe they didn't dare to spend too much time here,' I suggested.

'Maybe you are right, my white brother. They could have been inexperienced. I don't mind if we follow their tracks for a while.'

Rollins protested vehemently.

'Oh, no!' he cried, 'There's no use for us to go after them.'

'For us, no.' I replied. 'But for them probably a lot.'

'We don't want to waste time!' said Rollins

'We are not so pressed for time that we wouldn't help people who need it,' I replied

I added my last words with sharpness in my voice. While continuing his grumbling, Rollins got on his horse, and rode after us. I did not like his behaviour at all. I found him antipathetic, but I did not suspect then how crafty and mean he was.

The tracks led out of the forest to a bush, then to the open prairie. They were fresh, and after an hour's ride we spotted the men at about a mile from us. They walked on foot, I could say, struggled. One looked back, noticed us, and warned his companions. They stopped visibly frightened. Then quickly changed their mind, and started to run away. Being on horseback, it was easy to catch up with them.

They were completely unarmed, they did not have a knife even, which I deduced from the fact that the branches on which they leant were broken rather than cut. However, their clothing was in surprisingly good condition. One tied his forehead with a handkerchief, the other tied up his left hand, the third was not wounded.

'Why are you running like this, gentlemen?' I asked.

'We couldn't know who you were,' responded the oldest in a grouchy voice.

'Still running away is meaningless. Don't worry, we are honest people, and we followed you only to ask if we could help you as we suspected that you were in trouble.'

'You are right, Sir. We are happy that we have our life.'

'What happened to you?'

'The Oohenonpa Sioux attacked, and robbed us!'

'When did it happen?'

'Yesterday morning.'

'Where?'

'At the Turtle River. But I still don't know who you are.'

'It's not a secret,' I replied. 'This redskin gentleman is Winnetou, the chief of the Apache. This white gentleman is

Mr Rollins, an employee of a trader, and he is with us for a business deal. I'm known as Old Shatterhand.'

'Excellent! Then we really don't have to be anxious! What luck that we have met you!

'Tell me what happened.'

'My name is Warton. This is my son and the other man is my cousin. We heard that the settlers make a good living by the Turtle River, so we came here too.'

'Didn't you think of the Indians?'

'We heard that they were friendly. But they attacked us. Took everything: our horses, weapons, everything.'

'This is quite bad,' I said. 'You should be happy that they didn't take your clothing.'

'They seemed to be preparing for something. I don't know their language, but their leader used the frontiers' language, and I heard him say "Corner". Probably this is why they were contented with what they took from us.'

'That's right,' I said, 'they attacked Corner's farm, but they failed because we were there. So, you can thank your life to this event.'

'But what a life! They took our food, and we don't have any weapon to hunt something. We haven't eaten anything but berries and roots since yesterday morning. We can hardly stand.'

'And where are you heading to?'

'To Fort Berthold.'

'Why?'

'Our family is waiting for us there. We went forward to look around. We agreed with our relatives that we would meet them in the fort. But we don't know where it is.'

'You are lucky, because we are heading there,' I replied. 'If you want, you can join us.'

'We can walk only slowly. It would cost you a lot of time.'

'Well, I have to accept it. Sit down for a short rest. I'll give you some food.'

Rollins did not like this turn of the events. He mumbled something angrily about useless charity, and unnecessary loss of time. However, we did not care with him. We jumped off, took out our food, and gave the three men plenty. They did not stop thanking us. They wanted to enter into a conversation with us, but they were cooled by the fact that Winnetou and I were not very talkative. However, Rollins was even more sparing with words. He gave brief answers to the questions of the settlers, and he did not hide that he wished the three men to be somewhere else. I found his manners more and more repulsive, thus I watched him with a certain hostility.

Time to time I noticed a mocking smile fleeting across his lips when he thought he was unobserved, and he cast impertinently superior glances at me or at Winnetou. It meant something, it was certainly not beneficial to us. I was even more suspicious, because whenever Rollins talked to one of the three men, and their eyes met, they quickly moved their look away. Was it possible that these men had known each other? I could imagine any meanness about Rollins, but the other three? I rushed to help them, thus they should be grateful to me. However, they were clearly dishonest with me?

Then a strange thing happened, which showed the great understanding between Winnetou and me.

'You are surely tired of walking, my white brother,' said Winnetou to the old Warton. 'Ride on my horse for a while and Old Shatterhand will give his horse to your son. We are good runners, we won't lag behind too much.'

Rollins should have offered his horse to the third man, but he had no such an intention. Thus Warton's son rode on Swallow in turns with the cousin. We started off. The three riders were in the front with Warton's cousin next to them. Winnetou and I made it sure that we would be at the back.

'You did not offer your horse from sympathy, Winnetou,' I said quietly in the language of the Apache. 'You must have another reason.'

'You are right,' he replied.

'Has you also watched these four men, Winnetou?'

'I saw that you had become suspicious, my brother, and I kept my eyes open. I also spotted something before that.'

'Something suspicious?'

'Yes. One tied his head, the other his arm. They say that were wounded yesterday morning, when the Oohenonpa attacked them. Can you believe it, my white brother?'

'Do you think that the injuries are fake, Winnetou?'

'It's more than that! I know it! We have passed by some water twice since we met them. But they did not stop for washing out or cooling their wounds. If their wounds are lies, then the rest are lies too. The Oohenonpa have never attacked them. Did you watch how they behaved during the meal, my brother?'

'They ate a lot,' I replied.

'But not as greedily as those would, who lived on berries and roots since yesterday morning. And there is something else. Apparently they were attacked at the upstream of the Turtle River, how can they be here?'

'I don't know.'

'They obviously have never been there. What do you think, my white brother, of the trader's assistant? Is he hostile to the three?'

'No, he only plays this role.'

'Correct. He has known them for some time. Maybe he belongs to them.'

'But then why do they do this? What's their goal?'

'I don't know, but I think, we'll learn it soon.'

'Should I tell them that we can see through them?'

'No,' said Winnetou decidedly.

'Why not?'

'Because their role playing could be for a reason, which is not our concern. We could also be wrong, and I wouldn't like to hurt innocent people.'

'Hm!' I hummed. 'You sometimes make me ashamed with your goodwill, Winnetou.'

'Do you reproach me for this, Old Shatterhand?'

'No, Winnetou,' I replied.

'Haw! It's better to suffer a little injustice than making it. What does this Rollins plan against us?'

'I don't know. He wants to see the furs. Burton will make a good deal with Old Firehand. What else does he want?'

'He wanted to know the place of the cache. Does he want to steal it? In any case, whatever evil plan he has, we don't have any reason to be anxious until he learns the place of the cache. Do you agree with me, my white brother?'

'Yes. I do and the three men, who claim to be settlers ...'

'Your thought met mine. The four men are in cahoots. Maybe all the four are Burton's assistants.'

'Quite possibly. Corner mentioned it yesterday that the trader worked with four or five helpers. Rollins disappeared during the evening. Maybe he informed his master, and he sent his other three men. With good or bad intentions?'

'There cannot be a good intention,' asserted Winnetou. 'I'm afraid we are dealing with wicked people. We will learn their real intentions, which is probably robbery, and murder, when we get close to the fort. However, we are safe until they learn where the cache is.'

'In any case we have to be alert,' I said. 'We must watch them during the night too. Only one of us can sleep at any time, while the other must be ready for a fight.'

During the afternoon the supposed settlers wanted to give our horses back a number of times, but we insisted on the previous arrangements. In the evening we wanted to camp on the open prairie, because we thought it was important that we had a good view. Unfortunately a sharp wind rose that brought rain, and so we hurried to a forest. There we found some old trees whose foliage protected us from the rain.

We were running short of food as we planned provisions only for two people. However, Rollins also brought some food with him, thus there was enough for everybody, and we could put some away for breakfast.

We wanted to lie down after dinner, but the others did not feel like going to sleep. They started a lively talk, quite

529

loudly. Even Rollins participated. He related some stories, adventures that had happened to him during his business travels. We were not interested in their conversation, and did not participate in it, but we could not sleep.

Something told me that the loud conversation was not accidental. Was it a way to distract our attention from our environment? Or did they want to give a signal to someone? I glanced at Winnetou, and I saw that he was also suspicious as he kept all his weapons near his hands, and was watching in all direction. The others could not know of his alertness. His eyes were closed as if he had fallen asleep, but I knew that he was watching everything from under his eyelashes.

The rain stopped, and the wind eased too. We would have liked to retreat to the prairie, and sleep there, away from the others, but we could not do this without showing that we did not trust them. We did not make a campfire, and did not allow them to make one. The fact that we were on the land of hostile Sioux Indians was a good excuse. We had the advantage in the dark, because our eyes had been trained to see even in these conditions. However, we could not use our ears to listen to the noises of the forest because of the loud conversation.

As we sat at the edge of the forest, under the trees, we made it sure that we were facing the forest because an enemy could have approached us only from that direction. The loud conversation of the other four continued, it was quite clearly artificial. Winnetou stretched out in the grass, and rested his head on his hand. I noticed that he slowly pulled in his right leg, and raised his knee. Did he intend to do the famous knee-shot that only the best can carry out?

Indeed, he grabbed his gun, and rested its barrel, as if accidentally, on his thigh. Now I also looked to the direction where the gun pointed. Behind the third tree from us there was a bush and among its branches I spotted two fluorescent dots. It was a pair of eyes. Somebody was watching us from the bush. Winnetou, while avoiding all suspicious motions, attempted the aiming. He still had to raise his knee a little bit and I excitedly waited for the shot. Winnetou had never missed the target, not even in the night, and I was sure that even this extremely difficult shot would be successful. I saw that he put his finger on the trigger, but immediately let it go. He put the gun in the grass and stretched out his leg.

The pair of eyes disappeared.

'Skilful man!' he whispered to me in the language of the Apache.

'He knows the knee-shot,' I nodded.

'He was a paleface.' whispered Winnetou.

'Yes,' I replied. 'A Sioux would not have opened his eyes so much. We know that an enemy is near.'

'But he also knows that we know it. But it won't help him, because I'll get behind him.'

'It's dangerous!'

'For me?'

'He'll see that you get up.'

'I will pretend that I'm checking the horses. It won't be obvious to him.'

'Let me do it, Winnetou!'

'No! As it's dangerous, I can't shy away. Anyway I spotted him first, thus I'm entitled to his scalp. You should help me, my brother, so that I can do it.'

I waited a bit, and then cried over to the four men, 'What about sleeping, gentlemen? We have to leave early, and we should rest a bit! Have you tied your horse well, Mr Rollins?'

'Yes, of course!' said Rollins indignantly.

'My horse is still free,' said Winnetou. 'I'll tie it, but on a long lasso, so it can graze if it wants to. Should I tie your horse too, Old Shatterhand?'

'Yes, yes, thank you,' I replied in a voice as if it had really been about horses only.

Winnetou slowly got to his feet, and put his blanket on his shoulder. He walked to the horses. I knew that he would soon throw himself on the ground, and crawl into the forest. Of course, he did not need the blanket; he took it only to mislead the enemy.

531

The loud conversation continued. It was partly good, partly bad for us. If Winnetou's movements caused a little noise, the conversation would suppress it, but he could not listen either. I closed my eyes as if nothing interested me, but I was watching the edge of the forest.

Five minutes had gone, then ten, and even half an hour. I started to get anxious for Winnetou, but I also knew that approaching someone quietly was not easy, and it required patience. Finally I heard steps from the direction where Winnetou led the horses. I slightly turned my head. His blanket was on his neck, thus he had probably finished off the hiding enemy. I was relieved, and waited for him to sit down next to me, and tell me what had happened. The footsteps approached, and finally stopped behind me. Then I heard a voice, but it was not Winnetou's.

'Now this one too!'

I turned back, and saw the blanket again. It was not on Winnetou's shoulder, but on the shoulder of a bearded man, whose face seemed familiar. He put the blanket on only to mislead me. While he pronounced the four words, he lifted his gun by the barrel, and hit me. I rolled aside quickly to avoid the blow, but it was too late. The butt of the gun hit my neck instead of my head, and it paralysed me. Then a second blow was delivered on my skull, and I lost my consciousness.

I must have been unconscious for five or six hours. With a huge effort I opened my lead-weight eyelids. It was dawn. I immediately closed my eyes. I was in a state that was not sleeping, but not awaken either. I felt as if I was dead, and heard the voices from the conversation next to my dead body. For some time I could not understand the words, but finally a voice entered my consciousness that would have awoken me from death.

'The Apache dog doesn't speak, and I killed the other one! Damn, I was clumsy. Had I hit him gentler, I could get all the information I need!'

My dizziness had gone in a moment, and I looked at the bearded, disgusting face of the man. I would have thought many things, but not that I would meet Santer at this place, and so unexpectedly! I thought that I should close my eyes so that he would continue to believe that I was dead, but my eyes did not obey my will. Something forced me to stare at him until he would spot it. He did, and jumped up joyously.

'He's alive!' he shouted. 'He didn't kick the bucket! Can you see, his eyes are open! Now we will see!'

He asked me something, but I did not answer. For this he knelt next to me, grabbed my throat, shook me hard and banged my head several times to the stony-grassy ground. I could not defend myself as I was tied up.

'Are you answering, you dog?' he yelled at me. 'I can see that you're alive and conscious! If you don't want to speak, I will make you!'

While he banged my head to the ground again and again, I could turn it a little bit, and looked to the right. I caught sight of Winnetou, not far from me. He was tied up in a ring. Even a contortionist would have suffered in this position. Probably he had been like this for hours. Apart from him and Santer, I could also see Warton with his son and his cousin. But I could not see Rollins anywhere.

'Are you going to talk or what?' continued Santer threateningly. 'Should I make you talk with my knife? I want to know if you recognised me! Can you hear me?'

I would not have achieved anything with remaining silent, only making our situation more difficult. I did not know if I could speak. I was stuttering, but understandable words broke out from my throat.

'I know you ... You are Santer.'

'Oh, so you recognised me!' laughed Santer in my face mockingly. 'I hope you are happy! You are happy that you can see me again, aren't you? A wonderful surprise, isn't it?'

For this mocking remark I did not feel like answering. Santer pulled his knife, pointed it to my heart, and said, 'Say "yes"! Loudly! Otherwise I stab the knife in your heart!'

Winnetou, in spite of his pains, said, 'Old Shatterhand won't say "yes" even if you kill him.'

'Shut up, dog!' shouted Santer to him. 'I'll tighten your belts so much that you bones will break! Leave it to your friend what he would say! Let's hear you, you hero! Are you happy to see me again?'

'I'm happy,' I said loud not caring with Winnetou's words.

'Did you hear it?' turned Santer to the other three whites grinning victoriously. 'Old Shatterhand, the famous Old Shatterhand doesn't want to know the tip of my knife, he rather humiliates himself!'

Maybe his mocking laugh made me fully alert or I just then completely recovered from my dizziness, because I also laughed in his face.

'You are wrong! I'm not afraid of your knife! I'm really happy for this meeting.'

'Really? And why?'

'It's enough to say that I'm very happy!'

'You must have a concussion! Did you lose your marbles?'

'No, not at all. I know what I'm saying.'

'Do you dare to be insolent? I'll tie you up like Winnetou! Or hang you up by your legs!'

'You'll reconsider it!' I replied with smiling face.

'Why? Would you tell me why?'

'Because if you kill me, you would never know where it is what you want to get!'

Santer pulled up his eyebrows. He turned to Warton, and remarked, 'We thought that he was dead, but he pretended even the faint. He heard what I asked from Winnetou!'

'You are wrong!' I shouted at him. 'I was unconscious, I didn't hear anything. But I can see through you!'

'And what can you see? What would I like to know?'

'Something that's worth more than our life to you! But you waste your time, you won't get anything out of me.'

'We will see! You boasted about your mind! If you have a brain, you won't make me angry, because I'll torture you so much that you would wish that you had never been born. But if you answered my questions honestly, I may pardon you. Did you notice me in the bushes last night?'

534

'Of course. I saw the glowing of your eyes.'

'Yes. Winnetou wanted to shoot me, but he was too late. Then he wanted to get behind me. Wanted to surprise me, hahaha! What a stupidity. First I knocked him out with the butt of my rifle, then I mislead you, and knocked you out exactly in the same way. I tricked both of you as if you were babies! Look at the three men for whom you fell so easily! They are my men! I sent them your way to lure you. What do you say? At least you know who you are dealing with!'

I knew perfectly well whom I had to deal with, but it was better to keep quiet about it, and I only answered, 'You are the biggest villain in the world, and you'll remain that.'

'Thank you,' he grinned mockingly. 'You said it honestly. The nicest in the whole thing is that I don't trample on your face. You insulted me, and it won't go unpunished. I'll put it on your account, and you'll pay for it with interest if you understand me. But for the time being let's talk in a friendly way. So, you think I'm a villain? You are right. I don't like working. I'd rather harvest the produce of others' work. I have to say it's tiring, but hopefully I can retire soon.'

'Really? And what does it depend on?'

'On a big deal. I'll do this last one, and then I won't have to do anything till the end of my life.'

'Wonderful. Congratulations!' I said mockingly.

'Thank you,' he replied. 'And you can help me.'

'In what?'

'To find the land that I can harvest.'

'You don't know where it is? Quite unfortunate.'

'It cannot be far.'

'Then search for it!'

'Will you help me?'

'I don't know what you mean.'

'I'll remind you. It's not about land or meadow, but a cache that I'd like to empty.'

'What is in it?'

'Skins, furs and alike.'

'I don't know about it.'

535

'Don't lie! Why did you go to the Turtle River? Have you forgotten what you told the old Corner? That you wanted to offer furs to Burton, the trader.'

'You have excellent information.'

'You see! I know everything. I also know that it's a huge stock that Old Firehand collected with a group of hunters.'

'So what?'

'You didn't find the trader, but you talked to his assistant. He started off with you to look at the pelts, and value them. When we learnt it, we went after you to catch you, but the third man, I think his name is Rollins, has slipped away. He escaped while I was dealing with you and Winnetou. Do you understand it now?'

The good prairie habit of watching every detail, even those that appeared unimportant, was useful again. During the last words Santer involuntarily glanced at the bush where we had seen his eyes on the previous night, then he quickly turned his head. The whole thing lasted for a second, but I drew important conclusions form it.

'Damn him!' continued Santer. 'But I don't need him. The most important is that I have you. Do you know Old Firehand?'

'Of course!'

'And the place of his cache?'

'That too.'

'Oh, I'm very happy that your mind works appropriately, my friend, and you respond so well to me.'

'In fact, what do you want from me?' I asked politely.

'Only to betray the place of the cache.'

'To betray it? This is the problem! Old Shatterhand has never been, and will never be a traitor.'

'Do you also want to be tied up like Winnetou?' he snarled at me angrily.

I could see that the friendly conversation was coming to an end, and I replied, 'I'm following his example. I believe he didn't say as much as I did, because he's much more proud to talk to a rascal like you!'

'I'll torture you!'

'You won't achieve anything.'

'I'll find the furs without you!'

'Never! If we don't return by an agreed time, Old Firehand will move the furs to an even more secure place.'

He mused for a very long time, while he turned his knife between his fingers. I was not afraid, because I knew that there was no major danger. I could see through the double trick of the bandit. His first was to make me speak with threats, and he failed. He was embarrassed. Now he wanted to try the second version. It was obvious that he hated me, and he would have been happy to kill me, but his greed was stronger than his hatred. He would have even let us go for Old Firehand's cache.

'Are you attracted by Winnetou's example? Then die in the same way as he will!'

He signalled to his three accomplices. They ran to me, grabbed me, and tied me in a ring, then threw me next to Winnetou. We lay next to each other. However, while they carried me there, I had an opportunity to look at the place where I had sat with Winnetou on the previous night. I was right. Behind the bush a man stooped. It seemed that he was interested what was being done to me, because he pushed out his head a little. This moment was enough to recognise Rollins's ugly face.

I suffered, and lay next to Winnetou for three full hours without exchanging a word, but we did not betray to our torturers with a flinch of our facial muscles our pain. Santer came every quarter of an hour, and asked if we were willing to speak. We did not even answer.

At noon Santer came again, and made one more attempt. When it failed, he sat over with his accomplices, and started to discuss something with them quietly. Later he raised his voice as if he wanted us to hear what he said.

'I believe too that he's somewhere near,' he said. 'He'd like to get his horse back, as he's lost without it. Search the area again! I'll stay to keep an eye on the prisoners.'

Firstly, Santer would have said it quieter that he wanted to capture the man, if he had really believed that the man was near. Secondly, Rollins, hearing it would have to escape very quickly. They overplayed their roles again. The three accomplices picked up their weapons, and left. Santer stretched out by the bush. Winnetou now started to speak.

'Do you know, my white brother, what will happen now?' he whispered quietly.

'They'll find Rollins, and bring him here.' I replied.

'Yes, Rollins will be our supporter to gain our trust. They'll play something that they had learnt by heart. Like in those nice big houses that the palefaces call theatres.'

'Clear,' I replied. 'Santer and Burton are the same person. Rollins is the deputy of the gang, and also his spy. When he learnt who we were, and what we wanted he reported it to his boss, who decided that he would rob Old Firehand.'

'Your thoughts are exactly the same as mine. Santer sent the Oohenonpa against Corner's house. As the Oohenonpa refused to wage a war against us, Santer ordered Rollins to accompany us, and try to find out our secret. He sent the three other assistants on foot in our way, and he followed us.'

We exchanged these thoughts with barely moving lips, and Santer could not see that we were talking. In any case he turned away from us, and looked at the forest. Soon a loud cry came from the thicket, and then some bigger noise that kept on approaching, and becoming louder and louder. Finally Warton and the others stepped out having Rollins between them. He was clearly resisting, and the three others pushed him towards Santer.

'Did you catch him?' asked Santer jumping up. 'I told you that he was nearby. Tie him up, and push him to the ...'

He suddenly stopped, looked at Rollins astonished, and then he cried out joyously, 'Is it you, Rollins? Or a twin?'

'No, Mr Santer!' exclaimed Rollins, and he tore himself away from the other three, and rushed to Santer. 'What a luck! Mr Santer is here! Then everything is fine!'

'That's right, Mr Rollins, you don't have to be afraid of anything as long as I'm around. What a surprise! I want to catch a man, and it is you. So, you are working for Burton? Is it a good job?'

'Very good, Mr Santer. I had struggled before, but this is a good job. Mr Burton trusts me, and we do good business together. We were on a business trip yesterday evening ...'

He suddenly stopped, and looked at Santer with a shock. He had held Santer's hand before, but now he was confused.

'I don't understand ...' he stuttered. 'Did your men attack us, Mr Santer?'

'It looks like,' replied the bandit.

'Good Lord! A man whose life I have saved a number of time attacks me in the forest! What does it mean?'

'Nothing. How could I have known that it was you? I couldn't see you in the dark. And you disappeared anyway.'

'That's true! My first thought was saving my own skin, and only after then I thought of my two companions. This is why I stayed around. Where are they?' he asked with stupid astonishment, and then exclaimed if he had spotted us only now. 'But they are lying there, the poor men! Tied up like this! No, I can't watch it! I'll untie them!'

He was rushing towards us, but Santer caught his arm.

'What are you doing, Mr Rollins? These two men are my mortal enemies!'

'But they are my friends!'

'This is none of my concern! I've been waiting for the opportunity to settle the bill with them for a very long time. This is why I attacked them, but then I didn't know that you belonged with them.'

'Damn! Mortal enemies? What did they do against you?'

'Enough to execute them ten times!'

'What do you mean, Mr Santer? Do you know who these people are? Winnetou and Old Shatterhand! They are very famous people, and my friends! I ask you to release them!'

'Impossible!'

'Not even for my sake?'

'You can ask anything but this.'

'When I saved your life, you spoke differently! You spoke about eternal gratitude!'

'I know, I know, and I don't want to take back my words. But understand it! These two people ...'

'Come Mr Santer, let's discuss this thing as friends. It's impossible that ...'

He took Santer by the arm, and they went towards the trees while he was explaining something with wide gestures. They overplayed this comedy. Less would have been more convincing. Soon Rollins came back alone, and hurried to us.

'I hope I can rescue you. You can see I do everything I can. So far I achieved only that I can ease your suffering.'

He loosened the belts so we could lie more comfortably. Then he left. However, soon he returned with Santer, who told us, 'You are born under a lucky star! This gentleman obliged me once so much that I cannot refuse his request. He insists on you being released. This is the biggest stupidity in my life, but I'll do it. I give you your life back, and keep only your weapons and other belongings.

As Winnetou did not reply, I also remained silent.

'What's that?' asked Santer. 'Aren't you happy? Don't you thank me for my generosity?'

'They are half dead of their pain,' said Rollins excusing us. 'I'll cut their belts.'

'Stay where you are, Mr Rollins,' I snarled at him.

'I don't understand it. Why?'

'Everything or nothing!' I replied.

'What do you mean?'

'We would rather die, but we won't leave our weapons!'

'Aren't you happy that ...'

'You are wasting your words,' I interrupted. 'What I said I won't change.'

'I haven't seen such!' complained Rollins. 'I want to save your life, and you create obstacles.'

He grabbed Santer by the arm again, and took him. Soon the Wartons were also invited to the discussion.

'You did the right thing,' whispered Winnetou. 'I think they will oblige in the hope that they would get everything at the end.'

I was also sure that I would achieve my aim. Santer, of course, resisted the request for the sake of appearances, but finally gave in, returned to us, and made a statement.

'My friend insisted that I keep my word, and as I'm a gentleman, I cannot break it. Maybe you will laugh at me, but we'll see who laughs at the end. I give you back all your properties, including your weapons. But till the evening you'll stay here, tied to these trees, so that you could chase me only tomorrow morning. We will ride away now, and we will take Mr Rollins, so that he wouldn't be able to release you earlier. We will make sure that he only returns at the right time. You can thank your life to him, it's up to you how you return the favour to him.'

There were no more words. We were tied to two trees, and everything was put down next to us that they had taken on the previous night. I could hardly hide my joy when I saw my weapons. They tied our horses to another tree, a few steps from us, and then the five bandits rode away.

We kept quiet for an hour, and listened to the smallest noise. Finally Winnetou remarked, 'They are still near, even if not very near. They'll cut our bonds in the evening so that we are unable to see that they follow us. But all these tricks won't help Santer. What do you think my brother, how should we capture him?'

'Not by luring them to Old Firehand's fort.'

'You are right. He mustn't know the place. If we rode all night, by tomorrow evening we would arrive to the fort. But we won't go so far, we'll stop much earlier. Rollins will come with us to that point, and there we will sort him out. Then we'll wait for the rascals who follow our tracks. Haw, I have spoken!'

He pronounced the "Haw" with a deep satisfaction. The man who had evaded his clutches for so long could now be captured.

The Sun advanced with the pace of a snail until sunset. Then we heard the hooves of a horse. It was Rollins. He dismounted, and then released us. He kept on talking in the belief that his words would make us dizzy, and grateful. We pretended as if he was our saviour, but we were reserved. We got on the horses, and started off. Rollins rode next to us. We noticed that he often made his horse pounce. We knew that it was for leaving obvious tracks. Occasionally he broke off twigs, and threw them on the ground.

In the morning we had a short rest, and at noon a longer one. We made this rest last for three hours. We knew that Santer could follow our tracks only from dawn, and thus we wanted him to catch up with us. After lunch we rode for two hours. We were about two hours from the fort. It was time to settle the account with Rollins. We stopped, and dismounted. Rollins was behind us, and now he approached us surprised.

'Why did you stop again, gentlemen? For the third time today! We cannot be far from Old Firehand's place. Wouldn't it be better to make the remaining distance in one go?'

'No,' I replied.

'Why?'

Now Winnetou spoke, 'Because Old Firehand doesn't want to see rascals!'

'What do you mean? Who's the rascal?'

'You!'

"I? Do you talk about your saviour in such an ungrateful way, Winnetou?'

'Enough of your lies! Do you really think that you misled Winnetou and Old Shatterhand? But we know everything. Burton is Santer, and you are his spy and accomplice! You left signs all the way so that they could find Old Firehand's cache! You didn't know that we watched you! Santer left it to us how we would return your goodwill. Well, we will return it as it's just!'

He stretched out his hand to hold the bandit. Rollins jumped on his horse to ride away, but I grabbed the bridle just as quickly. Winnetou jumped behind Rollins to grab his throat. Rollins considered me a more dangerous enemy. He pulled his double barrelled pistol from his belt, and shot at me. I immediately stooped down, and at the same time Winnetou grabbed Rollins's right arm. The second shot went off, but it also missed me. In the next moment Winnetou pulled Rollins from the saddle, and in one more minute he was on the ground tied and disarmed. For the time being we did not have time to deal with him, thus we tied him to a tree, and his horse to another one. Once we dealt with Santer, we could return to sort him out.

We got on our horses, and galloped back not directly on our track, but parallel with it. Reaching a bush we decided that we would wait for Santer there. Our tracks led by this bush, and Santer had to pass by there. We hid our horses, and sat down to wait for the ones who wanted to kill us.

They had to come from the West. There was an open prairie there, and we considered it very advantageous as it made it possible to spot Santer well before he would reach our position. He could not be very far. Only about one and a half hours were left till sunset, and we were sure that he would arrive before dark. I sat next to Winnetou in silence. We understood each other so well that there was no need to agree on the tasks. We had our lasso in our hand. Santer and his three companions would be well received, that was sure!

A quarter of an hour passed, then the second, the third, but nothing had happened. Almost an hour had gone, when in the southern end of the prairie I saw a small dot that moved quickly to Southwest.

'Uff'!' murmured Winnetou. 'A rider!'

'Only one? Strange!'

'Uff! He goes to the place from where we expect Santer in a big arc. Can you see the colour of the horse, my brother?'

'I think it was a bay.'

'Rollins's horse was a bay too,' said Winnetou gloomily.

'It's impossible, Winnetou. We tied him so well that he could not have escaped.'

Winnetou's eyes flashed. The light bronze colour of his face darkened. He soon regained his control, and only said calmly, 'We wait for another quarter of an hour.'

These fifteen minutes had passed. The rider had long gone, but Santer had not turned up either. Winnetou clinched his hand into a fist.

'You should gallop to the place where we left Rollins, my white brother!'

'And if the four arrive?'

'Winnetou will finish them alone.'

I led my horse out of the thicket, and rode away. In ten minutes I got to the place where we tied Rollins to the tree. He was not there, and his horse had gone too. I spent five more minutes there to examine the tracks, and then I rode back to Winnetou to report. He jumped up like s spring when he heard that Rollins had disappeared.

'And what did the tracks show?' he asked.

'He turned back, and he's now going to the South after he rode to the West to warn Santer.'

'How did he get away? Who cut his bonds?'

'A rider arrived from the East, and released him.'

'Who could it have been? A soldier from Fort Berthold?'

'No. I could recognise the prints of the old, huge Indian boots of Sam Hawkins. I could even see the tracks of the hooves of his old mule, Mary.'

'Uff! Let's go after Santer!'

We jumped on the horses, and galloped to the West like a storm. Winnetou was quiet, but I could see in his eyes what a storm was in his heart. Woe to Santer if he caught him!

The Sun had disappeared beyond the horizon. After five minutes we left the prairie. In another five minutes we found Rollins's tracks. We got to the place where Rollins met Santer and the Wartons. The tracks showed that they stood there only for a few minutes to hear Rollins's report, and then they quickly turned around, and rode away. They rode in different directions, and we did not know which one was Santer's. They had also left the path on which they had arrived, thus we could not pursue them. Winnetou had not said a word. He turned his horse around, and we continued our journey to the East. We passed the bush where we hid waiting for Santer, and then we advanced to the fort.

The Moon had just rose on the sky when we arrived to the valley of the White Earth River. The guard was in his place, and he demanded the password. After we gave the clues, he apologised, 'Don't take it wrong that I'm so strict today. I have to be more careful than other times.'

'Why?' I asked.

'Something has happened. I don't know what, but Sam Hawkins came back very excited.'

I didn't have to ask anything more. I did not have any doubt now that Sam had spoilt our plan.

When we arrived to the yard, they received us with the bad news that Old Firehand's condition had deteriorated. There was no danger to his life, but I would have to accompany him to the fort, thus I would have to part with Winnetou.

We jumped off, and hurried to the campfire, where Old Firehand sat wrapped in soft blankets. Next to him were Harry, Sam Hawkins, and the officer from Fort Berthold.

'Have you have arrived! asked Old Firehand in a fading voice, but joyously. 'Have you found the trader?'

'We found him, and lost him,' replied Winnetou. 'Have you been out in the valley, my brother Hawkins?'

'Yes, I' have,' replied Sam unsuspecting.

'Do you know, my white brother, who you are?'

'I'm a hunter, and one of the best,' said Sam with high self-esteem.

'And also the stupidest man whom I've ever met!' broke out from the normally calm and polite Winnetou. 'Haw, I have spoken!' he added, turned around, and he hurried away.

Everybody stared after him, but they understood his anger only after I had sat down by the fire, and told them what happened. I was also very angry with Sam, but I had already felt sorry for him for taking it so much on his heart.

'Winnetou is right!' he cried desperately, he tore off his taupe from his head with his hat, and crumpled them. 'I'm the biggest ass in the world!'

He continued naming himself as various animals, even greenhorn, when I stopped him

'Tell me, Sam, how did this unfortunate story happen?'

'I heard two shots from the distance. I rode there, and I found a man at the edge of the forest tied to a tree. His horse was nearby. I asked him who he was, what he wanted, and how he got there. He said he was the trader who wanted to visit Old Firehand to buy the furs, but suddenly he was surrounded by Indians, he was robbed, and tied to a tree.'

'But there were no traces of Indians!'

'True! True! It seems that my mind went for a walk. I swallowed the bait, cut the belts to bring the bloke here. But right away he jumped on his horse, and rode away. He rode not towards our camp, but to the opposite direction. Then I got suspicious too, and hurried back to warn the men to be alert. But at tomorrow dawn I'll get up, and find the rascal! I'll follow him even to the hell!'

'You should stay here, my brother Sam,' said Winnetou, who had returned to the camp. 'Winnetou will start off after the murderer Santer. You should stick together, my white brothers, because it's possible that the greedy rascal would try to break in, and every clever, brave man will be necessary for the defence.'

Later, when everybody calmed down, I found Winnetou lying by the stream in the grass, while his horse grazed nearby. When he noticed me, he jumped up, and stretched out both of his hands to me.

'Winnetou knows what you want to say. You want to join me to catch Santer together.'

'Yes, Winnetou, this is what I want.'

'But it's impossible, Charlie. Old Firehand cannot stand on his feet, Harry is a child, and as we could see, we cannot rely on Sam. The soldiers are strangers. Old Firehand needs you more than I do. Who should stand by him if the fort is

546

attacked? In the name of our sacred friendship I ask you to protect Old Firehand! Do you promise this to Winnetou?'

I had to promise it, but with the condition that at dawn we would ride together for a while.

It happened. When we arrived to the point where Santer and his accomplices turned around Winnetou stopped.

'We will part here,' he said sadly but decisively. 'This is the order of the Good Spirit, and if he allows it, we'll meet again. I'm chased by hatred, and you are held here by love. But friendship will bring us together again. Old Shatterhand and Winnetou cannot be separated from each other. Haw, I've spoken!'

He leant over me, squeezed my arm, kissed me, and with a shrill cry to his horse he galloped away.

I looked after Winnetou. His black hair fluttered in the wind like a glorious mane. I kept on looking after him until he disappeared in the distance. When will I see you again, my dear, beloved brother?

VOLUME III

THE GREAT WESTERN RAILWAYS

I HAD ridden since dawn, and I must have made a long way. The Sun was on its zenith, and its rays made me quite sleepy. I decided that I would have a rest, and eat my lunch. Around me the infinite prairie stretched, whose chains of hills were like the frozen waves of a sea. It had been five days since a large Oglala band had dispersed our little group. Since then I had not met a single human being. I had got used to the loneliness of the forest, but it started to become too much. I was longing for someone to talk to, if for nothing else, to see if I had not forgotten how to speak.

There were no streams or springs, thus I did not have to look for a resting place with water, and I could stop where I felt like. At the bottom of one of the hillocks I tethered my horse, took the blanket from him, and went to the top of the hillock to rest. I left my horse at the bottom so that a potential enemy could not spot it, and I took the highest point to be able to see far, while remaining invisible.

I had enough reasons for being careful. Twelve of us left the Northern Platte along the eastern side of the Rocky Mountains to get to Texas. We knew that many Sioux tribes had gone on the warpath. Some of their warriors were killed, and they wanted revenge. Even though we tried to avoid them, they unexpectedly attacked us. In the battle they killed all but five of us, and dispersed the surviving ones to all directions. They could see from our tracks that we were heading to the South, and surely they would continue to pursue us. In such circumstances it could happen that one wrapped himself in his blanket in the evening, and awoke on the happy hunting grounds, scalped.

I took out a piece of dried bison meat, and rubbed it with gunpowder as I had run out of salt. Then I started to chew it with the hope that with the industrious work of my jaws I could swallow it. After eating in so torturously, I stretched out on my blanket, and lit a self-made cigar as I had run out of real cigars much earlier.

As I was smoking I noticed a moving dot on the horizon, and it was coming towards me. I sat up to have a better view. Soon I recognised that it was a rider who sat on the saddle in the Indian way, that is, leaning forward. He was about one and half miles from me. He rode slowly, so at his speed it would have taken half an hour until he would get close to me.

As I watched him, I noticed, to my surprise, four more moving dots, much further behind the rider. This rider, judging from his clothing was a white man. And the other four? Were they Indians who pursued the white rider? I took out my telescope, and it confirmed my assumptions. I could even see their weapons, and the colours on their faces. They were Oglala, the most warlike Sioux. They rode on great mustangs, while the white man was on a fairly lazy, and shapeless animal. He was now close enough for me to observe him thoroughly.

He was a small, gaunt man. He wore a shabby felt hat. One of the brims of the hat was missing. This would not have been particularly surprising on the prairie, but it emphasised one of the characteristics of the white rider: he did not have ears. Only red marks showed where his ears had been cut off. He had a blanket on his back that covered him so much that only his legs were visible. On his legs he had strange boots, the ones known only in South-America. There, when the *guacho* kills a horse, he immediately skins it, and puts the skin on his feet fresh and warm. When the skin cools, it shrinks, and excellently covers the foot and the leg of the *guacho*, except for his soles. This does not bother him as he is always on horseback.

This rider had a gun, but it was rather old. His horse had a disproportionately large head, and terribly long ears, but it did not have a tail. It had the impression of a mixture of a donkey and a camel. While it walked, it hung its head, and even more its ears like a Newfoundland water dog. He had a comic impression, but I did not laugh. The West had taught me not to judge people by their appearance, but by the character. It seemed that this man was oblivious to the danger behind him, otherwise he would not have ridden so slowly and comfortably. In his absent-mindedness he did not even look back.

When he got to a hundred steps from me, he noticed me, or maybe his horse noticed my mustang. In any case, his horse suddenly pulled back its ears, then let them drop again. For this signal his master wanted to dismount to examine the tracks that his sad animal found. However, before he got off, I shouted to him, 'Good man! Come closer!'

I sat up so that he could see me. Two heads turned to me, the rider's and the horse's. The horse's ears came forward as if they wanted to greet me.

'Shout quieter, young man,' he replied. 'It's not advisable to shout in such a place. Come, Tony!'

The mare continued, but then stopped by my mustang.

'Where are you going, good man?' I asked.

'None of your business!' he replied briefly.

'You are rude!' I complained. 'You know, I'm used to being answered in a polite way. Why don't you want to tell me where you have come from, and where you are going?'

'I can tell you if you are so curious, Mr Distinguished Gentleman! Look, I came from there, and I'm going there!' he replied, and pointed first back, and then forward.

I saw that he looked at me with such a contemptuous disgust. He probably thought that I was a Sunday hunter who was broken off from his company, and considered himself a true Westerner. I understood him well. Two weeks earlier I had bought my equipment, and a new suit in Fort Randall. My clothing was still relatively clean. As to my weapons, I always kept them clean. This was contrary to the habits of the hunters.

'Then just carry on with your business,' I said. 'But you could look back, because four Indians are pursuing you. It's unfortunate that you haven't noticed them.'

'I haven't noticed them? Don't tell me! Four Indians are after me, and I don't notice them! Well, young gentleman, you are mistaken. I noticed them so much that now I'll start a big arc, and get behind them. So far the landscape wasn't right, but among these hills I can do it. If you want to learn something, hide here for ten minutes, and then you'll see how an old hunter sorts out four reds who follow him. Come on, Tony!'

He did not care with me anymore, and rode away. In a few minutes he disappeared behind a hill. I understood his plan. He wanted to ride around the hills to get behind the Indians. He could not have done it on the flat plains, because the Indians would have seen through his plan. In any case, there were four of them against one, thus, to be on the safe side, I took my gun out, and waited for the events.

The Indians came in a file. The one who rode in front suddenly stopped. He was astonished that the man had disappeared. Now the four Indians were next to each other, and they were discussing something.

I could have shot at them with my bear slayer, and I was considering whether I should do it, when a gun went off, and it was immediately followed by another shot. Two Indians fell off their horses dead, and an ear-piercing scream resounded at the same time, 'Hi-hiy-hiyyy!' It sounded like the victory cry of the Indians, but it came from the throat of the strange, small hunter whom I now noticed at the end of the valley.

He had disappeared behind me, and now he was in front of me. After the two shots he pretended to be fleeing. His mare ran with great endeavour, and its long ears were fluttering in the wind. The rider loaded his gun while galloping. It was obvious that it was not the first time that he had been in such a situation. He was calm, quick, and skilful. I appreciated him more and more.

The two remaining Indians sent bullets after him, but they did not hit him. They yelled, grabbed their tomahawks, and galloped after the paleface. He did not care with them for a while, then he suddenly jerked the reins, and with this he turned his horse. The mare stood motionless. The small man lifted his gun, aimed, and in the next moment two shots

554

popped. The two Indians crashed on the ground with bullets in their heads.

The man got off his horse to examine his enemies. I also hurried there.

'Well, Sir, do you know now how four Indians can be sent to hell?' he asked.

'Thank you, Master,' I replied. 'It was a good lesson.'

'I wonder what you would have done,' he remarked in a superior tone.

'I wouldn't have thought of ...'

'You wouldn't, would you?' A smile appeared on his face. It was ambiguous, but it was a smile. 'And what did you learn?' he asked.

'I learnt that I wouldn't have thought of riding around half a world,' I continued. 'It's necessary only on the open prairie. In this hilly area, like this, you could have solved the problem with some craftiness.'

'Look at him! He knows it! Who are you?'

'I'm a writer,' I replied.

'Writer? What's that? Do you have a problem here?' he asked, and tapped on his head.

'You can be sure that the answer is no.'

'Then I don't understand you,' he said. 'What is it you are writing and for whom? '

'For others to read,' I replied.

'I still don't understand,' he said. 'One does something for himself. For example, I kill a bison, because I'm hungry, and I want to eat. I don't do it for others.'

'The same is about writers, but there is a difference. Writers write because they want to eat. But they can eat only if others gobble up their books.'

'Let's say it's true. But then what are you doing on the prairie? You can't write here!'

'I don't write here; I write at home. Here I only collect experiences. Then I go home, and write them up.'

'Will you write about me too?'

'Of course.'

The little man grabbed his Bowie knife, and pointed it at me with his left hand, and he said, 'There is your horse! Get on it, and get out of my sight if you don't want to feel several inches of cold blade between your ribs!'

He came towards me threateningly, however, I was not frightened, and only laughed in his face. How could I have taken him seriously when he reached only to my shoulder!

'Right, I won't write about you, if you don't want to!'

'I don't trust you! Mad men can promise everything, but you can't expect them to keep their words! Move young man until I'm gentle!'

'And if I don't?'

'Then you'll see!' he replied, and pulled his knife.

With one motion I pulled back both his arms, put my left arm between his two arms and his back, and squeezed his wrist with my right hand so hard that he dropped his knife. By the time he recovered from the shock, I had tied both of his hands behind his back.

'Hell!' he shouted. 'What's this? How dare you!'

'Shout quieter, young man! It's not advisable to shout in such places,' I quoted his own words. I let him go, and with a quick motion I picked up his knife and his gun that he had put down in the grass when he examined the dead. He tried to release his hands, his face was red of the effort, but my belts were stronger than him.

'You are wasting your energy! You can only escape from these belts if I want you to. You promised a few inches of cold blade between my ribs, but it may end up between your ribs.'

'Stab me!' he said gloomily. 'I don't deserve anything else as I was so careless! It has never happened to Sans-ear.'

'Sans-ear?' I exclaimed astonished. 'Are you Sans-ear?'

I had heard many times about this famous hunter, who was a lone wolf as he had not appreciated anyone good enough to accept him as a company. Many years earlier he had been caught by the Navajo, who cut off his ears. He had escaped, and since then he had this strange half English half French name.

'My name is none of your business,' his voice bubbled angrily. 'Finish me off.'

I stepped up to him, and removed the belts.

'Here are you knife and gun,' I said. 'It was only a joke. You are free, and do whatever you want.'

'Don't make stupid jokes,' he replied. 'How can I now live without shame after a greenhorn, who perhaps has been on the prairie for the first time in his life, captured me like this. Had it been one of the famous hunters, like Winnetou, the long Haller, Old Firehand or Old Shatterhand, I could cope with it.'

I felt sorry for him that he took the stupid joke so much to heart. But it felt good that he knew my name, because it offered me an opportunity.

'Why do you think that I'm a greenhorn?'

'Why? Because your clothing is so right!' he said, while pouting his lips. 'And your gun is so sparkly that it blinds me.'

'It's not only sparkly,' I replied, 'but it can do many things. Just watch!'

I picked up a stone, about twice the size of a dollar coin, and threw it in the air. I immediately aimed with my gun. When the stone reached the highest point I hit it with my bullet so it flew even higher. It was nothing special, but I had exercised it a thousand times until I was sure that I could do it at any time. There was true astonishment in the little man's eyes.

'My word! Excellent shot! Can you always do it?'

'Nineteen out of twenty.'

'You can be proud of it! What's your name?'

'Around here they call me Old Shatterhand.'

'But you aren't old at all!'

'You forget that the "Old" can also be an affectionate attachment.'

'This is true! I'm sorry that I'm still doubtful. Once I was told that a grizzly attacked Old Shatterhand in his sleep, and tore off the flesh from his shoulder to his ribs. He recovered, but surely the wound has its marks.'

I opened my coat, and my shirt.

'Look!'

'Damn it! It had indeed attacked you! I'm surprised that you could recover from it.'

'I wouldn't have believed it either. It happened at the Red River. I lay there for two weeks next to the bear until Winnetou, the chief of the Apache, found me.

'Then you are Old Shatterhand. Tell me, are you laughing at me?'

'Not at all. You made the mistake of considering me some greenhorn with whom you didn't need any precaution. I didn't defeat Sans-ear; you became the victim of surprise.'

'Yes, yes. There are very few people who are as strong as a bison. I'm not ashamed of being defeated by you. By the way, my real name is Sam Hawerfield, but I would be honoured if you called me Sam.'

'And you could call me Charlie as my best friends do. Let's shake hands.'

'Don't think that Sans-ear easily makes friendships, but in this case I'm happy to shake hands with you. Please don't squeeze it so much that it would become a mush. I may need it at some point.'

'Don't be afraid, Sam! You can rely on these hands in trouble. But now can I repeat my question: where are you coming from, and where are you heading to?'

'I'm coming from Canada, where the lumberjacks are on strike, and I helped them. I'm heading to Texas and Mexico where there are so many bandits that one is happily thinking of all the bullets and knives that he has to face with.'

'My plans are almost the same! I'm also heading to Texas and then to California. But it's not a problem if I make a detour to Mexico. Do you want me to join you?'

'Do I? I'll dance in my joy! But tell me, Charlie, do you really write books?'

For my nod he said, 'Well, then Old Shatterhand is really a very different person from what I expected. But anyway, what do you know of the Oglala?

I told him what I had experienced.

'Hm,' he hummed musing. 'Then we should really leave this area soon. Yesterday I was on a clearance where I saw the tracks of at least sixty horses. The four blokes whom I finished must be the scouts of a larger group. Do you know this area?'

'No. I have never been here before.'

'At about twenty miles to the West the Rolling Prairie ends, and the land becomes completely flat. Then after ten miles there is a river where the Indians water their horses. But we will avoid them, and head to the South, although in this way we will only reach the river tomorrow afternoon. If we leave soon, we will reach the rail tracks before evening. If we are lucky we could even see a train. It's a change anyway.'

'We can leave right now as far as I'm concerned. But what do we do with the bodies?'

'Nothing at all. We will leave them here, but first I cut off their ears.'

I looked at him horrified.

'Wouldn't it better to bury them? If they find them, they will know that we were here.'

'This is what I want, Charlie!'

He pulled the bodies up to the top of the hill, laid them next to each other, and cut off their ears one by one. Then he put them in their hands.

'From this they will know that Sans-ear was here,' he said contented. 'Don't look at me like this, Charlie! Everything has a cause. Do you know how unpleasant it is when one's ears are cold in the winter, but he doesn't have ears? What can I do? I was so careless that I was captured by the Indians? I killed some of them, but with my tomahawk I accidentally cut off an ear of one of them. As a revenge and mockery they cut off my ears too. They wanted to torture me, but I didn't wait for that. And I have compensated for my lost ears.' He showed me his gun. There were notches on the butt of it. 'Every notch is a hostile Indian whom I dispatched as a revenge. Now I have to add four more.'

559

He made four more notches, and then continued, 'These are the Indians. Above them you can see eight notches. They are white men whom I shot dead. I will tell you once why. I have two more notches to make. Father and son. The two worst bandits who came to this earth. If I could kill them, I wouldn't have any more desires in this life.'

His weather-worn face twitched, and it seemed that his eyes were filled with tears. I suspected that there had been some dark tragedy in the past of the old hunter. If he enjoyed so many murders, he must have had a reason. It could not just be cruelty, but rightful revenge. He loaded his gun again. It was a terribly old one with the grooves on the butt, and rust on the barrels. Another person would not have been able to hit any target, or even get close to it with this gun, while he had never missed it.

'Tony!' shouted the little man.

The mare was grazing nearby, and for the calling word she leapt next to the little man, so that he could get on her comfortably.

'You have an excellent horse, Sam,' I remarked. 'When I first saw her I thought I wouldn't give a dollar for her, but now I know that you wouldn't sell it for a thousand.'

'For a thousand? Not even for a million! Not to mention that I don't need money. I know one or two places in the mountains where I could fill my bag with gold, but what for? Of course, once it was different, when I still had a happy life. I was a young farmer, who carried his wife and child, whom he loved, to the house on a wonderful mare. The mare was called Tony, and when she had a filly, I called that Tony too. Are you listening, Charlie?'

'Very much so!' I replied. I was very touched.

'Yes ... Then the ten bandits came whom I mentioned.

They were cruel, and everybody was afraid of them. They burnt down my house, killed my wife and my child, and shot my mare, because they couldn't get on it. Only the filly survived, because she wandered away. When I returned from hunting, everything that had tied me to life disappeared.

560

Only the filly remained, and the revenge. I've killed eight members of the gang with this shabby gun. Two are still alive, but I'll catch them! This is why I'm heading to Texas and Mexico. The filly has grown up, and doesn't look like a horse any more, but it is just as brave when arrows and bullets whistle or tomahawks flash. If she died, I would die after her.'

He became quiet, and wiped his eyes. Then, without any signal, he jumped on his horse.

'But let's leave the past alone, Charlie!' he exclaimed once he was on the horse. 'You are the first person I've spoken to about this. Maybe to show you that I consider you a brother. You have probably heard of me that I live for the revenge. It is true. It has often come to my mind to put these bandits in the fire for quarter of an hour. '

I untied my mustang, and mounted it. Sam said that we would go to the South, but he turned to the West. I did not ask why, he surely knew why, and why he took the spears of the four killed Indians. This little man reminded me to Hawkins in many ways, and the fact that both were called Sam made the similarity even stronger.

We rode silently for a long time when he stopped his horse, got off, and erected one of the spears on the top of a hill. I now understood his purpose. He put out markings to lead the Indians to their killed companions so that they could see that Sans-ear's revenge had caught up with four more.

Sam opened his bag, and took out eight thick strips of a rug. He gave me four of them.

'Get off, Charlie, and tie these on the hooves of your mustang. They won't leave any print then, and the Indians will think that we flew. Ride straight to the South until you find the railway tracks. Wait there for me. I have to put the other three spears out to the best places. I'll find you, but just in case let's agree that my signal is the vulture screech at daytime, and coyote barking at night.

We parted. I was riding in steps, while I was deep in my thoughts. The strips on Swallow's hooves slowed me down a lot, so after five miles I took them off, as there was no need for them anymore. Their purpose was not to leave marks around the spears.

My mustang joyously switched to a gallop. The prairie became flatter, and the Sun had not yet set, when I noticed a bright line on the horizon that stretched from the East to the West. This was the railway track that Sam mentioned. It was on the top of a man-high embankment.

I had a strange feeling. For some time this was my first encounter with civilisation. It would have been enough to lift my hand, and the train would have slowed down, and I could have boarded, and I could have gone to the East or the West, saying good-bye to the infinite prairie.

I got off my mustang, and collected wood to make a camp fire. One of the bushes grew directly by the embankment. When I leant forward to pick up twigs I caught sight of a hammer. Its head was bright, thus it had been used recently, because otherwise the marks of the morning dew would have rusted it.

I examined the nearside of the embankment, but I could not find anything suspicious. I went to the other side, and searched there too, without a result. Then I spotted a tuft of fragrant grama grass. It caught my attention, because it was unusual in this area. I leant forward, and spotted a footprint on it. The footprint was fresh, not more than a few hours' old. It was a moccasin print. Was it possible that Indians were around? But how did they have a hammer? Whites could also wear moccasins. Maybe it was a railway man who had examined the tracks, and he wore moccasins. However, I could not rely just on assumptions. I needed certainty.

The examination of the embankment was dangerous. On either side, in any of the bushes, there could have been an enemy. I would not have cared with a hammer in other circumstances, but I knew that the Oglala were around, and it made me more cautious. I put my gun on my back, and held my revolver ready. I advanced from bush to bush on one side, and then back on the other side. However, still there was no result. As I climbed over the tracks on all fours I felt something wet. It seemed that sand and pebbles had been put there on purpose. With my fingers I started to dig in, and I got frightened for a moment, because my hand was covered with blood. The red colour started to sip up to the surface. I stretched out on the ground to be able to see it better, and got to the conclusion that the sand was used to cover a pool of blood.

It had to be a murder, because nobody would have tried to cover up the blood of an animal. But who was the victim, and who was the murderer? On the other side of the embankment I noticed more footprints, and also two parallel lines as if somebody had been pulled by his arms. As the blood was still fresh, I did not dare to follow the tracks as the murderer could have still been near the embankment. Instead, I crawled for some distance on the nearside before crossing the railway tracks again.

All these took a lot of time. Fortunately I found bushes on the other side too, and under their cover I advanced. Ten steps from me there was a wild current bush that obstructed my view. As I tried to peer through, it seemed to me that somebody lay in the bush. Was it the murderer or the body of the victim? I had to find it out.

Although I could have waited for Sam, and ridden away with him, I undertook this risky task, because every hunter knew that the seemingly most unimportant details could be crucial, because important conclusions could be deduced from them. Sometimes he could gallop for forty or fifty miles without stopping, other times he could not advance for half a mile because of the dangers.

I threw a twig towards the bush to test if somebody stirred for the noise, but nothing happened. Either it was such an experienced enemy, who was not lured with such a trick, or there was nothing in the bush. I decided to act.

With two leaps I was there, my knife in my right hand, and I thrust my left hand into the bush. There was a man on the ground, but he was dead. I lifted the branches, and I could see a scalped skull. He was a white man. There was a war arrow in his back, thus the Indians, who had killed him, were on warpath.

Had they gone or were they still around? Their tracks led to the prairie. I followed them knowing that I could be shot at any moment. From the tracks I could establish that there had been four Indians, two older and two younger. I followed the tracks on all fours, or rather on my fingers and my toes. This was difficult, but I had the strength and experience. The Indians must have felt safe, because they did not make any attempt to erase their tracks.

The wind blew from the South-east, that is, towards me. Thus, when I heard the snorting of a horse, I was not frightened, as the horse could not have smell me. I continued crawling. Finally I arrived to a clearance that was surrounded by thickets from all directions. There were at least sixty horses on the clearance. Two Indians guarded the horses. One of them, a very young warrior, wore leather boots. Probably he had pulled them off from the murdered white man. I remembered that the victim was completely naked, so the murderers took all his belongings, and then probably they shared them between themselves. This guard must have been one of the four whose tracks led here.

As the Indians and the white men had to communicate with each other without knowing each other's languages, a kind of sign language developed at the frontiers, and people often used them even when they talked in their mother tongue. From the motions and gestures of the Indians I could understand that they expected a train from the West, and that they would tear up the railway tracks, and then kill the passengers. I had seen enough, so I retreated quickly while erasing my tracks.

It took a long time until I got to Swallow. Next to him Sam's mare grazed, while Sam comfortably rested behind a bush, and chewed a huge piece of dried meat.

'How many are there, Charlie?' he asked.
'Who?'

564

'The Indians.'

'What do you mean?'

'Do you really think I'm a greenhorn, hehehe?' Even his laughter was similar to Sam Hawkins's. 'I saw the hammer when I arrived. What would you have done in my place?'

'I would have waited.'

'I don't think so! And if Old Shatterhand got into trouble? I cannot let my friend down!'

'But your presence could have put both of us in danger. How far did you come after me?'

'Where the white man was murdered by the Indians. When I found the body, I was sure that you also saw it, and you went on scouting. So I returned to here. So, how many?'

'At least sixty.'

'Interesting. Then it must be the group whose tracks I spotted yesterday. Are they on the warpath?'

'Undoubtedly.'

'Are they camping?'

'Yes, but only for a short time.'

'Damn them! What do they want?'

'I think they want to tear up the tracks, and then rob the passengers of the derailed train.'

'Are you mad, Charlie? How do you know this?'

'From their conversation.'

'Do you understand the Oglala's language?'

'I do, but anyway, they used sign language.'

'That's easy to misunderstand. What did you see?'

I described the motions and gestures of the Indians. Sam jumped up excitedly, but then regained his self-control, and sat back in the grass.

'Yes, you understood it well, Charlie! We must help the passengers, but we cannot take too much of a risk! Let's discuss it. Did you say sixty of them? Unpleasant! There's no room on the butt of my gun for more than ten notches!'

The situation was dangerous, but I had to smile. This little man was prepared to face sixty Indians, but he was anxious only because of the lack of room for his notches.

'How many of them do you want to kill?' I asked.

'I don't know … two or three. I don't think I can do more, because they'll escape as soon as they recognise that they had to fight with twenty or thirty white men.'

I smiled again because I could see that Sam accounted for the train crew and the passengers just as I did.

'The trouble is that we don't know which train they want to attack. It would be terrible to go to the wrong direction.'

'I think they meant the train from the West from the signs that you described. I'm quite surprised because mainly the trains from the East bring goods that the Indians want. If we cannot find it out, one of us will go to the East, and the other to the West.'

'Unfortunately we don't know the timetable,' I said.

'I'm not interested in it at all,' said Sam. 'I've never sat in a cage that they call a wagon. I wouldn't survive in a place where I couldn't stretch out my legs. Tony and I need the free prairie! What do you think? When will they attack?'

'I guess, in the night. We have half an hour till dark. If we scouted again then, we may learn something.'

'I say, we should wait until after it's dark. Let's rest until then, shall we?'

'Just rest, I'll be the guard.'

'Unnecessary, Charlie. We can trust Tony.'

'Tony?'

'Yes. I never tie her. She's very clever, and her smell sense is excellent. Have you seen a horse that doesn't snort when an enemy approaches?'

'Never.'

'There's only one such a horse, and it's Tony. The snorting calls the attention of the master, but also tells the enemy two things. Firstly, where the master is; secondly that the master has been warned. Thus I trained Tony to come to me if she senses enemies, and nudge me with her nose. With her ears she can hear an Indian from a thousand steps, and her eyes are so sharp like the eyes of an eagle. So you can lie down too.'

'Well, I do need some rest,' I replied, and stretched out on the grass. I started to smoke one of my self-made cigars. Sam just watched me. His nostrils expanded as I smoked. It was difficult to get tobacco on the prairie, and cigars were especially appreciated.

'This is wonderful,' said Sam sniffing. 'How did you get this wonderful cigar, Charlie?'

'I always have dozens with me. Do you want some?'

'Want? I beg you!'

I gave him a cigar, he lit it, breathed it deeply, moreover, he swallowed the smoke as the Indians do. His satisfaction was written all over his face.

'Glorious cigar! I can tell you the brand!'

'You know such things, Sam?'

'Of course!'

'Then tell me!'

'It's from either Virginia or Maryland!'

'No.'

'Then, for the first time in my life, I was wrong. But it's the type, because I know this smell and taste!'

'No.'

'Brazilian?'

'No!'

'From Bahia?'

'Still no.'

'Then tell me!'

'Look at it better,' I said and I opened one cigar.

'Are you mad, Charlie! Destroying a wonderful cigar like this! You could get five to eight beaver pelts for such a cigar!'

'I don't care. I'll have new stock in two or three days.'

'From where?'

'From my factory.'

'Do you have a cigar factory?'

'Yes, here,' I replied, and pointed at my mustang.

'If you were not Old Shatterhand, I would think that you have some little problem in your head,' said Sam with an unbelieving face. 'Or, if you make a joke, make a good one!'

For this I took a filled bag from Swallow.

'Just check it!'

Sam dived in, and took out a handful of leaves.

'But these are cherry and lentil leaves!'

'Not quite, but similar. There's also a little wild hemp in it. And the whole thing is wrapped in plantain leaves. I collect appropriate leaves, and put them in this bag. I keep it under my saddle. In the warmth it starts to ferment, and this is the secret. It's not a delicatessen, but it easily cheats the palate of a Westerner, who hasn't been able to smoke for months, as your example shows. '

'Indeed,' agreed Sam.

Apparently he did not lose his liking for my cigars, because he smoked it until it burnt his fingers. Meanwhile the Sun had gone behind the horizon, and it was time for action.

'Now?' asked Sam.

'Yes. We'll go together to the clearance with the Indians' horses. We will separate there, go around their camp, and meet at the other side.'

'Right,' said Sam. 'But if something happens then we meet by the river to the South. There's a forest before that. Its southern edge is wedged in the prairie. The place that I have in mind is two miles from there.'

While I did not expect any such surprises, it was right to be prepared for all possibilities.

We started off. After reaching the point, where the white man was killed, we advanced to our goal more carefully with a knife in hand.

'Now we part! You go to the right, and I'll go to the left,' whispered Sam, and he disappeared.

I went around the horses and got to another clearance that was surrounded by trees and bushes. Indians lay on the ground but so motionlessly and silently that I could hear the crawling bugs in the grass. At the edge of the bush I spotted three men some distance from the other Indians. It seemed that they were talking, and I decided that I would get closer.

568

I lay low under a bush five or six steps from them. I noticed with astonishment that one of the three men was white. What was he doing among the Indians? He could not be a prisoner, because he moved freely. He could not be a hunter who married a woman from the tribe, because his clothing was more similar to mine than to the Indians'.

The other two were chiefs as they had eagle feathers in their hair. Apparently two different tribes or villages joined forces for the enterprise.

I was close enough to them to hear every word, but when I arrived there was a lull in the conversation. However, a few minutes later the conversation restarted. They talked in the language of the frontiers.

'Are you sure, my white brother, that the Fire Mustang will bring a lot of gold?'

'I am. A man told me who lives near the stable of the Fire Mustang.'

'And the Great White Father wants to make coins of it?'

'Indeed.'

'He won't,' said the chief. 'Will there be many people on the Fire Mustang?'

'I don't know, but it doesn't matter, the Indian warriors will defeat them.'

'And the Oglala warriors will take many scalps home, and it will be a glory to them. Will the Fire Mustang bring things that the Indians need: weapons, leather, and clothing?'

'Plenty of it.'

'Then you will get the gold and silver, my white brother, that the Fire Mustang will bring. We don't need it. We have enough of them in our mountains. I, Ka-vo-mien, the chief of the Oglala, met a clever and brave pale face who said that the gold brought troubles to everyone.'

'That paleface was mad,' said the white man

'The Oglala believed the same at first,' replied the chief, 'because he was only observing the animals and plants of the prairies and the forests. Our warriors wanted to raid and kill trappers who caught many beavers on the hunting lands of the Oglala. But this paleface was wise and brave. His arms were strong, and his bullets always hit the target. He wasn't even afraid of the grizzly. He warned the trappers about us, but they laughed at him scornfully. The trappers were punished. We killed, and scalped all of them. But it had been a long struggle until we could overcome this one, as he stood his ground bravely, and killed many of our warriors. But there were many of us, and finally we defeated him. Then we tied him up, and took him to our village. Ma-ti-ru, the greatest chief of the Oglala, wanted to give him his daughter to be his squaw. But this paleface stole the chief's horse and weapons, killed several warriors, and escaped.

'When did this happen?' asked the white man

'The Sun has defeated the winter four times since then.'

'What was the name of this paleface?'

'The whites call him Old Shatterhand, because his fist is strong like the bear's paws, and he can knock out any enemy with one blow.'

I recognised the two chiefs now. Ko-vo-mien related one of my adventures, and Ma-ti-ru nodded to it.

'Old Shatterhand!' exclaimed the third man. 'My path has crossed his! I have an account to settle with him!'

Indeed, our paths had crossed when a group of bandits attacked us to steal our cache, but we defeated them, and only three escaped. He was more dangerous than any Indian, because enticed the Indians to robbery.

Ma-ti-ru now lifted his hand and said, 'He killed many brave Oglala warriors, stole my best horse, and refused the most beautiful girl of the tribe! If I Ma-ti-ru can capture him, he will tie Old Shatterhand to the torture stake, and peel off the flesh from his bone piece by piece.'

Had these three men known that the man whom they talked about lay only a few steps from them!

'He won't be captured by the Oglala,' said Ka-vo-mien. 'I heard that he crossed the Great Water to the land where the sun burns like the fire, the prairie is hot, and lions roar.'

I had mentioned a number of times by the campfires that I would go to the Sahara to look around. Now I knew that the even the Indians knew about it.

'If he went, he'll come back,' stated Ma-ti-ru. 'Anyone who has breathed the fresh air of the prairie, will be thirsty for it forever!'

He was right. Just as the mountain man feels the best among the cliffs, the seaman on the sea, I felt at the home on the prairie, and I had returned.

Ka-vo-mien pointed at the stars.

'Can you see the stars, my white brother? It's time to go. Is the iron hand, which my warriors took from the servant of the Fire Mustang, strong enough?'

From this question I learnt that the murdered man was a railway employee who checked the tracks.

'Stronger than the hands of twenty Oglala warriors,' said the white bandit. 'It'll be easy to tear up the tracks.'

'Do you know, my white brother, how to do it?'

'Yes. Your warriors can follow me. The train will arrive in an hour's time. But remember, my brother, that the gold and silver is mine.'

'Ma-ti-ru never lies!' announced the chief proudly. 'The gold is yours, the scalps and the belongings of the palefaces will be taken by the brave Oglala warriors.'

'You also promised that you'll give me mules, and some warriors to accompany me to the Canadian River.'

'Even further! My warriors will accompany you to the border of Mexico. If the Fire Mustangs brings many things that Ma-ti-ru likes, my warriors will accompany you all the way to the city where your son waits for you as you said.'

The chief gave a signal, for which the warriors stood up. I quickly retreated, when I heard some noise behind my back. 'Sam!' I breathed when I recognised my companion.

'Charlie!' he whispered happily.

'What did you see?' I asked.

'Nothing, but you did, didn't you?'

I nodded.

'Let's go back to the embankment,' I whispered. 'I'll tell you everything then.'

When we climbed over, I reported to him.

'Sam, you hurry to the horses, ride a mile to the West, and wait for me by the embankment. I still want to scout around a bit.'

'Wouldn't you let me do it? I would rather like if you went for the horses.'

'I can't do it, Sam. My mustang obeys you, but I wouldn't be able to move Tony from her place.'

'You are right, Charlie. Then I will go.'

As soon as he had gone, Indians appeared on the other side. I followed them under the cover of the embankment. At the place where I found the hammer they stopped, and climbed up. I retreated to the bush. I soon heard the clinking of the iron. The bandit had obviously started his work with the tools they took from the railway man.

Once I ascertained that I had not misunderstood their intentions, I quickly stole to the West, and ten minutes later I met Sam.

'They are already working on the tracks,' he said.

'How do you know?'

'I put my ear on the tracks, and I could hear the blows.'

'The train is here in forty-five minutes, Sam. We have to stop it before the Indians can spot its lamps.'

'Listen Charlie! I won't go with you.'

'Why?'

'Because you can do it alone. If I stay, I can learn more, and can inform you about what's happening when you return.'

'True. Then we'll meet here.'

'Yes, you will find me here.'

I mounted my horse, and rode towards the train. I would have liked to meet it as far as I could so that the Indians would not see that the train had stopped. It was a starry night and the light of the stars lit the prairie. I was able to gallop quicker and, without stopping, I made three miles.

I dismounted, and tied my horse so that the approaching train would not frighten it away. Then I tore up a lot of dry grass, and with the help of twigs I made a torch.

I put my ear on the tracks, and listened. Ten minutes later I heard a quiet murmur that was becoming stronger. Soon I spotted some light just above the horizon. It could not be a star as it kept on growing. The train was approaching.

The time of action had arrived, so I lit the torch. The roaring of the train kept on increasing. I swung the torch. The train driver understood that somebody was giving the signal for stopping. Two whistles cut in the quietness of the night, the brakes screeched and finally the engine stopped right by me. The train driver leant out, and asked, 'What do you want? Do you want to get on?'

'No, Sir, I prefer that you and your passengers all got off.'

'No way!'

'You'll reconsider it if you knew that a few miles from here the tracks were destroyed!'

'Who did it?'

'Indians. They want to attack the train.'

'Are you serious?'

'I don't joke.'

'What's up? What happened?' asked the conductor who came to the front of the train. He was the head of the crew.

'Apparently there are Indians in front of us,' replied the train driver.

'Really? Have you seen them?'

'I have, and I eavesdropped. They are Oglala.'

'How many?'

'About sixty!'

'Hell! This is the third ambush of the train this year. But now we'll give them a lesson. How far are they?'

'About three miles.'

'Then cover the light!' he ordered the train driver, and then he turned to me. 'You are a prairie hunter, aren't you? '

'Something like that,' I replied.

'Thank you for your warning.'

'There are two of us,' I said. 'My friend stayed near the Indians to watch them.'

'Very good,' said the head of the crew. 'It's good that you didn't lose your head.'

'Not even our scalps,' I replied smiling, 'because that was the main danger.'

Meanwhile the doors opened, and the passengers came up to us. They asked about the reason for stopping.

'An Indian attack can be expected,' said the conductor. 'Everyone must remain silent. I'm responsible for this train. I give the orders, and everybody must follow them. '

'Is it true that you transport gold and silver?' I asked.

'Who said it?'

'The Indians are led by a white bandit. He agreed with them that he would get the gold of which he heard from a railway employee. The rest of the cargo, and your scalps will go to the Indians.'

'I'll give them a lesson!' said the conductor. 'I wish we could capture the white bandit, Mr ...'

'My friend, is called Sans-ear and I ...'

'Sans-ear! He's worth twenty! And who are you? '

'They call me Old Shatterhand,' I replied.

'Old Shatterhand! The man, who three months ago, after being chased by more than a hundred Sioux warriors made the distance between the Yellowstone River to Fort Union on snow-slippers in three days? And who also saved a train some time ago?' enthused the conductor.

'The same. Then I was with Winnetou, the chief of the Apache. But now, Sir, you have to make a decision, because the Indians know the arrival time of the train, and if it's delayed, they'll be suspicious.'

'If you follow my command, everything will be fine,' he replied. 'You and your friend are too few for sixty Indians!'

'Well,' I answered, 'Sans-ear dispatched four Indians today at broad daylight, and I can shoot twenty-five times without loading with my Henry rifle. The number is not the most important in such a situation.'

'Look! We have sixteen track workers on the train, and also twenty militia men who are going to Fort Niobrara. I'm sure that many passenger gentlemen would like to join us.'

Indeed, they all agreed. I had to warn them that some would have to stay with the ladies and children to protect them. Eight passengers volunteered. I looked at them. They were traders, who knew a lot about maize, wine, tobacco, and hemp, but little about the handling of a Bowie knife.

'Do you have a plan then?' I asked the conductor. 'Are you experienced in Indian warfare?'

'That's unnecessary,' he replied, 'because these Injuns will flee. They always seek safety in a battle.'

'These are Oglala warriors, Sir!' I exclaimed. 'And two chiefs lead them!'

'Are you saying that I should be more cautious? But we have forty men!' he said in the tone of a great general. 'Listen! We will go as far as the damaged tracks. The Indians will believe that we don't know of their plans, and that we'll wait for them with weapons in our hand. We'll sort out these sixty Indians easily, restore the track, and continue our travel with an hour or two delay.'

'It's a plan worthy of a cavalry colonel,' I said mockingly. 'Only that you ignore certain circumstances, and you are leading the forty men to certain death!'

'Are you a coward then, or are you angry because you can't be the leader?'

'Cowardice? Sir, as you have heard of me, you know that your words were very hasty as they may entice me to show you the meaning of my name on your head.'

He wanted to interrupt, but I continued, 'As to anger, it's quite indifferent to me to whom your scalps will belong to, that is, to you or to the Indians. But I'm not indifferent to whom my scalp belongs to. Good night!'

I turned around, but the conductor grabbed my arm.

'I'm the commander, and it will happen what I consider right. Everybody must return to their place. If we are squeezed by the reds, we can find refuge on the train until another train arrives either from the East or from the West. You should also get on, and show to us how far we can go.'

While he was talking I untied my mustang, and mounted.

'Very good,' I said. 'You are the commander, and I have already obeyed.'

'I meant next to the train driver!'

'I won't get on there, but you can, if you want!' I replied. 'I can even help you.'

I leant forward on the saddle, grabbed him by his collar, lifted him, and put him on the locomotive, then I rode away.

After ten minutes' riding I found Sam.

'Are you alone?' he asked when I dismounted. 'I thought you would bring the railwaymen with you.'

I briefly told him what had happened, and why I had let the head of crew, who wanted to be a general, to do whatever he wanted.

'You did the right thing, Charlie,' said Sam. 'He's stupid! He wanted to command instead of asking you for help. We'll see how he gets on without you, hehehe.'

While he laughed he made the sign of scalping on his head.

'Have you gone on scouting, Sam?'

'Of course. The Indians split into two groups, and they hide on the two sides of the embankment. They left their horses on the clearance with two guards. The question is what we should do, Charlie. Should we continue our journey, and leave the train to its fate?'

'We can't do that, Sam. We must help them.'

'I don't think they would care a lot if we were in trouble, but anyway. Let's help them. If for nothing else, because I'd like a couple of notches on my gun and leave some earless Indians behind. What do you think of a stampede, Charlie?'

'I'd agree if our aim was to massacre the Indians. Because if their horses ran away, they would have to fight until their last drop of blood. But I'd like to avoid spilling too much blood, and leave the Oglala a path to escape.'

'But I'd really like to see the face of these Indians when they run to the clearance, and cannot find their horses there. Shouldn't we try, Charlie?'

'I don't mind as you want it so much. Let's sneak to the clearance then.'

First, of course, we had to secure our own horses so that the escaping herd would not take them. We took Swallow and Tony in the depth of a thicket, and tied them up. Then we quickly returned to the embankment. We looked in vain to the West. There was no sign of the train. It seemed that the conductor had not yet decided on starting the engine.

We approached the clearance crawling on all fours. First we had to finish off the two guards. I wanted to avoid bloodshed, but I considered the situation as self-defence. Sam's knife flashed, and the guard was dead. The other guard met the same fate.

While Sam turned his back to me, my look fell on one of the horses that was near me. A comfortable Spanish saddle was on it; the type they use in South and Central America. Who owned this horse? Maybe the white bandit who had planned this attack on the train? I stepped closer, and spotted small, deep pockets on the two sides of the saddle. I took out folded papers from one pocket and two bags from another. I put them in my pocket as we did not have time to examine them.

This was the moment when I noticed the light of the train in the distance.

'Look Sam! The train is coming!'

'Indeed! I'm curious as to what will happen.'

They tried to carry out the conductor's plan. The light of the engine approached, but only slowly so that the train driver could spot the place where the tracks were torn. The noise of the wheels came closer and closer, and then suddenly stopped.

The Indians must have been extremely angry when they saw that the most important condition of their victory, the surprise, failed. Maybe they understood that somebody

577

warned the train. I hoped that the passengers and the crew would not leave the train as the wagons were easy to defend, but it did not happen. As soon as the train stopped, men jumped off from every door, and in one crowd they went for the attack. They did not even care to remain in the shadow, but rushed to the front of the train, and made themselves excellent targets for the Indians. The odd shots of the whites were returned in volleys by the Indians. I had never heard such blood curling screaming that followed.

The Indians rushed out from their places swinging their guns. They only found the dead and the seriously wounded there, because the other whites fled back to the wagons. Some Indians tried to scalp the fallen, but such a strong gun fire came from the windows of the first wagon they had to retreat.

I hoped that the train would reverse, but the train driver had also sought safety in the first wagon.

'It will be a slow siege,' opined Sam. 'Like that of a castle.'

'I don't think so,' I said. 'The Indians know that they have only time until the next rain arrives. They have to hurry. '

'Shouldn't we intervene?' asked Sam.

'Of course, we should, but rationally. We will make the stampede with a prairie fire!'

'How?'

'We'll light the prairie in twenty or thirty places around the train in a ring. But first we make the stampede so that the Indians couldn't escape. This will decide the battle.'

'Excellent plan! Won't the wagon burn?'

'I don't think so. Although I don't know if they have any inflammable cargo, like oil or tar, because then they are finished! Otherwise the wagons are strong enough to resist the prairie fire. The Indians can escape only if they light a counter-fire. I hope they do, because I don't want them to be burnt alive. If they do this, you can be sure that they'll light the grass near the train, and I wouldn't be surprised if they sought refuge under the wagons.'

'And how do we set the prairie alight? With punk it's a bit slow, and we can't use torches as they would see us.'

'For a situation like this I always have some matches,' I replied, and took two boxes of matches from my pocket. I gave one of them to Sam.

'Great! Then I'll bring Swallow and Tony,' said Sam.

'What for? They are safe where they are. The fire won't reach that far. We'll go for them later. For the time being we are fine on these Indian horses. I'll sit on this bay. '

'And I on this fox.'

'All right! Let's start the stampede!'

We cut the horses loose, lit a pile of dry grass at the edge of the clearance then jumped on the two selected mustangs.

'You go to the right, and I will ride to left,' I shouted. 'We'll meet at the tracks. We'll break through in the opening between the two fires.'

'Go on!' cried Sam.

The horses were restless. They were already excited because we cut their tethers, but now they smelt the burning grass. Their manes stood up. Some horses were rising, and we could expect the stampede at any moment. I headed to the prairie on the left, and made an arc whose radius was about a mile. I stopped time to time, jumped off, and lit the dry grass. I was already near the embankment, when I remembered Swallow, and I had bad premonitions. Maybe the thicket would catch fire too, and the good, faithful animal would be in trouble. As I finished my task, I galloped towards the thicket without hesitation.

The fire was already high, and cast a frightening light at each of the bushes. From the prairie a thundering sound came: the ground was thundering under the stampeding mustangs. This was followed by a horrifying yelling. It was the outburst of the anger and fright of the Indians.

Under the wagons small fires were lit. The Oglala recognised that only a counter-fire could save them.

A few minutes later I was in the thicket, and soon found Swallow and Tony. To my surprise and joy Sam appeared on the other side. He had the same anxiety as I, and hurried to find his Tony.

The problem was that the Indians also spotted our horses, and at least ten rushed towards them. The front two almost reached the horses. I tightened the belt of my gun, rose in the saddle, and grabbed my tomahawk. The bay horse, for the pressure of my knees, leapt forward quickly. I arrived to Swallow at the same time as the two quickest Indians. I immediately recognised the two chiefs.

'Back, Ma-ti-ru! The horse is mine!' He turned to me, and recognised me.

'Old Shatterhand!' he cried. 'Die, you paleface toad!'

He pulled his knife. With one more leap I was next to Swallow. Ma-ti-ru lifted his arm to stab me, but my tomahawk hit his head, and he collapsed. The other chief jumped on Swallow's back, and only then did he notice that the horse was tethered.

He saw that the horse would not save him, thus he slipped off, and tried to disappear in the thicket. I threw my tomahawk after him, and the heavy weapon hit his skull. Ka-vo-mien also crashed on the ground. I jumped off from the looted horse, aimed with my Henry rifle, and shot at the attacking Oglala warriors several times in quick succession. I stretched out three, but I could not continue, because the fire was dangerously approaching. I quickly untied Swallow, and got on him. The bay horse ran away.

This is when Sam got to Tony. With a jump he changed from the fox to his own mare, then he leant forward, and cut off the tether. We were galloping towards a gap where the flames had not yet reached each other. Fortunately we got through the flame-sea, and stopped at a place where the fire had burnt the ground already. It was black from the cinder, but started to cool. The flames on the right and left created such a heat that it was difficult to breathe, not to mention that the fire used up a lot of oxygen from the air.

But this oppressed feeling did not last long, and improved by the minute. The air cooled quickly as the fire rushed away, but the horizon was still glowing red even after a quarter of an hour. The prairie was black around us, and the stars were shrouded by smoke-clouds.

'That was hellishly hot,' exclaimed Sam. 'I wouldn't be surprised if the wagons had melted.'

'I don't think so. The wagons are built so that they could withhold a lot. It happens often that the train has to cross burning forests or prairies.'

'The problem is that the Indians saw us.'

'They can still see us. We have to make them believe that we have had enough, and we are leaving. Maybe they think that we belong to some military column, and now we are riding back to make a report. Let's move to the North and then return to the tracks in a big arc from the East.'

'This is an excellent plan. And we can rest a bit. Your tomahawk worked hard.'

'Though I made it sure that it wouldn't kill anyone.'

'I don't understand you.'

'Whoever I hit only lost their consciousness.'

'Don't tease me, Charlie! They were the two chiefs! They didn't deserve mercy!'

'I have my own reasons, but you wouldn't understand them, Sam. When I was their prisoner, they could have killed me, but they didn't, and I repaid this with ingratitude when I escaped. So, I was careful now not to crack their heads.'

'I'm sorry, Charlie, but it was very stupid! These blokes don't know how you think, and they will say that Old Shatterhand is so weak that he couldn't even kill someone with a tomahawk.'

This conversation went on for a while as we were galloping. The old mare kept up with my mustang. After the arc we got back to the embankment, at about a mile from the place where the train stood. There we tied our horses, and stole to the place on foot. The air was filled with a burnt smell, and the ground was covered with ash. The wind swirled this ash, and threw it in our face. I barely could suppress coughing, but it was important to remain quiet.

Soon we caught sight of the lamp of the locomotive, but we could not see any Indians around. Only when I got closer could I see that what I had expected to happen: the Indians climbed under the wagons, and did not dare to come out because of the gun fire from the windows.

'Sam! Go back to the horses so that the Indians wouldn't be able to capture them!'

'What do you mean? The Indians won't come out from under the wagons!'

'I will make them!' I replied, and told him my plan that came from the spur of the moment.

'Excellent, Charlie!' grinned Sam. 'It will succeed. I'll be there with the horses at the right moment, you can be sure!'

With a knife in my hand I rushed along the embankment to the train. From the wheels I could not see if there were Indians under the locomotive. I stole up to the embankment, and then with two leaps I got on the locomotive.

My sudden appearance was greeted with surprised cries, but I did not care. I reversed the train, and it started. Now there was real yelling from under the wheels. We made about thirty yards, and then I turned it forward again.

'You dog!' an angry voice rasped somewhere near, and a muscular figure climbed up on the engine with a knife in his hand. It was the white bandit. His head appeared above the ladder, but I got rid of him with a huge kick.

'Charlie!' a sharp cry reached my ear. 'I'm here!'

Sam had arrived. He calmly sat on his Tony leading Swallow with one hand, and defending with the other against two Indians. I jumped off from the engine, and hurried to help him. Other Oglala warriors were running in front of me hoping to find their horses in spite of the fire. Sam's opponents started to flee when I appeared.

I suddenly heard Sam's yell, 'Fred Morgan! You Satan! You'll die, you wretch!'

I could see that he lifted his tomahawk high, but his opponent avoided the blow with a quick movement, and disappeared among the fleeing Indians. Sam rode after him, but I could not follow the events, because some brave Oglala blocked my way, and I had to look after myself in the following minutes.

The battle was over. I did not participate in the chase. I thought enough blood had been spilled, and the Indians' desire to participate in such adventures had been cooled sufficiently. I would have liked to find Sam, and thus imitated the howling of the coyote a number of times.

By now everybody had got out of the train. They pulled the dead and wounded from under the wagons. When the conductor noticed me, he yelled at me angrily, 'How dare you touch the engine! It's fortunate that you didn't make a bigger disaster! Had you not intervened, we would have caught the Indians, but now most of them escaped.'

'It's easy to show off now!' I replied. 'It could have ended much worse.'

'Who set fire to the prairie?'

'I did.'

'You did! And what would you say if I arrested you, and took you to court?'

'Try it! I'm really interested if you could manage it!' The conductor stepped back embarrassed.

'I didn't mean it seriously,' he replied. 'You made a stupid move, but I forgive you!'

'It's wonderful that the mighty of this Earth show such a goodwill towards me,' I replied. 'What will you do now?'

'We'll repair the tracks, and will continue our journey. Or do you think there will be a second attack?' I started to have enough of this man.

'Very unlikely after your excellently executed plan, Sir!' I said contemptuously.

'Why are you teasing me? Excuse me! I couldn't have known what good skills these Indians had!'

'But I told you! Look around! Of the sixteen railway workers and twenty militia men nine are dead. You have to take the responsibility for their deaths. If you had listened to me, there would have been fewer casualties!'

He wanted to argue, but the passengers gathered around us, and they agreed with me.

'What's your advice now?' he asked meekly.

'You have to restore the tracks, of course. You need some light. There's enough grass and twigs to make a big fire. You also have to set up guards so that the Indians couldn't surprise you, although it's unlikely.'

'Wouldn't you undertake the guarding, Sir?'

'If I was so stupid! I have had enough of you, and I have my own things to look after.'

Sam arrived at this moment, but his face was so upset that it was frightening to look at him.

'Did you hear my signal?' I asked.

He merely nodded, and then he turned to the conductor,

'Was it you who contrived this beautiful battle plan?' For the nod of the conductor, he continued, 'Then my old mare has more grits in her head than you, Sir!'

The railway official stood there in amazement. I was also curious what could have put Sam in such an extraordinarily bad mood. He obviously missed the white bandit who planned the whole robbery. It seemed that he had known the villain, because he called him out his name: Fred Morgan! He was the one whom I kicked off from the locomotive.

'I'm fed up! Let's go!' Sam shouted at me.

We walked along the embankment far from the people leading our horses by the reins.

'I'm sorry that I got you involved in this stupid thing, Sam,' I remarked grumpily.

'And what about me!' exclaimed Sam. 'As if everything was against me! Everything is bad! The two chiefs, whom you caressed with your tomahawk, escaped! But it's nothing! Fred Morgan, whom I have chased for years, has escaped!'

'Why were you chasing him?'

'You still don't know who is he? I thought you would have found it out a long time ago!'

I looked in his eyes. Deep anger mixed with bitterness reflected in them.

'The murderer of your wife and child?'

'Who else!'

'Damn it,' I swore now too. 'Can we still catch him?'

'No, he's escaped! I missed the opportunity! He either got away among the Indians or he hid in the bushes, and I rode past him. I'd tear off my ears if I had them!'

Somehow his angry words made me suddenly remember something. I pulled out the papers and bags that I had taken from the Spanish saddle.

'Look, Sam!' I said. 'I took these from the saddle of his horse. Maybe we can learn something from these.'

The light of one of the campfires by the railway tracks reached us, so I could see what I was doing.

I opened the bags, and exclaimed in my surprise, 'Gems! What beautiful diamonds! Sam! Look! These bags are worth a fortune!'

How did these diamonds get to the prairie? How did this bandit get them? I was sure not by honest means. Having these diamonds in my possession meant that I would have to find the rightful owner.

'Show me, Charlie!' said Sam. 'I haven't had such things in my hand. If one considers that a few such pebbles are worth a fortune ...'

'Although they are nothing else, but pure carbon.'

'To me they are that,' shrugged Sam. 'I wouldn't give my old gun for the whole lot. What do you want to do with them?'

'I'll give them back to their owner, of course.'

'And who's that?'

'I don't know, but we may find out somehow! The newspapers must have been written about them. When we get to a town, we'll enquire.'

'Then we have to subscribe, hehehe!' said Sam.

'Maybe we don't. These pieces of paper may give us more information,' I replied. 'Let's see!'

Among the papers, I found a detailed map of the United States. Then there was a letter without an envelope.

... Galveston

Dear Father,

I need you! Come as soon as you can whether you can get the diamonds or not. There's a bigger loot here. I'll meet you at the Sierra Blanca, by Head Peak, at the source of the Pecos River. I'll tell you the rest when we meet.

Your loving son

Patrick

The date at the top was torn off, thus it was impossible to determine when it had been written. I read it to Sam.

'This is what was sent to him, indeed,' said Sam. 'I know that his son is called Patrick. These are the two that are missing from my gun to have the ten notches. But where's the place of which he wrote about?'

'Head Peak? It's the highest mountain near Santa Fe. I've seen it when I hunted bears in the Sierra Blanca.'

'Do you know the Pecos River too?'

'I know that really well.'

'Then you're my man. We were heading to Texas and Mexico, so it's only a small detour to New Mexico. Will you come with me to capture this evil man, Fred Morgan?'

'Of course! I'll have a word or two with him too. I have to know to whom these expensive pebbles belong to.'

'Then put them away, and let's see what the railway men are doing!'

The workers were repairing the tracks. Some passengers were watching them, while others laid the dead bodies. When they spotted us, they approached, and thanked us for our help. They were wiser than the conductor, and they understood that they could thank their lives to us. One asked how they could express their gratitude. I said that we would be happy to buy gunpowder, lead, tobacco, bread, and matches as it was difficult to get these things on the prairie. Soon they packed everything, and did not allow us to pay for the goods. Meanwhile the workers had finished the repair works. The conductor came to me, and asked, 'Do you want to join us? I would take you as far as you want to go.'

586

'No, thank you. We'll stay here.'

'I won't forget to mention your important role in this raid. You will have your reward.'

'Thank you, but it won't help us as we don't stay here.'

He mused for a few moments, and then asked, 'And what will happen to the loot?'

'According to the law of the prairie,' I said, 'it belongs to the victor.'

'Then I'll take a few things as a souvenir,' said the head of the crew.

'To do that, first show the Indian whom you defeated!' said Sam.

'What do you mean?'

'You can take anything from the man whom you killed, but if you touch another, you are just a common ghoul.'

'Leave him alone, Sam!' I warned him quietly. 'We don't need these arguments.'

'Right! But he has to admit that we defeated the Indians.'

The conductor disappeared. The fallen white men were put in one of the wagons. Everybody boarded, the engine whistled, and the train started off. The passengers waved good-bye to us with their handkerchiefs. We remained alone.

THE STAKEMEN

AT THE border of New Mexico, by the headwaters of the Pecos River and the Red River, enclosed by the Colorado River, the Brazos River, and the Trinity River there is a barren plateau that could be called the Sahara of the United States.

Hot sand hills, barren cliffs, and chalk layers rule here. There is not enough resources for life. The hot days are replaced by freezing nights without a transition. There is no oasis, only some mesquite shrubs that break up the barren landscape. Apart from these, there was only a cactus species that could live on this ground, and could even develop into a thicket. Woe to the rider who entered such a thicket. The transparent, hard spikes of the cactus could wound him, and this could even result in his death.

Even though this barren land was horrible, people attempted to cross it. There were roads through it to the prairies of Texas, and to the towns of Santa Fe and El Paso del Norte. These roads were not real roads, but paths marked by a line of stakes that showed the way. Lonely hunters, adventurers, migrants with ox-driven wagons, and smaller Indian groups followed these stakes if they did not want to go around the plateau.

The journey was long and dangerous. There were more victims there than in the deserts of Africa or Central-Asia. Skeletons of men and animals, wrecks of wagons lay along the path suggesting horrific stories. Above the land vultures circle, and follow every living being as if they were sure that they would become their feed.

This terrible desert has many names in different languages, but most often it was called Llano Estacado, the Staked Plain.

Two riders were riding from the Red River to the Sierra Blanca. The two horribly emaciated horses looked like ill, dishevelled birds that one would expect to find dead in their cage the following morning. They advanced tottering, their eyes blinked tired, their dried out tongue hanged out from their muzzle. In spite of the burning heat there was not a drop of sweat or foam on them, which suggested that their bodies had dried out completely.

The two horses were Swallow and Tony, and the riders, of course, Sans-ear and I. We had been wandering across the Llano Estacado for the fifth day, we had not had water for so long that we had forgotten its taste.

Poor Sam just hung on the saddle, leaning on the neck of his mare, and his tired face showed that he sank into a state of indifference. I also felt as if my eyelids were made of lead, and my throat was so dry that it was difficult to squeeze out a word. I thought I could cope with this for one more hour, before I would fall off the saddle, and crash on the ground accepting death.

'Water!' sighed Sam.

I looked at him, but remained silent. Even if I could speak, what could I have said to him? My horse stumbled, and stopped. He refused to move his feet no matter what I did.

Tony immediately followed Swallow's example.

I got off from the saddle, grabbed my horse's rein, and this is how I led him. Without my weight he was relieved somewhat, and walked next to me. Sam followed my example. I lumbered like this for half a mile, when I heard a loud sigh behind my back. I turned around. Sam lay in the dust with his eyes closed. I sat next to him, and stared into the air silently.

"This is the ugly end," I thought, "of my adventures, travels, and young life!" I wanted to think of my parents, siblings, I wanted to say good-bye to my Germany, but my thoughts refused to obey. My head rattled empty. It was not that I had not prepared for this hard and long journey. For my shame, I have to admit that I fell for the debased and cruel trick that had caused many a death in the Staked Plain.

Gold prospectors, who had been lucky in California, often crossed here from Santa Fe and El Paso to travel to the eastern cities to enjoy the fruits of their hard work. Here in the Staked Plain a danger lurked, which was the ugliest example of human meanness. In the desert debased bandits, recruited mainly from failed prospectors and adventurists, hid. They did not stop short of any crime, and they hated any honest work. They wanted nuggets that the prospectors carried in bags around their neck. These prospectors were strong men who showed their bravery and endurance in many difficult situations. The bandits did not dare to attack them, but they developed a most cruel plan: they took out the stakes that showed the road across the Llano Estacado, and drove the in the ground to point to the wrong way, that is, to the depth of the desert, where the mislead people would definitely die. Then it was easy to steal the property of the dying or dead men. The bones of the prospectors marked the misleading path.

So far we had followed the stakes with trust, but at noon we had recognised that we had lost our way. We did not know where it happened, and we could not have turned back even if our condition had allowed it. Now we could not move forward or backward.

I heard the screeching of a vulture above my head. As if it had wanted to tell me that only a miracle could help me. Its movement suggested that a victim of the stakemen could not be far from us.

As I looked around, and in spite of my swollen eyes, I noticed small dots about five hundred steps from me. I took my gun, and headed that way. Soon I could discern the scene. Three coyotes sat near some black thing that could have been a human or an animal body. Whatever it was, it had to be alive, because otherwise they would have devoured it.

My hand was shaking from weakness, and I had to aim for a long time, resting the gun on my knee, to hit the coyotes. The second shot was not very good, but it broke the first two legs of the coyote. With my knife I opened the vein of the first animal, and I moistened my lips with the blood of these animals. I was disgusted, but I gained some strength.

I took my cup, and filled it with the blood of the animal.

Now I turned to the body. It was a black man, whose face was grey from exhaustion. He lay in the sand. In another situation I would have exclaimed seeing this familiar face, but now I could only stutter, while I almost dropped the cup.

'Bob!'

For this he slightly raised his head, and opened his eyes.

'Water!' he groaned.

I knelt down next to him, and moistened his lips too with blood. Seeing that he gained some strength from it, I went to the second coyote. I grabbed it by the neck, I pulled it to Sam. I opened one of the coyote's veins, filled my cup, and offered Sam some of the disgusting liquid.

'Horrible!' he exclaimed. 'Blood! Pfie! But it's good!'

He drank a second cup. In the meantime the third coyote returned to devour the coyote next to the black man. I shot it dead, and it provided enough blood so that Bob could completely regain his ability to move his limbs.

I was musing the caprice of fate that had created this encounter. In Louisville I had often visited the house of a rich jeweller called Marshall. I became a friend of his two sons, Bernard and Allan, and went hunting with them to the mountains, and to the prairie several times. I was on good terms with their servant, Bob, who now lay in front of me.

How did he get here, to the Llano Estacado?

'Are you very unwell, Bob?' I asked.

'I feel better,' he replied, and he smiled. I remembered that he had always been good humoured, and this smile was only a shadow of his real personality. But at least it showed that he recognised me. I pulled him up to a sitting position.

We sat next to each other silently for one or two minutes.

'I feel better,' repeated Bob. You saved me, 'Mr Charlie. Save Mr Bernard too, please!'

'Bernard? Where is he?'

'There,' he cast a look to one direction. 'No! No! There,' he looked now to the opposite direction. 'I don't know! I don't know anything!'

'What is Mr Bernard doing in the Llano Estacado?'

'He wants to go to California. He's travelling with many, many people.'

'What kind of people?'

'Hunters ..., traders ..., I don't know ...'

'Why is he going to California?'

'To his brother, Mr Allan, to San Francisco. He bought lots of gold for Mr Marshall there, but he doesn't need gold anymore as he's dead.'

'Mr Marshall died?' I asked surprised as he was a strong, and healthy man. 'What was the illness?'

'Not illness ..., wicked men murdered Mr Marshall.'

'Who?'

'I don't know ... The sheriff doesn't know ... nobody knows. It happened in the night. He was stabbed in the heart with a knife, and all the money and jewellery were stolen!'

'When did it happen?'

'Five months ago. Mr Bernard became poor, and was alone, because Mr Allan had gone to California earlier. He wrote to Mr Allan, but didn't get an answer.'

I was shocked by this terrible news. The old Marshall was a simple, good, and humorous man. Who would have thought that he would become a victim of a murder! The murderer disappeared with the money and jewellery ... I suddenly remembered the diamonds that I found in Fred Morgan's saddle. Could he have been in Louisville?

'And how come that you are alone here, Bob?' I asked.

'I was tired, my horse was tired, everybody was tired,' he explained. 'I fell off the horse, and the others continued. I was left here!'

'You said the others. How many?'

'Nine.'

'You have a knife, and a sword. Were the others armed?'

'Better than I. With guns and revolvers.'

'And who was their guide?'

'His name is Williams.'

I thought that the company with which Bob had arrived so far, had to be just as tired, and exhausted as we were, because Bernard Marshall would not have abandoned his old, faithful servant. Even if they had gone further, they could not be far. Unfortunately, Bob could not show the direction, but maybe I could find their tracks.

The liquid, the blood of the coyotes, had made a wonder of difference to us. Sam got up, and came over to us. With a few words I told him who Bob was, and what I had learnt from him.

'Listen, Sam,' I continued. 'Stay with the horses. I'll go forward, and look around a bit. But if I don't return in two hours, come after me.'

'As you wish,' replied Sam woozily. 'We will go as far as this coyote juice carries us.'

I searched the ground for the track of the company. The tracks led to the North, and I could read from them that they were at the limit of their strength.

I went for about a mile when I noticed some cacti bushes, and soon I was in a thicket of cacti. Of course, I did not penetrate it, but went around it at the edge. Then I suddenly had an idea that filled me with hope.

Once I had been on the plains of Florida, where it was so hot that the sky appeared to be glowing iron, and the ground glowing lead. Then I saw something interesting. The natives lit the dried out reed, and after the huge fire there was soon rain. I did not know the scientific explanation, but still I could use it. I immediately knelt down by the cacti, and cut one up to thin pieces to make tinder. Soon the fire caught on, and it rushed through the thicket. A few minutes later I stood next to fire-sea whose end went beyond the horizon. I had experienced several prairie fires, but this was something different. The burning cacti produced cracking noises like gun fire, and then as if a whole regiment, with all its weapons, entered a battle. The flames rose to the sky, and the thorns of the cacti flew up like sparks.

I did not know if it was effective, but hoped that the heat of the burning thicket would create some change. I turned around, and headed back. I met Sam and Bob half way.

'What happened, Charlie?' asked Sam pointing to the direction from which I arrived. 'I first thought that it was an earthquake. Then that the sand caught fire.'

The sand can't, but the cacti could, and I made this fire.'

'You made it? Why?'

'To get rain.'

'Rain? I'm sorry, Charlie, but I think you have lost your mind a bit.'

'Then talk to me with some respect,' I said. 'Don't you know, Sam, that the Indians respect the madmen?'

'You don't want to say that you did something clever, do you? The fire only increases the heat.'

'It could have other effects. Electricity, for example,' I replied calmly. 'You may kiss my hand if some thunderstorm and rain arrives!'

'Poor Charlie! You have heat stroke!' said Sam

He looked at me with such anxiety that I could see that he was not joking. I looked up at the sky.

'Can you see the vapour up there? It now starts to concentrate! What would you say if it becomes a cloud?'

'If you really make rain, Charlie, I'll not only kiss your hands, but also your feet! And will announce that you're the cleverest man in the world, and I'm the stupidest.'

'Stop this, Sam. It's not a big deal. I saw it in Florida, and I only imitated their practice. Look how beautiful that cloud is! By the time the fire stops, there'll be rain. If you don't believe me, look at your Tony! Her nostrils are open, and she looks happy. Swallow also smells rain. Come on, let's hurry so that we wouldn't miss it.

We ran, and our horses did not need encouragement. Their instincts chased them to the rain.

My prediction came to truth. Half an hour later the cloud was so big that it covered half of the sky, and five minutes it fell like fists hammering on our bodies! We immediately got as wet as after swimming. The two horses stood motionless. They snorted happily as they enjoyed the refreshing rain. Then they opened their muzzle, and drank the rain, and

594

their strength began to return. Our joy was not less. We collected the rain in stretched blankets, and poured it in our water bags. Bob joyously jumped around it the water.

'How much water! Good water, tasty water! I'm strong again. Does Mr Bernard also get some of this water?'

'If he's not too far from here. But stop talking, and drink! The rain won't be long!'

He held his hat under the rain, and when it was filled, he drank with long sips.

'How great it is! The best water ever!'

However, when he held his hat again to the sky, the rain had stopped. Until then it constantly thundered, but at the moment when the thunder stopped, the rain stopped too. Fortunately we did not need it anymore. We quenched our thirst, and our water-bags were full with this glorious water that we could really appreciate only after such a long thirst.

'Now let's eat,' I proposed to the other two. 'Then we will find Bernard Marshall.'

The lunch lasted only a few minutes. It was dried meat. Then we got on the horses, and rode ahead. Bob was an excellent runner, so he easily kept up with the horses.

Although the rain washed away the tracks, I knew which way they had gone. Soon I saw a carved gourd in the dust. It was probably used instead of a water bag, and then discarded.

The cactus thicket stretched very long from the West to the East, because the burnt ground was still next to us. I was glad for this, because then probably Marshall and his company had the rain too. Eventually the line of burnt bushes stopped, and we caught sight of a group in the distance. I took out my telescope, and saw that nine men and ten horses camped there. Eight men sat on the ground, but the ninth mounted on his horse, and started towards us. I soon recognised Bernard Marshall. He was leading another horse by the reins, and I knew why. In his exhaustion before the rain he did not notice or ignored that Bob had disappeared.

After the refreshing rain his strength and moral sense returned. As soon as he recovered, and his first thing to do was to find his faithful servant. Nobody joined to help him.

When Bernard spotted us, he stopped his horse, and looked towards us suspiciously, then turned back, and waved to his companions, who immediately grabbed their guns, and jumped on their horses.'

'Run to them Bob and tell them who we are!'

Bob ran, while Sam and I comfortably rode after him in steps. We could hear as he was shouting from the distance to Bernard, 'Don't shoot! It's Bob! Don't shoot! I'm bringing good men! Mr Charlie is here!'

Bob's words dissolved their suspicion, and they all waited calmly for us. Bernard held his hand above his eyes, and looked towards me.

'Impossible!' he cried. 'It can't be Charlie!'

In Louisville I certainly looked more like a gentleman, but if one spent a long time on the prairie and had given up on shaving, he could not be surprised if his friends could not recognise him. When I got twenty or thirty steps to him, he rode to us, and offered his hand to me.

'Charlie! It's really you! I thought you were going to Fort Benton, and the high mountains! How did you get here to the South?'

'I've been in the high mountains, Bernard, but I don't like being cold, so I came to the South. Who would have thought that we would meet here, in this damned Estacado! Would you like to introduce me to your company?'

'Of course! I haven't yet recovered from the surprise. I'm glad that we are together again. Come!'

He jumped off his horse, and I followed his example. He introduced me to each of the men, and then he had so many questions that I could hardly keep up with the answers. In the meantime, in secret, I watched his companions. Three of them were traders. It was easy to recognise them, because they held their weapons in a way that it was unlikely that they could use them in trouble. The other five looked more like Westerners. They said they were voyageurs, that is buyers of a large fur company, but my impression of them was different: greedy adventurists, who would not be too concerned using any means to get what they wanted. Their leader introduced himself as Williams. He had a rather patronising manner.

'We know where you've been,' he said, 'now I'm interested where you are going.'

'Maybe El Paso del Norte, or even further depending on how we feel like then,' I replied.

My instinct told me to give this evasive answer, after all, it was none of his business.

'I'm envious,' remarked Williams. 'But what's the purpose of your travel?'

'Nothing special. Seeing the world.'

'That's pleasant and interesting, especially if one doesn't have other duties, and has enough money for the travels.

From your gun I see that you must be quite well-off.'

'I thought that in the Estacado money doesn't matter,'

'You are right, Sir. Half an hour ago I thought I wouldn't see tomorrow if a miracle had not happened.'

'What miracle?'

'The rain, of course. Or you didn't get of it?'

'Why wouldn't we? We made it!'

'What? The rain?'

'Of course! The cloud, the thunder, the lightning, the rain, everything.'

'Listen Loudmouth! Do you think we are people whom you can take for a ride? Or have you been in Great Salt Lake, among the Mormons, and they taught you their miracles?'

'I've been there, but I'm not interested in the Latter Day, only today, and also if you would allow us to join you.'

'With joy! What a question! Why wouldn't we welcome Mr Marshall's acquaintances! But tell me, how were you so brave to come to the Llano Estacado, just two of you?'

Something told me again to pretend to be reckless and inexperienced rather than answering him honestly.

'Why do you say brave?' I asked. 'The road is marked by stakes, one walks in one end, and leaves at the other.'

'Good Lord! What a simpleton! Have you never heard of the stakemen?'

'No! Who are they?'

'You see! Let's not talk about the devil, because he will appear! I can tell you if you were such an experienced hunter like Old Firehand or Old Shatterhand, or crafty and smart as Sans-ear, you wouldn't say such stupid things. Or maybe you've never heard of them!'

'I might have heard these names, but I can't remember,' I replied. 'Tell me, how many days' ride is it to get out the Llano Estacado?'

'Two more days.'

'And are we in the right way?'

'Of course, why do you ask?'

'Because it seems that the stakes pointed to the Southeast so far, and now they turn to South-west.'

'You are imagining it! You can trust an experienced voyageur like me. I know the Llano Estacado like the back of my palm.'

I was happy that my trick worked, and he really thought that I was a simpleton. However, my suspicion also grew. If he was so experienced, he should have noticed the change of the direction. Thus I risked, with apparent naivety, another question, 'How comes that a fur company sends his buyers to the South? I thought that the trappers work in the North.'

'You think you are wiser than you are, my friend. Apart from the many black and grey opossum, we expect a lot of leather from the autumn migration of the bison.'

'I see,' I nodded. 'And you don't have to be afraid of the Indians either, because all tribes like the buyers of the furs. I heard that the identity cards issued by the fur companies are the best passport among Indians as they know the stamp of the companies. If the voyageur has it, the Indians protect, and even welcome him. Is it true or just a legend?'

'Very true! The Indians help us in everything.'

'And have you got such an identity card too?'

'Of course!'

'Oh, how much I'd like to see one! Show me that stamp!'

I noticed that he was embarrassed, and he became angry.

'What do you mean? I can show it only to Indians!'

'And if you have to identify yourself to whites?'

'Then I do it with my gun! Remember this well!'

I went silent as if I had become frightened by the threat. Sam did not even wink at me so as not to betray his thoughts. He understood that we had to be smart. I quickly turned away from Williams, and started to talk to Bernard.

'I heard what happened. Have you found the murderer?'

'Not. But I'm sure that there were more than one.'

'Is Allan still in Frisco?'

'I hope so. He sent his letters from there.'

'Are you continuing your journey or will you camp here?'

'We agreed that we will camp here.'

I took the saddle off from my mustang, and gave him a few handful of maize. Sam did the same. We did not talk to each other. It was not needed anyway as we had spent several weeks with each other, and so we could understand each other from the other's eyes. The rest of the day was spent with indifferent talks.

'Allocate the guards, Sir!' I told Williams when it became dark. 'We are tired and we would like to sleep.'

Williams did, but he made it sure than neither Bernard nor Sam nor I was paired with the voyageurs.

'Sleep among them, so that they can't speak among each other in secret!' I whispered to Marshall, who looked at me surprised, but obeyed the strange order.

People lay down in a circle, and everybody used their saddle as a pillow. I, however, lay down outside the circle, resting my head on the neck of my mustang. Sam, who had understood my intentions, lay down among the voyageurs.

The stars appeared, but maybe because of the rain, there was haze, and it dimmed their light. Two merchants were in the first pair, and their time passed without any event. The next two were Williams and the youngest voyageur. They were still up when their time arrived. They stood up, and started their walk around the camp, each in a half circle. I identified the two points where they met each other. One was near Bob's horse, which was good for me as it was acquainted with me.

From my place I could not see if the two talked to each other when they met, but the years on the prairie made my hearing sharper. From the noise of their steps it seemed to me that before turning, they exchanged a few words. Now I needed to know what they talked about.

With slow, careful motions I crawled to Sam's horse. The good animal did not show that I was approaching. I hid behind it, and stared into the night. Soon I spotted the two guards. Williams was arriving from the right, the young man from the left. Before they turned, I heard the following words, clearly: "You him and I the Nigger!" Williams said. At the next meeting it was him again.

His voice was commanding, 'Yes, the two idiots too, of course.'

This not very flattering remark was obviously about Sam and me. I thought that the young voyageur put his questions at the other meeting point, and Williams answered here. I hearkened even harder. When they arrived again, I heard, 'Come on! One is a midget, and the other is a simpleton. And we'll finish them off in their sleep!'

The midget was Sam, and the simpleton was I. It was clear that they wanted to murder us. I did not know why, but it was enough. Soon they passed by me, and the following command reached my ears: "Of course! All the three!"

The young man obviously asked if the three merchants would be murdered. Thus the five voyageurs prepared to murder their five companions, and Sam and me in addition. They perhaps would have succeeded with it had I not eavesdropped.

I was with villains! At the next turn Williams said, 'Not one minute earlier, but then quickly!'

It seemed that they had agreed on everything, and the last words were about the timing. When would it be? Then I remembered that I had heard earlier: "We'll finish them off in their sleep!". Thus we could expect it during the night. The two bandits had not more than quarter of an hour left of their guarding duty, thus I had to hurry if I wanted to pre-empt their plans.

At the next turn there was no conversation. They turned at the same time to start a new half-circle. At the moment when Williams passed by me, I jumped up, grabbed his neck with my left hand, and I hit his temple with my right fist. He collapsed without a sound.

I stood up and took his place in the half circle. The young voyageur approached unsuspecting, as he believed that Williams was coming. I grabbed his throat from the front, and knocked him out too. I knew that they would be unconscious for ten minutes. I hurried to the sleepers. Two were awake, Sam and Bernard. Sam because he knew I would need him, and Bernard was too excited because of my words earlier.

I took my lasso, and Sam followed my example.

'Only the three voyageurs,' I whispered, and then I shouted. 'Get up men!'

Everybody jumped up, but they were not really awaken when we tied up two of the voyageurs. Bernard Marshall, although he did not know what it was about, instinctively jumped on the third, and held him until we tied him up with his own lasso. All this happened so quickly that we finished by the time one of the merchants gathered his bravery, and snatched for his gun.

'Let's defend ourselves! We are betrayed!' he cried.

'Put it down! You can't shoot with it!' laughed Sam.

The crafty fellow took the cartridge fuse from their guns so that they could not cause any problem. This showed how well we understood each other without words.

'Calm down, gentlemen, we don't want anything from you! Just the opposite; it all happened in your interest. Your

601

companions are bandits, and wanted to kill you during the night, but we intervened.'

Now they really were frightened and joyous at the same time. The tied up prisoners were silent, they probably hoped that the two guards would rescue them.

'Bob!' I called. 'Next to your horse there is William, and at the other end the young voyageur. Bring them here.'

Bob put one of the unconscious bandit on his shoulder, and brought him to the middle of the circle, then he did the same with the other. We immediately tied them up. Now we could talk, and I told the three merchants what I had learnt, and how we had prevented murder. The three merchants angrily demanded the immediate hanging of the bandits.

'No, gentlemen!' I said. 'The prairie has its own laws. Had they attacked us, we could have shot them dead in self-defence. But now it would be murder. We have to organise a jury to make a judgement.'

'That'll do!' exclaimed Bob. 'The jury will sentence them to death, and I'll hang them. All the five!'

'Let's wait till the morning,' I proposed. 'There are seven of us, and if two are on guard, the other five could rest. Of course, in turns.'

At dawn we had our breakfast, the horses got their food, and then we organised the court. Sam pointed at me, and said, 'My friend will be the sheriff.'

'No, Sam, you should be!'

'What do you mean? You can write books, thus you will be the sheriff!'

'But I'm not an American citizen,' I replied. 'You are older, and you've lived on the prairie longer than me. If you don't do it, I'll propose Bob.'

'That's too much of a joke, then I have to do it.'

He lifted his right hand, and said, 'Sit down in a circle, gentlemen. You'll be the jury. Only Bob should stand as he'll be the policeman.'

When everybody took their place, Sam continued, 'The policeman should remove the bondage from the prisoners!

We live in a free country, not even murderers should stand in front of a court tied up.'

'And if they escape?' asked Bob.

'We have guns, and they are unarmed. If they tried, they would have bullets in their heads in ten steps!' stated Sam.

Bob untied the prisoners, and lined them up in front of the jury.

'You, said Sam, starting the investigation,' call yourself Williams. What's your real name?'

'I won't answer!' said the accused stubbornly. 'You have no right to question us. You attacked us, and you should be put on trial!'

'Just jabber on, son!' replied Sam. 'You won't deter us. If you don't answer my questions, I will consider your silence as "yes". Now, let's start! Are you really voyageurs?'

'Yes.'

'Prove it! Where's your identify card?'

'I haven't got one.'

'I thought so. Tell me what did you talk about with your fellow bandit while you were on guarding duty?'

'Nothing. Not a word.'

'This gentleman heard what you talked about. You aren't voyageurs, or hunters. A true hunter wouldn't plan such a debased act, and if he did, he would have done it better.'

'What do you want from us? We didn't hurt anyone! You greenhorns attacked us, and now you are playing court?'

'Lower your voice, rascal,' snapped Sam at him. 'Do you know who knocked both of you out during the night? You could have found it out that it couldn't be anybody else, but Old Shatterhand! And I'm Sans-ear, whose ears were cut off by the Navajo, and I always repay everything with interest!'

The two names created a shock and astonishment. The bandits stared at the ground frightened. Williams was the only one, who did not lose his head, moreover he became more hopeful.

'If you really are those, you cannot be unjust!' he shouted insolently. 'You asked my name before. I can tell you that

I'm not Williams. So what? It's not a sin here in America, where everybody can choose his name as he wants. Your real names aren't Old Shatterhand or Sans-ear!'

'The name is irrelevant! We have charged you with something very different!' replied Sam.

'What? Murder? Did we murder or did we try to murder someone?'

'You didn't try it, but planned it! You discussed it during the night!'

'Yes, we exchanged some words, I admit,' said Williams. 'But how do you know we talked about you? Did we say names?'

'You didn't. But it was easy to deduce it!' said Sam after some angry musing.

'Deduce! That's not evidence. Ridiculous! You can't make judgement on this basis! Or you'll kill innocent people! It will be talked about from the Mississippi to the Rocky Mountain, from the Slave River to the Mexican Gulf.'

I had to admit that the rascal defended himself well. He rolled over Sam with his arguments.

'May the devil take you!' said Sam jumping up. 'I don't care if the jury lets you go! There are enough bandits about, a few more won't make a difference.'

Also the merchants did not insist on the punishment of the accused men. They could have had evil intentions, but it was not enough for a punishment.

'They can go to hell,' said Bernard too. 'Williams is right, suspicion or assumption are not evidence.'

Only Bob's face showed deep disappointment. He could not understand that we would let these villains go freely. His hand was itching to hang them. As far as I was concerned, I did not have an objection to such a turn. I had insisted on the postponement of the judgement to the morning so that everybody would calm down. On the prairie one had to be prepared that somebody would attack him. These five men were obviously bandits, but whatever they had planned, they had not attacked anyone. I was not led by revenge, I was more interested in my friends' safety, and the rest did not interest me. Of course, I was a bit peeved that Williams so easily rolled the "sheriff" over. Sam was an excellent hunter; he was brave, skilful, enduring, and crafty, but he did not know how to cross examine someone. I could not resist to tease him a bit.

'I don't think that there's a meeker sheriff than you, Sam,' I told him.

'What can I do?' he replied. 'I'm not a lawyer! Don't you agree with letting them go?'

'I accept it about the murder attempt. But there is something else. Listen, Williams! I have one question, but be careful with the answer, because your fate depends on it. What direction is the quickest way to get to the Pecos River?'

'Straight to the West. It will take two days.'

'Yesterday I talked to you as if I hadn't known that there are bandits who lure the travellers to the depth of the Llano. I can tell you now that I suspected that you belonged to the stakemen already in the first moment we met. I'll let you go only when we arrive to the Pecos River without any trouble. Until then you are our prisoners. Tie them to the horses, and let's go!'

'Very good!' said Bob happily. 'If we can't find the river, I'll hang them all.'

A quarter of an hour later we were already on the way. The prisoners were kept in the middle of the column. Bob did not move from the prisoners, and kept his eyes on them. He obviously did not give up his role as a policeman. I rode in the front with Bernard and Sam at the back.

The conversation between me and Marshall was first about the events of the previous day, but I refused to go too deeply in it. Finally he understood it, and changed the subject.

'Is it true what Sans-ear said that you made the rain?'

'Yes.'

'It's unbelievable, although I know that you are telling the truth.'

'I made the rain in order to save our lives and yours.'

I explained how it was done, and then changed the subject of the conversation again.

'What was the name of the supposed voyageur, who was the guard with Williams?'

'He called himself Mercroft,' replied Bernard.

'He's the youngest of them, and also the most suspicious. His face, even if it's young, doesn't promise anything good. He reminds me to somebody, but I don't know who. A villain. His name is not real either.'

We rode silently next to each other, and only then did I ask Bernard how his father had lost his life.

'Allan wasn't at home by then,' replied Bernard. 'He went to San Francisco on business. Apart from myself and my father, only Bob and the cook lived in our house. As you know, my father enjoyed company, and went out almost every evening. One morning we found him murdered. My father had a key that opened all the doors of the house, and the workshop, where the valuable things were kept. When he was murdered, the key was taken from him, and they robbed the workshop and the office.'

'Was anybody suspected?'

'Only one of the employees knew about the key, but not even the police got anywhere with him. They had to let him go. Most of the stolen jewellery wasn't ours, but brought for repair or as a deposit. Of course, I compensated our clients, this made me bankrupt. I had just enough money to travel to California to discuss the situation with my brother. We used to correspond frequently, but I haven't had a letter from him for some time.'

'Is there no hope that the murderers would be captured, and you would be compensated at least to some extent?'

'No! I put some advertisements in the most important newspapers both in the USA, and in Europe with the exact description of the jewels, but nothing came from it.'

'I'd like to see such an advert,' I said.

'You can, because the Morning Herald is always with me.'

He gave me the newspaper. I studied it while riding, folded it up and gave it back to him.

'What would you say if I could name the murderers or at least one of them?'

'How comes, Charlie?' he asked surprised.

'And what would you say,' I continued, 'if I could help you to recover some of your losses?'

'What joke is it, Charlie? You were on the prairie when the murder happened. How could you help me?'

Without saying a word I took two bags out, and gave them to him.

His hands were shaking when he opened the bag. In the next moment he exclaimed, 'Good Lord! But these are ...'

'Quiet!' I warned him quietly, but sternly. 'It's quite unnecessary for those behind us to know what we are talking about. If these came from your father's workshop, put them away, and don't show your joy!'

It was difficult for Bernard, because he was in such a joy. I shared his feelings, but I also felt sorry for his father who had been murdered for these accursed stones, and could not be brought back to life.

'Where did you get these diamonds, Charlie? Tell me!'

'It's not a joy to talk about it,' I replied. 'The murderer was almost in my hand, but he got away. I kicked him off from the locomotive, and Sam also couldn't catch him. But I hope I'll meet him at the Pecos River. Because he's heading there for another crime.'

'Who is he? How did you come across him?'

I told him everything, the Oglala's attack against the train, the white bandit who planned it, the stampede, the clearance, and the bandit's horse. Finally I showed him the letter that Patrick wrote to Fred Morgan.

'Then he's the murderer!' exclaimed Bernard.

I had to quieten him again. It took him time until he collected himself and we continued the talking quietly.

'Do you know that these diamonds are worth a fortune?' asked Bernard.

607

'I suspected it,' I answered.

'And you give them to me, without any reward?'

'Of course, it belongs to you!'

'Charlie, you are an exceptional man! But I don't want to abuse your goodwill,' said Bernard, and untied one of the bags again. He took out the largest diamond. 'Take this, at least, as a souvenir from me!'

'I won't! Put it back right now! Remember that you didn't lose only the diamonds in this, but your father too. I'd accept some souvenir from you, but not this. Something that is dear to you, and thus will be dear to me too, but not something very expensive! Now stay here in the front, I have to talk to Sam.'

I waited until the group passed me, and then joined Sam.

'What was that big negotiation, Charlie?' he asked. 'It had to be exciting, because you both gesticulated a lot. You beat the poor air dead.'

'Do you know who murdered Bernard's father?'

'I don't! Do you?'

'I know it. Fred Morgan.'

'Impossible. Morgan is a rascal of whom I can assume anything, but he has been in the prairie for a very long time. He couldn't be in the East and the West at the same time. How would he get to Louisville?'

'I don't know. But those diamonds that I found in the saddle belonged to Marshall. I gave them back to him.'

'I would have done the same. So, his father is also Fred Morgan's victim. One more reason to capture him. I'd really like to make the two remaining notches on my gun!'

'I hope it'll happen soon. What will you do after that?'

'I came here, to the South, only because of Morgan. I would have gone all the way to Mexico or Brazil if I had to. When I have finished with him, I'm free. Maybe I'll go to California, I have heard many interesting things about it.'

'If you go that way, we can go together. I don't have any urgent affairs either, so I thought I'd go with Bernard to San Francisco.'

'Agreed,' nodded Sam. 'If we could get rid of these five! I dislike the youngest the most. My hand is itching whenever I look at his insolent face.'

We continued our journey all day undisturbed. In the evening we settled, chewed some dried meat, and then went to sleep. We tied the prisoners up for the night, and set up a guard for them. Early morning we continued our travel. At noon we noticed that the landscape started to change. The cacti were less dry, and there was some grass here and there that the horses tried to graze. Soon we arrived to a meadow. We tied the horses to a short rope so that they would not be able to graze too much, and get bloated. Now we were sure that we would get to water soon, and became less sparing with our water bags.

While I was contented that the frightening desert was behind us, Williams addressed me, 'Now you believe me, Sir, that we said the truth? We led you out from the Llano Estacado, didn't we?'

'It looks like.'

'Then keep your promise, and give back our horses and weapons. We didn't hurt you, and you have no reason to keep us as prisoners.'

'I can't make the decision alone,' I replied. 'I'll discuss it with the others.'

I gathered Sam, Bernard, Bob, and the three merchants.

'Gentlemen,' I told them, 'we are out of the desert, and we aren't dependent on each other anymore. The question is your plans. Where are you going to?' I asked the three merchants.

'We go to El Paso del Norte,' they replied. 'And you?'

'We go to Santa Fe,' I replied without hesitation. 'Thus we will part from each other. The only thing we have to decide is what we do with our prisoners.'

We agreed that we would release them. The merchants proposed that we should not wait with it for another day. I did not protest, thus we gave them their weapons, and belongings. I asked them where they were heading to, and

Williams said that they would follow the Pecos River to the valley of the Rio Grande, where they wanted to hunt bison. They rode away. The merchants waited half an hour, and then they said good-bye. Soon both groups disappeared on the horizon. We looked after them musing.

'Well, Charlie?' asked Sam, breaking the silence.

'You mean what do I think?' I asked. 'That they won't go to the Rio Grande. They'll ride in a big arc to block our way to Santa Fe.'

'I thought the same. I praised your brain in myself that you said that we were heading to Santa Fe. Thank God, we have nothing to do there. I'd like to know if we should wait here, or continue our journey.'

'I vote for staying,' I replied. 'I don't think that our horses have rested enough after the tiring ride. Let's stay here for the night.'

'It would be good,' said Bernard, 'but I'm afraid they'll return as soon as it's dark to attack us.'

'Even better as we could settle the bill with them,' I opined. 'But I'll go out scouting. You stay here, and wait for me. By the time it's dark, hopefully I'll be back.'

I did not listen to Sam's arguments, but got on my horse, and rode away. I first followed the merchants' tracks to the South-west. The three went to the same direction, but then they turned right to the South.

Swallow was fresh, and in half an hour I caught sight of the voyageurs. It seemed that their journey was not urgent, because they rode very comfortably. I knew that they did not have a telescope, so if I stayed at the right distance, they could not see me, while I could watch them.

To my surprise one of the riders separated from the rest, and galloped to the West. I turned my telescope there, and caught sight of a thicket that stretched into the prairie. What was I to do? Whom did I have to follow? The four or the one? My instinct suggested that the latter had some evil plan, and thus I would have to check it. I had nothing to do with the other four. We had let them go, and they went on their way. But what did the fifth want? After a short hesitation I started to follow him.

After about three quarters of an hour I watched as he disappeared among the bushes. Now I really galloped on my mustang, and in a large arc got behind the bushes so that he would not see me if he turned back. I entered the thicket not where he disappeared, but further away from there, and soon I got to a clearance that was surrounded by lush, green bushes. There had to be a spring there, and I found it. I jumped off from my horse, and tied it so that it could also drink to its liking. I also drank from the excellent, cold water of the spring, and then made a few steps to the direction where I expected to find the rider.

Examining the ground, to my surprise, I found a lot of tracks as if a lot of riders had been there. Their tracks had made a whole path to the spring. It was possible that the path was watched. I crawled through the thicket, parallel with the path until I stopped because I heard a snorting. I wanted to put out my head among the branches to check where the horse was, but I immediately withdrew, because at this point I also noticed the guard who lay among the bushes, and watched the path. There had to be a larger camp nearby.

Fortunately the guard did not see me. I retreated, and continued my scouting a bit further away. In ten minutes I came to understand the terrain. The path led to a bigger clearance whose centre was covered with bushes. The bushes were overgrown with so much wild hops that nobody could see through them. I heard the snorting of the horse from there. Lying low at the edge of the clearance I was listening, and I could hear a man. He was talking to someone. There were some men behind the bushes.

I decided that I would get closer. It was dangerous, but I risked it. With a few leaps I jumped over the clearance that was only a ring around the thicket. There the bushes were intertwined so much that it was impossible to climb in.

Finally I found an opening where I could sneak through. Now I could see into the thicket properly. Behind the bushes there was another round clearance whose diameter was about sixty yards. It had probably been a thicket too, but it was cleared. I saw eighteen horses, and seventeen men who were sitting or lying around the horses. I also saw many things, all kinds of stocks covered by bison leather. I had the impression that I had arrived to the bandit's site where they kept the loot.

One man was talking. I immediately recognised that it was Williams. So it was he who parted with the rest. He was reporting on his adventures. I could hear every word.

'Of the two, one apparently eavesdropped, because I felt that I was hit, and stretched out. Then ...'

'Why didn't you notice him earlier?' asked another man sternly. 'Because you are a useless donkey! They watched, and listened to you, as if you were a greenhorn!'

'Don't be so stern, *capitano*!' said Williams. 'If you knew who it was, you wouldn't be so surprised!'

'What? Do you want a bullet? You were knocked out with one blow! You simpleton!'

The veins swelled up on Williams's forehead. 'You know very well that I'm not afraid of my own shadow. The man who knocked me out would have done the same to you.'

The leader of the gang laughed mockingly.

'Don't jabber!' he shouted at Williams. 'Continue!'

'The other guard was Patrick, who used the name of Mercroft. He was knocked out too.'

'What? The bull-head? And what happened after then?'

Williams related all the events up to their release.

'I'll whip you, you dog!' raged the head of the gang. 'You were tied up! You may even have kissed the hands of those two tramps.'

'They weren't tramps, *capitano*! If they entered here with a gun, and a knife in their hands, I wouldn't be the only one who was anxious. Do you know who knocked me out? Do you know who the people were who were introduced as Charlie and Sam? One was Old Shatterhand, and the other Sans-ear!'

'You're lying! You only want to excuse your cowardice!'

'Stab me, *capitano*! You'll see that my eyes won't finch!'

'So you are telling the truth?'

'You can be sure!'

'*Per todos los santos*! Then they will die with the other two, otherwise they wouldn't rest until they finish us off!'

'They don't care with us! I heard when they said that they were going to Santa Fe.'

'Shut up! You are stupider than I thought! Do you think that they revealed their destination to you? There's more craftiness in their little finger than in your head! I wouldn't be surprised if they had followed you. Maybe one is hiding in these bushes, and listens to us.'

I have to admit I felt the heat hearing these words.

'I know these brave prairie hunters,' continued the leader of the gang. 'I stayed with Florimont, who's also called Track Sniffer, for a whole year. I learnt a lot of tricks from him. You can cut off my head if they are going to Santa Fe. I bet they haven't yet left their camp. They know that they would find your tracks tomorrow morning, and can pursue you with renewed energy. I heard that this Shatterhand has such a gun with which he can shoot for a week without charging. He sold his soul to the devil, and got this gun in exchange. We have to attack them tonight. Can you find the way back?'

'Of course,' replied Williams.

'Then be ready! We have to be there by midnight. We will go on foot, and surprise them. Not one of them can survive!'

On the one hand the *capitano* underestimated us, on the other hand he believed every legend that had been said about us. In this respect the prairie was similar to the gossips of the towns: overstatement was rife. We, could stand up for ourselves, and could compete with anyone in terms of bravery, endurance, and tricks. But these qualities were not talked about by the campfires. My rifle, with which I could shoot twenty-five times without loading, became the devil's present! I had to smile to myself

'Where has Patrick gone with the others?' asked the head of the gang.

'Towards Head Peak, where he's meeting his father. On the way he'll finish off the three merchants, who have a lot of money, and excellent weapons.'

'And will he send the loot here?'

'Naturally. He will send it with two men, and he takes the third with him.'

At that moment I heard the barking of the prairie dog nearby. It was a badly chosen signal as there were no prairie dogs in this area.

'Antonio is bringing the stakes,' remarked the leader of the gang. 'Tell him to bring them here. As long as those hunters are alive, we must be very careful.'

These words reinforced my suspicion that we faced with the well-organised gang of stakemen, and this was their hiding place, the cache of their loot.

The bushes opened just opposite me. Three riders appeared under the lifted trailing vegetation. They pulled a large pile of stakes that were hooked on straps on the two sides of their horses, that is, in the same way as the Indians transported their tents.

Their arrival attracted so much attention from the gang that I had the opportunity to retreat. However, I could not resist to take s souvenir.

The leader of the gang put his broad belt in the grass. It was so close to me that I could reach it with my outstretched hand. Apart from his Bowie knife, there were two double-barrelled pistols in it, richly decorated with copper. I waited until he turned away, and then took one of the pistols.

Now I really had to retreat. Very slowly, removing my tracks on the way, I crawled out of the bush. I succeeded in crossing the barren ring without being noticed. I got to the outer thicket. Leaning on my toes and fingers, I continued the withdrawal until I was far enough away to stand up. From there I ran to my mustang. Making a big detour, I rode back to our camp.

It was quite dark when I arrived. I could see from my companions' faces how anxious they were for me, and how impatient they were.

'Mr Charlie arrived!' exclaimed Bob happily. 'It's so good! I was so anxious!'

'What's the news?' asked Sam.

'They murdered the three merchants.'

'I'm not surprised. What else?'

'I know now who this Mercroft is.'

'I thought that it wasn't his real name,' shrugged Sam.

'His real name …is Patrick Morgan.'

'Pat … rick … Mor … gan!' stuttered Sam in complete shock. 'God! What an ass I am! The damned bastard was in my hands, and I let him go! I told you that I'm not good to be the sheriff!'

'Now I understand why he looked so familiar,' I said.

'Yes, I do too. But it's too late!' groaned Sam.

'But he's heading to the Head Peak to meet his father,' I said trying to calm him

'I'll catch him at Head Peak then! Let's go now!'

'Wait Sam! I forgot to tell you that there will be guests tonight. Should we wait for them?'

'Guests? Who?'

'Patrick is a member of a gang. Their camp is where I've been until now. Their leader is a Mexican whom they call *capitano*. He worked with the old Florimont, thus he had a good school. I was there when Williams made his report. They decided that they would attack us at midnight.'

'Do they think that we spend the night here?'

'They do.'

'I don't mind it, let them enjoy it!' said Sam. 'We'll make sure that there will be a reception. How many are they?'

'Twenty-one.'

'Huh. Quite a few. Twenty-one guests and four hosts. You know what? We'll make a big fire, and put coats around it as if were sleeping. We will hide a bit further away, and they'll be by the fire, so they will become excellent targets.'

'Excellent plan!' enthused Bernard Marshall.

'Then I'm going to gather wood,' said Sam.

'Stay!' I cried out to him. 'Do you think that you can sort out twenty-one men with this trick?'

'Why not? After the first shots they'll lose their head, and they will run away.'

'And if they figure out our plan, and counterattack?'

'Well, there are all kinds of dangers in a hunter's life.'

'If you lose, how will you find the two Morgans?'

'You are right! Then what do you think? Should we escape, Charlie, and let these stakemen continue their crimes? Give them the Llano Estacado?'

'Not at all! I have a plan that could be better than yours.'

'Let's hear it!'

'While they visit us, we'll visit their camp, and take their horses with all their loots, and stocks.'

'Will they leave their horses there?'

'Yes. The *capitano* ordered that the gang should come on foot here. Thus they would have to leave at ten o'clock to get here by midnight.'

'Did you hear it well?'

'Like you now! If we wait for them here, we are risking our life. If we take their horses and stocks, they are finished.'

'You're very clever, Charlie! Let's try it! But then we have to go soon.'

'It's already dark. We can leave in fifteen minutes,' I replied.

After a quarter of an hour it was so dark that one could see only as far as ten steps. We set off. I rode in front, the others followed me in a file as Indians do. We approached their camp in a big arc. At about a mile beyond our goal we stopped in the thicket, and left our horses there. We then approached the place on foot. Although Marshall and Bob did not have experience in such a stalking, we arrived to the edge of the clearance, opposite the path where the guard had lay in the afternoon.

616

There was some light behind the ring showing that there was a campfire or at least a torch there, but around us it was so dark that we could easily get to the place where I had eavesdropped earlier. I just stooped down when I could hear the voice of the head of the gang. I pushed forward, and saw that the whole gang was ready in the middle of the clearance. The *capitano* was speaking, 'If there had been the slightest track, I would have thought that one of the two famous hunters had been here, and heard us. Where could that pistol be? Maybe I lost it in the morning, and did not notice it when I put my belt down? Damn it! Are you sure Hoblin that you saw all the four together?

'Yes they sat next to each other, and their horses grazed nearby. One of the horses doesn't have a tail. It looks like a goat without horns!'

'I know. Sans-ear's mare is just as famous as her master. I hope they didn't notice you.'

'No. Williams and I got off the horses far enough, and crawled forward until we could see them.'

Old Florimont's apprentice thus sent out scouts before the attack. Fortunately the two scouts arrived after I had returned.

'Then it's fine. Williams, you must be tired. Stay with the horses. You, Hoblin, will guard the path. The rest will come with me!'

In the light of the fire I could see how they opened the entrance, and the nineteen men left. By the time they had disappeared from view, I was next to Sam.

'What's up, Charlie? I think they have gone.'

'Yes, except for two. There's a guard on the path with a gun. Williams is next to the fire, but he doesn't have his gun near him. Let's not move for a while because one of the bandits may come back if he had forgotten something. When everything is quiet, we will start.'

We waited for a quarter of an hour, and then I gave the commands in a whisper, 'Sam, you come with me. You two stay here until we call you.'

Sam and I crept to the path, and watched the guard. He walked so calmly and comfortably up and down which showed that he felt secure. When he turned his back on us, I went to the other side of the path, while Sam, understanding my intention, stayed. We waited until the guard walked between two of us. Then Sam grabbed his throat, and I gagged him. In a minute he was tied up with his own lasso.

'Now, let's get the other.'

We went to the entrance where I pushed the wild hops aside a bit. Williams sat by the fire. He was frying a piece of meat. He sat with his back to us. I could get very close to him without being noticed.

'Keep the meat higher, Williams, lest it will burn,' I said.

Williams turned around very quickly, then looked at me paralysed by fear.

'Good evening,' I continued. 'I'm sorry I almost forgot to say hello.'

'O … O … Old Shat … Shatterhand!' he stuttered, and his eyes goggled. 'What do you want?'

'I only brought back the *capitano's* pistol that I accidentally took in the afternoon, when you reported to him.'

He pulled up his knee as if he wanted to jump up. He looked for his gun, but only his knife was near.

'Just sit calmly, because the smallest motion could cost you your life! Don't forget that the *capitano's* pistol is loaded, and if you look in the direction of the entrance, you will see that you can get a couple of bullets in your head from that direction also.'

'Damn! Then I'm finished!'

'You have some hope if you obey,' I replied. 'Bernard! Bob! Come here!'

The two arrived immediately.

'Bob! Bring the lasso from his saddle, and tie him up!'

'Damn! You won't tie me up again alive!' he exclaimed, and stabbed his Bowie knife into his heart.

'There! He went headlong to hell!' I remarked, and shook my head.

'He belongs there!' replied Sam. 'He must have murdered or helped to murder at least a hundred innocent men.'

Then I ordered Bob to bring over Hoblin. When he did, we took the gag from the bandit's mouth. He breathed heavily. Only after then he noticed his accomplice's body. His face became distorted from fright.

'You will also die if you don't answer to my questions!' I shouted at him.

'I'll do everything you want!' said the frightened bandit.

'Where's the hidden gold?' I asked, guessing.

'We hid it behind the flour bags.'

We lifted the bison skins and checked their cache.

There were stocks of everything that had even been transported across the Estacado: all kinds of weapons, lead, ammunition, gun powder, lassos, saddles, blankets, trapper suits, woollen and calico material rolls, fake corral necklaces, glass beads, tools, pemmican in large boxes, and other food stuff. It was obvious that all these were loots from robberies.

Bob lifted, and threw the bags out of the cache. Soon we found a lot of gold dust, and nuggets. I was horrified by the thought of the victims, whose fates had been sealed by the "deadly dust". The prospectors usually took bank notes, banker's drafts, and certificates of deposit with them. Where were these?

'And where is all the looted money?' I asked Hoblin.

'It has a separate cache, far from here,' he replied. 'The *capitano* hid it elsewhere, because he did not trust all the members of the gang.'

'Is it only he who knows the cache?'

'He and our lieutenant.'

'Who's your lieutenant?'

'Patrick Morgan.'

I suddenly remembered some words of Patrick's letter. "An even bigger loot"! Why did the villain write it to his father? Did he want to rob his accomplices?

'Do you know anything about that cache?'

'Only that the *capitano* doesn't trust the lieutenant who left with one men to the Pecos River, towards Head Peak. I was ordered to follow him with two men tomorrow.'

'Aha! Then the *capitano* gave you exact instructions, didn't he?'

Hoblin became confused, and remained silent.

'If you don't speak or mislead me, you can say good-bye to your wretched life! But if you speak honestly, I'll pardon you, although we should execute you.'

'Question me, Sir!'

'Where's the place?'

'It's a little valley that I know well because I have been there before. But you won't find it alone. I was ordered to go there, and shoot the lieutenant dead if I find him there.'

'Did he tell you only the valley or the exact place?'

'Only the valley. The *capitano* wouldn't tell it to anyone.'

'Right! If you lead us to that valley, you will be pardoned.'

'I will.'

'You'll be released only if I'm convinced that you didn't mislead us. Until then you are a prisoner.'

'What do we do with all these?' asked Sam.

'We will take the gold,' I replied. 'Of the rest only what we need, some weapons, ammunition, tobacco, and food. Gather these things, and in the meantime I'll check the horses.'

I chose four bony horses appropriate as pack horses, and three mustangs. These were better than Bernard's and Bob's horses. I gave them two. The third was for Hoblin.

We wrapped the things that we wanted to take with us in blankets. We put together eight packages, two for each pack horse. We piled up the rest of the stuff, and then mixed gun powder in it.

'What should we do with the other horses?'

'Bob will chase them to the prairie. It would be wiser to kill them, but I can't bring myself to do that. You' will lead. I'll stay behind, and put the loot to the fire.'

'Why not now?' asked Marshall curiously.

'Because the gang may come back earlier than we expect them, and if they see the fire from the distance, they'll chase us. Thus I want to leave this to the last moment. When you are far enough, I'll do it, and gallop after you,'

'Then let's go!' said Sam giving the order.

He rode away leading one of the pack horses by the reins. The other three pack horses followed them cleverly. At the back Marshall and Bob rode keeping Hoblin, who was tied to his horse, between them. I waited for a quarter of an hour and then carefully put the loot to the fire. I cut up a blanket to strips and made a kind of fuse from them. Using this fuse, I was far enough from the gun powder when I lit it. The gun powder exploded. There were bullets in the pile, these also exploded. This noise was the farewell of the Estacado. The flames rose high, and devoured the loot of the stakemen stained by a lot of blood and tears.

AMONG THE COMANCHE

OUR JOURNEY led us through a romantic landscape where Texas, Arizona and New Mexico met. The tributary rivers of the Rio Grande cut through the mountains, and they created valleys. The mountain ranges, the southern end of the Rocky Mountains, raised the thought in me that once giants had lived there, and even they tottered about helplessly in these huge Labyrinths. The mountain sides, covered with dark forests, heightened into sky-reaching, barren cliffs; the slightly sloping valleys entered gorges with vertical cliffs on both sides. The mountains were cut through by canyons whose bottom the Sun never reached. The mountain tops, and the cliff terraces were so varied as if a fantasy-rich artist had devised them.

How empty and deserted was this wonderful landscape. From the silence I imagined that one would never meet a human or an animal here, and at the higher points, not even a plant. But it was not true. The wind took the pollen from the legs of the cliffs, and on the plateau wild flowers bloomed. Black and grey bears wandered around the cliffs. The migration of thousands and thousands of bison broke the silence of the forest in springs.

There were also humans there sometimes. A hunter with a gun on his shoulder; a strong trapper with his traps on his back; an escapee who fled there; sometimes an Apache or Comanche as this forest was their last refuge. The Indians were in war with the world that wanted to destroy them. This deserted area was a battlefield for survival. The mountains are formed in such a way that if an enemy appeared, one could not avoid him unless he was without a horse, but being without a horse meant death.

One more day was needed, and we would reach the valley of the Pecos River. When I had ridden along it for the first time, we were a large group, and we were safe. Now there were only four of us, and the prisoner. He did not make us stronger, just the opposite, as we had to guard him. Hoblin rode freely in the day, but he was tied up in the night.

It was a beautiful morning. The Sun gilded the tops of the mountains on the other side of the river. It was mid-August, and we enjoyed the Sun's rays as the nights were cold in the mountains, and the dawns were so humid that we did not feel like getting out of the blankets.

'Is that peak far?' asked Marshall.

'Head Peak? We'll get there tomorrow except if we turn to the right to the cache where Hoblin leads us.'

'Wouldn't it better to go first to the peak where we could catch Fred Morgan?'

'We will find him tomorrow, because he was to meet his son in the middle of August, and today is the 14th. We can find Patrick today. I think he's only a few hours ahead of us.'

'Look out!' exclaimed Sam. 'That branch on the ground at the edge of the forest! It was broken off not long ago.'

'You are right,' I replied. 'We may find footprints as well.'

After some examination we identified the tracks of two riders. They led to the forest. Suddenly Sam, who was in front, stopped. The ground was disturbed there. It seemed that somebody was digging there, and then covered the marks with moss. Sam leant forward, and picked up the moss directly in front of him.

'A print of a pick axe!' he cried.

'You are right!' I replied. 'There was a pick axe here.'

'But it was taken. Why was it here and why was it taken?'

'This is easy,' I said. 'When the *capitano* buried the treasure with the lieutenant, after a while they had enough of carrying the tool. Thus they buried it, but marked the place as it was their intention to come back for the fortune, and then they would have needed the pick axe.'

I put back the moss as it was, and then I examined the trees nearby. I did not have to look long. On the right and the left of the path there were two trees opposite each other. There were symbols engraved in them with a knife, and the bottom branches of the trees were torn off.

'Patrick was here,' said Sam. 'The question is: did he go to the valley first, or to meet his father.'

'We can find it out easily,' I said, and asked Hoblin, 'How far is the place where the path turns to the valley?'

'About two hours from here if I remember right.'

'So, if he goes this way, he's heading for the cache. If he diverts, he's going to meet his father first. So let's ride, but carefully. Or even better, we should rest a bit as we are too close to the bandits. I don't want them to catch sight of us.'

'Right, Charlie. Let's move the horses to the forest, and eat something, because I'm really hungry.'

We sat down in the soft moss. We had been sitting there for a few minutes only, when Hoblin exclaimed, and pointed towards the river.

'Look at the other side of the river! I'm sure that I saw something gleaming at the edge of the gorge. Was it the tip of a lance?'

'Impossible!' opined Sam. 'One cannot see such a small thing from this distance.'

'It is possible, Sam, if the rays of the Sun reflect from them,' I replied. 'If they are Indians, we are very lucky that we have retreated into the forest.'

I took out my telescope. What I saw made me anxious.

'Indians! A lot of them! At least a hundred and fifty!'

Sam took the telescope from me, looked in it, and then passed it to Bernard.

'Look at it, Mr Marshall! It's probably the first time in your life that you see Comanche.'

'Are you sure that they are Comanche?'

'They could be Apache, but they tie their hair differently. Can you see those blue and red stripes on their faces? They are on the warpath. They sharpened their spears, this why they are so bright. I bet that they have some poison arrows in their quivers too. What do you think, Charlie, if they cross the river, will they find us?'

'They will. We were careless when we didn't remove our tracks,' I replied. 'We even left broken branches.'

'We could probably still do something about it,' said Sam.

'I'll try,' I replied.

There was a small pine tree next to me. I cut it off, and pulled it back to the edge of the forest. I also collected a few handfuls of needles, and threw them on the tracks where we turned into the forest.

'It may help, Sam.'

'This? It wouldn't trick me.'

'Why not?'

'Since when does the maple tree drop pine needles?'

I looked up. Indeed there was a maple tree above the tracks. But I did not have time to think about it, because the Indians took up all of my attention. They had stopped at the bottom of the gorge, and sent out scouts.

'Thank God, they won't come in this way!' said Sam.

'How do you know it?' asked Bernard.

'Tell him, Charlie; he's your friend.'

'Look, Bernard! They sent out three men. Two ride on the edge of the gorge, along the river, and the third went down to the water. If they wanted to cross the river upstream, they would be interested in the other direction. The two riders in front scout for the enemy, while the third is looking for a ford.'

The scouts soon returned, and the whole group started off towards the water. By naked eye we could count them, and we could see that we had underestimated their numbers. They were probably from two villages, because there were two chiefs at the front.

'I always thought chiefs ride on a white horse,' remarked Bernard.

'Never! Not even on a grey one!' said Sam. 'The Indians don't like light coloured horses, because they frighten away the game, and such colours are even worse in war.'

'Yes,' I continued Sam's remark, 'the only time they use white horses is in the winter, but if they don't have white horses, they put white blankets on them. I tried this method when hunting with a reasonable success.'

In the meantime the Indians entered the river at a place where it very fast. They crossed with hard swimming so that they would not to be swirled downstream too much. They then continued their journey downstream. We watched it relieved.

'What will happen to Patrick if he meets the Comanche?' asked Sam.

'Nothing,' said Hoblin.

'Why?'

'Because these belong to the Comanche band with whom the *capitano* smoked the peace pipe.'

I put my head out from the branches. The Comanche had disappeared by the bend of the river. I turned to the opposite direction to see what was happening upstream, but in the next moment I pulled back my head quickly. Sam noticed it, and asked, 'What's that? Did you see Indians that way too? '

'Unfortunately,' I replied. 'I saw at least one.' Sam picked up my telescope.

'Yes,' he said, 'One Indian. But he's different from the others. I think he's an Apache.'

'Really?'

'Yes, and a chief! He has long hair.'

'Give me that telescope!'

I took it from his hand, but I was too late, the Indian was covered by a small hillock on this side of the river.

'You know what's going on here, Charlie?' Sam said. 'The Comanche are chased by the Apache, and the Apache chief has gone ahead to scout. He has to pass by us. It's better if you clip the nostrils of your horses, because they snort when an Indian is approaching. My horse has more brain. But now we must be quiet.'

In five minutes we could clearly hear the noise of the hooves of an approaching horse. Then the noise stopped suddenly. Did the Indian recognise our tracks? Through the bushes I saw that he glanced at the needles on the ground, and he grabbed his tomahawk.

'Shoot, Charlie!' said Sam.

Instead of shooting I jumped out of the bush. The Indian raised his muscular arm to hit me.

'Winnetou! Do you want to kill your white brother?' He let his arm drop, and his dark eyes flashed.

'Charlie!' he exclaimed with joy forgetting the reserved behaviour of the Indians. In the next moment we were embracing each other. I was overfilled with joy because of this unexpected meeting.

'What are you doing, my Apache brother, at this section of the Pecos River?'

'The Comanche dogs bare their teeth to the Apache warriors,' he said, as he put away his tomahawk. 'I had to see what they were doing. But what are you doing here, my white brother, in this valley? Many moons have been swallowed since I saw you last. You told me then that you would cross the Great Water to visit your father, and then you would visit the big desert that is more frightening than the Mapimi or the Estacado!'

'These have all happened, Winnetou. I visited my father, and I've been in the Sahara. But the spirit of the prairie called me, and this is why I came back.'

'You couldn't do anything else, my white brother!' nodded Winnetou. He was leading his horse by its reins. He noticed my companions only now, but his face did not show any surprise. He took out a pipe and tobacco, and sat down.

'Winnetou has been in the North, by the Great Lakes, to bring the sacred clay from which the peace pipe could be burnt,' he said. 'You are the first, my white brother, to whom I give this calumet.'

'Don't you want to smoke the calumet with my friends?'

'I don't know them. I honour only those warriors with the peace pipe whose heart is clean. But I know that you would have only this type of friends.'

'Have you heard of Sans-ear's name, my brother?'

'Winnetou does not know him, but has heard of him. He's wise like a serpent, cunning like a fox, and he's also brave. He kills red men because of his ears. His wife and child were murdered, and he lives only for the revenge of their death. Why doesn't he show himself to Winnetou?'

Sam approached the great Apache chief shyly. The Indian measured him up, and then gave him the pipe. Sam knew what he had to do, and blew the smoke to the six directions ceremoniously.

I called Bernard.

'The Apache chief should look at this paleface! His father was a rich man, but he couldn't reach his old age. Bandits murdered him in his own house, and robbed his property. His murderer is now here at the Pecos River. The son of the victim came here to take revenge.'

'He has the responsibility to take revenge,' nodded the chief of the Apache. 'Winnetou will help him.'

Bernard's face brightened. He knew that the help of the Apache chief meant a lot in his quest. Winnetou gave him the calumet too, and waited until the ceremony was completed.

'Did you bring many warriors, my brother?' asked Sam.

Winnetou looked at me, and instead of an answer he asked him, 'How many bears are needed to trample over an ant-hill? How many alligators to swallow hundreds of toads?'

'Only one,' he replied smiling.

'Uff!' nodded Winnetou. 'For the extermination of the Comanche ants and toads one Apache warrior is enough. Winnetou does not need help, but it's enough if he raises his hand and hundreds of Apache warriors would come to follow his command, because Winnetou is not just a chief of an Apache village, but the great chief of all Apache. The Comanche will regret that they dug up the war hatchet. But enough of the words. Men talk with action! My white brothers can follow me if they want to.'

He led his horse out of the thicket and jumped on it. We followed his example. We continued our journey. I rode next to Winnetou and briefly told him what had happened to me and why I was at the River Pecos. Sam in the meantime watched Winnetou's horse. It was a strong boned, brown animal. A superficial person would have considered it a beast of burden, but I knew that it was an excellent mustang. It was enduring in steps, fast in gallop and unparalleled in intelligence. He followed all the motions of his master obediently, even finding out his thoughts.

When we followed the tracks of the Comanche we were extremely surprised by their carelessness, because they had not tried to remove any of their tracks. They felt they were safe. We had been following their tracks for an hour when Winnetou suddenly stopped his horse. He pointed forward with his clinched fist indicating that we needed to be quiet and careful. I leant forward and peered, but could not see anything suspicious. Winnetou hung his gun on his saddle, pulled out his knife, jumped off his horse and disappeared among the trees.

'What's happened, Charlie?' asked Sam.

'I don't know.'

'Your Apache chief is strange! He disappears without informing us of what he wanted.'

'You heard him, the man acts. It seems that he noticed something and he's going after it.'

'Why didn't he tell us what we need to do?'

'Because we know it. We have to wait until he returns or gives a signal to follow him. This is natural, because ...'

'Mister! Mister!' interrupted Bob excitedly. 'I heard a cry. A man cried.'

'Where?'

'In the thicket.'

I looked at my companions with a questioning look, but none of them heard anything and I almost believed that Bob had only imagined it. But at that moment the song of a mocking bird resounded. The others believed that it was a bird, but I knew it was Winnetou's signal because he had used it many times in our excursions.

'Funny!' said Sam. 'I'm curious how this bird got here.'

'It didn't,' I replied. 'Winnetou is calling us. Look, he's at the edge of the forest!'

I grabbed the reins of Winnetou's horse and started off towards Winnetou, who stood a few hundred steps from us, under the trees of the edge of the forest. When he saw that we noticed him, he withdrew to the forest again. Soon we saw the chief who leant against a tree. There was a young man by his feet. He was tied up with his own belt. He groaned quietly and blinked frightened at Winnetou.

'A coward!' said the chief and contemptuously turned away his head. The prisoner was a white man. When he noticed me, his face brightened up, because the approach of a white man filled him with hope especially when Sam also arrived.

'A paleface!' exclaimed Sam surprised. 'Why does my brother treat him as an enemy?'

'His eyes are wicked!' replied Winnetou briefly.

I looked at Winnetou astonished, when I heard another voice, 'Holfert! For God's sake, how did you get here?'

Bernard Marshall rushed to the tied up man. His face showed a real shock.

'Mr Marshall!' replied the tied up man. He obviously knew Bernard, but he did not seem happy for the meeting.

'Who's this man?' I asked.

'His name is Holfert. He was an assistant in our shop,' replied Bernard.

An assistant of the Marshalls' company at the bank of the Pecos River, where we expected Morgan to appear. Suddenly I had an idea.

'Was he with you when you wound up the business?' I asked Bernard.

After the affirmative answer, I turned to the stranger, 'Mr Holfert, I have been looking for you for some time. Could you tell me where your friend, Fred Morgan, is right now?'

Holfert's face became pale.

'Are you a detective, Sir?' he asked.

'You'll soon know who I am,' I replied. 'But you don't have to be fearful. I know that your sin is only that you fell under the wrong influence. But you can redeem yourself if you answer all my questions honestly. Where's Morgan?'

'Untie me, Sir, then I'll tell you everything.'

Bernard's astonishment heightened hearing these words.

'There's no way!' I replied sternly. 'But we can loosen it a bit. Bob!'

Bob leant forward to follow my instruction.

'Bob! Are you here too?' exclaimed Holfert.

'Yes, I am! Where Mr Bernard is, this is where I am! But why aren't you, Mr Holfert, in Louisville? Why did you come to the mountains? Why are you bound?'

He loosened the belt as much as it was necessary for Holfert to sit up. I continued the cross examination.

'I ask you for the third, and last time: where's Morgan.'

'At the Head Peak.'

'How long have you been with him?'

'Almost for a month.'

'Where did you meet him?'

'In Austin. He called me there in a letter.'

'He called you? So you've known him for some time, haven't you?'

The prisoner was quiet. I took out my revolver, and started to play with it.

'Look at this little toy, Holfert! Do you think that I don't know everything? I'm only questioning you to check my information that I gathered about the death of your boss. I know the facts, I'm only interested in the details. If you help me, you won't regret it. But if you keep quiet or try to lie, this toy can go off! Do you understand? Here, in the West we don't waste much time on a murderer and robber!'

'I'm not a murderer and robber!' cried out Holfert almost screaming.

'But you aren't innocent either,' I replied. 'I told you that I don't consider you a real criminal. The question is if you show repentance. How do you know Morgan?'

'He's my relative.'

'Did he visit you in Louisville?'

'He lived there for some time.'

'Carry on, I don't feel like pulling every word out of you! Think of the revolver.'

'If Mr Marshall leaves, I'll tell you everything.'

In the interest of the goal, I gave way to the desire of this gentle soul, and waved to Bernard to go a bit further away. He did, but I saw that he returned in a large arc, and was hiding behind a thick trunk not too far from us. I could understand his curiosity, and his upset state of mind.

'I'm listening!'

'Morgan often visited me, and I played cards with him. At first I won, and I became a gambler. Then I started to lose. I lost more and more. Finally I had several thousand dollars debt. I signed promissory notes for him on which I forged my boss's signature. I was in his hands then. I had to tell him where my boss kept the key to the house and the office.'

'Did you know his plans?'

'No. I thought he would only break in. We agreed that if he succeeded, we will share the loot and we would escape to Mexico.'

'Who murdered the jeweller?'

'Morgan. He told me that he would only knock the old man out, but he stabbed him. I had no part in it.'

'Only in the loot?'

'He shared it with me right after the murder. As a jeweller, I could easily sell my share.'

'I see, and then he wanted this money. Did he take it from you?'

'He did.'

'It was stupid of you that you came to Austin! How could you think that such a man would be fair with his accomplice? How did he take the money?'

'Yesterday night he was the guard, and I slept. I woke up because I felt that he was searching my pockets. He had already taken my purse and my weapons. He was about to stab me. The fright and despair doubled my strength, I pushed him away and ran for my life. He chased me, but it was dark. I ran all night, because I knew that he would follow my tracks in the morning. When I arrived to this forest, I hid so I could sleep a bit. This is all.'

He closed his eyes. I could see how exhausted he was, and probably this was why he confessed everything. However, I could hear in his voice only tiredness, but not genuine remorse.

'I give this man to you,' I told Bernard. 'Do whatever you want with him.'

Bernard put a few more questions to Holfert, then he pulled me aside.

'He deserves death. There's no doubt about this,' he said.

'But don't laugh at me when I say that I can't kill him. Let God be his judge.'

'If you let him go without weapons and supply, it's the same as killing him,' I replied.

'Then let's take him with us until we can release him.'

'We already have a prisoner. It would be inconvenient. Let's ask Winnetou!'

The Apache chief listened to our conversation with some contempt on his face. He came to us, and took off the belt from Holfert.

'Get up!' he ordered.

The prisoner rose. Winnetou pointed at his hands.

'Has the paleface washed his hands since the murder?' he asked.

'Of course!' replied Holfert.

'Yet, I can see the blood that cannot be washed off with water,' said Winnetou in a stern voice. 'The Great Spirit will decide on the fate of the paleface. Can the white man see that branch of the tree at the bank of the river that leans over the water?'

'I can.'

'Then go there and bring it. If he can break it off, he will live, because that branch is the symbol of mercy.'

As we listened to these strange words, we were baffled.

Holfert started off towards the river that was about four hundred steps from us. We were sure that Winnetou wanted to pardon him, this is why he had set such an easy condition for him. Holfert already stretched out for the branch, when

Winnetou raised his gun. The shot resounded, and Holfert fell in the river.

Winnetou calmly reloaded his gun.

'The paleface did not bring the branch, so he died. The law of the prairie is just, and doesn't pardon a murderer. If he wasn't killed now, he would be killed by the Comanche or the stakemen, and his body would have been devoured by the coyotes.'

After these words he jumped on his horse, and rode away without looking at us. We followed him in a gloomy, and silent mood.

The Comanche were on the warpath, there was no doubt about that. Yet, they did not try to remove their tracks, which suggested that they expected the enemy to be further away, otherwise they would have been more cautious. What was their aim and plan? Winnetou certainly knew it, but he was more reserved to speak about it. I was about to leap forward on my horse next to him, when two shots resounded. Winnetou stopped his horse, slipped off it, and carefully sneaked among the bushes to the bend of the path.

A few minutes later he returned and said, 'Comanche and two palefaces!'

After this he returned to the bushes. We followed him after leaving Bob behind to guard the horses and Hoblin.

By the bend of the path we had an excellent view of the river. It was very broad there. The Comanche camped at this spot. The two chiefs stuck their spears in the ground, and put their shield to it. They were sitting on the ground, and were smoking the calumet with the two white men who sat next to them. The horses of these four men were grazing nearby. A bit further away we had a view that was peaceful and warlike at the same time. The Comanche were exercising their battle skills. They showed excellence in riding and using their weapons.

I put my telescope to my eye, and exclaimed, 'Look who's there, Sam!'

Sans-ear took the telescope from my hand.

'Hell! Fred Morgan with his son, damn them! How did they get among the Indians?'

'Why are you surprised? Patrick has always been ahead of us, while his father was chasing Holfert, and this is how he got here. They didn't have to hide from the Comanche.

You heard from Hoblin how friendly they are with them.'

'Terrible!'

'Why?'

'How will we get them from the Indians?'

'Don't worry, they won't stay with them for very long. It's not in their interest to show them their cache. We can wait here for the developments.'

'And if Morgan comes this way after Holfert?'

'What for? The Comanche came on this path, and went to the valley, and they didn't meet anyone. Morgan obviously asked them, thus he has no reason to come up here. Let's find a good hiding place for our horses.'

Winnetou nodded in agreement. Because we were likely to spend several hours there, with our horses we went to the depth of the forest, and unloaded the pack horses.

When Hoblin looked down, he remarked, 'The gorge on which I wanted to lead you to the cache is down there.'

'That's quite unfortunate!' I exclaimed peeved. 'The Morgans are closer, and can act earlier.'

'But the Morgans don't know this path. Only the *capitano* and I know it. The lieutenant will go along a stream that enters the Pecos River.'

'Then that's fine,' I said relieved. 'We can watch what they are doing there.'

The Comanche split into two groups, and played war games. The warriors were on their horses without a saddle, as these were substituted by some leather or blanket. On the sides of these blankets they fixed a strong, broad belt that they threw over the neck of the horse, thus it became a kind of hook in which the rider could push through his arm if he wanted to slip down to one or the other side of the horse. This made it possible to change position while galloping, using the horse as a cover, yet being able to shoot at the enemy, even from under the horse. This required much skills and craft.

The game attracted our attention so much that we forgot about everything else. Fortunately I accidentally glanced back on the path on which we had arrived, and, for my shock, I saw two men who were approaching us.

'Look out!' I told my companions. 'Look back!'

They all turned back. Hoblin spoke first, 'The *capitano* and Conchez!'

'Indeed! Quickly! Let's move to the forest, and remove our tracks!'

A few minutes later our little group disappeared in the thicket without a sign. Only Winnetou and I stayed near the path. We hid behind a bush from where we could see everything, but nobody could see us.

The two riders soon passed me by, and reached the bend of the path when the Comanche broke out in war cries. The two men were taken by surprise, and they stopped. They peered carefully for a while, and then withdrew. Two maple trees hid them from my view. I lay down, and crawled behind the two trees, with my tomahawk in my hand. I got so close that I could hear their conversation.

'Comanche,' said the *capitano*. 'We don't have to be afraid of them. We could go down to them, but we should know first who the two whites are with them. I can't recognise their countenance from this distance.'

'Can you see the four horses, *capitano*? One of them, the fox, is very familiar!'

'Carramba! The lieutenant's horse!'

'I think so too. So one of them is the lieutenant.'

'That's for sure! Can you see his scarf? The lieutenant had a very similar one. What should we do now?'

'If I knew your goal, I would say something, but ...'

'You are right. I'll tell you. The most valuable part of our loot is hidden here. Nobody knows the place, only I, and the lieutenant. He agreed that he would meet his father, not at our place, but here, by the Pecos River. This is why I suspected him. I'm afraid he wants to take the loot. He probably met the Comanche accidentally. The only question is if I should go there, and settle the bill with him, or wait until I can catch him in action?'

'The latter will be better,' said Conchez, who obviously wanted to know the place of the cache. 'Otherwise he could excuse himself. And also, you cannot rely on the redskins.'

'You are right. We'll wait until the Indians move on. Then Patrick will obviously go to the cache. But we will be there before him, because I know a shorter way. He won't have the loot, if it's still there!'

'Why wouldn't it be there?'

'Hm! We got some lessons from Old Shatterhand and Sans-ear, didn't we?'

'How would they know the secret?'

'From Hoblin,' said the *capitano* gloomily.

'From Hoblin? How?'

'It's very simple. I made the mistake that I sent Hoblin here. I wanted him to watch out for Patrick. But Hoblin disappeared, and I'm afraid he was captured by the two great hunters. Maybe he told them everything to save his skin.'

'That's bad! What should we do, *capitano*? Should we go to the Comanche then?'

'And tell them about our treasures? They may take it from us. Look! The Comanche are taking out their provisions. Let's do the same, and eat something. We can think in the meantime. Bring the meat!'

Conchez started off towards the horses, and I quickly crawled back to my companions to report on what I had heard.

'Have they mentioned the three, who acted as voyageurs?' asked Sam. 'Patrick took one of them. Where's he?'

'I don't know,' I replied, 'because they didn't talk about that. Probably Patrick killed him. None of our business. '

'What should we do with the *capitano*?' asked Sam.

'Nothing, he can do what he wants.'

Winnetou, who had not said a word so far, now shook his head.

'You forget, my white brother, that you have only one scalp,' he said.

'Do you think it's endangered? I'll be careful.'

'You are a clever hunter, and a brave warrior, but you don't know the customs of the Comanche. This band goes to the mountains once a year to the grave of their chief, Chuga-chat, always on the day when Winnetou killed him in a duel.'

Now I understood why he had followed the Comanche.

'It doesn't make any difference,' opined Sam.

'I don't really want to spill more blood either,' I agreed.

Winnetou shook his head again.

'You can do whatever you want, my white brothers, but those who spare the enemies, the robbers and murderers, will pay with their own blood. Haw, I have spoken!'

It was a conflict between moral convictions. While I was musing about it, I heard shouts from the valley. I sneaked forward to the bend of the path, and looked out.

The Comanche were on the bank and with their spears they pulled something from the water. They looked at it, and then pushed it back to the river. Then they surrounded the two chiefs and the white men. Soon they all started off in gallop. I returned to my companions.

'What was it?' asked Sam.

'They found something in the river, maybe Holfert's body.'

'It can't be,' said Winnetou. 'The body could not have floated so far. The water would have put it on the bank far from here.'

'Not necessarily,' I replied. 'The river is deep here and the current is very strong. The bank is tall and steep.'

Winnetou looked at me, then stood up, and without a word he disappeared among the trees. I knew what his decision was. He wanted to advance in the forest, go to the river, and check if they really had found Holfert's body.

I knew that it was a dangerous undertaking, and my bad premonitions were soon confirmed. The *capitano* also heard the shouts from the valley, and he hurried to the bend of the path with Conchez. They watched and noticed Winnetou who appeared from the forest as he rushed to the river. The two bandits brought their horses out of the forest, and hurried to the valley. I could not do anything against it. I thought Winnetou needed about half an hour to get to the water, and swim to the place where the Comanche found the body.

A quarter of an hour had passed, thus Winnetou could have been captured by the two bandits. After telling the others to wait at the place, I hurried to the bend of the path, and I saw Winnetou as he threw off his clothing and jumped in the water. He left his gun at the bank, and took perhaps only his knife, thus he was very disadvantaged against the two bandits. However, I could only watch the events.

Winnetou had not yet reached the point where the body was found when the *capitano* lifted his gun, and shot. He did not hit Winnetou, who immediately dived. A minute later he appeared at the bank, and climbed out. He jumped on his attacker. But then the other bandit aimed at him. Winnetou had only as much time to knock upwards the barrel of the gun, thus the bullet went somewhere in the air. In the meantime the *capitano* turned his gun, and wanted to hit Winnetou with the butt. He jumped away at the right time, twisted the gun out of the *capitano's* hand, and threw it in the water. I could hear galloping horses from the other bank. The Comanche must have heard the shots, and returned.

The two bandits had not yet recovered from their surprise when Winnetou had already disappeared.

I hurried back to my companions.

'We must go!' I told them. 'The Comanche saw Winnetou, and may come in this way. We also have to help him.'

We went in the direction where Winnetou had gone. We led our horses at the edge of the forest, under the foliage of the trees, thus we could advance very slowly. I stayed behind, and removed our tracks. Twenty minutes later I heard the crackling of twigs, and Winnetou stepped out from among the trees. He was wet, and he held his gun and clothing in his hand.

'Uff!' he said. You were right, my white brother, to come after me. The Comanche jackals are following my tracks. Where are your companions?'

'I sent them deeper into the forest.'

'That was wise.'

He quickly dressed, and then took the reins of his horse from me.

'What did you see in the river, my brother?' I asked.

'The paleface's body. It was a mistake to shoot him into the river. Winnetou was hasty today.'

I downcast my eyes. It was unusual that the proud Winnetou admitted his mistake like this.

We crossed the forest to get to the gorge that Hoblin had spoken about. On the first clearance we wrapped the horses' hooves in strips that we cut from the blankets that we had brought from the bandits' camp.

I decided that while the others could advance, I would stay behind, and scout on our enemies activities.

I gave the reins of my horse to Bernard, and I crawled into the bushes. I did not have to wait long before I heard hoof-beats. The Comanche arrived, or at least half of them. They rode very slowly, and looked at the ground for tracks. At the point where we wrapped the hooves of our horses they stopped. One of the Indians jumped off his horse, and picked up an object from the ground. I could not see what it was. They discussed something, and then the chief sent some warriors to scout around. Although it was a very dangerous situation for me, it was also important to know the plans of the Comanche. When they had passed by me, I could see that what they had found was a piece of cloth from one of our blankets. We probably lost it when we cut it up for wrapping the horses' hooves. The scouts returned, and reported that they could not find any track.

As they were riding past me, I heard Fred Morgan's words, 'It was our own track that we found.'

'Who was the Injun and the two whites whom we saw?' his son asked.

'We'll find out, because they will be found. I'm …'

I could not hear any more as they were now at a distance. We were in relative safety for the time being, and I also learnt that the *capitano* had chosen not to go to the Comanche. The question was whether the Comanche would find him and Conchez.

It took me half an hour to catch up with my companions, and I reported to them what I had seen.

'So, our trick worked,' said Sam.

'The Comanche are blind and deaf,' added Winnetou. 'We can take off the moccasins from the horses.'

It was very good that we could relieve the animals, because the landscape became worse. It was difficult to break through the forest, but the gorge was even worse. We tottered in this dried out river bed for many hours. At sunset we camped at an appropriate place, and we spent the night there. Although it was unlikely that anybody could come after us in this gorge, we still set up guards. The night passed without any event, and in the morning we continued our journey.

We rode in the valley towards the West. As we advanced, the valley became gentler because the cliffs became less steep, and not as high as earlier. We arrived to another valley that was about one and a half miles long. There had to be water in it, because the vegetation was lush. However, we could not allow the animals to graze, because it would have betrayed our presence.

Hoblin cried out. 'This is the valley!'

'Are you sure?'

'Definitely, Sir! I can recognise the huge beech tree down there. This is where we had some rest when I came with the *capitano*.'

'Then let's go to a side valley where our horses can graze, and then we can return to here, and guard the pass.'

'And if we suddenly need our animals?' asked Sam.

'You are right,' I replied. 'We must examine the area thoroughly first.'

'Right,' nodded Winnetou. 'I'll go to the right, and Old Shatterhand will go to the opposite direction. The others should wait here until we return.'

'Good,' I said, 'but I'm also taking Bob.'

I got off my horse, and started off to the forest with my gun in my hand. Bob followed me. It was not easy to advance among the trees and rocks, thus we got separated from each other a bit. Suddenly I heard a frightened cry from Bob.

'Oh! Come quickly here!'

I turned around, and I saw that Bob was holding on a branch of a tree, and pulled himself up. He kept on climbing upwards.

'What happened, Bob?'

'Come quickly! No, run away! There's a monster here!'

He did not have to say what monster he talked about, because I saw it approaching. A huge grey bear was clomping towards me from the thicket.

I had heard the roar of the lion in Africa, I had heard the roar of the tiger in Bengal, but neither of them had been so horrifying and blood curling than the deep, mean growl of the grizzly. It was about eight steps from me when it rose on its hind legs, and opened its terrible muzzle. "One of us will die," I thought, "either the grizzly or I!" I aimed at its eyes, pulled the trigger. The next moment I targeted its heart, and shot for the second time. After this I threw the gun away, pulled my knife, and jumped aside so that I could stab it with more strength. The gigantic animal was still approaching me, and it was as if the two shots had not meant anything to it. It made two, three, five, six steps, and I was lifting my knife when its front paws fell, it groaned sadly, stood for half a minute, and then crashed to the ground. One of the bullets entered its eye, the other its heart. A panther or a jaguar would have died immediately, but this grizzly made six more steps. Had he had the strength for two more steps, it would have been the end of me!

'Is it really dead?' I heard from the tree.

'Yes, Bob. You can come down.'

'Are you sure?'

'Yes, I'm sure!'

Bob came down from the tree, and approached with caution. I leant over the bear, and to make it sure I stabbed my knife between its second and third ribs

'How huge it is!' said Bob astonished. 'He didn't eat me!'

'No, Bob. We will eat him. Or at least its paws, and its ham. They are very tasty. Everybody will get some of it. But wait here until I return.'

'With the bear? No, no! It may rise again!'

'Then you'll climb up on the tree again.'

'No! I'll climb right now,' he said, and followed his words with action. He was not a coward, he stood up against men, but the grizzly filled him with such terror that it lasted even after the death of the animal.

I scouted around if it was a lonely bear or a member of a whole bear family, and thus I had to be alert. I could not find any other track.

Bob did not have to be alone for long. The sound of the gun alerted my companions, and they hurried to help me. Then they admired my loot. They all stated that they had never seen such a size grizzly. Winnetou leant forward, and dipped his medicine bag in the blood of the grizzly.

'You shot it at the right place, my white brother,' he said. 'The soul of the bear will be grateful, because he didn't have to suffer for long, and could move to the happy hunting grounds quickly.'

He said it because the Indians believed that in every grizzly there was the soul of a famous hunter who suffered for his sins in this form, and he only could take his place in the happy hunting grounds when the grizzly was dead.

Winnetou helped me to skin the grizzly, and cut out the most valuable pieces from its meat. We covered the rest with branches, stones, soil, and moss so that the body would not attract the vultures, and thus become our traitor.

The scouting of the Apache chief was also reassuring. He found a big cave where we could all camp, including our horses. We decided to stay there for the night. As it was still light, and a fire could not be seen from the distance, we roasted the paws of the bear, and had an excellent dinner. When it got dark, we agreed on the guarding, and lay down for the night. The night passed undisturbed.

Our cave opened to a steep slope from where we could see far into the valley. In the morning Sam rushed to me excitedly.

'They are coming!' he reported.

'Who?'

'You see, I can't tell you that, because I couldn't see their faces.'

'How many?'

'Two riders.'

'Well, I'll check it.'

With my telescope I soon spotted the two Morgans. They were still a quarter of an hour from the cave. As we erased our tracks, and we had more men, we calmly waited for their approach. We were about to return to the cave, when the bushes cracked far above us on the slope. Was it another bear? We listened, and concluded that two beings were heading downhill.

'What could they be, Charlie?'

'We will know it, let's hide!'

A few minutes later we learnt that not wild animals approached, but two humans, who were pulling their horses by the reins. I almost exclaimed in my surprise, when I recognised the *capitano* and Conchez. It was visible on the men and their horses that they had had a tiring journey, and they were barely able to advance. They stopped near our cave, and stared down into the valley.

'At last!' sighed the *capitano* relieved. 'It was a hellish journey. I wouldn't like to do it again! But we arrived on time, nobody has been here.'

'How do you know?' asked Conchez.

'Because nobody dug here. The Morgans have not been here, and nobody would come to this Godless place.'

'Have you forgotten Sans-ear and Old Shatterhand?'

'They were probably captured by the Comanche.'

'And the naked Indian whom we saw in the Pecos River?'

'Yes, he was suspicious. This is why I shot at him, but what can I do if he escaped?'

'Who knows why he was there?'

'Not important! He was probably after the Comanche. He wouldn't have come up here.'

'*Capitano*!' cried Conchez. 'I can see two men down there!'

'Carramba! It's them!'

'They think that they have the loot already!' said Conchez.

'I'll sort them out!' hummed the *capitano* gloomily. 'I'll dissuade Patrick from robbing his comrades!'

'And what will happen to the treasure?'

'We'll take it, naturally.'

'And whom will it belong to?'

'To us!'

'How do you mean this, *capitano*? Two of us or the whole gang?'

'What do you think?'

'It's difficult to answer *capitano*. If I think it over, maybe it's not worth to return to the gang. If somebody struggled so much as I did, he deserves some rest and comfort. If something comes from this treasure to me, I'll say good-bye to the prairie. I'll settle in a town, and start a new life.'

'I don't say that you are wrong,' replied the *capitano*. 'We'll discuss it. But for the time being our task is to give a lesson to the traitor. Let's go downhill, and hide near the treasure.'

They talked so loud that even my friends could hear it, and they came out of the cave. The shock on the faces of the two bandits was indescribable when they faced the Indian whom they had seen in the Pecos River. It increased when they saw Hoblin behind Winnetou.

'Hoblin!' exclaimed Conchez. 'What are you doing here?'

'Hoblin!' echoed the *capitano*. 'What are you doing on the side of the Sierra Blanca? And who are these people?'

I stepped out of the bush, and put my hand on his shoulder.

'All good acquaintances, *capitano*!' I said.

'You are wrong, señor!' he replied. 'I don't know you.'

'Then I'll introduce myself, but let me I'll introduce my friends first. This black gentleman was a fellow traveller of Mr Williams of whom you must have heard. This gentleman is Mr Marshall from Louisville, who wants to exchange a few words with Mr Morgan, whose name you have also heard. Now look at this gentleman. His name is Winnetou. I don't have to say any more about him. Then here's one of the most famous hunters, Sans-ear. I'm known as Old Shatterhand.'

The *capitano* went pale in his fright, and he could only stutter, 'It's impossible.'

'Why would it be impossible? Only difficult to believe. It's also difficult to believe that a few days ago I was an invisible guest in your camp, and I took your pistol as a souvenir. Bob! Disarm these gentlemen, and tie their hands and legs!'

'Señor!' flared up the *capitano*.

'Do you want to protest? Be considerate, because for the slightest resistance you can say good-bye to your life!'

The two bandits recognised that they had to surrender. Bob was grinning as he tied them up.

'Tell me, *capitano*,' I continued, 'where have you hid those things that Patrick wants so much?'

'They are mine!'

'Do you think so? Well, I won't force you. But let me ask you another question. What happened to those voyageurs whom Patrick took with him?'

'Two returned to the camp, and Patrick killed the third.'

'I thought so,' I answered. 'But now we'll gag you so that you won't frighten the other two birds away.'

We had just finished the work, when Fred Morgan and his son arrived nearby. There was a blackberry bush about thirty steps from us on the bottom of the slope, and Patrick was heading there.

'This is the place, father!'

'Then let's start the work!' said the other.

They tied their horses to one of the trees, put down their weapons, and then knelt down to tear out the weed. When they cleared the ground in a place, they started to dig with their knives, and lifted out the soil with their hand.

'It's here!' exclaimed Patrick after a short time and pulled out a packet sewn into bison leather.

'Is it all?'

'It's not too big, but even more valuable. Bank notes, certificates of deposit, and gems. We'll fill the hole, and then leave quickly.'

'Don't hurry so much! Stay a little bit!'

These words came from Sam's lips, who had sneaked up to them, and with one leap got between the two bandits and their weapons. He stood there like a tiger before leaping on his victim. The two Morgans were at first paralysed in their surprise, and by the time they recovered I was also there aiming my revolver at the older Morgan.

'Hands up!' I shouted. 'I'll shoot for the first suspicious move!'

'Who are you?' asked Fred Morgan.

'You son will tell you.'

'Why are you attacking us?'

'I have more right to attack you than you had when you killed Marshall in Louisville or Sam Hawerfield's family. Lie down on the ground!'

'I won't!'

'You will reconsider it when you know whom you are faced with! Look around. Here's Winnetou, Sam Hawerfield, Bernard Marshall, not to mention myself. Your son will tell you my name! I count to three. If you don't obey, I'll shoot! One ... Two ...'

With grinding teeth and clinched fists they jumped on the ground.

'Bob tie them up!'

He carried out the task with great endeavour. Bernard Marshall was shaking with anger, but controlled himself, and did not say anything.

'Bob! Bring the other two!' ordered Sam. 'Let's finish them all at the same time!'

Bob brought the *capitano* and Conchez.

'Who will make the judgement?' asked Bernard.

'You, Charlie,' said Sam.

'No,' I replied. 'We are all affected. The only neutral party is Winnetou. He should speak!'

Everybody agreed with me, and Winnetou also nodded.

'The chief of the Apache knows the law of the prairie. He will be a just judge of the palefaces. What's the name of this man?' he pointed at Hoblin who had just come up to us.

'Hoblin,' replied Sam.

'What's his sin?'

'He used to belong to the stakemen.'

'Did he kill someone?'

'As far as I know, nobody.'

'Did he help you?'

'Yes.'

'Then Winnetou pardons him with the condition that he will move to the right path.'

We all agreed, and I gave Hoblin Fred Morgan's knife and rifle.

'Thank you, gentlemen' said Hoblin with joy. 'You won't be disappointed.'

'Who is this paleface?' continued Winnetou.

'The leader of the stakemen.'

'That's enough. He deserves death. Who speaks for him?' Everybody was silent, thus it confirmed the judgment. 'And this man, next to him? '

'Conchez,' replied Sam.

'Even his name is a lie,' said Winnetou contemptuously. 'What's his sin?'

'Nothing better than that of the *capitano*,' opined Sam.

'Then he should die too! But none of us should soil his hand with them. What's the name of this young man?'

'Patrick.'

'He joined the murderers quite young. So probably he's skilful in killing. Let him do it. We don't want to give him any weapon, thus he should throw them in the water tightly bound.'

'Bob! Untie him, but keep an eye on him!' ordered Sam.

Bob untied Patrick. Several guns pointed at him, but there was no need for any threat. He willingly carried out the role of the executioner. The *capitano* and Conchez could not, and did not want to defend themselves. In a few minutes he completed the death sentences. Then Bob tied him up again.

'Now it's him and his father,' said Winnetou. 'What are the accusations?'

'They murdered my wife and my child,' announced Sam gloomily.

'They are murderers and robbers,' added Bernard. 'They murdered my father and robbed him.'

'The older attacked the railways, and organised the murder of a railway worker,' I said. 'The younger wanted to kill us. There's no need to go any further in their numerous crimes.'

'Then they deserve the rope too. Bob should hang them.'

'No!' cried Sam. 'For years I've been in pursuit of the rascals, and I won't let others do it! I'll make two more notches on my gun, and then I can die in peace either in the forest or in the prairie, where the bones of thousand and thousand hunters have become dust.'

'Your request is just, my brother,' stated Winnetou. 'You can execute the two murderers.'

'Sam,' I whispered, 'let Bob do it!'

Sam looked at the ground gloomily, and he did not reply. To give him time, I turned away, and went to Fred Morgan's horse. I searched his saddle, but did not find anything. Then I searched Morgan. I found a packet under his shirt. There

649

was money in it, the money that he took from Holfert. I gave it to Bernard, who put it in his pocket without a word.

At that moment, from the direction of our horses I heard snorting. I stepped to that direction, and I saw how my mustang's mane fluttered, and his eyes sparkled. Either there was a predator or Indians in the area. I let out a cry of warning; but this was suppressed by a terrifying war cry, because with a wild yelling Indians jumped forward from behind the bushes and trees. While we were dealing with the two Morgans, the Comanche, who followed the *capitano* and Conchez, sneaked up to us, and attacked. They first overcame Sam, then they threw a lasso on Winnetou. Hoblin crashed on the ground dead, because a tomahawk split his skull. I did not see what happened to Bob. Bernard was surrounded by five Indians, but I could not see what happened to him either, because I jumped on the ground, and crawling in the grass I reached my mustang. I quickly untied it, and pulling him after me, I hiked uphill. It was painful to leave my companions behind, but this was the only way to help them later. The overwhelming number of Comanche made all resistance meaningless. I could only hope that those whom they captured alive, would be taken as prisoners, and I could do something for them.

Reaching the ridge of the mountain I jumped on my horse, and rode away. I knew that the Comanche would pursue me, and I made it sure that my tracks would lead them astray. I rode until I got to a stream whose shallow water ran down in a hard rock bed to the valley. I continued my journey in the stream to erase my tracks. Then I tied strips of cloths on Swallow's hooves, and with a big detour I returned to the forest. In the meantime the night fell, and I was looking for a moss-grown place to rest for the night.

How quickly everything had changed! I was lying under a tree, being torn away from my companions, I was hungry and tired. I thought I would never fall asleep, but I closed my eyes, and when I opened them again, the Sun was high on the sky.

I found a good place for my horse, and then headed to the battlefield on my feet. It was a dangerous undertaking. I advanced very carefully. The ten-minute route took almost two hours. I was about to pass by a huge, old oak tree, when I heard a strange sound, "Ssh!"

I looked around, but I could not see anything. When the sound was repeated, I recognised that it came from above, and looked up. There was a hole among the branches of the oak. From this Bob's face grinned.

'Wait, I'm coming!' he whispered.

I heard a scrubbing sound. Soon the hazelnut branches on the tree moved, and I could hear Bob's voice from nearer.

'Come in to my room. Nobody will find us here!'

I climbed in the rotten inside of the trunk of the tree, and Bob pulled back the hazelnut branches carefully.

'Excellent place!' I said. 'How did you find it?'

'A small animal came in and I went after it.'

'What animal?'

'I don't know. It had four legs, two eyes and a tail.'

"It was probably a racoon," I thought, "and Bob did right to follow it."

'So, you've been hiding here since yesterday. What have you seen and heard?'

'I saw and heard many Indians. They were looking for me, but they could not find me. Then they made a fire, and roasted ham.'

'What ham?'

'Of the bear that you killed! Can they eat our bear?'

Although his indignation was perfectly just, I could not enforce it.

'Then?'

'They left at dawn.'

'Where?'

'I don't know, but I could see everything from the window. They went out of the valley, and they took Mr Winnetou, Mr Sam and Mr Bernard. They were all tied up.'

'None of them stayed? '

'Yes, they did!' nodded Bob.

'Where are they?'

'Where we covered the bear. I could see everything from the window.'

I looked up, and I saw that one could climb up in the trunk. I tried, and succeeded. I looked out of the hole that Bob called window. From this I could see the whole valley. I saw the tree on which Bob climbed up when the bear surprised us. An Indian sat under it. He was left there obviously, maybe with some others, to catch us if we returned.

I climbed down, and told Bob, 'Wait for me here. I'll come back for you.'

'Where are you going? Aren't you staying with me?'

'Don't you want to save our friends?'

'Save Mr Bernard? Of course! And also Mr Sam and Mr Winnetou!'

'Then keep quiet and wait for me!'

I climbed out of the tree. It was a good feeling that somebody else had also escaped, and I could rely on him. I sneaked forward extremely carefully. The Indians obviously knew that two of their enemies escaped, and were hiding nearby. They were clever to set up guards by the bear as the escapees were likely to be hungry, and thus would have tried to get to the meat.

An hour later, after getting around to the other side of the valley, I was hiding behind the Indian guard. He was very young, eighteen years old at the most. Perhaps this was his first warrior undertaking. His clean clothing and good weaponry showed that he was probably the son of a chief. There was a whistle on his neck. Perhaps he would have to give a signal with that. I should have killed him in this situation, but I had no such an intention.

I quietly got closer to him, and knocked him out. I tied the young man up, gagged him, and then tied him to a tree that was surrounded with thick bushes. I took the whistle from him, and blew it. For this an old Indian stepped out from a near bush, and rushed towards us. He had the same treatment as the young one, but I used the handle of my revolver instead of my fist. I knew that more Indians were around, maybe three or four, and I could not sort all of them out like this. It would be better to deprive them from their horses. The question was where were they. I imitated the neighing of a horse, and immediately got an answer.

I tied up the old Indian, and took the young one to the direction from where the horses responded to my neighing. I found the horses. There were six of them, thus I knew that four more Indians were nearby. I could have driven away their horses, but first my young prisoner had to be secured.

After a short musing I picked him up again, and took him to the oak tree where Bob lived for the time being. When he noticed me from the window, he came down to me.

'Oh! You captured an Indian!' said Bob happily. 'Is he dead or alive?'

'Alive, and do you know why, Bob? Because he will help us to rescue Bernard.'

'I will do anything,' he said. 'Tell me what to do.

'Can you see the hickory tree there? Take this young Indian there, and guard him until I come. Make sure he remains bound, otherwise he'll kill you.'

He easily picked up the Indian, and started off with him. I went back to the horses. I knew that on this terrain I could not get away with the horses very simply. After some musing I tied the tail of the first horse to the head of the second, and continued with the rest. Finally the six horses were in one chain. Then I took the first horse by its reins, and the rest followed him. I was terribly lucky that their neighing, and their steps did not betray me. By achieving my aim, I deprived the Indians from their horses which was almost the equivalent of depriving them from their weapons.

In ten minutes I was by the hickory tree where my prisoner lay. Bob was clearly relieved when I returned.

He told me that the Indian was groaning, and that he smacked the Indian's mouth.

'That's not right, Bob!' I told him. 'He may want to revenge this insult!'

'Then it's better if I kill him,' he said, and already pulled out his knife.

'No Bob! We need him to rescue the others!' I took out the cloth that I used for gagging him.

'You can take a deep breath, my young brother, but you can talk only if I ask you.'

'Ma-ram speaks whenever he wants,' he said stubbornly. 'Why should he be quiet? You would kill him in any way, and then scalp him.'

'Ma-ram will live and won't lose his scalp,' I replied. 'Old Shatterhand kills only in battle.'

'Are you Old Shatterhand? Uff!'

'Yes. You aren't my enemy, Ma-ram, but my brother. Old Shatterhand will take you to your father's tent.'

'Ma-ram's father is To-key-Choun, Horned Bull, the great chief of the Comanche. If he sees Ma-ram, he will kill him because he was captured.'

'Do you want your freedom, my young brother?'

The young Indian looked at me surprised. 'Do you release a Comanche warrior who is your prisoner, Old Shatterhand?'

'I will release you, if you promise that you won't escape but lead me to your father, because I want to talk to him. If you promise this, I'll give you back your horse and weapons.'

'Uff! Your fist is strong, Old Shatterhand, and your heart is generous, but isn't your tongue mean like that of the other palefaces'?'

'Old Shatterhand never lies,' I replied. 'If you promise that you keep to these conditions, you are free.'

'I promise.'

'Then we'll smoke the calumet.'

My horse was not far from the hickory tree.

I led it there, and took out two cigars from my saddle. These were real cigars that I found at the camp of the bandits. I cut off the bondage of the Indian, and gave him one of the cigars, and I lit the other one. I gave fire to my prisoner, and we blew the smoke exactly as if it had been a calumet.

'Can't the palefaces make calumet?'

'We can, but we smoke pipes only at home, and carry these instead of the calumet, because these need less room.'

Bob, remembering the possibility of revenge, also insisted on participating in the "smoking of peace".

The Comanche identified his horse, and got on it. Bob also chose an Indian horse, while I got on my mustang. We led the other four Indian horses by the reins.

We got to the valley, but we were still at a high point. Suddenly a wild howling resounded. The Indians obviously found out that their horses had been taken. However, we were safe. Ma-ram controlled himself so much that not even a muscle flinched on his face.

Soon we got to another slope, and we reached another valley. This is how we descended, step by step to the river. It was almost evening when we arrived to the bank of the Pecos River, and found an appropriate place where we could spend the night.

Among the blankets of the Indian horses there was enough dried meat to have a proper dinner. Ma-ram lay down to sleep, while Bob and I took the guarding in turns. At dawn we took off the blankets from the four additional horses, and chased the animals into the river. They swam across, and soon disappeared into the forest on the other bank. They were mustangs, they had regained their freedom, so they could easily become wild horses again. The Indian watched it without saying a word.

We continued our journey on the right bank of the Pecos River following tracks of a large group that had ridden there two days earlier. At the bend of the river I was surprised that the tracks split into two. One led forward, while the other to the Guadalupe Mountains. I got off from my horse, and examined the tracks. I recognised the hoof prints of Tony.

I turned to Ma-ram, and asked, 'Did the Comanche move to the mountains to the grave of the great chief?'

'You are right, my white brother,' he said hesitatingly.

'But some went on this path. Did they take the prisoners to the village of the Comanche?'

'They followed the chiefs' order,' was the evasive answer.

I counted the hoof prints, and I saw that sixteen continued along the river. Thus Winnetou, Sam and Bernard were guarded by thirteen warriors to the village. In such circumstances they could not escape. By now they were certainly in the village. I could save them only by some trick.

I got on my horse again, and followed the tracks of the smaller group. To my surprise this path also left the bank, and turned to the forest. It took me some time until I recognised the reason for this: the Comanche wanted to cut through the bend of the river, and wanted to shorten their way. Their path would lead to the river sooner or later. Ma-ram was not very willing to give me any information, and did everything to dissuade me to take the shortcut. Still I asked him, and he had to admit that we were heading to the village the shorter way.

The route was shorter, but harder, especially for those who did not know it. We tottered on the rocky ground until we crossed the bend, and got back to the Pecos River. We stopped at a stream that entered the river. The tracks showed that the Comanche had rested there, and we followed their example.

For security I did not settle on the bank of the stream, but much further in the thicket. Soon it became clear that the carefulness was necessary. Bob wanted to have a wash in the stream, but suddenly turned back, and alerted me with the news that six riders were approaching along the bank of the river.

I went to the edge of the bushes, and looked down at the bank. Six horses rode towards us, but only two riders. There were two pack horses behind each rider. I did not know what I should think, especially when I saw that the two riders were not Indians, but white men. They were too far for me to recognise them.

My surprise heightened, when further behind the six animals a small group of riders appeared. There were five of them. The way in which they rode showed that they were Indians. It was also obvious that they were chasing the white men. I took my telescope to see what was happening.

'Hell! I cursed involuntarily when I recognised the two escaping whites, Fred Morgan and his son, Patrick.

What should I do? Should I shoot at them or try to capture them? I did not want to stain my hand with their blood. I had only a little time to lift my gun. The two rascals were in front of me, while the Indians five hundred steps behind them. I did not aim at the heads of the two bandits, but at the horses on which they sat. The two animals collapsed. The pack horses tried to escape frightened, and almost trampled on the riders. I rushed forward to jump on the two rascals, when an ear piercing yelling stopped me.

'O-hiiiiii!' The battle cry of the Comanche, in which Ma-ram also participated, resounded. Three tomahawks, and two knives flashed above my head.

'*Cha*!' shouted Ma-ram, and lifted his arm above my head. 'This paleface is Ma-ram's friend!'

Now I understood the situation. The five Indians who chased the white riders spotted me, and charged to finish me off first. Although they obeyed Ma-ram, their mistake could not be repaired. The two riders had enough time to get up from the ground, and escape. They had already disappeared in the bushes on the bank. The pack horses had bolted because of the two shots and the battle cry, and they fell in the river. As they carried heavy packs, and also because of the vortex in the river bend, the animals could not swim, and disappeared under the water. I just noticed that these were our pack horses, thus with them the loots from the bandits' camp were swallowed by the river.

Four of the five Indians galloped after the escapees, but I held back the fifth.

'Can you tell me, my red brother, why you chase your paleface allies?'

'The palefaces have two tongues. They smoked the peace pipe with us, but in the night they killed the guard, and escaped with their treasure.'

'Was it their treasure?'

'We don't know. The chiefs were to decide it.'

'Was it gold?'

'Gold and medicine papers.'

After these words he left me, and rushed after his companions. This is how I learnt that the Morgans did not feel secure among their allies. They were anxious that the Comanche would want their treasure, and they had escaped. The colourful papers were banknotes and certificates of deposit, but the Indians thought that these were magic talismans. There was no hope that the treasures would ever come to the surface. The damned gold stained by so much blood was swallowed by the river!

I had a new dilemma. The desire of revenge urged me to chase the two bandits, but my anxiety for my friends was stronger. My most urgent task was to hurry after them, and maybe I could help them. The other two were chased by five Comanche, they could catch them without my contribution.

'Why did you shoot at the horses, my white brother, and not the riders?' asked Ma-ram. 'Can't you aim well?'

'I wanted to talk to them, this is why I didn't kill them.'

'You can talk to them if you join the pursuing Comanche warriors,' said the young man pouting his lips.

I almost laughed out loud for this attempt of the Indian. Then I started to count. Thirteen riders were with my friends. Two of them were the whites, five of them were now chasing the Morgans, one was killed, thus there were only five warriors left for guarding my companions. I turned back to Ma-ram.

'Five quick and brave Comanche warriors are chasing them. They'll capture the two rascals themselves, and I can face them in the Comanche village.'

The events made me so excited that I did not have the patience to rest, and we started off. Although Ma-ram was earnest to find a night camp, he had to follow me for four more miles. Then it became so dark that we had to settle for the night. However, at dawn we started off again. The path soon turned from the river towards the plains. There we could advance quicker. After a few miles we arrived to a meadow, where I saw the tracks of many horses. At least forty paths led to the same direction, to the South-east.

'Uff!' exclaimed Ma-ram.

He did not say anything else, and while his face remained motionless, his eyes brightened up.

'How far are we from the Comanche village?'

'If we ride faster, we'll reach the village before sunset.'

At twilight I saw dark lines on the horizon. I took out my telescope, and I could see the long lines of tents. This Comanche village was one of the largest Indian settlements I had ever seen. Many Comanche bands joined for bison hunting. I stopped my horse.

'Are these the tents of the Comanche?' I asked.

'They are,' replied Ma-ram.

'Is To-kei-choun, the chief of the Comanche, there now?'

'Yes, my father is always with his tribe.'

'Would you ride there with a message, my brother?'

'What message?'

'That Old Shatterhand would like to speak to him.'

He looked at me surprised.

'Are you not afraid, Old Shatterhand?' he asked. 'Your fist is strong, you can knock out the grizzly, but you cannot kill as many Comanche warriors as many are in the village.'

'Old Shatterhand doesn't want to kill them. He doesn't kill the brave Sioux, Kiowa, and Comanche, or any other red men. He only fights the bad people, but he's a friend of all good Comanche warriors. You should speak to the great chief, my brother! I'll wait here for the answer.'

'But Ma-ram is your prisoner. Aren't you afraid that you'd lose him?'

'Ma-ram is not my prisoner. I smoked with him the signal of peace and friendship. Ma-ram is free!'

'Uff!' exclaimed the young Indian, and rode away. Bob and I dismounted and let the horses graze.

We did not have to wait long. Half an hour later a large group was heading towards us from the village. A hundred steps from us they split to two groups, and with loud yelling, and swinging their weapons they surrounded us. Bob lay down on the ground in his fright. I, however, did not lose my head, and calmly sat in the grass as if I had not seen them.

Four riders came forward from the ring, and from their eagle feathers I could see that they were chiefs. The oldest rode next to me, and said, 'Why don't you stand up, white hunter, when you see that the chiefs of the Comanche approach?'

'The white hunter wants to show how happy he is for them,' I replied. 'Would you sit down with me, my Comanche brothers?'

'The Comanche chief would sit down only with another chief. Where are your tents, paleface? Where are your warriors?'

I lifted my tomahawk, and said, 'You can recognise the chief by his bravery and strength. If you don't believe that I'm a chief, you can fight with me, and you will see that I'm telling the truth.'

'What's your name, paleface?'

'The warriors and hunters call me Old Shatterhand.'

'You are boasting, and you gave yourself the name!'

'If the Comanche chiefs want to fight with me, they can have their knife and tomahawk and I'll fight with bare hand.'

'You speak proudly, paleface, but you should show us if you are brave! Get on your horse, and follow the Comanche warriors.'

'Will you smoke the calumet with me?'

'We don't yet know it. We'll have a council to decide it.'

'You have to. I came with peaceful intentions to you.'

I got on my horse, and Bob followed my example. The chiefs rode on my two sides, and we galloped to the village.

We stopped by a larger tent, and the Comanche jumped off their horses. Of course I did the same. Bob disappeared from my vision. The warriors surrounded me, and the chief whom I had talked to, stretched out for my gun.

'You have to give over your gun, paleface!'

'I won't because I'm not your prisoner. I came to you of my own volition.'

'You have to give it over until we know what you want.'

'So your bravery stretches only to that much? You are so many against one man, and you still want to take his weapons?'

The chief, hurt in his martial honour, replied indignantly, 'The Comanche warriors aren't afraid of anyone! The paleface can keep his gun!'

'This is right for you! I'd be happy to know your name.'

'I'm To-kei-choun, whom is feared by all enemies.'

'Then I ask the great chief, my brother To-kei-choun, to give me a tent until the council decides on Old Shatterhand.'

'You speak right. You will get a tent until the Comanche chiefs make a decision.'

He started off, and waved for me to follow him. I grabbed the reins of my mustang, and followed him. The Indians opened a way for us. Many old and young squaws peeped out of the tents to stare at the paleface who was brave enough to come voluntarily to the Comanche. These were Western Comanche, that is, different from those whom Winnetou had fought in the Mapimi.

I looked around, and immediately saw that the life of this village was the same as others'. The men were involved only in hunting, fishing, and war, while the women did everything else. The tents were erected, and furnished by the women, they cut the leather pieces for the tents, they carried these, and the poles to the place where they wanted to erect the tent. There they dug a two-feet deep round hole, and put the poles around this. They then tied these together with young hazelnut branches. When the skeleton of the tent was ready, they fixed heavy leather sheets on the poles.

Sometimes they split the inside of the tent to separate sections with animal skins.

I was led to a smaller tent that had no inhabitants. I tied up my mustang, and entered the tent. The chiefs did not follow me. After five minutes a very old Indian woman came with a huge pile of twigs on her back. She threw it on the ground, and disappeared. However, she returned soon with a big earthenware pot in which there was water and something else. She made a fire in the middle of the tent. The smoke rose to the opening in the top. When there was enough embers, she put the pot in it.

I lay down, and watched her work silently. I knew that I was not supposed to talk to a squaw, and also knew that I was watched invisibly.

The water started to boil, and the smell told me that there would be bison meat for dinner. When it was ready, the old woman put the hot dish next to me, and she left. I gave myself over to the joy of eating. I was hungry, and I ate with good appetite even though they made the meat without salt, and the pot was not particularly clean. I recognised that I was treated well. I was sure that the pot came from one the chiefs' tent, and it was respectful that they cooked for me separately.

After dinner I saw that they fed my horse, and that there were two guards by my tent. I put a blanket under my head, and wrapped myself in another. I immediately fell asleep, because I knew that there would be exciting events on the following day. In the morning I woke up for a hissing sound. The old woman was there making fire, and put the pot on the fire. The breakfast was the same type of meat as the dinner, and my appetite was also similar. Then I decided that I would look around. I had barely put my head out when one of the guards charged at me with his spear as if he wanted to poke me through.

I knew that I could not accept this behaviour without damaging my reputation. I grabbed the spear with two hands just under the tip, and jerked it towards myself. The guard had to let go of the spear, he lost his balance, and crashed on the ground.

'Uff!' he shouted angrily. He got up, and pulled out his knife from his belt.

'Uff!' I replied in the same tone, and grabbed my knife, while with my other hand I threw the spear in my tent.

'Give back my spear, paleface!' yelled the guard.

'You can go in for it if you want!' I answered.

The guard did not think it was advisable to enter my tent, thus he called the other guard for help.

'You must go back to your tent, paleface!' he yelled at me pointing at me with his spear. I could not resist the temptation, and repeated the previous action. The second guard also crashed to the ground, and I threw the second spear in my tent.

There was a much bigger tent opposite mine. There were three shields by its side. For the shouting of the guards a girl's head appeared, and her dark eyes looked at me curiously, then she disappeared. Soon four men stepped out of the tent, the four chiefs.

'What are you doing outside your tent, paleface?' asked To-kei-choun sternly.

'Did I hear it right?' I replied. 'You probably wanted to ask what the two guards were doing outside my tent.'

'They were there so that you would not be harmed.'

'Isn't the order of the great chief enough for this? Because if it isn't, Old Shatterhand can look after himself. You don't have to be anxious for me, my brother. I will just walk a bit, and look around in the village.'

I returned to my tent to take my weapons. When I stepped out again, a dozen spears pointed at me. "So, I'm a prisoner," I concluded. I went back, cut a hole at the back of the tent with my tomahawk, and stepped out. The guards were waiting at the front, and were taken aback when I appeared behind them.

In the next moment they rushed towards me yelling. If I had tried to defend myself with weapons, I would have been killed. I did not know why, but I grabbed my telescope and lifted it to my eye.

'Not one more step!' I shouted. 'Or you'll die!'

They had never seen a telescope; they did not know what it was, and thought that it was some magic.

'What is it in your hand?' asked To-kei-choun.

'Something that is more dangerous than a gun! Old Shatterhand is a great magic man among the palefaces,' I replied. 'But let me show you what my gun can do. I closed the telescope, put it away, and took my Henry rifle.

'Can you see that pole there?' I asked pointing at a pole standing by a faraway tent.

I lifted my gun, and shot without aiming. My bullet hit the pole just under its tip. There was an appreciating murmur, because the Indians recognised skills and bravery even in their enemies. My second bullet hit the pole an inch lower. The third again an inch lower. Instead of the murmur, there was an astonished silence, and also consternation on the faces. The Indians had seen many double barrelled guns, but not a repeating rifle. I sent one bullet after the other in deadly silence. I stopped at the twentieth. The holes were at equal distances on the pole. After putting my rifle on my back, and said, 'You can see that Old Shatterhand is a great magic man. Woe to those who attack him. Haw, I've spoken!'

I started off, and everybody stepped back to give me way. Women and girls appeared in the front of the tents, and stared at me with great respect. I was perfectly contented with the result of my show.

There was a guard next to another tent. Who could have been guarded there? I did not have to think for long, because I heard Bob's voice.

'Oh Mister Shatterhand! Save me! The Indians want to roast and eat me!'

I stepped to the entrance, and waved to Bob to come out. The guard who saw the previous scene did not dare to contradict me.

'Come with me, but stay behind me!' I ordered Bob.

I saw that To-kei-choun was hurrying towards me. I stretched my hand for my gun, but he waved that he did not have hostile intentions. I waited until he reached me.

'Where are you going, my white brother?' he asked. 'The chiefs are waiting for you!'

I liked this. So far he had called me "paleface", now he called me "white brother". He turned back, and I followed him. We passed by my tent. A bit further away I saw Tony tied to a tent next to Winnetou's and Bernard's horses. My friends could not be in that tent, otherwise there would have been a guard there.

We got to a small square among the tents. Three chiefs sat in the middle, and To-kei-choun sat down with them. Soon other older warriors stepped forward as well as some younger ones, probably the leading warriors. I did not hesitate, and sat down next to the chiefs. I waved to Bob to sit down behind me.

'Why do you sit down, when you came to listen to our judgements?' asked To-kei-choun in a sharp voice.

'If I cannot sit down, then I'll leave!' I replied loudly, and decidedly.

'You can remain seated,' said the great chief, 'but the black man must go.'

'The black man is my servant, and he has to be with me. We can start the council,' I answered the challange without flinching my eyes.

I knew that some tribes were not exempt of racial prejudices. But I also knew that I had to be unbending, because the slightest allowance could have cost my downfall. To-kei-choun stared into my eyes, then lit his calumet, and blew a big smoke from it. He then passed it to the next man. The calumet went around, but it was not offered to me.

When the pipe returned to the great chief, he looked me in the eye, and started to speak.

'Many summers have passed since the Indians and the palefaces lived separately on the two sides of the Great Water. Our tribes lived happily in their villages. The forest, the prairie, the sunshine, the rain, the day, and the night belonged to them. The women and children were happy, and well fed. Then the palefaces came. Their skin was white like the snow, but their soul was black like soot. First only a few came, and the Indians accepted them. They returned our hospitality with kind words and presents. But they also brought other things: fire water, firearms, treason, illnesses, and death. More and more came over the Great Water. Their tongue was deceitful, and their soul viperish. We believed them, but they cheated us. They chased us away from our fathers' lands, they burnt down our tents, and they created quarrels among the tribes so that it would be easier for them to defeat us! As many curses are cried against them as many leaves are in a forest, and stars on the sky!'

Cries of agreement interrupted the speech of the chief. He waited until everybody became quiet, and then continued, 'One of the palefaces came to the village of the Comanche. He showed friendship, but we cannot see into his heart. The council of the elders decided that they would listen to him, and make a judgement over him. I allow the paleface to speak.'

I wanted to reply, but now the three chiefs spoke, one after the other, and they also raised the complaints of the Indians.

As I could not speak, I took out my little notebook, and started to draw. I drew all the four chiefs with the warriors and the tents in the background.

After the last speech, and the cries of agreement To-kei-choun asked me, 'What are you doing, while the chiefs of the Comanche speak?'

I tore the page out of my notebook, and gave it to him.

'Uff!' he exclaimed when he glanced at the drawing.

'Uff! Uff! Uff!' cried the three other chiefs.

'This is a secret!' said To-kei-choun. 'The paleface put the soul of the Comanche on this thin white skin. This is To-kei-choun. These are the three chiefs. These are the tents, and the warriors. What do you want to do with this?'

I had not had any intention with it, but seeing his shock it came to me that I could use it for my advantage. I took the paper from him, crumpled it, and put it in my gun.

'Your soul, as you said, is now in the barrel of my gun,' I said. 'If I shoot, its pieces will be taken by the wind, and then your soul cannot reach the happy hunting grounds!'

I had always known that many peoples identify the depiction of the person with the person, but I had not expected such an effect of my drawing or my words. The four chiefs jumped up frightened, and there was horror on the faces of the warriors. I hurried to dissolve their fears.

'My brothers can sit down, and smoke the peace pipe with me! Then I'll give back your souls, and there won't be any problem!'

To-kei-choun quickly sat down, and took out his calumet. All eyes were on me expectantly, and thus I also made a short speech.

'The Great Spirit gave this land to his red skin children. The whites also have their own country, and it's not just that they take others' land. But why are my red brothers angry with all palefaces? Don't they know that there are whites, who don't hate the Indians, don't want to grab their land, burn their forests, annihilate their bison and mustangs? My brothers should look at Old Shatterhand! Can they see any Indian scalp on his belt? Has he killed any Indian who had not attacked him? He captured Ma-ram, the son of the great chief, he could have killed him, but instead he sent him back to his tribe. Old Shatterhand is a great magic man, but doesn't want to be hostile with the Comanche. He wants to live in peace with them, this is why he now smokes the peace pipe with them!'

With this I blew the smoke to the six directions, and passed the pipe to To-kei-choun who, taken by surprise, did the same. The three other chiefs followed his example.

'Am I now a brother of the Comanche?' I asked.

'You are our brother, Old Shatterhand, and you can do what you want,' replied To-key-chun.

'Then I want to choose my tent,' I said, and started off.

The four chiefs joined me. As I walked along the tents, I saw four guards by one of the tents. I lifted my hand to my mouth, and imitated the howling of the coyote for which a similar answer came from the tent.

'This will be my tent!'

'You can't have this one. We guard our enemies here.'

'Who are they?'

'Winnetou, the chief of the Apache and two palefaces.'

'Old Shatterhand wants to see them,' I announced, and entered the tent with the four chiefs behind me.

'This is my tent,' I said, 'and these three men are my guests. Bob! Untie them! Start with Winnetou!'

Bob had already went to Bernard, but he also recognised that Winnetou could be more help for us. As he was cutting through the bondage, one of the chiefs jumped on him, and twisted the knife out of his hand. I intervened and the chief stabbed my arm. I knocked him out, and the falling body crashed onto another chief. I grabbed the third by the throat, and Winnetou had already overcome To-kei-choun in spite of his swollen wrists. In two minutes the four chiefs were bound and gagged.

'Good Lord!' said Sam rubbing his limbs to quicken the restoration of his circulation. 'How did you do this, Charlie?'

'I will tell you later, but now we have to act quickly.'

We armed ourselves from the chiefs, and agreed that we would immediately kill them if we were attacked. After this I stepped out of the tent. There was a guard there, and quite a few Comanche who were curious about the events. I went to the guard.

'Have you heard, my brother, that Old Shatterhand became a son of the Comanche?'

He downcast his eyes as an affirmative answer.

'Guard my tent, my brother, until I come back,' I said, and turned to another warrior asking him to call a council.

While the council was called, I cleaned my wound, and went to the place where ten minutes earlier I had sat with

668

the four chiefs. When the warriors arrived, I started to speak, 'You all know that Old Shatterhand has become a son of the Comanche. He was offered that he could choose his tent, and he chose one, the tent of the prisoners. Has it become his property?'

'It has,' they agreed

'And yet the chiefs refused to recognise it. Are the chiefs of the Comanche liar? The prisoners sought my protection. Could he refuse them? I told the chiefs that the prisoners were my guests. Was I allowed to do that?'

'You had this right, but you also have to allow us to put them to our court. You can defend them, but then you may have to die with them.'

'Was I allowed to untie them if I vouched for them?' There was an agreement on the faces.

'So I only acted within my rights, yet one of the chiefs wanted to kill Old Shatterhand! The blade bounced harmlessly off my arm. What can a Comanche do when another man wants to kill him in his own tents? '

'He may kill him.' said one of the warriors.

'And all his accomplices? '

'All!' he said but now quieter.

'You are wise and just. The chiefs wanted to murder me. I didn't kill them, only bound them. I demand the freedom of my guests for the freedom of the chiefs! You should discuss this, my brothers, and I will wait. You should also know that if someone enters my tent, the chiefs will be killed instantly.'

With these words I withdrew so that they could discuss the proposal among each other. After a long discussion three warriors approached me.

'So, you have our four chiefs in your tent, white brother.'
'I do.'

'Give them over to the Comanche so we could judge them.'

'You are wrong, my brother,' I contradicted him, 'I captured them in a fight in my own tent, thus I'm the only one who can judge them.'

'And what's your judgement, Old Shatterhand?'

'Death if my guests are not freed.'

'Do you know these guests?' asked the Comanche.

'I do.'

'One of them is Sans-ear, who has killed many red men!'

'Have you ever heard that he had killed a Comanche?'

'No,' he admitted, 'but there's also Winnetou the Pimo dog. He must have killed hundreds of Comanche!'

'But none of the Western Comanche!' I stated, and he had to agree. 'The third man came from the city, and has never killed any red man.'

'If you kill the chiefs, you'll be killed with your guests.'

I laughed out loud, 'Killing Old Shatterhand? You saw my gun, and you also know that the soul of the Comanche is in the barrel of his gun!'

He could not argue any further, and after returning to the council the discussion restarted. There was no hatred or anger against me on their faces as they recognised my bravery, and so they could negotiate with me. This discussion had lasted for half an hour, when the three warriors came to me again.

'You can leave with your guests freely for as long as what the white men call six hours.'

While it was a dangerous offer for us, I recognised that if we were to leave in the evening, they would not be able to follow us, thus we would have twice as much advantage, and so I would be a fool if I did not accept it. However, I still had to show restraint.

'Old Shatterhand will accept this, providing that the guests get back their weapons, and all their belongings.'

I had in mind the valuables that Bernard carried, because I had not had the time to ask him about it.

'They will have everything,' they agreed.

'However, the bargain is still not fair, because the chiefs wanted to kill me, and I was stabbed.'

'So what do you want, my white brother?'

'For the stab I want to choose three horses of the Comanche, and they can have our three horses.'

I could see on his face that he knew that I asked this because our horses were tired, but he agreed.

'When will you release the chiefs?'

'When we leave, and you will have the magic drawing too.'

With this the agreement was made. I calmly walked back to the tent. When I entered I told them that we had six hours advantage.

'Well,' said Sam, 'I cannot really ask more for getting out from this hellish mess! What about Tony?'

'You can have her. Winnetou, Marshall and Bob will receive a good horse each. I will retain my mustang.'

At this point the old woman stepped in, and informed me that I should go over to Ma-ram. I obeyed. He waited for me with a magnificent black horse.

'This is the best horse of the Comanche,' he started. 'Ma-ram got it from his father. I give it to you, Old Shatterhand, in exchange of my scalp.'

As we were walking across the village, he stopped by a tent, and said, 'Would you come in my tent for a word, my white brother?'

I could not refuse this invitation. In the tent a girl came to me. She was Ma-ram's sister. Her name was Hih-lah-dih, Pure Stream. She wanted to thank me for saving her brother's life. I offered my hand, and said, 'May the Great Spirit give you a long life, flower of the prairie. Your eyes are bright, and your forehead is clear. May your life be joyous and sunny!'

As we left there was not one Indian outside their tent. I knew that they were getting ready for the persecution. In the village more than a hundred hearts longed for revenge, but there were at least two that longed for our escape, and this is what happened.

IN CALIFORNIA

WE CROSSED the Colorado River, and through the endless savannahs, high mountains, and salt plains we got to California. It was a long and difficult journey, which exhausted men and animals. What drove us? Bernard Marshall was driven by the hope of seeing his brother, Sam by the desire of revenge. He was sure that the two Morgans, after losing their loot by the Pecos River, would try to get compensation in the gold fields of California. I shared Sam's views. Winnetou did not care with anything, he only wanted to be with us.

After leaving the Comanche village we rode all afternoon and through the night. We crossed the Rio Grande a few days later, thus we escaped the Comanche.

We got to the southern end of the Sierra Nevada without trouble, except for a little adventure we had there. We rested on the side of the mountain, when Winnetou climbed up on a cliff from where there was a good view to all directions, and he suddenly exclaimed, 'Uff!'

He jumped on the ground, and quickly crawled to us like a lizard. Obviously we immediately grabbed our weapons.

'What happened?' I asked.

'Red men,' replied Winnetou.

'How many?'

Winnetou showed eight fingers.

'Are they on warpath?'

'They have their weapons, but their faces aren't painted.'

'How far are they?'

'They'll be here in quarter of an hour,' replied Winnetou. 'I suggest that we split into two groups. Sans-ear should go to the front with me, Marshall with Bob to the back behind the cliffs. My brother Charlie should stay here with his horse.'

He took the other horses to an opening in the cliff where they could not be seen. The two pairs went as agreed, and I sat down on the ground facing the direction from where we expected the Indians. My gun was next to me.

A quarter of an hour later the Indians appeared. They stopped, and their leader shouted to me, 'What are you doing here, paleface?'

'I had a long journey and I'm now having a rest.' I replied.

'Where have you come from?'

'I left the Pecos River three days ago.'

'Uff!' exclaimed one of the Indians. 'I know this paleface! He was with Ma-ram, when we chased the two palefaces! He shot their horses.'

I also recognised the young Indian now. He had been with four other Comanche who had chased Fred and Patrick Morgan when they tried to escape with their pack horses.

I entered a conversation with them in which I calmly told them that I saved their three prisoners, Winnetou, Sans-ear and Bernard. For this the leader of the group immediately pulled his knife.

'You must die, paleface!'

'You are wrong, red man,' I replied. 'You will die if you continue like this.'

A sharp whistle resounded at that moment. The Comanche turned back. Winnetou and Sans-ear appeared from the bush a hundred steps from him. Bernard and Bob came out on the other side. The leader of the Indians considered that it was better to negotiate. There were eight of them, but our weapons were superior.

'What do you want from me, my white brother?' he asked in a friedlyt tone. 'You can see that we aren't on the warpath.'

'Still you wanted to kill me,' I answered. 'If you have peaceful intentions, we don't want to attack you. Dismount, and smoke the peace pipe with us. Do you know who that warrior is behind you?'

'I know,' he replied. 'Winnetou, the chief of the Apache.'

'You see! And who am I?'

'I don't know.'

'Old Shatterhand! You might have heard my name!'

'Uff!' exclaimed the Comanche, then he jumped off his horse, and hurried to take out his calumet. His companions also dismounted, and sat down on the ground. In the meantime my friends approached. Only Winnetou pulled away a few steps. The calumet went from hand to hand. Bernard made the mistake of offering it to Winnetou, but he refused it.

'My white brothers want peace, and for their sake Winnetou also sits down with the Comanche,' he said, 'but the chief of the Apache won't touch their calumet. After this occasion, if Winnetou meets them again, their bones will be gnawed by jackals.'

The leader of the Comanche pretended as if he had not heard these words.

'Will my Comanche brothers continue to pursue the two palefaces?' I asked.

'This is why we crossed the Rio Grande, and the Colorado River,' he replied, 'but we won't continue, and return to our brothers. The two coyotes slipped away.'

'How could they flee when I killed their horses?'

'We gathered at the grave of our great chief, and left our horses behind with a guard. The two coyotes murdered the guard, and stole two horses.'

This was the only way they could escape, and they needed bravery. It reinforced my view again that these were desperate bandits. I glanced at Sam, and I saw that he ground his teeth, and stared at the ground gloomily. Yes, we will pursue them to the end of the world if necessary!

'How far were you, my Comanche brothers, from the two traitors when you abandoned the chase?'

'Half a day's ride,' replied the Comanche. 'But we had to turn back, because these are the hunting grounds of the Navajo, who are our enemies.'

'Report to To-kei-choun that you met us, and we continue the chase of the two rascals. They'll receive their punishment from our hands. Return in peace, and we'll continue our journey.'

'Won't the chief of the Apache attack us?' asked the Comanche glancing at Winnetou.

'No,' stated Winnetou. 'The Comanche warriors are my enemies, but as they smoked the peace pipe with my friends, they can go in peace.'

I was happy that we had met these Comanche, because we now knew that we followed the two Morgans tracks. We did not have to be afraid of the Navajo, because Winnetou maintained a good relationship with them, and in case of necessity we could even go to any of their villages.

We were riding in one of the valleys of the Sierra Nevada, and this was where we found the tracks of a bison herd which enthused us as we had lived on dried meat for days.

Bernard had never been on bison hunting, and he was happy that he could participate in one. On the right hand side there was a thicket on the river bank. I led Bernard there in the hope that we would see the bison soon as they liked cooling in the water or rummaging near water.

My plan was good, because we soon saw four big animals approaching. Unfortunately the wind blew from our directions thus the animals noticed us. I prepared my lasso that had a ring. The noose was smoother in this way than on those that the Indians made.

We put our horses into a gallop, and soon we caught up with the small herd. A huge bull was escaping with three cows. I separated one cow from the rest, because it seemed to be young, and threw my lasso.

My horse behaved excellently when the lasso flew. The mustang bent ahead, and stretched its legs. The noose tightened on the neck of the cow. The huge jerk almost pulled my horse over, but it kept itself straight, and finally the cow collapsed. I jumped off from the saddle, and stabbed the cow in the neck with my knife. The horse came after me slowly. Bernard also jumped off from his horse, and hurried to me. He helped me to turn the animal. This is when I noticed the branding on the cow's side.

'Huh!' I exclaimed. 'It's not a wild bison! It's a huge, but common cow. It must belong to the herd of a nearby estanzia or hacienda or ranch.'

'Damn it!' said Bernard. 'Then we can expect trouble with the owner.'

'I don't think so,' I replied. 'Here there's no value to the meat of the animal, only its skin. If we don't take its skin, they won't think we are thieves. Only we have to report to the house where we left the skin.'

I could not even finish my words, when I heard a rustling sound, and at the same moment Bernard cried out. I looked up from my work as I had already started the skinning of the cow. I could only see that a lasso held Bernard's waist, and pulled him along the edge of the thicket. I grabbed my gun, and jumped up. I saw a rider in Mexican dress as he galloped, and pulled the unfortunate Bernard after him.

I could not hesitate, otherwise the ground would have rubbed Bernard to death. I aimed at the horse, and pulled the trigger. The horse made a couple of steps, and then collapsed. The rider fell over. I rode there. The Mexican got up from the ground, and when he noticed me, he ran away frightened.

I could not chase him, because first I had to look after Bernard. He could not move at as the noose held his arms so tightly. I quickly cut off the lasso. Fortunately none of Bernard's bones were broken, and he got to his feet.

'Damn it! It was a gliding!' he cried out. 'What did he want from me, Charlie?'

'I don't know.'

'Why didn't you shoot at his head instead of his horse?'

'First of all, because he is a human, and the horse is an animal, Bernard! Secondly, because the lasso was tied to the saddle thus the animal would have dragged you even if I had killed the rider.'

'You are right, Charlie! Why didn't it come to my mind?'

He felt his body.

'Let's go back to the cow!' I proposed. 'Let's finish with it because this place is not particularly friendly.'

'I don't understand it! If there was a ranch here, then we don't have to be afraid of Indians.'

'Well, there are very few *indios bravos* around here, but there are more than enough bandits. I'm afraid we will have many affairs with them!'

We cut out the best pieces of the meat of the cow, and tied them on our horses. After then we got on our horses, and we were soon with our friends, which was easy as they waited for us. When Bob saw the huge pieces of meat, he was very contented.

'You bring the meat,' he cried, 'and I'll make the fire! It will be an excellent dish.'

We had experienced that he was a good cook, so we entrusted him with the task. While I talked about our unpleasant experience to Sam and Winnetou, the meat was ready. We ate with good appetite, especially Bob. Thus it was surprising that it was Bob who was the most alert.

'Mister!' he cried out. 'Riders? Or only horses?'

I took out my telescope.

'Riders,' I said. 'Three, six, eight ... Yes, eight!'

'Have they noticed us?' asked Sam.

'Naturally, they saw the smoke. They are heading straight here.'

'What kind?'

'Judging from their sombreros and high boots, Mexicans.'

'Then we should keep our guns ready, because this company is probably coming because of the lasso-man.'

The riders were approaching, and then suddenly stopped a small distance from us. It seemed to me that a Mexican gentleman led them, while the others were some kind of servants. The man whose horse I had shot was also among them. They had a short council, and then they split, and got around us in two directions.

'They look at us very angrily,' remarked Sam with some superiority in his voice. 'I hope you aren't afraid. Because I could deal with the whole company alone.'

When the circle was closed, their leader stepped forward, and addressed us in a mixed Spanish and English languag ecommonly used in the North of the Mexican border.

677

'Who are you?'

Sam replied on our behalf, 'We are Mormons from Salt Lake City, and came to convert people in California.'

'And who's this Indian?'

'He's not an Indian, but an Eskimo from the Netherlands whom we will show for money if the conversion doesn't go well.'

'And the black man?'

'He's not a black man, but a solicitor from Kamchatka, who will represent his client at the court in San Francisco.'

Clearly the Mexican took all Sam's replies seriously.

'Nice company, I might say!' he mocked us. 'Three Mormons, one Eskimo Indian and an African solicitor unite to steal a cow from me, and attempt to kill one of my *vaqueros*. But you'll see! I'm arresting all of you! You'll come to my ranch!'

Sam looked at me and put on a clown face.

'What can we do Charlie? The order is an order, we have to obey.'

'I agree,' I nodded.

Sam tried to negotiate.

'You don't want to punish us for such a trifle as a *vaquero* and a cow, señor?'

'I'm not a señor, but a Spanish grand! My name is Don Fernando de Vanango e Colonna de Molynates de Gajalpa y Rostero! Remember this!'

'Fine. But I'll need some time until I learn all these,' replied Sam with a serious face.

I put out the fire, got on my horse, and followed the stranger obediently. We rode at such a speed that is common only in Mexico. Still we could look at these riders.

They had sombrero made of black or brown cloth. They had a short vest whose sleeves were richly decorated with embroidery, and even golden fringes. They had a black scarf tied around their neck. The two corners of the scarf reached their belt. Their trousers were tight by the waist, but broad by the legs. The side of the trousers, just as the sleeves of the vests, were slit. These slits were covered with a silk underlining that had a different colour. They also had fine boots with huge spurs, some probably weighed two pounds.

Their horses were well trained, and the Mexican rode on their richly decorated saddles with great skills. I did not have any doubt that they would be able to use their weapons securely in the fastest gallop. Their pistols were short rifles really. They were deadly weapons from a hundred and fifty steps because the high rifle barrel twist rate ensured that the bullet had a strong axis rotation, thus it did not deviate from the target. They all had a lasso with which they could stop even the charging bull. These lassos were sixty yards long, and I had no doubt that they would throw it securely and safely. It was a dangerous weapon in experienced hands, and these men had practised lasso throwing from their childhood.

After a half an hour ride we got to a large house. We turned to a big yard, and jumped off the saddles.

'Señora Eulalia, Señorita Alma, come and see whom I've brought!' cried the rancher turning to the windows. For this the door opened, and two ladies hurried out, an older and a younger. If I had not known that the lady and the maiden of the house came out, I would have thought that they were unkempt servants. They were barefoot, and their hair was like a strange maze. Their shirts had probably been white once, but now they looked like cloths for cleaning the fireplace. Obviously they had not expected guests.

'Whom did you bring to the house, Don Fernando de Venango e Colonna?' screamed the elder lady. 'You don't think that we would host five strangers? Feed them, water them, entertain them, and make beds for them? I would run away instead, and leave you here in this accursed ranch! Why did I listen to you, and leave the beautiful San Jose!'

'Mama!' cried out the younger lady pointing at Bernard. 'Can't you see how similar this caballero is to Don Allano?'

'Similar or not, I can't allow strangers brought to my house without notice.'

'But these are not guests, Señora Eulalia!' exclaimed the rancher.

'Not guests? Then who are they, Don Fernando de Venango e Colonna?'

'Prisoners, Señora Eulalia.'

'Prisoners? What did they do?'

'They murdered three *vaqueros* and five cows, dear Señora Eulalia!'

He slightly exaggerated our sins, but I did not feel it necessary to correct his statement.

'Three *vaqueros* and five cows!' exclaimed the lady slapping together her hands. 'This is terrible! Horrible! And did you catch them in action Don Fernando de Venango e Colonna?'

'I arrested them when they roasted it, and ate it!' replied the don.

'Whom? The cow or the *vaquero*?' asked the Dona.

'For the time being only the cow, Señora Eulalia. But I don't know what else they planned because I disturbed them in action.'

'I know the rest,' nodded the lady. 'You arrested them, and brought them here. And what do you want to do with them now?'

'I'll hang them!' stated the don pugnaciously. 'Call all our men, Señora Eulalia!'

'All? But they are here, except for Betty, but she's coming too. But then we don't have a man missing! How could they have killed three *vaqueros*, Don Fernando?'

'We'll investigate it, Señora Eulalia, and we'll see!' replied the Don.

Three chairs were put out. The trial was in preparation, but we did not care much about it. When the master and the mistresses took their seat, I stepped forward, bowed and said, 'Dona Eulalia, let me ask for your support. I've always respected ladies, especially if their beauty was coupled with justice. If I have to bear the responsibility for my actions, I want Dona Eulalia to be my judge!'

680

'Oh!' sighed the lady melting.

'Our appearance is a bit untidy,' I continued, 'but don't forget Dona Eulalia, that we have been in the wilderness for months, but if we could arrange ourselves a bit, the beautiful and noble Dona will see that we are gentlemen.'

'I let you introduce yourself, señor, and you can introduce your companions too.'

'The Indian gentleman is Winnetou, this man is called Sans-ear, my name is Old Shatterhand, and my friend on my left is called Bernard Marshall.'

I could not continue because Señorita Alma interrupted by saying, 'Mama! Don Allano was also called Marshall!'

'Interesting!' said the lady of the house. 'We know a Señor Allano Marshall who stayed with my sister in San Francisco.'

'Was he from Louisville?'

'Indeed, he was!'

'And my friend here, Dona Eulalia, is Bernard Marshall, a jeweller from Louisville, the brother of your acquaintance.'

'*Santa Laureta*! Allano is also a jeweller! You were right Alma! They are brothers! Are they your friends, Señor Bernardo?'

'All of them!' replied Bernard. 'Old Shatterhand has saved my life many times!'

'Oh! You had all these adventures! How exciting!'

'And the cow? And our *vaquero's* horse?' asked Don Fernando. 'Have you forgotten about them, Dona Eulalia?'

'Stop this silliness, Don Fernando!' exclaimed the lady impatiently. 'Making such a fuss about a cow! Can't you see that these are gentlemen?'

'And we would have brought the hide into the ranch.'

'As it's the custom,' agreed the Dona. 'But how come you are Mormons?'

'We aren't Mormons, Dona Eulalia, we were only joking.'

'You see, Don Fernando! They aren't murderers, robbers and they aren't Mormons! They are the guests of our house. Alma! Bring a bottle of mintjulep from the kitchen!'

681

For the word mintjulep Don Fernando's face also brightened up. It was clear that he got of it only on festive days. Alma returned with a big bottle and glasses. We all had a glass, except for Winnetou, who had never touched Fire Water. The Don poured a rather good portion for himself. The Dona immediately took the bottle from him.

'Not so much, Don Fernando de Venango de Rostredo y Colonna! You know that I have only two bottles left of this brand. Take the señores to their rooms,' said Dona Eulalia, and then turning to us, continued, 'Please excuse us, because we have to retreat to change. We'll meet at lunch. Come Alma! Adios, señores!'

The ladies disappeared behind a door, and Don Fernando led us to a rather simply furnished room. There was a bench running along the walls, which offered a good resting place for the night as we could not continue our journey on that day. We washed, and by lunch time we felt we looked more acceptable. The two ladies had gone through a whole transformation too, and they could have even gone to a court as they looked.

The Mexican ladies did not wear hat. They wore rebozo, a scarf of about four yards that they put on their shoulders, but sometimes when they went out for a walk or, when they went to visit someone, they covered their head with it. They left their faces uncovered, but the rebozo could also be worn instead of a veil. The rebozo is an Indian handcraft piece, whose preparation takes two years and expensive.

The ladies of the house appeared in such rebozo by the table. They had also brushed their hair, and put on stockings and shoes. They sat down by the table that was laid by an old black woman who had also made the lunch.

It was a true Mexican lunch: beef with rice that was red of the Spanish pepper; young ox meat that was black of the common pepper, chicken with garlic and onion, and pasta with pepper and onion. We felt as if we had eaten fire. The ladies were not concerned with the fiery food, and cooled their palates with odd sips of mintjulep.

The ladies kept on talking about Señor Allano, and I had the suspicion that Señorita Alma fell for Allan Marshall, and she would have liked to marry him. We also learnt that the sister of the lady of the house was the wife of the owner of a hotel in San Francisco. Señorita Alma had spent several weeks there, and met Allan who had stayed in the same hotel.

In such circumstances it was not surprising that the lady of the house gave a special attention to me. This is how Old Shatterhand became Señor Carlos, and later Don Carlos. After lunch Dona Eulalia leant over to me, and whispered. 'I'd like to talk to you, Don Carlos.'

'I'm open to listen, Dona Eulalia!'

'Not here, but in the garden, where we can talk in confidence. Let's meet in a quarter of an hour under the plantain trees!'

Thus the many times murderer of cows and *vaqueros,* who had about to be hanged, was invited to a secret meeting with the lady of the house. I let fate take its way.

I slipped out to the garden without attracting attention, and walked up and down there. Soon I heard the whirling of a dress then I saw a big lady who approached me wrapped in her rebozo.

'Thank you, Don Carlos!' she said. 'I asked you to come here, because it's about a secret that I didn't want to mention in front of the others.'

'I'm listening,' I replied.

'Señor Bernardo mentioned that you were pursuing two robbers. I think that those two were here.'

'Ah! When?'

'They left the day before yesterday. In the morning.'

'Where to?'

'Over the Sierra Nevada to San Francisco. I talked so much about Señor Allano that they wanted to visit him.'

This was an interesting piece of news to me, and I was not particularly surprised. The lady liked to talk in general, but about Allan in particular as her daughter fell in love

683

with him. We followed the Morgans' tracks, thus they also passed by Don Fernando's ranch. When they learnt that Allan was in San Francisco, they probably decided that they would rob him, and also take revenge.

'Why do you think, Dona Eulalia, that these two men were the same?'

For this she described the two men in details, and by this I could have no doubt.

'They also asked a lot about my sister,' continued the lady. 'They asked for a letter of introduction, but I didn't feel like writing it, so I gave them a letter that my brother-in-law sent me once to San Jose.'

'What's his name?'

'Henrico Gonzales. They own Hotel Valladolid on Sutter Street.'

'Did Señorita Alma stay there?'

'Naturally.'

'When was this?'

'Three months ago.'

I thanked the lady for her valuable information, and then we returned to the house separately. She could have said all these by the table, but it was more romantic in this way, and Dona Eulalia liked to show off anyway.

We left the house in the early morning. Don Fernando came with us for some of the way, and said good-bye in such a friendly manner you would think he had never threatened us with hanging. Our horses were well rested, and they endured the long and difficult journey through the Sierra Nevada to Stockton and to San Francisco excellently.

The city was built at the edge of a peninsula. To the West it was the Pacific Ocean, to the East the beautiful San Francisco Bay, the biggest port of the world that could probably receive all the fleet of the world at the same time. The traffic in the streets was frantic, and made up of many nations, the English, the French, the Mexican, the Japanese, and the red men, who brought their game to the market, and perhaps for the first time were not cheated with the price.

There were also Indians and Chinese. The Chinese were the most industrious. They made textile, carved wooden things, cooked, washed, sewed, carried burden, and did all these often for only very little wage. However, it was still more than they had in their homeland.

Not only the Chinese, but everybody was industrious. They worked constantly as their motto was: time is money. They did not stop for anything, and only cared for themselves.

We easily found Stutter Street, and got to the Hotel Valladolid through the basking street. It was a hotel only of the then standards. It was a wooden house, built in the Californian manner, stretching deep into the yard. The ground floor was a bar and restaurant. We gave over our horses to a servant, who led them to the stables. We entered the bar, where we managed to grab a table, which was not easy because in spite of the early hour, the bar was full. We ordered drinks and once the waiter brought them, I asked, 'Is Señor Gonzales in?'

'Yes, Sir.'

'Can I talk to him?'

'I'll let him know.'

Soon a tall, stern-faced, well-dressed man came to our table, and asked what we wanted.

'We are looking for Mr Allan Marshall,' I replied. 'Could you tell me if he's still in the hotel?'

'I don't know señor. I don't know him, I can't remember any of our guests, and I don't know anything that happens in this hotel. It's the señora's business.'

'Could I talk to her?'

'Try it!' he said rather curtly, and left.

I saw that the situation was the same as in Don Fernando's house. The lady of the house was the commander. I stood up, and set off after my nose, that is, from where the smell of the roasts came from. I grabbed the arm of one of the girls.

She looked at me with angrily flashing eyes.

'*Vous êtes un âne!*'

Aha! A French woman. I turned to another one, 'Mademoiselle, could I talk to the Señora?'

'I'm not a mademoiselle!'

After several other attempts I finally got an answer.

''I don't think you can talk to her,' the girl said, 'It's not her office hour.'

'What?' I said surprised.

'Yes. She has office hours twice a day. At eleven in the morning, and at six in the evening. Otherwise she locks herself up in her office.'

'But I have to talk to her urgently.'

'I'll ask her,' she replied graciously.

The girl led me to a small hall, and told me to wait. She disappeared behind a door, but soon returned with the news that the señora, exceptionally, would receive me right away. She also told me that I must call her Dona Elvira if I wanted to gain her goodwill.

I entered the lady's room that looked like a furniture storage. It was so full that there was no empty space. Dona Elvira sat on the chaise lounge surrounded by an open book near her hand, an open fan, a guitar, a started embroidery, and a small mirror. In front of her there was an easel and two sketches. I could not decide if the first one was a tomcat or the head of a woman. The other one was definitely some sort of animal. It could have been a sperm whale in a homeopathic dilution, or a tapeworm in the light of an oxyhydrogen lamp.

I bowed, and wanted to introduce myself, but the lady did not let me speak. She put the question to me, 'How far is the Moon from the Earth?'

I did not know why she had asked this, but replied without hesitation, 'Fifty-two thousand miles on Monday, but on Saturday, when it's closer, fifty thousand miles.'

'Right,' she nodded, and looked up to one point of the ceiling without blinking. I also turned my head there, but I could not see anything special.

'What is raisin made of? she asked suddenly.

'Of grape, of course.'

'Then one more question! What's *Poil de Chevre*?'

'A fabric. Quite expensive if it's not too worn.'

'Thank you, señor,' the lady said with a friendly smile, and stretched out her hand which I kissed with respect. 'Maybe you considered it strange that I had this little examination, but I have my reasons. During my office hours I have to talk to so many common, rough people, so I decided that in my resting time I talk only to gentlemen. With my questions I wanted to find out if you were one of them. From your answers I can see that you are an educated man, and thus I'm happy to help you. Sit down, señor!'

I sat down on a round, padded chair that did not have a back and I said, 'I have a big request to ask of you, Dona Elvira de Gonzales!'

'You'd like to get a room in my hotel, don't you?'

'Yes, that one too, Dona Elvira, but also ...'

'Let's stay with the room. You surely have heard that we are very selective with our guests. But we are happy to see you in our house. With some care, I'm sure your appearance will improve too. Have you been to Spain?'

For my nod, she handed me a piece of tissu paper had been traced after a bad map, and asked, 'Then what do you say of this?'

'Very accurate, Donna Elvira!'

She took my comment as a praise.

'Yes, you can see that ladies are catching up with men in all fields, from science to arts. Look at this painting. Look at the unsurpassed grandiosity of the object. The fineness of the lines, the play of lights! I'm sure that you are a connoisseur, but I have to test you. What is this?'

Fortunately the expression "grandiosity of the object" gave a sufficient hint, and I replied with cold audacity, 'The sea serpent, of course.'

"That's right! Although nobody has ever seen it, the artist's eyes can penetrate the depth of the oceans.'

The lady pointed to the table. There's ink, pen and the guest book. Put your name in it.'

I did, and then asked, 'Can I put my friends' names down as well?'

'Who are they, if I may ask.'

'First of all, a black man called Bob.'

'Doesn't matter. Naturally, a caballero, who can recognise the sea serpent, cannot travel without a servant.'

'Then another coloured gentleman, an Indian, called Winnetou.'

'The great Winnetou of whom we have also heard?'

'It cannot be anybody else.'

'I'm happy to see famous people in my house. You will introduce him to me,' nodded the lady. 'Who else?'

'Another famous hunter, Sans-ear.'

'I've heard about him. So there are four of you.'

'Five, Dona Elvira. A jeweller from Louisville, Bernard Marshall is the fifth.'

The lady had leant back on the worn chaise lounge earlier, but now she sat up.

'Surely not Señor Allano's relative?' she asked.

'His brother, Dona Elvira,' I replied.

'Oh, my premonitions! My wonderful premonitions!' exclaimed Dona Elvira. 'When I saw you, something told me that you aren't an everyday man! The brother of Señor Allano and his friends are of course my guests! You will dine with me in my private room.'

'I'd like to turn to my other request, if you allow me. Is Allan Marshall still in Hotel Valladolid?'

'No, unfortunately not. He moved out three months ago.'

'Where to?'

'To a prospector settlement in Sacramento.'

'Did he write to you from there?'

'Yes, he did once, and gave me his address to forward any mail to him.'

'What's the name of the place?'

'Yellow Wood.'

'And did you forward any mail there?'

'Yes. There were some letters, and I sent them there. And I also gave the address to those who looked for him for some business reason.'

'When was it?'

'The day before yesterday. They continued their journey yesterday morning.'

'An older and a younger?'

'Yes, yes,' nodded Dona Elvira. 'I think father and son. They referred to my brother-in-law, Don Fernando. Do you know him?'

'Don Fernando de Venango e Colonna? Of course! I know even his wife, Dona Eulalia! They sent me here.'

'Wonderful!' exclaimed Dona Elvira. 'Tell me about them, señor! When were you with them, and how was it in the ranch?'

I reported in details, but without disclosing my impressions too faithfully. Dona Elvira listened with great interest, and then said, 'Thank you, señor, a thousand thank you! You are the first Westerner who knows how to speak to a Spanish dona. I expect you at dinner! Adios, señor!'

I returned to my table, where my companions waited for me impatiently. San Francisco was an international city, where non-whites and trapper suits were common, but in this large room, openly or hidden, everybody watched us, especially Winnetou, but also Sans-ear. This did not make me happy.

'Well?' asked Bernard.

'Your brother has gone,' I replied. 'He moved to Yellow Wood three months ago, and wrote only once from there. But his post was forwarded to him, I believe including yours.'

'Where's that Yellow Wood?'

'In the Sacramento Valley if I remember well. I think in a side valley where they found a lot of gold. It used to be swarming with prospectors, but the gold ran out, and people moved upstream to try to find luck there.'

'Did he leave something behind?' he asked eagerly.

'I didn't ask it. But you can, as we are invited to dinner with Señora Gonzales.'

Soon a maid hurried to our table, and informed us that dinner was at nine o'clock, and that we would have to be punctual.

'And now I'm showing you your rooms,' she said. 'They are in a small house, which is empty. Normally the relatives stay there.'

'Did Señorita Alma stay here?' I asked.

'I heard so,' replied the maid, 'but then I wasn't here.'

She led us to the little house where there were only two rooms. One was for me and Bernard, and the other for Winnetou, Sans-ear and Bob. The good Sam immediately lay down on his bed, but, in a quarter of an hour, he got up, and left the house, because in the room he felt like he was in a prison. He had got used to the free air of the prairie.

I did not stay in my room for long either. With Bernard we visited the banker who had been in business contact with the Marshalls for decades. We learnt the same from him as from Dona Elvira. Allan visited him several times while he had been in San Francisco. He had a farewell visit three months earlier with the intention of going to the mines. He took a large sum from the banker for buying gold.

The banker had not heard from Allen, he had not received a letter, but he attributed it to the fact that Allan was in places where it was difficult to send a letter.

After this visit we went for a walk, and during the wandering Bernard pushed me into a department store where they were selling clothing. There was everything available from Mexican to Chinese outfits.

It was not difficult to find out Bernard's intentions. Although our clothing was made of good material, they were worn out by the long journey. We shaved in Hotel Valladolid, even cut our hair, but our clothing was quite dirty. Bernard put together a dress for himself that was half Indian, half trapper. He looked good in it.

'Now it's your turn, Charlie,' he said. 'Choose something for yourself.'

'These prices are quite high,' I replied. 'I don't have hundreds of dollars in my pocket.'

'Then I'll choose.'

My protest was in vain, the good Bernard insisted of leaving my rags in the shop. Instead of them he chose the following pieces from the shelves: deer-skin shirt tanned to snow-white with red embroidery; trousers made of similar, but thicker material decorated with fringes; bison skin jacket that was as soft as a squirrel-skin, high bear-skin boots whose sole was made of the most enduring material, the tail-skin of an old alligator; and finally a wonderful beaver-skin hat whose rim was decorated with the skin of a rattle snake.

I refused it, but Bernard insisted that I had to try it at least, and by the time I came out from the booth, he had paid for it.

'I'll charge you for it,' he said, 'there's a lot to put on the accounts.'

He also wanted to buy something for Sans-ear, but knowing Sam's antics, I advised him not to.

Arriving to the hotel, Bob admired our appearance, but Sam did not even look at us. He sat by a table in the bar, and when he saw us, he only waved to join him.

'Listen!' he said. 'At the next table they speak about things that interest us.'

'What's that?'

'Somebody talks about the security at the prospectors' settlements. The returning prospectors are attacked by bandits who often murder too. There's somebody by that table who has come from there, and he talks about his adventures. Just listen!'

There were several people by that table, and on their faces it was visible that they had tried one or two things in their lives. They listened with great attention to the words of a red faced, strong man.

'Well,' he said, 'I grew up in Ohio and I learnt everything that one needs on the water and on the land, on the savannah and in the mountains. I fought with the pirates of the Mississippi, the bandits of the prairie, and I'm not a man who's afraid of his own shadow. But what I experienced in the valley of Sacramento, on the busiest road in broad daylight is beyond all imagination!'

'I'm surprised!' remarked another man, 'because you said that there were fifteen of you. Couldn't you deal with eight bandits?'

'Yes, there were fifteen of us,' agreed the man, 'that is nine miners and six *tropeiros*, that is, drovers. You should know that the latter one cannot be relied on. Of our nine, three were ill with such high fever that they could barely hold themselves in the saddle. Are you still saying that there were fifteen of us?'

'That's different. It sounds plausible,' said another man. 'But it's a busy road. Didn't you get help from others?'

'The bandits waited until nobody was nearby. Then attacked very swiftly.'

'How?'

'I'll tell you. We worked at the Pyramid Lake, and we were lucky. We found such a bonanza that in two months we made a fortune. Each of us had two hundred weights of nugget and gold dust. We could have got more, but we had had enough. Our limbs ached, and our joints were in constant pain. It's not easy to stand in the water from the dawn to the night and shake the *batea*, the sieve. So, we packed up, and went to Yellow Wood, where we found a Yankee, who paid a good price for both the nuggets and the gold dust. He wasn't a rascal who offered a pound of bad flour and half a pound of even worse tobacco for an ounce of gold. Even in his honest way he made a good business. His name was Marshall and I think he came from Kentucky.'

Bernard turned quickly.

'Did you say Marshall?'

'Yes, yes … Allan Marshall, if I remember well.'

'Is he still in Yellow Wood?'

'God knows! None of my business! If I have to answer unnecessary questions, I'll never get to the end of my story! I promised this man,' he pointed at one man in the audience,' that I'll tell him my story. So, we sold all the gold to this Marshall, and decided that we would live well for a while. It was stupid! If he had thought, we would have left immediately, but we were tired, and some of us needed medical help, thus we kept on postponing the departure. Then we heard also of prospectors, who left but had never arrived to San Francisco ...'

'Was it true?'

'You will learn it. We waited for a few weeks for the opportunity to join a bigger company. But life was damned expensive. Also there were some card sharpers who sucked on our blood. There were four of us, and we got acquainted with five others, who were also lucky, and wanted to get back home. So, there were nine of us. We hired mules with their drivers, and so there were fifteen of us. All of us had weapons, even the *tropeiros*, who looked so rough that we believed they would keep the bandits away. We started off. We advanced well, but then the rain started. For days we were wet and cold. The road was so soft that we could not progress at all. We set up our tents at the edge of the road, and stayed there. The sick got worse, and at end we tied them to the mules, because otherwise they would have fallen off. On the last day we made only eight miles; this is when we set up our tents.'

'It must have been a damned situation,' nodded a man. 'It happened to me as well. I can imagine it.'

'So, we have made two thirds of the journey, but we had to stop. We made a fire, big enough to cast light around, and then from somewhere a volley was shot at us. I was kneeling in the shadow of one of the tents, and I was tying the canvass to the pole. This is why they didn't see me. I looked up, and saw that the drivers jumped on their mules, and left us. They rode so comfortably that the bandits could have shot them dead, but nothing happened to them. Obviously they were in cahoots with the bandits. The bandits shot well. First they shot the five men, and then the three sick men. What could I have done against a whole gang?'

'Damn it! I would have shot at them!'

'I wasn't so stupid! It would have been mad! Of course it was important for them not to leave any witness. If they had noticed that I survived, they would have killed me too. My skin is worth more to me than shooting one or two of them.'

'So what did you do?'

'All my wealth was in my pocket in bank notes and certificates of deposit. My mule was tied near the tent. I was about to take it, when one of the bandits whistled, and the *tropeiros* returned for their share. I sneaked away with my mule, and rode away in the dark. Fortunately it wasn't as stubborn as most of the mules, so I could get away.'

'And then?'

'I arrived to San Francisco and I'm sitting here, and I'm drinking my beer. I'm happy that I saved my skin.'

'The bandits could be here.'

'Well, they wore black masks so I wouldn't recognise them except for one. He was their leader. When he whistled to the *tropeiros*, he had to move that black cloth from his face. He was a mulatto with a scar on right side of his face. Surely made by a knife.'

'And the *tropeiros*?' asked somebody.

'I would recognise them, but I won't go back to that hell. Their leader was called Sanchez, but surely he changes his name quite often. The bandits, the mule drivers, the innkeepers all belong to the gang they call the "Pack". The members are called "Dogs". San Francisco and the mining settlements should put together law enforcement agencies against them. Now you know everything. If you have any question, I'm willing to answer.'

'Then let me ask you again about Allan Marshall,' said Bernard, 'because he's my brother.'

'Yes, you look a bit like him. What do you want to know?'

694

'Everything! When did you see him last?'

'When? At least five weeks ago!'

'Do you think he's still in Yellow Wood?'

'I don't know. In the bonanza land people easily move. It could be the same with the jeweller, today here, tomorrow there!'

'He hasn't responded to any of my letters.'

'Not necessarily. Maybe you haven't received them. Don't rely on the post! Many letters are lost, or end up in the wrong hands. If you go to an inn, the barman is a Dog. If you go to a shop, the shopkeeper belongs to the Pack. You sit down to play cards, your opponent is a Dog. If you find a good bonanza, the Pack will be there to take the fruits of your work. Even the sheriff is a Dog, why couldn't the postman be one?'

'Nice!' sighed Bernard.

'Are you going to your brother?'

'I am!'

'Then I can give you an advice, and it's up to you whether you accept it or not. There are two roads to the mining area from here. One goes to the South around the bay, and leads to the Sacramento valley along the San Joaquin River. If you don't have much to carry, you can make it in five days. There anyone can tell you how you can get to Yellow Wood, because I guess you don't know much about it apart from its name.'

'No, I only heard that it's a side valley of the Sacramento.'

'That's right. You'll find it. Still, I advise you not to take this way.'

'Why?'

'Firstly, because although it's more comfortable, it's not shorter than the other. Also, the Dogs watch that road. They normally attack the returning prospectors, but they may attack you. Thirdly, it's a terribly expensive journey. Culture has arrived to the inns: they now give you a bill. But it's easier to read them than paying them. You pay a dollar for the room, but you are sleeping in the yard. You pay a dollar for a bed, but you'll be given two handfuls of hey. You will pay a dollar for lighting, but it'll be the Moon. You'll pay a dollar for the service, but there's no staff. You'll be charged a dollar for the wash basin, but it's the river, and a dollar for the towel, but it's your own coat. The only thing that you get what you paid for: is the bill, because for that you'll be charged a dollar too. Now, how do you like it Mr Marshall?'

'Crafty, I have to say!'

'You see! This is why I suggest a different route in which you can get to Yellow Wood in four days. You cross the bay on the ferry, and without passing by San Joaquin you head directly to the North. It's a difficult road, because you have to cross mountains. However, if you have a good horse, you'll get through. You also gain a day, and you won't meet the Pack. But if you caught sight of a mulatto, who has a scar on his right cheek, don't ask anything, only stab him, or shoot him dead. You'll provide a good service to everyone, and make the travellers of the Sacramento valley grateful.'

'Thank you. I'll follow your advice.'

We could hardly wait for the morning, but first we had to go to dinner. At the head of the table Dona Elvira sat with such a *grandezza*, like the princess of Spain. I introduced everybody very formally. The dinner was good, and we had a high-brow conversation between the courses about literature, art, and science. After we had paid the due respect with our listening, the conversation turned to our adventures.

Finally, Dona Elvira said, 'Señores, you are excellent guests, I hope you'll stay with us for a very long time.'

'Dona Elvira de Gonzales,' I replied, 'unfortunately we'll leave early in the morning.'

'Where to, Don Carlos?'

'To the Sacramento valley to find Allan Marshall and bring him with us.'

'That's different, then I don't want to hold you up. You take what you need. We'll settle the bill later. Good luck señores! Adios!'

The following morning the ferry took us to the other side of the bay, and we continued our journey on horseback. On the fourth day we arrived to the Sacramento valley, where everybody was busy. Hundreds and thousands of people were struggling for the yellow dust stained by so much tear and blood. I watched with pity these sunken faced, feverish eyed, ragged men. They risked their life and health for a hope that, even if they realised it, would not have brought happiness, only temporary and very low joys. But even in these very few of the prospectors had a part. Most worked for months without a result, and left the place cursing only to start work at another place where new disappointments waited for them. The pale ghosts of hunger, illness, and despair surrounded them, and they did not stop shaking the *batea* until the accursed tool fell from their hands.

We arrived to the side-valley of the Sacramento. In the end of the long and narrow valley there was the gullet by which a great many mud huts, sheds, and tents provided some accommodation for the prospectors. This was Yellow Wood, a sad place, whose golden age had gone.

In the middle of the valley there was a long and low wooden house. Written in chalk on it was:

HOTEL, RESTAURANT, BAR & STORE

After dismounting we left the horses with Bob, and entered the long, big room where unplaned tables and chairs were lined up. There were some miserable, rough looking customers sitting on the benches.

'New miners,' laughed one. 'Come here, redskin, and have a drink with me!'

Winnetou acted as if he did not hear the call. The man stood up with a glass in his hand, and it was clear on his face that he would challenge Winnetou.

'You rascal, refusing to drink is the biggest insult! I ask it again: are you having a drink with me or else!'

'I won't drink fire water, but I don't want to offend you.'

'Damn you,' the miner was raging. He threw the drink in Winnetou's face, and with a knife in his hand jumped on Winnetou. However, he staggered back with a loud cry, and crashed to the floor. The Apache chief also had a knife in his hand, and a second earlier it entered the man's heart. The miner's companions rose also with knife in hand, but by then we stood with rifles in our hand.

'Stop,' cried the innkeeper. 'Sit down! The matter is settled, and it was only between Jim and the redskin. Nell! Take the body!'

The miners sat down.From behind the bar the bartender emerged, and took the body on his shoulder. We could see later that he threw it to an abandoned mining pit, and threw some soil over the body.

'What do you drink, gentlemen?' asked the innkeeper.

'Beer. What is your best?'

'The ale! It's a true Burton Ale from Staffordshire.'

I was a little curious about this ale that came directly from England, but before I could say anything Bernard ordered, "Five bottles of beer!'

'Have you got money?' asked the innkeeper suspiciously.

Bernard indignantly dived in his pocket, but Sam grabbed his arm.

'Just leave it to me,' he said and turning to the barman he asked, 'How much is the beer?'

'Three dollars a bottle,' he replied without blinking.

'Cheap,' nodded Sam. 'Have you got a scale?'

'Do you want to pay with gold?'

'Naturally.'

Sam took out an egg-sized nugget.

'Wow!' exclaimed the barman. 'This is nice! Where did you find it?'

'In my bonanza.'

'Where is it?'

'In America,' replied Sam with a bored face, 'I can't tell you more precisely, because my memory often lets me down. But if I need money, I can find it even blindfolded.'

The barman understood the rebuke. Nobody would have told him where his bonanza was, and it was impolite to ask about it. He brought a scale. He exchanged the nugget at a very low price, and the scale was suspect too, but Sam so indifferently put away the money as if it was unimportant to him whether he had been cheated by a few ounces or not. The barman's face reminded me to a hawk. In his eyes greed flashed.

He brought the beer. Had we came from the savannah, we might have enjoyed it. But after Dona Elvira's hosting our palette protested against this terrible liquid. For three dollars we could have bought champagne elsewhere, and here we had to accept a home-made brew. It was a good taster, not only of the beer, but also of the manner in which the prospectors were exploited here.

The barman returned to our table because his curiosity could not let him rest. He asked, 'Is you bonanza far from here?'

'Which one?' asked Sam indifferently.

'What do you man? You have more than one?'

'I don't know if it's four or five,' replied Sam. 'The fifth is good too, but I don't feel like working on it.'

'Four bonanza! I don't believe it! Then you wouldn't have come to this sad Yellow Wood!'

'It's your business whether you believe it or not, it doesn't matter to me.'

'Why don't you sell at least the fifth?'

'What for?' asked Sam shrugging his shoulder. 'I don't need money.'

'Great! You don't need money! If you are lazy, take a partner, who knows how to do it. Like the famous Allan Marshall who came here with a thousand dollars, and made ten thousands.'

'What?'

'This is true! He had a helper, whom he fired, because he stole from him. This is why Marshall left, but the helper stayed here, and I heard from him what businesses Marshall made. They say that he buried huge nuggets in his tent. Then one day he disappeared, and nobody knows where.'

'Didn't he have a horse?'

'He had, of course. The day before yesterday three men were looking for him. Two whites and a mulatto.'

'What did they want from him?'

'I don't know! They looked for the place where his tent stood. When they returned they sat for a long time by this table, and studied some paper. I think they dug it out by the place of the tent. I didn't want to ask them, but I think it was some sort of map, or a similar drawing.'

'And then?'

'They asked where Short Rivulet was. I told them.'

'It's difficult to find that place after a description.'

'Have you been there?'

'Yes, once.'

'Tell me, my friend,' said Bernard turning to the innkeeper smiling, 'would you show me the place where the tent stood? Maybe I could find something there.'

'I doubt it!' answered the innkeeper, 'But you can see the place from here. On the hill side, behind the hawthorn bushes.'

'I may check it out,' said Bernard. 'And what's the name of that helper whom he fired?'

'Fred Buller. The second allotment from the top is his.'

I nudged Bernard. We stood up, and left the place. Along the stream we walked up to the hill, and stopped by the second allotment, where two men worked.

'Good morning, gentlemen! Do you know where can I find Mr Buller?'

'I'm Buller,' said one of them.

'Could I talk to you?'

'Why not, if you pay for it? Time really is money here.'

'How much do you want for ten minutes?'

'Three dollars.'

Marshall paid him.

'Thank you, Sir. What can I do for you?'

His eyes were twinkling craftily, and I saw that we had to be alert, and thus I took over the conversation.

'Come out of there,' I told him. 'Let's go to the side here.'

He did not do it willingly, and glanced at our weapons. He did not seem to have a clear conscience.

'What is it about?' he asked.

'Three men visited you the day before yesterday, didn't they?'

'Yes.'

'Two whites and a mulatto?'

'Yes, why?'

'The two whites were father and son.'

'Yes and the mulatto is an old acquaintance.'

Something came to my mind and immediately I said, 'Yes, mine too, if it's the same person. He's got a scar on the right side of his face made by a stab.'

'Yes, yes! So you know the capi..., I mean, Shelley! How do you know him?'

'We had good business together, but then I lost him, and I'd like to know where he is.'

'I don't know,' he said.

I saw that he was telling the truth, and continued the enquiries.

'What did they want?'

'Sir, the ten minutes have gone!'

'Not yet, but you don't have to reply, I know that they were asking about your old boss, Mr Marshall. Let's extend the talk, and you get five more dollars, right?'

Bernard immediately paid.

'Thank you, Sir. You aren't so mean as Shelley and the two Morgans! I don't know where they have gone, but they went over to the place of Marshall's tent, and dug about until they found something. It was a valueless piece of paper. Had Shelley talked to me cleverly, like you, they could have got very different papers.'

'What kind of papers?' I asked.

'Letters.'

'Written to whom?'

'Sir, that's not in the few dollars that you paid!'

'What's the price?'

'A hundred dollars.'

'That's a bit brave price! You didn't give it to the *capitano* because he didn't offer you money, and now you want to make some profit. How about fifty?'

'I can see that you really know Shelley. Right. You get them for fifty dollars. Come to my tent!'

We returned to the hut that he called "tent". It had three mud walls, and a torn tar-board acted as a roof. In the corner there was a hole. Buller pulled out a bundle from it. From this he took out two letters. When I stretched out for it, he pulled it back quickly.

'First the money!' he said.

'Show the address at least!'

'Right, but only from here!'

Bernard cast a look at the envelope and paid. The letters were from Allen to his father. Bernard smiled bitterly. He was hurt by paying for the letters that this rascal stole, and held back. Buller nodded contented, and put the money in his pocket. He was about to tie up his bundle, when something gleamed in it. Bernard immediately snatched it. It was a double cover golden watch.

'What do you want with that watch?' snarled Buller.

'Nothing special,' replied Bernard, 'just I want to know the situation.'

'What do you mean? It isn't wound up. Give it back!'

'Just a moment!' I shouted at him, and grabbed his arm. 'What kind of watch is it?'

'Allan's watch,' replied Bernard. 'How did you get it?'

'None of your business!' said the man sulkily.

'Not quite!' I said. 'This gentleman is Allan Marshall's brother. How did you get this watch?'

'He gave it to me.'

'He's a liar.' said Bernard. 'This is a three-hundred-dollar watch. One doesn't give it to a servant.'

I grabbed Buller's other arm too. He tried to jerk it out, but failed.

'What do you want from me?' he cried. 'How dare you search my tent? Do you want me to shout for help?'

'Calm down, because I'll squeeze your throat if I must!' I replied.

'He stole the watch,' said Bernard.

'Of course,' I nodded.

'I'll take it back.'

'Of course,' I said again. 'He also stole the letters, and he has to give them back to us.'

'And his punishment?'

'We'll take back the money. Just get in his pocket, I'm holding him. Take the fifty dollars, the five dollars and the three. Then he can go!'

He kicked and bucked in vain. We took back the money, and then I let him go. He rushed towards the bar cursing.

We followed him slowly, and soon arrived there. Our horses were there, but we could not see Bob. There was a big noise in the bar. We quickly entered, and saw a real battle. In the corner Winnetou stood. With his left hand he held Buller by his throat, and with his gun in his right he tried to keep the others away. Next to him stood Sans-ear who defended himself in a similar way. Bob's gun was twisted out of his hand, but he kept the attackers away with his knife and fist. Later I learnt that Buller enticed the prospectors with the tale that we wanted to rob him. The angry prospectors attacked our friends, and as there were many, they pushed them back. We arrived just at the right time.

'We'll work with the butt of the gun, Bernard!' I said. 'We'll shoot only if there's no other way!'

We started it. First we rescued Bob from the threatening arms of five men, and then pushed away Sam's attackers. Fortunately they did not have firearms.

'Are you here, Charlie?' asked Sam joyously. 'I had enough of the butt of the gun. Let's us the tomahawk! But only with the flat end!'

In five minutes we put the whole company to flight. Only Buller and the innkeeper remained in the room apart from us. Buller wanted to escape too, but I caught his coat.

'Did he really steal the clock and the money, Charlie?' asked Sam.

'And the letters,' I replied.

'Well, it's none of my business,' said Sam, 'but he raised all these gold prospectors against us. So, he must pay for it.'

'You won't kill him Sam!' I exclaimed.

'No,' replied Sam. 'Hold him tight Winnetou!'

When it was done, Sam aimed and cut Buller's nose off. After a short discussion with the innkeeper in which Sansear promised a similar treatment to him if he put his nose in things that was not his business, and forcing the innkeeper to drink five bottles of his "ale" in one go that must have made him ill, we left the bar.

In a few minutes we were riding along the river to Short Rivulet. It was just in time as the prospectors were already gathering with their shotguns. When we got some way away, Bernard cried out, 'Let's stop for a moment! I have to read these letters at long last!'

We jumped off the horses, and sat next to him on the grass. Bernard opened the letters.

'Allan's last two letters,' he remarked when he had read them. 'He complained that he hadn't received an answer. But in the last letter there's a part that I have to read to you. Listen! "I'm making much better deals than I would have thought. I sent the nuggets to Sacramento and San Francisco with a reliable man. I can get more for them there than for the price I bought them here. I've already doubled my capital, but I'm saying good-bye to Yellow Wood, because production dropped here, and the security is so bad that I don't dare to send my goods to the town. From certain signs it seems to me that the bandits want to search my tent. Thus I decided that I would disappear from here unexpectedly. With about a hundred pound of nuggets I'll move to Short Rivulet where they started to work on an even better bonanza, thus the business would be better there too. I'll spend a month there, then I'll find a ship that takes me to San Francisco.'

'So, Short Rivulet is not a fairy tale,' nodded Sam. 'Allan has gone there. And the two Morgans knew it. But how?'

'Probably the paper that they found in the place of Allan's tent,' I opined.

'That's possible,' said Bernard. 'There's a sentence in the letter, listen to this! "... As I don't go with a larger group. I don't need guides either, because after the map I've made a good outline in which I marked the direction well, thus I cannot lose my way ..."'

'Maybe he threw away a draft when he completed his outline.' I said, 'which was careless.'

'It cannot happen to a real Westerner,' remarked Sam, 'because one's life may depend on such a small detail. I'm really anxious for Allan. Even if he could get to the Short Rivulet, it's still a problem to deal with the Snake Indians, who have their hunting grounds there.'

'Are they worse than the Comanche?' asked Bernard wrinkling his forehead.

'They are like the others. They are noble to their friends, and cruel to their enemies,' replied Sam. 'I don't have to be afraid of them, because I lived with them for some time, and every Snake Indians know Sans-ear's name.'

'The chief of the Shoshone is my friend,' remarked Winnetou. 'The Shoshone are good, honest warriors. They haven't forgotten that the chief of the Apache smoked the peace pipe with them.'

The important thing was that both Sam and Winnetou smoked the peace pipe with the Shoshone, thus there were no concerns about them. I was also happy that both knew the route to the Short Rivulet well.

We advanced on a more and more difficult landscape, because we were going on the paths from the valley of Sacramento to the San Jose Mountains to catch up with the bandits. They had two days advantage even if they could not advance as fast as we did. Of course, our advancing was only relatively fast, because the journey was still long.

After a whole week of struggling we arrived to an interesting place. Among the mountains an even higher mount rose. It was like a huge ungula. In the bottom it was covered by the thick waving of the foliage of trees, while higher there was an almost impenetrable forest of pine trees. The top of the mount was a plateau with a lake in the middle. This was the Black Eye Lake that was named by its gloomy surroundings. The Short Rivulet entered this lake.

It seemed unbelievable that in such a height one could find gold. How could the gold come there? The river could not have brought it from the higher Western mountains. It was more likely that the bonanza was the leftover of a volcanic change when the powers of nature moved whole mountains. There were more hopes in this place than in the famous valley of the Sacramento.

Heading to the mountain there was a jungle in front of us, but when we got higher, the scene became friendlier. We felt as if we were in an endless huge hall, whose ceiling was made of closely knitted, yet transparent, green foliage that were held by thousands of columns. The tree trunks were so thick that not even three men could have embraced them.

We slowly advanced higher and higher until we got to the plateau. Now we could quicken up, and by sunset we arrived to the southern end of the Black Eye Lake. The deep, motionless water was fluorescent in the evening sunshine. It was mysterious like death.

In the valley the sun had long gone, but up where we were the sunset was a long process, and it allowed us to scout around the shores of the lake.

'Should we continue?' asked Bernard, who was the most impatient of all of us.

'We should make our camp here for tonight,' said Winnetou in his decisive and brief way.

'Yes, this is the best,' agreed Sam. 'There's thick moss here, on which we can sleep well, and there's water and grass for our horses. Let's find a small hidden place where we can make a small fire on which we could roast the wild turkey that Bob shot.'

Yes, on that day Bob gave us our dinner, perhaps for the first time in our journey, and he was very proud of this. After a short search we found the place that satisfied both Winnetou and Sam. Soon the fire was lit, and Bob started to make the dinner. In the meantime it became completely dark, but our fire lit only the nearby trees and bushes. Soon the wild turkey was ready, and we consumed it happily.

After a good night's rest we got on our horses, and did not stop until the valley of Short Rivulet. It was not even a river, only a stream that was fed by brooks from the hills. It was dry in the hot season. We expected to find a lively scene with struggling and hopeful people, but we found only destroyed tents, collapsed holes, and thrown away tools. These were the signs of some desperate, death-or-life struggle. There was no doubt that the prospectors were attacked by robbers, but we could not find any bodies.

After some searching we found a larger tent on the other bank of the river among the trees. It had also been damaged, but it had not been destroyed completely. We searched it thoroughly, but we could not find any evidence of the owner of the tent.

It was a terrible disappointment for Bernard who hoped that he would see Allan here.

'Something tells me that Allan lived in this tent,' he said with a sigh.

We rode around the river surrounded by the jungle, and we found the tracks of riders on the western shore.

'Allan wanted to leave in this direction to get to a port from where he could have travelled further. The bandits followed him,' opined Bernard.

'It's possible,' as I did not want to challenge his hopes, 'assuming that he had escaped. Strange that we did not find any bodies. It seems that the bandits threw their victims into the lake.'

707

Yes, it was probably the fate of people who had dreamt of fortune, happiness, and the joys of life, and now they rest in the water of the Black Eye Lake. Had they had more modest desires, they would have had a different fate.

'Who murdered them?' asked Bernard.

'The two Morgans and the mulatto,' I replied. 'Nobody else could have been.'

'Then we will catch them now!' exclaimed Sam, and threatened with his fist the forest to where the tracks led.

'Then let's go!' I also cried.

The tracks there were still vague, but once we got lower, they became deeper, and were also visibly dispersed. I watched the tracks for a long time, and I then shared my conclusions with my companions.

'Sixteen riders, and four well packed mules went here. The prints of the mules' hooves are sharp, and they also show that the mules stopped several times, and refused to advance. The bandits could not go as fast as we do, and thus hopefully we can catch them before they attack Allen.'

By the afternoon we arrived to the place where the gang spent their night. This was their first resting place. We followed the tracks without stopping, and rested only at sunset. At dawn we continued our journey, and in the morning we found the second camp of the gang. Thus we made up one day on them.

We wanted to reach the upper branch of the Sacramento to be sure that we would catch up with the bandits on the following day. But there was an unpleasant surprise. The tracks suddenly split to two. The Sacramento had a big arc there, and we were heading to the middle of this bend. The tracks of the four mules turned to the left to cut through the bend and six riders went with them. The rest followed the direction of the previous tracks.

'Damn!' exclaimed Sam annoyed. 'Was it a trick or not?'

'I think it wasn't a trick,' I replied. 'I don't think they had us in their mind.'

'Then why did they split?'

'It's easy. They put the loot on the back of the mules. These couldn't keep up with the riders. They wanted to catch Allen, thus they sent the loot with six bandits to the left, and the rest galloped forward. They surely agreed on a place along the Sacramento where they would meet.'

'Then let the mules go where they go, and we gallop after the other riders. My Tony is really bored by this slow riding.'

'Slow?' I laughed. 'Before you ride faster, you have to decide which Morgan you want to catch.'

'What do you mean? Both, of course!'

'You can't do that!'

'Why?'

'Most of the burden on the mules is gold. If Fred Morgan departs from them, whom would he send with them?'

'Whom?' asked Sam, surprised.

'His son, naturally,' I replied

'Damn it! I now understand it! You are right, Charlie!'

'So, who's your choice?'

'The elder.'

'Right! Then let's ride!'

As we calculated, by the evening we reached the Upper Sacramento. We crossed the river, and made our camp on the other side.

On the following morning we continued the chase. At noon we got to the plains, where the tracks were so fresh that we were sure not more than five miles separated us from the bandits.

Excitedly we rode forward. Then suddenly we slowed down astonished. We looked at the ground with goggling eyes. What was it? There were so many tracks that suggested at least a hundred riders. The ground showed a hard battle. There were even blood stains on the grass.

We examined the ground thoroughly. The tracks of three horses pointed towards the plains, while the rest of the tracks forward.

We followed the broadest tracks in the fastest possible gallop. It was possible that as Allan had not had enough lead on his pursuers, he had been captured by Indians. A mile later we caught sight of an Indian village.

'Shoshone!' exclaimed Winnetou.

'Snake Indians,' nodded Sam, and we rode into the camp without stopping.

In the middle of the camp at least a hundred warriors stood around the chief. For our approach they grabbed their guns and tomahawks, and they opened the circle to give way to us.

'Ko-tu-cho!' shouted Winnetou as he was galloping towards the chief as if he wanted to wade through him. However, he stopped his horse suddenly at one or two steps from the Shoshone chief.

The chief waited for the end of this equestrian show, and then lifted both of his arms.

'Winnetou, the chief of the Apache! Joy fills the hearts of the Shoshone warriors, and Ko-tu-cho is full of happiness that he could see again his brave brother!'

'And I?' shouted Sam. 'Can't you recognise your old friend, Sans-ear?'

'Ku-ta-cho doesn't forget any of his friends. Our tents are open to your guests.'

At this moment I heard a blood curling scream from the right, I turned, and saw that Bernard was prostrated on a human shape on the ground. I quickly went there. The man was dead as his lungs were shot through. He was a white man, and his countenance was similar to Bernard's. I understood the situation.

My companions also hurried to him, and none of them said a word. They looked at Bernard with deep sympathy. He kissed the dead body's eyes, face, and then suddenly stood up.

'Who killed him?' he asked.

The chief of the Shoshone answered, 'Ko-tu-cho sent out his warriors to have some equestrian exercise. They saw that three palefaces were approaching, and behind them other palefaces who were chasing the three. It wasn't brave for fourteen to chase three, thus the red warriors hurried to help the three warriors. But the others started to shoot, and they hit this paleface. Our warriors attacked the chasing palefaces, and captured eleven, but three have escaped. The warriors brought the shot man to the camp, but he died. His two companions are resting in our tents.

'I have to talk to them! This man is my brother! My father's son!' cried Bernard.

'You arrived with Winnetou and Sans-ear, my brother, thus you are our friend. Follow me!'

First he led us to a large tent, where the prisoners lay tied up. The mulatto was among them, but not the two Morgans.

'What do you want to do with these palefaces, my Shoshone brothers?' I asked the chief.

'Do you know them, my white brother?'

'I know that they are bandits, and many innocent people's death is on their souls.'

'Then you can make the judgement about them.'

I looked at my companions, and then I said, ''They deserve death, but we don't have time to do it now. We leave it to you to carry out their judgement.'

'You made the right decision, my brother.'

'Where are the two palefaces who accompanied the dead man?'

'Follow me, I'll show them to you.'

He led us to another tent where two men were sleeping, and their clothing suggested that they were *tropeiro*. We woke them up, and started to question them, but soon it became clear that they did not know anything important. Allan recruited them, and they served him well. We returned to the dead man.

Bernard had gone through a difficult learning in the last few months, and had become strong physically as well as psychologically, but his hand was shaking when he searched his brother's pockets. With tearful eyes he looked at the well-known objects. When the notebook of the dead came to his hand, and he saw the notes of his beloved brother, his handwriting, he kissed every page, and broke out in sobbing. I stood by him, and I could not hold him back from allowing the free flowing of his tears.

The Shoshone were around us. Despise appeared on Ko-tu-cho's face seeing Bernard's weakness. Winnetou had to remark, 'You shouldn't think that these palefaces are squaws. The brother of the dead man fought against the Comanche and the bandits bravely, and you have heard the name of the other paleface. He's Old Shatterhand.'

There was a quiet murmur among the Shoshone. The chief came up to me, and offered his hand.

'The Shoshone will celebrate this day,' he said. 'You can stay with us, my brothers. You can eat of the game that our warriors hunted. Let's smoke the calumet, and you can also watch the war exercise of the Shoshone.'

'My heart is joyous that I could be the guest of my Shoshone brothers,' I replied, 'but I cannot stay with you today. We will return soon. We'll leave our dead with you. Our most urgent task is to catch his murderers, and punish them.'

'Yes, we cannot miss a moment!' cried out Bernard recovering from his lethargy. 'Who comes with me?'

'I, for example,' said Sam.

'All of us, of course,' I added.

Winnetou was heading to his horse. The Shoshone chief gave orders quietly. Soon they led out a wonderful mustang.

'Ko-tu-cho will go with you. The Shoshone will take the belongings of the dead to the tent of the chief, and the squaws will mourn for him.'

Our short but sad visit to the Shoshone was finished. With renewed energy we continued the chase. It was easy to follow their tracks, and their advantage was not more than two hours. Our horses, as if they understood our intention, almost flew over the plains.

It was mid-afternoon, and we had to catch up with the murderers before sunset otherwise they could have escaped. We galloped for three hours without stopping. I jumped off the saddle to examine the prints of the hooves, as they were sharply visible in spite of the short and thick grass. As none of the blades of the grass had yet risen, the murderers could not be more than a mile away.

I took out my telescope, and turned to the direction where the tracks led. Finally I noticed three spots that apparently moved slowly.

'There they are!'

'Then forward!' cried Bernard, and spurred his horse.

'No!' I protested. 'We have to surround them. My horse, and the mustang of the chief of the Shoshone can still run fast. I will go to the right, Ku-tu-cho to the left, and we will get ahead of them in twenty minutes. You will charge at them from behind.'

'Uff!' exclaimed the chief of the Shoshone, and turned to the left in gallop. I did the same, but to the right.

In ten minutes my companions disappeared from my view, though they also rode fast. I thought that by then I was riding parallel with the three bandits. My horse, in spite of the trials of the past days, was still fresh. It was not sweating, and its muzzle was not foaming.

After another ten minutes I turned to the left. Five minutes later I could see through my telescope that the bandits were behind me and the Shoshone chief. The Indian turned at that moment, and rode towards the three men. I did the same, and I was contented how well Ko-tu-cho understood my plan.

As the bandits noticed us, they turned back, and saw that they were pursued from there too. They had only one option: to break through in one of the directions. They chose the Shoshone's.

I emitted that shrill cry that the Indians use to urge the mustang to put all its energy into the gallop. I stood up in the stirrup to help the breathing of my horse. Westerners ride like this only when the prairie is on fire.

One of the bandits stopped his horse, and lifted his gun. I immediately recognised Fred Morgan. He was aiming at the

Shoshone chief, and at the moment when the gun popped, Ko-tu-cho crashed on the ground with his horse. I shouted in my anger, because I thought that either the chief or his mustang was mortally wounded. But I was wrong. In the next moment they jumped up, and the Shoshone chief was galloping towards the bandits while swinging his tomahawk. What I had seen was one of the wonderful results of the Indian horse training. The mustang had been taught that for a certain noise it should lie down, thus the bullet whistled well above their heads.

Ko-tu-cho crushed the head of one of the bandits at the moment when I charged at Fred Morgan. I decided that I would catch him alive not caring with the fact that the other barrel of his gun was still loaded, and he was aiming at me. His horse was restless, and the bullet only grazed the sleeve of my jacket.

'Hurrah! Here's Old Shatterhand!' I screamed, and threw my lasso. My horse raised, turned, and galloped back. I felt the jerk, even if it was not as strong as the one I had felt when I stopped Don Fernando de Venango e Colonna's cow. The noose of my lasso held Fred Morgan's body and arms. He crashed to the ground, and I dragged him behind my horse. Soon Sam and the others arrived. The third bandit shot at Bernard, but in the next moment he fell from his horse dead, because Sam's bullet, and the Shoshone's tomahawk killed him at the same time.

I jumped off my horse. At last! At last! We captured Fred Morgan! When he crashed from his horse, he lost his consciousness. I took my lasso off him, and tied him up with his own lasso. My friends were running there. Bob was the first. He pulled his knife to stab the bandit.

'How many times should I stab him?' he asked.

'Stop!' shouted Sam to him grabbing his arm. 'This man is mine!'

'What happened to the other two?' asked Bernard.

'They kicked the bucket,' I replied without any pity. I looked at him. His trousers were blood soaked.

'What about you? Are you wounded?'

'Only a graze.'

'That's bad, because we aren't yet ready as we have to capture Patrick with the mules. What should we do with Morgan?' I asked.

'Morgan is mine!' stated Sam decisively. 'I should smash up his head right now, but that's too easy! I'd like to talk to him first. Bernard and Bob could take him to the Shoshone village, and guard him. As Bernard is wounded and has to arrange his brother's funeral, he will need Bob. Three of us, Winnetou, Old Shatterhand and I, are enough to deal with the six men. I don't know if the chief of the Shoshone wants to come with us.'

'The chief won't desert you, my white brothers,' said Ko-tu-cho.

'Then four of us. More than enough!'

'Then let's do it!' I cried.

We tied Fred Morgan on his horse. Bernard and Bob rode either side of him, and set off to the Shoshone village.

'Let's not waste time,' I opined. 'Let's use the time until it's light.'

'Where do you want to go, my brothers?' asked the Shoshone.

'To the valley of the Sacramento,' replied Sam.

'Then we can let our horses graze,' said Ko-tu-cho. 'I know the route well. I can lead you even in the night.'

'We shouldn't have sent Morgan back so quickly,' remarked Sam. 'We should have questioned him.'

'About what?'

'For example the exact meeting place with his son. If we knew it, we could get there earlier.'

'Come on! You don't imagine that he would have told you!'

'I would have beaten it out from him!'

'Never! He wouldn't have helped you to get his son and his treasures. Especially as he knows that it wouldn't change his own fate anyway.'

715

'You are right, Charlie,' said Winnetou. 'The eyes of the chief of the Shoshone and my eyes are sharp enough to find the tracks of the mules.'

'Who are these people?' asked the chief of the Shoshone. This was out of character to be curious about other people's affairs, but he felt he was in the company of warriors who were equal to him, thus he became less introverted.

'The accomplices of those bandits whom the Shoshone warriors captured.'

'How many of them?'

'Six.'

'Are these men the six of whom my brother just talked about? We will find them, and capture them.'

By sunset our horses were sufficiently rested to continue the chase. The chief of the Shoshone led us. He confidently rode in front all night.

Soon the prairie was behind us. We had to climb up on mountains, and descend to valleys. We had to break through forests and thickets. At dawn we stopped for an hour, ate something, and then continued our journey. We had not stopped until we reached the valley of the Sacramento. We rode into the valley, and soon reached a place where a side-valley led to the left and to the right. At this crossing there was a blockhouse. According to the board above its door it was a "hotel". The owner found an excellent place for his inn. Many carts, wagons, horses and pack horses stood outside the house. There was not enough room inside, thus the owner set up tables and benches for the excess guests outside.

'Should we go in to enquire?' asked Sam.

'Have you got nuggets for Burton Ale?' I laughed.

'I have a lot of them,' replied Sam. 'Let's sit down, but outside,' replied Sam. 'You know that I prefer the fresh air.'

We tied our horses to the fence, and sat down in a booth that the owner called "terrace". It was an excellent place. We were outside, yet in the inn as the walls of the booth hid us.

'What are you drinking?' asked the barman.

'How much is the beer?' asked Sam carefully after the lesson in Yellow Wood.

'Half a dollar for a bottle.'

'This is good! Four bottles, please!'

In a few minutes the beer arrived. Sam was about to start his enquiries, when he spotted a small company through one of the gaps of the wall of the box. They were arriving from the side-valley, and stopped by the house. Two men led four mules, and behind them there were three riders. In front one of the men rode. I also looked out, and squeezed Sam's arm so that he would not exclaim as the leading rider was Patrick Morgan.

The six men tied the horses to the fence and sat down by a table just in front of our booth.

The first thing that caught my attention was that there were no packs on the mules. The bandits obviously hid the loot somewhere, and were heading to the meeting place. They ordered brandy, and started to talk not suspecting that we could hear every word.

'I wonder if your father is already there.'

'Very likely,' replied Patrick. 'They had less to carry. Sorting out the stupid Marshall couldn't take much time as he only had two men.'

'Stupid indeed! Such a dangerous journey with two men! And all those treasures!'

'It's good to us! He should have been more careful with the draft of his journey plan that he left in his tent. But damn it! What's that!'

'What? Why are you frightened?'

'Look at those four horses!'

'Three of them are excellent animals, but the fourth is ridiculous.'

Sam clinched his hand. 'I'll make you laugh soon!' he murmured.

Patrick had a very similar view, because he remarked, 'You won't laugh if you know about that horse. It's famous in the West! Do you know her master?'

717

'I don't.'

'Sans-ear!'

'Damn it! How comes that he's here?'

'Doesn't matter! Let's drink up. I have met him before, and I don't want him to recognise me!'

'Let's go then!' said one of the accomplices, and in the next minute the whole company disappeared.

'These are the men,' I told the Shoshone chief. 'You with Winnetou can easily catch up with them, while if we two cut off their retreat, we surround them.'

'Haw!' said the Indian and stood up. Winnetou and he got on their horses and galloped to the valley after Patrick and his accomplices. Sam paid for the beer that was cheaper and better than the one in Yellow Wood, and we left too, in pursuit.

The bandits had not even recognised that they were surrounded. Winnetou and Ko-tu-cho appeared in front of them, and behind them Sam and I galloped.

'Damn you!' swore Patrick after glancing back.

He picked up his gun, but crashed from his horse before he could have taken aim. It was Winnetou's lasso that caused it. His five accomplices fled to five directions.

'Let them go!' I shouted. 'The main rascal is caught!'

But my companions did not listen to me. They shot them off their horses one by one. The last was killed by the Shoshone chief's tomahawk.

'It was too hasty!' I scolded Sam. 'We should have found out from them where they hid the loot.'

'Morgan will tell us.'

'I doubt it.'

I was right. He remained quiet. The gold, that caused so many deaths, was lost.

We tied Patrick on the horse, and, to avoid the "hotel", we crossed the Sacramento that was not particularly deep there. We had not squeezed a word out of our prisoner until Bernard, in his impatience, rode towards us. The bandit's face distorted, and he swore. When we arrived to the camp I pushed him in the tent where his father lay with the other prisoners.

'Here's your son, Mr Morgan!' I told him. 'He hardly could wait to meet you, so I brought him here!'

Fred Morgan looked at me with eyes glowing of hatred, but did not respond. We arrived in the evening, thus the judgement had to wait till the morning. The Shoshone chief hosted us in his own tent. There was a sumptuous dinner, then we smoked the peace pipe, and finally everybody retired to his tent.

The trials of the last few days exhausted me too, and I slept deeper than usual. However, my sleep was not calm. I was fighting with determined enemies who surrounded me from every side, and threatened my life. I was hitting about, and knocked out many of them, but their numbers kept on increasing. The cold sweat poured from me when I thought my last hour came. For the first time in my life I was in mortal fear. Of course, it was all only a nightmare. However, when I woke up I heard a terrible noise from outside.

I jumped up, grabbed my weapons, and rushed out of the tent half naked. I immediately understood what happened. In some way the prisoners escaped from their bondage, and broke out of their tent. They attacked the guards. Immediately Indians jumped out of the tents, some with guns, some with tomahawks, but most with knives. Winnetou also appeared, and with a quick glance measured up the situation.

'Surround the camp!' he thundered, and sixty or eighty warriors immediately took positions at the edge of the camp.

I saw that I was not needed. The prisoners countered the Shoshone without weapons, and there were ten times as many Indians as bandits. I also heard Sam's voice from the turmoil, and it calmed me. The struggle lasted only for ten minutes. All the prisoners were massacred. The death cry of the last bandit hit my ear. I looked in that direction, and recognised his pale face from the distance. It was Fred Morgan. Sam's knife finished his life.

Sam caught sight of me, and hurried to me.

'What's up, Charlie? Did you withdraw?'

'I thought there were enough of you.'

'Yes, it's true. But if I hadn't been up all night with the guards in front of the tent of the prisoners, they could have escaped.'

'But I hope none of them escaped.'

'None. I counted them. But you know, I imagined the minute in which I settle the bill with the Morgans differently.'

He stooped down next to me and engraved the last two, so much longed for, notches on his gun.

'Yes, Charlie, I revenged the death of my dearests. Now I can die, I have no other aim in life.'

'Don't speak like this, Sam! Once you calm down, you will think differently. Knock it out from your head that you have lived only for the revenge!'

'I'll see Charlie ...'

'Yes, you will. Revenge and hatred doesn't lead anywhere.'

Sam slowly got up, and returned to his tent silently.

On the following day we buried Allan Marshall. It was a Christian funeral. As there was no coffin, we wrapped the body in several bison hides.

After the funeral the Shoshone did not leave time for Bernard to indulge dark thoughts. They organised a big hunt in which we had to participate. A week passed like this, and then we returned to San Francisco.

RAILWAY BANDITS

THE MOST beautiful and most interesting part of the American West is the huge area from the source of the Yellowstone River and Snake River all the way to Green River. It comprises of the whole of Wyoming and some parts of Montana, Idaho, Nevada, Utah and Colorado. It is between the 40th lateral to the 45th. Grim and pleasant landscapes alternate here with natural wonders. The United States created the Yellowstone National Park with other national parks here. Such mountains rise here like the triple Teton Mountain and the mountain ranges that create the valley of Wind River.

I returned to Europe, and I thought I would stay there. Once I had to travel to Hamburg, and I accidentally met an old acquaintance whom I had met in the Wild West. We had hunted together in the swamps of the Mississippi. Later he became a very rich businessman, and settled in Saint Louis. He came over to Europe for a few weeks, and he was ready to return to America. He asked me if I wanted to accompany him. For this pleasure he was ready to pay my fare.

I felt the call of the prairies. I telegrammed for my guns and other equipment, and five days later we were sailing to America.

We spent a few weeks in the forests of the lower Missouri. Then he had to return to Saint Louis, while I travelled on the Missouri to Omaha. I wanted to take the Pacific Railway train to travel to the West, exactly to the area of the Yellowstone Park. My only problem was that I did not have a horse, however, I was convinced that I would find one once I needed it.

The Pacific Railways had not yet been finished. Along the railway lines one could often see workers as they were repairing the bridges and viaducts, or making more permanent constructions in the place of the provisional ones. Wherever the railway passed new settlements mushroomed. These settlements were mainly camps for the workers. Most of them had some fortification against the attacks of the

Indians, who considered the construction of the railways an infringement of their rights.

The fortifications were necessary for another enemy that was more dangerous than the Indians, the white rabble. These people, who could not settle in the East, now moved to the West to make a living from their crimes. The common criminal intention brought these people to gangs that were feared even by the most militant Indian tribes. One of their favourite targets were these new settlements and camps. As these bandits knew that they could not expect any mercy if they were caught, they murdered everyone they caught irrespective of age or sex.

I sat down in a coach in Omaha, and I thought I would go to Ogden, where I wanted to look around in the homeland of the Mormons a little bit. It was Sunday afternoon when the train left Omaha. There was nobody in the coach who attracted my attention, but on the following morning, in Fremont, a man boarded who raised my interest. He sat down next to me, thus I could observe him.

He was a short, stout, round man. His clothing was more comical than trustworthy, but I knew that when one makes judgement by appearance, it could be a major error. He wore a sheepskin coat on his shoulder with fur on the outside, but it was bare in places. It became obvious why he had it on his shoulder: he could not button the coat anymore. His trousers, jacket, and shirt were made of leather. From the appearance of the trousers it was clear that the owner used it as wiping cloth and serviette. Below the trousers his naked ankle was visible, while he wore shoes cut from double sole cowhide boots. These shoes were further reinforced by numerous nails. They seemed to be strong enough to trample a crocodile to death. Half of his hat was missing, and it was impossible to say what had been the original colour of his scarf. There was an ancient pistol and a Bowie knife in his belt. Between these, a pipe and an ammunition bag hung, not to mention a mirror and another pouch that contained, as I learnt later, shaving equipment.

This latter one appeared to me the most unnecessary thing in the West. His small eyes craftily winked from his round, rosy cheeked, shaven face. He reminded me to my old friend Sam Hawkins in many ways.

'Good morning, Sir!' he greeted me, when he sat down.

I returned the greeting, and for a couple of hours we were both silent.

'Do you mind if I smoke?' he asked.

'You have the right,' I replied, 'You don't have to ask permission.'

I also took out my cigar case, and offered him one.

'Thank you,' he said, 'I'll stick with my pipe.'

His pipe hung from his neck. He filled it, and lit it with a punk. Our conversation stopped with this, and he paid his attention to the scenery. When we arrived to the next bigger station, North Platte, which was also a junction, my stout fellow passenger went forward to the coach where his horse travelled. He stroked the animal, and made sure that it had everything it needed, and then returned to our coach. The train started to move again.

We reached Cheyenne in the Black Hills, when the conversation restarted.

'Are you changing here to the Denver train?' he asked.

'No.'

'Then we remain neighbours.'

'Indeed, one can travel with the Pacific far,' I remarked.

'And how far are you travelling, Sir?' he asked.

'For the time being to Ogden,' I answered. 'I will visit the Mormons around the Great Salt Lake and Salt Lake City, then I will head to the Wind River Mountains and the Teton!'

'Huh!' he exclaimed. 'Do you have any company to do this with?'

'No, just alone,' I replied calmly.

'Isn't it a bit too much? Or too hard? The Tetons! Among the Sioux and the grizzlies! What's your job, if I may ask?'

'I'm a writer.'

'Oh! And you want to write a book on the Tetons?'

'Perhaps.'

He laughed.

'And you perhaps have also read about the Indians and the grizzly in books?'

'Indeed I have.'

'And you have your shotgun in that canvass?' he asked with craftily gleaming eyes.

'You are right.'

'Then, my friend, I give you an advice. Return to your home, because although you look like a strong fellow, I doubt that you could shoot even a squirrel let alone a bear! It would be a pity to shorten your life because the books have confused your mind.'

He giggled, and did not suspect that I was just as amused as he was.

'Have you heard of the famous Westerners,' he continued, 'like Winnetou, Old Firehand, Old Shatterhand?'

'I have,' I nodded

'You see, Winnetou, the chief of the Apache, would be able to defend himself against a thousand devils. Old Firehand would be able to shoot every mosquito in a swarm. Old Shatterhand hasn't missed a shot in his life, and can knock out anyone with a single blow. If any of these three said to me that they were going up to the three Tetons, I would believe them. But you, Mr Writer!'

He paused a bit, and then asked, 'Have you got a horse?'

'I don't have one, but I'll get one.'

'Where?'

'In the mountains. I heard that good mustangs can be caught there. One tames it, and it's free.'

The stout man laughed so much that his belly shook.

'You want to catch a mustang! Excellent! Maybe with hooks as fish? You need only patience and nothing else! Good Lord, these townees! It's not a Sunday excursion, Sir,' he said. 'It's a serious challenge.'

'Why do you think that I'm a townee?'

'That's easy! Because everything is so nice and clean on you. Your boots are new! Your leggings are made of the finest elk leather. Your shirt is a masterpiece from the hand of an Indian squaw. Your hat must have cost you at least twelve U.S. dollars.'

'I'll get on with it somehow,' I replied, and with this the conversation stopped.

Our train had passed Sherman Station, and it was dark. In the morning we arrived to Rawlins. This is where the barren mountains started on which apart from wormwood, no other plant can live. There are no rivers or streams in this stone desert. The few men who had struggled there could not suspect what a buzzing life would develop soon when they would start the excavation of the coal from these mountains.

We had travelled almost nine hundred miles from Omaha, when the gloomy landscape started to change, and we could see more green, more plants. The slopes of the mountain were covered with lush grass. The train crossed a beautiful valley and then arrived to large, open plains. The engine gave out several short whistles in quick succession that warned of dangers. We jumped up from our seats, the brakes and wheels screeched, and the train stopped suddenly.

The passengers got off, and their first feeling was the joy of standing on solid ground. Our joy did not last very long, because when we looked around, we could see a horrible scene. The side of the tracks was covered by the remains of a derailed, burnt out freight and workers' train. It was obvious that the train had been attacked by bandits. During the night they tore up the railways, and the wagons fell down from the high embankment. Only the iron pieces survived, because the bandits robbed the wagons, and then burnt them.

There were many bodies among the remains of the wagons. Some died in the catastrophe, but most were killed by the bandits. No one survived.

We were lucky that the train driver caught sight of the derailed train, otherwise we would have had the same fate. The engine stopped only a few yards from the gap in the tracks. The crew and the passengers were terribly excited. With cries, shouts, curses they ran up and down, and searched the still smoking remains of the train. They wanted to help, but unfortunately there was nobody to help.

They could do only one thing: starting the repair of the tracks. At those time all American trains carried the necessary tools. The head of the crew announced that he would make a report at the next station, but this was all he could do. The rest, chasing and capturing the bandits, was the task of the law enforcement office.

While the others with goodwill, but unnecessarily and without result searched the remains, I decided that I would examine the tracks of the bandits. The railways were by the grassy prairie whose monotony was broken only by a few bushes. I made a good distance next to the railways, then turned to the right, and thus made a large half circle around the scene of the tragedy.

At about three hundred steps from the derailed train I found trampled grass. Not long earlier many people sat or lay in the grass. The tracks led to another place that was surrounded by bushes. Many signs suggested that horses were tied there. I examined the place thoroughly to establish the number of the horses, and then returned to our train.

Along the tracks I met my stout fellow passenger who was doing the same thing, but on the other side. He looked at me surprised.

'Are you walking here, Sir? What are you doing?'

'The same thing as every Western hunter would do in such a situation: I was looking for tracks.'

'You do that in vain! The bandits were clever, and they erased their tracks. I couldn't find one, and I don't think that a greenhorn would outdo me in this.'

'Maybe the greenhorn has better eyes,' I replied, 'and thought that there were more bushes on the right hand side, thus it would be more advantageous for the bandits, while you went to the left.'

He looked at me astonished, and said, 'Hm … not a bad thought! And, Mr Writer? Did you find something?'

'Yes.'

'What?'

'I established that they camped three hundred steps from here among the wild cherry, and they hid their horses among the hazelnut grows.'

'Aha! And do you know how many of them?'

'Twenty-six.'

'How do you know it so precisely?'

'Not from the sky, but from the tracks, Sir,' I replied laughing. 'There were eight shod horses and eighteen unshod. But most of the riders were Indians, there were only three whites among them. The leader of the riders was a white bandit, who hobbled on his right leg. His horse is a brown mustang. The chief of the Indians rode on a black stallion, and I think he belonged to the great Sioux tribe, or to be precise, Oglala.'

'Hah!' he exclaimed. 'You have a strong fantasy, Sir!'

'Check it if you don't believe me!'

'How do you know this so precisely? Explain it!'

'Come with me, I'll show you.'

He hurried to the wild cherry bushes almost angrily, and I followed him at a slower pace. When I arrived, he was stooping over the tracks, and dived so much in their study that he did not care with me. In ten minutes he stood up, and came up to me.

'You are right, Sir!' he said in an appreciating voice. 'Eighteen unshod and eight shod horses. But the rest is pure fantasy, you see! They camped here, and left from here, this is the fact, and we don't know anything else.'

'Then I show you how a greenhorn thinks, who has not only fantasy, but also logic.'

'I'm interested,' he said.

His face showed amazement.

'The tracks show that only three horses were tied by their hips as the Indians tie them, the rest were tied by their neck, weren't they?'

He stooped down, examined the tracks, and then said in agreement, 'I can see … only three riders were Indians.

'Now, come to this little puddle! This is where the Indians washed, and then painted their faces again. They took off the paint with bear fat, and then put on new paint. Can you see these round marks on the ground? This is where the paint cups stood. It was hot and the paint was thin. Can you see this black, then this red, and the two blue spots?

'Wow! You are right!'

'And you surely know that the black-red-blue are the war colours of the Oglala, don't you?'

He nodded only but his face showed his increasing astonishment. I held a short pause, and then continued, 'Let's see the rest. When the group arrived here, they stopped by the puddle. You can see that the hoof prints are wet. Only two riders went ahead, obviously the two leaders, to scout the area. Let's see their tracks. One horse was shod as its prints are deeper at the front. The other was unshod as its prints are deeper at the back. You know the riding style of the Indians, don't you? Obviously one of the leaders was an Indian, the other white.'

'Yes, yes, but how do you know …'

'Just wait! Here the two horses bit each other. Stallions do this at the end of a tiring, long journey.'

'How can you see that they bit each other?'

'Firstly from the direction of the tracks. You can see that here they turned to each other. Then look at this hair that I picked up from the ground. Four strings from the mane of a brown mustang, two from the tail of a black stallion. The Indian's horse bit a few hairs from the mane of the mustang, but its master drove it further, and then the brown mustang bit in the tail of the black stallion.'

'Now I understand it, but …'

'The white rider jumped off from the saddle to climb up to the railways. You can see that he walks with one of his legs harder than with the other. He hobbles.'

'Yes! Hobbles with his right leg.'

'The Indian riders did not care with erasing their tracks. It seems they felt completely secure. Why? Either because they thought that they would have sufficient advantage. This is because they knew that reinforcements of the railway company wouldn't arrive, or because they belonged to a larger group This group came for scouting, and this is when they met the whites.'

The stout man looked at me with wide open mouth, and could not speak.

'Man!' he cried out finally. 'Who are you?'

'A greenhorn as you stated earlier. A writer of books. But you didn't ask me, so I did not tell you that I have travelled the prairies through and through.'

'I apologise! Your Sunday clothing, and your sparkling boots mislead me. You looked like an actor who plays a role in a Wild West show, while he doesn't know the Wild West at all. You said that you will catch a mustang, and tame it. As the herds are moving to the North, I believe it. Can you also shoot?'

'Do you want to examine me?' I laughed.

'Maybe … I have a purpose,' he answered seriously.

'What is it?'

'I'll tell you later … Let me see how you can shoot!'

I went to the carriage for my gun. By the time I took it out of its cover, not only the stout fellow, but other passengers surrounded me, because Americans of the West had always been interested in guns.

'Look! A Henry rifle!' exclaimed the stout man. 'How many shots can you shoot with it without loading?'

'Twenty-five.'

'Wow! Man, I envy you for this rifle!'

'But this gun,' and I showed him the bear slayer, 'is equally dear to me.'

He looked at the mark of the gunsmith and stepped back in his surprise.

'Forgive me, sir," he cried, 'This is rare. I have heard that Old Shatterhand has one. Is it a fake one? I'm asking because it looks new. I doubt that it had been used many times.'

'Right. Let's try it. Give me a target.'

'How about you shoot with the shotgun at that bird in the bush?'

I sat down, took out my glasses and put them on my nose. There was laughter.

'What are you laughing at, gentlemen? If you are reading and writing books for thirty years, your eyesight would also suffer.'

'This is a fair point,' said the stout man, 'but the redskins won't wait for you to put your glasses on, and would scalp you. You see you can't even shoot at the bird as it has flown away!'

Although I was a little annoyed, I remained calm especially as I brought this whole thing on myself by not declaring my name.

'So we are looking for another target,' I said.

The bird in question had been sitting at a distance of perhaps two hundred yards, which would have made a very common shot. However at this point I heard a lark above our head, and looked up.

'Can you see the lark up there, gentlemen?" I asked. 'That's the target!'

'That is quite impossible,' exclaimed someone. 'You will hit only the air. Not even Sans-ear or Old Firehand could bring it down!'

'Let's see!'

I raised my gun, and shot.

'It went,' the stout passenger laughed. 'The shot scared it away!'

'You perhaps need glasses too,' I said, 'Cross the embankment, and you will see that the lark fell down about eighty steps from here.'

Some of the passengers immediately rushed over, and brought the lark. The stout man looked at the lark and at me, and repeated this several time.

'You hit it and with a bullet, and not with shots!' he said finally.

'Only boys and Sunday hunters would shoot with shots to such a height, Sir,' I said seriously.

'Was it a lucky shot?'

'Do you want to give me a new target?'

He pulled me aside from the crowd.

'I can see you tricked me,' he shook his head.

'I'm sorry, but it was your fault, because you laughed when I said that I wanted to go up to the Tetons.'

'I now believe that you can climb them! Devilish bloke! I'm really happy that we have met. You said you wanted to visit Salt Lake City. I ask you, is it so important for you?'

'Not at all. What do you propose instead?'

'Have you heard of Fred Walker?'

'A very capable Westerner. The best guide in the mountains, and he speaks several Indian languages.'

'He does,' he replied, 'and here's his hand.'

We shook hands. 'What are you after now, Fred?' I asked.

'Well, there is a man called Haller. He's a bandit. I have followed him and his gang across the West. Look!' he showed me a paper 'This is an exact drawing of the two rear hooves of his horse. They correspond to the one you found. Also Haller limps on his right leg ...'

'Haller!' I exclaimed. 'What's his first name?'

'Sam, Samuel. But he changes his names frequently.'

'Samuel Haller? I have heard of someone by that name. He was the accountant of Rallow, the Oil Prince. He got away with a lot of money.'

'The same man. He seduced the cashier to clear the cash, then shot her. He was pursued by the police, and he killed two constables. In New Orleans, he was caught when he wanted to embark on a ship, but escaped again. This is when he moved to the West. His crimes must stop.'

731

'And you want to catch him?'

'Dead or alive.'

'So you have a personal account to settle with him?'

His eyes were downcast as he looked at the ground. Finally he lifted his head, and replied, 'I don't like talking about it. I may tell you once. Once, when we know each other better. I hope we will know each other better.'

He paused, and then continued, 'I have lost his track, but you found it for me. I'll take my horse from the train, and follow the tracks of the bandits. Will you accompany me, Sir?'

'It's never been my habit to mix myself in other people's business. This Samuel Haller is nothing to me, and I don't know whether I would go with you.'

He blinked at me with his small little eyes and said, 'You have concerns about me, or about yourself? You shouldn't. The stout Walker, if he is ready to connect with someone, that person must be a great guy.'

'In this one I'm similar to you. One cannot be careful enough when choosing a companion. He can go to bed as a comrade, and awake, or rather doesn't awake, as a corpse.'

'You think I'm such a rascal?'

'No. You are an honest fellow. I can see that. Even more, I think you belong to the police, which is a better voucher than the countenance.'

He blushed, and his look was questioning.

'Mr Walker, your behaviour is not police-like, but could be very useful for a detective. As you can see, I have seen through you, so you should be more guarded in the future, because if the news spreads in the West that stout Walker is a secret police agent, you would have your last shot.'

'You are mistaken, sir,' he tried to reassure me.

'Oh come on! Your adventure appeals to me, and I would like to join you immediately to punish these bandits. The risk could not stop me because it lurks everywhere. However, your role-playing does bother me, and before I commit myself, I must know where I stand with you.'

He looked at the ground thoughtfully again, then he raised his head, and looked straight in my eyes.

'Well, Sir, you shall know where you stand with me. You have something in you that creates trust. I already felt it in the carriage. So, I'll be honest with you. Yes, I am a private detective of Dr Sumter in St Louis. My job is to trace escaped prisoners. It's not an easy job, but I do it. I'll tell you once why. It's a sad story. Now it's your turn. Will you join me?'

'I will. Here is my hand; we want to be faithful comrades, and share all the hardship and danger together, Mr Walker!'

His face brightened up.

'This is wonderful! But don't call me Mr Walker. Those who are close to me call me Fred, which is short and sweet.'

'Good, and you can call me Charlie.'

'Then I'll go and bring Victory. Don't get frightened by him, when you see him. He's not a show horse, but he has served me well for twelve years and I would not exchange it for any Arabic stallion. I'll also bring your baggage.'

'Good. Will you tell the others that we won't go with them?'

'Unnecessary. The less they talk about it, the better it is.'

He hurried to the wagon where his horse stood. The ground was not appropriate to put the bridge to the wagon on which the horses could be led down, but Victory did not need it. For his master's word he put out his clever head to investigate the ground, then pushed his ears back, and with a brave and well calculated jump he was next to Walker. Many passengers watched the scene, and they applauded. The clever horse, as if he understood it, neighed loudly.

I smiled. The horse was called Victory, but he was at least twenty years old, and very lean. But I could also appreciate it, because I could see that he did not allow any stranger near. Fred mounted the horse, and rode to me.

'It's quite unfortunate that you don't have a horse, Charlie!' he said.

'I will have,' I replied. 'With Victory's help I'll catch a mustang.'

'I don't think so. He won't accept anybody else on his back but me, otherwise we could ride in turns. Unfortunately you'll have to walk next to me. Look! The train is leaving.'

Indeed, this is what happened. The wheels started to move, and the train disappeared to the West.

'Give me your guns at least, I'll hang them on the saddle,' said Fred.

'Unnecessary,' I replied, 'I can carry them.'

I put the rifle on my back, the bear slayer on my shoulder, and started off alongside Victory. We started the chasing of the train robbers.

The tracks led almost straight to the North, and we followed them without stopping for half a day. Then we had a short break, and ate something that we had with us. We could have had more provisions had we bought food on the train, but neither of us expected that we would need it. As long as the hunter had bullets, he could not die of hunger in the savannah, and my waterproof belt was full of ammunition. Late afternoon I shot a fat raccoon, which is not a delicacy, but edible, and we roasted it for dinner.

On the following morning we found the place where the train robbers spent the night. From the ash and charcoal we saw that they made several camp fires, thus they had not expected anyone would pursue them. The tracks led along a little creek, first through a plain, then into a forest.

It was already evening, but we had not seen anyone. We entered the forest when suddenly an Indian rider appeared in front of us. He was sitting on a black horse, and led a pack horse by the reins.

As soon as the Indian caught sight of us, he slipped off from the saddle, and hiding behind his horse, he lifted his gun to his shoulder. All this happened so quickly that I did not have time to examine his carriage or his face.

Fred also found cover behind his horse, just as quickly and skilfully as the Indian. I jumped behind the thick trunk of a red beech tree. As soon as I reached it, the Indian's gun had gone off, and the bullet scratched the bark of the tree.

Had I hesitated for two more seconds, he would have hit me. Not only the Indian's hand was quick, but his mind too. He immediately recognised that I was the more dangerous enemy, because from behind the trees I could get behind him.

I also lifted the gun to my shoulder, when the Indian's gun went off again. Hearing this I put down my gun. Every gun has its own sound, but it is difficult to differentiate them. One needs good hearing and practice. The refined hearing is the skill of excellent hunters, and the prairie and the forest are good schools to develop such skills.

Although I had not had time to look at the Indian, I immediately recognised the sound of his gun. Only one gun had this popping, Winnetou's silver gun! I shouted to him in Apache language from behind the tree.

'Don't shoot! I'm your friend.'

'I don't know who you are,' he replied. 'Show yourself!'

'Aren't you Winnetou, the great chief of the Apache?'

'I am,' he answered.

For this I jumped out from behind the tree, and ran towards him.

'Charlie!' he exclaimed with joy.

He opened his arms, and we embraced.

'Charlie! My friend and brother!' he kept on repeating, and his eyes were tearful.

The sudden meeting made me happy too, and it took minutes until I could speak normally.

'Who's this man?' Winnetou asked pointing at Fred.

'The stout Walker,' I replied. 'He's a good friend, and very good man.'

'I almost killed you but fortunately you, my brother, recognised the sound of my gun. Charlie's friends are my friends,' said Winnetou and offered his hand to Fred. 'What are you doing here, my white brothers?'

'We are pursuing a rascal, who is our enemy,' I replied. 'You can see his and his accomplices' tracks.'

'What kind?'

'Whites and Oglala,' I said.

Winnetou knitted his eyebrows, and put his hand on his tomahawk in his belt.

'The Oglala are toads,' he said. 'If they dare to come out of their holes, I trample on them. Do you allow me, Charlie, to join you against the Oglala.

'Allow?' I cried out. 'The chief of the Apache could not give me a greater joy.'

Fred was listening to these words raptured, and could not stop admiring this wonderful Indian whom he had met by accident. Winnetou was not a giant or some muscular show piece, but his proportionate body, his proud carriage, springy walking, serious face, calm and open look, bluish-black hair immediately showed that he was not a common man. He wore the same clothing as when we met at the River Pecos or later, when we said good-bye to each other in the camp of the Snake Indians. He was the same as always: clean, kempt, brave and calm, modest, yet made for commanding. He was the great chief of the Apache.

'Let's sit down to smoke the peace pipe with my brother Charlie's friend,' said Winnetou.

After the ceremony he turned to me and said, 'Tell me, my brother, what has happened since we last saw each other.'

I told him everything, and then asked him to do the same. Winnetou stared at the ground in the front of him, and said, 'The dew evaporates and feeds the clouds. These send rain on the ground, and the heat dries it up. Human life is the same circular process. Days come and days go; one does what he has to. What should Winnetou say about the past days and moons?'

I knew that he was talking about the years and months, because in the language of most Indian tribes the day means year and the moon means month.

'I'm interested in everything that has happened to you,' I encouraged him. 'Even the smallest things, Winnetou!'

'The chief of the Dakota of the Sioux insulted me, and I had to revenge it. I followed him until he was forced to duel with me. I defeated him, and took his scalp. His warriors chased me. I misled them, and while they sought me, I returned to their village, and brought the proofs of my victory from his tent. His horse is carrying them.'

He said all these simply, with a few short words. Others might have talked about it for hours. Winnetou did not like to boast with his successes, although this was a heroic deed too. He chased his enemy for months from the bank of the Rio Grande to the huge Sioux land's northern border, through mountains, forests and prairies, until he had caught up with him, and defeated him in an honest duel. He even entered the village of his enemy, and brought away the symbols of his victory that were worth more than any loot.

'I can see that you don't have a horse, Charlie,' Winnetou continued. 'How do you want to catch up with the Oglala and their white allies? You should accept the horse of the Dakota chief from me! It's a perfectly trained horse.'

He had given me once a wonderful mustang, and I did not want to use his generosity again.

'Let me, my brother, catch a mustang for myself,' I replied. 'The purpose of the Dakota chief's horse is different: to carry the loot to the tent of the victor.'

Winnetou shook his head.

'We don't have time to catch mustangs,' he replied, 'because the Oglala would slip out of our hand. I'll bury the loot somewhere, and I will come back for it. The horse belongs to you, Charlie!'

I had to accept the present, which was not too difficult, because it was a beautiful animal. It was a small, but strong dun, it had a long main, and its tail almost reached the ground. In its nose I could see the reddish mark that the Indians appreciated so much. Its nice big eyes were fiery, but clever as well. In one word, it was a horse that was a joy to look at, and it was very reliable.

'And what about the saddle?' asked Fred. 'You can't ride on a pack saddle!'

'That's not a problem,' I replied smiling. 'Have you seen how the Indians make a saddle from the freshly killed game's skin? You'll see, I'll have a very comfortable saddle tomorrow.'

'Right,' nodded Winnetou. 'Not far from the river I saw the tracks of prairie wolves. Before the Sun sets, we will kill them and you'll have a saddle. At dawn we will follow the tracks of the bandits. The Great Spirit is angry with them, and will deliver them to us. They offended the law of the prairie, and they'll be punished according to the law of the prairie.'

In an hour everything was done. We killed the coyote, skinned it and made a saddle of its skin. We buried Winnetou's loot that consisted of the weapons, a medicine bag, and blankets of the Dakota chief, at an appropriate place, and marked the nearby trees with our knives to find the cache later. We put out the fire and went to sleep.

PUNISHING THE RAILWAY BANDITS

AT DAWN we continued our journey. I could now really appreciate the character of my horse. Those who do not understand the taming of Indian horses would not have been able to stay on the horse for a minute. It tried to throw me off once or twice, but then it recognised the futility of its actions. An hour later we had got used to each other, and became friends. Fred was glancing at me secretly, and I could see that he appreciated me much, much more. It was mysterious to him that such a famous Indian chief as Winnetou knew me, and called me his friend and brother. Now he also saw that I knew horses so well that he would never have imagined. He did not understand the situation.

Old Victory kept up well, and by noon we had made a long distance. This is when we found the last camp site of the train robbers. They had only a few hours advantage on us. The tracks diverted from the creek, and followed a dried out stream's bed upstream. We rode behind each other on the narrow path. Winnetou suddenly stopped, and turned back.

'Uff!' he said. 'What do you think, Charlie, of this path? Where does it lead to?'

'Up to the ridge of the mountain,' I replied.

'And then?'

'Then down on the other side where the bandits are heading to.'

'Why? What's there?'

'Probably the Oglala's pasture.'

Winnetou nodded.

'Your eyes, my white brother, are still as sharp as that of an eagle's, and your sniffing is like that of the fox's. You are right.'

'What is it about?' enquired Fred. 'Tell me, Charlie!'

'I can see Fred that we have swapped roles,' I replied smiling. 'Now you speak like a greenhorn, and I'm telling you that you are one.'

'Why? Did I make a mistake?'

'You didn't make a mistake, but you don't understand the situation. What do you think, what are these white bandits doing among the Oglala?'

'They are in cahoots.'

'Naturally, but you can go further.'

'To where?'

'We keep on forgetting that in the West there are still more Indians than white men. This is the case here too. This group of bandits, even if there are more than twenty of them, have to rely on the Indians. They put themselves under the protection of a tribe. What do you think, would they do it free of charge? They hate all palefaces, even those who are their allies. They make the whites pay for the protection. And what do the bandits pay with? With the loot. The lion share of the loot belongs to the Oglala. They transport the blood-stained loot to their village, and agree on the next crime.'

'The next? What will that be?'

'I don't know, but I can suspect it.'

'This is too much!' exclaimed Fred. 'You suspect it! Don't you think that you keep your nose a little bit too high?'

'There's no magic in this. You only have to think, Fred. If we want to find out what our enemies want to do, we have to put ourselves in their place.'

'This is wise. Let's see what comes out of it?'

'They know that the next train repaired the railway tracks, and will report at the next station. Which is the next station?'

'Echo Canyon,' replied Fred. 'I know this line.'

'What will the chief of Echo Canyon station do? He will hurry to the derailed train, and will take all the men to capture the gang, won't he?'

'He can't do anything else,' nodded Fred.

'Then Echo Canyon will be unprotected. It can be ransacked without any risk.'

'You are right, Charlie!'

'You see! But as we have to climb up on this path, let's not talk.'

The terrain was difficult, and we had to be careful with our steps. We climbed uphill for hours. It was almost sunset when we reached the ridge of the mountain. Winnetou stopped his horse, and pointed with his stretched out hand.

'Uff!' he said in a muffled voice.

We stopped, and looked to the direction that Winnetou had indicated. The ground descended steeply to a broad, grassy plain where tents stood. Horses grazed on the green meadow, and Indians were busy around the tents. We could see that they were drying meat. There were a few bison carcasses around the tents, and on ropes large pieces of meat were being dried.

'Oglala!' said Fred unbelieving.

'Thirty-two tents,' I counted.

'Two hundred warriors,' nodded Winnetou.

'Let's count the horses,' I said, 'it's the best way.'

We counted two hundred and five horses from the ridge, thus Winnetou's estimate was quite precise. The Oglala were not out hunting, but on the warpath, as they had their shields with them, which were unnecessary for hunting. The largest tent stood a bit aside from the others, and its top was decorated with eagle feathers.

'What do you think, my brother Charlie, do they want to stay for a longer time?' asked Winnetou.

'I don't think so,' I replied. 'The bones of the bison are quite white. They have been under the sun for at least four or five days. The meat must be dry by now. There is no reason for the Oglala to stay here for very long.

'Look!' said Fred. 'Somebody stepped out of that large tent. Who could it be?'

Winnetou took out a telescope. We looked at him astonished as we had not seen such a modern tool in an Indian's hand. Winnetou had visited the large Eastern towns, and bought a telescope for himself. He set it up expertly, looked into it, and then offered it to me.

'Ko-itse, the traitorous rascal!' Winnetou cried angrily. 'I will chop his head into two with his tomahawk.'

With the telescope I could examine the Oglala chief thoroughly. Ko-itse meant Fiery Mouth. I had heard of him. I knew that he was a great orator, a brave warrior, and a mortal enemy of all white men.

'We have to be careful,' I said, and offered the telescope to Fred, so he could see the village too. 'I can see quite a few people around the tent, but some could be nearby.'

'You should wait here, my brothers,' said Winnetou. 'I'll find a good place to hide.'

He disappeared among the trees, and returned only after some time. He led us to a hollow in the ridge of the mountain, where the bushes were so thick that we could barely break through it. In the depth of the bushes we found a clearance that was big enough for three of us, and for our horses. The Apache chief carefully erased our tracks near the bushes, and we lay down. We rested in the scented grass in silence until evening. Winnetou then slipped away again, and soon returned with the news that the Oglala had made a number of campfires.

'They don't suspect anything,' said Fred. 'If only they knew that we were so close to them!' he added gleefully.

'I think they want to move on tomorrow. And with them the paleface bandits too,' opined Winnetou. 'I go down, and will try to find out something more.'

'I'll go with you,' I said. 'Fred Walker will stay here, and look after the horses. We leave our guns behind, the knives and tomahawks will be enough. We can also use our revolvers if we need to.'

The fat Walker happily agreed to stay with the horses. He was not a coward, but he did not want to risk his life if he could avoid it. It was clearly a dare-devil enterprise to go down to the valley, and scout the Oglala from such a close distance. If the scout was spotted, he was finished.

It was three or four days to the new moon, the sky was cloudy, there was not a single star in the sky, thus the circumstances were advantageous for our purpose. We got out of the bush, and returned to the place from where we looked down into the valley for the first time.

'Winnetou will go to the right, and you should go to the left, my brother,' whispered the Apache chief, and in the next moment he silently disappeared among the trees.

Following the command of my friend, I went to the left, and descended on the quite steep hillside. I crawled to the bottom of the valley like a snake until I caught sight of the camp fires. Now, holding my Bowie knife between my teeth, I lay down in the grass, and slipped slowly forward towards the chief's tent that was about two hundred steps from me. There was a fire in front of it, but the wall of the tent cast a shadow at me.

I advanced inch by inch, slowly and carefully with infinite patience. I was lucky, because the wind blew in my face, thus I did not have to be afraid of the horses smelling me, and calling the attention of their masters with their restless behaviour. Winnetou had a more difficult task in this respect.

It took me more than half an hour to make the two hundred steps. I was right behind the back wall of the chief's tent, about twenty yards from those who sat by the fire. They were talking quite loudly and in English. When I risked to lift my head a bit, I could see five white men, and three Indians around the fire. The Indians were quiet, only the whites were loud. Indians would have only whispered, or used sign language near such a high fire.

One of the whites was a tall, bearded man with the mark of a knife stab on his forehead. He talked very loudly, and his companions listened to him with some respect, which suggested that even if he was not the leader of the gang, he must have been at least a deputy. I could clearly hear his words and that of the others'.

'Is Echo Canyon far from here?' asked one of them.

'About a hundred miles,' replied the tall man. 'We will be there in three days.'

'And if they don't go out for pursuing us, and all of them will be at the station? We cannot attack so many armed men.'

The tall man waved contemptuously, 'Poppycock! Thirty men died on the derailed train. They cannot leave it unrevenged. They'll go there!'

'Then our plan will work!' said the other man. 'What do you think, Rollins, how many people work at Echo Canyon?'

'About a hundred and fifty,' replied the tall man. 'It's a big station with many workers. There are some good stores and bars too, and what's the most important: the cash till of the whole construction department is there! It provides the supplies to the whole line from Promontory and Green River. That's two hundred and thirty miles, so you can imagine that they must have a lot of cash.'

'Great! What do you think, won't they find our tracks?'

'They will, but they won't be happy with it. I think our persecutors will be here tomorrow lunch time. But we will have already left tomorrow morning. We will continue to the North for a while, then we break up, and go in all directions. When they find these tracks, they will be confused, and won't know which one they should follow. We will meet at Green Fork.'

'Won't we send out scouts?'

'We will, naturally! Our scouts will go tomorrow to the canyon in the shortest way, and they will wait for us on Painter Hill, next to the station.'

I was really lucky to arrive there at the right time. I had learnt everything that was necessary. I had nothing else to do there. I slowly started to retreat. It was quite tiring, because I had to erase my tracks. I did it on my all fours, and could stand up only when I was at the edge of the forest again.

I lifted my hands to my mouth, and imitated the sound of the toad. This was an agreed signal, and I hoped that Winnetou heard and understood it. The Oglala could not suspect anything as there were numerous toads in the wet grass, and this was the hour when they made their sounds.

I was glad that I could signal to Winnetou. I wanted to let him know that he could retreat, and that there was no more reason for staying in the valley. I quickly climbed up on the slope, and I breathed freely only when I returned to the bush.

'What's the news, Charlie?' asked Fred.

'Wait until Winnetou arrives,' I replied.

'Huh! I'm very curious!'

'Then be! I don't feel like saying the same thing twice.'

He sulked a little, but accepted that he had to wait. It took a long time until Winnetou returned. Finally the bush cracked, and in the next moment Winnetou was sitting next to me.

'Did you signal to me, my white brother?' he asked.

'Yes, I was lucky. What did you learn?'

'Nothing. It was very difficult to advance along the horses, and by the time I got to the camp fire, I heard the sound of the toad. In the meantime the stars appeared, and I also had to erase my tracks. What did you hear?'

'Everything I wanted.'

'You are always lucky, my white brother, when you scout the enemy. What did you hear this time?'

I reported in detail. Fred also listened, and remarked with appreciation, 'You were right again, Charlie! They are going to raid the Echo Canyon. You mentioned the man with a scar on his forehead and beard. What was his name?'

'Rollins,' I replied.

'It could be the man I know of, who got such a scar when raiding a farm near Leavenworth. Although that one didn't have a beard, and called himself by another name.'

After some musing he also added, 'We will intervene in this raid. None of them will escape alive!'

'I'm against it. I'm not as blood thirsty as you are, Fred. I've always held that blood is a very expensive liquid. I'm not happy when I have to kill an enemy. It's enough if I give him a lesson, and disarm him. I kill only if there's no other means of self-defence.'

745

'You speak like Old Shatterhand!' replied Fred Walker. 'They say that he hates killing just as much as you do!'

'Uff!'

With this word Winnetou expressed his surprise. He understood the situation immediately. Walker did not know that Old Shatterhand sat next to him. But I still did not consider it necessary to enlighten him.

'Don't worry, Fred!' I consoled him. 'We will settle the account with them in Echo Canyon.'

'How?'

'First of all, we will be there earlier than them, and we will warn the workers to be alert.'

'The problem is that most of them won't be there. They went to the derailed train.'

'I'll warn them to return to Echo Canyon quickly.'

'Warn them? How?'

'I'll write a note, and put it on a tree that's on their way if they follow the tracks.'

'Will they believe it?' Fred was still doubtful.

'The railway people must have told them that two men left the train. I will also write it in a way that they would believe it. I will also tell them to avoid Green Fork, where the Sioux will be gathering, and Painter Hill, where their scouts will be.'

'You are right, my white brother' said Winnetou. 'But let's go right now if we want to be there before the bandits.'

He went to his horse, and untied it. We followed his example. We led the horses out of the bush, mounted, and started off. We had to forgo sleeping that night.

We did not get off our horses, because we knew that the horses could find their way better than us, so we would rely on them, and we did not regret it. Winnetou rode in front, through all kinds of terrains. He never hesitated, and never lost the way.

By dawn we were ten miles from the camp of the Oglala, and we could gallop freely. We stopped at an appropriate place. I took a sheet of paper from my notebook, and wrote a short message on it. With a carved twig I pinned it on the trunk of the tree. If someone was coming from the South, they must notice it. We rode towards the South-west.

At noon we crossed Green Fork, a few miles from where the Oglala wanted to gather again. The Indians had to avoid the open space so that they would not be spotted, but we could advance straight.

After the crossing we kept on galloping, and rested only at sunset. During the day we had advanced at least forty miles, and I could not stop admiring Victory's endurance as he kept up with us. Winnetou had said that if we continued at such a pace, we would arrive to Echo Canyon on the following evening or afternoon.

In the front of the canyon there was a broad, fertile valley with cultivated corn fields. Brave squatters lived in a small village or rather homestead that they called Holy Village. We arrived there before dark. The small homestead consisted of five block houses not counting the stables and other outhouses. The squatters received us in a friendly manner. Their kindness affected Winnetou. They willingly offered us accommodation for the night, and they gave us a hot dinner.

'How many families live in Holy Village?' I asked the old squatter who offered his room to us.

'Five families,' he replied. 'Thirty-nine souls.'

'How many of them are men?'

'Sixteen.'

'Aren't you afraid of the Indians?'

'We have a good relationship with them,' he replied, 'or at least they haven't yet disturbed us. We have enough weapons. The women and children know something about guns too. Hopefully they won't need this knowledge.'

'Hopefully,' I agreed. For a moment it came to my mind that I should let them know of the raids of the Oglala, but I changed my mind. Why should I make them anxious, when the bandits were after a much bigger loot than the one they could find in Holy Village.

I had long forgotten how it felt sleeping in a bed, but after the long ride, this comfort was pleasant.

At dawn we said good bye to our hosts, and continued our journey. Beyond the valley the path kept on ascending. After hours of riding in the mountains, in the late afternoon, we arrived to a cliff from where we see the canyon.

The Echo Canyon was not as frightening as those near the Yellowstone in the North, and near the Colorado in the South, where the Sun reaches the bottom only at lunch time. The railway tracks led into the canyon. The workers were busy with replacing the provisional tracks with permanent ones. They lived near the station at the entrance of the canyon.

From our position we could see the railway tracks, the barracks, and the station that we wanted to rescue.

A side-gorge provided the route on which we could enter the settlement. The first workers whom we met were preparing to blow up some rock. They were surprised when they saw us, two well-armed strangers and an Indian. After a short hesitation they put down their tools, and grabbed their weapons.

I waved to them in the friendliest way to calm them, and rode directly towards them.

'Good afternoon!' I said greeting them. 'You won't need your guns. We are friends.'

'What do you want?' asked one of the workers.

'We are hunters, and we brought some very important news to you. Who's the head of the station?'

'Engineer Rudge. They call him Colonel Rudge.'

'Where can I find him?'

'He's not here. There was some problem on the track. He rode out with some men to check it.'

'Who is his deputy?'

'Mr Ohlers, the paymaster. You can find him in the large barrack.'

I thanked them for the information, and hurried forward with Fred and Winnetou. In five minutes we arrived to the camp of the workers. It consisted of huts and blockhouses, but there were also two stone-built barracks, one larger and one smaller. The camp was encircled with wall made of piled up stones. It looked strong, and was about five feet tall. A strong wooden gate led to the yard. The gate was open, and some workers were busy with their tasks there. For my enquiry they pointed towards the large stone barrack.

We got off our horses at the front of the house, and entered the barrack. Even this larger building was only a large hall full of boxes, bags and barrels. It was a storage. A little, thin man leant over a box.

'What do you want?' he asked in his weak voice when he caught sight of us. 'Good Lord! An Indian!'

'I can assure you, Sir, you don't have to be afraid!' I said in a calming voice. 'I'm looking for Mr Ohlers.'

'That's me,' he replied, and blinked at me frightened from behind his glasses.

'I would have liked to talk to Colonel Rudge,' I continued, 'but I heard that he's not here.'

'I'm his deputy,' said Ohlers, and glanced at the door longingly.

'Did the colonel go to pursue the train robbers?' I asked.

'Y … es.'

'How many men did he take?'

'Why do you want to know?'

'You will learn it in a moment. How many men are here?'

'That's really none of your business!'

'This is true, but listen. It is …'

I stopped because I just noticed that I was talking to the air. Mr Ohlers, like a snake, passed me by, and rushed out of the door. In the next moment the door banged, and I heard the creaking of the padlock, and the movement of the bolts. I did not understand the situation, but it was clear that we were prisoners. I turned around, and looked at my two companions. The always serious Winnetou smiled, and his snow white, healthy teeth flashed. Fred showed a sour face, and I broke out in a laughter.

749

'This midget thought that we are spies of the bandits!' exclaimed Fred. 'Damn it!'

Outside a whistle was blown. I went to a narrow window, and looked out. I saw that the workers from outside the camp rushed in, and locked the gate. I counted them. There were sixteen of them. Ohlers explained something to them with animated gestures, and gave orders. The men hurried to the block houses, obviously for their guns.

'They'll soon execute us,' I said. 'What should we do in the meantime?'

'Let's smoke,' said Fred

There was a box of cigars on the table. Fred took one, lit it, and I followed his example. I offered one to Winnetou too, but he shook his head.

Soon the door opened, and we could hear the high pitched voice of the paymaster.

'Don't shoot you scoundrels, because you'll regret it!'

With these words he entered the room in front of his men who stood by the door with gun in hand. Ohlers jumped behind a large barrel, and started to talk to us while aiming at us with a shotgun.

'Who are you?' he asked sternly. 'Now you can speak!'

'Stop this stupidity!' growled Fred at him. 'You called us scoundrels, and now you are asking who we were!'

'We'll see who's stupid! Who are you? Are you telling us or not?

'Hunters!' said Walker, who clearly wanted to lead the conversation.

'And why did you come to Echo Canyon?'

'To help you.'

'We don't want such help! You are spies of the bandits! Men! Tie them up!'

'Just a moment,' said Fred, and dived into his pocket.

I suspected that he wanted to verify his identity with some detective card, and intervened.

'Wait, Fred,' I said. 'Seventeen men won't overcome three Westerners. Whoever touches us will die!'

I pulled both of my revolvers with the most menacing manner I could put on, and started towards the door with Fred and Winnetou behind me. The paymaster immediately stooped down behind the barrel, while the workers opened the way to us, thus we got to the door without any trouble. There I turned back, and said, 'Let's understand each other! The Oglala and the white bandits are about to attack Echo Canyon. We heard their plans. We came to warn you. This gentleman accuses us, and doesn't listen to the clever words. If you don't come to your mind, you'll be massacred by the Indians!'

For this Ohlers came out from behind the barrel. His face was white, like chalk, and his voice trembled when he spoke to us.

'I'm sorry, gentlemen, if I misunderstood your intentions. But it happened because you refused to name yourself. Who are you?'

'It's enough if I tell you that this is Winnetou, the great chief of the Apache,' I said and pointed at my friend.

'Wow!' I could hear from every direction.

'Oh!' exclaimed the paymaster. 'I'm glad to meet you Mr Winnetou! I've heard many good things about you!'

'And this is stout Walker, the famous guide,' I continued.

The paymaster bowed to him too, and then asked my name. I gave him my birth name rather than my prairie name. Then I told him what I had heard in the Oglala camp, and also that we had left a message for the railway men.

'And if the Oglala arrive before the colonel?' asked Ohlers in a new panic. 'I have only forty men. It would be better to evacuate Echo Canyon, and retreat to the next station.'

'I don't know if it's better,' I replied, 'but it would be a shame. Anyway if your superiors learn about it, they would fire you I think.'

'So what? My life is more important than my job! How many redskins are coming?'

'About two hundred, including the white bandits.'

'They'll massacre us!' The paymaster could barely stand now in his panic.

Pull yourself together! Which is the largest station on this line?'

'Promontory. At least three hundred workers are employed there.'

'Then send them a telegram, and ask them to send a hundred armed men here!'

Ohlers looked at me with goggling eyes, and then hit his forehead.

'You are right!' he exclaimed. 'Excellent idea! How could I not think of this!'

'Perhaps you are a good paymaster, but not a great strategist,' I replied. 'Also include in the telegram that they should bring a lot of ammunition and food. And that they have to do everything in secret. How far is Promontory?

'Ninety-one miles.'

'Will they have a free engine?'

'Of course. And wagons too.'

'Very good! The scouts of the Oglala will arrive only tomorrow evening, but the help could be here by the morning. We have time for the preparations. First of all, the height of the wall has to be increased by three feet. It's important that the Indians cannot not look in, and see how many men we have. In order that they couldn't see our real strength from the hills, I'll go out, and will give you the signal when they arrive. Then you and your men should retreat to the blockhouses, and keep quiet.'

'I see,' nodded Ohlers now enthusiastically. 'And how should we raise the fence?'

'You ram poles in the ground on this side of the fence, and nail boards and beams on them. Also make benches, so that our men can stand on them, and shoot at the enemy. We'll give them a good lesson to take away their appetite to attack the station again!'

'Right!' cried the paymaster. 'Bing-bang! And if they run away, we'll chase them!

'We'll see that,' I replied smiling. 'But let's start. For the time being you have three tasks: telegram to Promontory, building the fence, and looking after us.'

'Of course, of course! What do you need?'

'Some accommodation, some food, and fodder for the horses.'

'Everything will be arranged, just leave it to me! I'm cooking for you! I'm good in that! Then we will make the bandits dance so much that they'll collapse!'

Early in the morning the train arrived with the hundred men. They had plenty of weapons, ammunition, and food. They immediately joined in the work, and the wall was ready by noon. I also instructed them to fill in every empty barrel with water, and stand them by the fence. So many men would need a lot of water, and we had to be prepared for a long siege. The water would be also be useful if there was fire. We informed the nearby stations of the situation, and told them to let the trains run by the timetable so that there would not be anything unusual that would make the enemy suspicious.

After lunch the three of us left the station to find the Oglala scouts. We agreed that if any of us catch sight of the scouts, he should return to the station, and with an explosion he would send the signal to the others. It was necessary, because we looked for the scouts in three different directions. I went to the West, Walker to the East and Winnetou to the North.

From the canyon I climbed up on a steep rock wall, and advanced along the edge of the forest. An hour later I arrived to a hill on which there were two trees next to each other: a huge oak tree, and a slim pine tree. I climbed up on the latter, and then jumped over to a strong branch of the oak tree, where the trunk was slim enough for me to climb up further. I was soon on the top of the tree. The foliage covered me well. I could see as far as the grassland, and the hills around the forest. I sat down as comfortably as it was possible, and watched the forest.

I had sat there for hours patiently without seeing anything interesting. Finally I noticed a flock of crows rising from the green. They did not fly away in one group, but dispersed in the air, and flew around for a few minutes hesitatingly before settling back on the trees. It could not be accidental; the crows had been disturbed by something or somebody.

The scene was repeated twice. Somebody was approaching among the trees towards me. I quickly climbed down, erased my tracks, and slipped into a nearby thicket. I went in deep, and lay down on the ground. Soon I noticed something. I could not see it, I could not hear it, but still I noticed it: one, two, three, four, five, six ghosts passed by me noiselessly. Not a single twig cracked under their feet. Only Indians could walk like this.

Of course, they were the scouts. Finally, I could see one of them. His face was painted in war colours.

I waited until they were in the distance, and I started my retreat. I knew the area better than they, and I did not have to hide in the thickest bushes. Thus I overtook the Oglala scouts, and in half an hour I was descending on the rock wall to the canyon.

I was crossing the railway tracks when I noticed Winnetou who was descending on the other side of the canyon. I waited for him, and I asked him, 'Have you seen anything, my brother?'

'Nothing,' he answered. 'After you, Charlie, spotted the scouts, I returned immediately.'

'Oh! How do you know, Winnetou, that I spotted them?'

'I climbed on a tree, and watched the area through my telescope. I noticed you on the top of a tree. I also saw the crows. Then I saw you coming down from the tree. You wouldn't have done this without a reason.

I smiled to myself that Winnetou showed his unparalleled perceptive abilities again.

Before we arrived to the fence a middle aged man approached us.

'I'm Colonel Rudge,' he said. 'First of all, I'd like to thank you for the great service that you did for the workers of this station.'

'We'll have time for this later, colonel,' I replied. 'Right now, the scouts of the Oglala have arrived. There has to be an explosion for recalling one of our men.'

'I'll give the instructions,' said the colonel. 'Come in, we'll continue the talk in a minute.'

Soon there was a loud bang to call Walker back, as we had agreed. The workers quickly retreated into the blockhouses, and only one or two stayed near the railways as if they were carrying out their daily duties. Colonel Rudge soon found us in the large store barrack.

'Have you found my note in the forest?' I asked.

'I did, and immediately returned. What do you think when will the Oglala attack?'

'It's very likely that it will happen towards the end of the next night, before dawn.'

'Then we have time for a chat,' laughed the colonel. 'Be my guest, and bring your Indian friend too.'

He had military manners, and he was a decisive man. He probably got his rank in the civil war, and retained it after the demobilisation as it was customary then. He led us to the smaller stone building. This is where his quarters were.

'Take a seat, gentlemen,' he started. 'I have heard about the great chief of the Apache many times, and I consider it as an honour that he's my guest. I'll open a good bottle of wine. I'll arrange that the third gentleman would be led here too, when he arrives.'

We did not have to wait very long. Fred heard, and understood the signal, and immediately returned from his watch place from where he did not, and could not see anything. The time was spent talking and eating until midnight. The night passed without any event, just as did the following day. The evening was very dark as it was new moon. However, later, when the stars appeared, the landscape was dimly lit by their light.

The armament of our little army looked satisfactory. Everybody had a knife and a gun, but many had revolvers or pistols. As the Indians normally attacked between midnight and dawn, it was sufficient to set up some guards, while the others could lie down in the grass to talk or sleep. The air was perfectly still, but this great calmness did not mislead me. For my command the men grabbed their weapons, and positioned themselves behind the fence on the benches. I was guarding the gate with Winnetou. My Henry rifle was in my hand.

Colonel Rudge distributed his men evenly on the four sides of the fence. He had two hundred and ten men, while thirty workers guarded the horses in a hidden opening to the canyon.

Time passed very slowly. Many started to believe that the whole thing was a false alarm, and we only imagined the Oglala. But suddenly we heard a small noise as if stones had hit the rail tracks. This almost inaudible noise caught my attention. For an inexperienced man it would have appeared as the sigh of the breeze, but I knew then that the enemy were coming.

'Look out!' I whispered to my neighbour.

He passed on the warning, and we were all ready. It seemed that ghostly shadows passed in the night, and soon a hostile line surrounded the camp. In a few moments the battle would break out.

The shadows were approaching noiselessly. Now they were only twenty steps from the fence, Then ten … five. At this moment a sharp voice resounded in the night.

'Death to the Oglala! This is Winnetou, the chief of the Apache. Fire!'

He lifted his gun to his shoulder, and pulled the trigger. His shot was followed by the popping of two hundred guns. I was the only one who had not yet shot, because I wanted to see the effect of the volley first. There was a nerve racking silence, and then a blood churning battle cry resounded. The unexpected volley crippled the Oglala for a minute, but then such a sound of anger and pain rose as if all the devils of hell had been released.

'Another volley!' commanded the colonel in such a thundering voice that overpowered even the hellish yelling.

The valley resounded. Then Rudge's new command came, 'Now after them! With the butts of the rifles!'

The workers rushed out of the camp, and chased the escaping Oglala, whose number was significantly reduced by the two volleys. Their only hope was fleeing from the place. Dark shadows flitted towards the forest, and I spotted a white man among them, then another. The bandits were on the wing where I stood, next to the gate, and they were good targets in the twilight.

Now I aimed. I had the advantage that I could shoot twenty five times without the need to spend valuable moments for reloading the gun. I shot eight times then stopped because there were no more targets. Those enemies who were not wounded sought refuge in fleeing, while the rest either lay on the ground or tried to crawl away. The latter was useless, because they were surrounded, and those who did not surrender were massacred.

Ten minutes later several fires were lit outside, and one could see the horrific harvest of death. I did not want to look at it. I turned around, and went to the colonel's room. Soon Winnetou followed me. I looked at him surprised.

'Are you already here, my brother?' I asked. 'Didn't you scalp the fallen Sioux?'

'Why should Winnetou collect scalps, when his white brother spared the life of the paleface murderers? I saw that you shot only in their legs. All the eight are caught. They could not escape.'

All the eight! So all my bullets hit the target as I wanted. I hoped that Haller was among them.

At this moment Walker entered the room.

'Charles, Winnetou! Come out! We caught him!'

'Whom?' I asked.

'Haller.'

'Ah! Who caught him?'

'Nobody. He was wounded, and could not escape. You have never seen such a miracle! Eight white bandits lay helplessly by the gate. All the eight got the same wound: a bullet in their pelvis.'

'It is strange, Fred!'

'None of the wounded Oglala surrendered, but these eight white bandits are begging for their life humbly.'

'Is their wound mortal?'

'I don't know. I haven't had time to look at them yet. But there are many dead. Not more than eighty Oglala escaped.'

I thought of the many dead with horror. My only consolation was that they could thank it to themselves, and they did not deserve better. I went out, and turned away my head so that I would not see the pile of bodies in the early morning sunshine. I remembered that I had once read in some book that humans were the mightiest, but also the most dangerous beasts.

The doctor arrived with the afternoon train, and examined the wounded. I heard him saying that Haller's wound was the most dangerous, and it was mortal. The bandit listened to it indifferently, and did not show any regret. I went back to the colonel's room to rest, however, already after ten minutes Fred Walker rushed in.

'Charles! Get ready!' he cried excited. 'We have to go!'

'Where to?'

'To Holy Village!'

'Why?' I asked feeling the premonition.

'The escaped Oglala want to burn it down.'

'How do you know?'

'From Haller. I stood next to him with the colonel, and I told him that we stayed there, and how kind they were. For this Haller laughed mockingly and remarked that we won't see those kind people anymore. After long questioning he said that the Oglala had decided on a raid on the farm.'

'That would be terrible! I don't believe it!. I have to talk to him. Ask Winnetou in the meantime to bring the horses.'

I ran to the blockhouse where the wounded prisoners were kept. Haller lay on the blood stained blanket. His face was deadly pale, and he looked at me with stubborn hatred.

'What is your real name? Rollins or Haller?' I asked.

'It's none of your business.'

'It is!' I replied. 'My bullet brought you down, this is why I'm interested in you.'

His eyes goggled, and on his forehead the old scar became red suddenly.

'You are lying, you dog!' he rattled.

'I didn't want to kill you, only making your escape impossible,' I answered calmly. 'But I don't mind that you kick the bucket. I freed the world from a debased villain. You won't murder anymore!'

'Do you think so?' he asked with mocking in his voice, and bared his teeth. 'Go over to Holy Village, and you'll see!'

'What?'

'I think only smouldering ruins. The Oglala did not know about that small settlement, but I did. We agreed that we destroy the station first, and then the village. We failed here, but the Oglala will take their revenge on the settlement. The settlers will experience a terrible, torturous death!'

'Are you mad, Haller? Such enormity is in your mind even at the threshold of death?'

'Stop this sermon! If I had the strength, I'd tear your tongue out!'

Another wounded man lifted his head, and said, 'Stop boasting, Rollins! You don't know whom you are talking to. This is Old Shatterhand!'

Haller was raging. He tried to rise leaning on his two palms, but fell back. He swore blasphemously.

I wanted to hurry away, but Colonel Rudge, who listened to the conversation grabbed my arm.

'Is it true what this man says?' he asked with awe. 'Are you really Old Shatterhand?'

'Yes, I am.'

'Why did you keep it a secret?'

'I don't have time, colonel! I have to hurry to Holy Village. Come with me with your man.'

'Unfortunately I can't because I'm on duty. I cannot leave my post and officially I cannot order the men either. But whoever volunteers, and wants to go with you, can go. I'll give horses, weapons, and food if you promise that you'll return the horses and guns.'

'Thank you, colonel,' I replied. 'This is all I need.'

Two hours later Winnetou, Walker, and I rode in front of forty well-armed men to the Holy Village. Winnetou was silent, but I could read from his eyes that it was woe to the Oglala if they massacred the innocent and peaceful settlers.

We rode almost without a word all night, and in the morning. I did not say more than a hundred words during this time. Our horses were soaking in their sweat when we arrived to the gorge where the houses of the settlement had stood … a day earlier. We arrived too late. We found only smouldering ruins.

We jumped off the horses, and searched the ruins, and the tracks, but we could not find any sign of life. We did not find wounded or dead either. It was a bit encouraging. After further investigation we found out what happened. The settlement was attacked, and raided during the night. There was no serious battle. They captured the settlers, and carried them to the direction where Idaho and Wyoming's borders met.

'Men!' I shouted, 'let's not waste time! Let's follow the tracks, we may be able to save them.'

Winnetou's face was extremely determined. There were only forty of us against eighty Oglala, but in such a situation not even this numeric superiority of the enemy could deter me. We had three hours till sunset, and we utilised the time well. We only rested when it was completely dark.

On the following day we established that the Oglala had only a day advantage or not even that much, even though they rode all night. The reason for this hurry was that they knew Winnetou was pursuing them. The Apache chief named himself in the beginning of the battle, and it was enough for the Oglala to try to increase the distance from him. Our horses were completely exhausted, and thus we had to slow down.

'The settlers' situation is hopeless,' remarked Walker disheartened.

'Not at all!' I replied. 'The Oglala are angry for the defeat at Echo Canyon and want to take revenge on the settlers. They want to execute them on the torture stake. But for that they would have to call three or four Oglala villages together.'

'And where are those villages?'

'In the northern corner of Wyoming or even over the border,' replied Winnetou. 'We'll catch up with them well before that.'

On the third day we faced a difficult choice because the tracks split. Some continued to the North, the rest turned to the West. Most of the tracks led to North.

'My white brothers should stop,' said Winnetou, 'and keep their horses away from the tracks.'

He looked at me, and I knew what he wanted. I continued along the northern tracks, and he along the western tracks, while the others stopped.

I rode for about a quarter of an hour watching the ground. I could not establish the number of horses, because they rode behind each other, but from the shape and depth of the prints of the hooves I concluded that about twenty riders passed there. I also found footprints. I quickly rode back, and by the time I arrived to the workers, Winnetou also returned.

'What did you see, my brother?' he asked.

'They took the prisoners this way,' I replied. 'Forward!'

I turned my horse to the North.

'Uff!' exclaimed Winnetou, driving his horse next to me.

He was a bit surprised by my decisiveness, and thought that I had found the tracks of the settlers. After a short time I stopped, and turned to Walker who caught up with us.

'You are an experienced path finder, Fred. Look at these footprints, and tell me what they tell you.'

'Footprints?' he asked surprised. 'Where?'

'Here!'

'This is not a footprint. Only the wind blew the sand.'

'Really? I bet that Winnetou will read more from it.'

The Apache chief jumped off his horse, leant forward, and examined the ground for some time. Finally he said, 'You chose the right way, my brother. The prisoners were taken this way.'

'Damn it!' exclaimed Walker. 'How can you see this?'

'You should look at this barely visible print, my brother,' Winnetou pointed at the edge of the path. 'A very strange one. Smaller than a footprint, but larger than a hoof. And next to it as if some sack was pulled on the ground. And there are these small red dots. It's blood.'

'And what does it mean?' burst out Fred.

'Not difficult to find out. A child fell off the horse here and hit his nose,' I replied.

'I don't believe it.'

'We will see! Forward!'

We continued for ten more minutes when we arrived to a rocky place where the tracks disappeared. We had to stop, and investigate the ground carefully. Winnetou stooped down. Suddenly he exclaimed in joy. He stood up and gave me a yellow piece of cloth.

'What can it be?' asked Fred surprised.

'This cloth was torn off from a blanket,' I said.

'Yes,' nodded Winnetou. 'They cut up blankets and put it on the hooves of the horses so that no tracks would be left. It seems that they were arriving to a place that they wanted to keep it secret.'

We continued our journey, and soon found the prints of an Indian moccasin on a sandy spot. The direction of the toes showed that he advanced in the same direction as us. From the tracks we could see that the Oglala were progressing extremely slowly and carefully. Soon the tracks became clearer. They abandoned caution, and took off the rugs from the hooves of the horses to be quicker. It was quite mysterious. While I was musing about this, Winnetou suddenly stopped his horse, and pointed to the distance.

'Uff!' he exclaimed with a tone that suggested that something had come to his mind that he had not considered earlier. 'The Hitchcock Mount! Where the sacred cave of the Sioux is!'

'I haven't heard about this.'

'Now I understand everything,' continued Winnetou gloomily. The Sioux sacrifice their prisoners to the Great Spirit in that cave. The Oglala split. The larger group turned to the left to get to the villages of the Oglala in the quickest possible way. The smaller group takes the prisoners to the cave. They put two or three prisoners on each horse, while the Oglala went on foot.'

'I can't see that mountain. Is it far from here?'

'We will be there by the evening.'

'Have you been in this cave, my brother?'

'Once, when I made an alliance with Ko-itse's father, who kept his word, but his son, this mangy dog, dug out the hatchet without any reason. We'll abandon these tracks, and Winnetou will lead.'

He spurred his horse, and galloped away. We followed him. We had ridden through mountains, valleys, and gorges for many hours until finally we arrived to a plain. On the horizon a dark mountain rose above the land.

'This is not a common prairie,' remarked Winnetou without stopping his horse. 'This is the Y-akom Akomo, the Blood Field, as the Tehua Indians in the South call it.'

I had heard about it. This was the place of execution where the Dakota took their prisoners, and after torturing them, they executed them. Thousands and thousands victims died on the torture stakes here. Members of other tribes, not to mention the whites, rarely dared to advance this far, but we galloped calmly through the prairie of sighs and curses because Winnetou was our guide.

Our horses started to tire, still we rode without stopping until we reached the steep southern side of the lonely mount. The side was grown over by thick bushes.

'This is the Hitchcock Mount,' said Winnetou quietly.

'And the cave?' I asked.

'It's on the other side, on the northern slope. You will see it in an hour, Charlie. Now follow me on foot, my brother, and leave your guns here.'

'I alone?'

'Yes. This is the land of death. Only strong soul men can enter. The rest should hide in the bushes, and wait for us.'

It was a volcanic mount, and it would have taken an hour to go around it. I put my guns in the grass, and then followed Winnetou who started to climb the steep southern slope. He climbed first to the right then to left, and to the right again. It was a difficult and dangerous climb, and required care and attention. It had taken an hour until we reached the summit.

'Be extremely quiet!' whispered Winnetou while he lay down and carefully slipped through between two bushes.

I followed him and as soon as I put my head through I pulled it back frightened, because I was just at the edge of the deep crater. Another movement, and I would have fallen in. The edge was rimmed by bushes, and the depth of the crater was about a hundred and fifty feet. In the bottom of the crater I spotted the settlers tied up. When I recovered from my surprise, I counted the prisoners. There were thirty-nine of them, thus they were all there guarded by many Oglala warriors.

I examined this burnt out volcano crater to find out if I could get down from where I lay. It was possible if one was brave enough, had a long and strong rope, and could remove the guards. There were many small shelves on the cliff, so someone would be able to rest on the way down.

I saw that Winnetou pulled back and I happily followed his example.

'Is it the one?' I asked.

'It is. Not really a cave, but this is how they call it.'

'And where is the entrance?'

'On the eastern side of the mount, but it's guarded so strongly that it's impossible to get through there.'

'Then we'll descend from here. We'll go back to our men, and bring them up here. We have enough lassos and ropes.'

Winnetou nodded, and started off downhill. The Sun was halfway down on the horizon. When we arrived, we told the railway men in a few words what we had seen. They were all ready to save the settlers. We collected all our ropes, and tied them together. Winnetou chose the twenty most skilful men to take with us, and left the rest to guard the horses. Some of these guards were told that a quarter of an hour after our leaving they should ride to the eastern side of the mountain, light big fires, and then return to this place. With this Winnetou wanted to distract the Oglala's attention from the side of the crater where we wanted to descend.

Purple flames lit up the sky, everything became golden, and then suddenly it was dark. It suddenly occurred to me that in the last few hours Winnetou had been different. His steady, calm eyes had been flickering restlessly. He had often wrinkled his forehead, and it seemed that he had lost the equilibrium of his inner life.

When he saw me he said, 'You came to check on Winnetou, my brother. You did the right thing, because you won't see me for much longer.'

'What is my brother thinking of?' I asked him.

'My sun sets too,' he replied sadly.

'Do you have bad premonitions? Don't listen to them. I know our task is dangerous, but how many times have we had to face death! The physical and emotional extortions of the last days made you exhausted, this is why you talk like this now.'

'No, Charlie. There's no tiredness that would make Winnetou downhearted. But look at those clouds on the sky! A long night will come.'

'But the Sun will rise again, Winnetou!'

'But my eyes won't see it,' he replied. 'I will be on the happy hunting grounds tomorrow. I've always said that I could only be killed by a bullet. Knife and tomahawk cannot touch me. I'm strong and skilful enough to defend myself against these. But the bullet …'

He became silent and he wanted to turn away from me, but I grabbed his arm.

'I'd like to ask you something, Winnetou,' I said. 'Do it for me! Stay with the horses and the guards. I'll lead the men to the cave. There are enough of us, we can do the job without you.'

He shook his head quietly.

'You don't mean this seriously, Charlie.'

'I do. You have had enough deeds. You can rest for once.'

'I? To retreat from the battle? Not to be where my friends fight? So that it would be said that Winnetou, the chief of the Apache, is afraid of death?'

'Nobody would dare to say that!'

'It's enough if I thought this of myself. Cowardice is a shame, and shame is worse than death! Don't talk about it!'

It was an argument for which I did not have an answer. Had I continued to ask him to stay with the horses, he would have considered it an insult.

After a short pause Winnetou continued, 'You have been a faithful comrade, Charlie. We have faced death together many times. You have been ready for it, my brother. I know that there's a small book in your pocket in which you noted what should happen if you had fallen in the battle. Then I would have taken the little book, and would have carried out your will. Winnetou also made a will even if he had never talked about it. But it's now time for it. Are you promising to me that you'll execute my will?'

'I am, Winnetou. But believe me, your premonitions are wrong. I know that you'll have many days and nights before you move to the happy hunting grounds. And I'll be here, and carry out your will.'

'Even if it's dangerous and difficult?'

766

'How can you ask such a thing, Winnetou? You are my true friend; I'd go through fire, water, death for you!'

'I know, Charlie. You'll do what I ask, and what nobody else would do. Can you remember when in the beginning of our friendship I talked to you about gold …'

'I haven't forgotten it, Winnetou.'

'I thought you were interested in money then. What's your opinion now?'

'In our world we need it. But I know that there are higher joys in life than those that can be bought for money.'

'I'm happy that you talk like this, Charlie. You know that I know many places, where gold is in abundance. But I won't tell you them. The Great Spirit didn't create you for being a slave of common joys. Your strong body and soul are created for better. For tasks that are right for a man. You'll find the goal in your life for which it's worthwhile to live.'

'Talk about your will, Winnetou.'

'I am. It is about a huge treasure. I want to give it to you, but not for your own purposes. You will find the purposes in my will. When I die, go to my father's grave. If you dig on the Western side of the grave, you will find my will. You'll read it, and carry it out.'

'I give you my word!' I replied. 'There's nothing that could hold me back from carrying out your will.'

'Thank you Charlie! This is it. The time of the attack is approaching, and I know that I won't survive it. Let's say good-bye to each other as is right for men. Bury me in the Gros Ventre Range, at the bank of the little creek, where you and I have been once, according to the Indian customs. I wish you were rewarded for your friendship, and you have a long life, Charlie. Don't forget Winnetou, and think sometimes of me.'

I felt that my eyes were burning but I suppressed my tears. I grabbed Winnetou's hand, and squeezed it in silence.

'And now, let's do our duty!' said Winnetou in a shaky voice, and he quickly turned away from me so that I could not see his face.

I was thinking feverishly how I could persuade him not to participate in the next battle, to avoid the danger for the first and only time in his life, but I knew that it was useless.

'It's dark now, we can go!' I heard Winnetou's voice. 'You can follow me!'

We started off. Winnetou was in the front, I followed him, Fred was behind me, and then came the railway workers. It was more difficult to climb the mount in the darkness than at the first time. It took almost one and a half hours until we arrived to the edge of the crater in the quietest possible way. In the bottom of the crater a huge fire was lit, and by its light we could see the prisoners as well as their guards. We could not hear anything.

We attached one end of the rope to a rock sticking out. It was long enough to reach the next shelf on the cliff. Then we waited for the lighting of the fires that our men had to do. Soon three, four, five fires were lit on the East, on the prairie. We looked down into the crate excitedly. Soon an Indian appeared by the entrance, and shouted something to the guards. They jumped up and hurried out. Obviously they were about to check the strange fires.

It was time. I grabbed the end of the rope to go down first, but Winnetou took it from my hand.

'The Apache chief is the leader,' he said. 'You can only come after me, my brother.'

We had agreed that once the first man descended, the rest would follow him in a way that not more than four would be on the rope at any time. I did not wait until Winnetou was on the ground. I followed him soon and Fred came after me. The rope was let down slowly, and we got to the ground.

The only problem was that we rubbed off a lot of stones because in the dark we could not be careful enough. One pebble fell on a child's head, and the child started to cry. One of the Indians came back, heard the noise of the rubbed off stones, looked up, and warned his companions.

'Look out Winnetou!' I cried. 'We are spotted.'

Our men recognised the danger, and come down on the rope quickly. In half a minute we were all on the ground. At the same time several shots flashed towards us from the opening.

Winnetou collapsed.

I became paralysed in my fright.

'Winnetou! My dear friend! Have you been hit?'

'I'm dying …' he replied barely audibly.

I recovered from my paralysis, and was raging so much that I would have taken on the whole world.

'Winnetou is dying!' I shouted to Walker who had just arrived.

I did not lose time with taking my gun from my back or pulling my knife or grabbing my revolver. I jumped at the five Indians who were rushing at me from the entrance. The first one, I recognised him immediately, was the chief.

'Die Ko-itse!' I screamed at him. My fist hit his temple, and Ko-itse collapsed like a sack. The Oglala next to him had already raised his tomahawk to hit me when the light of the fire fell on my face. The Oglala dropped his hatchet.

'Old Shatterhand!' he cried frightened.

'I am!' I replied. 'You die too!'

My fist knocked him out.

'Old Shatterhand!' cried the other Indians.

'Old Shatterhand!' exclaimed Walker too. 'You, Charlie? Then I understand everything!'

I felt a stab on my shoulder, but I did not care. Fred shot two Indians, and I knocked out the third. In the meantime more railway workers arrived and I could leave the rest of the Oglala to them.

I turned to Winnetou, knelt next to him, and asked, 'Where are you wounded?'

'Here,' he said a muffled voice, and put his hand on his chest. Blood sipped from his right hand side.

I cut off his clothing to get to his wound. Yes, the bullet entered his lung.

My heart ached as never before.

'Lift my head,' whispered Winnetou, 'so I can see the battle …'

I took his head on my lap. He could see that all the enemies were killed. Our men were around me now. They had released the prisoners who expressed their gratitude loudly. I only glanced at them, and turned back to my best friend, the dying man whose wound had stopped bleeding. I knew what it meant. He was bleeding internally. I looked at his closed eyes and bronze face with infinite sadness.

'Do you have any wish, my brother?' I asked.

'Yes, don't forget the Apache.'

Walker came up to me and reported, 'We killed them to the last man.'

'But Winnetou is also dead!' the sobbing broke out of me. 'Not a thousand lives of the Oglala equal his!'

The railwaymen and the settlers stood around the dying man, and looked at him in silence, and deeply touched. Winnetou's body jerked, blood sipped from his mouth. His hand moved, and then it fell lifelessly. The great, young chief of the Apache was dead.

I kept wake all night next to him in silence, motionless, and with dry burning eyes. I cannot speak about my feelings and my thoughts.

Early morning we left the mount before the Sioux could have taken a revenge on us. We wrapped Winnetou's body in a blanket, and tied it to his horse. We headed to the Gros Ventre Range that was about two days' ride from us. We hurried as much as we could, but we also had to erase our tracks.

At the end of the second day we arrived to the valley of the creek, and buried Winnetou by the leg of the mount with the ceremonies due to a chief. We buried him with his horse and weapons, and raised a little hump of earth over his grave and reinforced it with stones.

There rests the noblest chief of the Apache.

WINNETOU'S WILL

WINNETOU was dead! These three words were sufficient to describe my state of mind. I felt I could not get away from his grave. I sat at the grave burying my face in my two hands, and recalled all the times that we had spent together in battles, hunts, by camp fires, in the forest, in talking. As if I had been hit, I looked in front of me dizzy, and could not see, could not hear what happened around me. It was lucky that the Sioux did not find our tracks, because in my shock I would not have been able to defend myself.

My grieving lasted for two weeks, and then I convinced myself that I could not stay there any longer. I had to make my journey to Nuggets' Hill, where we had buried Inchu Chunna, and his beautiful daughter, Nsho-chih. First though I had another important task: to ride to the Pecos River to inform the Apache of the death of their outstanding chief. I knew that the news of such an important event would spread like lightning, but as a witness of the sad event, I had to report on it in details. I said good-bye to the good settlers, and the railway workers. I also said good-bye to Fred Walker, who decided to stay with the settlers for a while.

I got on my dun, and started off to the South-east. It was a long and dangerous route as I had to cross the hunting grounds of the Comanche and the Kiowa, from whom I could expect hostility. Apart from smaller adventures, in which I saved several whites from the Comanche, I arrived near the Canadian River without a problem. There, for my surprise, I found the track of a rider who headed in the same direction as me. My first thought was to make a detour as I did not want to meet anyone, either white or Indian. However, it would have meant some loss of time, and I was already impatient, so I followed the track that was so fresh that I was sure it had been left behind less than an hour earlier.

Soon I had to recognise that I had not paid enough attention to the track, because not one, but three riders left them. I found the place where they had a break. One dismounted maybe to tighten some belt. His footprints showed that he wore a boot, thus he was a white man. Since it was most unusual that a white man would ride with two Indians in the forest, I concluded that there were three palefaces.

Now I was determined to follow the tracks. After all, if I did not like them, I did not have to stay with them. They were riding in steps, and in two hours I caught up with them by the river at which I wanted to spend the night.

If the three strangers had the same plan, it was none of my business. They could not force me to spend the time in their company. There was one more thicket until I could get to the river, and by the time I got out of it I saw that the three riders were getting off from their horses. They had excellent equipment, but for some reason I did not like them.

They were frightened when I suddenly appeared, but calmed down immediately when they saw that I was alone. I greeted them from the distance, and they returned the greeting. I stopped at a certain distance from them, and they approached me.

'You frightened us!' said one of them.

'Do you have a bad conscience that you are frightened so easily?' I asked smiling.

'Our conscience is clean,' said the stranger, 'but we are in the Wild West, and one never knows, who the other is. Can I ask you where you have come from?'

'From the Beaver Fork.'

'And where are you going?'

'To the Pecos River.'

'Then your journey is longer than ours. We only go as far as the Mugwort Hill.'

My words stuck in my throat. Mugwort Hill was the same as Nuggets Hill. Why were these people going there? And what should I do? Should I join them as I was going there? I decided that I would try to find out their intentions. For this I had to pretend a bit.

'Mugwort Hill?' I asked. 'What's that place?'

'A very nice one. They call it such because of the plants there. But we don't go there for the mugwort, but for something else.'

'What for?'

'You would like to know, wouldn't you? But it's a secret!'

'You gossiping old woman!' the other scolded him. 'You have spoken enough.'

'Well, if someone is excited by something, he will talk about that. But tell me, my friend, who are you?'

The little company interested me more and more, and I decided that I would get to the bottom of why they were going to Mugwort Hill. The only way to do it was if I stayed with them.

'I'm a trapper,' I replied. 'I catch smaller animals with a trap if you don't mind.'

'Why would I? The forest belongs to everybody! And your name? Or you want to keep it in secret?'

'I have no reason for that,' I replied. 'My name is Jones.'

'A rare name, I have to say,' he laughed. 'But at least it's easy to remember. And where are your traps?'

'The Comanche took them with my two-months of loot.'

'That's a problem.'

'Yes, it is. But at least I survived.'

'Yes, these reds kill every white man whom they can capture. Especially now.'

'Are the Kiowa bad too?' I asked in an anxious voice.

'They are worse than the Comanche,' replied my acquaintance.

'And you still dared to come here?'

'Our situation is different. We don't have to be afraid of the Kiowa. Their chief, Tangua, likes Mr Santer, our boss, very much.'

Santer! I could not speak. It took me a great effort to show an indifferent face, and hide my surprise. These men knew Santer, and he was their boss. It was sure that it was our Santer as he was friendly with Tangua.'

773

'This Mr Santer must be a great man that the Indians appreciate him.'

'At least the Kiowa,' he answered. 'But why don't you get off your horse? It's evening now, and you surely want to stay by the river where there is water and grass for you horse, don't you?'

'You are right, but one has to be careful. I don't know you.'

'Are we so frightening?'

'I wouldn't say that, but I think it's strange that you are questioning me, but you don't tell me your names.'

'My name is Gates, this is Mr Clay and he is Mr Summer. Are you happy now?'

'Thank you.'

'And I don't want to persuade you to anything. You can continue your riding, or you can stay as you feel like.'

'If you don't mind, I would join you. Here, the more that are together, the better it is.'

'Right. You don't have to be afraid of us. Santer's name gives us safety.'

'What kind of gentleman is this Mr Santer?' I enquired while I jumped off my horse.

'He's a gentleman. We should be grateful to him if everything happens as he promised.'

'Have you known him for a long time?'

'No. We met him a short while ago for the first time.'

'Where?'

'In Fort Smith, by the Arkansas River. Why are you asking so many questions? Do you know him?'

'If I knew him, would I ask so many questions?'

'You are right,' said Gates.

'You said, Mr Gates, that Santer's name gives us protection. Then, if I may say, I'm also under his protection, so I have to know about him, don't I?'

'All right. Then sit down with us. Have you got dinner?'

'I have a piece of meat.'

'We have plenty of everything. If you don't have enough, you can have some of our provisions.'

For the first sight I had thought that they were tramps, but then I recognised that they were relatively honest people, at least in a Western sense as the criteria were different there than in more civilised places.

We took water from the river, sat down, and ate. During dinner they started to enquire about me. Gates, who appeared to be the leader of the men, asked me, "If you lost your traps, how do you want to survive?'

'Maybe from hunting.'

'Are your guns good? I can see you have two.'

'Quite good. I load the larger with bullets and the smaller with shots.'

I could say this as I had made a cover for both of my guns, otherwise anybody could have recognised me by them.

"Why do you need two guns for that?' asked Gates. You could just have a double-barrelled gun, and load one barrel with bullet and the other with shot.'

'You are perfectly right, but I got used to my old gun.'

'And what do you want to do at the Pecos River, Mr Jones?'

'Nothing special. They say that it's a good place for a trapper.'

'This is stupid! If you believe that the Apache will leave you in peace, you are wrong. Must you go there?'

'Not at all.'

'Then come with us!'

'With you?' I asked surprised.

'With us.'

'To Mugwort Hill?'

'Yes.'

'What for?'

'Hm! I don't know if I can tell you. What do you say Clay? And you Summer?'

The two men shrugged their shoulders.

'I don't know,' opined Clay. 'Mr Santer told us many times not to talk about it, but he also said that he wouldn't mind if we could find some appropriate men. Do as you want, Gates.'

'So, you are free, Mr Jones?' asked Gates.

'I don't have any obligations right now.'

'Would you participate in work from which good money could be made?'

'Why not? But first I have to know what it is about.'

'Naturally! It's a secret, but I like you. You have such an honest, simpleton face. You won't trick us, will you?'

'I'm an honest man.'

'This is what we need. Well, we go to Mugwort Hill to find nuggets.'

'Wow!' I exclaimed. 'So there's gold there!'

'Not so loud! I can see you like it. Yes, there's gold there.'

'Who told you?'

'Mr Santer.'

'Did he find it?'

'No, because then he wouldn't need our help.'

'So it's just a guess! Hm!'

'It's a bit more than that. Santer knows that there's gold there, only he doesn't quite know the place.'

'Strange!'

'Yes, it is, but this is how it is. I'll explain it to you. Have you heard of Winnetou?'

'The Apache chief? Of course!'

'And did you hear about another man called Old Shatterhand?'

'Yes, somebody mentioned him.'

'Well, these two are friends, and they went together to Mugwort Hill. Winnetou's father was also there. Mr Santer eavesdropped once, and learnt that they went for gold there. Santer, of course, wanted to find out where the bonanza was. I don't know exactly what happened, but Santer shot Winnetou's father, the then chief of the Apache.'

'Unpleasant!' I shook my head.

'Well, yes. But if you consider that the Indians cannot do anything with their gold … I don't know how this quarrel happened, or if they talked at all, but Winnetou's sister died there too. Winnetou himself would have kicked the bucket

776

had this Old Shatterhand not intervened. As a result, Santer had to flee, and found refuge with the Kiowa. This is when he made a friendship with Tangua, the chief of the Kiowa, who is a mortal enemy of Winnetou and Old Shatterhand.'

'Terrible story!' I remarked.

'Our interest is only that the gold is there. Santer had been there several times, but failed. But you know, more eyes can see more. And if we find it, we will share it. Maybe we can find it in a few days, but it's possible that it takes weeks or even months. But it pays in the end. What do you say?'

'I don't really feel like having that gold,' I replied.

'Why?'

'Because it's stained with blood.'

'Don't say silly things! It's none of our business. Two Indians don't matter. In a few decades none will survive. It's really not our business. The gold belongs to the one who finds it. If we find it, we can live like millionaires.'

Now it was clear what kind of men these three were. They did not belong to the scum of the West, who would not have stepped back from any crime, but their consciences were quite loose. To them an Indian was not more than a game that anybody could shoot at. But there was one common point between them and me. They were interested in the gold, and nothing else. I was interested in finding Santer with their help, thus I had to continue my role playing. Luck gave me this opportunity, and I could not miss it. I was determined to catch Santer.

I shook my head, and remarked with uncertainty in my voice, 'It's all very good, but I'm afraid …'

'Afraid? What? Whom?'

'Santer.'

'I told you he's a gentleman. He doesn't want to cheat us. We asked about him in the fort, and got the best references.'

'Then where is he? Why isn't he with us?'

'We parted with him yesterday. He told us to ride to Mugwort Hill, because he had to go to Salt Fork, to the largest village of the Kiowa, where Tangua, the chief, lives.'

777

'What for?'

'He wanted to make Tangua happy by taking him the news that Winnetou is dead. The Sioux shot him dead. Tangua will be happy when he hears it, and this is why Santer is making the detour. But we agreed that we would meet on Mugwort Hill.'

'Let's hope …' I hummed.

'You are so suspicious!' exclaimed Gates visibly peeved. 'What's your problem?'

'Nothing, nothing. I told you that I'd go with you, but I'll keep my eyes open.'

'Why?'

'I can't trust someone who killed two people in cold blood for a few nuggets. Who can assure me that he wouldn't kill us too if we found the gold?'

'What? What are you saying? Mr Jones, but this is …'

He did not finish his sentence, only stared at me. The same shock was visible on Clay's and Summer's face.

'Why are you so surprised?' I continued. 'Maybe he introduced you to his secret only because he's sure that he would kill you too.'

'You are seeing ghosts!'

'I think I can see the situation very well! What do you expect from a man who is Tangua's friend?'

'So what?'

'Tangua hates every paleface. If he makes an exception for Santer, he must have a good reason. Maybe he helps the chief to kill palefaces.'

'I don't care!' shrugged Gates. 'I'm only interested in the nuggets. We'll find them, and nicely share them.'

'In what proportions?' I asked.

'Equally, of course. Santer promised this.'

'After he has taken the lion share?'

'He didn't say this.'

'I believe so,' I replied. 'Why shouldn't Santer be so generous with promises when he wants to take everything from us at the end?'

'Enough of this!' burst out Gates impatiently. 'You are full of doubts and suspicions. I thought I do you a favour when I offered that you could join us. But if you don't want to, you may go!'

'I didn't say that I don't want to, and I thank you for your kindness,' I answered, 'but I was only led by good intentions when I warned you.'

'Then let's finish this subject,' he said half-heartedly.

Soon we went to sleep. Before lying down, I scouted around a bit, but I could not find anything suspicious. The night passed without any event. On the following day we continued our way towards Nuggets' Hill together.

The night found us on the open prairie. Gates wanted to light a fire, but he could not find twigs. I was happy for this. The three men considered all caution unnecessary. They believed that it would be enough to say Santer's name, and for this magic word they would be welcomed by the Kiowa. I, however, had no inclination to meet the Kiowa again, because I was quite certain that they would recognise me. Fortunately we had not met anyone.

In the morning we used up all our provisions.

'Now we really need some prey,' remarked Gates.

'I'll help,' I replied.

'You aren't a hunter, Mr Jones, only a trapper. Would you be able to hit a rabbit from a hundred steps?'

'From a hundred steps?' I asked with doubt in my voice. 'That's quite a distance, isn't it?'

Gates laughed with superiority. 'Is it? But don't worry, we are hunters, and we will shoot something for you too.'

'Here in the prairie?' I showed my doubt. 'There are only antelopes, but they are too far.'

'I don't mean here, but Mugwort Hill. There's forest there, and game. Mr Santer told us so.'

'When will we get there?'

'At around noon if we are on the right track.'

I knew that we headed in the right direction as in fact I led the group invisibly. The Sun has not yet reached the zenith, when the contours of the hills appeared on the horizon.

'Is that Mugwort Hill?' asked Clay.

'Yes, we have arrived,' nodded Gates. 'Mr Santer described precisely what we would see if we arrived from the North.'

'You forgot something,' intervened Summer. 'Santer also said that one cannot get to Mugwort Hill from the North on horseback.'

'Then we ride around it, and approach it from the South. There is a gorge there that leads to a clearance between two mountains. We'll have to wait for Santer on that clearance.'

I could see that Santer described the place very precisely for them, but I tried to be a nag.

'I don't know how we can get to that clearance,' I said, 'as there's no path or road.'

'Of course, there's no road,' replied Gates, 'but there's a gorge, and we can totter up if we get off the horses, and lead them up.'

'We could leave the horses at the bottom,' I proposed.

'Stupid! I can see that you're a trapper, and not a hunter. It could be a whole week until we find what we are looking for and we cannot leave the horses that long. Or are you staying with them?'

'I don't know,' I said hesitatingly.

'Then just come with us! At least you can see something interesting. The graves of Winnetou's father and daughter are on that clearance.'

'We won't camp by the graves, will we?'

'We will!' replied Gates.

'In the night too?' I asked perplexed.

I deliberately put this stupid question. I had to dig next to Inchu Chunna's grave to find Winnetou's will, and I did not need anyone nearby when I would do this. It was unpleasant that they wanted to camp there. With my comment I tried to frighten them away as many people have superstitions about staying at graves. But I failed with my plan.

'In the night?' echoed Gates mockingly. 'Are you afraid?'

'I'm not afraid, but it's not pleasant to sleep next to graves.'

'Can you hear this, Clay? What do you say, Summer? Our friend, Jones, is afraid of the dead! He's afraid that they would climb out of their graves in the night, hahaha!'

His companions laughed with him, and I listened with downcast eyes and embarrassment.

Gates laughed, and calmed me in a mocking tone, 'Are you superstitious? It's silly, believe me! The dead don't come out from their graves, and they don't want to frighten us. Especially as these are Indians, who enjoy the happy hunting grounds, where they can eat bison from the morning to the evening. If you can still see ghosts, just let us know, and we'll chase them away!'

In the meantime we arrived to the hills that really could not be hiked from our side. Going to the South we found the narrow gorge between two mountains. We got off our horses, and walked uphill. Gates suddenly cried out, 'We are here! There are the two graves, can you see them? We'll wait for Santer here.'

Yes, we had arrived to the sad clearance where we buried Inchu Chunna and Nsho-chih. With Winnetou I had visited this place many times, and everything had been in order every time, nobody had disturbed the graves. Winnetou had stood next to the graves with bowed head at these times, and was silent, but I knew what had occupied his mind, and what emotions had filled his heart. He wanted to punish the murderer. He took his revenge to the grave, and if he had an heir for this, it was me. I inherited the boiling desire of vengeance, this just feeling, and I did not want to forget about it. I owed this to the memory of the three dead.

'Why are you staring at those dirt hillocks?' shouted Gates at me, and I felt his voice rougher than at any other times. 'Are you already seeing the ghosts? Wait until midnight at least! You should know that it's forbidden for them to come out from their grave!'

781

I did not say anything, only dismounted, and let my horse graze as it wanted. Then, as it was my habit, I scouted around. When I returned, Gates and his companions were already comfortable. They were sitting by Inchu Chunna's grave, exactly at the spot where I wanted to dig.

'Why are you so industrious?' asked Gates. 'Are you already seeking the nuggets? Stop it if you don't want an argument! We will be seeking the gold together, so that if one finds something, he could not hide it from the others. Do you get it?'

I was happy that he meant only this, but his voice made me angry, and I protested sharper than I wanted.

'I'm not a child to be spoken to like this!'

'Even if you aren't a child, you have to adjust to us!' replied Gates.

'Do you think you can command me?'

'Yes, I do!'

'You are wrong! If somebody is a commander, it is Santer.'

'Santer is not here. I'm his deputy. I tell you, stop snooping around!'

'Right! I stop it. But I did it in your interest, and this was the thank you I got.'

'For us?'

'You are such excellent hunters that you did not know this? If one camps in the forest, he shouldn't rest until scouting about. I went to check if there was any danger.'

'Aha! So you sought tracks!'

'Yes, and thank God, I didn't find any.'

'Do you know path finding?'

'I do, indeed.'

'And I thought you were hunting for nuggets.'

'Not at all!' I replied. 'I don't really think that there are nuggets here.'

'Are you starting it again? Why don't you think?'

'Because Winnetou surely took the nuggets somewhere else, when he saw that someone else knew about them. Would you have left them there?'

'Let's wait for Mr Santer. He will explain everything. Tomorrow, or the day after tomorrow at the latest, he will be here. Let's think about our dinner as we have ran out of food.'

'If we go hunting,' I replied. 'I'll join you.'

'You stay!' said Gates stopping me. 'You don't know how to hunt, and you would only make our task more difficult. It's enough if Clay comes with me. Two of us would get something. Summer will stay with you.'

I failed. My only purpose with this conversation was to be left alone. I offered myself for the hunt, but I did not mean it seriously. I knew that they considered me unskillful, and thus would not take me. My plan had almost succeeded, but then Summer would stay. It could be that Gates did not trust me, and hence he did not want to leave me without supervision. Whatever it was, I had to accept it.

Gates and Clay took their guns, and disappeared among the trees. They were in the forest all afternoon, and the only result was that in the evening they brought a lean rabbit. It was not enough for four people.

On the following day Gates took Summer. This time the prey was a few old wood pigeon. Their meat was so tough that we could barely cope with them.

'I'm afraid,' I said while chewing, 'that it's the same pigeon that Noah sent out for scouting during the Deluge.'

'Are you mocking me?' flared up Gates. 'Bring something better if you can!'

'I will!' I replied, and taking both of my weapons on my shoulders I headed to the forest.

'Look at the hero!' laughed Gates. 'He wants to show that he's a hunter. You'll see he'll come back empty handed!'

I did not hear anything more. I should have stayed to eavesdrop! But I learnt only later what happened. They were so hungry that a few minutes after my leaving, they also left to find some game. I headed for the canyon to which we had wanted to lure the Kiowa many years earlier. It seemed that nobody had visited the place since, and it was not difficult to shoot two turkey hens.

I stepped on the clearance with a proud face hoping for success, but there was nobody there. Where were they? Did they hide to make a fun of me? I searched the area, but I could not find them.

My principle had always been to think first, and then act. But this time I was so happy for my luck that I decided that I would not miss these valuable moments. It was a hasty decision, but I started to work.

I took out my knife, and on the western side of Inchu Chunna's grave I cut out a rectangular shaped turf of grass nicely so that I could put it back later. Not one clod of earth should show that somebody had dug there. I laid down my blanket, and put the earth on it so that I could use it later to fill the hole. I worked very fast as they could return at any time, and surprised me. Time to time I listened if steps were approaching. In such an excited state of mind it was easy to make an error. I could not concentrate on anything else, but my task.

The hole became deeper and deeper, and I could barely reach the bottom. At this point my knife hit a stone. I lifted out the stone and there was another stone under it. I found a perfectly dry, cubic shaped cache made of smooth stones. In this cache a strong leather holder came to my hand, obviously Winnetou's will. I put it in my pocket, and quickly filled up the hole.

This work was much quicker. From my blanket I threw the earth in the hole, and with my fist I pressed it down. Finally I put the turf of grass in its place. Nobody could see that somebody had dug there.

I thought I had arranged everything well. I listened again, but I could not hear any noise. "Excellent," I thought, "then I can even open the leather holder." It was not a real holder, but a square soft leather whose corners were folded like an envelope, and were slipped into four incisions. I found another envelope in it that Winnetou had sewed with the sinew of a deer. I opened it, and saw the will for the first time. There were many densely written page.

"Should I hide it or should I start reading it?" I asked myself. I decided that there was no risk in reading it, because if the others came back, they could only see that I was reading something, and that was all. They would not know what it was about. It could be an old letter. They did not have any right to ask about it, and if they still enquired, I could say anything.

I could not really think, I was so immersed in Winnetou's writing. Klekih-Petra taught him writing, and Winnetou understood its importance. He had exercised it until he perfected it. He had a notebook in which he had often made notes. I knew his writing.

It was not pretty, but characteristic. It was like the writing of a fourteen years old pupil who attempts to write very nicely.

I sat down and put the papers on my knee. In the will Winnetou's personality was manifest. His regular lines showed orderly and logical thinking. Where could he have written these lines, and what did he think and felt when he wrote it? My eyes were filled with tears when I started to read it.

My dear brother,

You are alive and Winnetou, your loving brother is dead. But his soul is by you because it's alive on these papers, and you can enclose it in your heart.

You will learn the last will of your Apache brother when you read these papers, and you mustn't forget it. Especially remember the most urgent task. Winnetou has another will that he implanted in his warriors' heart, but this one, on these papers are only for you.

I entrust you with a lot of gold, and you have to do with it what I prescribe to you here. We hid the treasure on Nuggets' Hill, but when Santer, the murderer, stretched his blood stained hand for it, I took it to Deklil-to, where you have been with me. Now remember the place where you can find the gold. You ride over the Indelche-chil, all the way to Tse-Shosh. There you get off your horse, and climb up to ...

785

I got thus far in the reading when a voice sounded behind my back. 'Good morning, Mr Shatterhand! What are you reading so diligently?'

I turned around, and immediately recognised that I made the stupidest mistake in my life. What a light-headedness!

When I threw the two wild turkeys on the ground, I put my guns next to them. They were ten steps behind me. But this was not all. When I sat down on the grass to read the will, I turned my back to the path that led from the forest to the clearance. Thus I could not notice that somebody sneaked up behind me, cut my way to my guns, and aimed at me with my own gun. I jumped up immediately because the man was Santer.

I quickly moved my hand to my waist to grab my knife or revolver, but I forgot that when I had dug, I took off my belt as it obstructed me in my work. The belt with my weapons was a few steps from me. I was completely disarmed.

Santer noticed my involuntary motion, because he laughed out mockingly, and snarled at me threateningly, 'Not one step! If you go for your weapons, I'll shoot you dead! It's not a joke!'

His eyes were flashing, and I saw that for one movement he would shoot. His sudden appearance had paralysed me for a minute, but now I recovered, and my mind worked. I looked coldly in the mean eyes of the rascal.

'You are in my hands!' he shouted. 'Can you see my finger on the trigger? Just a little pull, and a bullet goes in your head! You didn't expect it, did you?'

'No,' I replied calmly.

'You believed that I would arrive only tomorrow evening. You were wrong!'

He knew this, so he had obviously talked to the other three. Where were they now? I regretted that they were not present, because although they had dubious moral values, they were not murderers, and Santer probably would not have dared to kill me in front of them. I thought that he would not kill me even in the current situation, but I should not provoke him.

Santer watched me with glowing hatred, and continued, 'I was heading to Salt Fork, because I wanted to talk to Tangua. I wanted to tell him that your friend, the Apache dog had died at long last. But on the way I met some Kiowa warriors, and sent the message to Tangua with them. Thus I arrived back earlier. In the forest I met Gates. He told me that a man called Jones had joined them. He also told me that this man had two guns a long and a short. I immediately thought of you. This bloke, I thought, pretends to be a simpleton, but he cannot be anybody else, but Old Shatterhand. I sneaked up here, and watched as you made a hole and then buried it. What is that paper in your hand?

'A tailor's bill.'

'Don't be insolent, because you'll regret it. I ask you again: what is it?'

'Come here, and look at it!'

'I'm not stupid. I will do that when we have tied you up. What did you look for in the hole?'

'Buried treasures.'

'Ah! I thought so! But you found only a tailor's bill, didn't you. I'll check it. You were wrong! What do you think? How will it end?'

'One of us will die,' I replied.

'One of us? You insolent dog! You still bark when you know that this is the last time that you can bark? You growl at me in vain, you won't escape this time! And the treasure that you wanted will be mine!'

'I don't know what you are talking about,' I replied shrugging my shoulder. 'There's no treasure here.'

'Have they moved it? Where to? I know! The paper in your hand will tell me. You will give it to me! Boys, here! Tie him up!'

For this order Gates, Clay and Summer appeared among the trees where they had so far hidden. Gates took out belts from his pocket, and approached me in an excusing manner.

'It's not my fault, Sir!' he said. 'Aren't you called Jones? Why did you want to mislead me? You lost.'

'Why are you jabbering so much?' Santer shouted at him. 'Tie his hands, and that's it! And you,' he turned to me, 'throw those papers on the ground, and stretch your arms forward!'

Now that the other three were there, he felt secure, and became more hopeful. I was sure that there would an advantageous moment, and I would be able to grab it.

'So?' yelled Santer. 'You either throw that paper down or I'll shoot!'

I dropped the papers, and offered my two hands to Gates to tie. The man stepped up to me in a hurry and stood between me and Santer.

'Go to the side,' shouted Santer. 'You are in the way if I had to shoot! Go ...'

He could not finish the sentence, because I impertinently interrupted him. I grabbed Gates by his waist, lifted him, and threw him at Santer. He jumped aside but it was too late. Gates crashed on him, knocked him over, and the gun fell out of Santer's hand. I leapt there, and knelt on Santer. With one blow I knocked him out. I pulled his revolver from his belt, quickly stood up, and now thundered at the other three while aiming at them with the revolver, 'You can see that I'm Old Shatterhand! Throw down all weapons, because I'll shoot! I'm not joking!'

They immediately obeyed.

'Sit down there, on the grave of the Indian girl, but quickly!'

I told them this because there was no weapon near there. They obeyed.

'Just stay calm! You won't be harmed! But if you try to resist or flee, you can say good-bye to life!'

'This is terrible!' moaned Gates rubbing his limbs. 'I think my bones are broken.'

'Look out, because it can happen! Whose belts are these?'

'I got them from Mr Santer.'

'Are there more of them?'

'Yes.'

'Throw them to me.'

He took some belts out from his pocket, threw them to me, and I tied Santer's legs and hands behind his back.

'Now, he can try to move,' I laughed contented. 'Should I tie you too?'

'It's unnecessary, Sir,' replied Gates. 'We won't move until you allow us, Old Shatterhand! And we thought that you were a meek trapper.'

'Did you shoot something?'

'Nothing.'

'Look at those two wild turkeys. If you behave well, we'll roast it, and eat it together. I hope you can see what a rascal this Santer is.'

As if his name helped him to regain his consciousness, Santer opened his eyes suddenly.

'What is it?' he cried frightened. 'Who tied me?'

'I, if you don't mind,' I replied smiling. 'The situation has changed as you can see. You have to accept it.'

'Damned dog,' he rattled, and ground his teeth.

'I advise you to watch your words. In the previous situation I accepted your tone of conversation because I had no other option, but now I demand the polite tone. Do you get it, Mr Santer?'

He glanced at his men and asked, 'Did you speak?'

'Not a word,' replied Gates.

'Then remain silent!'

'What is it about? What shouldn't you speak about?'

They were all quiet.

'Speak, Gates!' I shouted. 'Don't wait until I open your mouth! What is it about?'

'About the gold,' he said apparently unwillingly.

'Not about the Kiowa whom Santer met in the valley? If you have any brain, you won't mislead me! Is it true that he met the Kiowa?'

'True.'

'So he wasn't at Salt Fork?'

'No.'

'How many Kiowa?'

'He said that there were sixty warriors.'

'Who was their leader?'

'Pida, Tangua's son.'

'Where are they now?'

'They returned to their village.'

'Are you sure?'

'I'm telling you the truth, Sir,' said Gates.

I looked at him musingly. I did not like the tone of his voice, and it seemed to me that there was guile in his eyes.

'Right, Mr Gates. One chooses his own path, and he's responsible for the choice. If you misled me, you'll pay for it.'

I picked up the papers from the ground, put them in the two leather envelopes, and the envelope to my pocket.

'Are you still trusting this rascal, Mr Gates?' I asked.

'I don't know,' he replied hesitatingly, and after glancing at Santer, he added, 'He promised we would share the gold.'

'He doesn't know where it is.'

'But you do, it seems.'

I left the question unanswered.

'So you do. Tell us!'

'I can't,' I replied as I was surprised by the request.

'You see, Sir, you are against us and not for us.'

'The gold does not belong to you.'

'But it will be ours, because Mr. Santer will find it, and share it with us.'

'He won't be able to keep his promise, even if he wanted,' I said. 'I tied him well.'

'He can still free himself,' answered Gates and his eyes met Santer's again.

'I doubt it,' I stated gloomily.

Santer had a derisory laugh. 'We'll talk about this, Old Shatterhand!' he said challengingly.

'And if I shoot you dead right now like a rabid dog?' I asked angrily.

'I'm not afraid of that,' grinned Santer. 'Old Shatterhand is repulsed by killing.'

"What an insolence!" I thought. I had his life in my hands, and he dared to tease me. I was about to decide to show him that he was wrong, but then I just waved.

'You are right, Santer. To me human life is worth more than to you. But look out! Murder and punishing a murderer are different. It would be a shame if such a rascal like you would escape the judgement!'

'Only a judge has the right to make a judgement!' he shouted. 'If you take revenge, you can call it whatever you want, but it will be murder.'

'Right, I don't care. I'll take you to the nearest fort, and give you over to the authorities.'

'Really? Or vice versa! And I don't have such high moral values as you have! Hahaha!'

His mocking laughter was overpowered by the wild battle cries of Indians. Kiowa warriors with war paint on their faces jumped out from behind the trees, and flooded the clearance. They had crawled there like snakes, and surrounded the clearance. Gates cheated me. He knew, but did not tell me that Santer had brought the Kiowa to Nuggets' Hill. When they had learnt Winnetou's death, they had decided that they would celebrate it by his father's and sister's grave. Although it matched their way of thinking, Santer must have enticed them too.

While it was a surprise attack, I did not lose my mind. In the first moment I wanted to defend myself, and already lifted my revolver, but when I saw that I was surrounded by sixty warriors, I put the revolver back to my belt. I knew that I could not escape, and resistance was meaningless. It would only have made my situation worse. The only thing I did was pushing away some Indians who came too close to me, and wanted to put their hands on me.

'Stop!' I cried. 'Old Shatterhand surrenders to the Kiowa warriors. Where's the young chief? I surrender only to him, nobody else.'

The Indians stepped back a bit, and looked for Pida, who did not participate in the attack, but stood under a tree nearby to wait for the outcome of the events.

'Only to him?' screeched Santer. 'Who cares what you want. If you don't surrender, we'll smash your head.'

He was only a loud mouth, he did not come any closer to me. However, for his enticement the Kiowa attacked me again, not with weapons, only with their hands as they wanted to capture me alive. I defended myself, and knocked out several warriors, when they overpowered me. At that moment Pida shouted at them, 'Stop it! He wants to surrender!'

Santer yelled at him angrily, 'Why do you spare him? Beat him to death! I order it!'

The young chief stepped up to him and said, 'You cannot order anybody here. Don't you know who the commander of the Kiowa warriors is?'

'You.'

'And who are you?'

'The friend of the Kiowa and I hope my words count for something to them.'

'The friend of the Kiowa? Who said so?'

'Your father.'

'Not true. Tangua, the great chief of the Kiowa has never called you a friend. You are a paleface whom we tolerate. This is all.'

I would have liked to use this opportunity to attempt an escape. It could have succeeded as the warriors watched Santer and Pida. But then I would have to leave my weapons behind, and I could not make a peace with this.

I could not think about this any longer, because Pida approached me, and asked, 'Old Shatterhand is my prisoner. Is he giving me all his belongings?'

'I do,' I replied.

'And let us tie him up?'

'I won't defend myself.'

'Then give me your weapons!'

I was happy that he talked to me like this, because it showed that he was afraid of me. I gave him my knife and revolvers without a word.

Santer leant forward and picked up my two guns.

'How dare you touch them?' said Pida. 'Put them down right now!'

'No way! These are mine!'

'Not true! Mine!'

'Why?' asked Santer challengingly.

'Because Old Shatterhand surrendered himself to me, thus all his belongings are mine.'

'But without me you could not have caught him! I could have done with him whatever I wanted.'

Pida lifted his hand threateningly.

'Put them down immediately!' he commanded.

'No!' replied Santer.

'Take them from him!' said Pida turning to his warriors.

'Don't you touch me!' shouted Santer, and lifted his fist defensively.

'Take it from him!' repeated Pida.

Seeing that many hands stretched towards him, Santer threw down the guns, and shouted, 'Here they are! Take it for the time being! But I'll complain to Tangua!'

'Do!' replied Pida contemptuously.

The warriors took the two guns to Pida, and I offered my hands to be tied. At this moment Santer came to me, and said, 'I don't mind, you can have the guns, but everything else that is in his pockets is mine, especially this ...'

He stretched for the pocket of my shirt in which I put Winnetou's will.

'Away from me!' I snarled at him in such a voice that he stepped back frightened, but quickly collected himself, and grinned in my face mockingly.

'What an insolence! He knows that he's finished, and still growls at me like a rabid dog! Give me that paper! I want to read it!'

'Take it if you dare!'

793

'If I dare! Hahaha!'

He came closer and with both hands he grabbed me. However, my hands had not yet been tied fully as the belts were only on one of my wrists, and they wanted to hook it on the other only now. With a quick motion I released my hands, grabbed Santer's shoulder with my right, and hit his head with my left. He immediately collapsed, and was stretched out.

'Uff!' exclaimed the Indians.

'And now tie me up again,' I said calmly, and held my two wrists to them.

'Old Shatterhand deserves his name,' nodded Pida with appreciation. 'What did Santer want to take from you?'

'A piece of paper,' I replied, but I was quiet about the content of the paper.

'He said that it was about some treasure.'

'Come on! How could he know what it is about? And whose prisoner am I? Yours or his?'

'Mine.'

'Then why do you allow him to go into my pocket?'

'We want only your weapons, we don't want other things.'

'Still, don't let him near me! I can't accept that such a rascal would go into my pocket. I surrendered to you, because you are a good warrior. But don't forget that I'm a good warrior too, and this Santer is not good enough even to kick him!'

The Indians highly appreciate bravery and pride even in their enemies. Pida looked at me with respect.

'Old Shatterhand is the bravest hunter among the palefaces,' he said. 'The other paleface has two tongues and two faces. I don't believe him, and I won't let him go into your pocket.'

'Thank you!' I answered. 'You are worthy of three eagle feathers! A real warrior kills his enemy, but doesn't humiliate him.'

I could see that my words felt good to him, and he replied almost apologetically.

'Yes, kills him … you will also have to die. You will have a nice death … you'll suffer a lot!'

'I don't mind, torture me, you won't hear a single woe from me. But keep this rascal away from me.'

After they tied my hands, I had to lie down on the ground so that they could tie my legs too. In the meantime Santer had recovered. He stood up, hurried to me, and kicked me.

'You hit me, you dog!' he yelled. 'You'll pay for it! I'll strangle you!'

He leant forward to grab my throat.

'Away from him!' brayed Pida at him. 'I forbid you to touch him!'

'You can't forbid me to anything!' replied Santer angrily. 'The prisoner dared to touch me! I'll teach him a lesson!'

Then something happened that he did not expect. I suddenly pulled up my knees, and with my tied feet I kicked Santer so hard that he rolled backwards, stretched out again, and hit his head. He screamed in anger, and wanted to charge at me again, but he barely could stand up. His head and his limbs were aching. He pulled out his revolver, aimed it at me, and shouted, 'You'll die, you dog!'

The Indian next to him grabbed his arm, the revolver popped but the bullet missed me.

'Let go of my arm!' shouted Santer at the Indian. 'This dog hit me, kicked me! I'll shoot him dead. He's an old enemy; I can do whatever I want with him!'

'You can't!' warned Pida lifting his hand threateningly. 'I command Old Shatterhand. If you kill him … you will die!'

'What do you want to do with him?' asked Santer more humbly, and visibly frightened.

'I'll discuss it with my warriors.'

'Why do you need to discuss anything? Kill him, and that's it! You came here to celebrate the death of Winnetou, your greatest enemy. This dog was his friend. He should be tortured to death here, at this place!'

'And I'm saying that Tangua, the great chief of the Kiowa, should decide what should happen to him.'

'You don't want to take him to your village, do you? It would be a big mistake! Old Shatterhand has escaped many times. He may escape again.'

'I'll make sure that he can't escape,' replied Pida. 'My father and the whole tribe should enjoy his death. But until then we'll treat him as it's right with a famous warrior.'

'What? You will be tender with him? Why don't you give him garlands and medals?'

'I don't know what garlands and medals are, but I tell you that I'll treat him differently than I'd treat you if you were in his place.'

'Thank you, at least I know where I stand. He's not only your prisoner, but mine too. I want to be there when he dies. I'll go with you to the village.'

'I cannot forbid that,' said Pida coldly, 'but if you touch Old Shatterhand, I'll kill you. And now I want to hold council with my old and wise warriors.'

'I'll be there too!' exclaimed Santer.

'You won't. You have no word in our council!'

He chose the elder warriors, and sat down with them to discuss the issues. The younger warriors stooped near me on the grass, and talked quietly. Although I could not understand the words, I suspected that they were talking about me. They were clearly proud that Old Shatterhand was their prisoner. If they could ceremonially torture me to death, it would be such a glory that other tribes would envy. I pretended to be indifferent, but watched them unnoticeably. I looked at one face after the other, and I tried to find out what their facial expressions meant. I felt that they did not have a real hatred towards me. They certainly did not look at me with the same vengeance as at that time when I had crippled their chief.

Since then years had passed, and passions had calmed. I had become a famous hunter, such a warrior that had proved many times that he considered the Indian to be the same as the whites. Only Tangua hated me with the same passion, which was a natural outcome of his destroyed knees. He thought of me as the cause of his disability, not considering that he had been the real cause.

The Kiowa also knew that I had Pida's life in my hand, but I did not harm him. They thought of this, rather than the time when Tangua had forced me to aim at his knees. Sometimes they glanced at me, and there was respect in these glances. It would have been a mistake though if I had tried to find hope in this. I could not expect mercy from them. They had high expectations about my execution. They would talk for years about the heroism with which Old Shatterhand coped with the sufferings before his death.

I knew all these, but still I was not afraid, and not even anxious. I had been in dangerous, hopeless situations so many times, and yet I came out alive from them. This is how it would be now! I did not want to give up. On has to put all the effort, even until the last moment to realise his hopes. Sitting helplessly, and waiting for good luck is silly, while struggling till the last moment is appropriate for a man, and often leads to success.

Santer now sat down with the three whites, and quietly but passionately explained something to them. I suspected what the subject was. They had heard of Old Shatterhand, and knew that I was an honest man. They might even regret that they entrapped me, because they must have known that my death would be their doing. They had lied to me, deliberately misled me, they had not told me that the Kiowa came. Santer was trying to put their conscience to sleep, and entice them against me with all kinds of lies.

The council was not long. The old warriors stood up, and Pida made the announcement, 'The Kiowa warriors will return to their village, and after a meal we will start off immediately. Everybody must prepare!'

I expected this, but Santer, who did not know the customs and thinking of the Indians, felt disappointed. He jumped up, and hurried to Pida.

'Are you going?' he asked ardently. 'But the decision was that we would stay here for a few days!'

'But we changed the decision,' replied Pida calmly.

'Won't you celebrate Winnetou's death?'

'We will, but not now.'

'Then when?'

'Tangua will decide on that.'

'I don't understand. Why have you changed the decision?'

'I don't owe you any explanation, but I tell you because I want Old Shatterhand to hear it.'

I looked at Pida curiously. He turned to me, and continued, 'When we arrived here, we did not know that we would capture Old Shatterhand. This event doubles our joy and victory. Winnetou was our enemy, and a red man, Old Shatterhand is our enemy, and he is a paleface. His death will be an even bigger joy for us than Winnetou's death. All members of the Kiowa tribe will want to participate in this double celebration. This is why we return to our village where the whole tribe can gather, and Tangua, the greatest and eldest chief, can make the judgement on the prisoner.'

'Still, this is the best place for his death,' argued Santer. 'He became your enemy for the people who are buried here. Execute,. and bury him by these graves.'

'I know. And he doesn't have to die somewhere else. We can bring him back.'

'You said that Tangua wants to watch his torture. But Tangua cannot come here as he cannot get on a horse.'

'But two horses could bring him here. He must decide where Old Shatterhand has to die. Wherever he dies, we'll bury him here.'

'And who will bring him here?'

'I will.'

'Strange!' laughed Santer. 'Why would a Kiowa warrior bother with the body of a paleface?'

Pida tossed up his head proudly, and replied, 'Why? I tell you. Old Shatterhand is our enemy, but not a mean enemy. He could have killed Tangua by the Pecos River, but he did not do that. Only crippled him. He fought against the red men, but he respected them. If he dies, we won't throw his body to the fish or the coyotes or the vultures. Pida has heard that Nsho Chih, the daughter of the Apache, gave her heart to him. This is why we'll bury him next to her. They can meet on the happy hunting grounds. This will be Pida's gratitude to him for not killing him, but exchanging him for a paleface prisoner. My Kiowa brothers heard my words. Tell me if you agree with me.'

He looked at his warriors with a questioning expression on his face.

'Haw!' came the exclamations unanimously.

The noble behaviour of the young chief affected me. Who would have expected such gentleness from this young Indian? Santer was grinding his teeth in anger, and sought consolation by mocking me.

'Does it matter?' he said. 'Whether you die here or by the Red River, the importance is that you'll kick the bucket, and I'll be at your funeral.'

'Or I will be at yours!' I replied.

'What are you talking about? It seems that you mean that you'd escape! But it won't happen. I'll keep an eye on you all the time!'

The Kiowa soon started off. They went to the valley where they had left their horses. They unbound my legs so I could walk, but there was an Indian on both of my sides. Pida had both of my guns on his shoulder. Santer and his three accomplices led their horses, and my horse was led by a Kiowa warrior.

When we arrived to the valley, we had a break. The Kiowa made a fire, and roasted meat although they also brought dried meat. I got a big piece of meat, so big that I could hardly eat it, but still I consumed it, because I wanted to be in good strength. They had to release my hands for my meal, but they watched me closely so that I could not escape. After the meal they tied me to the back of my horse, and the group started off towards the Kiowa village.

When we got to the plains I turned my head to have one more glance on Nuggets' Hill. Maybe a farewell glance. Will

799

I see the graves of Inchu Chunna and his daughter again? Or will it be as Pida had said that they would bring me back for my funeral?

On the route to Salt Fork and Red River, nothing happened. The Kiowa were very alert, and even if they were not, I could not have escaped, because Santer was always nearby. He did everything to make the journey more difficult for me, and grabbed all the opportunities to annoy me. As to the latter one, I have to say that all his efforts were in vain because I let his mocking comments go, and listened to his words with indifference. I did not do him the favour to respond to him even once. He could not have any physical contact with me as Pida would not have tolerated it.

The Indians treated Gates, Clay, and Summer as air, thus they had to stick with Santer. Although I noticed that sometimes they would have liked to talk to me, and Pida did not care about it, Santer always obstructed them. He was afraid that I would open the eyes of his three companions and it did not suit his plans. He talked to them rough and impatiently. They were unnecessary for him now. As long as he had hoped that they would help him to find the treasure, he was kind to them. But now the situation had changed. He learnt that Winnetou had probably taken the treasure to a better place. Thus he wanted to get the papers, but he could not. He now needed the papers, and not helpers. He would have killed Gates, and the other two if he could.

The papers! These were his thoughts, desires, and goal. He could not get them from me openly, Pida would not have allowed it. He could get them only in two ways: stealing them while I was asleep or waiting for our arrival to the village, and persuade Tangua to give them to him. He knew which pocket I kept the papers in, and as my hands were tied, I could not put them to a different place or hide them better. It was a cause of anxiety, but not because of fearing for my life, but because of my inability to fulfil Winnetou's will.

The Kiowa village still stood at the confluence of the two rivers. We crossed the Red River at a ford where the water was low. There were only a few hours left until our arrival. Pida sent two warriors forward to report it. I could imagine the joy with which the news was received that Pida had captured Old Shatterhand.

We were still riding on the prairie, far from the forest that covered the banks of the river, but already riders galloped towards us. They did not form a group, some arrived alone or in couples or in trios. They were the youth of the Kiowa who were not patient enough to wait for Pida, and would have liked to see the famous prisoner, Old Shatterhand. They greeted the returning warriors with sharp, screeching cries, and cast curious glances at me. Then they joined the group at the back. If I had had a similar celebrity status in a town, then they would have stared in my face insensitively. But this was different. The Kiowa were much too proud to betray their excitement and interest.

Our group became bigger and bigger, but I was left in peace. When we finally arrived to the forest, which was only a narrow strip of woods at the bank of the river, I was surrounded by at least four hundred Indians, mainly adult warriors. It seemed that the village became bigger since I had seen it last.

Under the trees there was a long line of tents. They were empty now as everyone came out to watch our arrival. I saw many women, old and young, also adolescent boys and girls. These were not as reserved as the serious warriors, and they made such a noise that I would have liked to press my hands on my ears, but my hands were bound. The yelling, screaming, laughing showed not only their lack of restraint, but also the importance that they attached to me.

Pida rode at the front of the group. He lifted his hand, and made a quick motion horizontally for which the noise stopped immediately. He gave another signal for which the riders made a big arc. In the middle of this arc I stood with Pida, and the two Kiowa warriors who had had the task of guarding me for days and nights. Santer also pushed there, but the young chief ignored him, and pretended he did not exist. This is how we rode in step to a big tent whose top was decorated with the feathers of a chief. In the front of the tent Tangua waited for us in a half sitting half lying position. He had become very old, and was lean like a skeleton. From his sunken eyes he cast such a look at me that almost cut and pricked. It was full of boiling hatred. Tangua's hair was long and white like the snow. He had become completely grey since I last saw him.

Pida jumped off his horse, and the warriors followed his example. Everybody came closer, because they all wanted to hear Tangua's words with which he would receive his old enemy, Old Shatterhand. They untied me from my horse, and cut the belts on my legs so I could stand in the front of Tangua. I was also interested in the words of the chief, but he was silent for a very long time.

First he measured me up from my head to feet, and then from my feet to head. He repeated this examination twice. His look was stern, and it was meant to frighten me. Then he closed his eyes. Everybody was silent. It started to become uncomfortable, and I was about to break it when Tangua slowly and ceremonially started to speak without opening his eyes.

'The flowers long for the dew, but the dew doesn't come. The flower bows its head, withers, but the dew doesn't come. The flower is almost dead when the dew arrives!'

He was quiet for some time, and then continued, 'The bison ploughs the snow, but there is no grass under it. It roars hungrily to call the spring, but the spring doesn't come. The bison becomes lean, its strength wither, it is about to die. Then it feels the warm breeze, and the spring arrives.'

He paused again.

How strange! This Indian had always hated me, persecuted me, insulted me, and wanted my demise. I could have killed him, but I only aimed at his knees. I made him a cripple, but only because I had to. He became old, rattling bones in skin, a mummy; his voice sounded as if it came from the grave, but he thought only of revenge and gloating. I was not afraid of him, and, I do not know why, I felt sorry for him.

He started to speak again. Nothing moved on his face, but his bloodless lips.

'Tangua was the flower, Tangua was the starving bison. He wanted the revenge, but the revenge did not come. He hoped day after day, week after week, month after month, but in vain. Yet he can take his revenge at the threshold of his death.'

He suddenly opened his eyes, rose as much as his paralysed legs allowed, stretched out his two lean arms, and pointed at me.

'It is coming! It is coming!' he exclaimed. 'It's here now, I can see it. The revenge has arrived! Dog! What death should I measure out to you?'

He sank back exhausted, and closed his eyes. Nobody dared to break the silence. After a long pause Tangua opened his eyes again, and asked, 'How did you capture this stinky toad? I want to know!'

Santer immediately grabbed the opportunity. He did not wait for Pida, who should have made the report, but jumped in front of Tangua.

'I know it the best!' he cried. 'Should I tell it to you?'

'Speak!'

Santer reported in detail, but his goal was to emphasise his own merits. Nobody interrupted him. Pida was far too proud to correct his words, and I could not care with Santer's boasting. When he finished, he added, 'Everybody can see that you can thank me if you can take your revenge on him. Do you recognise it?'

Tangua nodded.

'Will you give me what I ask as a reward?'

'Maybe. If it's possible.'

'It depends only on you.'

'Then tell me what you want.'

'There's something in Shatterhand's pocket that I need.'

'What is it?'

'Talking papers.'

'Did he steal it from you?'

'No, he found it. I rode to Mugwort Hill only to find this paper, but he arrived there before me.'

'Right. You can have it. Take it from him.'

Santer was rubbing his hands in his joy that he achieved his goal, and stepped closer to me. I did not say anything, did not move, but looked at him so threateningly that he did not dare to touch my pocket.

'Did you hear what the chief commanded, Sir?'

He called me "Sir"! But it did not affect me, and I did not reply. Because of this, he continued. 'Look, Mr Shatterhand, it's the best for you too if you don't resist. Accept it, and let me go into your pocket.'

He stepped closer and stretched his arm, but my hands were already in fist and with my bound hands I hit him on his chin so hard that he crashed backward. The Indians liked it.

'Uff!' exclaimed many, but Tangua thought differently.

'This bound dog dares to defend himself!' he shouted angrily. 'Tie him up so that he could not move, and take the talking papers from his pocket!'

This is when Pida spoke for the first time.

'Father, the great chief of the Kiowa is wise and just, and will listen to his son's words.'

The old man's faraway look suddenly become livelier.

'What does my son say?' Isn't it just what this paleface, Santer, asks from me?'

'No.'

'Why?'

'Because I defeated Old Shatterhand, and not Santer. Old Shatterhand surrendered to me. Whose prisoner is he?'

'Yours.'

'To whom do his horse, weapons, and other properties belong?'

'To you.'

'Then why do you give him those talking papers?'

'Because they belong to him. Only Old Shatterhand got there before him.'

'Then make him prove it! If the talking papers are his, he can tell us what the papers talk about! Does the great chief think that it's correct?'

'Yes it is,' nodded Tangua. 'Santer must tell us what the papers talk about. If he knows it, then I'll give it to him.'

Santer was embarrassed. He suspected that it was about Winnetou's treasure, but he could not be sure, so he gave an evasive answer.

'Nobody is interested in what the paper talks about only me. Otherwise I wouldn't have come here for it.'

'You spoke wisely, the papers are yours,' said Tangua.

It was time that I would enter the discussio as I clearly saw on Pida's face that he would not continue to contradict his father.

'Santer spoke wisely, but he lied!' I exclaimed.

The old man's shoulder jerked. His passion flared up by hearing my voice, and hissed angrily, 'The rabid dog dares to bark! It won't help him!'

'Pida said that the great chief of the Kiowa is wise and just. Then he should listen to both parties. Then I'll accept the will of the great chief,' I replied,

'You are right,' Tangua nodded.

'Would Tangua tell me if I had ever lied to him?'

'No,' he answered. 'You, Old Shatterhand, are the most dangerous paleface, but you don't have two tongues.'

'Then believe me that Santer doesn't know what the paper talks about. I rode a long journey for the papers, not Santer. He only wanted the gold that he has been searching for in Mugwort Hill for years. He only came for the gold.'

'He is lying!' yelled Santer.

'I'm telling the truth as always,' I replied calmly. 'Tangua could ask the other three palefaces. Santer brought them here to help him find the treasure.'

Tangua asked the three men, and they did not dare to deny it.

'Yes, I came for the gold, but also for the papers.'

'He has never seen the papers,' I replied. 'Ask him if they are valuable to him.'

Santer did not wait for Tangua's question, but answered immediately, 'Of course, they are valuable to me! Otherwise I wouldn't have come for them!'

'If they are valuable for him,' I said, 'then he can tell us how many papers are in my pocket: two, three, four or five?'

Santer was quiet. He was afraid of not giving the correct number.

'He's silent!' I said. 'He doesn't know it!'

'I forgot it!' exclaimed Santer. 'One doesn't pay attention to such an unimportant thing.'

'If the papers are important for him, he couldn't call it unimportant,' I turned to Tangua. 'But let's make another attempt. He should tell us whether the papers were written by pen or by pencil. You'll see that he will remain silent.'

I said the last words mockingly so that he would answer quickly, and would not have time to think. I hoped he would not choose the option good for me. In the West one could find ink only in the forts, while everybody carried pencils.

I was right, because Santer replied in a hurry, 'By pencil, of course!'

'Are you sure?'

'By pencil! Not ink!' he repeated angrily.

'Right,' I said. 'There must be someone among the Kiowa warriors who have seen talking papers, and can differentiate ink from pencil. If the young chief takes the papers from my pocket, and gets them examined, we will see if Santer told the truth or lied.'

Pida did so and said, 'Here are the three palefaces, they can look at it.'

He called Gates, Clay, and Summer, and showed them the papers but in a way that they would not have time to read it. All the three stated that it was ink.

'Idiots!' yelled Santer angrily.

'It is ink, I can't say anything else,' said Gates, excusing himself.

Pida put the papers back in the leather envelop, and turned to his father.

'Old Shatterhand showed that Santer lied. Now the great chief should decide.'

'The papers belong to Old Shatterhand,' replied Tangua, 'and as he's your prisoner, the talking papers belong to you.'

'If the two palefaces struggle for them so much, these papers must be important,' said Pida. 'I'll keep them in my medicine bag.'

He put the papers away. I did not know if I should be happy or sad for this. If I had the opportunity to escape, how would I get the papers? But Santer could not get them either. If the papers stayed with me, Santer would have made an attempt to steal them from me when I was asleep or when I could not defend myself.

It seemed that Santer had the same thoughts because his face became very gloomy. He wanted to protest, but then changed his mind and said, 'Right, you can have the papers. You cannot do anything with it as you can't read. Let's not talk about it. Come my friends, we have nothing to do here, and we need to find accommodation.'

He waved to his three accomplices and left with them. Nobody tried to hold them back.

Tangua asked Pida, 'How is it possible that the papers remained with Old Shatterhand? Didn't you empty his pockets?'

'No,' replied Pida. 'Old Shatterhand is a great warrior: we will kill him, but won't humiliate him. I took his weapons, but did not search his pockets. When he dies, everything will belong to me anyway.'

I thought Tangua would disagree, but I was wrong. He cast a proud, loving glance at his son, and said to the audience, 'Pida, the young chief of the Kiowa, is a noble warrior. He kills his enemies, but doesn't humiliate them.

807

His name will be more famous that Winnetou's, the Apache dog. As a reward I will let him stab his knife in Old Shatterhand's heart when the last moment arrives. Then he will be known as the warrior who dispatched the most famous paleface. Now, call the elder warriors. We will hold council on the execution of this paleface. In the meantime, hang him on the death tree.'

I learnt what the death tree was in a few minutes. They led me to a thick pine tree. They drove short poles around it in groups of four. They called the tree death tree, because they tied the prisoners whom they wanted to torture to death there. On the lowest branches of the tree many belts hung down. After I was tied, two warriors sat on my left and on my right to guard me. By the tent of the chief the elder warriors sat in a half circle to decide on the details of my fate. Before they started the council Pida came to me, and examined the belts.

I was bound extremely tight. Pida did not like it, and loosened the belts a bit.

'Guard him, but don't torture him!' he told the guards. 'He's a great warrior, famous hunter, and a chief among the palefaces. Also, he has never treated the red men cruelly.'

After these words he left, and joined the council.

I was tied to the tree in a standing position with my back to the trunk. Women, girls, and children came to the death tree to see me. The warriors kept their distance, and even the boys were too proud to show their curiosity. I could not see hatred on any of their faces. They wanted to see the great white hunter of whom they had heard so much, and whose death was entertainment for them.

I noticed a young Indian woman who could not yet be a squaw. She was slightly away from the others, and looked at me only secretly as if she felt ashamed for being with the spectators. She was not beautiful, but not ugly either. I could call her face sweet. Her soft countenance, serious, open look, and her large black eyes reminded me to Nsho-chih, although she was not similar. For some reason I nodded to her in a friendly way. She blushed, quickly turned around, and left. After a few steps she stopped for a moment, looked at me, and then disappeared behind the entrance of a larger, more decorated tent.

'Who is this Kiowa girl who stood alone, and now left?' I asked my guards.

Nobody forbade them to talk to me, and one of them replied, 'Kaho-oto, Sus-homasha's daughter. Her father is a great warrior. He achieved fame already as boy, and thus he's allowed to wear one feather in his hair. He's sitting in the council there. Do you like her?'

'Yes,' I answered, although it was strange that the Indian asked me this in my current situation.

I understood the Kiowa language a bit, and I knew that Sus-homasha meant One Feather, and his daughter's name meant Black Hair.

'The squaw of the young chief is her sister,' continued the guard.'

The council had lasted almost for two hours, and then I was taken to them to be informed about their decision. I knew that I would have to listen to long speeches, and this is what happened. Tangua listed all my sins that cried for the biggest punishment. One or two old men spoke of the complaints of the Indians. I was sentenced to selected tortures that probably no other had had to endure. I should have been proud of this as it showed that they highly respected me as their enemy. There was one good thing in the decision: they postponed the execution. A part of the tribe were on the way, and they wanted to wait for their arrival. They could not deprive them from the joy to watch Old Shatterhand's slow death.

Of course, I listened to the judgement like a man who was not afraid of death. I was very short in my response, and I avoided any insulting words about my judges. This contradicted the Indian customs. They normally considered a sign of bravery if the accused behaved in a challenging way, and enticed the judges. However, I did not want to do

809

this partly because of Pida, who behaved in a noble way with me, but also because of the other Kiowa, who were much more friendly than I expected. I was not afraid that they would explain my reservation with cowardice. Nobody could accuse Old Shatterhand with it.

When they took me back to the death tree, I passed by the tent of One Feather.

His daughter stood at the entrance, and I asked her, 'Is my younger sister happy that the wicked Old Shatterhand was captured?'

She blushed again, and after a short hesitation she replied, 'Old Shatterhand is not wicked.'

'How do you know it?'

'Everybody knows it.'

'Then why do you want to kill me?'

'Because you crippled Tangua, and you aren't a paleface anymore but an Apache.'

'If one is born paleface, he remains that,' I answered.

'But you didn't,' she said seriously. 'Inchu Chunna accepted you as an Apache, and made you a chief. And aren't you a blood brother of Winnetou?'

'I am. Yet I have never hurt the Kiowa if I didn't have to. Black Hair shouldn't forget it!'

'How do you know my name, Old Shatterhand?'

'I asked, and learnt that you are the daughter of a great warrior. May the Great Spirit give you as many nice years as many hours as I have left.'

Then I walked off. My guards did not obstruct me talking to the girl. They would not have allowed it to other prisoners. I thanked this to Pida's words and behaviour. Not even old Tangua appeared to be as spiteful as in the first moments. The young offspring can make the old tree noble.

When I was tied up again only two guards remained with me. It seemed that the women and the children were instructed not to disturb me. It was glad for this because it was not a pleasant feeling being stared at when I was hanging on the tree. Later I saw that Black Hair stepped out of her tent, and she was approaching with a shallow earthenware dish in her hands.

'My father allows me to feed you,' she said. 'Do you accept it?'

'Willingly,' I replied, 'but I cannot use my hands because they are tied.'

'That's not a problem. I will help you.'

There was chopped roast bison meat in the dish. Black Hair brought a knife with her, and she spiked the pieces on that. She put the pieces in my mouth one by one. A young Indian woman fed Old Shatterhand like a baby. I almost laughed out aloud for this thought. But I did not have a reason for being ashamed as the person who fed me like this was not a priggish white lady, but an Indian girl for whom this could have been natural. I was not the first prisoner whom she had seen.

The two guards watched the scene with a serious face, but it seemed that they had to suppress their smiles. When I swallowed the last piece, one of the guards, maybe to express his appreciation of the girl's behaviour, remarked, 'Old Shatterhand said that he liked Black Hair.'

The girl looked at me searchingly, and I think I blushed just as much as she had done earlier. Then she turned around, and left. But after a few steps she turned back, and asked, 'Did this Kiowa warrior tell the truth?'

'He asked me if I liked you, and I answered that I did,' I told her truthfully.

The girl left without a word, and I gently scolded my guard for his gossiping, but he only laughed.

Later in the afternoon I caught sight of Gates as he was walking among the tents.

'Can I talk to this paleface?' I asked the guard.

'I don't mind it,' he replied, 'but you can't talk about escaping.'

I waved to Gates to approach, and he obeyed unwillingly like a child who was forbidden of doing something, and was afraid that somebody could see him doing it.

'Just come!' I encouraged him. 'Why are you so hesitant?'

'Mr Santer doesn't like it,' he replied honestly.

'Did he say so?'

'He did.'

'I'm not surprised. He's afraid that I would enlighten you as to what sort of man you are dealing with.'

'A very good man,' he answered. 'I know you have a bad opinion of him, but you are wrong.'

'If I was wrong! But it cannot be. Santer is a criminal.'

'It's your problem, Mr Shatterhand. It's nothing to do with me. I don't take sides in this.'

'If you are so impartial, why did you mislead me? Why did you keep numb about the Kiowa at Mugwort Hill? I became a prisoner because of you!'

'You weren't honest with us either. You didn't tell us who you were, and called yourself Jones.'

'So what? Is it fraud?'

'Naturally.'

'No, Mr Gates! Fraud is when someone unlawfully misappropriates something from another. But if one keeps his real name secret for personal safety, it's simply a trick. Santer is a murderer, and a dangerous man. I knew that he would kill me. I also knew that he was your ally. So I couldn't possibly tell you that I wanted to go to Mugwort Hill.'

'I don't know why you think that Santer wants to kill you, Mr Shatterhand. He told me that he could kill you, but he doesn't want to.'

'Oh! The good Samaritan! When has he told you this?'

'Just now, in our tent.'

'You have a tent already?'

'Tangua told Santer that he could choose one.'

'And which one did he choose?'

'The one next to Pida's tent.'

'Interesting! He moved next to Pida who does not like him as much as his father. I can tell you, Mr Gates, look after yourself. You can fall down with Santer!'

'How?'

'For example he disappears suddenly, and leaves you in trouble. The Kiowa tolerate you just now, but if they become angry with Santer, they won't hesitate about you! I don't know if I have the opportunity then to help you.'

'What? You? Us? I don't understand it, Mr Shatterhand. You speak as if you were a free man, a friend of the Kiowa, and not a bound prisoner who will be executed soon.'

'A lot of things may happen. Don't forget that ...'

'Damn!' he interrupted. 'He saw that I'm talking to you!'

Santer came out of the tents, and hurried towards us.

'Why are you so frightened,' I asked Gates. 'You said that Santer is the best man in the world! And you fear him?'

'I don't want to argue with him.'

'Then kneel in front of him, and apologise!' I said angrily.

'What's this?' shouted Santer when he got closer. 'What are you doing here Gates? Don't you have anything better to do than talking to this man?'

'I came this way, and he called me,' said Gates excusing himself.

'You shouldn't have answered him! Get lost from here!'

'But Mr Santer, I'm not a child to be talked to ...'

'Shut up! You have nothing to do here! Come with me!'

He grabbed Gates's arm, and pulled him. Gates obeyed without protestation. What had Santer said and lied to these people that they had become his slaves?

Naturally, the Kiowa chose guards who spoke English, and thus they had understood the quarrel. I could see again that the Kiowa looked at me with greater respect than at their guest, Santer. After Santer and Gates had gone, one of the guards remarked, 'One is a wolf, the other is a lamb. The wolf sooner or later will eat the lamb. Why didn't he listen to Old Shatterhand?'

Soon Pida visited me to examine my bondage, and asked if I had any complaints. After my answer he pointed at the poles that surrounded the death tree in groups of four.

'If you get tired of standing for so long, you can lie down among the poles. You will spend the night there anyway.'

'I can cope with standing,' I replied.

'Good, then he you lie down after dinner,' nodded Pida. 'Do you have any other request?'

'Yes, I have one.'

'Tell me and I'll fulfil it.'

'I'd like to warn you of Santer.'

'That nobody? What can such a worm do to Pida, the young chief of the Kiowa?'

'You are right, he is a worm. But one has to be aware of worms too. I've heard that he is in the tent next to yours.'

'Yes, that tent was empty.'

'Then look out that he won't enter your tent.'

'If he tries, I'll throw him out.'

'Of course, if he comes openly. But if he sneaks in, and you don't notice it?'

'It's impossible!'

'And if you aren't in your tent?'

'Then my squaw will chase him away.'

'He wants to get the talking papers that you have.'

'He won't get them.'

'I know that you won't give them to him, and that he cannot get them with violence. But if he steals them?'

'Even if he could sneak into my tent, he won't find them. I hid them very well.'

'Would you allow me to look at them again?'

'But you have read it, haven't you?'

'Only half way through.'

'You can look at them, but it's getting dark. Tomorrow morning, when it's light again, I'll bring them to you.'

'Thank you! And something else. Santer longs for not only the talking papers, but my weapons too. They are famous weapons, and he would like to get them very much. Where are they?'

'In my tent.'

'Look after them!'

'I hid them very well. Even if he entered my tent at broad daylight, he wouldn't be able to see them. I wrapped

814

them in two blankets, and hid them under my bed so that they wouldn't rust. They are now my weapons. I'll inherit the glory of the Henry rifle. But I can do something with it only if Old Shatterhand fulfils one of my requests.

'I will do if I can,' I replied similarly as Pida had done earlier.

'I looked at our weapons. I can shoot with the bear slayer, but not with the rifle. Would you show me how to load it and shoot with it before your death?'

'I will.'

'Thank you. I wouldn't be able to force you to betray this secret to me, and if you denied my request I couldn't do anything with the rifle. But as you have always been good to me, and you are good to me now, I'll make it sure that all your requests are fulfilled before your torture starts.'

After his words he left, and he did not suspect what hopes he created in me. I had hoped before, but only vaguely, without a plan. Maybe I had expected help from Gates, Clay, and Summer. Even if they were not my friends, as white men they should have felt that they should try to save me from the torture if they could. Maybe there would have been some opportunity to escape from the death tree. If somebody cut my bonds, there was no power that could have held me back from escaping. But I had to recognise that I had only deluded myself with hoping in Gates's and his friends' help. Gates's last words had shown clearly that I could not expect anything from him. Thus I had to rely on myself. I did not see any hope, yet I was not disheartened. I felt that there must be an opportunity, only I had to find the way to it. If my bondage was undone, and I had a knife in my hand! After removing Gates from my calculations, I started to think of Black Hair. I saw that she felt sympathy for me, and I knew that many white prisoners had escaped utilising this. Before death, the most horrible death, one cannot be choosy with the means! And then Pida had come to me and asked me to teach him how to use the rifle. There was nothing better than this. If he wanted me to teach him the loading of the rifle, and the shooting with it then he would have to untie my hands. I could grab his knife ... one more motion and there would not be bondage on my legs. And then I would be free! Free! Even if there were a thousand Kiowa, I would have the Henry rifle in my hand! It would be a death-daring enterprise, of course, but one would risk everything if it is about his life. If he did not use the chance, he would die anyway, but at least there would be a chance in acting.

It would have been better to escape through some trick, and not by being exposed to the guns, arrows and tomahawks of the Kiowa, but I could not find any way. I hoped that I could come up with some solution.

I leant that I would spend the night lying between the poles. They drove sixteen poles in the ground by the tree: four on each side, enough for four prisoners. After some investigation I recognised how the sons of the death tree slept there. The poles stood in a narrow rectangular shape. The prisoner's legs and arms were tied to the poles, and he would lie there with stretched limbs, very uncomfortably which makes sleeping almost impossible. The Indians could be sure that their prisoner could not escape even if the guards fell asleep.

As I was musing, and investigating my situation, it had become dark, and they lit fires in the front of the tents. I saw that the squaws were busy with making the dinner. My dinner was brought by Black Hair, and she also brought water so I could refresh myself. Probably she asked her father to intervene for me with Tangua or maybe Pida acted. We did not talk, but when she left I thanked her for her goodwill. They changed my guards, and the new ones were just as friendly as the previous ones. I asked when I would have to lie down among the poles, and they said that Pida would come because he wanted to check it personally. However, instead of the young chief, an elder warrior approached me with slow, ceremonial steps. It was One Feather. He stopped in front of me, looked at me for two minutes, and then ordered my guards.

'My brothers can leave until I'm here. I'll call you back. I have something to talk about with the paleface.

They immediately obeyed which suggested that, although he was not a chief, he commanded great respect. When the guards had left, he sat down on the ground in front of me. He was quiet for a while again, and then started to speak in a ceremonial tone.

'The palefaces used to live on the other side of the Great Water. Their country is big, and they had enough land. They were still caming over the Great Water to rob our plains, mountains, and forests.'

He became quiet again. His words, according to the Indian customs, were the introduction, and I knew that he had a much more important thing on his mind. What could he talk about with me? I suspected it. He expected some response, but I remained silent, thus he continued, 'The red men received the palefaces with friendly hospitality, but it was returned with robbery and murder!'

He paused again.

'And they still devise ways in which they can cheat the red men. They won't rest until they can crowd us out from our own country. Their actions demand revenge!'

I remained silent.

'If a red man meets a paleface, he always faces a mortal enemy. Or are their palefaces who don't hate us?'

Now I could see where he was heading to with his introduction. He would have liked to talk about me, but he could not start with this. As I remained stubbornly silent, he had to ask me openly, 'Don't you want to answer, Old Shatterhand? Doe you deny what I said? Do you think that the palefaces aren't in fault against us?'

'What you said, One Feather, is true,' I replied.

'So you admit that the palefaces are our enemies?'

'Most of them.'

'Most of them? Are there such who don't want to kill us, who don't want to rob us?'

'Yes there are.'

'Could Old Shatterhand name at least one?'

'I could list you names, but it is unnecessary. You want to know of one. If you open your eyes, you can see that one in front of you.'

'I can see only Old Shatterhand.'

'I meant him.'

'So you think that you are such a paleface, who doesn't hate our people and he is not in fault against us?'

'No!' I replied.

He could not make sense of my answer, so he asked, 'Which one did you mean? That you are not such a paleface? Or that you don't hate us, and you aren't in fault against us?'

'Almost the second.'

'Why almost?'

'My brother's words don't quite fit me. It's not enough that I don't hate the Indians, because I'm their friend. It's not enough that I'm not in fault against them, because I want to help them.'

'Have you never killed a single red man?'

'As a warrior I cannot say that. But I can say that I have never attacked an Indian, but I fought with him only if I had to, and if I killed him, it was only for self-defence.'

'You said you are our friend.'

'I have demonstrated it many times. I was always on the side of the Indians, and if I could I protected them against the transgressions of the whites. If you are just, you have to admit this.'

'One Feather has always been just!'

'Think of Winnetou then! We loved each other like two brothers. Winnetou was an Indian, wasn't he?'

'He was, even if he was our enemy.'

'He wasn't your enemy, only you treated him as an enemy. He liked all Indian peoples as much as the Apache. He wanted you to live in peace with each other, and struggle against the whites as a united one. But you didn't listen to him, and hated and fought with each other. This was the great sadness of Winnetou until the last minute of his life.

And how he felt and thought is the same as I feel and think. He loved the Indian peoples, and I do too. This led his steps and this leads my steps.'

I spoke just as slowly and ceremonially as he had done. When I became quiet One Feather bowed his head, and mused for a long time. Finally he lifted his head and said, 'You spoke the truth, Old Shatterhand. One Feather can see the good even in his enemies. If all red men were like Winnetou, and all palefaces like Old Shatterhand, the two peoples could live in peace with each other, they would love and help each other as the Earth is big enough, and all its children have enough place on it. But it's very dangerous to give an example that nobody wants to follow. Winnetou is dead, and Old Shatterhand will finish his life on the torture stake.'

Now he arrived to the point that he wanted. I was deliberately silent because I did not want to meet him half way, yet we got to the subject about which he wanted to talk.

'You, Old Shatterhand, are a great hero,' nodded the old man. 'This is why you will have to suffer a lot before your death.'

'I will cope with it as a man,' I replied, 'if it happened.'

'You said, "if it happened"! Aren't you sure?'

'No!'

'You are very honest!'

'Would you like me to lie instead?'

'No. But admitting that you still have hopes is fool hearted.'

'Old Shatterhand has never been a coward.'

'Are you hoping to escape?'

'I don't deny it.'

'Uff! Uff!' he exclaimed because of my openness. 'It seems they have been too permissive with you. We'll guard you more seriously in the future.'

'Still I have to say what I think.'

'Every warrior is proud of his bravery. But being fool hearted is different from bravery.'

'Only those are fool hearted who misunderstand the situation or who don't have anything to lose.'

'And what is the cause of your honesty?'

'It comes from something completely different.'

'And what is it?'

'I can't tell you, you have to find it out.'

What I could not tell him was very simple. One Feather came to me to save my life. He could do it only in one way, if he gave me his daughter. Then I would be free, and I would be accepted in the Kiowa tribe. But I did not want to become a Kiowa. However, if I refused One Feather, I would have insulted him, and made him a mortal enemy. I did not want to do this. This is why I talked to him so openly, and admitted that I was hoping to escape. It was the same as if I had said to him: "don't give me your daughter, because I can save my life in a different way". If he understood this hint, he would not be insulted, and would not have to take a revenge on me.

I was proud that I thought so quickly and so well. Unfortunately it did not work as I expected. One Feather was musing for some time, and then with a crafty countenance he started to argue with me.

'You are ashamed to admit that your position is hopeless, and this is why you speak about escaping, Old Shatterhand. But One Feather cannot be so easily mislead. You know well that you are finished!'

'I don't.'

'Escaping is impossible. If there was the smallest chance, I would sit here day and night to guard you. You can escape only with my help.'

'I don't need any help!'

'I know that you are proud. Much prouder than I thought. But if someone in your position pushes away the helping hand, it is not pride, but silliness. I don't ask any gratefulness from you, but I help you. Has Black Hair looked after you?'

'Yes, and I thanked her.'

'I know. She feels sorry for you.'

'Then Old Shatterhand is a very pitiful being. For a warrior the woman's sorry is an insult!'

I talked so rough and coldly deliberately. I tried to deter him from his intentions. But it was all in vain.

'I don't want to insult you,' he answered mildly. 'My daughter has heard of you many times. She knows that Old Shatterhand is the greatest white warrior, and wants to save your life.'

'This only shows that Black Hair is a good hearted being. But she cannot save me. It's impossible.'

'It's not impossible. It's easy.'

'My brother is wrong.'

'I'm not wrong. You know the customs of the red men, but it seems that you don't know something. Black Hair will save you. You'll have a good life. You said that you are attracted to her.'

'This is also wrong. I didn't say anything like this.'

'My daughter told me, and Black Hair has never said anything else but the truth.'

'What happened was the following. She brought food for me. Then one of the guards asked me if I liked the girl. I said yes, I liked her. But I did not say this to Black Hair.'

'I see! But it doesn't matter if you told it to her or somebody else. You like her, and that's what's important. If somebody marries a girl of the tribe, the tribe would adopt the person, and he would belong to us. Do you understand?'

'I do.'

'Even if he was an enemy or a prisoner.'

'I know.'

'His sins are forgiven, and he regains his liberty.'

'I know this too.'

'Uff! Then you understand what I want.'

'I have understood it.'

'You like my daughter and my daughter likes you. Do you want her to be your squaw?'

'No.'

A long and uncomfortable silence followed.

One Feather did not expect this answer. I was the groom of death while Black Hair was a pretty, kind girl, the daughter of the most respected warrior of the tribe, and I refused her. Unimaginable!

Finally One Feather asked me very briefly, 'Why?'

Could I tell him the real reason? That I would destroy my life if I tied it to an Indian girl? That I could not expect from this what I expected from a marriage? That Old Shatterhand was not one of those rascals who seduce an Indian girl, and then leave her or have a squaw in every village? These things would have been beyond One Feather's perspectives, and he would not have understood them.

I had to bring up something that belonged to his culture and thus I answered, 'You, my brother, said that you consider Old Shatterhand a great warrior, but it seems to me that you didn't mean it seriously.'

'But I do!'

'Then how could you expect me to accept my life from a girl's hand as a present. Would you do it?'

'Uff!' he exclaimed, and then became quiet. It seemed that this explanation made sense to him. After a while he asked, 'What do you think of One Feather?'

'That you are a great, brave, and experienced warrior who is just as excellent in the council as on the warpath.'

'Would you like One Feather to be your friend?'

'Very much.'

'And what do you think of Black Hair?'

'She's the most beautiful flower of the tribe, and I haven't met a more kind-hearted being than her.'

'Is she good enough to be the squaw of a great warrior?'

'Even the greatest warrior would be proud of her.'

'So you didn't refuse me because you look down upon her or me?'

'Not at all! But Old Shatterhand can fight till the last drop of his blood, can face death, but he cannot live because of the mercy of a woman.'

'Uff! Uff!' he nodded in agreement.

'You cannot expect Old Shatterhand to do something that could be used to mock him or reproach him. You don't want him to do something for which everybody would frown upon if they hear it by the campfire.'

'Obviously not.'

'That it would be said that he escaped to the arms of a pretty squaw from death.'

'Not at all.'

'So isn't it my duty to defend my name and honour even at the cost of my life?'

'You are right.'

'Now you understand why I had to say no. But thank you for the respect, and your words, and I thank you for the goodwill of Black Hair. If I could show my gratefulness with actions!'

'Uff! Uff!' said One Feather enthusiastically. 'You are a man, Old Shatterhand. It's really a shame that you have to die. What I offered was the only way to save your life. But I can see that a brave warrior cannot choose this. And my daughter won't be angry when I tell her this.'

'Yes! Tell her! It would hurt me if she thought that there was another reason for my refusal.'

'She will love you, and appreciate you more than before. When you are tied to the torture stake, and everybody will stand around to see your death, my daughter will be in her tent, and cover her face. Haw!'

With this he stood up, and left and did not mention again that he would guard me day and night.

When he disappeared, the guards returned. They did not speak to me, and I was musing. For the time being I succeeded. Had I made One Feather my enemy and enticed his revenge, every plan would have failed even if I had found the best.

Soon Pida visited me, and I had to lie down. They stretched my limbs to the four poles, but they put a blanket under my head, and covered me with another.

After Pida I had another visitor, and I was very happy for this. My dun, who grazed nearby, did not join the herd, and now came to me, caressed me with his nose, and then lay down next to me. The guards did not chase him away as the horse could not untie me. The faithfulness of my horse meant a lot for me. If I could escape from my bonds in the night, my horse being near would have made my task easier. Otherwise I would have to spend the time to find him unless I jumped on the nearest horse.

For the time being I was in a difficult situation. As I suspected, I could not fall asleep. My stretched limbs soon started to ache, and then they became numb. If I dozed off, I soon awoke for the pain of my body. It was a real relief when finally the morning arrived, and I was tied to the death tree again.

Three or four such nights would have weakened me even if they fed me well. For the plan that started to develop in me I needed strength, freshness and suppleness! The worse was that I could not complain about the lack of sleep. Old Shatterhand could make himself ridiculous by asking for a more comfortable bed.

I was curious who would bring my breakfast. I would not have been surprised if it was not Black Hair after my refusal, but she came. She did not say a word, but I could see in her eyes that she was not angry with me, only deeply saddened.

Pida also checked me. I learnt from him that he would go for hunting with a small party, and would return only in the afternoon. Soon I could see him riding out to the prairie.

A few hours had passed without any event when Santer appeared from among the trees. He led his horse by the reins, and he had his gun across his back. He was coming towards me.

He stopped in front of me, and said, 'I'm also going for hunting, and I felt it was my obligation to tell you, Mr Shatterhand. Maybe I can meet Pida in the forest. He is very good willing towards you, and really hates me.'

He expected some answer, but I pretended that I did not see him, and did not hear him. 'Are you deaf?'

I was still quiet.

'I regret this, because I would have liked to talk to you. You are such a kind man,' he added mockingly and wanted to slap my shoulder.

'Away with you, you rascal!' I yelled at him.

'So you can speak! Maybe you recovered from deafness too? I would like that because I would like to ask you a few things.'

He stared in my face impertinently. I had to look at him, and on his face I saw some satanic joy, some victorious satisfaction. 'I think I would ask you something that you are also interested in, Mr Shatterhand,' he said, and looked at me expectantly, but I remained quiet.

'A very amusing scene, hahaha! Old Shatterhand is tied to the death tree, and the rascal Santer is free! This is nothing, Sir! Have you heard of a forest, some pine tree forest called Indelche-chill?'

I was shaken as if I had been electrocuted. I met this name in Winnetou's will for the first time. My eyes goggled, and stared at Santer like daggers.

'What are you staring at?' grinned Santer. 'You'd kill me with your look if you could, hahaha! Yes, yes, I'm talking about that forest.'

'Where did you get this name, you rascal?'

'Where I found the other, Tse-Shosh.'

'May the thunder hit you, you debased, you ...'

'Wait a bit! I haven't yet finished! There is another interesting place, some Deklil-to. I'd like to see it!'

'You Devil!' I shouted at him. 'So you got ...'

'Your papers?' he laughed. 'Of course. I've read them three times!'

'You stole it from Pida?'

'Stole it? Poppycock! I simply took it, because I needed it! It will be more useful for me than for Pida, don't you think so? It's in my pocket!'

He hit his chest boasting.

'Catch him! Take it from him!' I shouted at the guards almost mad.

'Catching me?' he laughed, and jumped on his horse. 'Just try it!'

'Don't let him go!' I yelled. 'He robbed Pida! Don't let him go!'

They probably did not understand my words, but the anger swelled up in me so much that I could not explain to them what I wanted. Santer galloped away, and the guards did not obstruct him. They jumped up, but not to block his way. They only stared after him uncomprehending. They did not know what it was about! Winnetou's will, my brother's will in the hands of his mortal enemy! The rascal was already riding on the open prairie, and there was nobody to chase him.

In my rage I tore the belts by which my hands were tied. I did not think that there was anyone who could have torn those belts, and even if I could do it, it was useless as my legs were tied too! I did not feel the pain when the belts cut into my flash, I kept on tearing, jerking my arms, and shouted. Then suddenly I fell forward. The belts were torn.

'Uff! Uff!' shouted the guards. 'He's escaping!'

They grabbed me.

'Let me go!' I yelled. 'I don't want to escape. I only want to catch Santer! He stole from the young chief!'

My yelling raised the whole village, and Kiowa were running towards me to hold me. It was easy because I could not move my legs, and I could only use my fist. A hundred hands stretched towards me to hold me back. It did not happen easily. I was beaten, and I distributed blows. The fight went on without any intention on either side. Finally they tied me to the tree even tighter than before.

The Kiowa were rubbing their bruises, but were not angry with me. They were only surprised that I could tear the belts.

'What a strength! Not even a bison could have done it!'

Such exclamations filled the air, while I ground my teeth in my helpless anger. Now I felt the pain in my wrist, because the belts that I tore cut into my flesh to my bone.

'What are you standing here, and staring at me for!' I shouted at them. 'You still don't understand it? Santer stole from Pida! Get on your horses, and ride after him!'

Nobody obeyed. For my yelling finally somebody came who would listen. One Feather cut his way through crowd. He came to me, and asked what had happened. With a few words I told him.

'So the talking paper was with Pida?' he asked finally.

'You were there when Tangua gave it to his son.'

'True! How do you know that Santer escaped?'

'He won't come back.'

'Then I have to ask Tangua what we should do.'

'Go! Ask him quickly! Don't hesitate! Don't lose time!'

But I encouraged him in vain, because I could not shake him out of his indifference. He kept on looking around, and finally he found the torn belts on the ground. He picked them up, shook his head, and asked one of the guards, 'Are these the ones he tore?'

'They are.'

'Uff! This is Shatterhand! And such a man must die! If he was a Kiowa warrior or any Indian, not only a paleface!'

Finally he went, and took the belts. The crowd followed him, and only my guards stayed with me.

I was waiting for the moment with tense excitement, and devouring impatience when would they start chasing Santer. But nothing showed such an intention. Soon the noise subdued, and life returned to normality. If my hands had been free I would have torn my hair out.

I begged the guards to ask what Tangua decided. They were shrugging their shoulders, and said that they could not leave their place. Finally I managed to call over another Kiowa. From him I learnt that Tangua forbade the chasing of Santer. If he took the papers, that did not matter as Pida could not read.

My face was a picture hearing this piece of news. The guards looked at my distorted countenance with anxiety. I groaned in my despair, and I almost started to tear the belts again. But my raging was in vain, and I had to accept what I could not change, and I forced external calmness on me. But I was determined that I would grab the smallest opportunity for escaping ignoring every obstacle and every danger.

Three hours had passed in this dark musing when a female scream hit my ears. I saw Black Hair stepping out of her tent, and hurrying somewhere, but I did not care. Now she rushed back screaming, and in a minute later she appeared again with her father. One Feather ran up and down, shouted, and the nearby Kiowa ran after him. Something must have happened, something exceptional. "Maybe it is something to do with the stolen papers," I thought, and listened carefully, but I did not learn anything.

Soon One Feather hurried to the tree, and shouted towards me, 'You know everything! Can you treat illnesses?'

'Of course!' I replied in the hope that I would be led to a sick person, and then I would be untied.

'Can you cure the sick?'

'I can.'

'But you can't raise the dead, can you?'

'Has somebody died? Who?'

'My daughter!'

'Black Hair?'

'No, the other one. The squaw of the young chief. We found her in the tent bound, and she doesn't move. The magic man examined her, and he says that she's dead. Santer killed her when he stole the talking papers. Would you come with me to raise her?'

'Lead me there!'

They untied me from the tree, and with loosened bonds I was led through the village to Pida's tent. At least I knew which tent it was. It was important for me as my weapons were in that tent. There was a big crowd around the tent, but they opened the way for me with respect.

Two of us entered the tent, One Feather and I. I glanced first at Black Hair who stared at her sister in despair. An old man, a gloomy, ugly man stooped by the lifeless woman. He was the magic man of the tribe. When he caught sight of me, he stood up, and gave me room next to the woman. With one look I measured up the tent. I could see my saddle and my blankets in a corner on the left. On one of the tent poles hanged my revolvers and Bowie knife. These objects were there, because Pida already considered them his property.

'I asked Old Shatterhand to examine the dead if he could raise her,' said One Feather.

I knelt down and examined the young woman as far as my bound hands allowed it. It took me some time until I could be sure that she still had circulation. Her father and sister watched all my motions anxiously.

'Unnecessary to examine her!' growled the magic man. 'She's dead, and nobody can raise her!'

'There is someone,' I replied. 'Old Shatterhand can do it.'

'Really?' exclaimed One Feather quickly and then added, 'I thought so!'

'Then do it!' begged Black Hair. 'Raise her quickly!'

She put both of her hands on my shoulder, and looked at me hopefully.

'I can do it, and I will do it,' I said decisively. 'But if you want her to recover, you have to leave me alone with her.'

'Should we go out?' asked One Feather.

'The magic will work only then.'

'Uff! Do you know what you want from us?'

'What are you afraid of?' I asked although I knew what he meant.

'Your weapons are here. If you get them, you are free. Promise that you won't touch them.'

It was difficult to answer. I looked at my knife longingly as I could have cut my bondage easily with it. And if I had my revolvers and my rifle, nobody could hold me up! But no! It would be a massacre! I was also repulsed by the thought to use the trouble of a woman for my advantage. The most important was to make her regain her consciousness. There was a stretched out piece of leather next to her. This is what she worked on. Her tools were also there: the needle, the drill and … two or three tiny knives. I knew these small, but very sharp knives. The Indian women used these for cutting out the strong animal sinews. If I could get one of them, I would not need my Bowie knife! Maybe this hope gave me the strength to say, 'I promise. And if you want you can take my weapons out from here.'

'No, it's unnecessary. Old Shatterhand always keeps his words. But it's not enough that you don't touch your weapons.'

'Why?'

'Because you can try to escape without weapons. Promise me that you won't.'

'Right, I promise.'

'So you will come back with me to the death tree, and let yourself bound again?'

'I give my word.'

'Then we'll leave you alone. You don't lie like Santer. We can trust you.'

When they left the tent I picked up one of the tiny knives first of all, and, with some difficulties, I hid it under my left sleeve. Then I turned my attention to the squaw.

It was not too difficult to find out what had happened to her. Pida had gone for hunting, and Santer used this opportunity to sneak into the tent. A long time had passed since then, and the woman was still unconscious. She was in this state either because of the fright or she was knocked out some way. I felt her head, and found that between the squamosal suture and the temple it was swollen. I pressed it for which the woman sighed with pain. I kept on pressing the swell until she opened her eyes. She looked at me uncomprehending at first, and then stuttered my name, 'Old Shatterhand.'

'Can you recognise me?' I asked.

'Yes.'

'Then can you remember what happened to you? Make sure that you don't faint again, because you'll be dead. I won't be able to raise you again.'

The threatening warning had its effect. The young woman gathered all her strength, sat up with my help, and took some deep breathes. She put her hand on her aching head, and said, 'I was alone ... He came in, and demanded Pida's medicine bag ... I didn't want to give it to him ... Then he hit me ...'

'And where's the medicine bag?'

She looked at one of the tent poles, exclaimed frightened as much as she could in her weakness.

'Uff! It's not there! He took it! When he hit me, I collapsed ... I don't know what happened after that.

I just remembered what Pida had told me a day earlier: he had hidden the papers in his medicine bag. So Santer took not only the papers, but the medicine bag too! It was a terrible blow to an Indian! Now I could be sure that they will start chasing Santer.

'Are you strong enough to remain sitting?' I asked. 'Or will you collapse again?'

'No, I won't collapse,' she replied. 'You, Old Shatterhand, gave me my life back. Thank you!'

I stood up and opened the entrance. One Feather and Black Hair stood there impatiently, and behind them half the village. 'Come in!' I told the father and the sister. 'The dead has risen!' I do not have to say what a joy my words raised. Everybody was convinced that I was a magic man, and I had made a miracle. I did not disappoint them in their belief.

Of course I did not order any other medicine but cold poultice, and I showed them how to do it. Their joy was great, but their anger and despair for the lost medicine bag even bigger. It had to be reported to Tangua who immediately sent a group of warriors after Santer and some scouts for finding Pida. One Feather did not forget about me in the turmoil. He led me back to the death tree, and tied me up again. He was profuse with praise and gratitude.

'You'll have a wonderful death!' he encouraged me with lots of goodwill. 'We'll find out such tortures that this tree has never seen. One has never suffered as much as you will! Few palefaces have got to the happy hunting grounds, but you will get there with glory.'

"Aren't I lucky!" I thought but I only said aloud, 'Had you gone after Santer right away as I told you, you would have caught him. Now you won't!'

'We will! We must catch him!' exclaimed One Feather. 'Especially if you helped us!'

'I?' I was surprised. 'With tied hands and legs?'

'We would let you go with Pida after Santer if you promise that you would return. Will you?'

'No. It would only postpone my death, and I don't like that. Let's get over it! I can hardly wait for it!'

'This is how a hero speaks! I know that you aren't afraid of death. It's bad that you aren't a Kiowa. Our warriors all say this.'

He left me alone before I could tell him that the excellent future that he had showed to me did not fill me with such enthusiasm as him. Why should I make him anxious? He would eventually learn what an ungrateful man I was.

The messengers found Pida. His horse was dripping with sweat when he galloped into the village. He first went to his tent, then to his father's, and finally visited me. He appeared to be calm, but I knew what a self-discipline he needed not to show his excitement.

'You gave back my squaw's life,' he said. 'I thank you for what you did for me. Do you know what has happened?'

'I heard about it. How is your squaw?'

'Her head aches, but the poultice that you gave her works. Soon she will be healthy. But my heart is ill, and won't recover until I get back my medicine bag.'

'You see, why didn't you listen to me?'

'You are always right, Old Shatterhand, and our warriors should have followed your advice to gallop after the thief.'

'Will you do it now, Pida?'

'Yes, right away. I only came to you to say good-bye. One Feather said that you are impatient, and you would like to die. But you have to wait until I return.'

'Then I'll wait,' I replied.

'I know that it's not good to face death for a long time,' said Pida. 'I ordered that you should be given everything that a prisoner can ask for. Then the waiting could be easier. It would be even easier if you did what I would like.'

'What is it?'

'Come with me, and let's catch Santer together! If you come with me, we will definitely capture him. Then I'll untie you, and I'll give you your weapons back. What do you say?'

'I'll go with you only if I can go as a free man.'

'Uff! You know that it's impossible!'

'Then I stay.'

'Why? As long as you are with me, you are a free man. It's enough if you give your word that you would come back.'

'I won't. You can use Old Shatterhand as a Beagle.'

'It's bad. I fear that without you I won't be able to catch Santer! What will happen if I can't recover my medicine bag?'

'That's your problem,' I replied. 'Everybody should be concerned with his own.'

There was a deep disappointment on Pida's face. He shook his head discontented, and then said, 'I thought you would be happy if I took you. This is how I wanted to thank you for giving back my squaw's life. I love my squaw.'

'If you want to thank me for this, fulfil one of my wishes.'

'What is it?'

'What happened to the three palefaces who came with Santer?'

'For the time being, they are in their tent.'

'Free?'

'No, we bound them.'

'It wasn't them who stole your medicine bag.'

'I don't know. But they were friends of the thief. And the friend of my enemy is my enemy. They will be tied to the torture stake, and will die with you.'

'Just what I suspected. It wouldn't be just to kill them. They didn't know anything about Santer's plans.'

'It's not my business! They should have listened to you. I heard that you warned them.'

'Pida, the noble young chief of the Kiowa, cannot commit injustice. I'm ready to die, and I'm not begging for my life. But pardon them!'

'Uff! This is your request?'

'Yes. Release them!'

'Impossible!'

'Do it for your squaw whom, as you said, you love.'

Pida turned away from me, and bowed his head. He was struggling with himself. Then he turned back to me.

'You are different from other palefaces,' he said, 'you are different from other people! I cannot understand you! If you had begged for your own life I would think how I could fulfil your request. We would have allowed you to fight with one of our warriors, of course the bravest and the strongest. And if you had won, we would have given you his life. But you, Old Shatterhand, don't accept presents from anyone, and you beg for others' life.'

'I hope not in vain.'

'No,' said Pida. 'I'll meet your request with one condition.'

'What is it?'

'That I don't owe you anything after then. You saved my squaw's life, and I fulfilled your request.'

'Right.'

'Then I let them go. But first I bring them here so that they could thank you for what you did for them. Haw!'

After this he left me with my guards. I saw that he went to his father's tent, obviously to report on our talk. He soon came out of the tent, and disappeared among the trees. When he appeared again, the three white men followed him on horseback. He sent them to me, but he did not join them.

'Mr Shatterhand,' started Gates, 'we have heard what happened. Is it really such a terrible thing if such a shabby medicine bag disappears?'

'The most terrible thing that can happen to an Indian. If he lost his medicine bag, he cannot enter the happy hunting grounds. What kind of Westerners are you that you don't even know this? Santer took it because of the papers. And the papers contained the description of the place that the gold was in.'

'The scoundrel!'

'But you should clear away from here as quickly as you can, right now!'

'Listening to you I understand now why Pida was so angry, and why we were tied up like we were. He let us go only because of you. He said that he did it for your request. Will he let you go too?'

'No. I have to die on the torture stake.'

'Really? I'm really sorry, Mr Shatterhand! Can't we help you at all?'

'No. You could have helped me on Mugwort Hill, but it's too late now. Go and you can tell everyone that Old Shatterhand finished his life on a Kiowa torture pole.'

Gates did not know what to say in his embarrassment. Clay and Summer, as usual, only hummed. They even forgot to say thank you for what I did for them. Soon they rode out, and their gratitude was expressed only by looking back once, and casting a pitying glance at me. Of course, I did not care about their gratitude and their pity.

They had not even disappeared when Pida galloped away. He did not say good-bye to me as he obviously expected to find me here when he would return. I hoped that if he followed Santer's tracks, I would meet both at the River Pecos.

Black Hair brought me lunch, and when I asked about her sister, she told me that her head did not ache that much, and she felt better. The good girl put so much meat in the dish that I hardly could eat it all. While I was eating, she looked at me with tearful and sad eyes. I saw that she would have liked to say something, and only shyness held her back, and she expected encouragement.

'My young sister is thinking about something now,' I said. 'I'd like to know what it is.'

'You didn't do the right thing,' she replied meekly.

'When?'

'When you didn't ride out with Pida.'

'I didn't have any reason to do so.'

'You would have had a very good reason. It's glory to die on the torture stake without a woe, but Black Hair thinks that it is much better to live in glory.'

'I wouldn't have lived even if I had gone with Pida,' I answered, 'as I would have to come back here with him.'

'Pida could not have said anything else only that the prisoner would have to die. But it could have happened differently, if on the way Pida and Old Shatterhand had become friends, and smoked the peace pipe with each other.'

'Then I wouldn't have to die?'

'I think so.'

'Would you like me to live?'

'Very much,' admitted the girl honestly. 'You gave my sister her life back!'

'Good, don't worry for me. Old Shatterhand always knows what he has to do.'

She was musing, and she cast a glance at the guards. Her right hand made an involuntary motion. I understood her thoughts.

She would have liked to talk to me about the escape, but she could not do it because of the guards. When she looked at me again, I nodded smiling, and said, 'Your eyes are clear and transparent like the water of the spring, my younger sister. Old Shatterhand can see in your heart and find out all your thoughts.'

'Really?'

'It is true. And I know that what you think will happen, my young sister.'

'When?'

'Soon.'

'Then Black Hair will be very happy.'

836

Her face brightened up, and this short conversation calmed her, and filled her with hope. At dinner she talked, and acted more bravely. Small fires were burning in the front of the tents just as in the previous night, but under the trees it was dark. While she was feeding me slowly and patiently she was very close to me. Then she stepped on my foot to call my attention for her next words.

'You are still hungry although there are only a few pieces of meat left. Would you like something else? Just tell me, and I'll procure it.'

The guards did not care with these words, but I immediately understood her. She wanted an answer that appeared to be about food, but she asked me if I needed anything for my escape. She promised that she would "procure" it.

'You are very good to me, my younger sister,' I replied, 'and I thank you for doing so much for me. I'm well fed and I don't need anything. How is the beautiful squaw of the young chief?'

'She is feeling better.'

'Good, but she still needs nursing. Who is with her?'

'I am.'

'Tonight as well?'

'Yes.'

'She shouldn't be left alone even during the night.'

'I'll stay with her till the morning,' she replied, and the tremor in her voice showed that she understood what I wanted to say.

'Till the morning?' I asked. 'Then we'll see each other!'

She nodded, and left. I could not have any doubt that she had immediately understood the double meaning of my words.

I would have to go to Pida's tent for my belongings. I now knew that Black Hair would be there, and wait for me. It gave me joy and anxiety at the same time. If I took my belongings in the presence of the two women, I could endanger them. They would be reproached or even punished.

Their gratitude dictated not to betray me, while their duty was to cry for help. How could I bridge this dilemma? There was only one way: if they agreed that I would tie them up. As soon as I escaped they could make a noise, and they would have to say only that I appeared, knocked them out, and tied them up. As soon as they recovered, they could say, they cried for help. Everybody would believe this. Black Hair promised me that she would help me in everything. And I was sure that her sister would act similarly.

My other anxiety, which caused me more trouble, was that I did not know if my rifle was still in the tent. Pida knew the value of this famous weapon, and probably took it. On the other hand he did not know how to use it, then why would he have taken it. Only time could tell me which assumption was correct. One was sure. I was so attached to the Henry rifle that I would have rather given up chasing Santer than abandoning my rifle.

Soon the time of the change of guards arrived. One Feather led the new guards to the death tree. He behaved very seriously, but in a friendly manner. He untied my bonds to avoid that the guards would be rough with my wounded wrist. I lay down among the four poles, and in an appropriate moment, when nobody could see it, I took the little knife from my sleeve. Only after then I offered my left hand to be tied. When it happened, and they wanted to tie my hand to the pole, I hissed, and jerked my hand as if the belt had hurt my wound. At the same time with my right hand I almost cut through the belt on my left wrist.

'Look out!' cried One Feather to the guard who was tying me up. 'Don't touch his wound! We'll torture him when the time arrives, but until then we have to be gentle with him!'

In the meantime I dropped the little knife to a place where they could not see, but I could reach it with my left hand. Now they tied my right hand too, and then my legs. I got two blankets as in the previous night: one under my head and one over me. When all these happened, One Feather made a remark that was very useful for me.

'We don't have to be afraid of his escape tonight. With such a wounded wrist it's impossible to tear the belt.'

After this he left, and the two guards sat down a few steps from me.

Most people would not be able to remain calm before such important events, but I got used to making myself even calmer in such situations. In such moments one needs a clear head.

Hours passed. The fires were put out except for the one in front of the chief's tent. The weather was chilly, and the guards pulled up their knees. However, this uncomfortable position exhausted them, thus they lay down more and more while facing me. They were quiet, and I knew that this was the right moment. With a slow, but strong, motion I tore the belt on my left hand. One of my hands was free! I searched for the knife and then cut the belt on my right wrist under the blanket. Now my two hands were free. But how would I free my legs? To reach my ankles I would have to sit up, and then my head would be too close to the two guards. Would they notice it? I made a few careful motions, but the guards did not move. Were they asleep?

Whatever they did, I had to act, and act quickly. I pushed off the blanket from my body, and sat up. The guards were asleep! With two cuts I freed my legs and with two blows the guards were knocked out. Now I tied them up, and with pieces of the blanket I gagged them. With this, even if they regained their consciousness, they could not sound an alarm. My horse was near me.

I stood up, and stretched my limbs. It was a very good feeling! When my arms regained their suppleness, I stooped down, and from tree to tree I approached Pida's tent. The village was quiet, and everybody was asleep. I reached the tent without a problem. I was about to enter the tent, when I heard some noise from the left. I held back my breathing, and listened. Quiet steps approached. Somebody stopped three steps from me without noticing me.

'Black Hair?' I asked.

'Old Shatterhand!'

I stood up and whispered, 'You aren't in the tent. Why?'

'Nobody is in the tent. It is empty. We came out so that we wouldn't be scolded tomorrow. My sister is ill, needs nursing, thus I took her to my father's tent.'

I had always appreciated tricks. This was an excellent one. 'Are my weapons there?' I asked.

'Exactly where they were.'

'I couldn't see my gun.'

'You'll find it under Pida's bed. And your horse?'

'He waits for me, and will come to me.'

'I'm happy.'

'You are very good to me,' I said. 'I can thank a lot to you.'

'You are good to everyone, Old Shatterhand,' she replied. 'Will you ever come back to us?'

'Maybe with Pida. Then we will be brothers and sisters.'

'Will you ride after him?'

'Yes, I hope I will find him.'

'Then don't talk to him about me. Nobody, but my sister must know what I did.'

'I know that you would have liked to do even more. Give me your hand.'

She offered her hand, and then said, 'I hope your escape will be successful. But I have to go, because my sister is anxious.'

Before I could have stopped her, she lifted my hand to her lips, and kissed it. In the next moment she glided away. I looked after her with a grateful heart.

After this I went to the tent, and groping around I found Pida's bed. Under it I found my guns wrapped in a blanket. I quickly found my knife and revolvers as well as my saddle. In five minutes I left Pida's tent. I crawled back to the death tree to saddle my horse. When I was ready, I leant over the two guards. They could not move or speak, but they had regained their consciousness.

'You won't see Old Shatterhand's death on the torture stake,' I whispered to them. 'I'm going after Pida, and help him to capture Santer. I'll be Pida's brother and friend, and I may return with him to you. Tell this to chief Tangua. Tell him not to be anxious for his son because I'll protect him. The sons and daughters of the Kiowa were good to me. Tell everyone that I want to be the friend of the Kiowa, and I won't ever forget their goodwill to me. Haw, I have spoken!'

I grabbed the reins of my horse, and led him in a way not to wake up anyone. I jumped on him only when I was at some distance from the village. The Kiowa had thought I would never be on a horse again, and now I was galloping like the wind out to the prairie, straight to the South. I did not look to the right or the left, and I did not care with Santer's tracks. I knew that Santer was heading to the Pecos River, and that was enough to me. I knew this from Winnetou's will.

Even though I could not read it through, there were three names in the part that I had read, each in the language of the Apache. One was Indelche-chil, and Santer understood the meaning of this name. But he did not know that Tse-shosh meant Bear Cliff, and he did not know about the Deklil-to. These were beyond the Santa Rita Mountains. I had been there with Winnetou and two old Apache warriors. Winnetou was dead, and the two Apache warriors, if they were still alive, would have been so old that they would not have left the pueblo at the bank of the Pecos River. Thus Santer had to hurry there, because if he wanted to get to the Deklil-to, he had to know where it was. And the only place where he could learn it was the pueblo, and he would have been sent to the two old men. No one else had ever been to the lake and the Blue Waterfall with Winnetou, but everyone knew that the two old warriors had.

Would he dare to show up in the pueblo? Everybody knew that he was Inchu Chunna's and Nsho-chih's murderer. However, knowing Santer's greed, I was sure that he would risk the journey. He probably hoped that nobody would recognise him. He could deny it, he could lie. Who could prove after so many years what a crime he had committed?

841

There was something else that I realised only now, and it made me anxious. On the leather envelope Winnetou had carved his totem. According to the Indian customs, this was the best affidavit. If Santer showed it, he could expect the help from all the Apache.

My plan was to get to the Apache's pueblo before Santer, and warn them. He would have been caught as soon as he stepped on the Apache's land. I just hoped that I would succeed as my dun was a quick, and enduring horse. This is why I did not care with the tracks as investigating them would have taken some time.

Unfortunately I had a little accident that crossed out my plans. My horse foundered for some reason. Only on the third day I noticed the inflammation on its leg caused by a long, pointed thorn. After I removed the thorn, I understood why my horse had foundered earlier, but the time could not be made up.

I had not reached the River Pecos, when two riders appeared on the barren savannah. They were Indians, and as they did not have to be afraid of a lone rider, they galloped towards me. When they got closer, one swung his gun, and cried my name. It was Yato Ka, Quick Feet, an Apache warrior whom I had known for some time. I had never seen the other before. After greetings I asked, 'I can see that you, my brothers, aren't on the warpath and aren't going for hunting. Where are you going?'

'To the North. We are going to the Gros Ventre Ridge to visit Winnetou's grave.'

'So you know that he has died?'

'We do. You will tell us everything, and you will be our leader when we go to take revenge for the death of the great Apache chief.'

'We will talk about it later. Only you two are heading to the North?'

'We are only the scouts, because the Comanche dogs dug out the war hatchet. The main group comes later.'

'How many?'

'Five times ten warriors.'

'Who's their leader?'

'Til Lata. We elected him as chief.'

'Til Lata,' I nodded. Bloody Hand was an excellent warrior, and I had heard good things about him.

'You couldn't have chosen a better one,' I said aloud. 'Have you seen strangers around?' I asked.

'Just one.'

'When?'

'Yesterday. It was a paleface and he wanted to know where the Tse-shosh. We couldn't tell him. We sent him to the pueblo to the old Inta, who has been there.'

'Uff!' I exclaimed. 'I'm pursuing that paleface. He was Inchu Chunna's murderer! I have to catch him.'

'Uff!' cried out both warriors who were almost paralysed from the information. 'The murderer! And we didn't know!'

'No problem. It's enough that you saw him. You cannot continue your journey. You have to come with me. Later I'll lead you to the Gros Ventre Ridge. Come!'

I galloped towards the pueblo.

'Yes, we come,' said Yato Ka. 'The most important is to catch the murderer.'

A few hours later we reached the Pecos River, and crossed it. We continued our journey on the bank. In the meantime I told the two Apache warriors how I met Santer on Nuggets' Hill, and what had happened in the great village of the Kiowa.

'So Pida, the young chief of the Kiowa, is chasing Santer?' asked Yato Ka, because this interested him the most.

'Yes, he is,' I replied.

'Alone?'

'He followed a group that his father had sent out. He must have caught up with them.'

'Do you know how many are in the group?'

'When they left the village, I counted them. There were ten warriors and Pida is the eleventh.'

'So few?'

'To catch the escapee ten warriors are rather too many than too few.

'Uff! There will be great joy in the Apache village because we'll catch Pida and his warriors, and we'll tie them to the torture stake!'

'No,' I replied briefly.

'Do you mean that we cannot catch them? But Santer rode to the pueblo, and they follow Santer, so we must be able to catch them.'

'That's for sure. But they won't go on the torture stake.'

'Why? They are our enemies, and they wanted to kill you on the torture stake!'

'Yet they were good to me, and Pida, although he wished my death, is now my good friend.'

'Uff!' they exclaimed surprised. 'You, Old Shatterhand, have always been a strange warrior and you are strange now. The only question is Til Lata's opinion. Will he allow this?'

'I'm sure.'

'You know that he has been a great warrior, and now he's the chief. He cannot start his office with being merciful to the enemies! He has to be sterner than ever.'

'I'm also a chief of the Apache, aren't I?'

'Yes, you have become our chief, Old Shatterhand, and you are a chief today.'

'I have become a chief before Til Lata.'

'Yes, many great days earlier.'

'So he must obey me. If he captures the Kiowa, he cannot harm him, because this is my will.'

He probably had other counter arguments, but our attention was attracted by prints of hooves that appeared on our left. A rider had crossed the ford, and continued his journey on the same bank as we did. After examining the track we recognised that it was not from one rider. Many passed there one behind the other. It was an Indian custom to ride like this when they were on enemy territory, and wanted to hide their number. As we were on Apache land, I assumed it was Pida who had passed.

After a short ride we arrived to a place where the group in front of us had had a break. We counted eleven horses from the prints of the hooves, so my assumption was correct. Yato Ka had the same opinion.

'Did the Apache group come on this side of the river?' I asked him.

'Yes. They'll meet the Kiowa who have eleven warriors, while the Apache five times ten.'

'How far are they?'

'They were half a day behind us when we met.'

'From the Kiowa's track I can see that they are only about half an hour ahead us. Let's catch up with them before they start a battle with the Apache. Quick!'

I started to gallop, because I was afraid that the two groups would attack each other before I had the time to make peace between them. Pida deserved my protection.

The river had a bend to the left at this point. The Kiowa knew this, and did not follow the river, but cut through the bend. Naturally we did the same, and soon noticed riders in front of us on the plain. They rode to the South one behind the other and each horse stepped in the hoof prints of the previous horse. They had not noticed us yet because none of them looked back.

Suddenly they stopped as if they were frightened by something. They turned their horses to ride towards us. This is when they noticed us, and they stopped again for two minutes. After a short council they continued their retreat, but not quite in our direction.

'Why did they turn back?' asked Yato Ka.

'Because they caught sight of the Apache warriors, and saw their number. We are only three men so they think they don't have to be afraid of us.

'Yes, I can see it. There come the Apache! They started to chase the Kiowa.'

'Then you two ride to them, and tell Til Lata that he should stop it until I arrive there.'

'Why aren't you coming with us?'

'I have to talk to Pida first. Go! Forward!'

They obeyed, and I turned to the left where the Kiowa wanted to pass. They were too far to recognise me, but when I approached in gallop they already knew who I was. Pida screamed in fright, and urged his horse more than ever. However, I directed my dun so that Pida could not avoid me. When I got closer, I shouted to him, 'Stop, Pida! I want to protect you from the Apache!'

It seems that his trust in me was bigger than his fear, because he stopped his horse, and ordered his warriors to do the same. The Indian warriors' self-control is legendary but now I saw that it took time for Pida to regain his calm, not to mention his men.

'Od ... Shat ... Shatter ... hand!' he stuttered. How is it possible? Who released you?'

'Nobody,' I replied. I released myself.'

'Uff! Uff! It's impossible!'

'Not for me. I knew that I would be free sooner or later, this is why I didn't ride with you. Why would I have accepted something as a present when I could achieve it myself? This is why I told you that everybody should look after his own problems. But you don't have to be afraid of me. I'm your friend, and I'll make sure that the Apache won't hurt you.'

'Will you do it? Really?'

'I give my word.'

'That's enough for me. What you say, I believe.'

'You can do that. Look behind! Can you see that the Apache have stopped, because I sent my companions with this order. They got off their horses, and they'll wait until I get there. Have you seen Santer's tracks?'

'We followed his tracks, but we couldn't catch up with him yet.'

'He's heading to the Apache's pueblo.'

'We thought so, because we saw the direction of his tracks. Still we followed it.'

'That was very brave! This is the homeland of the Apache! You were heading to certain death.'

'We knew it. But I have to risk my life to get my medicine bag back. We thought we would go behind the pueblo, and keep watch there to capture Santer.'

'Good. It will be easier now, because I'll protect you from the Apache. But I can do that only if you are my brother. Get off your horse! Let's smoke the peace pipe!'

'Uff! You, the great warrior, who escaped without any help, consider Pida worthy to be your brother and friend?'

'Yes. Hurry before the Apache lose their patience!'

We jumped off, and smoked the peace pipe. After this I rode to the Apache. They stood in an arc, and Til Lata, the new chief, stood in the middle. I knew that he was a very ambitious man, and would be happy for any opportunity to show his bravery. I was slightly anxious about his plans. I offered my hand, and said, 'Old Shatterhand came alone, without his friend, Winnetou. You, my brothers, would like to know how the great chief of the Apache died. I'll tell you everything. But first I have to talk about these Kiowa.'

'I know your request, Old Shatterhand' replied Bloody Hand. 'Yato Ka has already told me.'

'And what do you say?'

'You are one of the Apache chiefs. I respect his request. The ten Kiowa warriors should turn back right away. They can go home without harm.'

'And the young chief, Pida?'

'I saw that you smoked the calumet with him. He can be our guests as long as he wants, and can leave in peace. But as soon as he left he will be our enemy again.'

'Very good! The Apache warriors should join me to help in catching Inchu Chunna's and his daughter's murderer. After that I will lead the Apache warriors to Winnetou's grave. Haw!'

'Haw!' Til Lata nodded. I waved to Pida to join us, and we continued our journey along the Pecos River. We did not stop until the evening.

As we were on Apache land, we could make fire. We ate dried meat, and then, by the campfire, I told them how

847

Winnetou had died. They listened to my report with shock and deep sadness. There was a long silence then one and then another brought up some memories related to Winnetou: an action or a word of the beloved chief. Then the fire went out, but it took time until I could fall asleep. I had nightmare dreams, and woke up swimming in sweat.

At dawn we continued our journey. We had only a short break at noon so that we could get to the pueblo as soon as we could because we knew that Santer would not have stayed there for long.

We arrived near the pueblo late afternoon. On the right I saw the lone rock where Klekih-Petra had been buried, and I saw the large stones and the cross on his grave. On the left was the area, where I had jumped in the water, while Inchu Chunna had followed me with a tomahawk in his hand … This is how the duel had started that ended up with a huge change. How many times had I walked there with Winnetou! And Winnetou was no more!

It was twilight when we rode in the gorge where the pueblo was built. Smoke rose from every terrace as the women were making dinner. Til Lata formed a cone from his hands, and shouted up to the pueblo, 'Old Shatterhand is here! The Apache warriors should hurry to receive Old Shatterhand!'

A huge noise rose, and lots of activities developed. They let down the ladders, and by the time we jumped off the horses, hundreds and hundreds of hands stretched to me to greet me or at least touch me.

My heart was filled with even more sadness. I did not expect such a warm reception.

'Where's Inta?' I asked. 'I have to talk to him!'

'In this chamber,' they replied. 'We'll bring him out.'

'No! He's frail.' I protested. 'I will go to the old man.'

They led me to one of the small chambers carved into the cliff. The old man sat there, and cried out when he saw me. He wanted to put a lot of questions to me, but I had to interrupt him.

'I'm sorry for interrupting you. We can talk about everything later. But now I have to ask you: has a paleface visited you?'

'He did,' he replied.

'When?'

'Yesterday.'

'What's his name?'

'He said Winnetou had forbidden him to name himself.'

'Has he gone?'

'He has.'

'How long has he been in the pueblo?'

'Only as long as the paleface call an hour. He showed me Winnetou's totem. He said he came to carry out Winnetou's last order.'

'What did he want from you?'

'The route to Deklil-to.'

'Did you tell him?'

'Of course as Winnetou ordered it.'

'Did you give the precise directions?'

'I gave the description of the route, and the surroundings of the lake.'

'The pine forest, the Bear Cliff and the Blue Waterfall?'

'Everything.'

'The path that leads to the top of the cliff?'

'That too. It was good to talk about the old places where I've been with Winnetou. He's on the happy hunting grounds, and I'll soon move there too.'

Even if he made a mistake, I could not reproach him. The good old man was misled by Winnetou's totem. I asked him only, 'Did you see the horse of that paleface? Was it tired?'

'Not at all. It was fresh when he rode away.'

'Did his master eat anything?'

'I offered him food, but he said he didn't have time. He only asked for fibre to make a fuse.'

'Really? What for?'

'He didn't say. He also asked for gun powder. A lot of gun powder. It seems he wanted to blow something up.'

'Did you see where he put Winnetou's totem?'

'In a medicine bag. I was surprised, because palefaces don't wear such a thing.'

'Uff!' exclaimed Pida who stood next to me. 'My medicine bag! He stole it from me!'

'Stole?' Inta was shocked. 'Is this man a thief?'

'Even worse!'

'But he showed Winnetou's totem!'

'He stole that one too! Do you know who this paleface is? Santer! Inchu Chunna's and Nsho-Chih's murderer!'

I cannot describe Inta's shock. I would have liked to calm him or console him, but I had no time. I quickly said good-bye, and hurried to Til Lata.

'We are late,' I told him. 'Santer left yesterday.'

'We go after him!'

'Aren't you tired?'

'I don't need rest! There's moonlight, and we can ride in the night too.'

'Is Pida tired?' I asked.

'I can't rest until I get back my medicine bag!' he replied.

'Right. Then we eat something, and change horses. I'll leave my dun here.'

Two hours later, on fresh horses with supplies, we galloped out of the village with twenty Apache warriors. The Deklil-to was about seventy miles away, and the route was terribly difficult, horribly rocky, especially towards the end. I expected us to be able to cover six miles a day, thus the journey would take about twelve days.

For the time being we did not look for Santer's tracks as it would have been a waste of time. Only one path led to the Deklil-to, and Santer followed this. It was a tiring ride. Days passed without any event. It was only on the eleventh day when something important happened. Two Indian riders came towards us, an older and a younger; clearly father and son. I had known the older for some time, and when he caught sight of me, he greeted me joyously.

'Old Shatterhand! Are you alive? Didn't you die?'

'Why would I have died?'

'Because it's said that the Sioux shot you dead!'

I suspected that he had met Santer.

'Who told you this?' I asked.

'A paleface who told me in detail how the famous Old Shatterhand, and the famous Winnetou had died. I believed all his words as he showed Winnetou's totem, and his medicine bag.'

'He lied to you! As you can see I'm alive and here.'

'So is Winnetou also alive?'

'Unfortunately not,' I replied. 'Winnetou died.'

The Indian was quiet for a long time. He belonged to the Mimbreño Apache who knew Winnetou, and respected him.

'Where did you meet that lying paleface?' I asked him.

'In our camp. He wanted to exchange his tired horse for a fresh one, and looked for a guide to Deklil-to that we call Shish-tu. He offered Winnetou's medicine bag as a payment, and I accepted it. I gave him a good horse, and with my son I led him to the Dark Water.'

'Where's that medicine bag?'

'With me.'

'Show it to me!'

He took the bag out from his saddle. Pida screamed in joy, and wanted to get the bag, but the Mimbreño did not want to give it to him. They almost started a fight. I intervened, and said, 'This medicine bag belongs to the young Kiowa chief. Winnetou has never touched it.'

'You are wrong!' exclaimed the Mimbreño.

'There's no mistake!' I replied.

'Still, I won't give it to him! I made the long journey for the medicine bag with my son, and I gave a good horse too!'

'He lied to you, and cheated you. He needed the fresh horse because he knew he was pursued. He has committed many debased things. You cannot keep another man's medicine bag!'

'Do I have to give it back? If somebody else told me, I wouldn't do it. But for Old Shatterhand I'll do it.'

851

He gave the bag to Pida.

'You are an honest man!' I praised him.

'But I'll take revenge for my loss!' he cried. 'I'll turn around I'll find the rascal! I'll kill him!'

'This is what we want to do to him. Come with us!'

The Mimbreño joined us. On the way I told him several things from Santer's past. When he heard all these, he did not regret his loss, only that he helped such a man.

Pida was happy, he had got back his medicine bag. He achieved his goal, but when would I? I counted the minutes in my impatience.

On the following day we reached the lake, but only in the evening when nothing could be done. We settled in the forest, and lay quietly under the trees. We did not make a fire so that we would not show our presence to Santer. Where could he be? He had not told the Mimbreño where he was going. Once they had arrived to the lake, he told them that he knew his way, and he encouraged them in all manners to leave him.

Our journey from the Pecos River to this point led through the South-western corner of New Mexico, and now we were in Arizona where the hunting grounds of the Mimbreño and the Gileño met. As the Gileño were Apache too, we did not have to be afraid of them. We were in safety, but the landscape was barren. Wherever we looked we saw only stones and rocks. But the shore of the lake was different. The forest, where we camped for the night, was like an oasis in this rock-desert.

Imagine a valley whose depth is filled with a lake. It does not dry out. It is surrounded by steep cliffs, and these cast such a shadow that the water of the lake gleams almost black. This is why the Indian tribes called it Dark Water.

We spent the night on the South side of the lake, but the cliff on the North side was the tallest. A huge rock grew out of it almost horizontally over the lake, forming a kind of roof above it. On one of the side of this rock formation the water of the higher mountains rushed down thundering from about a hundred feet height. The rock probably contained cobalt, because the waterfall twinkled in a bluish colour. This is why the Indians called it Blue Waterfall.

On the other side of the rock, on the left at a lower height there was a rock shelf where Winnetou and I had killed a grizzly, and since then we called the place Tse-shosh, that is Bear Cliff. One could get up to this point on horseback, but I did not know the path any further. However, obviously, Winnetou had found it. Behind this strange rock formation there was a cave. I felt that the following day would bring decisive events. Unusually for me, I could not overcome my excitement, and I slept very little. After the restless night I was up at dawn, and was searching for Santer's footprints. My companions helped, but we did not find anything. I decided that I would climb up on the rock wall as Santer would have gone that way. I took only Pida and Til Lata with me.

We climbed through the pine forest mentioned in Winnetou's will until we arrived to the Bear Cliff where we stopped and looked around. "There you get off your horse and climb up ...," wrote Winnetou. This is how far I had read his will. Where should I climb? Probably to the cave up there. The rock wall was very steep there, but I tried to scale it. With a lot of effort I managed it. Finally I arrived, although not to the cave, but near the cave. If I looked up I could see the entrance of the cave on the left, high above my head. But from there I could not advance. There was no path and I could not find any place where I could put my foot. Maybe there was a hidden path, but without Winnetou's will I could not find it.

I was about to turn back when a shot popped near me, and above my shoulder a bullet hit the rock. Right after then I heard an angry voice from the height. 'Did you escape, you wretch! I thought the Kiowa were after me, and now I can see that it's you! You'll be in hell soon!'

Another shot went off but it also missed me. We turned our head up, and saw Santer at the entrance of the cave.

'You want the will, don't you?' he laughed mockingly. 'Do you want Winnetou's treasure? You are late! I came earlier, and the fuse is already burning! You won't get any gold! The noble aims that the will speaks about is stupid! None will go to them. I'll take everything!'

After a neighing, disgusting laugh he continued, 'I can see you don't know the path! And you don't know the other that leads down behind the cave! I will take the gold on that, and you won't be able to do anything! You climbed up in vain! I won!'

I really could not do anything. The treasure was in his hands, and we could not get up to the cave. Maybe we could have found the path, but he would have disappeared by then. He could go down on the other path that he mentioned. Except if a bullet stops him! From where I stood it was very difficult to shoot upwards or downwards. This is why he missed me. I made a few side steps, and stopped at a place that was more promising for aiming. I took the rifle from by back.

'Look at the dog! He wants to shoot!' shouted Santer teasingly. 'You can't imagine that you'll hit me, can you? Wait, I'll help you!'

He disappeared, and when he reappeared he stood on the outstretching rock. He was right at the edge. It was dizzy even to look at him. There was something white in his hand.

'Look!' he shouted. 'Do you know what it is? Winnetou's will. I don't need it, but you won't ever get it! Or you'll have to fish it out of the lake!'

He tore up the papers, and threw them down. The small pieces of paper floated in the air, and descended into the lake. The dear handwriting was lost! Winnetou's will! It is impossible to describe what I felt because it was more than anger. I was pale, I was shaking, and my blood was boiling.

'You rascal!' I yelled. 'Listen to me!'

'Just speak!' he laughed. 'I'm happy to listen to you.'

'Think of Inchu Chunna! He's greeting you!'

'Thank you,' he replied.

'Nsho-Chih too!'

'Thank you!'

'And I'm sending his bullet on behalf of Winnetou. I hope you won't thank this!'

I lifted the bear slayer as I could aim more securely with it. Aiming took normally a few seconds, but now ... What happened? Did my arm move? Or did Santer move? Or the cliff? I could not aim securely. I let the gun down to look at it properly. Good Lord! The cliff was swinging! A deep, dim crackling resounded. Smoke broke out from the cave, and the cliff, as if it was bent by the hand of a giant, moved forward with Santer. Santer pushed both his arms in the air, and cried for help, but the cliff with a thunderous noise fell in the depth, in the lake. In the next moment I could see only the broken stem of the cliff above my head ... Light dust fluttered around it.

I stood there in silent shock.

'Uff!' exclaimed Pida opening his arms. 'The Great Spirit made his judgement. He ordered the cliff to collapse under him!'

Til Lata pointed down in the foaming waves of the lake that looked like a huge cauldron in which boiling water swirled. The bronze coloured face of the Apache was pale.

'Yes, then the Wicked Spirit pulled him down into the vortex, and will hold him there until the end of times! He'll be damned forever!'

I could not speak. Joy and anger raged in my heart. Winnetou's treasure and his will were lost forever! But Santer was also punished! He carried out the death penalty that he deserved many times when he lit the fuse. He did not know that he would be his own executioner!

The Apache were waving on the shore of the lake. The two chiefs hurried down to see if the water threw up Santer's body. It did not happen. The huge rock buried him in the bottom of the lake.

I had had stable nerves, and nothing could take me out of my calm, but now I felt so weak that I had to sit down on the

855

ground. My legs were trembling, my head was dizzy. I closed my eyes, but I could still see the huge rock as it shook, and fell down, and I could hear Santer's scream.

How could it happen? I felt, suspected, I knew that it was Winnetou. His preparations made it sure that a thief would be punished. The same thing would not have happened to me. In the will I would have found the instructions to find the treasure. Winnetou would have written it with such words that only I could have understood. He mined the cave and the rock. The thief, misinterpreting the instructions, blew himself up! I could not find it out how, but this was the essence of it.

And the treasure? Was it in the collapsed cave or did it fall to the bottom of the lake where human hands could not find it? Whatever happened I was not interested in the treasure. I felt that my only loss was that the will of my brother and friend was torn up, and soaked in the lake. What did Winnetou want from me? What was his message? Could I never learn it? This thought gave me back my strength. I jumped up, and as quickly as I could I hurried down on the steep hillside to the lake hoping that I could save pieces of the will. I saw something white on the dark waves of the lake. I undressed, jumped in the water, and swam there. It was a piece of the will indeed. I swam in the lake in all directions, and found three further pieces. I dried these in the sun, and tried to read the blurred lines. Of course it was impossible to make full sense of these. With great effort I could read the following few words: "... *selling ... half of the sum ... for my Indian brothers ... reducing poverty ... blow up ... peace instead of revenge ...*".

This was all I could read, but it was enough to understand the essence of the will. I put away the pieces of paper as sacred.

Later, when my psychological state improved, we searched the area. Some of the Apache searched the forest looking for Santer's horse as we did not want the poor animal to die if he tied it to a tree. With the others I climbed to the height if I could find the way to the cave. We searched for it for hours in vain. Then I sat down, and rethought the last few words that I had read in the will. It said, "You get off your horse there, and climb up …". One can climb up on the rock wall, but also on a tree. Could Winnetou mean a tree? We searched, and noticed a strong pine tree. It grew slanted, and leant over a rock shelf. I climbed up, and from one of its highest branches I could step over to the rock. There was enough room for my feet, and I could make a few steps forward. There the path was in front of me! I tottered forward, and got to the place where the opening of the cave used to be.

The Apache came after me, and helped me search the area. We turned every stone, but we could not find any treasure. All the men were experienced, and would have noticed something that had to be noticed. But we did not find anything. When we returned to the lake in the evening the Apache, who searched the forest, also returned. They found Santer's horse, and brought it with them. I searched the saddle, but I could not find anything.

We spent four days by the Dark Water, and sniffed, searched around like dogs. I am convinced if the treasure was there, we would have found it. But it fell with the cliff in the lake, and was lost forever. We returned to the pueblo without treasure, but at least with the knowledge that Inchu Chunna's and Nsho-Chih's murderer got his deserved punishment.

Winnetou's will was destroyed, his treasures were lost. This would be the fate of his brothers whatever tribe they belonged to. The talented, noble Indian peoples were not given the opportunity to catch up with the earlier developed cultures. Their tragic meeting with the culture that the Europeans had taken over the Ocean was fatal to them.

If somebody finds Winnetou's grave in the Gros Ventre Ridge near the creek, he must say, "Winnetou rests here, a great red man." And decades later, when everything in the West has gone, an honest man, standing in front of the

Rocky Mountains and the prairies, must sigh, "The Indian people destined for great things, lived here, and disappeared because they could not become big enough!"

Printed by BoD™in Norderstedt, Germany

9 781910 47